"A TAUT THRILLER . . . FASCINATING . . ."

Crichton is a master at blending edge-of-the-chair adventure and a scientific seminar, educating his readers as he entertains them."

—*St. Louis Post-Dispatch*

"Crichton combines his knowledge of science with a great talent for creating suspense . . . Fast-moving."

—*San Francisco Chronicle*

"Crichton is remarkably realistic with his depictions of what it could be like if genetic engineering created a theme park full of carefully modified dinosaurs—and the terrible lizards got out of control."

—*USA Today*

"Crichton's notion is wonderful precisely because nothing about it is entirely outside the realm of possibility . . . He presents an astonishingly plausible case that a lot of money and a little bit of luck are all one would need to make this book's unlikely scenario become real."

—*The Cleveland Plain Dealer*

"Intellectually provocative, high-octane entertainment."

—*New York Newsday*

Please turn the page for more rave reviews . . .

Also by Michael Crichton:

Fiction:
THE ANDROMEDA STRAIN
THE TERMINAL MAN
THE GREAT TRAIN ROBBERY
EATERS OF THE DEAD
CONGO
SPHERE
RISING SUN
DISCLOSURE
THE LOST WORLD
AIRFRAME
TIMELINE
PREY
STATE OF FEAR
NEXT

Nonfiction:
FIVE PATIENTS
JASPER JOHNS
ELECTRONIC LIFE
TRAVELS

JURASSIC PARK

Michael Crichton

BALLANTINE BOOKS • NEW YORK

A Ballantine Book
Published by The Random House Publishing Group

Published in the United States by Ballantine Books, an imprint of The Random House Publishing Group, a division of Random House, Inc., New York, and simultaneously in Canada by Random House of Canada Limited, Toronto.

Ballantine and colophon are registered trademarks of Random House, Inc.

www.ballantinebooks.com

Cover illustration by Chip Kidd

Library of Congress Catalog Card Number: 90-52960

ISBN 0-345-37077-5

The edition published by arrangement with Alfred A. Knopf, Inc.

Manufactured in the United States of America

First International Ballantine Books Edition: September 1991
First Ballantine Books Edition: December 1991

OPM 33 32

For **A-M**
and
T

"*Reptiles are abhorrent because of their cold body, pale color, cartilaginous skeleton, filthy skin, fierce aspect, calculating eye, offensive smell, harsh voice, squalid habitation, and terrible venom; wherefore their Creator has not exerted his powers to make many of them.*"

LINNAEUS, 1797

"*You cannot recall a new form of life.*"

ERWIN CHARGAFF, 1972

INTRODUCTION

"The InGen Incident"

The late twentieth century has witnessed a scientific gold rush of astonishing proportions: the headlong and furious haste to commercialize genetic engineering. This enterprise has proceeded so rapidly—with so little outside commentary—that its dimensions and implications are hardly understood at all.

Biotechnology promises the greatest revolution in human history. By the end of this decade, it will have outdistanced atomic power and computers in its effect on our everyday lives. In the words of one observer, "Biotechnology is going to transform every aspect of human life: our medical care, our food, our health, our entertainment, our very bodies. Nothing will ever be the same again. It's literally going to change the face of the planet."

But the biotechnology revolution differs in three important respects from past scientific transformations.

First, it is broad-based. America entered the atomic age through the work of a single research institution, at Los Alamos. It entered the computer age through the efforts of about a dozen companies. But biotechnology research is now carried out in more than two thousand laboratories in America alone. Five hundred corporations spend five billion dollars a year on this technology.

Second, much of the research is thoughtless or frivolous. Efforts to engineer paler trout for better visibility in the stream, square trees for easier lumbering, and injectable scent cells so you'll always smell of your favorite perfume may seem like a joke, but they are not. Indeed, the fact that biotechnology can be applied to the industries traditionally subject to the vagaries of fashion, such as cosmetics and leisure activities, heightens concern about the whimsical use of this powerful new technology.

Third, the work is uncontrolled. No one supervises it. No federal laws regulate it. There is no coherent government policy, in America or anywhere else in the world. And because the products of biotechnology range from drugs to farm crops to artificial snow, an intelligent policy is difficult.

But most disturbing is the fact that no watchdogs are found among scientists themselves. It is remarkable that nearly every scientist in genetics research is also engaged in the commerce of biotechnology. There are no detached observers. Everybody has a stake.

The commercialization of molecular biology is the most stunning ethical event in the history of science, and it has happened with astonishing speed. For four hundred years since Galileo, science has always proceeded as a free and open inquiry into the workings of nature. Scientists have always ignored national boundaries, holding themselves above the transitory concerns of politics and even wars. Scientists have always rebelled against secrecy in research, and have even frowned on the idea of patenting their discoveries, seeing themselves as working to the benefit of all mankind. And for many generations, the discoveries of scientists did indeed have a peculiarly selfless quality.

When, in 1953, two young researchers in England, James Watson and Francis Crick, deciphered the structure of DNA, their work was hailed as a triumph of the human spirit, of the centuries-old quest to understand the universe in a scientific way. It was confidently expected that their discovery would be selflessly extended to the greater benefit of mankind.

Yet that did not happen. Thirty years later, nearly all of Watson and Crick's scientific colleagues were engaged in another sort of enterprise entirely. Research in molecular genetics had become a vast, multibillion-dollar commercial undertaking, and its origins can be traced not to 1953 but to April 1976.

That was the date of a now famous meeting, in which Robert Swanson, a venture capitalist, approached Herbert Boyer, a biochemist at the University of California. The two men agreed to found a commercial company to exploit Boyer's gene-splicing techniques. Their new company, Genentech, quickly became the largest and most successful of the genetic engineering start-ups.

Suddenly it seemed as if everyone wanted to become rich. New companies were announced almost weekly, and scientists flocked to exploit genetic research. By 1986, at least 362 scientists, including 64 in the National Academy, sat on the advisory boards of biotech firms. The number of those who held equity positions or consultancies was several times greater.

It is necessary to emphasize how significant this shift in attitude actually was. In the past, pure scientists took a snobbish view of business. They saw the pursuit of money as intellectually uninteresting, suited only to shopkeepers. And to do research for industry, even at the prestigious Bell or IBM labs, was only for those who couldn't get a university appointment. Thus the attitude of pure scientists was fundamentally critical toward the work of applied scientists, and to industry in general. Their long-standing antagonism kept university scientists free of contaminating industry ties, and whenever debate arose about technological matters, disinterested scientists were available to discuss the issues at the highest levels.

But that is no longer true. There are very few molecular biologists and very few research institutions without commercial affiliations. The old days are gone. Genetic research continues, at a more furious pace than ever. But it is done in secret, and in haste, and for profit.

In this commercial climate, it is probably inevitable that a company as ambitious as International Genetic Technologies, Inc., of Palo Alto, would arise. It is equally unsurprising that the genetic crisis it created should go unreported. After all, InGen's research was conducted in secret; the actual incident occurred in the most remote region of Central America; and fewer than twenty people were there to witness it. Of those, only a handful survived.

Even at the end, when International Genetic Technologies filed for Chapter 11 protection in United States Bankruptcy Court in San Francisco on October 5, 1989, the proceedings drew little press attention. It appeared so ordinary: InGen was the third small American bioengineering company to fail that year, and the seventh since 1986. Few court documents were made public, since the creditors were Japanese investment consortia, such as Hamaguri and Densaka, companies which traditionally shun publicity. To avoid unnecessary disclosure, Daniel Ross, of Cowan, Swain and Ross, counsel for InGen, also represented the Japanese investors. And the rather unusual petition of the vice consul of Costa Rica was heard behind closed doors. Thus it is not surprising that, within a month, the problems of InGen were quietly and amicably settled.

Parties to that settlement, including the distinguished scientific board of advisers, signed a nondisclosure agreement, and none will speak about what happened; but many of the principal figures in the "InGen incident" are not signatories, and were willing to discuss the remarkable events leading up to those final two days in August 1989 on a remote island off the west coast of Costa Rica.

PROLOGUE: THE BITE OF THE RAPTOR

The tropical rain fell in drenching sheets, hammering the corrugated roof of the clinic building, roaring down the metal gutters, splashing on the ground in a torrent. Roberta Carter sighed, and stared out the window. From the clinic, she could hardly see the beach or the ocean beyond, cloaked in low fog. This wasn't what she had expected when she had come to the fishing village of Bahía Anasco, on the west coast of Costa Rica, to spend two months as a visiting physician. Bobbie Carter had expected sun and relaxation, after two grueling years of residency in emergency medicine at Michael Reese in Chicago.

She had been in Bahía Anasco now for three weeks. And it had rained every day.

Everything else was fine. She liked the isolation of Bahía Anasco, and the friendliness of its people. Costa Rica had one of the twenty best medical systems in the world, and even in this remote coastal village, the clinic was well maintained, amply supplied. Her paramedic, Manuel Aragón, was intelligent and well trained. Bobbie was able to practice a level of medicine equal to what she had practiced in Chicago.

But the rain! The constant, unending rain!

Across the examining room, Manuel cocked his head. "Listen," he said.

"Believe me, I hear it," Bobbie said.

"No. *Listen.*"

And then she caught it, another sound blended with the rain, a deeper rumble that built and emerged until it was clear: the rhythmic thumping of a helicopter. She thought, *They can't be flying in weather like this.*

But the sound built steadily, and then the helicopter burst low

1

through the ocean fog and roared overhead, circled, and came back. She saw the helicopter swing back over the water, near the fishing boats, then ease sideways to the rickety wooden dock, and back toward the beach.

It was looking for a place to land.

It was a big-bellied Sikorsky with a blue stripe on the side, with the words "InGen Construction." That was the name of the construction company building a new resort on one of the offshore islands. The resort was said to be spectacular, and very complicated; many of the local people were employed in the construction, which had been going on for more than two years. Bobbie could imagine it—one of those huge American resorts with swimming pools and tennis courts, where guests could play and drink their daiquiris, without having any contact with the real life of the country.

Bobbie wondered what was so urgent on that island that the helicopter would fly in this weather. Through the windshield she saw the pilot exhale in relief as the helicopter settled onto the wet sand of the beach. Uniformed men jumped out, and flung open the big side door. She heard frantic shouts in Spanish, and Manuel nudged her.

They were calling for a doctor.

Two black crewmen carried a limp body toward her, while a white man barked orders. The white man had a yellow slicker. Red hair appeared around the edges of his Mets baseball cap. "Is there a doctor here?" he called to her, as she ran up.

"I'm Dr. Carter," she said. The rain fell in heavy drops, pounding her head and shoulders. The red-haired man frowned at her. She was wearing cut-off jeans and a tank top. She had a stethoscope over her shoulder, the bell already rusted from the salt air.

"Ed Regis. We've got a very sick man here, doctor."

"Then you better take him to San José," she said. San José was the capital, just twenty minutes away by air.

"We would, but we can't get over the mountains in this weather. You have to treat him here."

Bobbie trotted alongside the injured man as they carried him to the clinic. He was a kid, no older than eighteen. Lifting away the blood-soaked shirt, she saw a big slashing rip along his shoulder, and another on the leg.

"What happened to him?"

"Construction accident," Ed shouted. "He fell. One of the back-hoes ran over him."

The kid was pale, shivering, unconscious.

Manuel stood by the bright green door of the clinic, waving his arm. The men brought the body through and set it on the table in the center of the room. Manuel started an intravenous line, and Bobbie swung the light over the kid and bent to examine the wounds. Immediately she could see that it did not look good. The kid would almost certainly die.

A big tearing laceration ran from his shoulder down his torso. At the edge of the wound, the flesh was shredded. At the center, the shoulder was dislocated, pale bones exposed. A second slash cut through the heavy muscles of the thigh, deep enough to reveal the pulse of the femoral artery below. Her first impression was that his leg had been ripped open.

"Tell me again about this injury," she said.

"I didn't see it," Ed said. "They say the backhoe dragged him."

"Because it almost looks as if he was mauled," Bobbie Carter said, probing the wound. Like most emergency room physicians, she could remember in detail patients she had seen even years before. She had seen two maulings. One was a two-year-old child who had been attacked by a rottweiler dog. The other was a drunken circus attendant who had had an encounter with a Bengal tiger. Both injuries were similar. There was a characteristic look to an animal attack.

"Mauled?" Ed said. "No, no. It was a backhoe, believe me." Ed licked his lips as he spoke. He was edgy, acting as if he had done something wrong. Bobbie wondered why. If they were using inexperienced local workmen on the resort construction, they must have accidents all the time.

Manuel said, "Do you want lavage?"

"Yes," she said. "After you block him."

She bent lower, probed the wound with her fingertips. If an earth mover had rolled over him, dirt would be forced deep into the wound. But there wasn't any dirt, just a slippery, slimy foam. And the wound had a strange odor, a kind of rotten stench, a smell of death and decay. She had never smelled anything like it before.

"How long ago did this happen?"

"An hour."

Again she noticed how tense Ed Regis was. He was one of those eager, nervous types. And he didn't look like a construction foreman. More like an executive. He was obviously out of his depth.

Bobbie Carter turned back to the injuries. Somehow she didn't think she was seeing mechanical trauma. It just didn't look right. No soil contamination of the wound site, and no crush-injury component. Mechanical trauma of any sort—an auto injury, a factory accident—almost always had some component of crushing. But here there was none. Instead, the man's skin was shredded—ripped— across his shoulder, and again across his thigh.

It really did look like a maul. On the other hand, most of the body was unmarked, which was unusual for an animal attack. She looked again at the head, the arms, the hands—

The hands.

She felt a chill when she looked at the kid's hands. There were short slashing cuts on both palms, and bruises on the wrists and forearms. She had worked in Chicago long enough to know what that meant.

"All right," she said. "Wait outside."

"Why?" Ed said, alarmed. He didn't like that.

"Do you want me to help him, or not?" she said, and pushed him out the door and closed it on his face. She didn't know what was going on, but she didn't like it. Manuel hesitated. "I continue to wash?"

"Yes," she said. She reached for her little Olympus point-and-shoot. She took several snapshots of the injury, shifting her light for a better view. It really did look like bites, she thought. Then the kid groaned, and she put her camera aside and bent toward him. His lips moved, his tongue thick.

"Raptor," he said. *"Lo sa raptor . . ."*

At those words, Manuel froze, stepped back in horror.

"What does it mean?" Bobbie said.

Manuel shook his head. "I do not know, doctor. *'Lo sa raptor'*— *no es español.*"

"No?" It sounded to her like Spanish. "Then please continue to wash him."

"No, doctor." He wrinkled his nose. "Bad smell." And he crossed himself.

Bobbie looked again at the slippery foam streaked across the wound. She touched it, rubbing it between her fingers. It seemed almost like saliva. . . .

The injured boy's lips moved. "Raptor," he whispered.

In a tone of horror, Manuel said, "It bit him."

"What bit him?"

"Raptor."

"What's a raptor?"

"It means *hupia*."

Bobbie frowned. The Costa Ricans were not especially superstitious, but she had heard the *hupia* mentioned in the village before. They were said to be night ghosts, faceless vampires who kidnapped small children. According to the belief, the *hupia* had once lived in the mountains of Costa Rica, but now inhabited the islands offshore.

Manuel was backing away, murmuring and crossing himself. "It is not normal, this smell," he said. "It is the *hupia*."

Bobbie was about to order him back to work when the injured youth opened his eyes and sat straight up on the table. Manuel shrieked in terror. The injured boy moaned and twisted his head, looking left and right with wide staring eyes, and then he explosively vomited blood. He went immediately into convulsions, his body vibrating, and Bobbie grabbed for him but he shuddered off the table onto the concrete floor. He vomited again. There was blood everywhere. Ed opened the door, saying, "What the hell's happening?" and when he saw the blood he turned away, his hand to his mouth. Bobbie was grabbing for a stick to put in the boy's clenched jaws, but even as she did it she knew it was hopeless, and with a final spastic jerk he relaxed and lay still.

She bent to perform mouth-to-mouth, but Manuel grabbed her shoulder fiercely, pulling her back. "No," he said. "The *hupia* will cross over."

"Manuel, for God's sake—"

"*No.*" He stared at her fiercely. "No. You do not understand these things."

Bobbie looked at the body on the ground and realized that it didn't matter; there was no possibility of resuscitating him. Manuel called for the men, who came back into the room and took the body away. Ed appeared, wiping his mouth with the back of his hand, muttering, "I'm sure you did all you could," and then she watched as the men took the body away, back to the helicopter, and it lifted thunderously up into the sky.

"It is better," Manuel said.

Bobbie was thinking about the boy's hands. They had been covered with cuts and bruises, in the characteristic pattern of defense wounds. She was quite sure he had not died in a construction accident; he had been attacked, and he had held up his hands against his attacker. "Where is this island they've come from?" she asked.

"In the ocean. Perhaps a hundred, hundred and twenty miles offshore."

"Pretty far for a resort," she said.

Manuel watched the helicopter. "I hope they never come back."

Well, she thought, at least she had pictures. But when she turned back to the table, she saw that her camera was gone.

The rain finally stopped later that night. Alone in the bedroom behind the clinic, Bobbie thumbed through her tattered paperback Spanish dictionary. The boy had said "raptor," and, despite Manuel's protests, she suspected it was a Spanish word. Sure enough, she found it in her dictionary. It meant "ravisher" or "abductor."

That gave her pause. The sense of the word was suspiciously close to the meaning of *hupia*. Of course she did not believe in the superstition. And no ghost had cut those hands. What had the boy been trying to tell her?

From the next room, she heard groans. One of the village women was in the first stage of labor, and Elena Morales, the local midwife, was attending her. Bobbie went into the clinic room and gestured to Elena to step outside for a moment.

"Elena . . ."

"*Sí*, doctor?"

"Do you know what is a raptor?"

Elena was gray-haired and sixty, a strong woman with a practical, no-nonsense air. In the night, beneath the stars, she frowned and said, "Raptor?"

"Yes. You know this word?"

"*Sí.*" Elena nodded. "It means . . . a person who comes in the night and takes away a child."

"A kidnapper?"

"Yes."

"A *hupia*?"

Her whole manner changed. "Do not say this word, doctor."

"Why not?"

"Do not speak of *hupia* now," Elena said firmly, nodding her head toward the groans of the laboring woman. "It is not wise to say this word now."

"But does a raptor bite and cut his victims?"

"Bite and cut?" Elena said, puzzled. "No, doctor. Nothing like this. A raptor is a man who takes a new baby." She seemed irritated by the conversation, impatient to end it. Elena started back toward the clinic. "I will call to you when she is ready, doctor. I think one hour more, perhaps two."

Bobbie looked at the stars, and listened to the peaceful lapping of the surf at the shore. In the darkness she saw the shadows of the fishing boats anchored offshore. The whole scene was quiet, so normal, she felt foolish to be talking of vampires and kidnapped babies.

Bobbie went back to her room, remembering again that Manuel had insisted it was not a Spanish word. Out of curiosity, she looked in the little English dictionary, and to her surprise she found the word there, too:

raptor \ *n* [deriv. of L. *raptor* plunderer, fr. *raptus*]: bird of prey.

FIRST ITERATION

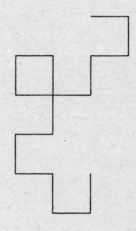

"At the earliest drawings of the fractal curve, few clues to the underlying mathematical structure will be seen."

IAN MALCOLM

ALMOST PARADISE

Mike Bowman whistled cheerfully as he drove the Land Rover through the Cabo Blanco Biological Reserve, on the west coast of Costa Rica. It was a beautiful morning in July, and the road before him was spectacular: hugging the edge of a cliff, overlooking the jungle and the blue Pacific. According to the guidebooks, Cabo Blanco was unspoiled wilderness, almost a paradise. Seeing it now made Bowman feel as if the vacation was back on track.

Bowman, a thirty-six-year-old real estate developer from Dallas, had come to Costa Rica with his wife and daughter for a two-week holiday. The trip had actually been his wife's idea; for weeks Ellen had filled his ear about the wonderful national parks of Costa Rica, and how good it would be for Tina to see them. Then, when they arrived, it turned out Ellen had an appointment to see a plastic surgeon in San José. That was the first Mike Bowman had heard about the excellent and inexpensive plastic surgery available in Costa Rica, and all the luxurious private clinics in San José.

Of course they'd had a huge fight. Mike felt she'd lied to him, and she had. And he put his foot down about this plastic surgery business. Anyway, it was ridiculous, Ellen was only thirty, and she was a beautiful woman. Hell, she'd been Homecoming Queen her senior year at Rice, and that was not even ten years earlier. But Ellen tended to be insecure, and worried. And it seemed as if in recent years she had mostly worried about losing her looks.

That, and everything else.

The Land Rover bounced in a pothole, splashing mud. Seated beside him, Ellen said, "Mike, are you sure this is the right road? We haven't seen any other people for hours."

"There was another car fifteen minutes ago," he reminded her. "Remember, the blue one?"

11

"Going the other way . . ."

"Darling, you wanted a deserted beach," he said, "and that's what you're going to get."

Ellen shook her head doubtfully. "I hope you're right."

"Yeah, Dad, I hope you're right," said Christina, from the backseat. She was eight years old.

"Trust me, I'm right." He drove in silence a moment. "It's beautiful, isn't it? Look at that view. It's beautiful."

"It's okay," Tina said.

Ellen got out a compact and looked at herself in the mirror, pressing under her eyes. She sighed, and put the compact away.

The road began to descend, and Mike Bowman concentrated on driving. Suddenly a small black shape flashed across the road and Tina shrieked, "Look! *Look!*" Then it was gone, into the jungle.

"What was it?" Ellen asked. "A monkey?"

"Maybe a squirrel monkey," Bowman said.

"Can I count it?" Tina said, taking her pencil out. She was keeping a list of all the animals she had seen on her trip, as a project for school.

"I don't know," Mike said doubtfully.

Tina consulted the pictures in the guidebook. "I don't think it was a squirrel monkey," she said. "I think it was just another howler." They had seen several howler monkeys already on their trip.

"Hey," she said, more brightly. "According to this book, 'the beaches of Cabo Blanco are frequented by a variety of wildlife, including howler and white-faced monkeys, three-toed sloths, and coatimundis.' You think we'll see a three-toed sloth, Dad?"

"I bet we do."

"Really?"

"Just look in the mirror."

"Very funny, Dad."

The road sloped downward through the jungle, toward the ocean.

Mike Bowman felt like a hero when they finally reached the beach: a two-mile crescent of white sand, utterly deserted. He parked the Land Rover in the shade of the palm trees that fringed the beach, and got out the box lunches. Ellen changed into her bathing suit, saying, "Honestly, I don't know *how* I'm going to get this weight off."

"You look great, hon." Actually, he felt that she was too thin, but he had learned not to mention that.

Tina was already running down the beach.

"Don't forget you need your sunscreen," Ellen called.

"Later," Tina shouted, over her shoulder. "I'm going to see if there's a sloth."

Ellen Bowman looked around at the beach, and the trees. "You think she's all right?"

"Honey, there's nobody here for miles," Mike said.

"What about snakes?"

"Oh, for God's sake," Mike Bowman said. "There's no snakes on a beach."

"Well, there might be. . . ."

"Honey," he said firmly. "Snakes are cold-blooded. They're reptiles. They can't control their body temperature. It's ninety degrees on that sand. If a snake came out, it'd be cooked. Believe me. There's no snakes on the beach." He watched his daughter scampering down the beach, a dark spot on the white sand. "Let her go. Let her have a good time."

He put his arm around his wife's waist.

Tina ran until she was exhausted, and then she threw herself down on the sand and gleefully rolled to the water's edge. The ocean was warm, and there was hardly any surf at all. She sat for a while, catching her breath, and then she looked back toward her parents and the car, to see how far she had come.

Her mother waved, beckoning her to return. Tina waved back cheerfully, pretending she didn't understand. Tina didn't want to put sunscreen on. And she didn't want to go back and hear her mother talk about losing weight. She wanted to stay right here, and maybe see a sloth.

Tina had seen a sloth two days earlier at the zoo in San José. It looked like a Muppets character, and it seemed harmless. In any case, it couldn't move fast; she could easily outrun it.

Now her mother was calling to her, and Tina decided to move out of the sun, back from the water, to the shade of the palm trees. In this part of the beach, the palm trees overhung a gnarled tangle of mangrove roots, which blocked any attempt to penetrate inland. Tina sat in the sand and kicked the dried mangrove leaves. She noticed many bird tracks in the sand. Costa Rica was famous for its birds. The guidebooks said there were three times as many birds in Costa Rica as in all of America and Canada.

In the sand, some of the three-toed bird tracks were small, and so faint they could hardly be seen. Other tracks were large, and cut deeper in the sand. Tina was looking idly at the tracks when she heard a chirping, followed by a rustling in the mangrove thicket.

Did sloths make a chirping sound? Tina didn't think so, but she wasn't sure. The chirping was probably some ocean bird. She waited quietly, not moving, hearing the rustling again, and finally she saw the source of the sounds. A few yards away, a lizard emerged from the mangrove roots and peered at her.

Tina held her breath. A new animal for her list! The lizard stood up on its hind legs, balancing on its thick tail, and stared at her. Standing like that, it was almost a foot tall, dark green with brown stripes along its back. Its tiny front legs ended in little lizard fingers that wiggled in the air. The lizard cocked its head as it looked at her.

Tina thought it was cute. Sort of like a big salamander. She raised her hand and wiggled her fingers back.

The lizard wasn't frightened. It came toward her, walking upright on its hind legs. It was hardly bigger than a chicken, and like a chicken it bobbed its head as it walked. Tina thought it would make a wonderful pet.

She noticed that the lizard left three-toed tracks that looked exactly like bird tracks. The lizard came closer to Tina. She kept her body still, not wanting to frighten the little animal. She was amazed that it would come so close, but she remembered that this was a national park. All the animals in the park would know that they were protected. This lizard was probably tame. Maybe it even expected her to give it some food. Unfortunately she didn't have any. Slowly, Tina extended her hand, palm open, to show she didn't have any food.

The lizard paused, cocked his head, and chirped.

"Sorry," Tina said. "I just don't have anything."

And then, without warning, the lizard jumped up onto her outstretched hand. Tina could feel its little toes pinching the skin of her palm, and she felt the surprising weight of the animal's body pressing her arm down.

And then the lizard scrambled up her arm, toward her face.

* * *

"I just wish I could see her," Ellen Bowman said, squinting in the sunlight. "That's all. Just see her."

"I'm sure she's fine," Mike said, picking through the box lunch packed by the hotel. There was unappetizing grilled chicken, and some kind of a meat-filled pastry. Not that Ellen would eat any of it.

"You don't think she'd leave the beach?" Ellen said.

"No, hon, I don't."

"I feel so isolated here," Ellen said.

"I thought that's what you wanted," Mike Bowman said.

"I did."

"Well, then, what's the problem?"

"I just wish I could see her, is all," Ellen said.

Then, from down the beach, carried by the wind, they heard their daughter's voice. She was screaming.

PUNTARENAS

"I think she is quite comfortable now," Dr. Cruz said, lowering the plastic flap of the oxygen tent around Tina as she slept. Mike Bowman sat beside the bed, close to his daughter. Mike thought Dr. Cruz was probably pretty capable; he spoke excellent English, the result of training at medical centers in London and Baltimore. Dr. Cruz radiated competence, and the Clínica Santa María, the modern hospital in Puntarenas, was spotless and efficient.

But, even so, Mike Bowman felt nervous. There was no getting around the fact that his only daughter was desperately ill, and they were far from home.

When Mike had first reached Tina, she was screaming hysterically. Her whole left arm was bloody, covered with a profusion of small bites, each the size of a thumbprint. And there were flecks of sticky foam on her arm, like a foamy saliva.

He carried her back down the beach. Almost immediately her

arm began to redden and swell. Mike would not soon forget the frantic drive back to civilization, the four-wheel-drive Land Rover slipping and sliding up the muddy track into the hills, while his daughter screamed in fear and pain, and her arm grew more bloated and red. Long before they reached the park boundaries, the swelling had spread to her neck, and then Tina began to have trouble breathing. . . .

"She'll be all right now?" Ellen said, staring through the plastic oxygen tent.

"I believe so," Dr. Cruz said. "I have given her another dose of steroids, and her breathing is much easier. And you can see the edema in her arm is greatly reduced."

Mike Bowman said, "About those bites . . ."

"We have no identification yet," the doctor said. "I myself haven't seen bites like that before. But you'll notice they are disappearing. It's already quite difficult to make them out. Fortunately I have taken photographs for reference. And I have washed her arm to collect some samples of the sticky saliva—one for analysis here, a second to send to the labs in San José, and the third we will keep frozen in case it is needed. Do you have the picture she made?"

"Yes," Mike Bowman said. He handed the doctor the sketch that Tina had drawn, in response to questions from the admitting officials.

"This is the animal that bit her?" Dr. Cruz said, looking at the picture.

"Yes," Mike Bowman said. "She said it was a green lizard, the size of a chicken or a crow."

"I don't know of such a lizard," the doctor said. "She has drawn it standing on its hind legs. . . ."

"That's right," Mike Bowman said. "She said it walked on its hind legs."

Dr. Cruz frowned. He stared at the picture a while longer. "I am not an expert. I've asked for Dr. Guitierrez to visit us here. He is a senior researcher at the Reserva Biológica de Carara, which is across the bay. Perhaps he can identify the animal for us."

"Isn't there someone from Cabo Blanco?" Bowman asked. "That's where she was bitten."

"Unfortunately not," Dr. Cruz said. "Cabo Blanco has no permanent staff, and no researcher has worked there for some time. You were probably the first people to walk on that beach in several months. But I am sure you will find Dr. Guitierrez to be knowledgeable."

Dr. Guitierrez turned out to be a bearded man wearing khaki shorts and shirt. The surprise was that he was American. He was introduced to the Bowmans, saying in a soft Southern accent, "Mr. and Mrs. Bowman, how you doing, nice to meet you," and then explaining that he was a field biologist from Yale who had worked in Costa Rica for the last five years. Marty Guitierrez examined Tina thoroughly, lifting her arm gently, peering closely at each of the bites with a penlight, then measuring them with a small pocket ruler. After a while, Guitierrez stepped away, nodding to himself as if he had understood something. He then inspected the Polaroids, and asked several questions about the saliva, which Cruz told him was still being tested in the lab.

Finally he turned to Mike Bowman and his wife, waiting tensely. "I think Tina's going to be fine. I just want to be clear about a few details," he said, making notes in a precise hand. "Your daughter says she was bitten by a green lizard, approximately one foot high, which walked upright onto the beach from the mangrove swamp?"

"That's right, yes."

"And the lizard made some kind of a vocalization?"

"Tina said it chirped, or squeaked."

"Like a mouse, would you say?"

"Yes."

"Well, then," Dr. Guitierrez said, "I know this lizard." He explained that, of the six thousand species of lizards in the world, no more than a dozen species walked upright. Of those species, only four were found in Latin America. And judging by the coloration, the lizard could be only one of the four. "I am sure this lizard was a *Basiliscus amoratus*, a striped basilisk lizard, found here in Costa Rica and also in Honduras. Standing on their hind legs, they are sometimes as tall as a foot."

"Are they poisonous?"

"No, Mrs. Bowman. Not at all." Guitierrez explained that the swelling in Tina's arm was an allergic reaction. "According to the literature, fourteen percent of people are strongly allergic to reptiles," he said, "and your daughter seems to be one of them."

"She was screaming, she said it was so painful."

"Probably it was," Guitierrez said. "Reptile saliva contains serotonin, which causes tremendous pain." He turned to Cruz. "Her blood pressure came down with antihistamines?"

"Yes," Cruz said. "Promptly."

"Serotonin," Guitierrez said. "No question."

Still, Ellen Bowman remained uneasy. "But why would a lizard bite her in the first place?"

"Lizard bites are very common," Guitierrez said. "Animal handlers in zoos get bitten all the time. And just the other day I heard that a lizard had bitten an infant in her crib in Amaloya, about sixty miles from where you were. So bites do occur. I'm not sure why your daughter had so many bites. What was she doing at the time?"

"Nothing. She said she was sitting pretty still, because she didn't want to frighten it away."

"Sitting pretty still," Guitierrez said, frowning. He shook his head. "Well. I don't think we can say exactly what happened. Wild animals are unpredictable."

"And what about the foamy saliva on her arm?" Ellen said. "I keep thinking about rabies. . . ."

"No, no," Dr. Guitierrez said. "A reptile can't carry rabies, Mrs. Bowman. Your daughter has suffered an allergic reaction to the bite of a basilisk lizard. Nothing more serious."

Mike Bowman then showed Guitierrez the picture that Tina had drawn. Guitierrez nodded. "I would accept this as a picture of a basilisk lizard," he said. "A few details are wrong, of course. The neck is much too long, and she has drawn the hind legs with only three toes instead of five. The tail is too thick, and raised too high. But otherwise this is a perfectly serviceable lizard of the kind we are talking about."

"But Tina specifically said the neck was long," Ellen Bowman insisted. "And she said there were three toes on the foot."

"Tina's pretty observant," Mike Bowman said.

"I'm sure she is," Guitierrez said, smiling. "But I still think your daughter was bitten by a common *basilisk amoratus*, and had a severe herpetological reaction. Normal time course with medication is twelve hours. She should be just fine in the morning."

In the modern laboratory in the basement of the Clínica Santa María, word was received that Dr. Guitierrez had identified the animal that had bitten the American child as a harmless basilisk lizard. Immediately the analysis of the saliva was halted, even though a preliminary fractionation showed several extremely high molecular weight proteins of unknown biological activity. But the night technician was busy, and he placed the saliva samples on the holding shelf of the refrigerator.

The next morning, the day clerk checked the holding shelf against the names of discharged patients. Seeing that BOWMAN, CHRISTINA L. was scheduled for discharge that morning, the clerk threw out the saliva samples. At the last moment, he noticed that one sample had the red tag which meant that it was to be forwarded to the university lab in San José. He retrieved the test tube from the wastebasket, and sent it on its way.

"Go on. Say thank you to Dr. Cruz," Ellen Bowman said, and pushed Tina forward.

"Thank you, Dr. Cruz," Tina said. "I feel much better now." She reached up and shook the doctor's hand. Then she said, "You have a different shirt."

For a moment Dr. Cruz looked perplexed; then he smiled. "That's right, Tina. When I work all night at the hospital, in the morning I change my shirt."

"But not your tie?"

"No. Just my shirt."

Ellen Bowman said, "Mike told you she's observant."

"She certainly is." Dr. Cruz smiled and shook the little girl's hand gravely. "Enjoy the rest of your holiday in Costa Rica, Tina."

"I will."

The Bowman family had started to leave when Dr. Cruz said, "Oh, Tina, do you remember the lizard that bit you?"

"Uh-huh."

"You remember its feet?"

"Uh-huh."

"Did it have any toes?"

"Yes."

"How many toes did it have?"

"Three," she said.

"How do you know that?"

"Because I looked," she said. "Anyway, all the birds on the beach made marks in the sand with three toes, like this." She held up her hand, middle three fingers spread wide. "And the lizard made those kind of marks in the sand, too."

"The lizard made marks like a bird?"

"Uh-huh," Tina said. "He walked like a bird, too. He jerked his head like this, up and down." She took a few steps, bobbing her head.

After the Bowmans had departed, Dr. Cruz decided to report this conversation to Guitierrez, at the biological station.

"I must admit the girl's story is puzzling," Guitierrez said. "I have been doing some checking myself. I am no longer certain she was bitten by a basilisk. Not certain at all."

"Then what could it be?"

"Well," Guitierrez said, "let's not speculate prematurely. By the way, have you heard of any other lizard bites at the hospital?"

"No, why?"

"Let me know, my friend, if you do."

THE BEACH

Marty Guitierrez sat on the beach and watched the afternoon sun fall lower in the sky, until it sparkled harshly on the water of the bay, and its rays reached beneath the palm trees, to where he sat among the mangroves, on the beach of Cabo Blanco. As best he could determine, he was sitting near the spot where the American girl had been, two days before.

Although it was true enough, as he had told the Bowmans, that lizard bites were common, Guitierrez had never heard of a basilisk lizard biting anyone. And he had certainly never heard of anyone being hospitalized for a lizard bite. Then, too, the bite radius on Tina's arm appeared slightly too large for a basilisk. When he got back to the Carara station, he had checked the small research library there, but found no reference to basilisk lizard bites. Next he checked International BioSciences Services, a computer database in America. But he found no references to basilisk bites, or hospitalization for lizard bites.

He then called the medical officer in Amaloya, who confirmed that a nine-day-old infant, sleeping in its crib, had been bitten on the foot by an animal the grandmother—the only person actually to see it—claimed was a lizard. Subsequently the foot had become swollen and the infant had nearly died. The grandmother described the lizard as green with brown stripes. It had bitten the child several times before the woman frightened it away.

"Strange," Guitierrez had said.

"No, like all the others," the medical officer replied, adding that he had heard of other biting incidents: A child in Vásquez, the next village up the coast, had been bitten while sleeping. And another in Puerta Sotrero. All these incidents had occurred in the last two months. All had involved sleeping children and infants.

Such a new and distinctive pattern led Guitierrez to suspect the presence of a previously unknown species of lizard. This was particularly likely to happen in Costa Rica. Only seventy-five miles wide at its narrowest point, the country was smaller than the state of Maine. Yet, within its limited space, Costa Rica had a remarkable diversity of biological habitats: seacoasts on both the Atlantic and the Pacific; four separate mountain ranges, including twelve-thousand-foot peaks and active volcanoes; rain forests, cloud forests, temperate zones, swampy marshes, and arid deserts. Such ecological diversity sustained an astonishing diversity of plant and animal life. Costa Rica had three times as many species of birds as all of North America. More than a thousand species of orchids. More than five thousand species of insects.

New species were being discovered all the time at a pace that had increased in recent years, for a sad reason. Costa Rica was becoming deforested, and as jungle species lost their habitats, they moved to other areas, and sometimes changed behavior as well.

So a new species was perfectly possible. But along with the excitement of a new species was the worrisome possibility of new diseases. Lizards carried viral diseases, including several that could be transmitted to man. The most serious was central saurian encephalitis, or CSE, which caused a form of sleeping sickness in human beings and horses. Guitierrez felt it was important to find this new lizard, if only to test it for disease.

Sitting on the beach, he watched the sun drop lower, and sighed. Perhaps Tina Bowman had seen a new animal, and perhaps not. Certainly Guitierrez had not. Earlier that morning, he had taken the air pistol, loaded the clip with ligamine darts, and set out for the beach with high hopes. But the day was wasted. Soon he would have to begin the drive back up the hill from the beach; he did not want to drive that road in darkness.

Guitierrez got to his feet and started back up the beach. Farther along, he saw the dark shape of a howler monkey, ambling along the edge of the mangrove swamp. Guitierrez moved away, stepping out toward the water. If there was one howler, there would probably be others in the trees overhead, and howlers tended to urinate on intruders.

But this particular howler monkey seemed to be alone, and walking slowly, and pausing frequently to sit on its haunches. The monkey had something in its mouth. As Guitierrez came closer, he saw it was eating a lizard. The tail and the hind legs drooped from the monkey's jaws. Even from a distance, Guitierrez could see the brown stripes against the green.

Guitierrez dropped to the ground and aimed the pistol. The howler monkey, accustomed to living in a protected reserve, stared curiously. He did not run away, even when the first dart whined harmlessly past him. When the second dart struck deep in the thigh, the howler shrieked in anger and surprise, dropping the remains of its meal as it fled into the jungle.

Guitierrez got to his feet and walked forward. He wasn't worried about the monkey; the tranquilizer dose was too small to give it anything but a few minutes of dizziness. Already he was thinking of what to do with his new find. Guitierrez himself would write the preliminary report, but the remains would have to be sent back to the United States for final positive identification, of course. To whom should he send it? The acknowledged expert was Edward H. Simpson, emeritus professor of zoology at Columbia University, in New York. An elegant older man with swept-back white hair, Simpson was the world's leading authority on lizard taxonomy. Probably, Marty thought, he would send his lizard to Dr. Simpson.

NEW YORK

Dr. Richard Stone, head of the Tropical Diseases Laboratory of Columbia University Medical Center, often remarked that the name conjured up a grander place than it actually was. In the early twentieth century, when the laboratory occupied the entire fourth floor of the Biomedical Research Building, crews of technicians worked to eliminate the scourges of yellow fever, malaria, and cholera. But medical successes—and research laboratories in Nairobi and São Paulo—had left the TDL a much less important place than it once was. Now a fraction of its former size, it employed only two full-time technicians, and they were primarily concerned with diagnosing illnesses of New Yorkers who had traveled abroad. The lab's comfortable routine was unprepared for what it received that morning.

"Oh, very nice," the technician in the Tropical Diseases Laboratory said, as she read the customs label. "Partially masticated fragment of unidentified Costa Rican lizard." She wrinkled her nose. "This one's all yours, Dr. Stone."

Richard Stone crossed the lab to inspect the new arrival. "Is this the material from Ed Simpson's lab?"

"Yes," she said. "But I don't know why they'd send a lizard to *us*."

"His secretary called," Stone said. "Simpson's on a field trip in Borneo for the summer, and because there's a question of communicable disease with this lizard, she asked our lab to take a look at it. Let's see what we've got."

The white plastic cylinder was the size of a half-gallon milk container. It had locking metal latches and a screw top. It was labeled "International Biological Specimen Container" and plastered with stickers and warnings in four languages. The warnings were in-

23

tended to keep the cylinder from being opened by suspicious customs officials.

Apparently the warnings had worked; as Richard Stone swung the big light over, he could see the seals were still intact. Stone turned on the air handlers and pulled on plastic gloves and a face mask. After all, the lab had recently identified specimens contaminated with Venezuelan equine fever, Japanese B encephalitis, Kyasanur Forest virus, Langat virus, and Mayaro. Then he unscrewed the top.

There was the hiss of escaping gas, and white smoke boiled out. The cylinder turned frosty cold. Inside he found a plastic zip-lock sandwich bag, containing something green. Stone spread a surgical drape on the table and shook out the contents of the bag. A piece of frozen flesh struck the table with a dull thud.

"Huh," the technician said. "Looks eaten."

"Yes, it does," Stone said. "What do they want with us?"

The technician consulted the enclosed documents. "Lizard is biting local children. They have a question about identification of the species, and a concern about diseases transmitted from the bite." She produced a child's picture of a lizard, signed TINA at the top. "One of the kids drew a picture of the lizard."

Stone glanced at the picture. "Obviously we can't verify the species," Stone said. "But we can check diseases easily enough, if we can get any blood out of this fragment. What are they calling this animal?"

" '*Basiliscus amoratus* with three-toed genetic anomaly,' " she said, reading.

"Okay," Stone said. "Let's get started. While you're waiting for it to thaw, do an X ray and take Polaroids for the record. Once we have blood, start running antibody sets until we get some matches. Let me know if there's a problem."

Before lunchtime, the lab had its answer: the lizard blood showed no significant reactivity to any viral or bacterial antigen. They had run toxicity profiles as well, and they had found only one positive match: the blood was mildly reactive to the venom of the Indian king cobra. But such cross-reactivity was common among reptile species, and Dr. Stone did not think it noteworthy to include in the fax his technician sent to Dr. Martin Guitierrez that same evening.

There was never any question about identifying the lizard; that would await the return of Dr. Simpson. He was not due back for several weeks, and his secretary asked if the TDL would please store the lizard fragment in the meantime. Dr. Stone put it back in the zip-lock bag and stuck it in the freezer.

Martin Guitierrez read the fax from the Columbia Medical Center/ Tropical Diseases Laboratory. It was brief:

SUBJECT: *Basiliscus amoratus* with genetic anomaly
                  (forwarded from Dr. Simpson's office)

MATERIALS: posterior segment, ? partially eaten animal

PROCEDURES PERFORMED: X ray, microscopic, immunological RTX for viral, parasitic, bacterial disease.

FINDINGS: No histologic or immunologic evidence for any communicable disease in man in this *Basiliscus amoratus* sample.

(signed)
Richard A. Stone, M.D., director

Guitierrez made two assumptions based on the memo. First, that his identification of the lizard as a basilisk had been confirmed by scientists at Columbia University. And second, that the absence of communicable disease meant the recent episodes of sporadic lizard bites implied no serious health hazards for Costa Rica. On the contrary, he felt his original views were correct: that a lizard species had been driven from the forest into a new habitat, and was coming into contact with village people. Guitierrez was certain that in a few more weeks the lizards would settle down and the biting episodes would end.

The tropical rain fell in great drenching sheets, hammering the corrugated roof of the clinic in Bahía Anasco. It was nearly midnight; power had been lost in the storm, and the midwife Elena Morales was working by flashlight when she heard a squeaking, chirping sound. Thinking that it was a rat, she quickly put a compress on the forehead of the mother and went into the next room to check on the newborn baby. As her hand touched the doorknob, she heard the chirping again, and she relaxed. Evidently it was just a bird, flying in the window to get out of the rain. Costa Ricans said that when a bird came to visit a newborn child, it brought good luck.

Elena opened the door. The infant lay in a wicker bassinet, swaddled in a light blanket, only its face exposed. Around the rim of the bassinet, three dark green lizards crouched like gargoyles. When they saw Elena, they cocked their heads and stared curiously at her, but did not flee. In the light of her flashlight Elena saw the blood dripping from their snouts. Softly chirping, one lizard bent down and, with a quick shake of its head, tore a ragged chunk of flesh from the baby.

Elena rushed forward, screaming, and the lizards fled into the darkness. But long before she reached the bassinet, she could see what had happened to the infant's face, and she knew the child must be dead. The lizards scattered into the rainy night, chirping and squealing, leaving behind only bloody three-toed tracks, like birds.

THE SHAPE OF THE DATA

Later, when she was calmer, Elena Morales decided not to report the lizard attack. Despite the horror she had seen, she began to worry that she might be criticized for leaving the baby unguarded. So she told the mother that the baby had asphyxiated, and she reported the death on the forms she sent to San José as SIDS: sudden infant death syndrome. This was a syndrome of unexplained death among very young children; it was unremarkable, and her report went unchallenged.

The university lab in San José that analyzed the saliva sample from Tina Bowman's arm made several remarkable discoveries. There was, as expected, a great deal of serotonin. But among the salivary proteins was a real monster: molecular mass of 1,980,000, one of the largest proteins known. Biological activity was still under study, but it seemed to be a neurotoxic poison related to cobra venom, although more primitive in structure.

The lab also detected trace quantities of the gamma-amino methionine hydrolase. Because this enzyme was a marker for genetic engineering, and not found in wild animals, technicians assumed it was a lab contaminant and did not report it when they called Dr. Cruz, the referring physician in Puntarenas.

The lizard fragment rested in the freezer at Columbia University, awaiting the return of Dr. Simpson, who was not expected for at least a month. And so things might have remained, had not a technician named Alice Levin walked into the Tropical Diseases Laboratory, seen Tina Bowman's picture, and said, "Oh, whose kid drew the dinosaur?"

"What?" Richard Stone said, turning slowly toward her.

"The dinosaur. Isn't that what it is? My kid draws them all the time."

"This is a lizard," Stone said. "From Costa Rica. Some girl down there drew a picture of it."

"No," Alice Levin said, shaking her head. "Look at it. It's very clear. Big head, long neck, stands on its hind legs, thick tail. It's a dinosaur."

"It can't be. It was only a foot tall."

"So? There were little dinosaurs back then," Alice said. "Believe me, I know. I have two boys, I'm an expert. The smallest dinosaurs were under a foot. Teenysaurus or something, I don't know. Those names are impossible. You'll never learn those names if you're over the age of ten."

"You don't understand," Richard Stone said. "This is a picture of a contemporary animal. They sent us a fragment of the animal. It's in the freezer now." Stone went and got it, and shook it out of the baggie.

Alice Levin looked at the frozen piece of leg and tail, and shrugged. She didn't touch it. "I don't know," she said. "But that looks like a dinosaur to me."

Stone shook his head. "Impossible."

"Why?" Alice Levin said. "It could be a leftover or a remnant or whatever they call them."

Stone continued to shake his head. Alice was uninformed; she was just a technician who worked in the bacteriology lab down the hall. And she had an active imagination. Stone remembered the time when she thought she was being followed by one of the surgical orderlies. . . .

"You know," Alice Levin said, "if this *is* a dinosaur, Richard, it could be a big deal."

"It's not a dinosaur."

"Has anybody checked it?"

"No," Stone said.

"Well, take it to the Museum of Natural History or something," Alice Levin said. "You really should."

"I'd be embarrassed."

"You want me to do it for you?" she said.

"No," Richard Stone said. "I don't."

"You're not going to do anything?"

"Nothing at all." He put the baggie back in the freezer and slammed the door. "It's not a dinosaur, it's a lizard. And whatever it is, it can wait until Dr. Simpson gets back from Borneo to identify it. That's final, Alice. This lizard's not going anywhere."

SECOND ITERATION

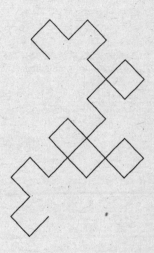

"With subsequent drawings of the fractal curve, sudden changes may appear."

IAN MALCOLM

THE SHORE OF THE INLAND SEA

Alan Grant crouched down, his nose inches from the ground. The temperature was over a hundred degrees. His knees ached, despite the rug-layer's pads he wore. His lungs burned from the harsh alkaline dust. Sweat dripped off his forehead onto the ground. But Grant was oblivious to the discomfort. His entire attention was focused on the six-inch square of earth in front of him.

Working patiently with a dental pick and an artist's camel brush, he exposed the tiny L-shaped fragment of jawbone. It was only an inch long, and no thicker than his little finger. The teeth were a row of small points, and had the characteristic medial angling. Bits of bone flaked away as he dug. Grant paused for a moment to paint the bone with rubber cement before continuing to expose it. There was no question that this was the jawbone from an infant carnivorous dinosaur. Its owner had died seventy-nine million years ago, at the age of about two months. With any luck, Grant might find the rest of the skeleton as well. If so, it would be the first complete skeleton of a baby carnivore—

"Hey, Alan!"

Alan Grant looked up, blinking in the sunlight. He pulled down his sunglasses, and wiped his forehead with the back of his arm.

He was crouched on an eroded hillside in the badlands outside Snakewater, Montana. Beneath the great blue bowl of sky, blunted hills, exposed outcroppings of crumbling limestone, stretched for miles in every direction. There was not a tree, or a bush. Nothing but barren rock, hot sun, and whining wind.

Visitors found the badlands depressingly bleak, but when Grant looked at this landscape, he saw something else entirely. This barren land was what remained of another, very different world, which had vanished eighty million years ago. In his mind's eye, Grant saw him-

31

self back in the warm, swampy bayou that formed the shoreline of a great inland sea. This inland sea was a thousand miles wide, extending all the way from the newly upthrust Rocky Mountains to the sharp, craggy peaks of the Appalachians. All of the American West was under water.

At that time, there were thin clouds in the sky overhead, darkened by the smoke of nearby volcanoes. The atmosphere was denser, richer in carbon dioxide. Plants grew rapidly along the shoreline. There were no fish in these waters, but there were clams and snails. Pterosaurs swooped down to scoop algae from the surface. A few carnivorous dinosaurs prowled the swampy shores of the lake, moving among the palm trees. And offshore was a small island, about two acres in size. Ringed with dense vegetation, this island formed a protected sanctuary where herds of herbivorous duckbilled dinosaurs laid their eggs in communal nests, and raised their squeaking young.

Over the millions of years that followed, the pale green alkaline lake grew shallower, and finally vanished. The exposed land buckled and cracked under the heat. And the offshore island with its dinosaur eggs became the eroded hillside in northern Montana which Alan Grant was now excavating.

"Hey, *Alan!*"

He stood, a barrel-chested, bearded man of forty. He heard the chugging of the portable generator, and the distant clatter of the jackhammer cutting into the dense rock on the next hill. He saw the kids working around the jackhammer, moving away the big pieces of rock after checking them for fossils. At the foot of the hill, he saw the six tipis of his camp, the flapping mess tent, and the trailer that served as their field laboratory. And he saw Ellie waving to him, from the shadow of the field laboratory.

"Visitor!" she called, and pointed to the east.

Grant saw the cloud of dust, and the blue Ford sedan bouncing over the rutted road toward them. He glanced at his watch: right on time. On the other hill, the kids looked up with interest. They didn't get many visitors in Snakewater, and there had been a lot of speculation about what a lawyer from the Environmental Protection Agency would want to see Alan Grant about.

But Grant knew that paleontology, the study of extinct life, had in recent years taken on an unexpected relevance to the modern world. The modern world was changing fast, and urgent questions about the weather, deforestation, global warming, or the ozone layer often seemed answerable, at least in part, with information from the past. Information that paleontologists could provide. He had been called as an expert witness twice in the past few years.

Grant started down the hill to meet the car.

The visitor coughed in the white dust as he slammed the car door. "Bob Morris, EPA," he said, extending his hand. "I'm with the San Francisco office."

Grant introduced himself and said, "You look hot. Want a beer?"

"Jesus, yeah." Morris was in his late twenties, wearing a tie, and pants from a business suit. He carried a briefcase. His wing-tip shoes crunched on the rocks as they walked toward the trailer.

"When I first came over the hill, I thought this was an Indian reservation," Morris said, pointing to the tipis.

"No," Grant said. "Just the best way to live out here." Grant explained that in 1978, the first year of the excavations, they had come out in North Slope octahedral tents, the most advanced available. But the tents always blew over in the wind. They tried other kinds of tents, with the same result. Finally they started putting up tipis, which were larger inside, more comfortable, and more stable in wind. "These're Blackfoot tipis, built around four poles," Grant said. "Sioux tipis are built around three. But this used to be Blackfoot territory, so we thought . . ."

"Uh-huh," Morris said. "Very fitting." He squinted at the desolate landscape and shook his head. "How long you been out here?"

"About sixty cases," Grant said. When Morris looked surprised, he explained, "We measure time in beer. We start in June with a hundred cases. We've gone through about sixty so far."

"Sixty-three, to be exact," Ellie Sattler said, as they reached the trailer. Grant was amused to see Morris gaping at her. Ellie was wearing cut-off jeans and a workshirt tied at her midriff. She was twenty-four and darkly tanned. Her blond hair was pulled back.

"Ellie keeps us going," Grant said, introducing her. "She's very good at what she does."

"What does she do?" Morris asked.

"Paleobotany," Ellie said. "And I also do the standard field preps." She opened the door and they went inside.

The air conditioning in the trailer only brought the temperature down to eighty-five degrees, but it seemed cool after the midday heat. The trailer had a series of long wooden tables, with tiny bone specimens neatly laid out, tagged and labeled. Farther along were ceramic dishes and crocks. There was a strong odor of vinegar.

Morris glanced at the bones. "I thought dinosaurs were big," he said.

"They were," Ellie said. "But everything you see here comes from babies. Snakewater is important primarily because of the number of dinosaur nesting sites here. Until we started this work, there were hardly any infant dinosaurs known. Only one nest had ever been found, in the Gobi Desert. We've discovered a dozen different hadrosaur nests, complete with eggs and bones of infants."

While Grant went to the refrigerator, she showed Morris the acetic acid baths, which were used to dissolve away the limestone from the delicate bones.

"They look like chicken bones," Morris said, peering into the ceramic dishes.

"Yes," she said. "They're very bird-like."

"And what about those?" Morris said, pointing through the trailer window to piles of large bones outside, wrapped in heavy plastic.

"Rejects," Ellie said. "Bones too fragmentary when we took them out of the ground. In the old days we'd just discard them, but nowadays we send them for genetic testing."

"Genetic testing?" Morris said.

"Here you go," Grant said, thrusting a beer into his hand. He gave another to Ellie. She chugged hers, throwing her long neck back. Morris stared.

"We're pretty informal here," Grant said. "Want to step into my office?"

"Sure," Morris said. Grant led him to the end of the trailer, where there was a torn couch, a sagging chair, and a battered end table. Grant dropped onto the couch, which creaked and exhaled a cloud of chalky dust. He leaned back, thumped his boots up on the end table, and gestured for Morris to sit in the chair. "Make yourself comfortable."

Grant was a professor of paleontology at the University of Denver, and one of the foremost researchers in his field, but he had never been comfortable with social niceties. He saw himself as an outdoor man, and he knew that all the important work in paleontology was done outdoors, with your hands. Grant had little patience for the academics, for the museum curators, for what he called Teacup Dinosaur Hunters. And he took some pains to distance himself in dress and behavior from the Teacup Dinosaur Hunters, even delivering his lectures in jeans and sneakers.

Grant watched as Morris primly brushed off the seat of the chair before he sat down. Morris opened his briefcase, rummaged through his papers, and glanced back at Ellie, who was lifting bones with tweezers from the acid bath at the other end of the trailer, paying no attention to them. "You're probably wondering why I'm here."

Grant nodded. "It's a long way to come, Mr. Morris."

"Well," Morris said, "to get right to the point, the EPA is concerned about the activities of the Hammond Foundation. You receive some funding from them."

"Thirty thousand dollars a year," Grant said, nodding. "For the last five years."

"What do you know about the foundation?" Morris said.

Grant shrugged. "The Hammond Foundation is a respected source of academic grants. They fund research all over the world, including several dinosaur researchers. I know they support Bob Kerry out of the Tyrrell in Alberta, and John Weller in Alaska. Probably more."

"Do you know why the Hammond Foundation supports so much dinosaur research?" Morris asked.

"Of course. It's because old John Hammond is a dinosaur nut."

"You've met Hammond?"

Grant shrugged. "Once or twice. He comes here for brief visits. He's quite elderly, you know. And eccentric, the way rich people sometimes are. But always very enthusiastic. Why?"

"Well," Morris said, "the Hammond Foundation is actually a rather mysterious organization." He pulled out a Xeroxed world map, marked with red dots, and passed it to Grant. "These are the digs the foundation financed last year. Notice anything odd about them? Montana, Alaska, Canada, Sweden . . . They're all sites in the north. There's nothing below the forty-fifth parallel." Morris pulled out more maps. "It's the same, year after year. Dinosaur projects to the south, in Utah or Colorado or Mexico, never get funded. The Hammond Foundation only supports cold-weather digs. We'd like to know why."

Grant shuffled through the maps quickly. If it was true that the foundation only supported cold-weather digs, then it was strange behavior, because some of the best dinosaur researchers were working in hot climates, and—

"And there are other puzzles," Morris said. "For example, what is the relationship of dinosaurs to amber?"

"Amber?"

"Yes. It's the hard yellow resin of dried tree sap—"

"I know what it is," Grant said. "But why are you asking?"

"Because," Morris said, "over the last five years, Hammond has purchased enormous quantities of amber in America, Europe, and Asia, including many pieces of museum-quality jewelry. The foundation has spent seventeen million dollars on amber. They now possess the largest privately held stock of this material in the world."

"I don't get it," Grant said.

"Neither does anybody else," Morris said. "As far as we can tell, it doesn't make any sense at all. Amber is easily synthesized. It has no commercial or defense value. There's no reason to stockpile it. But Hammond has done just that, over many years."

"Amber," Grant said, shaking his head.

"And what about his island in Costa Rica?" Morris continued. "Ten years ago, the Hammond Foundation leased an island from the government of Costa Rica. Supposedly to set up a biological preserve."

"I don't know anything about that," Grant said, frowning.

"I haven't been able to find out much," Morris said. "The island is a hundred miles off the west coast. It's very rugged, and it's in an area of ocean where the combinations of wind and current make it almost perpetually covered in fog. They used to call it Cloud Island. Isla Nublar. Apparently the Costa Ricans were amazed that anybody would want it." Morris searched in his briefcase. "The reason I mention it," he said, "is that, according to the records, you were paid a consultant's fee in connection with this island."

"I was?" Grant said.

Morris passed a sheet of paper to Grant. It was the Xerox of a check issued in March 1984 from InGen Inc., Farallon Road, Palo Alto, California. Made out to Alan Grant in the amount of twelve thousand dollars. At the lower corner, the check was marked CON-SULTANT SERVICES/COSTA RICA/JUVENILE HYPERSPACE.

"Oh, sure," Grant said. "I remember that. It was weird as hell, but I remember it. And it didn't have anything to do with an island."

* * *

Alan Grant had found the first clutch of dinosaur eggs in Montana in 1979, and many more in the next two years, but he hadn't gotten around to publishing his findings until 1983. His paper, with its report of a herd of ten thousand duckbilled dinosaurs living along the shore of a vast inland sea, building communal nests of eggs in the mud, raising their infant dinosaurs in the herd, made Grant a celebrity overnight. The notion of maternal instincts in giant dinosaurs—and the drawings of cute babies poking their snouts out of the eggs—had appeal around the world. Grant was besieged with requests for interviews, lectures, books. Characteristically, he turned them all down, wanting only to continue his excavations. But it was during those frantic days of the mid-1980s that he was approached by the InGen corporation with a request for consulting services.

"Had you heard of InGen before?" Morris asked.

"No."

"How did they contact you?"

"Telephone call. It was a man named Gennaro or Gennino, something like that."

Morris nodded. "Donald Gennaro," he said. "He's the legal counsel for InGen."

"Anyway, he wanted to know about eating habits of dinosaurs. And he offered me a fee to draw up a paper for him." Grant drank his beer, set the can on the floor. "Gennaro was particularly interested in young dinosaurs. Infants and juveniles. What they ate. I guess he thought I would know about that."

"Did you?"

"Not really, no. I told him that. We had found lots of skeletal material, but we had very little dietary data. But Gennaro said he knew we hadn't published everything, and he wanted whatever we had. And he offered a very large fee. Fifty thousand dollars."

Morris took out a tape recorder and set it on the endtable. "You mind?"

"No, go ahead."

"So Gennaro telephoned you in 1984. What happened then?"

"Well," Grant said. "You see our operation here. Fifty thousand would support two full summers of digging. I told him I'd do what I could."

"So you agreed to prepare a paper for him."

"Yes."

"On the dietary habits of juvenile dinosaurs?"

"Yes."

"You met Gennaro?"

"No. Just on the phone."

"Did Gennaro say why he wanted this information?"

"Yes," Grant said. "He was planning a museum for children, and he wanted to feature baby dinosaurs. He said he was hiring a number of academic consultants, and named them. There were paleontologists like me, and a mathematician from Texas named Ian Malcolm, and a couple of ecologists. A systems analyst. Good group."

Morris nodded, making notes. "So you accepted the consultancy?"

"Yes. I agreed to send him a summary of our work: what we knew about the habits of the duckbilled hadrosaurs we'd found."

"What kind of information did you send?" Morris asked.

"Everything: nesting behavior, territorial ranges, feeding behavior, social behavior. Everything."

"And how did Gennaro respond?"

"He kept calling and calling. Sometimes in the middle of the night. Would the dinosaurs eat this? Would they eat that? Should the exhibit include this? I could never understand why he was so worked up. I mean, I think dinosaurs are important, too, but not *that* important. They've been dead sixty-five million years. You'd think his calls could wait until morning."

"I see," Morris said. "And the fifty thousand dollars?"

Grant shook his head. "I got tired of Gennaro and called the whole thing off. We settled up for twelve thousand. That must have been about the middle of '85."

Morris made a note. "And InGen? Any other contact with them?"

"Not since 1985."

"And when did the Hammond Foundation begin to fund your research?"

"I'd have to look," Grant said. "But it was around then. Mid-eighties."

"And you know Hammond as just a rich dinosaur enthusiast."

"Yes."

Morris made another note.

"Look," Grant said. "If the EPA is so concerned about John Hammond and what he's doing—the dinosaur sites in the north, the amber purchases, the island in Costa Rica—why don't you just ask him about it?"

"At the moment, we can't," Morris said.

"Why not?" Grant said.

"Because we don't have any evidence of wrongdoing," Morris said. "But personally, I think it's clear John Hammond is evading the law."

"I was first contacted," Morris explained, "by the Office of Technology Transfer. The OTT monitors shipments of American technology which might have military significance. They called to say that InGen had two areas of possible illegal technology transfer. First, InGen shipped three Cray XMPs to Costa Rica. InGen characterized it as a transfer within corporate divisions, and said they weren't for resale. But OTT couldn't imagine why the hell somebody'd need that power in Costa Rica."

"Three Crays," Grant said. "Is that a kind of computer?"

Morris nodded. "Very powerful supercomputers. To put it in perspective, three Crays represent more computing power than any other privately held company in America. And InGen sent the machines to Costa Rica. You have to wonder why."

"I give up. Why?" Grant said.

"Nobody knows. And the Hoods are even more worrisome," Morris continued. "Hoods are automated gene sequencers—machines that work out the genetic code by themselves. They're so new that they haven't been put on the restricted lists yet. But any genetic engineering lab is likely to have one, if it can afford the half-million-dollar price tag." He flipped through his notes. "Well, it seems InGen shipped *twenty-four* Hood sequencers to their island in Costa Rica.

"Again, they said it was a transfer within divisions and not an export," Morris said. "There wasn't much that OTT could do. They're not officially concerned with use. But InGen was obviously setting up one of the most powerful genetic engineering facilities in the world in an obscure Central American country. A country with no regulations. That kind of thing has happened before."

There had already been cases of American bioengineering companies moving to another country so they would not be hampered by regulations and rules. The most flagrant, Morris explained, was the Biosyn rabies case.

In 1986, Genetic Biosyn Corporation of Cupertino tested a bio-engineered rabies vaccine on a farm in Chile. They didn't inform the government of Chile, or the farm workers involved. They simply released the vaccine.

The vaccine consisted of a live rabies virus, genetically modified to be nonvirulent. But the virulence hadn't been tested; Biosyn didn't know whether the virus could still cause rabies or not. Even worse, the virus had been modified. Ordinarily you couldn't contract rabies unless you were bitten by an animal. But Biosyn modified the rabies virus to cross the pulmonary alveoli; you could get an infection just inhaling it. Biosyn staffers brought this live rabies virus down to Chile in a carry-on bag on a commercial airline flight. Morris often wondered what would have happened if the capsule had broken open during the flight. Everybody on the plane might have been infected with rabies.

It was outrageous. It was irresponsible. It was criminally negligent. But no action was taken against Biosyn. The Chilean farmers who unwittingly risked their lives were ignorant peasants; the government of Chile had an economic crisis to worry about; and the American authorities had no jurisdiction. So Lewis Dodgson, the geneticist responsible for the test, was still working at Biosyn. Biosyn was still as reckless as ever. And other American companies were hurrying to set up facilities in foreign countries that lacked sophistication about genetic research. Countries that perceived genetic engineering to be like any other high-tech development, and thus welcomed it to their lands, unaware of the dangers posed.

"So that's why we began our investigation of InGen," Morris said. "About three weeks ago."

"And what have you actually found?" Grant said.

"Not much," Morris admitted. "When I go back to San Francisco, we'll probably have to close the investigation. And I think I'm about finished here." He started packing up his briefcase. "By the way, what *does* 'juvenile hyperspace' mean?"

"That's just a fancy label for my report," Grant said. " 'Hyperspace' is a term for multidimensional space—like three-dimensional tic-tac-toe. If you were to take all the behaviors of an animal, its eating and movement and sleeping, you could plot the animal within the multidimensional space. Some paleontologists refer to the behavior of an animal as occurring in an ecological hyperspace. 'Juvenile hyperspace' would just refer to the behavior of juvenile dinosaurs—if you wanted to be as pretentious as possible."

At the far end of the trailer, the phone rang. Ellie answered it. She said, "He's in a meeting right now. Can he call you back?"

Morris snapped his briefcase shut and stood. "Thanks for your help and the beer," he said.

"No problem," Grant said.

Grant walked with Morris down the trailer to the door at the far end. Morris said, "Did Hammond ever ask for any physical materials from your site? Bones, or eggs, or anything like that?"

"No," Grant said.

"Dr. Sattler mentioned you do some genetic work here. . . ."

"Well, not exactly," Grant said. "When we remove fossils that are broken or for some other reason not suitable for museum preservation, we send the bones out to a lab that grinds them up and tries to extract proteins for us. The proteins are then identified and the report is sent back to us."

"Which lab is that?" Morris asked.

"Medical Biologic Services in Salt Lake."

"How'd you choose them?"

"Competitive bids."

"The lab has nothing to do with InGen?" Morris asked.

"Not that I know," Grant said.

They came to the door of the trailer. Grant opened it, and felt the rush of hot air from outside. Morris paused to put on his sunglasses.

"One last thing," Morris said. "Suppose InGen wasn't really making a museum exhibit. Is there anything else they could have done with the information in the report you gave them?"

Grant laughed. "Sure. They could feed a baby hadrosaur."

Morris laughed, too. "A baby hadrosaur. That'd be something to see. How big were they?"

"About so," Grant said, holding his hands six inches apart. "Squirrel-size."

"And how long before they become full-grown?"

"Three years," Grant said. "Give or take."

Morris held out his hand. "Well, thanks again for your help."

"Take it easy driving back," Grant said. He watched for a moment as Morris walked back toward his car, and then closed the trailer door.

Grant said, "What did you think?"

Ellie shrugged. "Naïve."

"You like the part where John Hammond is the evil arch-villain?" Grant laughed. "John Hammond's about as sinister as Walt Disney. By the way, who called?"

"Oh," Ellie said, "it was a woman named Alice Levin. She works at Columbia Medical Center. You know her?"

Grant shook his head. "No."

"Well, it was something about identifying some remains. She wants you to call her back right away."

SKELETON

Ellie Sattler brushed a strand of blond hair back from her face and turned her attention to the acid baths. She had six in a row, at molar strengths from 5 to 30 percent. She had to keep an eye on the stronger solutions, because they would eat through the limestone and begin to erode the bones. And infant-dinosaur bones were so fragile. She marveled that they had been preserved at all, after eighty million years.

She listened idly as Grant said, "Miss Levin? This is Alan Grant. What's this about a . . . You have what? A *what*?" He began to laugh. "Oh, I doubt that very much, Miss Levin. . . . No, I really don't have time, I'm sorry. . . . Well, I'd take a look at it, but I can pretty much guarantee it's a basilisk lizard. But . . . yes, you can do that. All right. Send it now." Grant hung up, and shook his head. "These people."

Ellie said, "What's it about?"

"Some lizard she's trying to identify," Grant said. "She's going to fax me an X ray." He walked over to the fax and waited as the transmission came through. "Incidentally, I've got a new find for you. A good one."

"Yes?"

Grant nodded. "Found it just before the kid showed up. On South Hill, horizon four. Infant velociraptor: jaw and complete dentition, so there's no question about identity. And the site looks undisturbed. We might even get a full skeleton."

"That's fantastic," Ellie said. "How young?"

"Young," Grant said. "Two, maybe four months at most."

"And it's definitely a velociraptor?"

"Definitely," Grant said. "Maybe our luck has finally turned."

For the last two years at Snakewater, the team had excavated only duckbilled hadrosaurs. They already had evidence for vast herds of these grazing dinosaurs, roaming the Cretaceous plains in groups of ten or twenty thousand, as buffalo would later roam.

But increasingly the question that faced them was: where were the predators?

They expected predators to be rare, of course. Studies of predator/prey populations in the game parks of Africa and India suggested that, roughly speaking, there was one predatory carnivore for every four hundred herbivores. That meant a herd of ten thousand duckbills would support only twenty-five tyrannosaurs. So it was unlikely that they would find the remains of a large predator.

But where were the smaller predators? Snakewater had dozens of nesting sites—in some places, the ground was literally covered with fragments of dinosaur eggshells—and many small dinosaurs ate eggs. Animals like *Dromaeosaurus*, *Oviraptor*, *Velociraptor*, and *Coelurus*—predators three to six feet tall—must have been found here in abundance.

But they had discovered none so far.

Perhaps this velociraptor skeleton did mean their luck had changed. And an infant! Ellie knew that one of Grant's dreams was to study infant-rearing behavior in carnivorous dinosaurs, as he had already studied the behavior of herbivores. Perhaps this was the first step toward that dream. "You must be pretty excited," Ellie said.

Grant didn't answer.

"I said, you must be excited," Ellie repeated.

"My God," Grant said. He was staring at the fax.

* * *

Ellie looked over Grant's shoulder at the X ray, and breathed out slowly. "You think it's an *amassicus*?"

"Yes," Grant said. "Or a *triassicus*. The skeleton is so light."

"But it's no lizard," she said.

"No," Grant said. "This is not a lizard. No three-toed lizard has walked on this planet for two hundred million years."

Ellie's first thought was that she was looking at a hoax—an ingenious, skillful hoax, but a hoax nonetheless. Every biologist knew that the threat of a hoax was omnipresent. The most famous hoax, the Piltdown man, had gone undetected for forty years, and its perpetrator was still unknown. More recently, the distinguished astronomer Fred Hoyle had claimed that a fossil winged dinosaur, *Archaeopteryx*, on display in the British Museum, was a fraud. (It was later shown to be genuine.)

The essence of a successful hoax was that it presented scientists with what they expected to see. And, to Ellie's eye, the X ray image of the lizard was exactly correct. The three-toed foot was well balanced, with the medial claw smallest. The bony remnants of the fourth and fifth toes were located up near the metatarsal joint. The tibia was strong, and considerably longer than the femur. At the hip, the acetabulum was complete. The tail showed forty-five vertebrae. It was a young *Procompsognathus*.

"Could this X ray be faked?"

"I don't know," Grant said. "But it's almost impossible to fake an X ray. And *Procompsognathus* is an obscure animal. Even people familiar with dinosaurs have never heard of it."

Ellie read the note. "Specimen acquired on the beach of Cabo Blanco, July 16. . . . Apparently a howler monkey was eating the animal, and this was all that was recovered. Oh . . . and it says the lizard attacked a little girl."

"I doubt that," Grant said. "But perhaps. *Procompsognathus* was so small and light we assume it must be a scavenger, only feeding off dead creatures. And you can tell the size"—he measured quickly—"it's about twenty centimeters to the hips, which means the full animal would be about a foot tall. About as big as a chicken. Even a child would look pretty fearsome to it. It might bite an infant, but not a child."

Ellie frowned at the X ray image. "You think this could really be a legitimate rediscovery?" she said. "Like the coelacanth?"

"Maybe," Grant said. The coelacanth was a five-foot-long fish thought to have died out sixty-five million years ago, until a specimen was pulled from the ocean in 1938. But there were other examples. The Australian mountain pygmy possum was known only from fossils until a live one was found in a garbage can in Melbourne. And a ten-thousand-year-old fossil fruit bat from New Guinea was described by a zoologist who not long afterward received a living specimen in the mail.

"But could it be real?" she persisted. "What about the age?"

Grant nodded. "The age is a problem."

Most rediscovered animals were rather recent additions to the fossil record: ten or twenty thousand years old. Some were a few million years old; in the case of the coelacanth, sixty-five million years old. But the specimen they were looking at was much, much older than that. Dinosaurs had died out in the Cretaceous period, sixty-five million years ago. They had flourished as the dominant life-form on the planet in the Jurassic, 190 million years ago. And they had first appeared in the Triassic, roughly 220 million years ago.

It was during the early Triassic period that *Procompsognathus* had lived—a time so distant that our planet didn't even look the same. All the continents were joined together in a single landmass, called Pangaea, which extended from the North to the South Pole—a vast continent of ferns and forests, with a few large deserts. The Atlantic Ocean was a narrow lake between what would become Africa and Florida. The air was denser. The land was warmer. There were hundreds of active volcanoes. And it was in this environment that *Procompsognathus* lived.

"Well," Ellie said. "We know animals have survived. Crocodiles are basically Triassic animals living in the present. Sharks are Triassic. So we know it has happened before."

Grant nodded. "And the thing is," he said, "how else do we explain it? It's either a fake—which I doubt—or else it's a rediscovery. What else could it be?"

The phone rang. "Alice Levin again," Grant said. "Let's see if she'll send us the actual specimen." He answered it and looked at Ellie, surprised. "Yes, I'll hold for Mr. Hammond. Yes. Of course."

"Hammond? What does he want?" Ellie said.

Grant shook his head, and then said into the phone, "Yes, Mr. Hammond. Yes, it's good to hear your voice, too.... Yes ..." He looked at Ellie. "Oh, you did? Oh yes? Is that right?"

He cupped his hand over the mouthpiece and said, "Still as eccentric as ever. You've got to hear this."

Grant pushed the speaker button, and Ellie heard a raspy old-man's voice speaking rapidly: "—hell of an annoyance from some EPA fellow, seems to have gone off half cocked, all on his own, running around the country talking to people, stirring up things. I don't suppose anybody's come to see you way out there?"

"As a matter of fact," Grant said, "somebody did come to see me."

Hammond snorted. "I was afraid of that. Smart-ass kid named Morris?"

"Yes, his name was Morris," Grant said.

"He's going to see all our consultants," Hammond said. "He went to see Ian Malcolm the other day—you know, the mathematician in Texas? That's the first I knew of it. We're having one hell of a time getting a handle on this thing, it's typical of the way government operates, there isn't any complaint, there isn't any charge, just harassment from some kid who's unsupervised and is running around at the taxpayers' expense. Did he bother you? Disrupt your work?"

"No, no, he didn't bother me."

"Well, that's too bad, in a way," Hammond said, "because I'd try and get an injunction to stop him if he had. As it is, I had our lawyers call over at EPA to find out what the hell their problem is. The head of the office claims he didn't know there was any investigation! You figure that one out. Damned bureaucracy is all it is. Hell, I think this kid's trying to get down to Costa Rica, poke around, get onto our island. You know we have an island down there?"

"No," Grant said, looking at Ellie, "I didn't know."

"Oh yes, we bought it and started our operation oh, four or five years ago now. I forget exactly. Called Isla Nublar—big island, hundred miles offshore. Going to be a biological preserve. Wonderful place. Tropical jungle. You know, you ought to see it, Dr. Grant."

"Sounds interesting," Grant said, "but actually—".

"It's almost finished now, you know," Hammond said. "I've sent you some material about it. Did you get my material?"

"No, but we're pretty far from—"

"Maybe it'll come today. Look it over. The island's just beautiful. It's got everything. We've been in construction now thirty months.

You can imagine. Big park. Opens in September next year. You really ought to go see it."

"It sounds wonderful, but—"

"As a matter of fact," Hammond said, "I'm going to insist you see it, Dr. Grant. I know you'd find it right up your alley. You'd find it fascinating."

"I'm in the middle of—" Grant said.

"Say, I'll tell you what," Hammond said, as if the idea had just occurred to him. "I'm having some of the people who consulted for us go down there this weekend. Spend a few days and look it over. At our expense, of course. It'd be terrific if you'd give us your opinion."

"I couldn't possibly," Grant said.

"Oh, just for a weekend," Hammond said, with the irritating, cheery persistence of an old man. "That's all I'm talking about, Dr. Grant. I wouldn't want to interrupt your work. I know how important that work is. Believe me, I know that. Never interrupt your work. But you could hop on down there this weekend, and be back on Monday."

"No, I couldn't," Grant said. "I've just found a new skeleton and—"

"Yes, fine, but I still think you should come—" Hammond said, not really listening.

"And we've just received some evidence for a very puzzling and remarkable find, which seems to be a living procompsognathid."

"A what?" Hammond said, slowing down. "I didn't quite get that. You said a living procompsognathid?"

"That's right," Grant said. "It's a biological specimen, a partial fragment of an animal collected from Central America. A living animal."

"You don't say," Hammond said. "A living animal? How extraordinary."

"Yes," Grant said. "We think so, too. So, you see, this isn't the time for me to be leaving—"

"Central America, did you say?"

"Yes."

"Where in Central America is it from, do you know?"

"A beach called Cabo Blanco, I don't know exactly where—"

"I see." Hammond cleared his throat. "And when did this, ah, specimen arrive in your hands?"

"Just today."

"Today, I see. Today. I see. Yes." Hammond cleared his throat again.

Grant looked at Ellie and mouthed, *What's going on?*

Ellie shook her head. *Sounds upset.*

Grant mouthed, *See if Morris is still here.*

She went to the window and looked out, but Morris's car was gone. She turned back.

On the speaker, Hammond coughed. "Ah, Dr. Grant. Have you told anybody about it yet?"

"No."

"Good, that's good. Well. Yes. I'll tell you frankly, Dr. Grant, I'm having a little problem about this island. This EPA thing is coming at just the wrong time."

"How's that?" Grant said.

"Well, we've had our problems and some delays. . . . Let's just say that I'm under a little pressure here, and I'd like you to look at this island for me. Give me your opinion. I'll be paying you the usual weekend consultant rate of twenty thousand a day. That'd be sixty thousand for three days. And if you can spare Dr. Sattler, she'll go at the same rate. We need a botanist. What do you say?"

Ellie looked at Grant as he said, "Well, Mr. Hammond, that much money would fully finance our expeditions for the next two summers."

"Good, good," Hammond said blandly. He seemed distracted now, his thoughts elsewhere. "I want this to be easy. . . . Now, I'm sending the corporate jet to pick you up at that private airfield east of Choteau. You know the one I mean? It's only about two hours' drive from where you are. You be there at five p.m. tomorrow and I'll be waiting for you. Take you right down. Can you and Dr. Sattler make that plane?"

"I guess we can."

"Good. Pack lightly. You don't need passports. I'm looking forward to it. See you tomorrow," Hammond said, and he hung up.

COWAN, SWAIN AND ROSS

Midday sun streamed into the San Francisco law offices of Cowan, Swain and Ross, giving the room a cheerfulness that Donald Gennaro did not feel. He listened on the phone and looked at his boss, Daniel Ross, cold as an undertaker in his dark pinstripe suit.

"I understand, John," Gennaro said. "And Grant agreed to come? Good, good ... yes, that sounds fine to me. My congratulations, John." He hung up the phone and turned to Ross.

"We can't trust Hammond any more. He's under too much pressure. The EPA's investigating him, he's behind schedule on his Costa Rican resort, and the investors are getting nervous. There have been too many rumors of problems down there. Too many workmen have died. And now this business about a living procompsit-whatever on the mainland ...."

"What does that mean?" Ross said.

"Maybe nothing," Gennaro said. "But Hamachi is one of our principal investors. I got a report last week from Hamachi's representative in San José, the capital of Costa Rica. According to the report, some new kind of lizard is biting children on the coast."

Ross blinked. "New lizard?"

"Yes," Gennaro said. "We can't screw around with this. We've got to inspect that island right away. I've asked Hammond to arrange independent site inspections every week for the next three weeks."

"And what does Hammond say?"

"He insists nothing is wrong on the island. Claims he has all these security precautions."

"But you don't believe him," Ross said.

"No," Gennaro said. "I don't."

Donald Gennaro had come to Cowan, Swain from a background

49

in investment banking. Cowan, Swain's high-tech clients frequently needed capitalization, and Gennaro helped them find the money. One of his first assignments, back in 1982, had been to accompany John Hammond while the old man, then nearly seventy, put together the funding to start the InGen corporation. They eventually raised almost a billion dollars, and Gennaro remembered it as a wild ride.

"Hammond's a dreamer," Gennaro said.

"A potentially dangerous dreamer," Ross said. "We should never have gotten involved. What is our financial position?"

"The firm," Gennaro said, "owns five percent."

"General or limited?"

"General."

Ross shook his head. "We should never have done that."

"It seemed wise at the time," Gennaro said. "Hell, it was eight years ago. We took it in lieu of some fees. And, if you remember, Hammond's plan was extremely speculative. He was really pushing the envelope. Nobody really thought he could pull it off."

"But apparently he has," Ross said. "In any case, I agree that an inspection is overdue. What about your site experts?"

"I'm starting with experts Hammond already hired as consultants, early in the project." Gennaro tossed a list onto Ross's desk. "First group is a paleontologist, a paleobotanist, and a mathematician. They go down this weekend. I'll go with them."

"Will they tell you the truth?" Ross said.

"I think so. None of them had much to do with the island, and one of them—the mathematician, Ian Malcolm—was openly hostile to the project from the start. Insisted it would never work, could never work."

"And who else?"

"Just a technical person: the computer system analyst. Review the park's computers and fix some bugs. He should be there by Friday morning."

"Fine," Ross said. "You're making the arrangements?"

"Hammond asked to place the calls himself. I think he wants to pretend that he's not in trouble, that it's just a social invitation. Showing off his island."

"All right," Ross said. "But just make sure it happens. Stay on top of it. I want this Costa Rican situation resolved within a week." Ross got up, and walked out of the room.

* * *

Gennaro dialed, heard the whining hiss of a radiophone. Then he heard a voice say, "Grant here."

"Hi, Dr. Grant, this is Donald Gennaro. I'm the general counsel for InGen. We talked a few years back, I don't know if you remember—"

"I remember," Grant said.

"Well," Gennaro said. "I just got off the phone with John Hammond, who tells me the good news that you're coming down to our island in Costa Rica. . . ."

"Yes," Grant said. "I guess we're going down there tomorrow."

"Well, I just want to extend my thanks to you for doing this on short notice. Everybody at InGen appreciates it. We've asked Ian Malcolm, who like you was one of the early consultants, to come down as well. He's the mathematician at UT in Austin?"

"John Hammond mentioned that," Grant said.

"Well, good," Gennaro said. "And I'll be coming, too, as a matter of fact. By the way, this specimen you have found of a pro . . . procom . . . what is it?"

"Procompsognathus," Grant said.

"Yes. Do you have the specimen with you, Dr. Grant? The actual specimen?"

"No," Grant said. "I've only seen an X ray. The specimen is in New York. A woman from Columbia University called me."

"Well, I wonder if you could give me the details on that," Gennaro said. "Then I can run down that specimen for Mr. Hammond, who's very excited about it. I'm sure you want to see the actual specimen, too. Perhaps I can even get it delivered to the island while you're all down there," Gennaro said.

Grant gave him the information. "Well, that's fine, Dr. Grant," Gennaro said. "My regards to Dr. Sattler. I look forward to meeting you and him tomorrow." And Gennaro hung up.

PLANS

"This just came," Ellie said the next day, walking to the back of the trailer with a thick manila envelope. "One of the kids brought it back from town. It's from Hammond."

Grant noticed the blue-and-white InGen logo as he tore open the envelope. Inside there was no cover letter, just a bound stack of paper. Pulling it out, he discovered it was blueprints. They were reduced, forming a thick book. The cover was marked: ISLA NUBLAR RESORT GUEST FACILITIES (FULL SET: SAFARI LODGE).

"What the hell is this?" he said.

As he flipped open the book, a sheet of paper fell out.

Dear Alan and Ellie:

As you can imagine we don't have much in the way of formal promotional materials yet. But this should give you some idea of the Isla Nublar project. I think it's very exciting!

Looking forward to discussing this with you! Hope you can join us!

Regards,
John

"I don't get it," Grant said. He flipped through the sheets. "These are architectural plans." He turned to the top sheet:

VISITOR CENTER/LODGE	ISLA NUBLAR RESORT
CLIENT	InGen Inc., Palo Alto, Calif.
ARCHITECTS	Dunning, Murphy & Associates, New York. Richard Murphy, design partner; Theodore Chen, senior designer; Sheldon James, administrative partner.

ENGINEERS	Harlow, Whitney & Fields, Boston, structural; A. T. Misikawa, Osaka, mechanical.
LANDSCAPING	Shepperton Rogers, London; A. Ashikiga, H. Ieyasu, Kanazawa.
ELECTRICAL	N. V. Kobayashi, Tokyo. A. R. Makasawa, senior consultant.
COMPUTER C/C	Integrated Computer Systems, Inc., Cambridge, Mass. Dennis Nedry, project supervisor.

Grant turned to the plans themselves. They were stamped INDUSTRIAL SECRETS DO NOT COPY and CONFIDENTIAL WORK PRODUCT—NOT FOR DISTRIBUTION. Each sheet was numbered, and at the top: "These plans represent the confidential creations of InGen Inc. You must have signed document 112/4A or you risk prosecution."

"Looks pretty paranoid to me," he said.

"Maybe there's a reason," Ellie said.

The next page was a topographical map. It showed Isla Nublar as an inverted teardrop, bulging at the north, tapering at the south. The island was eight miles long, and the map divided it into several large sections.

The northern section was marked VISITOR AREA and it contained structures marked "Visitor Arrivals," "Visitor Center/Administration," "Power/Desalinization/Support," "Hammond Res.," and "Safari Lodge." Grant could see the outline of a swimming pool, the rectangles of tennis courts, and the round squiggles that represented planting and shrubbery.

"Looks like a resort, all right," Ellie said.

There followed detail sheets for the Safari Lodge itself. In the elevation sketches, the lodge looked dramatic: a long low building with a series of pyramid shapes on the roof. But there was little about the other buildings in the visitor area.

And the rest of the island was even more mysterious. As far as Grant could tell, it was mostly open space. A network of roads, tunnels, and outlying buildings, and a long thin lake that appeared to be man-made, with concrete dams and barriers. But, for the most part, the island was divided into big curving areas with very little development at all. Each area was marked by codes:

/P/PROC/V/2A,   /D/TRIC/L/5(4A+1),   /LN/OTHN/C/4(3A+1),   and
/VV/HADR/X/11(6A+3+3DB).

"Is there an explanation for the codes?" she said.

Grant flipped the pages rapidly, but he couldn't find one.

"Maybe they took it out," she said.

"I'm telling you," Grant said. "Paranoid." He looked at the big curving divisions, separated from one another by the network of roads. There were only six divisions on the whole island. And each division was separated from the road by a concrete moat. Outside each moat was a fence with a little lightning sign alongside it. That mystified them until they were finally able to figure out it meant the fences were electrified.

"That's odd," she said. "Electrified fences at a resort?"

"Miles of them," Grant said. "Electrified fences and moats, together. And usually with a road alongside them as well."

"Just like a zoo," Ellie said.

They went back to the topographical map and looked closely at the contour lines. The roads had been placed oddly. The main road ran north-south, right through the central hills of the island, including one section of road that seemed to be literally cut into the side of a cliff, above a river. It began to look as if there had been a deliberate effort to leave these open areas as big enclosures, separated from the roads by moats and electric fences. And the roads were raised up above ground level, so you could see over the fences. . . .

"You know," Ellie said, "some of these dimensions are enormous. Look at this. This concrete moat is thirty feet wide. That's like a military fortification."

"So are these buildings," Grant said. He had noticed that each open division had a few buildings, usually located in out-of-the-way corners. But the buildings were all concrete, with thick walls. In side-view elevations they looked like concrete bunkers with small windows. Like the Nazi pillboxes from old war movies.

At that moment, they heard a muffled explosion, and Grant put the papers aside. "Back to work," he said.

"Fire!"

There was a slight vibration, and then yellow contour lines traced across the computer screen. This time the resolution was perfect, and Alan Grant had a glimpse of the skeleton, beautifully defined, the long neck arched back. It was unquestionably an infant veloci-raptor, and it looked in perfect—

The screen went blank.

"I hate computers," Grant said, squinting in the sun. "What happened now?"

"Lost the integrator input," one of the kids said. "Just a minute." The kid bent to look at the tangle of wires going into the back of the battery-powered portable computer. They had set the computer up on a beer carton on top of Hill Four, not far from the device they called Thumper.

Grant sat down on the side of the hill and looked at his watch. He said to Ellie, "We're going to have to do this the old-fashioned way."

One of the kids overheard. "Aw, Alan."

"Look," Grant said, "I've got a plane to catch. And I want the fossil protected before I go."

Once you began to expose a fossil, you had to continue, or risk losing it. Visitors imagined the landscape of the badlands to be unchanging, but in fact it was continuously eroding, literally right before your eyes; all day long you could hear the clatter of pebbles rolling down the crumbling hillside. And there was always the risk of a rainstorm; even a brief shower would wash away a delicate fossil. Thus Grant's partially exposed skeleton was at risk, and it had to be protected until he returned.

Fossil protection ordinarily consisted of a tarp over the site, and a trench around the perimeter to control water runoff. The question was how large a trench the velociraptor fossil required. To decide that, they were using computer-assisted sonic tomography, or CAST. This was a new procedure, in which Thumper fired a soft lead slug into the ground, setting up shock waves that were read by the computer and assembled into a kind of X ray image of the hillside. They had been using it all summer with varying results.

Thumper was twenty feet away now, a big silver box on wheels, with an umbrella on top. It looked like an ice-cream vendor's push-cart, parked incongruously on the badlands. Thumper had two youthful attendants loading the next soft lead pellet.

So far, the CAST program merely located the extent of finds, helping Grant's team to dig more efficiently. But the kids claimed that within a few years it would be possible to generate an image so detailed that excavation would be redundant. You could get a perfect image of the bones, in three dimensions, and it promised a whole new era of archaeology without excavation.

But none of that had happened yet. And the equipment that worked flawlessly in the university laboratory proved pitifully delicate and fickle in the field.

"How much longer?" Grant said.

"We got it now, Alan. It's not bad."

Grant went to look at the computer screen. He saw the complete skeleton, traced in bright yellow. It was indeed a young specimen. The outstanding characteristic of *Velociraptor*—the single-toed claw, which in a full-grown animal was a curved, six-inch-long weapon capable of ripping open its prey—was in this infant no larger than the thorn on a rosebush. It was hardly visible at all on the screen. And *Velociraptor* was a lightly built dinosaur in any case, an animal as fine-boned as a bird, and presumably as intelligent.

Here the skeleton appeared in perfect order, except that the head and neck were bent back, toward the posterior. Such neck flexion was so common in fossils that some scientists had formulated a theory to explain it, suggesting that the dinosaurs had become extinct because they had been poisoned by the evolving alkaloids in plants. The twisted neck was thought to signify the death agony of the dinosaurs. Grant had finally put that one to rest, by demonstrating that many species of birds and reptiles underwent a postmortem contraction of posterior neck ligaments, which bent the head backward in a characteristic way. It had nothing to do with the cause of death; it had to do with the way a carcass dried in the sun.

Grant saw that this particular skeleton had also been twisted laterally, so that the right leg and foot were raised up above the backbone.

"It looks kind of distorted," one of the kids said. "But I don't think it's the computer."

"No," Grant said. "It's just time. Lots and lots of time."

Grant knew that people could not imagine geological time. Human life was lived on another scale of time entirely. An apple turned brown in a few minutes. Silverware turned black in a few days. A compost heap decayed in a season. A child grew up in a decade. None of these everyday human experiences prepared people to be able to imagine the meaning of eighty million years—the length of time that had passed since this little animal had died.

In the classroom, Grant had tried different comparisons. If you imagined the human lifespan of sixty years was compressed to a day, then eighty million years would still be 3,652 years—older than the pyramids. The velociraptor had been dead a long time.

"Doesn't look very fearsome," one of the kids said.

"He wasn't," Grant said. "At least, not until he grew up." Probably this baby had scavenged, feeding off carcasses slain by the adults, after the big animals had gorged themselves, and lay basking in the sun. Carnivores could eat as much as 25 percent of their body weight in a single meal, and it made them sleepy afterward. The babies would chitter and scramble over the indulgent, somnolent bodies of the adults, and nip little bites from the dead animal. The babies were probably cute little animals.

But an adult velociraptor was another matter entirely. Pound for pound, a velociraptor was the most rapacious dinosaur that ever lived. Although relatively small—about two hundred pounds, the size of a leopard—velociraptors were quick, intelligent, and vicious, able to attack with sharp jaws, powerful clawed forearms, and the devastating single claw on the foot.

Velociraptors hunted in packs, and Grant thought it must have been a sight to see a dozen of these animals racing at full speed, leaping onto the back of a much larger dinosaur, tearing at the neck and slashing at the ribs and belly. . . .

"We're running out of time," Ellie said, bringing him back.

Grant gave instructions for the trench. From the computer image, they knew the skeleton lay in a relatively confined area; a ditch around a two-meter square would be sufficient. Meanwhile, Ellie lashed down the tarp that covered the side of the hill. Grant helped her pound in the final stakes.

"How did the baby die?" one of the kids asked.

"I doubt we'll know," Grant replied. "Infant mortality in the wild is high. In African parks, it runs seventy percent among some carnivores. It could have been anything—disease, separation from the group, anything. Or even attack by an adult. We know these animals hunted in packs, but we don't know anything about their social behavior in a group."

The students nodded. They had all studied animal behavior, and they knew, for example, that when a new male took over a lion pride, the first thing he did was kill all the cubs. The reason was apparently genetic: the male had evolved to disseminate his genes as widely as possible, and by killing the cubs he brought all the females into heat, so that he could impregnate them. It also prevented the females from wasting their time nurturing the offspring of another male.

Perhaps the velociraptor hunting pack was also ruled by a dominant male. They knew so little about dinosaurs, Grant thought. After 150 years of research and excavation all around the world, they still knew almost nothing about what the dinosaurs had really been like.

"We've got to go," Ellie said, "if we're going to get to Choteau by five."

HAMMOND

Gennaro's secretary bustled in with a new suitcase. It still had the sales tags on it. "You know, Mr. Gennaro," she said severely, "when you forget to pack it makes me think you don't really want to go on this trip."

"Maybe you're right," Gennaro said. "I'm missing my kid's birthday." Saturday was Amanda's birthday, and Elizabeth had invited twenty screaming four-year-olds to share it, as well as Cappy the Clown and a magician. His wife hadn't been happy to hear that Gennaro was going out of town. Neither had Amanda.

"Well, I did the best I could on short notice," his secretary said. "There's running shoes your size, and khaki shorts and shirts, and a shaving kit. A pair of jeans and a sweatshirt if it gets cold. The car is downstairs to take you to the airport. You have to leave now to make the flight."

She left. Gennaro walked down the hallway, tearing the sales tags off the suitcase. As he passed the all-glass conference room, Dan Ross left the table and came outside.

"Have a good trip," Ross said. "But let's be very clear about one thing. I don't know how bad this situation actually is, Donald. But if there's a problem on that island, burn it to the ground."

"Jesus, Dan . . . We're talking about a big investment."

"Don't hesitate. Don't think about it. Just do it. Hear me?"

Gennaro nodded. "I hear you," he said. "But Hammond—"

"Screw Hammond," Ross said.

"My boy, my boy," the familiar raspy voice said. "How have you been, my boy?"

"Very well, sir," Gennaro replied. He leaned back in the padded leather chair of the Gulfstream II jet as it flew east, toward the Rocky Mountains.

"You never call me any more," Hammond said reproachfully. "I've missed you, Donald. How is your lovely wife?"

"She's fine. Elizabeth's fine. We have a little girl now."

"Wonderful, wonderful. Children are such a delight. She'd get a kick out of our new park in Costa Rica."

Gennaro had forgotten how short Hammond was; as he sat in the chair, his feet didn't touch the carpeting; he swung his legs as he talked. There was a childlike quality to the man, even though Hammond must now be . . . what? Seventy-five? Seventy-six? Something like that. He looked older than Gennaro remembered, but then, Gennaro hadn't seen him for almost five years.

Hammond was flamboyant, a born showman, and back in 1983 he had had an elephant that he carried around with him in a little cage. The elephant was nine inches high and a foot long, and perfectly formed, except his tusks were stunted. Hammond took the elephant with him to fund-raising meetings. Gennaro usually carried it into the room, the cage covered with a little blanket, like a tea cozy, and Hammond would give his usual speech about the prospects for developing what he called "consumer biologicals." Then, at the dramatic moment, Hammond would whip away the blanket to reveal the elephant. And he would ask for money.

The elephant was always a rousing success; its tiny body, hardly bigger than a cat's, promised untold wonders to come from the laboratory of Norman Atherton, the Stanford geneticist who was Hammond's partner in the new venture.

But as Hammond talked about the elephant, he left a great deal unsaid. For example, Hammond was starting a genetics company, but the tiny elephant hadn't been made by any genetic procedure; Atherton had simply taken a dwarf-elephant embryo and raised it in an artificial womb with hormonal modifications. That in itself was quite an achievement, but nothing like what Hammond hinted had been done.

Also, Atherton hadn't been able to duplicate his miniature elephant, and he'd tried. For one thing, everybody who saw the elephant wanted one. Then, too, the elephant was prone to colds, particularly during winter. The sneezes coming through the little trunk filled Hammond with dread. And sometimes the elephant would get his tusks stuck between the bars of the cage and snort irritably as he tried to get free; sometimes he got infections around the tusk line. Hammond always fretted that his elephant would die before Atherton could grow a replacement.

Hammond also concealed from prospective investors the fact that the elephant's behavior had changed substantially in the process of miniaturization. The little creature might look like an elephant, but he acted like a vicious rodent, quick-moving and mean-tempered. Hammond discouraged people from petting the elephant, to avoid nipped fingers.

And although Hammond spoke confidently of seven billion dollars in annual revenues by 1993, his project was intensely speculative. Hammond had vision and enthusiasm, but there was no certainty that his plan would work at all. Particularly since Norman Atherton, the brains behind the project, had terminal cancer—which was a final point Hammond neglected to mention.

Even so, with Gennaro's help, Hammond got his money. Between September of 1983 and November of 1985, John Alfred Hammond and his "Pachyderm Portfolio" raised $870 million in venture capital to finance his proposed corporation, International Genetic Technologies, Inc. And they could have raised more, except Hammond insisted on absolute secrecy, and he offered no return on capital for at least five years. That scared a lot of investors off. In the end, they'd had to take mostly Japanese consortia. The Japanese were the only investors who had the patience.

Sitting in the leather chair of the jet, Gennaro thought about how evasive Hammond was. The old man was now ignoring the fact that Gennaro's law firm had forced this trip on him. Instead, Hammond behaved as if they were engaged in a purely social outing. "It's too bad you didn't bring your family with you, Donald," he said.

Gennaro shrugged. "It's my daughter's birthday. Twenty kids already scheduled. The cake and the clown. You know how it is."

"Oh, I understand," Hammond said. "Kids set their hearts on things."

"Anyway, is the park ready for visitors?" Gennaro asked.

"Well, not officially," Hammond said. "But the hotel is built, so there is a place to stay. . . ."

"And the animals?"

"Of course, the animals are all there. All in their spaces."

Gennaro said, "I remember in the original proposal you were hoping for a total of twelve. . . ."

"Oh, we're far beyond that. We have two hundred and thirty-eight animals, Donald."

"Two hundred and thirty-eight?"

The old man giggled, pleased at Gennaro's reaction. "You can't imagine it. We have *herds* of them."

"Two hundred and thirty-eight . . . How many species?"

"Fifteen different species, Donald."

"That's incredible," Gennaro said. "That's fantastic. And what about all the other things you wanted? The facilities? The computers?"

"All of it, all of it," Hammond said. "Everything on that island is state-of-the-art. You'll see for yourself, Donald. It's perfectly wonderful. That's why this . . . *concern* . . . is so misplaced. There's absolutely no problem with the island."

Gennaro said, "Then there should be absolutely no problem with an inspection."

"And there isn't," Hammond said. "But it slows things down. Everything has to stop for the official visit. . . ."

"You've had delays anyway. You've postponed the opening."

"Oh, *that*." Hammond tugged at the red-silk handkerchief in the breast pocket of his sportcoat. "It was bound to happen. Bound to happen."

"Why?" Gennaro asked.

"Well, Donald," Hammond said, "to explain that, you have to go back to the initial concept of the resort. The concept of the most advanced amusement park in the world, combining the latest electronic and biological technologies. I'm not talking about rides. Everybody has *rides*. Coney Island has *rides*. And these days everybody has animatronic environments. The haunted house, the pirate den, the wild west, the earthquake—everyone has those things. So we set out to make biological attractions. *Living* attractions. Attractions so astonishing they would capture the imagination of the entire world."

Gennaro had to smile. It was almost the same speech, word for word, that he had used on the investors, so many years ago. "And we can never forget the ultimate object of the project in Costa Rica—to make money," Hammond said, staring out the windows of the jet. "Lots and lots of money."

"I remember," Gennaro said.

"And the secret to making money in a park," Hammond said, "is to limit your personnel costs. The food handlers, ticket takers, cleanup crews, repair teams. To make a park that runs with minimal staff. That was why we invested in all the computer technology—we automated wherever we could."

"I remember. . . ."

"But the plain fact is," Hammond said, "when you put together all the animals and all the computer systems, you run into snags. Who ever got a major computer system up and running on schedule? Nobody I know."

"So you've just had normal start-up delays?"

"Yes, that's right," Hammond said. "Normal delays."

"I heard there were accidents during construction," Gennaro said. "Some workmen died. . . ."

"Yes, there were several accidents," Hammond said. "And a total of three deaths. Two workers died building the cliff road. One other died as a result of an earth-mover accident in January. But we haven't had any accidents for months now." He put his hand on the younger man's arm. "Donald," he said, "believe me when I tell you that everything on the island is going forward as planned. Everything on that island is perfectly *fine*."

The intercom clicked. The pilot said, "Seat belts, please. We're landing in Choteau."

CHOTEAU

Dry plains stretched away toward distant black buttes. The afternoon wind blew dust and tumbleweed across the cracked concrete. Grant stood with Ellie near the Jeep and waited while the sleek Grumman jet circled for a landing.

"I hate to wait on the money men," Grant grumbled.

Ellie shrugged. "Goes with the job."

Although many fields of science, such as physics and chemistry, had become federally funded, paleontology remained strongly dependent on private patrons. Quite apart from his own curiosity about the island in Costa Rica, Grant understood that, if John Hammond asked for his help, he would give it. That was how patronage worked—how it had always worked.

The little jet landed and rolled quickly toward them. Ellie shouldered her bag. The jet came to a stop and a stewardess in a blue uniform opened the door.

Inside, he was surprised at how cramped it was, despite the luxurious appointments. Grant had to hunch over as he went to shake Hammond's hand.

"Dr. Grant and Dr. Sattler," Hammond said. "It's good of you to join us. Allow me to introduce my associate, Donald Gennaro."

Gennaro was a stocky, muscular man in his mid-thirties wearing an Armani suit and wire-frame glasses. Grant disliked him on sight. He shook hands quickly. When Ellie shook hands, Gennaro said in surprise, "You're a woman."

"These things happen," she said, and Grant thought: She doesn't like him, either.

Hammond turned to Gennaro. "You know, of course, what Dr. Grant and Dr. Sattler do. They are paleontologists. They dig up

63

dinosaurs." And then he began to laugh, as if he found the idea very funny.

"Take your seats, please," the stewardess said, closing the door. Immediately the plane began to move.

"You'll have to excuse us," Hammond said, "but we are in a bit of a rush. Donald thinks it's important we get right down there."

The pilot announced four hours' flying time to Dallas, where they would refuel, and then go on to Costa Rica, arriving the following morning.

"And how long will we be in Costa Rica?" Grant asked.

"Well, that really depends," Gennaro said. "We have a few things to clear up."

"Take my word for it," Hammond said, turning to Grant. "We'll be down there no more than forty-eight hours."

Grant buckled his seat belt. "This island of yours that we're going to—I haven't heard anything about it before. Is it some kind of secret?"

"In a way," Hammond said. "We have been very, very careful about making sure nobody knows about it, until the day we finally open that island to a surprised and delighted public."

TARGET OF OPPORTUNITY

The Biosyn Corporation of Cupertino, California, had never called an emergency meeting of its board of directors. The ten directors now sitting in the conference room were irritable and impatient. It was 8:00 p.m. They had been talking among themselves for the last ten minutes, but slowly had fallen silent. Shuffling papers. Looking pointedly at their watches.

"What are we waiting for?" one asked.

"One more," Lewis Dodgson said. "We need one more." He glanced at his watch. Ron Meyer's office had said he was coming up on the six o'clock plane from San Diego. He should be here by now, even allowing for traffic from the airport.

"You need a quorum?" another director asked.

"Yes," Dodgson said. "We do."

That shut them up for a moment. A quorum meant that they were going to be asked to make an important decision. And God knows they were, although Dodgson would have preferred not to call a meeting at all. But Steingarten, the head of Biosyn, was adamant. "You'll have to get their agreement for this one, Lew," he had said.

Depending on who you talked to, Lewis Dodgson was famous as the most aggressive geneticist of his generation, or the most reckless. Thirty-four, balding, hawk-faced, and intense, he had been dismissed by Johns Hopkins as a graduate student, for planning gene therapy on human patients without obtaining the proper FDA protocols. Hired by Biosyn, he had conducted the controversial rabies vaccine test in Chile. Now he was the head of product development at Biosyn, which supposedly consisted of "reverse engineering": taking a competitor's product, tearing it apart, learning how it worked, and then making your own version. In practice, it involved industrial espionage, much of it directed toward the InGen corporation.

In the 1980s, a few genetic engineering companies began to ask, "What is the biological equivalent of a Sony Walkman?" These companies weren't interested in pharmaceuticals or health; they were interested in entertainment, sports, leisure activities, cosmetics, and pets. The perceived demand for "consumer biologicals" in the 1990s was high. InGen and Biosyn were both at work in this field.

Biosyn had already achieved some success, engineering a new, pale trout under contract to the Department of Fish and Game of the State of Idaho. This trout was easier to spot in streams, and was said to represent a step forward in angling. (At least, it eliminated complaints to the Fish and Game Department that there were no trout in the streams.) The fact that the pale trout sometimes died of sunburn, and that its flesh was soggy and tasteless, was not discussed. Biosyn was still working on that, and—

The door opened and Ron Meyer entered the room, slipped into a seat. Dodgson now had his quorum. He immediately stood.

"Gentlemen," he said, "we're here tonight to consider a target of opportunity: InGen."

Dodgson quickly reviewed the background. InGen's start-up in 1983, with Japanese investors. The purchase of three Cray XMP supercomputers. The purchase of Isla Nublar in Costa Rica. The stockpiling of amber. The unusual donations to zoos around the world, from the New York Zoological Society to the Ranthapur Wildlife Park in India.

"Despite all these clues," Dodgson said, "we still had no idea where InGen might be going. The company seemed obviously focused on animals; and they had hired researchers with an interest in the past—paleobiologists, DNA phylogeneticists, and so on.

"Then, in 1987, InGen bought an obscure company called Millipore Plastic Products in Nashville, Tennessee. This was an agribusiness company that had recently patented a new plastic with the characteristics of an avian eggshell. This plastic could be shaped into an egg and used to grow chick embryos. Starting the following year, InGen took the entire output of this millipore plastic for its own use."

"Dr. Dodgson, this is all very interesting—"

"At the same time," Dodgson continued, "construction was begun on Isla Nublar. This involved massive earthworks, including a shallow lake two miles long, in the center of the island. Plans for resort facilities were let out with a high degree of confidentiality, but it appears that InGen has built a private zoo of large dimensions on the island."

One of the directors leaned forward and said, "Dr. Dodgson. *So what?*"

"It's not an ordinary zoo," Dodgson said. "This zoo is unique in the world. It seems that InGen has done something quite extraordinary. They have managed to clone extinct animals from the past."

"What animals?"

"Animals that hatch from eggs, and that require a lot of room in a zoo."

"What animals?"

"Dinosaurs," Dodgson said. "They are cloning dinosaurs."

The consternation that followed was entirely misplaced, in Dodgson's view. The trouble with money men was that they didn't keep up: they had invested in a field, but they didn't know what was possible.

In fact, there had been discussion of cloning dinosaurs in the technical literature as far back as 1982. With each passing year, the manipulation of DNA had grown easier. Genetic material had already been extracted from Egyptian mummies, and from the hide of a quagga, a zebra-like African animal that had become extinct in the 1880s. By 1985, it seemed possible that quagga DNA might be reconstituted, and a new animal grown. If so, it would be the first creature brought back from extinction solely by reconstruction of its DNA. If that was possible, what else was also possible? The mastodon? The saber-toothed tiger? The dodo?

Or even a dinosaur?

Of course, no dinosaur DNA was known to exist anywhere in the world. But by grinding up large quantities of dinosaur bones it might be possible to extract fragments of DNA. Formerly it was thought that fossilization eliminated all DNA. Now that was recognized as untrue. If enough DNA fragments were recovered, it might be possible to clone a living animal.

Back in 1982, the technical problems had seemed daunting. But there was no theoretical barrier. It was merely difficult, expensive, and unlikely to work. Yet it was certainly possible, if anyone cared to try.

InGen had apparently decided to try.

"What they have done," Dodgson said, "is build the greatest single tourist attraction in the history of the world. As you know, zoos are extremely popular. Last year, more Americans visited zoos than all professional baseball and football games combined. And the Japanese love zoos—there are fifty zoos in Japan, and more being built. And for this zoo, InGen can charge whatever they want. Two thousand dollars a day, ten thousand dollars a day . . . And then there is the *merchandising*. The picture books, T-shirts, video games, caps, stuffed toys, comic books, and pets."

"Pets?"

"Of course. If InGen can make full-size dinosaurs, they can also make pygmy dinosaurs as household pets. What child won't want a little dinosaur as a pet? A little patented animal for their very own. InGen will sell millions of them. And InGen will engineer them so that these pet dinosaurs can only eat InGen pet food. . . ."

"Jesus," somebody said.

"Exactly," Dodgson said. "The zoo is the centerpiece of an enormous enterprise."

"You said these dinosaurs will be patented?"

"Yes. Genetically engineered animals can now be patented. The Supreme Court ruled on that in favor of Harvard in 1987. InGen will own its dinosaurs, and no one else can legally make them."

"What prevents us from creating our own dinosaurs?" someone said.

"Nothing, except that they have a five-year start. It'll be almost impossible to catch up before the end of the century."

He paused. "Of course, if we could obtain examples of their dinosaurs, we could reverse engineer them and make our own, with enough modifications in the DNA to evade their patents."

"Can we obtain examples of their dinosaurs?"

Dodgson paused. "I believe we can, yes."

Somebody cleared his throat. "There wouldn't be anything illegal about it. . . ."

"Oh no," Dodgson said quickly. "Nothing illegal. I'm talking about a legitimate source of their DNA. A disgruntled employee, or some trash improperly disposed of, something like that."

"Do you have a legitimate source, Dr. Dodgson?"

"I do," Dodgson said. "But I'm afraid there is some urgency to the decision, because InGen is experiencing a small crisis, and my source will have to act within the next twenty-four hours."

A long silence descended over the room. The men looked at the secretary, taking notes, and the tape recorder on the table in front of her.

"I don't see the need for a formal resolution on this," Dodgson said. "Just a sense of the room, as to whether you feel I should proceed. . . ."

Slowly the heads nodded.

Nobody spoke. Nobody went on record. They just nodded silently.

"Thank you for coming, gentlemen," Dodgson said. "I'll take it from here."

AIRPORT

Lewis Dodgson entered the coffee shop in the departure building of the San Francisco airport and looked around quickly. His man was already there, waiting at the counter. Dodgson sat down next to him and placed the briefcase on the floor between them.

"You're late, pal," the man said. He looked at the straw hat Dodgson was wearing and laughed. "What is this supposed to be, a disguise?"

"You never know," Dodgson said, suppressing his anger. For six months, Dodgson had patiently cultivated this man, who had grown more obnoxious and arrogant with each meeting. But there was nothing Dodgson could do about that—both men knew exactly what the stakes were.

Bioengineered DNA was, weight for weight, the most valuable material in the world. A single microscopic bacterium, too small to see with the naked eye, but containing the genes for a heart-attack enzyme, streptokinase, or for "ice-minus," which prevented frost damage to crops, might be worth five billion dollars to the right buyer.

And that fact of life had created a bizarre new world of industrial espionage. Dodgson was especially skilled at it. In 1987, he convinced a disgruntled geneticist to quit Cetus for Biosyn, and take five strains of engineered bacteria with her. The geneticist simply put a drop of each on the fingernails of one hand, and walked out the door.

But InGen presented a tougher challenge. Dodgson wanted more than bacterial DNA; he wanted frozen embryos, and he knew InGen guarded its embryos with the most elaborate security measures. To obtain them, he needed an InGen employee who had access to the embryos, who was willing to steal them, and who could defeat the security. Such a person was not easy to find.

Dodgson had finally located a susceptible InGen employee earlier in the year. Although this particular person had no access to genetic material, Dodgson kept up the contact, meeting the man monthly at Carlos and Charlie's in Silicon Valley, helping him in small ways. And now that InGen was inviting contractors and advisers to visit the island, it was the moment that Dodgson had been waiting for—because it meant his man would have access to embryos.

"Let's get down to it," the man said. "I've got ten minutes before my flight."

"You want to go over it again?" Dodgson said.

"Hell no, Dr. Dodgson," the man said. "I want to see the damn money."

Dodgson flipped the latch on the briefcase and opened it a few inches. The man glanced down casually. "That's all of it?"

"That's half of it. Seven hundred fifty thousand dollars."

"Okay. Fine." The man turned away, drank his coffee. "That's fine, Dr. Dodgson."

Dodgson quickly locked the briefcase. "That's for all fifteen species, you remember."

"I remember. Fifteen species, frozen embryos. And how am I going to transport them?"

Dodgson handed the man a large can of Gillette Foamy shaving cream.

"That's it?"

"That's it."

"They may check my luggage. . . ."

Dodgson shrugged. "Press the top," he said.

The man pressed it, and white shaving cream puffed into his hand. "Not bad." He wiped the foam on the edge of his plate. "Not bad."

"The can's a little heavier than usual, is all." Dodgson's technical team had been assembling it around the clock for the last two days. Quickly he showed him how it worked.

"How much coolant gas is inside?"

"Enough for thirty-six hours. The embryos have to be back in San José by then."

"That's up to your guy in the boat," the man said. "Better make sure he has a portable cooler on board."

"I'll do that," Dodgson said.

"And let's just review the bidding. . . ."

"The deal is the same," Dodgson said. "Fifty thousand on delivery of each embryo. If they're viable, an additional fifty thousand each."

"That's fine. Just make sure you have the boat waiting at the east dock of the island, Friday night. Not the north dock, where the big supply boats arrive. The east dock. It's a small utility dock. You got that?"

"I got it," Dodgson said. "When will you be back in San José?"

"Probably Sunday." The man pushed away from the counter.

Dodgson fretted. "You're sure you know how to work the—"

"I know," the man said. "Believe me, I know."

"Also," Dodgson said, "we think the island maintains constant radio contact with InGen corporate headquarters in California, so—"

"Look, I've got it covered," the man said. "Just relax, and get the money ready. I want it all Sunday morning, in San José airport, in cash."

"It'll be waiting for you," Dodgson said. "Don't worry."

MALCOLM

Shortly before midnight, he stepped on the plane at the Dallas airport, a tall, thin, balding man of thirty-five, dressed entirely in black: black shirt, black trousers, black socks, black sneakers.

"Ah, Dr. Malcolm," Hammond said, smiling with forced graciousness.

Malcolm grinned. "Hello, John. Yes, I am afraid your old nemesis is here."

Malcolm shook hands with everyone, saying quickly, "Ian Malcolm, how do you do? I do maths." He struck Grant as being more amused by the outing than anything else.

Certainly Grant recognized his name. Ian Malcolm was one of the most famous of the new generation of mathematicians who were openly interested in "how the real world works." These scholars broke with the cloistered tradition of mathematics in several important ways. For one thing, they used computers constantly, a practice traditional mathematicians frowned on. For another, they worked almost exclusively with nonlinear equations, in the emerging field called chaos theory. For a third, they appeared to care that their mathematics described something that actually existed in the real world. And finally, as if to emphasize their emergence from academia into the world, they dressed and spoke with what one senior mathematician called "a deplorable excess of personality." In fact, they often behaved like rock stars.

Malcolm sat in one of the padded chairs. The stewardess asked him if he wanted a drink. He said, "Diet Coke, shaken not stirred."

Humid Dallas air drifted through the open door. Ellie said, "Isn't it a little warm for black?"

"You're extremely pretty, Dr. Sattler," he said. "I could look at your legs all day. But no, as a matter of fact, black is an excellent color for heat. If you remember your black-body radiation, black is actually best in heat. Efficient radiation. In any case, I wear only two colors, black and gray."

Ellie was staring at him, her mouth open.

"These colors are appropriate for any occasion," Malcolm continued, "and they go well together, should I mistakenly put on a pair of gray socks with my black trousers."

"But don't you find it boring to wear only two colors?"

"Not at all. I find it liberating. I believe my life has value, and I don't want to waste it thinking about *clothing*," Malcolm said. "I don't want to think about *what I will wear* in the morning. Truly, can you imagine anything more boring than fashion? Professional sports, perhaps. Grown men swatting little balls, while the rest of the world pays money to applaud. But, on the whole, I find fashion even more tedious than sports."

"Dr. Malcolm," Hammond explained, "is a man of strong opinions."

"And mad as a hatter," Malcolm said cheerfully. "But you must admit, these are nontrivial issues. We live in a world of frightful givens. It is *given* that you will behave like this, *given* that you will care about that. No one thinks about the givens. Isn't it amazing? In the information society, nobody thinks. We expected to banish paper, but we actually banished thought."

Hammond turned to Gennaro and raised his hands. "You invited him."

"And a lucky thing, too," Malcolm said. "Because it sounds as if you have a serious problem."

"We have no problem," Hammond said quickly.

"I always maintained this island would be unworkable," Malcolm said. "I predicted it from the beginning." He reached into a soft leather briefcase. "And I trust by now we all know what the eventual outcome is going to be. You're going to have to shut the thing down."

"Shut it down!" Hammond stood angrily. "This is ridiculous."

Malcolm shrugged, indifferent to Hammond's outburst. "I've brought copies of my original paper for you to look at," he said. "The original consultancy paper I did for InGen. The mathematics are a bit sticky, but I can walk you through it. Are you leaving now?"

"I have some phone calls to make," Hammond said, and went into the adjoining cabin.

"Well, it's a long flight," Malcolm said to the others. "At least my paper will give you something to do."

The plane flew through the night.

Grant knew that Ian Malcolm had his share of detractors, and he could understand why some found his style too abrasive, and his applications of chaos theory too glib. Grant thumbed through the paper, glancing at the equations.

Gennaro said, "Your paper concludes that Hammond's island is bound to fail?"

"Correct."

"Because of chaos theory?"

"Correct. To be more precise, because of the behavior of the system in phase space."

Gennaro tossed the paper aside and said, "Can you explain this in English?"

"Surely," Malcolm said. "Let's see where we have to start. You know what a nonlinear equation is?"

"No."

"Strange attractors?"

"No."

"All right," Malcolm said. "Let's go back to the beginning." He paused, staring at the ceiling. "Physics has had great success at describing certain kinds of behavior: planets in orbit, spacecraft going to the moon, pendulums and springs and rolling balls, that sort of thing. The regular movement of objects. These are described by what are called linear equations, and mathematicians can solve those equations easily. We've been doing it for hundreds of years."

"Okay," Gennaro said.

"But there is another kind of behavior, which physics handles badly. For example, anything to do with turbulence. Water coming out of a spout. Air moving over an airplane wing. Weather. Blood flowing through the heart. Turbulent events are described by nonlinear equations. They're hard to solve—in fact, they're usually impossible to solve. So physics has never understood this whole class of events. Until about ten years ago. The new theory that describes them is called chaos theory.

"Chaos theory originally grew out of attempts to make computer models of weather in the 1960s. Weather is a big complicated system, namely the earth's atmosphere as it interacts with the land and the sun. The behavior of this big complicated system always defied understanding. So naturally we couldn't predict weather. But what the early researchers learned from computer models was that, even if you could understand it, you still couldn't predict it. Weather prediction is absolutely impossible. The reason is that the behavior of the system is sensitively dependent on initial conditions."

"You lost me," Gennaro said.

"If I use a cannon to fire a shell of a certain weight, at a certain speed, and a certain angle of inclination—and if I then fire a second shell with almost the same weight, speed, and angle—what will happen?"

"The two shells will land at almost the same spot."

"Right," Malcolm said. "That's linear dynamics."

"Okay."

"But if I have a weather system that I start up with a certain temperature and a certain wind speed and a certain humidity—and if I then repeat it with almost the same temperature, wind, and humidity—the second system will not behave almost the same. It'll wander off and rapidly will become *very* different from the first. Thunderstorms instead of sunshine. That's nonlinear dynamics. They are sensitive to initial conditions: tiny differences become amplified."

"I think I see," Gennaro said.

"The shorthand is the 'butterfly effect.' A butterfly flaps its wings in Peking, and weather in New York is different."

"So chaos is all just random and unpredictable?" Gennaro said. "Is that it?"

"No," Malcolm said. "We actually find hidden regularities within the complex variety of a system's behavior. That's why chaos has now become a very broad theory that's used to study everything from the stock market, to rioting crowds, to brain waves during epilepsy. Any sort of complex system where there is confusion and unpredictability. We can find an underlying order. Okay?"

"Okay," Gennaro said. "But what is this underlying order?"

"It's essentially characterized by the movement of the system within phase space," Malcolm said.

"Jesus," Gennaro said. "All I want to know is why you think Hammond's island can't work."

"I understand," Malcolm said. "I'll get there. Chaos theory says two things. First, that complex systems like weather have an underlying order. Second, the reverse of that—that simple systems can produce complex behavior. For example, pool balls. You hit a pool ball, and it starts to carom off the sides of the table. In theory, that's a fairly simple system, almost a Newtonian system. Since you can know the force imparted to the ball, and the mass of the ball, and you can calculate the angles at which it will strike the walls, you can predict the future behavior of the ball. In theory, you could predict the behavior of the ball far into the future, as it keeps bouncing from side to side. You could predict where it will end up three hours from now, in theory."

"Okay." Gennaro nodded.

"But in fact," Malcolm said, "it turns out you can't predict more than a few seconds into the future. Because almost immediately very small effects—imperfections in the surface of the ball, tiny indentations in the wood of the table—start to make a difference. And it doesn't take long before they overpower your careful calculations. So it turns out that this simple system of a pool ball on a table has unpredictable behavior."

"Okay."

"And Hammond's project," Malcolm said, "is another apparently simple system—animals within a zoo environment—that will eventually show unpredictable behavior."

"You know this because of . . ."

"Theory," Malcolm said.

"But hadn't you better see the island, to see what he's actually done?"

"No. That is quite unnecessary. The details don't matter. Theory tells me that the island will quickly proceed to behave in unpredictable fashion."

"And you're confident of your theory."

"Oh, yes," Malcolm said. "Totally confident." He sat back in the chair. "There is a problem with that island. It is an accident waiting to happen."

ISLA NUBLAR

With a whine, the rotors began to swing in circles overhead, casting shadows on the runway of San José airport. Grant listened to the crackle in his earphones as the pilot talked to the tower.

They had picked up another passenger in San José, a man named Dennis Nedry, who had flown in to meet them. He was fat and sloppy, eating a candy bar, and there was sticky chocolate on his fingers, and flecks of aluminum foil on his shirt. Nedry had mumbled something about doing computers on the island, and hadn't offered to shake hands.

Through the Plexi bubble Grant watched the airport concrete drop away beneath his feet, and he saw the shadow of the helicopter racing along as they went west, toward the mountains.

"It's about a forty-minute trip," Hammond said, from one of the rear seats.

Grant watched the low hills rise up, and then they were passing through intermittent clouds, breaking out into sunshine. The mountains were rugged, though he was surprised at the amount of deforestation, acre after acre of denuded, eroded hills. "Costa Rica," Hammond said, "has better population control than other countries in Central America. But, even so, the land is badly deforested. Most of this is within the last ten years."

They came down out of the clouds on the other side of the mountains, and Grant saw the beaches of the west coast. They flashed over a small coastal village.

"Bahía Anasco," the pilot said. "Fishing village." He pointed north. "Up the coast there, you see the Cabo Blanco preserve. They have beautiful beaches." The pilot headed straight out over the ocean. The water turned green, and then deep aquamarine. The sun shone on the water. It was about ten in the morning.

"Just a few minutes now," Hammond said, "and we should be seeing Isla Nublar."

Isla Nublar, Hammond explained, was not a true island. Rather, it was a seamount, a volcanic upthrusting of rock from the ocean floor. "Its volcanic origins can be seen all over the island," Hammond said. "There are steam vents in many places, and the ground is often hot underfoot. Because of this, and also because of prevailing currents, Isla Nublar lies in a foggy area. As we get there you will see—ah, there we are."

The helicopter rushed forward, low to the water. Ahead Grant saw an island, rugged and craggy, rising sharply from the ocean.

"Christ, it looks like Alcatraz," Malcolm said.

Its forested slopes were wreathed in fog, giving the island a mysterious appearance.

"Much larger, of course," Hammond said. "Eight miles long and three miles wide at the widest point, in total some twenty-two square miles. Making it the largest private animal preserve in North America."

The helicopter began to climb, and headed toward the north end of the island. Grant was trying to see through the dense fog.

"It's not usually this thick," Hammond said. He sounded worried.

At the north end of the island, the hills were highest, rising more than two thousand feet above the ocean. The tops of the hills were in fog, but Grant saw rugged cliffs and crashing ocean below. The helicopter climbed above the hills. "Unfortunately," Hammond said, "we have to land on the island. I don't like to do it, because it disturbs the animals. And it's sometimes a bit thrilling—"

Hammond's voice cut off as the pilot said, "Starting our descent now. Hang on, folks." The helicopter started down, and immediately they were blanketed in fog. Grant heard a repetitive electronic beeping through his earphones, but he could see nothing at all; then he began dimly to discern the green branches of pine trees, reaching through the mist. Some of the branches were close.

"How the hell is he doing this?" Malcolm said, but nobody answered.

The pilot swung his gaze left, then right, looking at the pine forest. The trees were still close. The helicopter descended rapidly.

"Jesus," Malcolm said.

The beeping was louder. Grant looked at the pilot. He was concentrating. Grant glanced down and saw a giant glowing fluorescent cross beneath the Plexi bubble at his feet. There were flashing lights at the corners of the cross. The pilot corrected slightly and touched down on a helipad. The sound of the rotors faded, and died.

Grant sighed, and released his seat belt.

"We have to come down fast, that way," Hammond said, "because of the wind shear. There is often bad wind shear on this peak, and . . . well, we're safe."

Someone was running up to the helicopter. A man with a baseball cap and red hair. He threw open the door and said cheerfully, "Hi, I'm Ed Regis. Welcome to Isla Nublar, everybody. And watch your step, please."

A narrow path wound down the hill. The air was chilly and damp. As they moved lower, the mist around them thinned, and Grant could see the landscape better. It looked, he thought, rather like the Pacific Northwest, the Olympic Peninsula.

"That's right," Regis said. "Primary ecology is deciduous rain forest. Rather different from the vegetation on the mainland, which is more classical rain forest. But this is a microclimate that only occurs at elevation, on the slopes of the northern hills. The majority of the island is tropical."

Down below, they could see the white roofs of large buildings, nestled among the planting. Grant was surprised: the construction was elaborate. They moved lower, out of the mist, and now he could see the full extent of the island, stretching away to the south. As Regis had said, it was mostly covered in tropical forest.

To the south, rising above the palm trees, Grant saw a single trunk with no leaves at all, just a big curving stump. Then the stump moved, and twisted around to face the new arrivals. Grant realized that he was not seeing a tree at all.

He was looking at the graceful, curving neck of an enormous creature, rising fifty feet into the air.

He was looking at a dinosaur.

WELCOME

"My God," Ellie said softly. They were all staring at the animal
above the trees. "My *God*."

Her first thought was that the dinosaur was extraordinarily beautiful. Books portrayed them as oversize, dumpy creatures, but this
long-necked animal had a gracefulness, almost a dignity, about its
movements. And it was quick—there was nothing lumbering or dull
in its behavior. The sauropod peered alertly at them, and made a low
trumpeting sound, rather like an elephant. A moment later, a second
head rose above the foliage, and then a third, and a fourth.

"My God," Ellie said again.

Gennaro was speechless. He had known all along what to expect—
he had known about it for years—but he had somehow never believed it would happen, and now, he was shocked into silence. The
awesome power of the new genetic technology, which he had formerly considered to be just so many words in an overwrought sales
pitch—the power suddenly became clear to him. These animals were
so big! They were enormous! Big as a house! And so many of them!
Actual damned dinosaurs! Just as real as you could want.

Gennaro thought: We are going to make a fortune on this place. A
fortune.

He hoped to God the island was safe.

Grant stood on the path on the side of the hill, with the mist on his
face, staring at the gray necks craning above the palms. He felt
dizzy, as if the ground were sloping away too steeply. He had trou-

ble getting his breath. Because he was looking at something he had never expected to see in his life. Yet he was seeing it.

The animals in the mist were perfect apatosaurs, medium-size sauropods. His stunned mind made academic associations: North American herbivores, late Jurassic horizon. Commonly called "brontosaurs." First discovered by E. D. Cope in Montana in 1876. Specimens associated with Morrison formation strata in Colorado, Utah, and Oklahoma. Recently Berman and McIntosh had reclassified it a diplodocus based on skull appearance. Traditionally, *Brontosaurus* was thought to spend most of its time in shallow water, which would help support its large bulk. Although this animal was clearly not in the water, it was moving much too quickly, the head and neck shifting above the palms in a very active manner—a surprisingly active manner—

Grant began to laugh.

"What is it?" Hammond said, worried. "Is something wrong?"

Grant just shook his head, and continued to laugh. He couldn't tell them that what was funny was that he had seen the animal for only a few seconds, but he had already begun to accept it—and to use his observations to answer long-standing questions in the field.

He was still laughing as he saw a fifth and a sixth neck crane up above the palm trees. The sauropods watched the people arrive. They reminded Grant of oversize giraffes—they had the same pleasant, rather stupid gaze.

"I take it they're not animatronic," Malcolm said. "They're very lifelike."

"Yes, they certainly are," Hammond said. "Well, they should be, shouldn't they?"

From the distance, they heard the trumpeting sound again. First one animal made it, and then the others joined in.

"That's their call," Ed Regis said. "Welcoming us to the island."

Grant stood and listened for a moment, entranced.

"You probably want to know what happens next," Hammond was saying, continuing down the path. "We've scheduled a complete tour of the facilities for you, and a trip to see the dinosaurs in the park later this afternoon. I'll be joining you for dinner, and will answer any remaining questions you may have then. Now, if you'll go with Mr. Regis . . ."

The group followed Ed Regis toward the nearest buildings. Over the path, a crude hand-painted sign read: "Welcome to Jurassic Park."

THIRD ITERATION

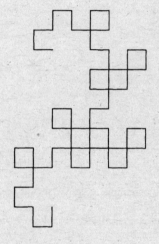

"Details emerge more clearly as the fractal curve is redrawn."

IAN MALCOLM

JURASSIC PARK

They moved into a green tunnel of overarching palms leading toward the main visitor building. Everywhere, extensive and elaborate planting emphasized the feeling that they were entering a new world, a prehistoric tropical world, and leaving the normal world behind.

Ellie said to Grant, "They look pretty good."

"Yes," Grant said. "I want to see them up close. I want to lift up their toe pads and inspect their claws and feel their skin and open their jaws and have a look at their teeth. Until then I don't know for sure. But yes, they look good."

"I suppose it changes your field a bit," Malcolm said.

Grant shook his head. "It changes everything," he said.

For 150 years, ever since the discovery of gigantic animal bones in Europe, the study of dinosaurs had been an exercise in scientific deduction. Paleontology was essentially detective work, searching for clues in the fossil bones and the trackways of the long-vanished giants. The best paleontologists were the ones who could make the most clever deductions.

And all the great disputes of paleontology were carried out in this fashion—including the bitter debate, in which Grant was a key figure, about whether dinosaurs were warm-blooded.

Scientists had always classified dinosaurs as reptiles, cold-blooded creatures drawing the heat they needed for life from the environment. A mammal could metabolize food to produce bodily warmth, but a reptile could not. Eventually a handful of researchers—led chiefly by John Ostrom and Robert Bakker at Yale—began to suspect that the concept of sluggish, cold-blooded dinosaurs was inadequate to explain the fossil record. In classic deductive fashion, they drew conclusions from several lines of evidence.

First was posture: lizards and reptiles were bent-legged sprawlers, hugging the ground for warmth. Lizards didn't have the energy to stand on their hind legs for more than a few seconds. But the dinosaurs stood on straight legs, and many walked erect on their hind legs. Among living animals, erect posture occurred only in warm-blooded mammals and birds. Thus dinosaur posture suggested warm-bloodedness.

Next they studied metabolism, calculating the pressure necessary to push blood up the eighteen-foot-long neck of a brachiosaur, and concluding that it could only be accomplished by a four-chambered, hot-blooded heart.

They studied trackways, fossil footprints left in mud, and concluded that dinosaurs ran as fast as a man; such activity implied warm blood. They found dinosaur remains above the Arctic Circle, in a frigid environment unimaginable for a reptile. And the new studies of group behavior, based largely on Grant's own work, suggested that dinosaurs had a complex social life and reared their young, as reptiles did not. Turtles abandon their eggs. But dinosaurs probably did not.

The warm-blooded controversy had raged for fifteen years, before a new perception of dinosaurs as quick-moving, active animals was accepted—but not without lasting animosities. At conventions, there were still colleagues who did not speak to one another.

But now, if dinosaurs could be cloned—why, Grant's field of study was going to change instantly. The paleontological study of dinosaurs was finished. The whole enterprise—the museum halls with their giant skeletons and flocks of echoing schoolchildren, the university laboratories with their bone trays, the research papers, the journals—all of it was going to end.

"You don't seem upset," Malcolm said.

Grant shook his head. "It's been discussed, in the field. Many people imagined it was coming. But not so soon."

"Story of our species," Malcolm said, laughing. "Everybody knows it's coming, but not so soon."

As they walked down the path, they could no longer see the dinosaurs, but they could hear them, trumpeting softly in the distance.

Grant said, "My only question is, where'd they get the DNA?"

Grant was aware of serious speculation in laboratories in Berkeley, Tokyo, and London that it might eventually be possible to clone an extinct animal such as a dinosaur—if you could get some dinosaur DNA to work with. The problem was that all known dinosaurs were fossils, and the fossilization destroyed most DNA, replacing it with inorganic material. Of course, if a dinosaur was frozen, or preserved in a peat bog, or mummified in a desert environment, then its DNA might be recoverable.

But nobody had ever found a frozen or mummified dinosaur. So cloning was therefore impossible. There was nothing to clone *from*. All the modern genetic technology was useless. It was like having a Xerox copier but nothing to copy with it.

Ellie said, "You can't reproduce a real dinosaur, because you can't get real dinosaur DNA."

"Unless there's a way we haven't thought of," Grant said.

"Like what?" she said.

"I don't know," Grant said.

Beyond a fence, they came to the swimming pool, which spilled over into a series of waterfalls and smaller rocky pools. The area was planted with huge ferns. "Isn't this extraordinary?" Ed Regis said. "Especially on a misty day, these plants really contribute to the prehistoric atmosphere. These are authentic Jurassic ferns, of course."

Ellie paused to look more closely at the ferns. Yes, it was just as he said: *Serenna veriformans*, a plant found abundantly in fossils more than two hundred million years old, now common only in the wetlands of Brazil and Colombia. But whoever had decided to place this particular fern at poolside obviously didn't know that the spores of *veriformans* contained a deadly beta-carboline alkaloid. Even touching the attractive green fronds could make you sick, and if a child were to take a mouthful, he would almost certainly die—the toxin was fifty times more poisonous than oleander.

People were so naïve about plants, Ellie thought. They just chose plants for appearance, as they would choose a picture for the wall. It never occurred to them that plants were actually living things, busily performing all the living functions of respiration, ingestion, excretion, reproduction—and defense.

But Ellie knew that, in the earth's history, plants had evolved as competitively as animals, and in some ways more fiercely. The poison in *Serenna veriformans* was a minor example of the elaborate chemical arsenal of weapons that plants had evolved. There were terpenes, which plants spread to poison the soil around them and inhibit competitors; alkaloids, which made them unpalatable to insects and predators (and children); and pheromones, used for communication. When a Douglas fir tree was attacked by beetles, it produced an anti-feedant chemical—and so did other Douglas firs in distant parts of the forest. It happened in response to a warning alleochemical secreted by the trees that were under attack.

People who imagined that life on earth consisted of animals moving against a green background seriously misunderstood what they were seeing. That green background was busily alive. Plants grew, moved, twisted, and turned, fighting for the sun; and they interacted continuously with animals—discouraging some with bark and thorns; poisoning others; and feeding still others to advance their own reproduction, to spread their pollen and seeds. It was a complex, dynamic process which she never ceased to find fascinating. And which she knew most people simply didn't understand.

But if planting deadly ferns at poolside was any indication, then it was clear that the designers of Jurassic Park had not been as careful as they should have been.

"Isn't it just wonderful?" Ed Regis was saying. "If you look up ahead, you'll see our Safari Lodge." Ellie saw a dramatic, low building, with a series of glass pyramids on the roof. "That's where you'll all be staying here in Jurassic Park."

Grant's suite was done in beige tones, the rattan furniture in green jungle-print motifs. The room wasn't quite finished; there were stacks of lumber in the closet, and pieces of electrical conduit on the floor. There was a television set in the corner, with a card on top:

> Channel 2: Hypsilophodont Highlands
> Channel 3: Triceratops Territory
> Channel 4: Sauropod Swamp
> Channel 5: Carnivore Country
> Channel 6: Stegosaurus South
> Channel 7: Velociraptor Valley
> Channel 8: Pterosaur Peak

He found the names irritatingly cute. Grant turned on the television but got only static. He shut it off and went into his bedroom, tossed his suitcase on the bed. Directly over the bed was a large pyramidal skylight. It created a tented feeling, like sleeping under the stars. Unfortunately the glass had to be protected by heavy bars, so that striped shadows fell across the bed.

Grant paused. He had seen the plans for the lodge, and he didn't remember bars on the skylight. In fact, these bars appeared to be a rather crude addition. A black steel frame had been constructed outside the glass walls, and the bars welded to the frame.

Puzzled, Grant moved from the bedroom to the living room. His window looked out on the swimming pool.

"By the way, those ferns are poison," Ellie said, walking into his room. "But did you notice anything about the rooms, Alan?"

"They changed the plans."

"I think so, yes." She moved around the room. "The windows are small," she said. "And the glass is tempered, set in a steel frame. The doors are steel-clad. That shouldn't be necessary. And did you see the fence when we came in?"

Grant nodded. The entire lodge was enclosed within a fence, with bars of inch-thick steel. The fence was gracefully landscaped and painted flat black to resemble wrought iron, but no cosmetic effort could disguise the thickness of the metal, or its twelve-foot height.

"I don't think the fence was in the plans, either," Ellie said. "It looks to me like they've turned this place into a fortress."

Grant looked at his watch. "We'll be sure to ask why," he said. "The tour starts in twenty minutes."

WHEN DINOSAURS RULED THE EARTH

They met in the visitor building: two stories high, and all glass with exposed black anodized girders and supports. Grant found it determinedly high-tech.

There was a small auditorium dominated by a robot *Tyrannosaurus rex*, poised menacingly by the entrance to an exhibit area labeled

WHEN DINOSAURS RULED THE EARTH. Farther on were other displays: WHAT IS A DINOSAUR? and THE MESOZOIC WORLD. But the exhibits weren't completed; there were wires and cables all over the floor. Gennaro climbed up on the stage and talked to Grant, Ellie, and Malcolm, his voice echoing slightly in the room.

Hammond sat in the back, his hands folded across his chest.

"We're about to tour the facilities," Gennaro said. "I'm sure Mr. Hammond and his staff will show everything in the best light. Before we go, I wanted to review why we are here, and what I need to decide before we leave. Basically, as you all realize by now, this is an island in which genetically engineered dinosaurs have been allowed to move in a natural park-like setting, forming a tourist attraction. The attraction isn't open to tourists yet, but it will be in a year.

"Now, my question for you is a simple one. Is this island safe? Is it safe for visitors, and is it safely containing the dinosaurs?"

Gennaro turned down the room lights. "There are two pieces of evidence which we have to deal with. First of all, there is Dr. Grant's identification of a previously unknown dinosaur on the Costa Rican mainland. This dinosaur is known only from a partial fragment. It was found in July of this year, after it supposedly bit an American girl on a beach. Dr. Grant can tell you more later. I've asked for the original fragment, which is in a lab in New York, to be flown here so that we can inspect it directly. Meanwhile, there is a second piece of evidence.

"Costa Rica has an excellent medical service, and it tracks all kinds of data. Beginning in March, there were reports of lizards biting infants in their cribs—and also, I might add, biting old people who were sleeping soundly. These lizard bites were sporadically reported in coastal villages from Ismaloya to Puntarenas. After March, lizard bites were no longer reported. However, I have this graph from the Public Health Service in San José of infant mortality in the towns of the west coast earlier this year."

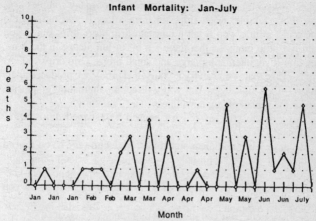

Infant Mortality: Jan-July

Month

∘ Infant deaths

"I direct your attention to two features of this graph," Gennaro said. "First, infant mortality is low in the months of January and February, then spikes in March, then it's low again in April. But from May onward, it is high, right through July, the month the American girl was bitten. The Public Health Service feels that something is now affecting infant mortality, and it is not being reported by the workers in the coastal villages. The second feature is the puzzling biweekly spiking, which seems to suggest some kind of alternating phenomenon is at work."

The lights came back on. "All right," Gennaro said. "That's the evidence I want explained. Now, are there any—"

"We can save ourselves a great deal of trouble," Malcolm said. "I'll explain it for you now."

"You will?" Gennaro said.

"Yes," Malcolm said. "First of all, animals have very likely gotten off the island."

"Oh balls," Hammond growled, from the back.

"And second, the graph from the Public Health Service is almost certainly unrelated to any animals that have escaped."

Grant said, "How do you know that?"

"You'll notice that the graph alternates between high and low spikes," Malcolm said. "That is characteristic of many complex systems. For example, water dripping from a tap. If you turn on the faucet just a little, you'll get a constant drip, drip, drip. But if you open it a little more, so that there's a bit of turbulence in the flow, then you'll get alternating large and small drops. Drip drip . . . Drip drip . . . Like that. You can try it yourself. Turbulence produces alternation—it's a signature. And you will get an alternating graph like this for the spread of any new illness in a community."

"But why do you say it isn't caused by escaped dinosaurs?" Grant said.

"Because it is a nonlinear signature," Malcolm said. "You'd need hundreds of escaped dinosaurs to cause it. And I don't think hundreds of dinosaurs have escaped. So I conclude that some other phenomenon, such as a new variety of flu, is causing the fluctuations you see in the graph."

Gennaro said, "But you think that dinosaurs have escaped?"

"Probably, yes."

"Why?"

"Because of what you are attempting here. Look, this island is an attempt to re-create a natural environment from the past. To make an isolated world where extinct creatures roam freely. Correct?"

"Yes."

"But from my point of view, such an undertaking is impossible. The mathematics are so self-evident that they don't need to be calculated. It's rather like my asking you whether, on a billion dollars in income, you had to pay tax. You wouldn't need to pull out your calculator to check. You'd know tax was owed. And, similarly, I know overwhelmingly that one cannot successfully duplicate nature in this way, or hope to isolate it."

"Why not? After all, there are zoos. . . ."

"Zoos don't re-create nature," Malcolm said. "Let's be clear. Zoos take the nature that already exists and modify it *very* slightly, to create holding pens for animals. Even those minimal modifications often fail. The animals escape with regularity. But a zoo is not a model for this park. This park is attempting something far more ambitious than that. Something much more akin to making a space station on earth."

Gennaro shook his head. "I don't understand."

"Well, it's very simple. Except for the air, which flows freely, everything about this park is meant to be isolated. Nothing gets in, nothing out. The animals kept here are never to mix with the greater ecosystems of earth. They are never to escape."

"And they never have," Hammond snorted.

"Such isolation is impossible," Malcolm said flatly. "It simply cannot be done."

"It can. It's done all the time."

"I beg your pardon," Malcolm said. "But you don't know what you are talking about."

"You arrogant little snot," Hammond said. He stood, and walked out of the room.

"Gentlemen, gentlemen," Gennaro said.

"I'm sorry," Malcolm said, "but the point remains. What we call 'nature' is in fact a complex system of far greater subtlety than we are willing to accept. We make a simplified image of nature and then we botch it up. I'm no environmentalist, but you have to understand what you don't understand. How many times must the point be made? How many times must we see the evidence? We build the Aswan Dam and claim it is going to revitalize the country. Instead, it destroys the fertile Nile Delta, produces parasitic infestation, and wrecks the Egyptian economy. We build the—"

"Excuse me," Gennaro said. "But I think I hear the helicopter. That's probably the sample for Dr. Grant to look at." He started out of the room. They all followed.

At the foot of the mountain, Gennaro was screaming over the sound of the helicopter. The veins of his neck stood out. "You did *what*? You invited *who*?"

"Take it easy," Hammond said.

Gennaro screamed, "Are you out of your goddamned *mind*?"

"Now, look here," Hammond said, drawing himself up. "I think we have to get something clear—"

"No," Gennaro said. "No, *you* get something clear. This is not a social outing. This is not a weekend excursion—"

"This is my island," Hammond said, "and I can invite whomever I want."

"This is a serious investigation of your island because your investors are concerned that it's out of control. We think this is a very dangerous place, and—"

"You're not going to shut me down, Donald—"

"I will if I have to—"

"This is a safe place," Hammond said, "no matter what that damn mathematician is saying—"

"It's not—"

"And I'll demonstrate its safety—"

"And I want you to put them right back on that helicopter," Gennaro said.

"Can't," Hammond said, pointing toward the clouds. "It's already leaving." And, indeed, the sound of the rotors was fading.

"God damn it," Gennaro said, "don't you see you're needlessly risking—"

"Ah ah," Hammond said. "Let's continue this later. I don't want to upset the children."

Grant turned, and saw two children coming down the hillside, led by Ed Regis. There was a bespectacled boy of about eleven, and a girl a few years younger, perhaps seven or eight, her blond hair pushed up under a Mets baseball cap, and a baseball glove slung over her shoulder. The two kids made their way nimbly down the path from the helipad, and stopped some distance from Gennaro and Hammond.

Low, under his breath, Gennaro said, *"Christ."*

"Now, take it easy," Hammond said. "Their parents are getting a divorce, and I want them to have a fun weekend here."

The girl waved tentatively.

"Hi, Grandpa," she said. "We're here."

THE TOUR

Tim Murphy could see at once that something was wrong. His grandfather was in the middle of an argument with the younger, red-faced man opposite him. And the other adults, standing behind, looked embarrassed and uncomfortable. Alexis felt the tension, too, because she hung back, tossing her baseball in the air. He had to push her: "Go on, Lex."

"Go on yourself, Timmy."

"Don't be a worm," he said.

Lex glared at him, but Ed Regis said cheerfully, "I'll introduce you to everybody, and then we can take the tour."

"I have to go," Lex said.

"I'll just introduce you first," Ed Regis said.

"No, I have to go."

But Ed Regis was already making introductions. First to Grandpa, who kissed them both, and then to the man he was arguing with. This man was muscular and his name was Gennaro. The rest of the introductions were a blur to Tim. There was a blond woman wearing shorts, and a man with a beard who wore jeans and a Hawaiian shirt. He looked like the outdoors type. Then a fat college kid who had something to do with computers, and finally a thin man in black, who didn't shake hands, but just nodded his head. Tim was trying to organize his impressions, and was looking at the blond woman's legs, when he suddenly realized that he knew who the bearded man was.

"Your mouth is open," Lex said.

Tim said, "I know him."

"Oh *sure*. You just met him."

"No," Tim said. "I have his book."

The bearded man said, "What book is that, Tim?"

"Lost World of the Dinosaurs," Tim said.

Alexis snickered. "Daddy says Tim has dinosaurs on the brain," she said.

Tim hardly heard her. He was thinking of what he knew about Alan Grant. Alan Grant was one of the principal advocates of the theory that dinosaurs were warm-blooded. He had done lots of digging at the place called Egg Hill in Montana, which was famous because so many dinosaur eggs had been found there. Professor Grant had found most of the dinosaur eggs that had ever been discovered. He was also a good illustrator, and he drew the pictures for his own books.

"Dinosaurs on the brain?" the bearded man said. "Well, as a matter of fact, I have that same problem."

"Dad says dinosaurs are really stupid," Lex said. "He says Tim should get out in the air and play more sports."

Tim felt embarrassed. "I thought you had to go," he said.

"In a minute," Lex said.

"I thought you were in such a rush."

"I'm the one who would know, don't you think, Timothy?" she said, putting her hands on her hips, copying her mother's most irritating stance.

"Tell you what," Ed Regis said. "Why don't we all just head on over to the visitor center, and we can begin our tour." Everybody started walking. Tim heard Gennaro whisper to his grandfather, "I could kill you for this," and then Tim looked up and saw that Dr. Grant had fallen into step beside him.

"How old are you, Tim?"

"Eleven."

"And how long have you been interested in dinosaurs?" Grant asked.

Tim swallowed. "A while now," he said. He felt nervous to be talking to Dr. Grant. "We go to museums sometimes, when I can talk my family into it. My father."

"Your father's not especially interested?"

Tim nodded, and told Grant about his family's last trip to the Museum of Natural History. His father had looked at a skeleton and said, "That's a big one."

Tim had said, "No, Dad, that's a medium-size one, a camptosaurus."

"Oh, I don't know. Looks pretty big to me."

"It's not even full-grown, Dad."

His father squinted at the skeleton. "What is it, Jurassic?"

"Jeez. No. Cretaceous."

"Cretaceous? What's the difference between Cretaceous and Jurassic?"

"Only about a hundred million years," Tim said.

"Cretaceous is older?"

"No, Dad, Jurassic is older."

"Well," his father said, stepping back, "it looks pretty damn big to me." And he turned to Tim for agreement. Tim knew he had better agree with his father, so he just muttered something. And they went on to another exhibit.

Tim stood in front of one skeleton—a *Tyrannosaurus rex*, the mightiest predator the earth had ever known—for a long time. Finally his father said, "What are you looking at?"

"I'm counting the vertebrae," Tim said.

"The vertebrae?"

"In the backbone."

"I know what vertebrae are," his father said, annoyed. He stood there a while longer and then he said, "Why are you counting them?"

"I think they're wrong. Tyrannosaurs should only have thirty-seven vertebrae in the tail. This has more."

"You mean to tell me," his father said, "that the Museum of Natural History has a skeleton that's wrong? I can't believe that."

"It's wrong," Tim said.

His father stomped off toward a guard in the corner. "What did you do now?" his mother said to Tim.

"I didn't do anything," Tim said. "I just said the dinosaur is wrong, that's all."

And then his father came back with a funny look on his face, because of course the guard told him that the tyrannosaurus had too many vertebrae in the tail.

"How'd you know that?" his father asked.

"I read it," Tim said.

"That's pretty amazing, son," he said, and he put his hand on his shoulder, giving it a squeeze. "You know how many vertebrae belong in that tail. I've never seen anything like it. You really *do* have dinosaurs on the brain."

And then his father said he wanted to catch the last half of the Mets game on TV, and Lex said she did, too, so they left the museum. And Tim didn't see any other dinosaurs, which was why they had come there in the first place. But that was how things happened in his family.

How things *used* to happen in his family, Tim corrected himself. Now that his father was getting a divorce from his mother, things would probably be different. His father had already moved out, and even though it was weird at first, Tim liked it. He thought his mother had a boyfriend, but he couldn't be sure, and of course he would never mention it to Lex. Lex was heartbroken to be separated from her father, and in the last few weeks she had become so obnoxious that—

"Was it 5027?" Grant said.

"I'm sorry?" Tim said.

"The tyrannosaurus at the museum. Was it 5027?"

"Yes," Tim said. "How'd you know?"

Grant smiled. "They've been talking about fixing it for years. But now it may never happen."

"Why is that?"

"Because of what is taking place here," Grant said, "on your grandfather's island."

Tim shook his head. He didn't understand what Grant was talking about. "My mom said it was just a resort, you know, with swimming and tennis."

"Not exactly," Grant said. "I'll explain as we walk along."

Now I'm a damned baby-sitter, Ed Regis thought unhappily, tapping his foot as he waited in the visitor center. That was what the old man had told him: You watch my kids like a hawk, they're your responsibility for the weekend.

Ed Regis didn't like it at all. He felt degraded. He wasn't a damn baby-sitter. And, for that matter, he wasn't a damned tour guide, even for VIPs. He was the head of public relations for Jurassic Park, and he had much to prepare between now and the opening, a year away. Just to coordinate with the PR firms in San Francisco and London, and the agencies in New York and Tokyo, was a full-time job—especially since the agencies couldn't yet be told what the resort's real attraction was. The firms were all designing teaser campaigns, nothing specific, and they were unhappy. Creative people needed nurturing. They needed encouragement to do their best work. He couldn't waste his time taking scientists on tours.

But that was the trouble with a career in public relations—nobody saw you as a professional. Regis had been down here on the island off and on for the past seven months, and they were still pushing odd jobs on him. Like that episode back in January. Harding should have handled that. Harding, or Owens, the general contractor. Instead, it had fallen to Ed Regis. What did he know about taking care of some sick workman? And now he was a damn tour guide and baby-sitter. He turned back and counted the heads. Still one short.

Then, in the back, he saw Dr. Sattler emerge from the bathroom.

"All right, folks, let's begin our tour on the second floor."

Tim went with the others, following Mr. Regis up the black suspended staircase to the second floor of the building. They passed a sign that read:

CLOSED AREA
AUTHORIZED PERSONNEL ONLY
BEYOND THIS POINT

Tim felt a thrill when he saw that sign. They walked down the second-floor hallway. One wall was glass, looking out onto a balcony with palm trees in the light mist. On the other wall were stenciled doors, like offices: PARK WARDEN ... GUEST SERVICES ... GENERAL MANAGER. ...

Halfway down the corridor they came to a glass partition marked with another sign:

BIOHAZARD

CAUTION
BIOLOGICAL
HAZARD

This Laboratory
Conforms to
USG P4/EK3
Genetic Protocols

Underneath were more signs:

CAUTION
TERATOGENIC SUBSTANCES
PREGNANT WOMEN AVOID EXPOSURE
TO THIS AREA

DANGER
RADIOACTIVE ISOTOPES IN USE
CARCINOGENIC POTENTIAL

Tim grew more excited all the time. Teratogenic substances! Things that made monsters! It gave him a thrill, and he was disappointed to hear Ed Regis say, "Never mind the signs, they're just up for legal reasons. I can assure you everything is perfectly safe." He led them through the door. There was a guard on the other side. Ed Regis turned to the group.

"You may have noticed that we have a minimum of personnel on the island. We can run this resort with a total of twenty people. Of course, we'll have more when we have guests here, but at the moment there's only twenty. Here's our control room. The entire park is controlled from here."

They paused before windows and peered into a darkened room that looked like a small version of Mission Control. There was a vertical glass see-through map of the park, and facing it a bank of glowing computer consoles. Some of the screens displayed data, but most of them showed video images from around the park. There were just two people inside, standing and talking.

"The man on the left is our chief engineer, John Arnold"—Regis pointed to a thin man in a button-down short-sleeve shirt and tie, smoking a cigarette—"and next to him, our park warden, Mr. Robert Muldoon, the famous white hunter from Nairobi." Muldoon was a burly man in khaki, sunglasses dangling from his shirt pocket. He glanced out at the group, gave a brief nod, and turned back to the computer screens. "I'm sure you want to see this room," Ed Regis said, "but first, let's see how we obtain dinosaur DNA."

The sign on the door said EXTRACTIONS and, like all the doors in the laboratory building, it opened with a security card. Ed Regis slipped the card in the slot; the light blinked; and the door opened.

Inside, Tim saw a small room bathed in green light. Four technicians in lab coats were peering into double-barreled stereo microscopes, or looking at images on high resolution video screens. The room was filled with yellow stones. The stones were in glass shelves; in cardboard boxes; in large pull-out trays. Each stone was tagged and numbered in black ink.

Regis introduced Henry Wu, a slender man in his thirties. "Dr. Wu is our chief geneticist. I'll let him explain what we do here."

Henry Wu smiled. "At least I'll try," he said. "Genetics is a bit complicated. But you're probably wondering where our dinosaur DNA comes from."

"It crossed my mind," Grant said.

"As a matter of fact," Wu said, "there are two possible sources.

Using the Loy antibody extraction technique, we can sometimes get DNA directly from dinosaur bones."

"What kind of a yield?" Grant asked.

"Well, most soluble protein is leached out during fossilization, but twenty percent of the proteins are still recoverable by grinding up the bones and using Loy's procedure. Dr. Loy himself has used it to obtain proteins from extinct Australian marsupials, as well as blood cells from ancient human remains. His technique is so refined it can work with a mere fifty nanograms of material. That's fifty-billionths of a gram."

"And you've adapted his technique here?" Grant asked.

"Only as a backup," Wu said. "As you can imagine, a twenty percent yield is insufficient for our work. We need the entire dinosaur DNA strand in order to clone. And we get it here." He held up one of the yellow stones. "From amber—the fossilized resin of prehistoric tree sap."

Grant looked at Ellie, then at Malcolm.

"That's really quite clever," Malcolm said, nodding.

"I still don't understand," Grant admitted.

"Tree sap," Wu explained, "often flows over insects and traps them. The insects are then perfectly preserved within the fossil. One finds all kinds of insects in amber—including biting insects that have sucked blood from larger animals."

"Sucked the blood," Grant repeated. His mouth fell open. "You mean sucked the blood of dinosaurs. . . ."

"Hopefully, yes."

"And then the insects are preserved in amber. . . ." Grant shook his head. "I'll be damned—that just might work."

"I assure you, it *does* work," Wu said. He moved to one of the microscopes, where a technician positioned a piece of amber containing a fly under the microscope. On the video monitor, they watched as he inserted a long needle through the amber, into the thorax of the prehistoric fly.

"If this insect has any foreign blood cells, we may be able to extract them, and obtain paleo-DNA, the DNA of an extinct creature. We won't know for sure, of course, until we extract whatever is in there, replicate it, and test it. That is what we have been doing for five years now. It has been a long, slow process—but it has paid off.

"Actually, dinosaur DNA is somewhat easier to extract by this process than mammalian DNA. The reason is that mammalian red cells have no nuclei, and thus no DNA in their red cells. To clone a mammal, you must find a white cell, which is much rarer than red cells. But dinosaurs had nucleated red cells, as do modern birds. It is one of the many indications we have that dinosaurs aren't really reptiles at all. They are big leathery birds."

Tim saw that Dr. Grant still looked skeptical, and Dennis Nedry, the messy fat man, appeared completely uninterested, as if he knew it all already. Nedry kept looking impatiently toward the next room.

"I see Mr. Nedry has spotted the next phase of our work," Wu said. "How we identify the DNA we have extracted. For that, we use powerful computers."

They went through sliding doors into a chilled room. There was a loud humming sound. Two six-foot-tall round towers stood in the center of the room, and along the walls were rows of waist-high stainless-steel boxes. "This is our high-tech laundromat," Dr. Wu said. "The boxes along the walls are all Hamachi-Hood automated gene sequencers. They are being run, at very high speed, by the Cray XMP supercomputers, which are the towers in the center of the room. In essence, you are standing in the middle of an incredibly powerful genetics factory."

There were several monitors, all running so fast it was hard to see what they were showing. Wu pushed a button and slowed one image.

```
   1  GCGTTGCTGG  CGTTTTTCCA  TAGGCTCCGC  CCCCCTGACG  AGCATCACAA  AAATCGACGC
  61  GGTGGCGAAA  CCCGACAGGA  CTATAAAGAT  ACCAGGCGTT  TCCCCCTGGA  AGCTCCCTCG
 121  TGTTCCGACC  CTGCCGCTTA  CCGGATACCT  GTCCGCCTTT  CTCCCTTCGG  GAAGCGTGGC
 181  TGCTCACGCT  GTAGGTATCT  CAGTTCGGTG  TAGGTCGTTC  GCTCCAAGCT  GGGCTGTGTG
 241  CCGTTCAGCC  CGACCGCTGC  GCCTTATCCG  GTAACTATCG  TCTTGAGTCC  AACCCGGTAA
 301  AGTAGGACAG  GTGCCGGCAG  CGCTCTGGGT  CATTTTCGGC  GAGGACCGCT  TTCGCTGGAG
 361  ATCGGCCTGT  CGCTTGCGGT  ATTCGGAATC  TTGCACGCCC  TCGCTCAAGC  CTTCGTCACT
 421  CCAAACGTTT  CGGCGAGAAG  CAGGCCATTA  TCGCCGGCAT  GGCGGCCGAC  GCGCTGGGCT
 481  GGCGTTCGCG  ACGCGAGGCT  GGATGGCCTT  CCCCATTATG  ATTCTTCTCG  CTTCCGGCGG
 541  CCCGCGTTGC  AGGCCATGCT  GTCCAGGCAG  GTAGATGACG  ACCATCAGGG  ACAGCTTCAA
 601  CGGCTCTTAC  CAGCCTAACT  TCGATCACTG  GACCGCTGAT  CGTCACGGCG  ATTTATGCCG
 661  CACATGGACG  CGTTGCTGGC  GTTTTTCCAT  AGGCTCCGCC  CCCCTGACGA  GCATCACAAA
 721  CAAGTCAGAG  GTGGCGAAAC  CCGACAGGAC  TATAAAGATA  CCAGGCGTTT  CCCCCTGGAA
 781  GCGCTCTCCT  GTTCCGACCC  TGCCGCTTAC  CGGATACCTG  TCCGCCTTTC  TCCCTTCGGG
 841  CTTTCTCAAT  GCTCACGCTG  TAGGTATCTC  AGTTCGGTGT  AGGTCGTTCG  CTCCAAGCTG
 901  ACGAACCCCC  CGTTCAGCCC  GACCGCTGCG  CCTTATCCGG  TAACTATCGT  CTTGAGTCCA
 961  ACACGACTTA  ACGGGTTGGC  ATGGATTGTA  GGCGCCGCCC  TATACCTTGT  CTGCCTCCCC
1021  GCGGTGCATG  GAGCCGGGCC  ACCTCGACCT  GAATGGAAGC  CGGCGGCACC  TCGCTAACGG
1081  CCAAGAATTG  GAGCCAATCA  ATTCTTGCGG  AGAACTGTGA  ATGCGCAAAC  CAACCCTTGG
1141  CCATCGCGTC  CGCCATCTCC  GAGCCGCGCA  CGCGGGCGAC  CTCGGGCAGC  GTTGGGTCCT
1201  GCGCATGATC  GTGCT ﬁﬀ CCTGTCGTTG  AGGACCCGGC  TAGGCTGGCG  GGGTGCCTT
1281  AGAATGAATC  ACCGATACGC  GAGCGAACGT  GAAGCGACTG  CTGCTGCAAA  ACGTCTGCGA
1341  AACATGAATG  GTCTTCGGTT  TCCGTGTTTC  GTAAAGTCTG  GAAACGCGGA  AGTCAGCGCC
```

"Here you see the actual structure of a small fragment of dinosaur DNA," Wu said. "Notice the sequence is made up of four basic compounds—adenine, thymine, guanine, and cytosine. This amount of DNA probably contains instructions to make a single protein—say, a hormone or an enzyme. The full DNA molecule contains *three billion* of these bases. If we looked at a screen like this once a second, for eight hours a day, it'd still take more than two years to look at the entire DNA strand. It's that big."

He pointed to the image. "This is a typical example, because you see the DNA has an error, down here in line 1201. Much of the DNA we extract is fragmented or incomplete. So the first thing we have to do is repair it—or rather, the computer has to. It'll cut the DNA, using what are called restriction enzymes. The computer will select a variety of enzymes that might do the job."

```
    1  GCGTTGCTGGCGTTTTTCCATAGGCTCCGCCCCCCTGACGAGCATCACAAAAATCGACGC
   61  GGTGGCGAAACCCGACAGGACTATAAAGATACCAGGCGTTTCCCCCTGGAAGCTCCCTCG
                         NspO4
  121  TGTTCCGACCCTGCCGCTTACCGGATACCTGTCCGCCTTTCTCCCTTCGGGAAGCGTGGC
  181  TGCTCACGCTGTAGGTATCTCAGTTCGGTGTAGGTCGTTCGCTCCAAGCTGGGCTGTGTG
                        □                              BrontIV
  241  CCGTTCAGCCCGACCGCTGCGCCTTATCCGGTAACTATCGTCTTGAGTCCAACCCGGTAA
  301  AGTAGGACAGGTGCCGGCAGCGCTCTGGGTCATTTTCGGCAGGGACCGCTTTCGCTGGAG
            434 DnxT1                     AoliBn
  361  ATCGGCCTGTCGCTTGCGGTATTCGGAATCTTGCACGCCCTCGCTCAAGCCTTCGTCACT
  421  CCAAACGTTTCGGCGAGAAGCAGGCCATTATCGCCGGCATGGCGGCCGACGCGCTGGGGT
  481  GGCGTTCGCGACGCGAGGCTGGATGGCCTTCCCCATTATGATTCTTCTCGCTTCCGGCGG
  541  CCCGCGTTGCAGGCCATGCTGTCCAGGCAGGTAGATGACGACCATCAGGGACAGCTTCAA
  601  CGGCTCTTACCAGCCTAACTTCGATCACTGGACCGCTGATCGTCACGGCGATTTATGCCG
                                             NspO4
  661  CACATGGACGCGTTGCTGGCGTTTTTCCATAGGCTCCGCCCCCCTGACGAGCATCACAAA
  721  CAAGTCAGAGGTGGCGAAACCCGACAGGACTATAAAGATACCAGGCGTTTCCCCCTGGAA
            924 Caoll1           DinoLdn
  781  GCGCTCTCCTGTTCCGACCCTGCCGCTTACCGGATACCTGTCCGCCTTTCTCCCTTCGGG
  841  CTTTCTCAATGCTCACGCTGTAGGTATCTCAGTTCGGTGTAGGTCGTTCGCTCCAAGCTG
  901  ACGAACCCCCCGTTCAGCCCGACCGCTGCGCCTTATCCGGTAACTATCGTCTTGAGTCCA
  961  ACACGACTTAACGGGTTGGCATGGATTGTAGGCGCCTATACCTTGTCTGCCTCCCC
 1021  GCGGTGCATGGAGCCGGGCCACCTCGACCTGAATGGAAGCCGGCGGCACCTCGCTAACGG
 1081  CCAAGAATTGGAGCCAATCAATTCTTGCGGAGAACTGTGAATGCGCAAACCAACCCTTGG
 1141  CCATCGCGTCCGCCATCTCCAGCAGCCGCACGCGGCGCATCTCGGGCAGCGTTGGGTCCT
                     1416 DnxT1
                     SSpd4
 1201  GCGCATGATCGTGCTAGCCTGTCGTTGAGGACCCGGCTAGGCTGGCGGGGTTGCCTTACT
 1281  ATGAATCACCGATACGCGAGCGAACGTGAAGCGACTGCTGCTGCAAAACGTCTGCGACCT
```

"Here is the same section of DNA, with the points of the restriction enzymes located. As you can see in line 1201, two enzymes will cut on either side of the damaged point. Ordinarily we let the computers decide which to use. But we also need to know what base pairs we should insert to repair the injury. For that, we have to align various cut fragments, like so."

Restriction Enzyme Sequence Alignment

codes : m=match e=extended match v=verified match f=finished

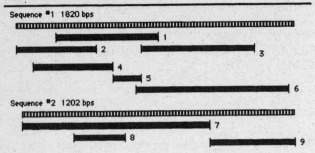

Sequence #1 1820 bps

Sequence #2 1202 bps

"Now we are finding a fragment of DNA that overlaps the injury area, and will tell us what is missing. And you can see we can find it, and go ahead and make the repair. The dark bars you see are restriction fragments—small sections of dinosaur DNA, broken by enzymes and then analyzed. The computer is now recombining them, by searching for overlapping sections of code. It's a little bit like putting a puzzle together. The computer can do it very rapidly."

```
   1  GCGTTGCTGGCGTTTTTCCATAGGCTCCGCCCCCCTGACGAGCATCACAAAAATCGACGC
  61  GGTGGCGAAACCCGACAGGACTATAAAGATACCAGGCGTTTCCCCCTGGAAGCTCCCTCG
 121  TGTTCCGACCCTGCCGCTTACCGGATACCTGTCCGCCTTTCTCCCTTCGGGAAGCGTGGC
 181  TGCTCACGCTGTAGGTATCTCAGTTCGGTGTAGGTCGTTCGCTCCAAGCTGGGCTGTGTG
 241  CCGTTCAGCCCGACCGCTGCGCCTTATCCGGTAACTATCGTCTTGAGTCCAACCCGGTAA
 301  AGTAGGACAGGTGCCGGCAGCGCTCTGGGTCATTTCGGCGAGGACCGCTTTCGCTGGAG
 361  ATCGGCCTGTCGCTTGCGGTATTCGGAATCTTGCACGCCCTCGCTCAAGCCTTCGTCACT
 421  CCAAACGTTTCGGCGAGAAGCAGGCCATTATCGCCGGCATGGCGGCCGACGCGCTGGGCT
 481  GGCGTTCGCGACGCGAGGCTGGATGGCCTTCCCCATTATGATTCTTCTCGCTTCCGGCGG
 541  CCCGCGTTGCAGGCCATGCTGTCCAGGCAGGTAGATGACGACCATCAGGGACAGCTTCAA
 601  CGGCTCTTACCAGCCTAACTTCGATCACTGGACCGCTGATCGTCACGGCGATTTATGCCG
 661  CACATGGACGCGTTGCTGGCGTTTTTCCATAGGCTCCGCCCCCCTGACGAGCATCACAAA
 721  CAAGTCAGAGGTGGCGAAACCCGACAGGACTATAAAGATACCAGGCGTTTCCCCCTGGAA
 781  GCGCTCTCCTGTTCCGACCCTGCCGCTTACCGGATACCTGTCCGCCTTTCTCCCTTCGGG
 841  CTTTCTCAATGCTCACGCTGTAGGTATCTCAGTTCGGTGTAGGTCGTTCGCTCCAAGCTG
 901  ACGAACCCCCCCGTTCAGCCCGACCGCTGCGCCTTATCCGGTAACTATCGTCTTGAGTCCA
 961  ACACGACTTAACGGGTTGGCATGGATTGTAGGCGCCGCCCTATACCTTGTCTGCCTCCCC
1021  GCGGTGCATGGAGCCGGGCCACCTCGACCTGAATGGAAGCCGGCGGCACCTCGCTAACGG
1081  CCAAGAATTGGAGCCAATCAATTCTTGCGGAGAACTGTGAATGCGCAAACCAACCCTTGG
1141  CCATCGCGTCCGCCATCTCCAGCAGCCGCACGCGGCGCATCTCGGGCAGCGTTGGGTCCT
1201  GCGCATGATCGTGCTAGCCTGTCGTTGAGGACCCGGCTAGGCTGGCGGGGTTGCCTTACT
1281  ATGAATCACCGATACGCGAGCGAACGTGAAGCGACTGCTGCTGCAAAACGTCTGCGACCT
1341  ATGAATGGTCTTCGGTTTCCGTGTTTCGTAAAGTCTGGAAACGCGGAAGTCAGCGCCCTG
```

"And here is the revised DNA strand, repaired by the computer.

The operation you've witnessed would have taken months in a conventional lab, but we can do it in seconds."

"Then are you working with the entire DNA strand?" Grant asked.

"Oh no," Wu said. "That's impossible. We've come a long way from the sixties, when it took a whole laboratory four *years* to decode a screen like this. Now the computers can do it in a couple of hours. But, even so, the DNA molecule is too big. We look only at the sections of the strand that differ from animal to animal, or from contemporary DNA. Only a few percent of the nucleotides differ from one species to the next. That's what we analyze, and it's still a big job."

Dennis Nedry yawned. He'd long ago concluded that InGen must be doing something like this. A couple of years earlier, when InGen had hired Nedry to design the park control systems, one of the initial design parameters called for data records with 3×10^9 fields. Nedry just assumed that was a mistake, and had called Palo Alto to verify it. But they had told him the spec was correct. Three billion fields.

Nedry had worked on a lot of large systems. He'd made a name for himself setting up worldwide telephone communications for multinational corporations. Often those systems had millions of records. He was used to that. But InGen wanted something so much larger. . . .

Puzzled, Nedry had gone to see Barney Fellows over at Symbolics, near the M.I.T. campus in Cambridge. "What kind of a database has three billion records, Barney?"

"A mistake," Barney said, laughing. "They put in an extra zero or two."

"It's not a mistake. I checked. It's what they want."

"But that's crazy," Barney said. "It's not workable. Even if you had the fastest processors and blindingly fast algorithms, a search would still take days. Maybe weeks."

"Yeah," Nedry said. "I know. Fortunately I'm not being asked to do algorithms. I'm just being asked to reserve storage and memory for the overall system. But still . . . what could the database be for?"

Barney frowned. "You operating under an ND?"

"Yes," Nedry said. Most of his jobs required nondisclosure agreements.

"Can you tell me anything?"

"It's a bioengineering firm."

"Bioengineering," Barney said. "Well, there's the obvious . . ."

"Which is?"

"A DNA molecule."

"Oh, come on," Nedry said. "Nobody could be analyzing a DNA molecule." He knew biologists were talking about the Human Genome Project, to analyze a complete human DNA strand. But that would take ten years of coordinated effort, involving laboratories around the world. It was an enormous undertaking, as big as the Manhattan Project, which made the atomic bomb. "This is a private company," Nedry said.

"With three billion records," Barney said, "I don't know what else it could be. Maybe they're being optimistic designing their system."

"Very optimistic," Nedry said.

"Or maybe they're just analyzing DNA fragments, but they've got RAM-intensive algorithms."

That made more sense. Certain database search techniques ate up a lot of memory.

"You know who did their algorithms?"

"No," Nedry said. "This company is very secretive."

"Well, my guess is they're doing something with DNA," Barney said. "What's the system?"

"Multi-XMP."

"*Multi*-XMP? You mean more than one Cray? Wow." Barney was frowning, now, thinking that one over. "Can you tell me anything else?"

"Sorry," Nedry said. "I can't." And he had gone back and designed the control systems. It had taken him and his programming team more than a year, and it was especially difficult because the company wouldn't ever tell him what the subsystems were for. The instructions were simply "Design a module for record keeping" or "Design a module for visual display." They gave him design parameters, but no details about use. He had been working in the dark. And now that the system was up and running, he wasn't surprised to learn there were bugs. What did they expect? And they'd ordered him down here in a panic, all hot and bothered about "his" bugs. It was annoying, Nedry thought.

Nedry turned back to the group as Grant asked, "And once the computer has analyzed the DNA, how do you know what animal it encodes?"

"We have two procedures," Wu said. "The first is phylogenetic mapping. DNA evolves over time, like everything else in an organism—hands or feet or any other physical attribute. So we can take an unknown piece of DNA and determine roughly, by computer, where it fits in the evolutionary sequence. It's time-consuming, but it can be done."

"And the other way?"

Wu shrugged. "Just grow it and find out what it is," he said. "That's what we usually do. I'll show you how that's accomplished."

Tim felt a growing impatience as the tour continued. He liked technical things, but, even so, he was losing interest. They came to the next door, which was marked FERTILIZATION. Dr. Wu unlocked the door with his security card, and they went inside.

Tim saw still another room with technicians working at microscopes. In the back was a section entirely lit by blue ultraviolet light. Dr. Wu explained that their DNA work required the interruption of cellular mitosis at precise instants, and therefore they kept some of the most virulent poisons in the world. "Helotoxins, colchicinoids, beta-alkaloids," he said, pointing to a series of syringes set out under the UV light. "Kill any living animal within a second or two."

Tim would have liked to know more about the poisons, but Dr. Wu droned on about using unfertilized crocodile ova and replacing the DNA; and then Professor Grant asked some complicated questions. To one side of the room were big tanks marked Liquid N_2. And there were big walk-in freezers with shelves of frozen embryos, each stored in a tiny silver-foil wrapper.

Lex was bored. Nedry was yawning. And even Dr. Sattler was losing interest. Tim was tired of looking at these complicated laboratories. He wanted to see the dinosaurs.

The next room was labeled HATCHERY. "It's a little warm and damp in here," Dr. Wu said. "We keep it at ninety-nine degrees Fahrenheit and a relative humidity of one hundred percent. We also run a higher O_2 concentration. It's up to thirty-three percent."

"Jurassic atmosphere," Grant said.

"Yes. At least we presume so. If any of you feel faint, just tell me."

Dr. Wu inserted his security card into the slot, and the outer door hissed open. "Just a reminder: don't touch anything in this room. Some of the eggs are permeable to skin oils. And watch your heads. The sensors are always moving."

He opened the inner door to the nursery, and they went inside. Tim faced a vast open room, bathed in deep infrared light. The eggs lay on long tables, their pale outlines obscured by the hissing low mist that covered the tables. The eggs were all moving gently, rocking.

"Reptile eggs contain large amounts of yolk but no water at all. The embryos must extract water from the surrounding environment. Hence the mist."

Dr. Wu explained that each table contained 150 eggs, and represented a new batch of DNA extractions. The batches were identified by numbers at each table: STEG-458/2 or TRIC-390/4. Waist-deep in the mist, the workers in the nursery moved from one egg to the next, plunging their hands into the mist, turning the eggs every hour, and checking the temperatures with thermal sensors. The room was monitored by overhead TV cameras and motion sensors. An overhead thermal sensor moved from one egg to the next, touching each with a flexible wand, beeping, then going on.

"In this hatchery, we have produced more than a dozen crops of extractions, giving us a total of two hundred thirty-eight live animals. Our survival rate is somewhere around point four percent, and we naturally want to improve that. But by computer analysis we're working with something like five hundred variables: one hundred and twenty environmental, another two hundred intra-egg, and the rest from the genetic material itself. Our eggs are plastic. The embryos are mechanically inserted, and then hatched here."

"And how long to grow?"

"Dinosaurs mature rapidly, attaining full size in two to four years. So we now have a number of adult specimens in the park."

"What do the numbers mean?"

"Those codes," Wu said, "identify the various batch extractions of DNA. The first four letters identify the animals being grown.

Over there, that TRIC means *Triceratops*. And the STEG means *Stegosaurus*, and so on."

"And this table here?" Grant said.

The code said XXXX-0001/I. Beneath was scrawled "Presumed Coelu."

"That's a new batch of DNA," Wu said. "We don't know exactly what will grow out. The first time an extraction is done, we don't know for sure what the animal is. You can see it's marked 'Presumed Coelu,' so it is likely to be a coelurosaurus. A small herbivore, if I remember. It's hard for me to keep track of the names. There are something like three hundred genera of dinosaurs known so far."

"Three hundred and forty-seven," Tim said.

Grant smiled, then said, "Is anything hatching now?"

"Not at the moment. The incubation period varies with each animal, but in general it runs about two months. We try to stagger hatchings, to make less work for the nursery staff. You can imagine how it is when we have a hundred and fifty animals born within a few days—though of course most don't survive. Actually, these X's are due any day now. Any other questions? No? Then we'll go to the nursery, where the newborns are."

It was a circular room, all white. There were some incubators of the kind used in hospital nurseries, but they were empty at the moment. Rags and toys were scattered across the floor. A young woman in a white coat was seated on the floor, her back to them.

"What've you got here today, Kathy?" Dr. Wu asked.

"Not much," she said. "Just a baby raptor."

"Let's have a look."

The woman got to her feet and stepped aside. Tim heard Nedry say, "It looks like a lizard."

The animal on the floor was about a foot and a half long, the size of a small monkey. It was dark yellow with brown stripes, like a tiger. It had a lizard's head and long snout, but it stood upright on strong hind legs, balanced by a thick straight tail. Its smaller front legs waved in the air. It cocked its head to one side and peered at the visitors staring down at it.

"*Velociraptor*," Alan Grant said, in a low voice.

"*Velociraptor mongoliensis*," Wu said, nodding. "A predator. This one's only six weeks old."

"I just excavated a raptor," Grant said, as he bent down for a closer look. Immediately the little lizard sprang up, leaping over Grant's head into Tim's arms.

"Hey!"

"They can jump," Wu said. "The babies can jump. So can the adults, as a matter of fact."

Tim caught the velociraptor and held it to him. The little animal didn't weigh very much, a pound or two. The skin was warm and completely dry. The little head was inches from Tim's face. Its dark, beady eyes stared at him. A small forked tongue flicked in and out.

"Will he hurt me?"

"No. She's friendly."

"Are you sure about that?" asked Gennaro, with a look of concern.

"Oh, quite sure," Wu said. "At least until she grows a little older. But, in any case, the babies don't have any teeth, even egg teeth."

"Egg teeth?" Nedry said.

"Most dinosaurs are born with egg teeth—little horns on the tip of the nose, like rhino horns, to help them break out of the eggs. But raptors aren't. They poke a hole in the eggs with their pointed snouts, and then the nursery staff has to help them out."

"You have to help them out," Grant said, shaking his head. "What happens in the wild?"

"In the wild?"

"When they breed in the wild," Grant said. "When they make a nest."

"Oh, they can't do that," Wu said. "None of our animals is capable of breeding. That's why we have this nursery. It's the only way to replace stock in Jurassic Park."

"Why can't the animals breed?"

"Well, as you can imagine, it's important that they not be able to breed," Wu said. "And whenever we faced a critical matter such as this, we designed redundant systems. That is, we always arranged at least two control procedures. In this case, there are two independent reasons why the animals can't breed. First of all, they're sterile, because we irradiate them with X rays."

"And the second reason?"

"All the animals in Jurassic Park are female," Wu said, with a pleased smile.

Malcolm said, "I should like some clarification about this. Because it seems to me that irradiation is fraught with uncertainty. The radiation dose may be wrong, or aimed at the wrong anatomical area of the animal—"

"All true," Wu said. "But we're quite confident we have destroyed gonadal tissue."

"And as for them all being female," Malcolm said, "is that checked? Does anyone go out and, ah, lift up the dinosaurs' skirts to have a look? I mean, how does one determine the sex of a dinosaur, anyway?"

"Sex organs vary with the species. It's easy to tell on some, subtle on others. But, to answer your question, the reason we know all the animals are female is that we literally make them that way: we control their chromosomes, and we control the intra-egg developmental environment. From a bioengineering standpoint, females are easier to breed. You probably know that all vertebrate embryos are inherently female. We all start life as females. It takes some kind of added effect—such as a hormone at the right moment during development—to transform the growing embryo into a male. But, left to its own devices, the embryo will naturally become female. So our animals are all female. We tend to refer to some of them as male—such as the Tyrannosaurus rex; we all call it a 'him'—but in fact, they're all female. And, believe me, they can't breed."

The little velociraptor sniffed at Tim, and then rubbed her head against Tim's neck. Tim giggled.

"She wants you to feed her," Wu said.

"What does she eat?"

"Mice. But she's just eaten, so we won't feed her again for a while."

The little raptor leaned back, stared at Tim, and wiggled her forearms again in the air. Tim saw the small claws on the three fingers of each hand. Then the raptor burrowed her head against his neck again.

Grant came over, and peered critically at the creature. He touched the tiny three-clawed hand. He said to Tim, "Do you mind?" and Tim released the raptor into his hands.

Grant flipped the animal onto its back, inspecting it, while the little lizard wiggled and squirmed. Then he lifted the animal high to look at its profile, and it screamed shrilly.

"She doesn't like that," Regis said. "Doesn't like to be held away from body contact. . . ."

The raptor was still screaming, but Grant paid no attention. Now he was squeezing the tail, feeling the bones. Regis said, "Dr. Grant. If you please."

"I'm not hurting her."

"Dr. Grant. These creatures are not of our world. They come from a time when there were no human beings around to prod and poke them."

"I'm not prodding and—"

"Dr. Grant. *Put her down*," Ed Regis said.

"But—"

"*Now*." Regis was starting to get annoyed.

Grant handed the animal back to Tim. It stopped squealing. Tim could feel its little heart beating rapidly against his chest.

"I'm sorry, Dr. Grant," Regis said. "But these animals are delicate in infancy. We have lost several from a postnatal stress syndrome, which we believe is adrenocortically mediated. Sometimes they die within five minutes."

Tim petted the little raptor. "It's okay, kid," he said. "Everything's fine now." The heart was still beating rapidly.

"We feel it is important that the animals here be treated in the most humane manner," Regis said. "I promise you that you will have every opportunity to examine them later."

But Grant couldn't stay away. He again moved toward the animal in Tim's arms, peering at it.

The little velociraptor opened her jaws and hissed at Grant, in a posture of sudden intense fury.

"Fascinating," Grant said.

"Can I stay and play with her?" Tim said.

"Not right now," Ed Regis said, glancing at his watch. "It's three o'clock, and it's a good time for a tour of the park itself, so you can see all the dinosaurs in the habitats we have designed for them."

Tim released the velociraptor, which scampered across the room, grabbed a cloth rag, put it in her mouth, and tugged at the end with her tiny claws.

CONTROL

Walking back toward the control room, Malcolm said, "I have one more question, Dr. Wu. How many different species have you made so far?"

"I'm not exactly sure," Wu said. "I believe the number at the moment is fifteen. Fifteen species. Do you know, Ed?"

"Yes, it's fifteen," Ed Regis said, nodding.

"You don't know for *sure*?" Malcolm said, affecting astonishment.

Wu smiled. "I stopped counting," he said, "after the first dozen. And you have to realize that sometimes we think we have an animal correctly made—from the standpoint of the DNA, which is our basic work—and the animal grows for six months and then something untoward happens. And we realize there is some error. A releaser gene isn't operating. A hormone not being released. Or some other problem in the developmental sequence. So we have to go back to the drawing board with that animal, so to speak." He smiled. "At one time, I thought I had more than twenty species. But now, only fifteen."

"And is one of the fifteen species a—" Malcolm turned to Grant. "What was the name?"

"Procompsognathus," Grant said.

"You have made some procompsognathuses, or whatever they're called?" Malcolm asked.

"Oh yes," Wu said immediately. "Compys are very distinctive animals. And, we made an unusually large number of them."

"Why is that?"

"Well, we want Jurassic Park to be as real an environment as possible—as authentic as possible—and the procompsognathids are

111

actual scavengers from the Jurassic period. Rather like jackals. So we wanted to have the compys around to clean up."

"You mean to dispose of carcasses?"

"Yes, if there were any. But with only two hundred and thirty-odd animals in our total population, we don't have many carcasses," Wu said. "That wasn't the primary objective. Actually, we wanted the compys for another kind of waste management entirely."

"Which was?"

"Well," Wu said, "we have some very big herbivores on this island. We have specifically tried not to breed the biggest sauropods, but even so, we've got several animals in excess of thirty tons walking around out there, and many others in the five- to ten-ton area. That gives us two problems. One is feeding them, and in fact we must import food to the island every two weeks. There is no way an island this small can support these animals for any time.

"But the other problem is waste. I don't know if you've ever seen elephant droppings," Wu said, "but they are substantial. Each spoor is roughly the size of a soccer ball. Imagine the droppings of a brontosaur, ten times as large. Now imagine the droppings of a *herd* of such animals, as we keep here. And the largest animals do not digest their food terribly well, so that they excrete a great deal. And in the sixty million years since dinosaurs disappeared, apparently the bacteria that specialize in breaking down their feces disappeared, too. At least, the sauropod feces don't decompose readily."

"That's a problem," Malcolm said.

"I assure you it is," Wu said, not smiling. "We had a hell of a time trying to solve it. You probably know that in Africa there is a specific insect, the dung beetle, which eats elephant feces. Many other large species have associated creatures that have evolved to eat their excrement. Well, it turns out that compys will eat the feces of large herbivores and redigest it. And the droppings of compys are readily broken down by contemporary bacteria. So, given enough compys, our problem was solved."

"How many compys did you make?"

"I've forgotten exactly, but I think the target population was fifty animals. And we attained that, or very nearly so. In three batches. We did a batch every six months until we had the number."

"Fifty animals," Malcolm said, "is a lot to keep track of."

"The control room is built to do exactly that. They'll show you how it's done."

"I'm sure," Malcolm said. "But if one of these compys were to escape from the island, to get away . . ."

"They can't get away."

"I know that, but just supposing one did . . ."

"You mean like the animal that was found on the beach?" Wu said, raising his eyebrows. "The one that bit the American girl?"

"Yes, for example."

"I don't know what the explanation for that animal is," Wu said. "But I know it can't possibly be one of ours, for two reasons. First, the control procedures: our animals are counted by computer every few minutes. If one were missing, we'd know at once."

"And the second reason?"

"The mainland is more than a hundred miles away. It takes almost a day to get there by boat. And in the outside world our animals will die within twelve hours," Wu said.

"How do you know?"

"Because I've made sure that's precisely what will occur," Wu said, finally showing a trace of irritation. "Look, we're not fools. We understand these are prehistoric animals. They are part of a vanished ecology—a complex web of life that became extinct millions of years ago. They might have no predators in the contemporary world, no checks on their growth. We don't want them to survive in the wild. So I've made them lysine dependent. I inserted a gene that makes a single faulty enzyme in protein metabolism. As a result, the animals cannot manufacture the amino acid lysine. They must ingest it from the outside. Unless they get a rich dietary source of exogenous lysine—supplied by us, in tablet form—they'll go into a coma within twelve hours and expire. These animals are genetically engineered to be unable to survive in the real world. They can only live here in Jurassic Park. They are not free at all. They are essentially our prisoners."

"Here's the control room," Ed Regis said. "Now that you know how the animals are made, you'll want to see the control room for the park itself, before we go out on the—"

He stopped. Through the thick glass window, the room was dark. The monitors were off, except for three that displayed spinning numbers and the image of a large boat.

"What's going on?" Ed Regis said. "Oh hell, they're docking."

"Docking?"

"Every two weeks, the supply boat comes in from the mainland. One of the things this island doesn't have is a good harbor, or even a good dock. It's a little hairy to get the ship in, when the seas are rough. Could be a few minutes." He rapped on the window, but the men inside paid no attention. "I guess we have to wait, then."

Ellie turned to Dr. Wu. "You mentioned before that sometimes you make an animal and it seems to be fine but, as it grows, it shows itself to be flawed. . . ."

"Yes," Wu said. "I don't think there's any way around that. We can duplicate the DNA, but there is a lot of timing in development, and we don't know if everything is working unless we actually see an animal develop correctly."

Grant said, "How do you know if it's developing correctly? No one has ever seen these animals before."

Wu smiled. "I have often thought about that. I suppose it is a bit of a paradox. Eventually, I hope, paleontologists such as yourself will compare our animals with the fossil record to verify the developmental sequence."

Ellie said, "But the animal we just saw, the velociraptor—you said it was a *mongoliensis*?"

"From the location of the amber," Wu said. "It is from China."

"Interesting," Grant said. "I was just digging up an infant *antirrhopus*. Are there any full-grown raptors here?"

"Yes," Ed Regis said without hesitation. "Eight adult females. The females are the real hunters. They're pack hunters, you know."

"Will we see them on the tour?"

"No," Wu said, looking suddenly uncomfortable. And there was an awkward pause. Wu looked at Regis.

"Not for a while," Regis said cheerfully. "The velociraptors haven't been integrated into the park setting just yet. We keep them in a holding pen."

"Can I see them there?" Grant said.

"Why, yes, of course. In fact, while we're waiting"—he glanced at his watch—"you might want to go around and have a look at them."

"I certainly would," Grant said.

"Absolutely," Ellie said.

"I want to go, too," Tim said eagerly.

"Just go around the back of this building, past the support facility, and you'll see the pen. But don't get too close to the fence. Do you want to go, too?" he said to the girl.

"No," Lex said. She looked appraisingly at Regis. "You want to play a little pickle? Throw a few?"

"Well, sure," Ed Regis said. "Why don't you and I go downstairs and we'll do that, while we wait for the control room to open up?"

Grant walked with Ellie and Malcolm around the back of the main building, with the kid tagging along. Grant liked kids—it was impossible not to like any group so openly enthusiastic about dinosaurs. Grant used to watch kids in museums as they stared open-mouthed at the big skeletons rising above them. He wondered what their fascination really represented. He finally decided that children liked dinosaurs because these giant creatures personified the uncontrollable force of looming authority. They were symbolic parents. Fascinating and frightening, like parents. And kids loved them, as they loved their parents.

Grant also suspected that was why even young children learned the names of dinosaurs. It never failed to amaze him when a three-year-old shrieked: *"Stegosaurus!"* Saying these complicated names was a way of exerting power over the giants, a way of being in control.

"What do you know about *Velociraptor*?" Grant asked Tim. He was just making conversation.

"It's a small carnivore that hunted in packs, like *Deinonychus*," Tim said.

"That's right," Grant said, "although *Deinonychus* is now considered one of the velociraptors. And the evidence for pack hunting is all circumstantial. It derives in part from the appearance of the animals, which are quick and strong, but small for dinosaurs—just a hundred and fifty to three hundred pounds each. We assume they hunted in groups if they were to bring down larger prey. And there are some fossil finds in which a single large prey animal is associated with several raptor skeletons, suggesting they hunted in packs. And, of course, raptors were large-brained, more intelligent than most dinosaurs."

"How intelligent is that?" Malcolm asked.

"Depends on who you talk to," Grant said. "Just as paleontologists have come around to the idea that dinosaurs were probably warm-blooded, a lot of us are starting to think some of them might have been quite intelligent, too. But nobody knows for sure."

They left the visitor area behind, and soon they heard the loud hum of generators, smelled the faint odor of gasoline. They passed a grove of palm trees and saw a large, low concrete shed with a steel roof. The noise seemed to come from there. They looked in the shed.

"It must be a generator," Ellie said.

"It's big," Grant said, peering inside.

The power plant actually extended two stories below ground level: a vast complex of whining turbines and piping that ran down in the earth, lit by harsh electric bulbs. "They can't need all this just for a resort," Malcolm said. "They're generating enough power here for a small city."

"Maybe for the computers?"

"Maybe."

Grant heard bleating, and walked north a few yards. He came to an animal enclosure with goats. By a quick count, he estimated there were fifty or sixty goats.

"What's that for?" Ellie asked.

"Beats me."

"Probably they feed 'em to the dinosaurs," Malcolm said.

The group walked on, following a dirt path through a dense bamboo grove. At the far side, they came to a double-layer chain-link fence twelve feet high, with spirals of barbed wire at the top. There was an electric hum along the outer fence.

Beyond the fences, Grant saw dense clusters of large ferns, five feet high. He heard a snorting sound, a kind of snuffling. Then the sound of crunching footsteps, coming closer.

Then a long silence.

"I don't see anything," Tim whispered, finally.

"Sssh."

Grant waited. Several seconds passed. Flies buzzed in the air. He still saw nothing.

Ellie tapped him on the shoulder, and pointed.

Amid the ferns, Grant saw the head of an animal. It was motionless, partially hidden in the fronds, the two large dark eyes watching them coldly.

The head was two feet long. From a pointed snout, a long row of teeth ran back to the hole of the auditory meatus which served as an ear. The head reminded him of a large lizard, or perhaps a crocodile. The eyes did not blink, and the animal did not move. Its skin was leathery, with a pebbled texture, and basically the same coloration as the infant's: yellow-brown with darker reddish markings, like the stripes of a tiger.

As Grant watched, a single forelimb reached up very slowly to part the ferns beside the animal's face. The limb, Grant saw, was strongly muscled. The hand had three grasping fingers, each ending in curved claws. The hand gently, slowly, pushed aside the ferns.

Grant felt a chill and thought, *He's hunting us.*

For a mammal like man, there was something indescribably alien about the way reptiles hunted their prey. No wonder men hated reptiles. The stillness, the coldness, the *pace* was all wrong. To be among alligators or other large reptiles was to be reminded of a different kind of life, a different kind of world, now vanished from the earth. Of course, this animal didn't realize that he had been spotted, that he—

The attack came suddenly, from the left and right. Charging raptors covered the ten yards to the fence with shocking speed. Grant had a blurred impression of powerful, six-foot-tall bodies, stiff balancing tails, limbs with curving claws, open jaws with rows of jagged teeth.

The animals snarled as they came forward, and then leapt bodily into the air, raising their hind legs with their big dagger-claws. Then they struck the fence in front of them, throwing off twin bursts of hot sparks.

The velociraptors fell backward to the ground, hissing. The visitors all moved forward, fascinated. Only then did the third animal attack, leaping up to strike the fence at chest level. Tim screamed in fright as the sparks exploded all around him. The creatures snarled, a low reptilian hissing sound, and leapt back among the ferns. Then they were gone, leaving behind a faint odor of decay, and hanging acrid smoke.

"Holy shit," Tim said.

"It was so *fast*," Ellie said.

"Pack hunters," Grant said, shaking his head. "Pack hunters for whom ambush is an instinct . . . Fascinating."

"I wouldn't call them tremendously intelligent," Malcolm said.

On the other side of the fence, they heard snorting in the palm trees. Several heads poked slowly out of the foliage. Grant counted three . . . four . . . five . . . The animals watched them. Staring coldly.

A black man in coveralls came running up to them. "Are you all right?"

"We're okay," Grant said.

"The alarms were set off." The man looked at the fence, dented and charred. "They attacked you?"

"Three of them did, yes."

The black man nodded. "They do that all the time. Hit the fence, take a shock. They never seem to mind."

"Not too smart, are they?" Malcolm said.

The black man paused. He squinted at Malcolm in the afternoon light. "Be glad for that fence, *señor,*" he said, and turned away.

From beginning to end, the entire attack could not have taken more than six seconds. Grant was still trying to organize his impressions. The speed was astonishing—the animals were so fast, he had hardly seen them move.

Walking back, Malcolm said, "They are remarkably fast."

"Yes," Grant said. "Much faster than any living reptile. A bull alligator can move quickly, but only over a short distance—five or six feet. Big lizards like the five-foot Komodo dragons of Indonesia have been clocked at thirty miles an hour, fast enough to run down a man. And they kill men all the time. But I'd guess the animal behind the fence was more than twice that fast."

"Cheetah speed," Malcolm said. "Sixty, seventy miles an hour."

"Exactly."

"But they seemed to dart forward," Malcolm said. "Rather like birds."

"Yes." In the contemporary world, only very small mammals, like the cobra-fighting mongoose, had such quick responses. Small mammals, and of course birds. The snake-hunting secretary bird of Africa, or the cassowary. In fact, the velociraptor conveyed precisely the same impression of deadly, swift menace Grant had seen in the cassowary, the clawed ostrich-like bird of New Guinea.

"So these velociraptors look like reptiles, with the skin and general appearance of reptiles, but they move like birds, with the speed and predatory intelligence of birds. Is that about it?" Malcolm said.

"Yes," Grant said. "I'd say they display a mixture of traits."

"Does that surprise you?"

"Not really," Grant said. "It's actually rather close to what paleontologists believed a long time ago."

When the first giant bones were found in the 1820s and 1830s, scientists felt obliged to explain the bones as belonging to some oversize variant of a modern species. This was because it was believed that no species could ever become extinct, since God would not allow one of His creations to die.

Eventually it became clear that this conception of God was mistaken, and the bones belonged to extinct animals. But what kind of animals?

In 1842, Richard Owen, the leading British anatomist of the day, called them *Dinosauria*, meaning "terrible lizards." Owen recognized that dinosaurs seemed to combine traits of lizards, crocodiles, and birds. In particular, dinosaur hips were bird-like, not lizard-like. And, unlike lizards, many dinosaurs seemed to stand upright. Owen imagined dinosaurs to be quick-moving, active creatures, and his view was accepted for the next forty years.

But when truly gigantic finds were unearthed—animals that had weighed a hundred tons in life—scientists began to envision the dinosaurs as stupid, slow-moving giants destined for extinction. The image of the sluggish reptile gradually predominated over the image of the quick-moving bird. In recent years, scientists like Grant had begun to swing back toward the idea of more active dinosaurs. Grant's colleagues saw him as radical in his conception of dinosaur behavior. But now he had to admit his own conception had fallen far short of the reality of these large, incredibly swift hunters.

"Actually, what I was driving at," Malcolm said, "was this: Is it a persuasive animal to you? Is it in fact a dinosaur?"

"I'd say so, yes."

"And the coordinated attack behavior . . ."

"To be expected," Grant said. According to the fossil record, packs of velociraptors were capable of bringing down animals that weighed a thousand pounds, like *Tenontosaurus*, which could run as fast as a horse. Coordination would be required.

"How do they do that, without language?"

"Oh, language isn't necessary for coordinated hunting," Ellie said. "Chimpanzees do it all the time. A group of chimps will stalk a monkey and kill it. All communication is by eyes."

"And were the dinosaurs in fact attacking us?"

"Yes."

"They would kill us and eat us if they could?" Malcolm said.

"I think so."

"The reason I ask," Malcolm said, "is that I'm told large predators such as lions and tigers are not born man-eaters. Isn't that true? These animals must learn somewhere along the way that human beings are easy to kill. Only afterward do they become man-killers."

"Yes, I believe that's true," Grant said.

"Well, these dinosaurs must be even more reluctant than lions and tigers. After all, they come from a time before human beings—or even large mammals—existed at all. God knows what they think when they see us. So I wonder: have they learned, somewhere along the line, that humans are easy to kill?"

The group fell silent as they walked.

"In any case," Malcolm said, "I shall be *extremely* interested to see the control room now."

VERSION 4.4

"Was there any problem with the group?" Hammond asked.

"No," Henry Wu said, "there was no problem at all."

"They accepted your explanation?"

"Why shouldn't they?" Wu said. "It's all quite straightforward, in the broad strokes. It's only the details that get sticky. And I wanted to talk about the details with you today. You can think of it as a matter of aesthetics."

John Hammond wrinkled his nose, as if he smelled something disagreeable. "Aesthetics?" he repeated.

They were standing in the living room of Hammond's elegant bungalow, set back among palm trees in the northern sector of the park. The living room was airy and comfortable, fitted with a half-dozen video monitors showing the animals in the park. The file Wu had brought, stamped ANIMAL DEVELOPMENT: VERSION 4.4, lay on the coffee table.

Hammond was looking at him in that patient, paternal way. Wu, thirty-three years old, was acutely aware that he had worked for

Hammond all his professional life. Hammond had hired him right out of graduate school.

"Of course, there are practical consequences as well," Wu said. "I really think you should consider my recommendations for phase two. We should go to version 4.4."

"You want to replace all the current stock of animals?" Hammond said.

"Yes, I do."

"Why? What's wrong with them?"

"Nothing," Wu said, "except that they're real dinosaurs."

"That's what I asked for, Henry," Hammond said, smiling. "And that's what you gave me."

"I know," Wu said. "But you see...." He paused. How could he explain this to Hammond? Hammond hardly ever visited the island. And it was a peculiar situation that Wu was trying to convey. "Right now, as we stand here, almost no one in the world has ever seen an actual dinosaur. Nobody knows what they're really like."

"Yes . . ."

"The dinosaurs we have now are real," Wu said, pointing to the screens around the room, "but in certain ways they are unsatisfactory. Unconvincing. I could make them better."

"Better in what way?"

"For one thing, they move too fast," Henry Wu said. "People aren't accustomed to seeing large animals that are so quick. I'm afraid visitors will think the dinosaurs look speeded up, like film running too fast."

"But, Henry, these are real dinosaurs. You said so yourself."

"I know," Wu said. "But we could easily breed slower, more domesticated dinosaurs."

"*Domesticated* dinosaurs?" Hammond snorted. "Nobody wants domesticated dinosaurs, Henry. They want the real thing."

"But that's my point," Wu said. "I don't think they do. They want to see their expectation, which is quite different."

Hammond was frowning.

"You said yourself, John, this park is entertainment," Wu said. "And entertainment has nothing to do with reality. Entertainment is antithetical to reality."

Hammond sighed. "Now, Henry, are we going to have another one of those abstract discussions? You know I like to keep it simple. The dinosaurs we have now are real, and—"

"Well, not exactly," Wu said. He paced the living room, pointed to the monitors. "I don't think we should kid ourselves. We haven't *re-created* the past here. The past is gone. It can never be re-created. What we've done is *reconstruct* the past—or at least a version of the past. And I'm saying we can make a better version."

"Better than real?"

"Why not?" Wu said. "After all, these animals are already modified. We've inserted genes to make them patentable, and to make them lysine dependent. And we've done everything we can to promote growth, and accelerate development into adulthood."

Hammond shrugged. "That was inevitable. We didn't want to wait. We have investors to consider."

"Of course. But I'm just saying, why stop there? Why not push ahead to make exactly the kind of dinosaur that we'd like to see? One that is more acceptable to visitors, and one that is easier for us to handle? A slower, more docile version for our park?"

Hammond frowned. "But then the dinosaurs wouldn't be real."

"But they're not real now," Wu said. "That's what I'm trying to tell you. There isn't any reality here." He shrugged helplessly. He could see he wasn't getting through. Hammond had never been interested in technical details, and the essence of the argument was technical. How could he explain to Hammond about the reality of DNA dropouts, the patches, the gaps in the sequence that Wu had been obliged to fill in, making the best guesses he could, but still, making guesses. The DNA of the dinosaurs was like old photographs that had been retouched, basically the same as the original but in some places repaired and clarified, and as a result—

"Now, Henry," Hammond said, putting his arm around Wu's shoulder. "If you don't mind my saying so, I think you're getting cold feet. You've been working very hard for a long time, and you've done a hell of a job—a *hell* of a job—and it's finally time to reveal to some people what you've done. It's natural to be a little nervous. To have some doubts. But I am convinced, Henry, that the world will be entirely satisfied. Entirely satisfied."

As he spoke, Hammond steered him toward the door.

"But, John," Wu said. "Remember back in '87, when we started to build the containment devices? We didn't have any full-grown adults yet, so we had to predict what we'd need. We ordered big taser shockers, cars with cattle prods mounted on them, guns that blow out electric nets. All built specially to our specifications. We've got a whole array of devices now—and they're all *too slow*. We've got to make some adjustments. You know that Muldoon wants military equipment: LAW missiles and laser-guided devices?"

"Let's leave Muldoon out of this," Hammond said. "I'm not worried. It's just a zoo, Henry."

The phone rang, and Hammond went to answer it. Wu tried to think of another way to press his case. But the fact was that, after five long years, Jurassic Park was nearing completion, and John Hammond just wasn't listening to him any more.

There had been a time when Hammond listened to Wu very attentively. Especially when he had first recruited him, back in the days when Henry Wu was a twenty-eight-year-old graduate student getting his doctorate at Stanford in Norman Atherton's lab.

Atherton's death had thrown the lab into confusion as well as mourning; no one knew what would happen to the funding or the doctoral programs. There was a lot of uncertainty; people worried about their careers.

Two weeks after the funeral, John Hammond came to see Wu. Everyone in the lab knew that Atherton had had some association with Hammond, although the details were never clear. But Hammond had approached Wu with a directness Wu never forgot.

"Norman always said you're the best geneticist in his lab," he said. "What are your plans now?"

"I don't know. Research."

"You want a university appointment?"

"Yes."

"That's a mistake," Hammond said briskly. "At least, if you respect your talent."

Wu had blinked. "Why?"

"Because, let's face facts," Hammond said. "Universities are no longer the intellectual centers of the country. The very idea is preposterous. Universities are the backwater. Don't look so surprised. I'm not saying anything you don't know. Since World War II, all the really important discoveries have come out of private laboratories. The laser, the transistor, the polio vaccine, the microchip, the hologram, the personal computer, magnetic resonance imaging, CAT scans—the list goes on and on. Universities simply aren't where it's happening any more. And they haven't been for forty years. If you want to do something important in computers or genetics, you don't go to a *university*. Dear me, no."

Wu found he was speechless.

"Good heavens," Hammond said, "what must you go through to start a new project? How many grant applications, how many forms, how many approvals? The steering committee? The department chairman? The university resources committee? How do you get more work space if you need it? More assistants if you need them? How long does all that take? A brilliant man can't squander precious time with forms and committees. Life is too short, and DNA too long. You want to make your mark. If you want to get something *done*, stay out of universities."

In those days, Wu desperately wanted to make his mark. John Hammond had his full attention.

"I'm talking about *work*," Hammond continued. "Real accomplishment. What does a scientist need to work? He needs time, and he needs money. I'm talking about giving you a five-year commitment, and ten million dollars a year in funding. Fifty million dollars, and no one tells you how to spend it. You decide. Everyone else just *gets out of your way*."

It sounded too good to be true. Wu was silent for a long time. Finally he said, "In return for what?"

"For taking a crack at the impossible," Hammond said. "For trying something that probably can't be done."

"What does it involve?"

"I can't give you details, but the general area involves cloning reptiles."

"I don't think that's impossible," Wu said. "Reptiles are easier than mammals. Cloning's probably only ten, fifteen years off. Assuming some fundamental advances."

"I've got five years," Hammond said. "And a lot of money, for somebody who wants to take a crack at it now."

"Is my work publishable?"

"Eventually."

"Not immediately?"

"No."

"But eventually publishable?" Wu asked, sticking on this point.

Hammond had laughed. "Don't worry. If you succeed, the whole world will know about what you've done, I promise you."

* * *

And now it seemed the whole world would indeed know, Wu thought. After five years of extraordinary effort, they were just a year away from opening the park to the public. Of course, those years hadn't gone exactly as Hammond had promised. Wu had had some people telling him what to do, and many times fearsome pressures were placed on him. And the work itself had shifted—it wasn't even reptilian cloning, once they began to understand that dinosaurs were so similar to birds. It was avian cloning, a very different proposition. Much more difficult. And for the last two years, Wu had been primarily an administrator, supervising teams of researchers and banks of computer-operated gene sequencers. Administration wasn't the kind of work he relished. It wasn't what he had bargained for.

Still, he had succeeded. He had done what nobody really believed could be done, at least in so short a time. And Henry Wu thought that he should have some rights, some say in what happened, by virtue of his expertise and his efforts. Instead, he found his influence waning with each passing day. The dinosaurs existed. The procedures for obtaining them were worked out to the point of being routine. The technologies were mature. And John Hammond didn't need Henry Wu any more.

"That should be fine," Hammond said, speaking into the phone. He listened for a while, and smiled at Wu. "Fine. Yes. Fine." He hung up. "Where were we, Henry?"

"We were talking about phase two," Wu said.

"Oh yes. We've gone over some of this before, Henry—"

"I know, but you don't realize—"

"Excuse me, Henry," Hammond said, with an edge of impatience in his voice. "I *do* realize. And I must tell you frankly, Henry. I see no reason to improve upon reality. Every change we've made in the genome has been forced on us by law or necessity. We may make other changes in the future, to resist disease, or for other reasons. But I don't think we should improve upon reality just because we think it's better that way. We have real dinosaurs out there now. That's what people want to see. And that's what they *should* see. That's our obligation, Henry. That's *honest*, Henry."

And, smiling, Hammond opened the door for him to leave.

CONTROL

Grant looked at all the computer monitors in the darkened control room, feeling irritable. Grant didn't like computers. He knew that this made him old-fashioned, dated as a researcher, but he didn't care. Some of the kids who worked for him had a real feeling for computers, an intuition. Grant never felt that. He found computers to be alien, mystifying machines. Even the fundamental distinction between an operating system and an application left him confused and disheartened, literally lost in a foreign geography he didn't begin to comprehend. But he noticed that Gennaro was perfectly comfortable, and Malcolm seemed to be in his element, making little sniffing sounds, like a bloodhound on a trail.

"You want to know about control mechanisms?" John Arnold said, turning in his chair in the control room. The head engineer was a thin, tense, chain-smoking man of forty-five. He squinted at the others in the room. "We have *unbelievable* control mechanisms," Arnold said, and lit another cigarette.

"For example," Gennaro said.

"For example, animal tracking." Arnold pressed a button on his console, and the vertical glass map lit up with a pattern of jagged blue lines. "That's our juvenile T-rex. The little rex. All his movements within the park over the last twenty-four hours." Arnold pressed the button again. "Previous twenty-four." And again. "Previous twenty-four."

The lines on the map became densely overlaid, a child's scribble. But the scribble was localized in a single area, near the southeast side of the lagoon.

"You get a sense of his home range over time," Arnold said. "He's young, so he stays close to the water. And he stays away from

126

the big adult rex. You put up the big rex and the little rex, and you'll see their paths never cross."

"Where is the big rex right now?" Gennaro asked.

Arnold pushed another button. The map cleared, and a single glowing spot with a code number appeared in the fields northwest of the lagoon. "He's right there."

"And the little rex?"

"Hell, I'll show you every animal in the park," Arnold said. The map began to light up like a Christmas tree, dozens of spots of light, each tagged with a code number. "That's two hundred thirty-eight animals as of this minute."

"How accurate?"

"Within five feet." Arnold puffed on the cigarette. "Let's put it this way: you drive out in a vehicle and you will find the animals right there, exactly as they're shown on the map."

"How often is this updated?"

"Every thirty seconds."

"Pretty impressive," Gennaro said. "How's it done?"

"We have motion sensors all around the park," Arnold said. "Most of 'em hard-wired, some radio-telemetered. Of course, motion sensors won't usually tell you the species, but we get image recognition direct off the video. Even when we're not watching the video monitors, the computer is. And checking where everybody is."

"Does the computer ever make a mistake?"

"Only with the babies. It mixes those up sometimes, because they're such small images. But we don't sweat that. The babies almost always stay close to herds of adults. Also you have the category tally."

"What's that?"

"Once every fifteen minutes, the computer tallies the animals in all categories," Arnold said. "Like this."

Total Animals	238		
Species	**Expected**	**Found**	**Ver**
Tyrannosaurs	2	2	4.1
Maiasaurs	21	21	3.3
Stegosaurs	4	4	3.9
Triceratops	8	8	3.1
Procompsognathids	49	49	3.9
Othnielia	16	16	3.1

Velociraptors	8	8	3.0
Apatosaurs	17	17	3.1
Hadrosaurs	11	11	3.1
Dilophosaurs	7	7	4.3
Pterosaurs	6	6	4.3
Hypsilophodontids	33	33	2.9
Euoplocephalids	16	16	4.0
Styracosaurs	18	18	3.9
Microceratops	22	22	4.1
Total	**238**	**238**	

"What you see here," Arnold said, "is an entirely separate counting procedure. It isn't based on the tracking data. It's a fresh look. The whole idea is that the computer can't make a mistake, because it compares two different ways of gathering the data. If an animal were missing, we'd know it within five minutes."

"I see," Malcolm said. "And has that ever actually been tested?"

"Well, in a way," Arnold said. "We've had a few animals die. An othnielian got caught in the branches of a tree and strangled. One of the stegos died of that intestinal illness that keeps bothering them. One of the hypsilophodonts fell and broke his neck. And in each case, once the animal stopped moving, the numbers stopped tallying and the computer signaled an alert."

"Within five minutes."

"Yes."

Grant said, "What is the right-hand column?"

"Release version of the animals. The most recent are version 4.1 or 4.3. We're considering going to version 4.4."

"Version numbers? You mean like software? New releases?"

"Well, yes," Arnold said. "It is like software, in a way. As we discover the glitches in the DNA, Dr. Wu's labs have to make a new version."

The idea of living creatures being numbered like software, being subject to updates and revisions, troubled Grant. He could not exactly say why—it was too new a thought—but he was instinctively uneasy about it. They were, after all, living creatures. . . .

Arnold must have noticed his expression, because he said, "Look, Dr. Grant, there's no point getting starry-eyed about these animals. It's important for everyone to remember that these animals are *created*. Created by man. Sometimes there are bugs. So, as we discover the bugs, Dr. Wu's labs have to make a new version. And we need to keep track of what version we have out there."

"Yes, yes, of course you do," Malcolm said impatiently. "But, going back to the matter of *counting*—I take it all the counts are based on motion sensors?"

"Yes."

"And these sensors are everywhere in the park?"

"They cover ninety-two percent of the land area," Arnold said. "There are only a few places we can't use them. For example, we can't use them on the jungle river, because the movement of the water and the convection rising from the surface screws up the sensors. But we have them nearly everywhere else. And if the computer tracks an animal into an unsensed zone, it'll remember, and look for the animal to come out again. And if it doesn't, it gives us an alarm."

"Now, then," Malcolm said. "You show forty-nine procompsognathids. Suppose I suspect that some of them aren't really the correct species. How would you show me that I'm wrong?"

"Two ways," Arnold said. "First of all, I can track individual movements against the other presumed compys. Compys are social animals, they move in a group. We have two compy groups in the park. So the individuals should be within either group A or group B."

"Yes, but—"

"The other way is direct visual," he said. He punched buttons and one of the monitors began to flick rapidly through images of compys, numbered from 1 to 49.

"These pictures are . . ."

"Current ID images. From within the last five minutes."

"So you can see all the animals, if you want to?"

"Yes. I can visually review all the animals whenever I want."

"How about physical containment?" Gennaro said. "Can they get out of their enclosures?"

"Absolutely not," Arnold said. "These are expensive animals, Mr. Gennaro. We take very good care of them. We maintain multiple barriers. First, the moats." He pressed a button, and the board lit up with a network of orange bars. "These moats are never less than twelve feet deep, and water-filled. For bigger animals the moats may be thirty feet deep. Next, the electrified fences." Lines of bright red glowed on the board. "We have fifty miles of twelve-foot-high fencing, including twenty-two miles around the perimeter of the island. All the park fences carry ten thousand volts. The animals quickly learn not to go near them."

"But if one *did* get out?" Gennaro said.

Arnold snorted, and stubbed out his cigarette.

"Just hypothetically," Gennaro said. "Supposing it happened?"

Muldoon cleared his throat. "We'd go out and get the animal back," he said. "We have lots of ways to do that—taser shock guns, electrified nets, tranquilizers. All nonlethal, because, as Mr. Arnold says, these are expensive animals."

Gennaro nodded. "And if one got off the island?"

"It'd die in less than twenty-four hours," Arnold said. "These are genetically engineered animals. They're unable to survive in the real world."

"How about this control system itself?" Gennaro said. "Could anybody tamper with it?"

Arnold was shaking his head. "The system is hardened. The computer is independent in every way. Independent power and independent backup power. The system does not communicate with the outside, so it cannot be influenced remotely by modem. The computer system is secure."

There was a pause. Arnold puffed his cigarette. "Hell of a system," he said. "Hell of a goddamned system."

"Then I guess," Malcolm said, "your system works so well, you don't have any problems."

"We've got endless problems here," Arnold said, raising an eyebrow. "But none of the things you worry about. I gather you're worried that the animals will escape, and will get to the mainland and raise hell. We haven't got any concern about that at all. We see these animals as fragile and delicate. They've been brought back after sixty-five million years to a world that's very different from the one they left, the one they were adapted to. We have a hell of a time caring for them.

"You have to realize," Arnold continued, "that men have been keeping mammals and reptiles in zoos for hundreds of years. So we know a lot about how to take care of an elephant or a croc. But nobody has ever tried to take care of a dinosaur before. They are new animals. And we just don't know. Diseases in our animals are the biggest concern."

"Diseases?" Gennaro said, suddenly alarmed. "Is there any way that a visitor could get sick?"

Arnold snorted again. "You ever catch a cold from a zoo alligator, Mr. Gennaro? Zoos don't worry about that. Neither do we. What we *do* worry about is the animals' dying from their own illnesses, or infecting other animals. But we have programs to monitor that, too. You want to see the big rex's health file? His vaccination record? His dental record? That's something—you ought to see the vets scrubbing those big fangs so he doesn't get tooth decay. . . ."

"Not just now," Gennaro said. "What about your mechanical systems?"

"You mean the rides?" Arnold said.

Grant looked up sharply: *rides*?

"None of the rides are running yet," Arnold was saying. "We have the Jungle River Ride, where the boats follow tracks underwater, and we have the Aviary Lodge Ride, but none of it's operational yet. The park'll open with the basic dinosaur tour—the one that you're about to take in a few minutes. The other rides will come on line six, twelve months after that."

"Wait a minute," Grant said. "You're going to have rides? Like an amusement park?"

Arnold said, "This is a zoological park. We have tours of different areas, and we call them rides. That's all."

Grant frowned. Again he felt troubled. He didn't like the idea of dinosaurs being used for an amusement park.

Malcolm continued his questions. "You can run the whole park from this control room?"

"Yes," Arnold said. "I can run it single-handed, if I have to. We've got that much automation built in. The computer by itself can track the animals, feed them, and fill their water troughs for forty-eight hours without supervision."

"This is the system Mr. Nedry designed?" Malcolm asked. Dennis Nedry was sitting at a terminal in the far corner of the room, eating a candy bar and typing.

"Yes, that's right," Nedry said, not looking up from the keyboard.

"It's a hell of a system," Arnold said proudly.

"That's right," Nedry said absently. "Just one or two minor bugs to fix."

"Now," Arnold said, "I see the tour is starting, so unless you have other questions . . ."

"Actually, just one," Malcolm said. "Just a research question. You showed us that you can track the procompsognathids and you can visually display them individually. Can you do any studies of them as a group? Measure them, or whatever? If I wanted to know height or weight, or . . ."

Arnold was punching buttons. Another screen came up.

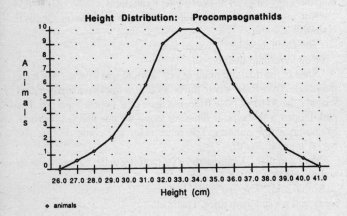

Height Distribution: Procompsognathids

Animals (y-axis): 0 1 2 3 4 5 6 7 8 9 10

Height (cm) (x-axis): 26.0 27.0 28.0 29.0 30.0 31.0 32.0 33.0 34.0 35.0 36.0 37.0 38.0 39.0 40.0 41.0

○ animals

"We can do all of that, and very quickly," Arnold said. "The computer takes measurement data in the course of reading the video screens, so it is translatable at once. You see here we have a normal Gaussian distribution for the animal population. It shows that most of the animals cluster around an average central value, and a few are either larger or smaller than the average, at the tails of the curve."

"You'd expect that kind of graph," Malcolm said.

"Yes. Any healthy biological population shows this kind of distribution. Now, then," Arnold said, lighting another cigarette, "are there any other questions?"

"No," Malcolm said. "I've learned what I need to know."

As they were walking out, Gennaro said, "It looks like a pretty good system to me. I don't see how any animals could get off this island."

"Don't you?" Malcolm said. "I thought it was completely obvious."

"Wait a minute," Gennaro said. "You think animals have gotten out?"

"I *know* they have."

Gennaro said, "But how? You saw for yourself. They can count all the animals. They can look at all the animals. They know where all the animals are at all times. How can one possibly escape?"

Malcolm smiled. "It's quite obvious," he said. "It's just a matter of your assumptions."

"Your assumptions," Gennaro repeated, frowning.

"Yes," Malcolm said. "Look here. The basic event that has occurred in Jurassic Park is that the scientists and technicians have tried to make a new, complete biological world. And the scientists in the control room expect to see a natural world. As in the graph they just showed us. Even though a moment's thought reveals that nice, normal distribution is terribly worrisome on this island."

"It is?"

"Yes. Based on what Dr. Wu told us earlier, one should never see a population graph like that."

"Why not?" Gennaro said.

"Because that is a graph for a normal biological population. Which is precisely what Jurassic Park is not. Jurassic Park is not the real world. It is intended to be a controlled world that only imitates the natural world. In that sense, it's a true park, rather like a Japanese formal garden. Nature manipulated to be more natural than the real thing, if you will."

"I'm afraid you've lost me," Gennaro said, looking annoyed.

"I'm sure the tour will make everything clear," Malcolm said.

THE TOUR

"This way, everybody, this way," Ed Regis said. By his side, a woman was passing out pith helmets with "Jurassic Park" labeled on the headband, and a little blue dinosaur logo.

A line of Toyota Land Cruisers came out of an underground garage beneath the visitor center. Each car pulled up, driverless and silent. Two black men in safari uniforms were opening the doors for passengers.

"Two to four passengers to a car, please, two to four passengers to a car," a recorded voice was saying. "Children under ten must be accompanied by an adult. Two to four passengers to a car, please . . ."

Tim watched as Grant, Sattler, and Malcolm got into the first Land Cruiser with the lawyer, Gennaro. Tim looked over at Lex, who was standing pounding her fist into her glove.

Tim pointed to the first car and said, "Can I go with them?"

"I'm afraid they have things to discuss," Ed Regis said. "Technical things."

"I'm interested in technical things," Tim said. "I'd rather go with them."

"Well, you'll be able to hear what they're saying," Regis said. "We'll have a radio open between the cars."

The second car came. Tim and Lex got in, and Ed Regis followed. "These are electric cars," Regis said. "Guided by a cable in the roadway."

Tim was glad he was sitting in the front seat, because mounted in the dashboard were two computer screens and a box that looked to him like a CD-ROM; that was a laser disk player controlled by a computer. There was also a portable walkie-talkie and some kind of a radio transmitter. There were two antennas on the roof, and some odd goggles in the map pocket.

The black men shut the doors of the Land Cruiser. The car started off with an electric hum. Up ahead, the three scientists and Gennaro were talking and pointing, clearly excited. Ed Regis said, "Let's hear what they are saying." An intercom clicked.

"I don't know what the hell you think you're doing here," Gennaro said, over the intercom. He sounded very angry.

"I know quite well why I'm here," Malcolm said.

"You're here to advise me, not play goddamned mind games. I've got five percent of this company and a responsibility to make sure that Hammond has done his job responsibly. Now you goddamn come here—"

Ed Regis pressed the intercom button and said, "In keeping with the nonpolluting policies of Jurassic Park, these lightweight electric Land Cruisers have been specially built for us by Toyota in Osaka. Eventually we hope to drive among the animals—just as they do in African game parks—but, for now, sit back and enjoy the self-guided tour." He paused. "And, by the way, we can hear you back here."

"Oh Christ," Gennaro said. "I have to be able to speak freely. I didn't ask for these damned kids to come—"

Ed Regis smiled blandly and pushed a button. "We'll just begin the show, shall we?" They heard a fanfare of trumpets, and the interior screens flashed WELCOME TO JURASSIC PARK. A sonorous voice said, "Welcome to Jurassic Park. You are now entering the lost world of the prehistoric past, a world of mighty creatures long gone from the face of the earth, which you are privileged to see for the first time."

"That's Richard Kiley," Ed Regis said. "We spared no expense."

The Land Cruiser passed through a grove of low, stumpy palm trees. Richard Kiley was saying, "Notice, first of all, the remarkable plant life that surrounds you. Those trees to your left and right are called cycads, the prehistoric predecessors of palm trees. Cycads were a favorite food of the dinosaurs. You can also see bennettitaleans, and ginkgoes. The world of the dinosaur included more modern plants, such as pine and fir trees, and swamp cypresses. You will see these as well."

The Land Cruiser moved slowly among the foliage. Tim noticed the fences and retaining walls were screened by greenery to heighten the illusion of moving through real jungle.

"We imagine the world of the dinosaurs," said Richard Kiley's voice, "as a world of huge vegetarians, eating their way through the giant swampy forests of the Jurassic and Cretaceous world, a hundred million years ago. But most dinosaurs were not as large as people think. The smallest dinosaurs were no bigger than a house cat, and the average dinosaur was about as big as a pony. We are first going to visit one of these average-size animals, called hypsilophodonts. If you look to your left, you may catch a glimpse of them now."

They all looked to the left.

The Land Cruiser stopped on a low rise, where a break in the foliage provided a view to the east. They could see a sloping forested area which opened into a field of yellow grass that was about three feet high. There were no dinosaurs.

"Where are they?" Lex said.

Tim looked at the dashboard. The transmitter lights blinked and the CD-ROM whirred. Obviously the disk was being accessed by some automatic system. He guessed that the same motion sensors that tracked the animals also controlled the screens in the Land Cruiser. The screens now showed pictures of hypsilophodonts, and printed out data about them.

The voice said, "Hypsilophodontids are the gazelles of the dinosaur world: small, quick animals that once roamed everywhere in the world, from England to Central Asia to North America. We think these dinosaurs were so successful because they had better jaws and teeth for chewing plants than their contemporaries did. In fact, the name 'hypsilophodontid' means 'high-ridge tooth,' which refers to the characteristic self-sharpening teeth of these animals. You can see them in the plains directly ahead, and also perhaps in the branches of the trees."

"In the *trees*?" Lex said. "Dinosaurs in the trees?"

Tim was scanning with binoculars, too. "To the right," he said. "Halfway up that big green trunk . . ."

In the dappled shadows of the tree a motionless, dark green animal about the size of a baboon stood on a branch. It looked like a lizard standing on its hind legs. It balanced itself with a long drooping tail.

"That's an othnielia," Tim said.

"The small animals you see are called othnielia," the voice said, "in honor of the nineteenth-century dinosaur hunter Othniel Marsh of Yale."

Tim spotted two more animals, on higher branches of the same tree. They were all about the same size. None of them were moving.

"Pretty boring," Lex said. "They're not doing anything."

"The main herd of animals can be found in the grassy plain below you," said the voice. "We can rouse them with a simple mating call." A loudspeaker by the fence gave a long nasal call, like the honking of geese.

From the field of grass directly to their left, six lizard heads poked up, one after another. The effect was comical, and Tim laughed.

The heads disappeared. The loudspeaker gave the call again, and once again the heads poked up—in exactly the same way, one after another. The fixed repetition of the behavior was striking.

"Hypsilophodonts are not especially bright animals," the voice explained. "They have roughly the intelligence of a domestic cow."

The heads were dull green, with a mottling of dark browns and blacks that extended down the slender necks. Judging from the size of the heads, Tim guessed their bodies were four feet long, about as large as deer.

Some of the hypsilophodonts were chewing, the jaws working. One reached up and scratched its head, with a five-fingered hand. The gesture gave the creature a pensive, thoughtful quality.

"If you see them scratching, that is because they have skin problems. The veterinary scientists here at Jurassic Park think it may be a fungus, or an allergy. But they're not sure yet. After all, these are the first dinosaurs in history ever to be studied alive."

The electric motor of the car started, and there was a grinding of gears. At the unexpected sound, the herd of hypsilophodonts suddenly leapt into the air and bounded above the grass like kangaroos, showing their full bodies with massive hind limbs and long tails in the afternoon sunlight. In a few leaps, they were gone.

"Now that we've had a look at these fascinating herbivores, we will go on to some dinosaurs that are a little larger. Quite a bit larger, in fact."

The Land Cruisers continued onward, moving south through Jurassic Park.

CONTROL

"Gears are grinding," John Arnold said, in the darkened control room. "Have maintenance check the electric clutches on vehicles BB4 and BB5 when they come back."

"Yes, Mr. Arnold," replied the voice on the intercom.

"A minor detail," Hammond said, walking in the room. Looking out, he could see the two Land Cruisers moving south through the park. Muldoon stood in the corner, silently watching.

Arnold pushed his chair back from the central console at the control panel. "There are no minor details, Mr. Hammond," he said, and he lit another cigarette. Nervous at most times, Arnold was especially edgy now. He was only too aware that this was the first time visitors had actually toured the park. In fact, Arnold's team didn't often go into the park. Harding, the vet, sometimes did. The animal handlers went to the individual feeding houses. But otherwise they watched the park from the control room. And now, with visitors out there, he worried about a hundred details.

John Arnold was a systems engineer who had worked on the Polaris submarine missile in the late 1960s, until he had his first child and the prospect of making weapons became too distasteful. Meanwhile, Disney had started to create amusement park rides of great technological sophistication, and they employed a lot of aerospace people. Arnold helped build Disney World in Orlando, and had gone on to implement major parks at Magic Mountain in California, Old Country in Virginia, and Astroworld in Houston.

His continuous employment at parks had eventually given him a somewhat skewed view of reality. Arnold contended, only half jokingly, that the entire world was increasingly described by the metaphor of the theme park. "Paris is a theme park," he once announced, after a vacation, "although it's too expensive, and the park employees are unpleasant and sullen."

For the past two years, Arnold's job had been to get Jurassic Park up and running. As an engineer, he was accustomed to long time schedules—he often referred to "the September opening," by which he meant September of the following year—and as the September opening approached, he was unhappy with the progress that had been made. He knew from experience that it sometimes took years to work the bugs out of a single park ride—let alone get a whole park running properly.

"You're just a worrier," Hammond said.

"I don't think so," Arnold said. "You've got to realize that, from an engineering standpoint, Jurassic Park is by far the most ambitious theme park in history. Visitors will never think about it, but I do."

He ticked the points off on his fingers.

"First, Jurassic Park has all the problems of any amusement park—ride maintenance, queue control, transportation, food handling, living accommodations, trash disposal, security.

"Second, we have all the problems of a major zoo—care of the animals; health and welfare; feeding and cleanliness; protection from insects, pests, allergies, and illnesses; maintenance of barriers; and all the rest.

"And, finally, we have the unprecedented problems of caring for a population of animals that no one has ever tried to maintain before."

"Oh, it's not as bad as all that," Hammond said.

"Yes, it is. You're just not here to see it," Arnold said. "The tyrannosaurs drink the lagoon water and sometimes get sick; we aren't sure why. The triceratops females kill each other in fights for dominance and have to be separated into groups smaller than six. We don't know why. The stegosaurs frequently get blisters on their tongues and diarrhea, for reasons no one yet understands, even though we've lost two. Hypsilophodonts get skin rashes. And the velociraptors—"

"Let's not start on the velociraptors," Hammond said. "I'm sick of hearing about the velociraptors. How they're the most vicious creatures anyone has ever seen."

"They are," Muldoon said, in a low voice. "They should all be destroyed."

"You wanted to fit them with radio collars," Hammond said. "And I agreed."

"Yes. And they promptly chewed the collars off. But even if the raptors never get free," Arnold said, "I think we have to accept that Jurassic Park is inherently hazardous."

"Oh *balls*," Hammond said. "Whose side are you on, anyway?"

"We now have fifteen species of extinct animals, and most of them are dangerous," Arnold said. "We've been forced to delay the Jungle River Ride because of the dilophosaurs; and the Pteratops Lodge in the aviary, because the pterodactyls are so unpredictable. These aren't engineering delays, Mr. Hammond. They're problems with control of the animals."

"You've had plenty of engineering delays," Hammond said. "Don't blame it on the animals."

"Yes, we have. In fact, it's all we could do to get the main attraction, Park Drive, working correctly, to get the CD-ROMs inside the cars to be controlled by the motion sensors. It's taken weeks of adjustment to get that working properly—and now the electric gearshifts on the cars are acting up! The gearshifts!"

"Let's keep it in perspective," Hammond said. "You get the engineering correct and the animals will fall into place. After all, they're trainable."

From the beginning, this had been one of the core beliefs of the planners. The animals, however exotic, would fundamentally behave like animals in zoos anywhere. They would learn the regularities of their care, and they would respond.

"Meanwhile, how's the computer?" Hammond said. He glanced at Dennis Nedry, who was working at a terminal in the corner of the room. "This damn computer has always been a headache."

"We're getting there," Nedry said.

"If you had done it right in the first place," Hammond began, but Arnold put a restraining hand on his arm. Arnold knew there was no point in antagonizing Nedry while he was working.

"It's a large system," Arnold said. "There are bound to be glitches."

In fact, the bug list now ran to more than 130 items, and included many odd aspects. For example:

The animal-feeding program reset itself every twelve hours, not every twenty-four hours, and would not record feedings on Sundays. As a result, the staff could not accurately measure how much the animals were eating.

The security system, which controlled all the security-card-operated doors, cut out whenever main power was lost, and did not come back on with auxiliary power. The security program only ran with main power.

The physical conservation program, intended to dim lights after 10:00 p.m., only worked on alternate days of the week.

The automated fecal analysis (called Auto Poop), designed to check for parasites in the animal stools, invariably recorded all specimens as having the parasite *Phagostomum venulosum*, although none did. The program then automatically dispensed medication into the animals' food. If the handlers dumped the medicine out of the hoppers to prevent its being dispensed, an alarm sounded which could not be turned off.

And so it went, page after page of errors.

When he had arrived, Dennis Nedry had been under the impression that he could make all the fixes himself over the weekend. He had paled when he saw the full listing. Now he was calling his office in Cambridge, telling his staff programmers they were going to have to cancel their weekend plans and work overtime until Monday. And he had told John Arnold that he would need to use every telephone link between Isla Nublar and the mainland just to transfer program data back and forth to his programmers.

While Nedry worked, Arnold punched up a new window in his own monitor. It allowed him to see what Nedry was doing at the corner console. Not that he didn't trust Nedry. But Arnold just liked to know what was going on.

He looked at the graphics display on his right-hand console, which showed the progress of the electric Land Cruisers. They were following the river, just north of the aviary, and the ornithischian paddock.

"If you look to your left," said the voice, "you will see the dome of the Jurassic Park aviary, which is not yet finished for visitors." Tim saw sunlight glinting off aluminum struts in the distance. "And directly below is our Mesozoic jungle river—where, if you are lucky, you just may catch a glimpse of a very rare carnivore. Keep your eyes peeled, everyone!"

Inside the Land Cruiser, the screens showed a bird-like head topped with a flaming red crest. But everyone in Tim's car was looking out the windows. The car was driving along a high ridge, overlooking a fast-moving river below. The river was almost enclosed by dense foliage on both sides.

"There they are now," said the voice. "The animals you see are called dilophosaurs."

Despite what the recording said, Tim saw only one. The dilophosaur crouched on its hind legs by the river, drinking. It was built on the basic carnivore pattern, with a heavy tail, strong hind limbs, and a long neck. Its ten-foot-tall body was spotted yellow and black, like a leopard.

But it was the head that held Tim's attention. Two broad curving crests ran along the top of the head from the eyes to the nose. The crests met in the center, making a V shape above the dinosaur's head. The crests had red and black stripes, reminiscent of a parrot or toucan. The animal gave a soft hooting cry, like an owl.

"They're pretty," Lex said.

"Dilophosaurus," the tape said, "is one of the earliest carnivorous dinosaurs. Scientists thought their jaw muscles were too weak to kill prey, and imagined they were primarily scavengers. But now we know they are poisonous."

"Hey." Tim grinned. "All *right*."

Again the distinctive hooting call of the dilophosaur drifted across the afternoon air toward them.

Lex shifted uneasily in her seat. "Are they really poisonous, Mr. Regis?"

"Don't worry about it," Ed Regis said.

"But are they?"

"Well, yes, Lex."

"Along with such living reptiles as Gila monsters and rattlesnakes, *Dilophosaurus* secretes a hematotoxin from glands in its mouth. Unconsciousness follows within minutes of a bite. The dinosaur will then finish the victim off at its leisure—making *Dilophosaurus* a beautiful but deadly addition to the animals you see here at Jurassic Park."

The Land Cruiser turned a corner, leaving the river behind. Tim looked back, hoping for a last glimpse of the dilophosaur. This was amazing! Poisonous dinosaurs! He wished he could stop the car, but everything was automatic. He bet Dr. Grant wanted to stop the car, too.

"If you look on the bluff to the right, you'll see Les Gigantes, the site of our superb three-star dining room. Chef Alain Richard hails from the world-famous Le Beaumanière in France. Make your reservations by dialing four from your hotel rooms."

Tim looked up on the bluff, and saw nothing.

"Not for a while, though," Ed Regis said. "The restaurant won't even start construction until November."

"Continuing on our prehistoric safari, we come next to the herbivores of the ornithischian group. If you look to your right, you can probably see them now."

Tim saw two animals, standing motionless in the shade of a large tree. Triceratops: the size and gray color of an elephant, with the truculent stance of a rhino. The horns above each eye curved five feet into the air, looking almost like inverted elephant tusks. A third, rhino-like horn was located near the nose. And they had the beaky snout of a rhino.

"Unlike other dinosaurs," the voice said, "*Triceratops serratus* can't see well. They're nearsighted, like the rhinos of today, and they tend to be surprised by moving objects. They'd charge our car if they were close enough to see it! But relax, folks—we're safe enough here.

"Triceratops have a fan-shaped crest behind their heads. It's made of solid bone, and it's very strong. These animals weigh about seven tons each. Despite their appearance, they are actually quite docile. They know their handlers, and they'll allow themselves to be petted. They particularly like to be scratched in the hindquarters."

"Why don't they move?" Lex said. She rolled down her window. "Hey! Stupid dinosaur! Move!"

"Don't bother the animals, Lex," Ed Regis said.

"Why? It's stupid. They just sit there like a picture in a book," Lex said.

The voice was saying, "—easygoing monsters from a bygone world stand in sharp contrast to what we will see next. The most famous predator in the history of the world: the mighty tyrant lizard, known as *Tyrannosaurus rex*."

"Good, *Tyrannosaurus rex*," Tim said.

"I hope he's better than these bozos," Lex said, turning away from the triceratops.

The Land Cruiser rumbled forward.

BIG REX

"The mighty tyrannosaurs arose late in dinosaur history. Dinosaurs ruled the earth for a hundred and twenty million years, but there were tyrannosaurs for only the last fifteen million years of that period."

The Land Cruisers had stopped at the rise of a hill. They overlooked a forested area sloping down to the edge of the lagoon. The sun was falling to the west, sinking into a misty horizon. The whole landscape of Jurassic Park was bathed in soft light, with lengthening shadows. The surface of the lagoon rippled in pink crescents. Farther south, they saw the graceful necks of the apatosaurs, standing at the water's edge, their bodies mirrored in the moving surface. It was quiet, except for the soft drone of cicadas. As they stared out at that landscape, it was possible to believe that they had really been transported millions of years back in time to a vanished world.

"It works, doesn't it?" they heard Ed Regis say, over the intercom. "I like to come here sometimes, in the evening. And just sit."

Grant was unimpressed. "Where is T-rex?"

"Good question. You often see the little one down in the lagoon. The lagoon's stocked, so we have fish in there. The little one has learned to catch the fish. Interesting how he does it. He doesn't use his hands, but he ducks his whole head under the water. Like a bird."

"The little one?"

"The little T-rex. He's a juvenile, two years old, and about a third grown now. Stands eight feet high, weighs a ton and a half. The other one's a full-grown tyrannosaur. But I don't see him at the moment."

"Maybe he's down hunting the apatosaurs," Grant said.

Regis laughed, his voice tinny over the radio. "He would if he

144

could, believe me. Sometimes he stands by the lagoon and stares at those animals, and wiggles those little forearms of his in frustration. But the T-rex territory is completely enclosed with trenches and fences. They're disguised from view, but believe me, he can't go anywhere."

"Then where is he?"

"Hiding," Regis said. "He's a little shy."

"Shy?" Malcolm said. "Tyrannosaurus rex is *shy*?"

"Well, he conceals himself as a general rule. You almost never see him out in the open, especially in daylight."

"Why is that?"

"We think it's because he has sensitive skin and sunburns easily."

Malcolm began to laugh.

Grant sighed. "You're destroying a lot of illusions."

"I don't think you'll be disappointed," Regis said. "Just wait."

They heard a soft bleating sound. In the center of a field, a small cage rose up into view, lifted on hydraulics from underground. The cage bars slid down, and the goat remained tethered in the center of the field, bleating plaintively.

"Any minute now," Regis said again.

They stared out the window.

"Look at them," Hammond said, watching the control room monitor. "Leaning out of the windows, so eager. They can't wait to see it. They have come for the danger."

"That's what I'm afraid of," Muldoon said. He twirled the keys on his finger and watched the Land Cruisers tensely. This was the first time that visitors had toured Jurassic Park, and Muldoon shared Arnold's apprehension.

Robert Muldoon was a big man, fifty years old, with a steel-gray mustache and deep blue eyes. Raised in Kenya, he had spent most of his life as a guide for African big-game hunters, as had his father before him. But since 1980, he had worked principally for conservation groups and zoo designers as a wildlife consultant. He had become well known; an article in the London Sunday *Times* had said, "What Robert Trent Jones is to golf courses, Robert Muldoon is to zoos: a designer of unsurpassed knowledge and skill."

In 1986, he had done some work for a San Francisco company that was building a private wildlife park on an island in North America. Muldoon had laid out the boundaries for different animals, defining space and habitat requirements for lions, elephants, zebras, and hippos. Identifying which animals could be kept together, and which had to be separated. At the time, it had been a fairly routine job. He had been more interested in an Indian park called TigerWorld in southern Kashmir.

Then, a year ago, he was offered a job as game warden of Jurassic Park. It coincided with a desire to leave Africa; the salary was excellent; Muldoon had taken it on for a year. He was astonished to discover the park was really a collection of genetically engineered prehistoric animals.

It was of course interesting work, but during his years in Africa, Muldoon had developed an unblinking view of animals—an unromantic view—that frequently set him at odds with the Jurassic Park management in California, particularly the little martinet standing beside him in the control room. In Muldoon's opinion, cloning dinosaurs in a laboratory was one thing. Maintaining them in the wild was quite another.

It was Muldoon's view that some dinosaurs were too dangerous to be kept in a park setting. In part, the danger existed because they still knew so little about the animals. For example, nobody even suspected the dilophosaurs were poisonous until they were observed hunting indigenous rats on the island—biting the rodents and then stepping back, to wait for them to die. And even then nobody suspected the dilophosaurs could spit until one of the handlers was almost blinded by spitting venom.

After that, Hammond had agreed to study dilophosaur venom, which was found to contain seven different toxic enzymes. It was also discovered that the dilophosaurs could spit a distance of fifty feet. Since this raised the possibility that a guest in a car might be blinded, management decided to remove the poison sacs. The vets had tried twice, on two different animals, without success. No one knew where the poison was being secreted. And no one would ever know until an autopsy was performed on a dilophosaur—and management would not allow one to be killed.

Muldoon worried even more about the velociraptors. They were instinctive hunters, and they never passed up prey. They killed even when they weren't hungry. They killed for the pleasure of killing. They were swift: strong runners and astonishing jumpers. They had lethal claws on all four limbs; one swipe of a forearm would disembowel a man, spilling his guts out. And they had powerful tearing jaws that ripped flesh instead of biting it. They were far more intelligent than the other dinosaurs, and they seemed to be natural cage-breakers.

Every zoo expert knew that certain animals were especially likely to get free of their cages. Some, like monkeys and elephants, could undo cage doors. Others, like wild pigs, were unusually intelligent and could lift gate fasteners with their snouts. But who would suspect that the giant armadillo was a notorious cage-breaker? Or the moose? Yet a moose was almost as skillful with its snout as an elephant with its trunk. Moose were always getting free; they had a talent for it.

And so did velociraptors.

Raptors were at least as intelligent as chimpanzees. And, like chimpanzees, they had agile hands that enabled them to open doors and manipulate objects. They could escape with ease. And when, as Muldoon had feared, one of them finally escaped, it killed two construction workers and maimed a third before being recaptured. After that episode, the visitor lodge had been reworked with heavy barred gates, a high perimeter fence, and tempered-glass windows. And the raptor holding pen was rebuilt with electronic sensors to warn of another impending escape.

Muldoon wanted guns as well. And he wanted shoulder-mounted LAW-missile launchers. Hunters knew how difficult it was to bring down a four-ton African elephant—and some of the dinosaurs weighed ten times as much. Management was horrified, insisting there be no guns anywhere on the island. When Muldoon threatened to quit, and to take his story to the press, a compromise was reached. In the end, two specially built laser-guided missile launchers were kept in a locked room in the basement. Only Muldoon had keys to the room.

Those were the keys Muldoon was twirling now.

"I'm going downstairs," he said.

Arnold, watching the control screens, nodded. The two Land Cruisers sat at the top of the hill, waiting for the T-rex to appear.

"Hey," Dennis Nedry called, from the far console. "As long as you're up, get me a Coke, okay?"

Grant waited in the car, watching quietly. The bleating of the goat became louder, more insistent. The goat tugged frantically at its tether, racing back and forth. Over the radio, Grant heard Lex say in alarm, "What's going to happen to the goat? Is she going to eat the goat?"

"I think so," someone said to her, and then Ellie turned the radio down. Then they smelled the odor, a garbage stench of putrefaction and decay that drifted up the hillside toward them.

Grant whispered, "He's here."

"She," Malcolm said.

The goat was tethered in the center of the field, thirty yards from the nearest trees. The dinosaur must be somewhere among the trees, but for a moment Grant could see nothing at all. Then he realized he was looking too low: the animal's head stood twenty feet above the ground, half concealed among the upper branches of the palm trees.

Malcolm whispered, "Oh, *my God*. . . . She's as large as a bloody building. . . ."

Grant stared at the enormous square head, five feet long, mottled reddish brown, with huge jaws and fangs. The tyrannosaur's jaws worked once, opening and closing. But the huge animal did not emerge from hiding.

Malcolm whispered: "How long will it wait?"

"Maybe three or four minutes. Maybe—"

The tyrannosaur sprang silently forward, fully revealing her enormous body. In four bounding steps she covered the distance to the goat, bent down, and bit it through the neck. The bleating stopped. There was silence.

Poised over her kill, the tyrannosaur became suddenly hesitant. Her massive head turned on the muscular neck, looking in all directions. She stared fixedly at the Land Cruiser, high above on the hill.

Malcolm whispered, "Can she see us?"

"Oh yes," Regis said, on the intercom. "Let's see if she's going to eat here in front of us, or if she's going to drag the prey away."

The tyrannosaur bent down, and sniffed the carcass of the goat. A bird chirped: her head snapped up, alert, watchful. She looked back and forth, scanning in small jerking shifts.

"Like a bird," Ellie said.

Still the tyrannosaur hesitated. "What is she afraid of?" Malcolm whispered.

"Probably another tyrannosaur," Grant whispered. Big carnivores like lions and tigers often became cautious after a kill, behaving as if suddenly exposed. Nineteenth-century zoologists imagined the animals felt guilty for what they had done. But contemporary scientists documented the effort behind a kill—hours of patient stalking before the final lunge—as well as the frequency of failure. The idea of "nature, red in tooth and claw" was wrong; most often the prey got away. When a carnivore finally brought down an animal, it was watchful for another predator, who might attack it and steal its prize. Thus this tyrannosaur was probably fearful of another tyrannosaur.

The huge animal bent over the goat again. One great hind limb held the carcass in place as the jaws began to tear the flesh.

"She's going to stay," Regis whispered. "Excellent."

The tyrannosaur lifted her head again, ragged chunks of bleeding flesh in her jaws. She stared at the Land Cruiser. She began to chew. They heard the sickening crunch of bones.

"Ewww," Lex said, over the intercom. "That's dis*gus*ting."

And then, as if caution had finally gotten the better of her, the tyrannosaur lifted the remains of the goat in her jaws and carried them silently back among the trees.

"Ladies and gentlemen, *Tyrannosaurus rex*," the tape said. The Land Cruisers started up, and moved silently off, through the foliage.

Malcolm sat back in his seat. "Fantastic," he said.

Gennaro wiped his forehead. He looked pale.

CONTROL

Henry Wu came into the control room to find everyone sitting in the dark, listening to the voices on the radio.

"—Jesus, if an animal like that gets out," Gennaro was saying, his voice tinny on the speaker, "there'd be no stopping it."

"No stopping it, no . . ."

"Huge, with no natural enemies . . ."

"My God, think of it . . ."

In the control room, Hammond said, "Damn those people. They are so *negative*."

Wu said, "They're still going on about an animal escaping? I don't understand. They must have seen by now that we have everything under control. We've engineered the animals and engineered the resort. . . ." He shrugged.

It was Wu's deepest perception that the park was fundamentally sound, as he believed his paleo-DNA was fundamentally sound. Whatever problems might arise in the DNA were essentially point-problems in the code, causing a specific problem in the phenotype: an enzyme that didn't switch on, or a protein that didn't fold. Whatever the difficulty, it was always solved with a relatively minor adjustment in the next version.

Similarly, he knew that Jurassic Park's problems were not fundamental problems. They were not control problems. Nothing as basic, or as serious, as the possibility of an animal escaping. Wu found it offensive to think that anyone would believe him capable of contributing to a system where such a thing could happen.

"It's that Malcolm," Hammond said darkly. "He's behind it all. He was against us from the start, you know. He's got his theory that complex systems can't be controlled and nature can't be imitated. I don't know what his problem is. Hell, we're just making a zoo here. World's full of 'em, and they all work fine. But he's going to prove his theory or die trying. I just hope he doesn't panic Gennaro into trying to shut the park down."

Wu said, "Can he do that?"

"No," Hammond said. "But he can try. He can try and frighten the Japanese investors, and get them to withdraw funds. Or he can make a stink with the San José government. He can make trouble."

Arnold stubbed out his cigarette. "Let's wait and see what happens," he said. "We believe in the park. Let's see how it plays out."

Muldoon got off the elevator, nodded to the ground-floor guard, and went downstairs to the basement. He flicked on the lights. The basement was filled with two dozen Land Cruisers, arranged in neat rows. These were the electric cars that would eventually form an endless loop, touring the park, returning to the visitor center.

In the corner was a Jeep with a red stripe, one of two gasoline-powered vehicles—Harding, the vet, had taken the other that morning—which could go anywhere in the park, even among the animals. The Jeeps were painted with a diagonal red stripe because for some reason it discouraged the triceratops from charging the car.

Muldoon moved past the Jeep, toward the back. The steel door to the armaments room was unmarked. He unlocked it with his key, and swung the heavy door wide. Gun racks lined the interior. He pulled out a Randler Shoulder Launcher and a case of canisters. He tucked two gray rockets under his other arm.

After locking the door behind him, he put the gun into the back seat of the Jeep. As he left the garage, he heard the distant rumble of thunder.

"Looks like rain," Ed Regis said, glancing up at the sky.

The Land Cruisers had stopped again, near the sauropod swamp. A large herd of apatosaurs was grazing at the edge of the lagoon, eating the leaves of the upper branches of the palm trees. In the same area were several duckbilled hadrosaurs, which in comparison looked much smaller.

Of course, Tim knew the hadrosaurs weren't really small. It was only that the apatosaurs were so much larger. Their tiny heads reached fifty feet into the air, extending out on their long necks.

"The big animals you see are commonly called *Brontosaurus*," the recording said, "but they are actually *Apatosaurus*. They weigh more than thirty tons. That means a single animal is as big as a whole herd of modern elephants. And you may notice that their preferred area, alongside the lagoon, is not swampy. Despite what the books say, brontosaurs avoid swamps. They prefer dry land."

"*Brontosaurus* is the biggest dinosaur, Lex," Ed Regis said. Tim didn't bother to contradict him. Actually, *Brachiosaurus* was three times as large. And some people thought *Ultrasaurus* and *Seismosaurus* were even larger than *Brachiosaurus*. *Seismosaurus* might have weighed a hundred tons!

Alongside the apatosaurs, the smaller hadrosaurs stood on their hind legs to get at foliage. They moved gracefully for such large creatures. Several infant hadrosaurs scampered around the adults, eating the leaves that dropped from the mouths of the larger animals.

"The dinosaurs of Jurassic Park don't breed," the recording said. "The young animals you see were introduced a few months ago, already hatched. But the adults nurture them anyway."

There was the rolling growl of thunder. The sky was darker, lower, and menacing.

"Yeah, looks like rain, all right," Ed Regis said.

The car started forward, and Tim looked back at the hadrosaurs. Suddenly, off to one side, he saw a pale yellow animal moving quickly. There were brownish stripes on its back. He recognized it instantly. "Hey!" he shouted. "Stop the car!"

"What is it?" Ed Regis said.

"Quick! *Stop the car!*"

"We move on now to see the last of our great prehistoric animals, the stegosaurs," the recorded voice said.

"What's the matter, Tim?"

"I saw one! I saw one in the field out there!"

"Saw what?"

"A *raptor*! In that field!"

"The stegosaurs are a mid-Jurassic animal, evolving about a hundred and seventy million years ago," the recording said. "Several of these remarkable herbivores live here at Jurassic Park."

"Oh, I don't think so, Tim," Ed Regis said. "Not a raptor."

"I did! *Stop the car!*"

There was a babble on the intercom, as the news was relayed to Grant and Malcolm. "Tim says he saw a raptor."

"Where?"

"Back at the field."

"Let's go back and look."

"We can't go back," Ed Regis said. "We can only go forward. The cars are programmed."

"We can't go back?" Grant said.

"No," Regis said. "Sorry. You see, it's kind of a ride—"

"Tim, this is Professor Malcolm," said a voice cutting in on the intercom. "I have just one question for you about this raptor. How old would you say it was?"

"Older than the baby we saw today," Tim said. "And younger than the big adults in the pen. The adults were six feet tall. This one was about half that size."

"That's fine," Malcolm said.

"I only saw it for a second," Tim said.

"I'm sure it wasn't a raptor," Ed Regis said. "It couldn't possibly be a raptor. Must have been one of the othys. They're always jumping their fences. We have a hell of a time with them."

"I know I saw a raptor," Tim said.

"I'm hungry," Lex said. She was starting to whine.

In the control room, Arnold turned to Wu. "What do you think the kid saw?"

"I think it must have been an othy."

Arnold nodded. "We have trouble tracking othys, because they spend so much time in the trees." The othys were an exception to the usual minute-to-minute control they maintained over the animals. The computers were constantly losing and picking up the othys, as they went into the trees and then came down again.

"What burns me," Hammond said, "is that we have made this wonderful park, this *fantastic* park, and our very first visitors are going through it like accountants, just looking for problems. They aren't experiencing the wonder of it at all."

"That's their problem," Arnold said. "We can't make them experience wonder." The intercom clicked, and Arnold heard a voice drawl, "Ah, John, this is the *Anne B* over at the dock. We haven't finished offloading, but I'm looking at that storm pattern south of us. I'd rather not be tied up here if this chop gets any worse."

Arnold turned to the monitor showing the cargo vessel, which was moored at the dock on the east side of the island. He pressed the radio button. "How much left to do, Jim?"

"Just the three final equipment containers. I haven't checked the manifest, but I assume you can wait another two weeks for it. We're not well berthed here, you know, and we are one hundred miles offshore."

"You requesting permission to leave?"

"Yes, John."

"I want that equipment," Hammond said. "That's equipment for the labs. We need it."

"Yes," Arnold said. "But you didn't want to put money into a storm barrier to protect the pier. So we don't have a good harbor. If the storm gets worse, the ship will be pounded against the dock. I've seen ships lost that way. Then you've got all the other expenses, replacement of the vessel plus salvage to clear your dock . . . and you can't use your dock until you do. . . ."

Hammond gave a dismissing wave. "Get them out of there."

"Permission to leave, *Anne B*," Arnold said, into the radio.

"See you in two weeks," the voice said.

On the video monitor, they saw the crew on the decks, casting off the lines. Arnold turned back to the main console bank. He saw the Land Cruisers moving through fields of steam.

"Where are they now?" Hammond said.

"It looks like the south fields," Arnold said. The southern end of the island had more volcanic activity than the north. "That means they should be almost to the stegos. I'm sure they'll stop and see what Harding is doing."

STEGOSAUR

As the Land Cruiser came to a stop, Ellie Sattler stared through the plumes of steam at the stegosaurus. It was standing quietly, not moving. A Jeep with a red stripe was parked alongside it.

"I have to admit, that's a funny-looking animal," Malcolm said.

The stegosaurus was twenty feet long, with a huge bulky body and vertical armor plates along its back. The tail had dangerous-looking three-foot spikes. But the neck tapered to an absurdly small head with a stupid gaze, like a very dumb horse.

As they watched, a man walked around from behind the animal. "That's our vet, Dr. Harding," Regis said, over the radio. "He's anesthetized the stego, which is why it's not moving. It's sick."

Grant was already getting out of the car, hurrying toward the motionless stegosaur. Ellie got out and looked back as the second Land Cruiser pulled up and the two kids jumped out. "What's he sick with?" Tim said.

"They're not sure," Ellie said.

The great leathery plates along the stegosaur's spine drooped slightly. It breathed slowly, laboriously, making a wet sound with each breath.

"Is it contagious?" Lex said.

They walked toward the tiny head of the animal, where Grant and the vet were on their knees, peering into the stegosaur's mouth.

Lex wrinkled her nose. "This thing sure is big," she said. "And *smelly.*"

"Yes, it is." Ellie had already noticed the stegosaur had a peculiar odor, like rotting fish. It reminded her of something she knew, but couldn't quite place. In any case, she had never smelled a stegosaur before. Maybe this was its characteristic odor. But she had her doubts. Most herbivores did not have a strong smell. Nor did their droppings. It was reserved for the meat-eaters to develop a real stink.

"Is that because it's sick?" Lex asked.

"Maybe. And don't forget the vet's tranquilized it."

"Ellie, have a look at this tongue," Grant said.

The dark purple tongue drooped limply from the animal's mouth. The vet shone a light on it so she could see the very fine silvery blisters. "Microvesicles," Ellie said. "Interesting."

"We've had a difficult time with these stegos," the vet said. "They're always getting sick."

"What are the symptoms?" Ellie asked. She scratched the tongue with her fingernail. A clear liquid exuded from the broken blisters.

"Ugh," Lex said.

"Imbalance, disorientation, labored breathing, and massive diarrhea," Harding said. "Seems to happen about once every six weeks or so."

"They feed continuously?"

"Oh yes," Harding said. "Animal this size has to take in a minimum of five or six hundred pounds of plant matter daily just to keep going. They're constant foragers."

"Then it's not likely to be poisoning from a plant," Ellie said. Constant browsers would be constantly sick if they were eating a toxic plant. Not every six weeks.

"Exactly," the vet said.

"May I?" Ellie asked. She took the flashlight from the vet. "You have pupillary effects from the tranquilizer?" she said, shining the light in the stegosaur's eye.

"Yes. There's a miotic effect, pupils are constricted."

"But these pupils are dilated," she said.

Harding looked. There was no question: the stegosaur's pupil was dilated, and did not contract when light shone on it. "I'll be damned," he said. "That's a pharmacological effect."

"Yes." Ellie got back on her feet and looked around. "What is the animal's range?"

"About five square miles."

"In this general area?" she asked. They were in an open meadow, with scattered rocky outcrops, and intermittent plumes of steam rising from the ground. It was late afternoon, and the sky was pink beneath the lowering gray clouds.

"Their range is mostly north and east of here," Harding said. "But when they get sick, they're usually somewhere around this particular area."

It was an interesting puzzle, she thought. How to explain the periodicity of the poisoning? She pointed across the field. "You see those low, delicate-looking bushes?"

"West Indian lilac." Harding nodded. "We know it's toxic. The animals don't eat it."

"You're sure?"

"Yes. We monitor them on video, and I've checked droppings just to be certain. The stegos never eat the lilac bushes."

Melia azedarach, called chinaberry or West Indian lilac, contained a number of toxic alkaloids. The Chinese used the plant as a fish poison.

"They don't eat it," the vet said.

"Interesting," Ellie said. "Because otherwise I would have said that this animal shows all the classic signs of *Melia* toxicity: stupor, blistering of the mucous membranes, and pupillary dilatation." She set off toward the field to examine the plants more closely, her body bent over the ground. "You're right," she said. "Plants are healthy, no sign of being eaten. None at all."

"And there's the six-week interval," the vet reminded her.

"The stegosaurs come here how often?"

"About once a week," he said. "Stegos make a slow loop through their home-range territory, feeding as they go. They complete the loop in about a week."

"But they're only sick once every six weeks."

"Correct," Harding said.

"This is boring," Lex said.

"Ssshh," Tim said. "Dr. Sattler's trying to think."

"Unsuccessfully," Ellie said, walking farther out into the field.

Behind her, she heard Lex saying, "Anybody want to play a little pickle?"

Ellie stared at the ground. The field was rocky in many places. She could hear the sound of the surf, somewhere to the left. There were berries among the rocks. Perhaps the animals were just eating berries. But that didn't make sense. West Indian lilac berries were terribly bitter.

"Finding anything?" Grant said, coming up to join her.

Ellie sighed. "Just rocks," she said. "We must be near the beach, because all these rocks are smooth. And they're in funny little piles."

"Funny little piles?" Grant said.

"All over. There's one pile right there." She pointed.

As soon as she did, she realized what she was looking at. The rocks were worn, but it had nothing to do with the ocean. These rocks were heaped in small piles, almost as if they had been thrown down that way.

They were piles of gizzard stones.

Many birds and crocodiles swallowed small stones, which collected in a muscular pouch in the digestive tract, called the gizzard. Squeezed by the muscles of the gizzard, the stones helped crush tough plant food before it reached the stomach, and thus aided digestion. Some scientists thought dinosaurs also had gizzard stones. For one thing, dinosaur teeth were too small, and too little worn, to have been used for chewing food. It was presumed that dinosaurs swallowed their food whole and let the gizzard stones break down the plant fibers. And some skeletons had been found with an associated pile of small stones in the abdominal area. But it had never been verified, and—

"Gizzard stones," Grant said.

"I think so, yes. They swallow these stones, and after a few weeks the stones are worn smooth, so they regurgitate them, leaving this little pile, and swallow fresh stones. And when they do, they swallow berries as well. And get sick."

"I'll be damned," Grant said, "I'm sure you're right."

He looked at the pile of stones, brushing through them with his hand, following the instinct of a paleontologist.

Then he stopped.

"Ellie," he said. "Take a look at this."

"Put it there, babe! Right in the old mitt!" Lex cried, and Gennaro threw the ball to her.

She threw it back so hard that his hand stung. "Take it easy! I don't have a glove!"

"You wimp!" she said contemptuously.

Annoyed, he fired the ball at her, and heard it *smack*! in the leather. "Now that's more like it," she said.

Standing by the dinosaur, Gennaro continued to play catch as he talked to Malcolm. "How does this sick dinosaur fit into your theory?"

"It's predicted," Malcolm said.

Gennaro shook his head. "Is anything *not* predicted by your theory?"

"Look," Malcolm said. "It's nothing to do with me. It's chaos theory. But I notice nobody is willing to listen to the consequences of the mathematics. Because they imply very large consequences for human life. Much larger than Heisenberg's principle or Gödel's theorem, which everybody rattles on about. Those are actually rather academic considerations. Philosophical considerations. But chaos theory concerns everyday life. Do you know why computers were first built?"

"No," Gennaro said.

"Burn it in there," Lex yelled.

"Computers were built in the late 1940s because mathematicians like John von Neumann thought that if you had a computer—a machine to handle a lot of variables simultaneously—you would be able to predict the weather. Weather would finally fall to human understanding. And men believed that dream for the next forty years. They believed that prediction was just a function of keeping track of things. If you knew enough, you could predict anything. That's been a cherished scientific belief since Newton."

"And?"

"Chaos theory throws it right out the window. It says that you can never predict certain phenomena at all. You can never predict the weather more than a few days away. All the money that has been spent on long-range forecasting—about half a billion dollars in the last few decades—is money wasted. It's a fool's errand. It's as pointless as trying to turn lead into gold. We look back at the alchemists and laugh at what they were trying to do, but future generations will laugh at us the same way. We've tried the impossible—and spent a lot of money doing it. Because in fact there are great categories of phenomena that are inherently unpredictable."

"Chaos says that?"

"Yes, and it is astonishing how few people care to hear it," Malcolm said. "I gave all this information to Hammond long before he broke ground on this place. You're going to engineer a bunch of prehistoric animals and set them on an island? Fine. A lovely dream. Charming. But it won't go as planned. It is inherently unpredictable, just as the weather is."

"You told him this?" Gennaro said.

"Yes. I also told him where the deviations would occur. Obviously the fitness of the animals to the environment was one area. This stegosaur is a hundred million years old. It isn't adapted to our world. The air is different, the solar radiation is different, the land is different, the insects are different, the sounds are different, the vegetation is different. Everything is different. The oxygen content is decreased. This poor animal's like a human being at ten thousand feet altitude. Listen to him wheezing."

"And the other areas?"

"Broadly speaking, the ability of the park to control the spread of life-forms. Because the history of evolution is that life escapes all barriers. Life breaks free. Life expands to new territories. Painfully, perhaps even dangerously. But life finds a way." Malcolm shook his head. "I don't mean to be philosophical, but there it is."

Gennaro looked over. Ellie and Grant were across the field, waving their arms and shouting.

"Did you get my Coke?" Dennis Nedry asked, as Muldoon came back into the control room.

Muldoon didn't bother to answer. He went directly to the monitor and looked at what was happening. Over the radio he heard Harding's voice saying, "—the stego—finally—handle on—now—"

"What's that about?" Muldoon said.

"They're down by the south point," Arnold said. "That's why they're breaking up a little. I'll switch them to another channel. But they found out what's wrong with the stegos. Eating some kind of berry."

Hammond nodded. "I knew we'd solve that sooner or later," he said.

"It's not very impressive," Gennaro said. He held the white fragment, no larger than a postage stamp, up on his fingertip in the fading light. "You sure about this, Alan?"

"Absolutely sure," Grant said. "What gives it away is the patterning on the interior surface, the interior curve. Turn it over and you will notice a faint pattern of raised lines, making roughly triangular shapes."

"Yes, I see them."

"Well, I've dug out two eggs with patterns like that at my site in Montana."

"You're saying this is a piece of dinosaur eggshell?"

"Absolutely," Grant said.

Harding shook his head. "These dinosaurs can't breed."

"Evidently they can," Gennaro said.

"That must be a bird egg," Harding said. "We have literally dozens of species on the island."

Grant shook his head. "Look at the curvature. The shell is almost flat. That's from a very big egg. And notice the thickness of the shell. Unless you have ostriches on this island, it's a dinosaur egg."

"But they can't possibly breed," Harding insisted. "All the animals are female."

"All I know," Grant said, "is that this is a dinosaur egg."

Malcolm said, "Can you tell the species?"

"Yes," Grant said. "It's a velociraptor egg."

CONTROL

"Absolutely absurd," Hammond said in the control room, listening to the report over the radio. "It must be a bird egg. That's all it *can* be."

The radio crackled. He heard Malcolm's voice. "Let's do a little test, shall we? Ask Mr. Arnold to run one of his computer tallies."

"Now?"

"Yes, right now. I understand you can transmit it to the screen in Dr. Harding's car. Do that, too, will you?"

"No problem," Arnold said. A moment later, the screen in the control room printed out:

Total Animals	238		
Species	Expected	Found	Ver
Tyrannosaurs	2	2	4.1
Maiasaurs	21	21	3.3
Stegosaurs	4	4	3.9
Triceratops	8	8	3.1
Procompsognathids	49	49	3.9
Othnielia	16	16	3.1
Velociraptors	8	8	3.0
Apatosaurs	17	17	3.1
Hadrosaurs	11	11	3.1
Dilophosaurs	7	7	4.3
Pterosaurs	6	6	4.3
Hypsilophodontids	33	33	2.9
Euoplocephalids	16	16	4.0
Styracosaurs	18	18	3.9
Microceratops	22	22	4.1
Total	**238**	**238**	

"I hope you're satisfied," Hammond said. "Are you receiving it down there on your screen?"

"We see it," Malcolm said.

"Everything accounted for, as always." He couldn't keep the satisfaction out of his voice.

"Now then," Malcolm said. "Can you have the computer search for a different number of animals?"

"Like what?" Arnold said.

"Try two hundred thirty-nine."

"Just a minute," Arnold said, frowning. A moment later the screen printed:

Total Animals	239		
Species	Expected	Found	Ver
Tyrannosaurs	2	2	4.1
Maiasaurs	21	21	3.3
Stegosaurs	4	4	3.9
Triceratops	8	8	3.1
Procompsognathids	49	50	??
Othnielia	16	16	3.1
Velociraptors	8	8	3.0
Apatosaurs	17	17	3.1
Hadrosaurs	11	11	3.1
Dilophosaurs	7	7	4.3
Pterosaurs	6	6	4.3
Hypsilophodontids	33	33	2.9
Euoplocephalids	16	16	4.0
Styracosaurs	18	18	3.9
Microceratops	22	22	4.1
Total	**238**	**239**	

Hammond sat forward. "What the hell is *that*?"

"We picked up another compy."

"From *where*?"

"I don't know!"

The radio crackled. "Now, then: can you ask the computer to search for, let us say, three hundred animals?"

"What is he talking about?" Hammond said, his voice rising. "Three hundred animals? What's he talking about?"

"Just a minute," Arnold said. "That'll take a few minutes." He punched buttons on the screen. The first line of the totals appeared:

Total Animals	239

"I don't understand what he's driving at," Hammond said.

"I'm afraid I do," Arnold said. He watched the screen. The numbers on the first line were clicking:

Total Animals	244

"Two hundred forty-four?" Hammond said. "What's going on?"

"The computer is counting the animals in the park," Wu said. "*All* the animals."

"I thought that's what it always did." He spun. "Nedry! Have you screwed up again?"

"No," Nedry said, looking up from his console. "Computer allows the operator to enter an expected number of animals, in order to make the counting process faster. But it's a convenience, not a flaw."

"He's right," Arnold said. "We just always used the base count of two hundred thirty-eight because we assumed there couldn't be more."

Total Animals	262

"Wait a minute," Hammond said. "These animals can't breed. The computer must be counting field mice or something."

"I think so, too," Arnold said. "It's almost certainly an error in the visual tracking. But we'll know soon enough."

Hammond turned to Wu. "They can't breed, can they?"

"No," Wu said.

Total Animals	270

"Where are they coming from?" Arnold said.

"Damned if I know," Wu said.

They watched the numbers climb.

Total Animals	283

Over the radio, they heard Gennaro say, "Holy shit, how much more?"

And they heard the girl say, "I'm getting hungry. When are we going home?"

"Pretty soon, Lex."

On the screen, there was a flashing error message:

ERROR: Search Params: 300 Animals Not Found

"An error," Hammond said, nodding. "I *thought* so. I had the feeling all along there must be an error."

But a moment later the screen printed:

Total Animals	292		
Species	**Expected**	**Found**	**Ver**
Tyrannosaurs	2	2	4.1
Maiasaurs	21	22	??
Stegosaurs	4	4	3.9
Triceratops	8	8	3.1
Procompsognathids	49	65	??
Othnielia	16	23	??
Velociraptors	8	37	??
Apatosaurs	17	17	3.1
Hadrosaurs	11	11	3.1
Dilophosaurs	7	7	4.3
Pterosaurs	6	6	4.3
Hypsilophodontids	33	34	??
Euoplocephalids	16	16	4.0
Styracosaurs	18	18	3.9
Microceratops	22	22	4.1
Total	**238**	**292**	

The radio crackled. "Now you see the flaw in your procedures," Malcolm said. "You only tracked the expected number of dinosaurs. You were worried about losing animals, and your procedures were designed to advise you instantly if you had less than the expected number. But that wasn't the problem. The problem was, you had *more* than the expected number."

"Christ," Arnold said.

"There can't be more," Wu said. "We know how many we've released. There can't be more than that."

"Afraid so, Henry," Malcolm said. "They're breeding."

"No."

"Even if you don't accept Grant's eggshell, you can prove it with your own data. Take a look at the compy height graph. Arnold will put it up for you."

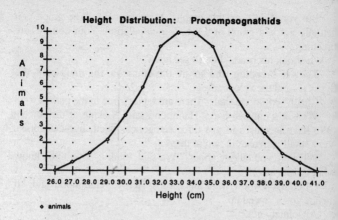

"Notice anything about it?" Malcolm said.

"It's a Gaussian distribution," Wu said. "Normal curve."

"But didn't you say you introduced the compys in three batches? At six-month intervals?"

"Yes . . ."

"Then you should get a graph with peaks for each of the three separate batches that were introduced," Malcolm said, tapping the keyboard. "Like this."

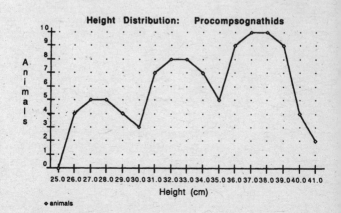

"But you didn't get this graph," Malcolm said. "The graph you actually got is a graph of a breeding population. Your compys are breeding."

Wu shook his head. "I don't see how."

"They're breeding, and so are the othnielia, the maiasaurs, the hypsys—and the velociraptors."

"Christ," Muldoon said. "There are raptors free in the park."

"Well, it's not that bad," Hammond said, looking at the screen. "We have increases in just three categories—well, five categories. Very small increases in two of them . . ."

"What are you talking about?" Wu said, loudly. "Don't you know what this means?"

"Of course I know what this means, Henry," Hammond said. "It means you screwed up."

"Absolutely not."

"You've got breeding dinosaurs out there, Henry."

"But they're all female," Wu said. "It's impossible. There must be a mistake. And look at the numbers. A small increase in the big animals, the maiasaurs and the hypsys. And big increases in the number of small animals. It just doesn't make sense. It must be a mistake."

The radio clicked. "Actually not," Grant said. "I think these numbers confirm that breeding is taking place. In seven different sites around the island."

BREEDING SITES

The sky was growing darker. Thunder rumbled in the distance. Grant and the others leaned in the doors of the Jeep, staring at the screen on the dashboard. "Breeding sites?" Wu said, over the radio.

"Nests," Grant said. "Assuming the average clutch is eight to twelve hatching eggs, these data would indicate the compys have two nests. The raptors have two nests. The othys have one nest. And the hypsys and the maias have one nest each."

"Where are these nests?"

"We'll have to find them," Grant said. "Dinosaurs build their nests in secluded places."

"But why are there so few big animals?" Wu said. "If there is a maia nest of eight to twelve eggs, there should be eight to twelve new maias. Not just one."

"That's right," Grant said. "Except that the raptors and the compys that are loose in the park are probably eating the eggs of the bigger animals—and perhaps eating the newly hatched young, as well."

"But we've never seen that," Arnold said, over the radio.

"Raptors are nocturnal," he said. "Is anyone watching the park at night?"

There was a long silence.

"I didn't think so," Grant said.

"It still doesn't make sense," Wu said. "You can't support fifty additional animals on a couple of nests of eggs."

"No," Grant said. "I assume they are eating something else as well. Perhaps small rodents. Mice and rats?"

There was another silence.

"Let me guess," Grant said. "When you first came to the island, you had a problem with rats. But as time passed, the problem faded away."

"Yes. That's true. . . ."

"And you never thought to investigate why."

"Well, we just assumed . . ." Arnold said.

"Look," Wu said, "the fact remains, all the animals are female. They can't breed."

Grant had been thinking about that. He had recently learned of an intriguing West German study that he suspected held the answer. "When you made your dinosaur DNA," Grant said, "you were working with fragmentary pieces, is that right?"

"Yes," Wu said.

"In order to make a complete strand, were you ever required to include DNA fragments from other species?"

"Occasionally, yes," Wu said. "It's the only way to accomplish the job. Sometimes we included avian DNA, from a variety of birds, and sometimes reptilian DNA."

"Any amphibian DNA? Specifically, frog DNA?"

"Possibly. I'd have to check."

"Check," Grant said. "I think you'll find that holds the answer."

Malcolm said, "Frog DNA? Why frog DNA?"

Gennaro said impatiently, "Listen, this is all very intriguing, but we're forgetting the main question: have any animals gotten off the island?"

Grant said, "We can't tell from these data."

"Then how are we going to find out?"

"There's only one way I know," Grant said. "We'll have to find the individual dinosaur nests, inspect them, and count the remaining egg fragments. From that we may be able to determine how many animals were originally hatched. And we can begin to assess whether any are missing."

Malcolm said, "Even so, you won't know if the missing animals are killed, or dead from natural causes, or whether they have left the island."

"No," Grant said, "but it's a start. And I think we can get more information from an intensive look at the population graphs."

"How are we going to find these nests?"

"Actually," Grant said, "I think the computer will be able to help us with that."

"Can we go back now?" Lex said. "I'm *hungry*."

"Yes, let's go," Grant said, smiling at her. "You've been very patient."

"You'll be able to eat in about twenty minutes," Ed Regis said, starting toward the two Land Cruisers.

"I'll stay for a while," Ellie said, "and get photos of the stego with Dr. Harding's camera. Those vesicles in the mouth will have cleared up by tomorrow."

"I want to get back," Grant said. "I'll go with the kids."

"I will, too," Malcolm said.

"I think I'll stay," Gennaro said, "and go back with Harding in his Jeep, with Dr. Sattler."

"Fine, let's go."

They started walking. Malcolm said, "Why exactly is our lawyer staying?"

Grant shrugged. "I think it might have something to do with Dr. Sattler."

"Really? The shorts, you think?"

"It's happened before," Grant said.

When they came to the Land Cruisers, Tim said, "I want to ride in the front one this time, with Dr. Grant."

Malcolm said, "Unfortunately, Dr. Grant and I need to talk."

"I'll just sit and listen. I won't say anything," Tim said.

"It's a private conversation," Malcolm said.

"Tell you what, Tim," Ed Regis said. "Let them sit in the rear car by themselves. We'll sit in the front car, and you can use the night-vision goggles. Have you ever used night-vision goggles, Tim? They're goggles with very sensitive CCDs that allow you to see in the dark."

"Neat," he said, and moved toward the first car.

"Hey!" Lex said. "I want to use it, too."

"No," Tim said.

"No fair! No fair! You get to do everything, Timmy!"

Ed Regis watched them go and said to Grant, "I can see what the ride back is going to be like."

Grant and Malcolm climbed into the second car. A few raindrops spattered the windshield. "Let's get going," Ed Regis said. "I'm about ready for dinner. And I could do with a nice banana daiquiri. What do you say, folks? Daiquiri sound good?" He pounded the metal panel of the car. "See you back at camp," he said, and he started running toward the first car, and climbed aboard.

A red light on the dashboard blinked. With a soft electric whirr, the Land Cruisers started off.

Driving back in the fading light, Malcolm seemed oddly subdued. Grant said, "You must feel vindicated. About your theory."

"As a matter of fact, I'm feeling a bit of dread. I suspect we are at a very dangerous point."

"Why?"

"Intuition."

"Do mathematicians believe in intuition?"

"Absolutely. Very important, intuition. Actually, I was thinking of fractals," Malcolm said. "You know about fractals?"

Grant shook his head. "Not really, no."

"Fractals are a kind of geometry, associated with a man named Mandelbrot. Unlike ordinary Euclidean geometry that everybody learns in school—squares and cubes and spheres—fractal geometry appears to describe real objects in the natural world. Mountains and clouds are fractal shapes. So fractals are probably related to reality. Somehow.

"Well, Mandelbrot found a remarkable thing with his geometric tools. He found that things looked almost identical at different scales."

"At different scales?" Grant said.

"For example," Malcolm said, "a big mountain, seen from far away, has a certain rugged mountain shape. If you get closer, and examine a small peak of the big mountain, it will have the same mountain shape. In fact, you can go all the way down the scale to a tiny speck of rock, seen under a microscope—it will have the same basic fractal shape as the big mountain."

"I don't really see why this is worrying you," Grant said. He yawned. He smelled the sulfur fumes of the volcanic steam. They were coming now to the section of road that ran near the coastline, overlooking the beach and the ocean.

"It's a way of looking at things," Malcolm said. "Mandelbrot found a sameness from the smallest to the largest. And this sameness of scale also occurs for events."

"Events?"

"Consider cotton prices," Malcolm said. "There are good records of cotton prices going back more than a hundred years. When you study fluctuations in cotton prices, you find that the graph of price fluctuations in the course of a day looks basically like the graph for a week, which looks basically like the graph for a year, or for ten years. And that's how things are. A day is like a whole life. You start out doing one thing, but end up doing something else, plan to run an errand, but never get there. . . . And at the end of your life, your whole existence has that same haphazard quality, too. Your whole life has the same shape as a single day."

"I guess it's one way to look at things," Grant said.

"No," Malcolm said. "It's the *only* way to look at things. At least, the only way that is true to reality. You see, the fractal idea of sameness carries within it an aspect of recursion, a kind of doubling back on itself, which means that events are unpredictable. That they can change suddenly, and without warning."

"Okay . . ."

"But we have soothed ourselves into imagining sudden change as something that happens outside the normal order of things. An accident, like a car crash. Or beyond our control, like a fatal illness. We do not conceive of sudden, radical, irrational change as built into the very fabric of existence. Yet it is. And chaos theory teaches us," Malcolm said, "that straight linearity, which we have come to take for granted in everything from physics to fiction, simply does not exist. Linearity is an artificial way of viewing the world. Real life isn't a series of interconnected events occurring one after another like beads strung on a necklace. Life is actually a series of encounters in which one event may change those that follow in a wholly unpredictable, even devastating way." Malcolm sat back in his seat, looking toward the other Land Cruiser, a few yards ahead. "That's a deep truth about the structure of our universe. But, for some reason, we insist on behaving as if it were not true."

At that moment, the cars jolted to a stop.

"What's happened?" Grant said.

Up ahead, they saw the kids in the car, pointing toward the ocean. Offshore, beneath lowering clouds, Grant saw the dark outline of the supply boat making its way back toward Puntarenas.

"Why have we stopped?" Malcolm said.

Grant turned on the radio and heard the girl saying excitedly, "Look there, Timmy! You see it, it's there!"

Malcolm squinted at the boat. "They talking about the boat?"

"Apparently."

Ed Regis climbed out of the front car and came running back

to their window. "I'm sorry," he said, "but the kids are all worked up. Do you have binoculars here?"

"For what?"

"The little girl says she sees something on the boat. Some kind of animal," Regis said.

Grant grabbed the binoculars and rested his elbows on the window ledge of the Land Cruiser. He scanned the long shape of the supply ship. It was so dark it was almost a silhouette; as he watched, the ship's running lights came on, brilliant in the dark purple twilight.

"Do you see anything?" Regis said.

"No," Grant said.

"They're low down," Lex said, over the radio. "Look low down."

Grant tilted the binoculars down, scanning the hull just above the waterline. The supply ship was broad-beamed, with a splash flange that ran the length of the ship. But it was quite dark now, and he could hardly make out details.

"No, nothing . . ."

"I can see them," Lex said impatiently. "Near the back. Look near the *back*!"

"How can she see anything in this light?" Malcolm said.

"Kids can see," Grant said. "They've got visual acuity we forgot we ever had."

He swung the binoculars toward the stern, moving them slowly, and suddenly he saw the animals. They were playing, darting among the silhouetted stern structures. He could see them only briefly, but even in the fading light he could tell that they were upright animals, about two feet tall, standing with stiff balancing tails.

"You see them now?" Lex said.

"I see them," he said.

"What are they?"

"They're raptors," Grant said. "At least two. Maybe more. Juveniles."

"Jesus," Ed Regis said. "That boat's going to the mainland."

Malcolm shrugged. "Don't get excited. Just call the control room and tell them to recall the boat."

Ed Regis reached in and grabbed the radio from the dashboard. They heard hissing static, and clicks as he rapidly changed channels. "There's something wrong with this one," he said. "It's not working."

He ran off to the first Land Cruiser. They saw him duck into it. Then he looked back at them. "There's something wrong with both the radios," he said. "I can't raise the control room."

"Then let's get going," Grant said.

In the control room, Muldoon stood before the big windows that overlooked the park. At seven o'clock, the quartz floodlights came on all over the island, turning the landscape into a glowing jewel stretching away to the south. This was his favorite moment of the day. He heard the crackle of static from the radios.

"The Land Cruisers have started again," Arnold said. "They're on their way home."

"But why did they stop?" Hammond said. "And why can't we talk to them?"

"I don't know," Arnold said. "Maybe they turned off the radios in the cars."

"Probably the storm," Muldoon said. "Interference from the storm."

"They'll be here in twenty minutes," Hammond said. "You better call down and make sure the dining room is ready for them. Those kids are going to be hungry."

Arnold picked up the phone and heard a steady monotonous hiss. "What's this? What's going on?"

"Jesus, hang that up," Nedry said. "You'll screw up the data stream."

"You've taken *all* the phone lines? Even the internal ones?"

"I've taken all the lines that communicate outside," Nedry said. "But your internal lines should still work."

Arnold punched console buttons one after another. He heard nothing but hissing on all the lines.

"Looks like you've got 'em all."

"Sorry about that," Nedry said. "I'll clear a couple for you at the end of the next transmission, in about fifteen minutes." He yawned. "Looks like a long weekend for me. I guess I'll go get that Coke now." He picked up his shoulder bag and headed for the door. "Don't touch my console, okay?"

The door closed.

"What a slob," Hammond said.

"Yeah," Arnold said. "But I guess he knows what he's doing."

* * *

Along the side of the road, clouds of volcanic steam misted rainbows in the bright quartz lights. Grant said into the radio, "How long does it take the ship to reach the mainland?"

"Eighteen hours," Ed Regis said. "More or less. It's pretty reliable." He glanced at his watch. "It should arrive around eleven tomorrow morning."

Grant frowned. "You still can't talk to the control room?"

"Not so far."

"How about Harding? Can you reach him?"

"No, I've tried. He may have his radio turned off."

Malcolm was shaking his head. "So we're the only ones who know about the animals on the ship."

"I'm trying to raise somebody," Ed Regis said. "I mean, Christ, we don't want those animals on the mainland."

"How long until we get back to the base?"

"From here, another sixteen, seventeen minutes," Ed Regis said.

At night, the whole road was illuminated by big floodlights. It felt to Grant as if they were driving through a bright green tunnel of leaves. Large raindrops spattered the windshield.

Grant felt the Land Cruiser slow, then stop. "Now what?"

Lex said, "I don't want to stop. Why did we stop?"

And then, suddenly, all the floodlights went out. The road was plunged into darkness. Lex said, "Hey!"

"Probably just a power outage or something," Ed Regis said. "I'm sure the lights'll be on in a minute."

"What the hell?" Arnold said, staring at his monitors.

"What happened?" Muldoon said. "You lose power?"

"Yeah, but only power on the perimeter. Everything in this building's working fine. But outside, in the park, the power is gone. Lights, TV cameras, everything." His remote video monitors had gone black.

"What about the two Land Cruisers?"

"Stopped somewhere around the tyrannosaur paddock."

"Well," Muldoon said, "call Maintenance and let's get the power back on."

Arnold picked up one of his phones and heard hissing: Nedry's computers talking to each other. "No phones. That damn Nedry. Nedry! Where the hell is he?"

* * *

Dennis Nedry pushed open the door marked FERTILIZATION. With the perimeter power out, all the security-card locks were disarmed. Every door in the building opened with a touch.

The problems with the security system were high on Jurassic Park's bug list. Nedry wondered if anybody ever imagined that it wasn't a bug—that Nedry had programmed it that way. He had built in a classic trap door. Few programmers of large computer systems could resist the temptation to leave themselves a secret entrance. Partly it was common sense: if inept users locked up the system—and then called you for help—you always had a way to get in and repair the mess. And partly it was a kind of signature: Kilroy was here.

And partly it was insurance for the future. Nedry was annoyed with the Jurassic Park project; late in the schedule, InGen had demanded extensive modifications to the system but hadn't been willing to pay for them, arguing they should be included under the original contract. Lawsuits were threatened; letters were written to Nedry's other clients, implying that Nedry was unreliable. It was blackmail, and in the end Nedry had been forced to eat his overages on Jurassic Park and to make the changes that Hammond wanted.

But later, when he was approached by Lewis Dodgson at Biosyn, Nedry was ready to listen. And able to say that he could indeed get past Jurassic Park security. He could get into any room, any system, anywhere in the park. Because he had programmed it that way. Just in case.

He entered the fertilization room. The lab was deserted; as he had anticipated, all the staff was at dinner. Nedry unzipped his shoulder bag and removed the can of Gillette shaving cream. He unscrewed the base, and saw the interior was divided into a series of cylindrical slots.

He pulled on a pair of heavy insulated gloves and opened the walk-in freezer marked CONTENTS VIABLE BIOLOGICAL MAINTAIN $-10°C$ MINIMUM. The freezer was the size of a small closet, with shelves from floor to ceiling. Most of the shelves contained reagents and liquids in plastic sacs. To one side he saw a smaller nitrogen cold box with a heavy ceramic door. He opened it, and a rack of small tubes slid out, in a cloud of white liquid-nitrogen smoke.

The embryos were arranged by species: Stegosaurus, Apatosaurus, Hadrosaurus, Tyrannosaurus. Each embryo in a thin glass container, wrapped in silver foil, stoppered with polylene. Nedry quickly took two of each, slipping them into the shaving cream can.

Then he screwed the base of the can shut and twisted the top. There was a hiss of releasing gas inside, and the can frosted in his hands. Dodgson had said there was enough coolant to last thirty-six hours. More than enough time to get back to San José.

Nedry left the freezer, returned to the main lab. He dropped the can back in his bag, zipped it shut.

He went back into the hallway. The theft had taken less than two minutes. He could imagine the consternation upstairs in the control room, as they began to realize what had happened. All their security codes were scrambled, and all their phone lines were jammed. Without his help, it would take hours to untangle the mess—but in just a few minutes Nedry would be back in the control room, setting things right.

And no one would ever suspect what he had done.

Grinning, Dennis Nedry walked down to the ground floor, nodded to the guard, and continued downstairs to the basement. Passing the neat lines of electric Land Cruisers, he went to the gasoline-powered Jeep parked against the wall. He climbed into it, noticing some odd gray tubing on the passenger seat. It looked almost like a rocket launcher, he thought, as he turned the ignition key and started the Jeep.

Nedry glanced at his watch. From here, into the park, and three minutes straight to the east dock. Three minutes from there back to the control room.

Piece of cake.

"Damn it!" Arnold said, punching buttons on the console. "It's all screwed up."

Muldoon was standing at the windows, looking out at the park. The lights had gone out all over the island, except in the immediate area around the main buildings. He saw a few staff personnel hurrying to get out of the rain, but no one seemed to realize anything was wrong. Muldoon looked over at the visitor lodge, where the lights burned brightly.

"Uh-oh," Arnold said. "We have real trouble."

"What's that?" Muldoon said. He turned away from the window, and so he didn't see the Jeep drive out of the underground garage and head east along the maintenance road into the park.

"That idiot Nedry turned off the security systems," Arnold said. "The whole building's opened up. None of the doors are locked any more."

"I'll notify the guards," Muldoon said.

"That's the least of it," Arnold said. "When you turn off the security, you turn off all the peripheral fences as well."

"The fences?" Muldoon said.

"The electrical fences," Arnold said. "They're off, all over the island."

"You mean . . ."

"That's right," Arnold said. "The animals can get out now." Arnold lit a cigarette. "Probably nothing will happen, but you never know. . . ."

Muldoon started toward the door. "I better drive out and bring in the people in those two Land Cruisers," he said. "Just in case."

Muldoon quickly went downstairs to the garage. He wasn't really worried about the fences' going down. Most of the dinosaurs had been in their paddocks for nine months or more, and they had brushed up against the fences more than once, with notable results. Muldoon knew how quickly animals learned to avoid shock stimuli. You could train a laboratory pigeon with just two or three stimulation events. So it was unlikely the dinosaurs would now approach the fences.

Muldoon was more concerned about what the people in the cars would do. He didn't want them getting out of the Land Cruisers, because once the power came back on, the cars would start moving again, whether the people were inside them or not. They might be left behind. Of course, in the rain it was unlikely they would leave the cars. But, still . . . you never knew. . . .

He reached the garage and hurried toward the Jeep. It was lucky, he thought, that he had had the foresight to put the launcher in it. He could start right out, and be out there in—

It was gone!

"What the hell?" Muldoon stared at the empty parking space, astonished.

The Jeep was gone!

What the hell was happening?

FOURTH ITERATION

"Inevitably, underlying instabilities begin to appear."

IAN MALCOLM

THE MAIN ROAD

Rain drummed loudly on the roof of the Land Cruiser. Tim felt the night-vision goggles pressing heavily on his forehead. He reached for the knob near his ear and adjusted the intensity. There was a brief phosphorescent flare, and then, in shades of electronic green and black, he could see the Land Cruiser behind, with Dr. Grant and Dr. Malcolm inside. Neat!

Dr. Grant was staring out the front windshield toward him. Tim saw him pick up the radio from the dash. There was a burst of static, and then he heard Dr. Grant's voice: "Can you see us back here?"

Tim picked up the radio from Ed Regis. "I see you."

"Everything all right?"

"We're fine, Dr. Grant."

"Stay in the car."

"We will. Don't worry." He clicked the radio off.

Ed Regis snorted. "It's pouring down rain. Of course we'll stay in the car," he muttered.

Tim turned to look at the foliage at the side of the road. Through the goggles, the foliage was a bright electronic green, and beyond he could see sections of the green grid pattern of the fence. The Land Cruisers were stopped on the downslope of a hill, which must mean they were someplace near the tyrannosaur area. It would be amazing to see a tyrannosaur with these night-vision goggles. A real thrill. Maybe the tyrannosaur would come to the fence and look over at them. Tim wondered if its eyes would glow in the dark when he saw them. That would be neat.

But he didn't see anything, and eventually he stopped looking. Everyone in the cars fell silent. The rain thrummed on the roof of the car. Sheets of water streamed down over the sides of the windows. It was hard for Tim to see out, even with the goggles.

"How long have we been sitting here?" Malcolm asked.

"I don't know. Four or five minutes."

"I wonder what the problem is."

"Maybe a short circuit from the rain."

"But it happened before the rain really started."

There was another silence. In a tense voice, Lex said, "But there's no lightning, right?" She had always been afraid of lightning, and she now sat nervously squeezing her leather mitt in her hands.

Dr. Grant said, "What was that? We didn't quite read that."

"Just my sister talking."

"Oh."

Tim again scanned the foliage, but saw nothing. Certainly nothing as big as a tyrannosaur. He began to wonder if the tyrannosaurs came out at night. Were they nocturnal animals? Tim wasn't sure if he had ever read that. He had the feeling that tyrannosaurs were all-weather, day or night animals. The time of day didn't matter to a tyrannosaur.

The rain continued to pour.

"Hell of a rain," Ed Regis said. "It's really coming down."

Lex said, "I'm hungry."

"I know that, Lex," Regis said, "but we're stuck here, sweetie. The cars run on electricity in buried cables in the road."

"Stuck for how long?"

"Until they fix the electricity."

Listening to the sound of the rain, Tim felt himself growing sleepy. He yawned, and turned to look at the palm trees on the left side of the road, and was startled by a sudden thump as the ground shook. He swung back just in time to catch a glimpse of a dark shape as it swiftly crossed the road between the two cars.

"Jesus!"

"What was it?"

"It was huge, it was big as the car—"

"Tim! Are you there?"

He picked up the radio. "Yes, I'm here."

"Did you see it, Tim?"

"No," Tim said. "I missed it."

"What the hell was it?" Malcolm said.

"Are you wearing the night-vision goggles, Tim?"

"Yes. I'll watch," Tim said.

"Was it the tyrannosaur?" Ed Regis asked.

"I don't think so. It was in the road."

"But you didn't see it?" Ed Regis said.

"No."

Tim felt bad that he had missed seeing the animal, whatever it was. There was a sudden white crack of lightning, and his night goggles flared bright green. He blinked his eyes and started counting. "One one thousand . . . two one thousand . . ."

The thunder crashed, deafeningly loud and very close.

Lex began to cry. "Oh, *no* . . ."

"Take it easy, honey," Ed Regis said. "It's just lightning."

Tim scanned the side of the road. The rain was coming down hard now, shaking the leaves with hammering drops. It made everything move. Everything seemed alive. He scanned the leaves. . . .

He stopped. There was something beyond the leaves.

Tim looked up, higher.

Behind the foliage, beyond the fence, he saw a thick body with a pebbled, grainy surface like the bark of a tree. But it wasn't a tree. . . . He continued to look higher, sweeping the goggles upward—

He saw the huge head of the tyrannosaurus. Just standing there, looking over the fence at the two Land Cruisers. The lightning flashed again, and the big animal rolled its head and bellowed in the glaring light. Then darkness, and silence again, and the pounding rain.

"Tim?"

"Yes, Dr. Grant."

"You see what it is?"

"Yes, Dr. Grant."

Tim had the sense that Dr. Grant was trying to talk in a way that wouldn't upset his sister.

"What's going on right now?"

"Nothing," Tim said, watching the tyrannosaur through his night goggles. "Just standing on the other side of the fence."

"I can't see much from here, Tim."

"I can see fine, Dr. Grant. It's just standing there."

"Okay."

Lex continued to cry, snuffling.

There was another pause. Tim watched the tyrannosaur. The head was huge! The animal looked from one vehicle to another. Then back again. It seemed to stare right at Tim.

In the goggles, the eyes glowed bright green.

Tim felt a chill, but then, as he looked down the animal's body, moving down from the massive head and jaws, he saw the smaller, muscular forelimb. It waved in the air and then it gripped the fence.

"Jesus Christ," Ed Regis said, staring out the window.

The greatest predator the world has ever known. The most fearsome attack in human history. Somewhere in the back of his publicist's brain, Ed Regis was still writing copy. But he could feel his knees begin to shake uncontrollably, his trousers flapping like flags. Jesus, he was frightened. He didn't want to be here. Alone among all the people in the two cars, Ed Regis knew what a dinosaur attack was like. He knew what happened to people. He had seen the mangled bodies that resulted from a raptor attack. He could picture it in his mind. And this was a rex! Much, much bigger! The greatest meat-eater that ever walked the earth!

Jesus.

When the tyrannosaur roared it was terrifying, a scream from some other world. Ed Regis felt the spreading warmth in his trousers. He'd peed in his pants. He was simultaneously embarrassed and terrified. But he knew he had to do something. He couldn't just stay here. He had to do something. *Something.* His hands were shaking, trembling against the dash.

"Jesus Christ," he said again.

"Bad language," Lex said, wagging her finger at him.

Tim heard the sound of a door opening, and he swung his head away from the tyrannosaur—the night-vision goggles streaked laterally—in time to see Ed Regis stepping out through the open door, ducking his head in the rain.

"Hey," Lex said, "where are you going?"

Ed Regis just turned and ran in the opposite direction from the tyrannosaur, disappearing into the woods. The door to the Land Cruiser hung open; the paneling was getting wet.

"He left!" Lex said. "Where did he go? He left us alone!"

"Shut the door," Tim said, but she had started to scream, "He left us! He left us!"

"Tim, what's going on?" It was Dr. Grant, on the radio. "Tim?"

Tim leaned forward and tried to shut the door. From the back-seat, he couldn't reach the handle. He looked back at the tyrannosaur as lightning flashed again, momentarily silhouetting the huge black shape against the white-flaring sky.

"Tim, what's happening?"

"He left us, he left us!"

Tim blinked to recover his vision. When he looked again, the tyrannosaur was standing there, exactly as before, motionless and huge. Rain dripped from its jaws. The forelimb gripped the fence. . . .

And then Tim realized: the tyrannosaur was holding on to the fence!

The fence wasn't electrified any more!

"Lex, *close the door!*"

The radio crackled. "Tim!"

"I'm here, Dr. Grant."

"What's going on?"

"Regis ran away," Tim said.

"He *what*?"

"He ran away. I think he saw that the fence isn't electrified," Tim said.

"The fence isn't electrified?" Malcolm said, over the radio. "Did he say the fence isn't electrified?"

"Lex," Tim said, *"close the door."* But Lex was screaming, "He left us, he left us!" in a steady, monotonous wail, and there was nothing for Tim to do but climb out of the back door, into the slashing rain, and shut the door for her. Thunder rumbled, and the lightning flashed again. Tim looked up and saw the tyrannosaur crashing down the cyclone fence with a giant hind limb.

"Timmy!"

He jumped back in and slammed the door, the sound lost in the thunderclap.

The radio: "Tim! Are you there?"

He grabbed the radio. "I'm here." He turned to Lex. "Lock the doors. Get in the middle of the car. And *shut up*."

Outside, the tyrannosaur rolled its head and took an awkward step forward. The claws of its feet had caught in the grid of the flattened fence. Lex saw the animal finally, and became silent, still. She watched with wide eyes.

Radio crackle. "Tim."

"Yes, Dr. Grant."

"Stay in the car. Stay down. Be quiet. Don't move, and don't make noise."

"Okay."

"You should be all right. I don't think it can open the car."

"Okay."

"Just stay quiet, so you don't arouse its attention any more than necessary."

"Okay." Tim clicked the radio off. "You hear that, Lex?"

His sister nodded, silently. She never took her eyes off the dinosaur. The tyrannosaur roared. In the glare of lightning, they saw it pull free of the fence and take a bounding step forward.

Now it was standing between the two cars. Tim couldn't see Dr. Grant's car any more, because the huge body blocked his view. The rain ran in rivulets down the pebbled skin of the muscular hind legs. He couldn't see the animal's head, which was high above the roofline.

The tyrannosaur moved around the side of their car. It went to the very spot where Tim had gotten out of the car. Where Ed Regis had gotten out of the car. The animal paused there. The big head ducked down, toward the mud.

Tim looked back at Dr. Grant and Dr. Malcolm in the rear car. Their faces were tense as they stared forward through the windshield.

The huge head raised back up, jaws open, and then stopped by the side windows. In the glare of lightning, they saw the beady, expressionless reptile eye moving in the socket.

It was looking in the car.

His sister's breath came in ragged, frightened gasps. He reached out and squeezed her arm, hoping she would stay quiet. The dinosaur continued to stare for a long time through the side window. Perhaps the dinosaur couldn't really see them, he thought. Finally the head lifted up, out of view again.

"Timmy . . ." Lex whispered.

"It's okay," Tim whispered. "I don't think it saw us."

He was looking back toward Dr. Grant when a jolting impact rocked the Land Cruiser and shattered the windshield in a spiderweb as the tyrannosaur's head crashed against the hood of the Land Cruiser. Tim was knocked flat on the seat. The night-vision goggles slid off his forehead.

He got back up quickly, blinking in the darkness, his mouth warm with blood.

"Lex?"

He couldn't see his sister anywhere.

The tyrannosaur stood near the front of the Land Cruiser, its chest moving as it breathed, the forelimbs making clawing movements in the air.

"Lex!" Tim whispered. Then he heard her groan. She was lying somewhere on the floor under the front seat.

Then the huge head came down, entirely blocking the shattered windshield. The tyrannosaur banged again on the front hood of the Land Cruiser. Tim grabbed the seat as the car rocked on its wheels. The tyrannosaur banged down twice more, denting the metal.

Then it moved around the side of the car. The big raised tail blocked his view out of all the side windows. At the back, the animal snorted, a deep rumbling growl that blended with the thunder. It sank its jaws into the spare tire mounted on the back of the Land Cruiser and, in a single head shake, tore it away. The rear of the car lifted into the air for a moment; then it thumped down with a muddy splash.

"Tim!" Dr. Grant said. "Tim, are you there?"

Tim grabbed the radio. "We're okay," he said. There was a shrill metallic scrape as claws raked the roof of the car. Tim's heart was pounding in his chest. He couldn't see anything out of the windows on the right side except pebbled leathery flesh. The tyrannosaur was leaning against the car, which rocked back and forth with each breath, the springs and metal creaking loudly.

Lex groaned again. Tim put down the radio, and started to crawl over into the front seat. The tyrannosaur roared and the metal roof dented downward. Tim felt a sharp pain in his head and tumbled to the floor, onto the transmission hump. He found himself lying alongside Lex, and he was shocked to see that the whole side of her head was covered in blood. She looked unconscious.

There was another jolting impact, and pieces of glass fell all around him. Tim felt rain. He looked up and saw that the front windshield had broken out. There was just a jagged rim of glass and, beyond, the big head of the dinosaur.

Looking down at him.

Tim felt a sudden chill and then the head rushed forward toward him, the jaws open. There was the squeal of metal against teeth, and he felt the hot stinking breath of the animal and a thick tongue stuck into the car through the windshield opening. The tongue slapped wetly around inside the car—he felt the hot lather of dinosaur saliva—and the tyrannosaur roared—a deafening sound inside the car—

The head pulled away abruptly.

Tim scrambled up, avoiding the dent in the roof. There was still room to sit on the front seat by the passenger door. The tyrannosaur stood in the rain near the front fender. It seemed confused by what had happened to it. Blood dripped freely from its jaws.

The tyrannosaur looked at Tim, cocking its head to stare with one big eye. The head moved close to the car, sideways, and peered in. Blood spattered on the dented hood of the Land Cruiser, mixing with the rain.

It can't get to me, Tim thought. It's too big.

Then the head pulled away, and in the flare of lightning he saw the hind leg lift up. And the world tilted crazily as the Land Cruiser slammed over on its side, the windows splatting in the mud. He saw Lex fall helplessly against the side window, and he fell down beside her, banging his head. Tim felt dizzy. Then the tyrannosaur's jaws clamped onto the window frame, and the whole Land Cruiser was lifted up into the air, and shaken.

"Timmy!" Lex shrieked, so near to his ear that it hurt. She was suddenly awake, and he grabbed her as the tyrannosaur crashed the car down again. Tim felt a stabbing pain in his side, and his sister fell on top of him. The car went up again, tilting crazily. Lex shouted *"Timmy!"* and he saw the door give way beneath her, and she fell out of the car into the mud, but Tim couldn't answer, because in the next instant everything swung crazily—he saw the trunks of the palm trees sliding downward past him—moving sideways through the air—he glimpsed the ground very far below— the hot roar of the tyrannosaur—the blazing eye—the tops of the palm trees—

And then, with a metallic scraping shriek, the car fell from the tyrannosaur's jaws, a sickening fall, and Tim's stomach heaved in the moment before the world became totally black, and silent.

In the other car, Malcolm gasped. "Jesus! What happened to the car?"

Grant blinked his eyes as the lightning faded.

The other car was gone.

Grant couldn't believe it. He peered forward, trying to see through the rain-streaked windshield. The dinosaur's body was so large, it was probably just blocking—

No. In another flash of lightning, he saw clearly: the car was gone.

"What happened?" Malcolm said.

"I don't know."

Faintly, over the rain, Grant heard the sound of the little girl screaming. The dinosaur was standing in darkness on the road up ahead, but they could see well enough to know that it was bending over now, sniffing the ground.

Or eating something on the ground.

"Can you see?" Malcolm said, squinting.

"Not much, no," Grant said. The rain pounded on the roof of the car. He listened for the little girl, but he didn't hear her any more. The two men sat in the car, listening.

"Was it the girl?" Malcolm said, finally. "It sounded like the girl."

"It did, yes."

"Was it?"

"I don't know," Grant said. He felt a seeping fatigue overtake him. Blurred through the rainy windshield, the dinosaur was coming toward their car. Slow, ominous strides, coming right toward them.

Malcolm said, "You know, at times like this one feels, well, perhaps extinct animals *should* be left extinct. Don't you have that feeling now?"

"Yes," Grant said. He was feeling his heart pounding.

"Umm. Do you, ah, have any suggestions about what we do now?"

"I can't think of a thing," Grant said.

Malcolm twisted the handle, kicked open the door, and ran. But even as he did, Grant could see he was too late, the tyrannosaur too close. There was another crack of lightning, and in that instant of glaring white light, Grant watched in horror as the tyrannosaur roared, and leapt forward.

Grant was not clear about exactly what happened next. Malcolm was running, his feet splashing in the mud. The tyrannosaur bounded alongside him and ducked its massive head, and Malcolm was tossed into the air like a small doll.

By then Grant was out of the car, too, feeling the cold rain slashing his face and body. The tyrannosaur had turned its back to him, the huge tail swinging through the air. Grant was tensing to run for the woods when suddenly the tyrannosaur spun back to face him, and roared.

Grant froze.

He was standing beside the passenger door of the Land Cruiser, drenched in rain. He was completely exposed, the tyrannosaur no more than eight feet away. The big animal roared again. At so close a range the sound was terrifyingly loud. Grant felt himself shaking with cold and fright. He pressed his trembling hands against the metal of the door panel to steady them.

The tyrannosaur roared once more, but it did not attack. It cocked its head, and looked with first one eye, then the other, at the Land Cruiser. And it did nothing.

It just stood there.

What was going on?

The powerful jaws opened and closed. The tyrannosaur bellowed angrily, and then the big hind leg came up and crashed down on the roof of the car; the claws slid off with a metal screech, barely missing Grant as he stood there, still unmoving.

The foot splashed in the mud. The head ducked down in a slow arc, and the animal inspected the car, snorting. It peered into the front windshield. Then, moving toward the rear, it banged the passenger door shut, and moved right toward Grant as he stood there. Grant was dizzy with fear, his heart pounding inside his chest. With the animal so close, he could smell the rotten flesh in the mouth, the sweetish blood-smell, the sickening stench of the carnivore. . . .

He tensed his body, awaiting the inevitable.

The big head slid past him, toward the rear of the car. Grant blinked.

What had happened?

Was it possible the tyrannosaur hadn't seen him? It seemed as if it hadn't. But how could that be? Grant looked back to see the animal sniffing the rear-mounted tire. It nudged the tire with its snout, and then the head swung back. Again it approached Grant.

This time the animal stopped, the black flaring nostrils just inches away. Grant felt the animal's startling hot breath on his face. But the tyrannosaur wasn't sniffing like a dog. It was just breathing, and if anything it seemed puzzled.

No, the tyrannosaur couldn't see him. Not if he stood motionless. And in a detached academic corner of his mind he found an explanation for that, a reason why—

The jaws opened before him, the massive head raised up. Grant squeezed his fists together, and bit his lip, trying desperately to remain motionless, to make no sound.

The tyrannosaur bellowed in the night air.

But by now Grant was beginning to understand. The animal couldn't see him, but it suspected he was there, somewhere, and was trying with its bellowing to frighten Grant into some revealing movement. So long as he stood his ground, Grant realized, he was invisible.

In a final gesture of frustration, the big hind leg lifted up and kicked the Land Cruiser over, and Grant felt searing pain and the surprising sensation of his own body flying through the air. It seemed to be happening very slowly, and he had plenty of time to feel the world turn colder, and watch the ground rush up to strike him in the face.

RETURN

"Oh damn," Harding said. "Will you look at that."

They were sitting in Harding's gasoline-powered Jeep, staring forward past the *flick flick* of the windshield wipers. In the yellow flare of the headlamps, a big fallen tree blocked the road.

"Must have been the lightning," Gennaro said. "Hell of a tree."

"We can't get past it," Harding said. "I better tell Arnold in control." He picked up the radio and twisted the channel dial. "Hello, John. Are you there, John?"

There was nothing but steady hissing static. "I don't understand," he said. "The radio lines seem to be down."

"It must be the storm," Gennaro said.

"I suppose," Harding said.

"Try the Land Cruisers," Ellie said.

Harding opened the other channels, but there was no answer.

"Nothing," he said. "They're probably back to camp by now, and outside the range of our little set. In any case, I don't think we should stay here. It'll be hours before Maintenance gets a crew out here to move that tree."

He turned the radio off, and put the Jeep into reverse.

"What're you going to do?" Ellie said.

"Go back to the turnout, and get onto the maintenance road. Fortunately there's a second road system," Harding explained. "We have one road for visitors, and a second road for animal handlers and feed trucks and so on. We'll drive back on that maintenance road. It's a little longer. And not so scenic. But you may find it interesting. If the rain lets up, we'll get a glimpse of some of the animals at night. We should be back in thirty, forty minutes," Harding said. "If I don't get lost."

He turned the Jeep around in the night, and headed south again.

Lightning flashed, and every monitor in the control room went black. Arnold sat forward, his body rigid and tense. Jesus, not now. Not now. That was all he needed—to have everything go out now in the storm. All the main power circuits were surge-protected, of course, but Arnold wasn't sure about the modems Nedry was using for his data transmission. Most people didn't know it was possible to blow an entire system through a modem—the lightning pulse climbed back into the computer through the telephone line, and—bang!—no more motherboard. No more RAM. No more file server. No more computer.

The screens flickered. And then, one by one, they came back on.

Arnold sighed, and collapsed back in his chair.

He wondered again where Nedry had gone. Five minutes ago, he'd sent guards to search the building for him. The fat bastard was probably in the bathroom reading a comic book. But the guards hadn't come back, and they hadn't called in.

Five minutes. If Nedry was in the building, they should have found him by now.

"Somebody took the damned Jeep," Muldoon said as he came back in the room. "Have you talked to the Land Cruisers yet?"

"Can't raise them on the radio," Arnold said. "I have to use this, because the main board is down. It's weak, but it ought to work. I've tried on all six channels. I know they have radios in the cars, but they're not answering."

"That's not good," Muldoon said.

"If you want to go out there, take one of the maintenance vehicles."

"I would," Muldoon said, "but they're all in the east garage, more than a mile from here. Where's Harding?"

"I assume he's on his way back."

"Then he'll pick up the people in the Land Cruisers on his way."

"I assume so."

"Anybody tell Hammond the kids aren't back yet?"

"Hell no," Arnold said. "I don't want that son of a bitch running around here, screaming at me. Everything's all right, for the moment. The Land Cruisers are just stuck in the rain. They can sit a while, until Harding brings them back. Or until we find Nedry, and make that little bastard turn the systems back on."

"You can't get them back on?" Muldoon said.

Arnold shook his head. "I've been trying. But Nedry's done something to the system. I can't figure out what, but if I have to go into the code itself, that'll take hours. We need Nedry. We've got to find the son of a bitch right away."

NEDRY

The sign said ELECTRIFIED FENCE 10,000 VOLTS DO NOT TOUCH, but Nedry opened it with his bare hand, and unlocked the gate, swinging it wide. He went back to the Jeep, drove through the gate, and then walked back to close it behind him.

Now he was inside the park itself, no more than a mile from the east dock. He stepped on the accelerator and hunched forward over the steering wheel, peering through the rain-slashed windshield as he drove the Jeep down the narrow road. He was driving fast—too fast—but he had to keep to his timetable. He was surrounded on all sides by black jungle, but soon he should be able to see the beach and the ocean off to his left.

This damned storm, he thought. It might screw up everything. Because if Dodgson's boat wasn't waiting for him at the east dock when Nedry got there, the whole plan would be ruined. Nedry couldn't wait very long, or he would be missed back at the control room. The whole idea behind the plan was that he could drive to the east dock, drop off the embryos, and be back in a few minutes, before anyone noticed. It was a good plan, a clever plan. Nedry'd worked on it carefully, refining every detail. This plan was going to make him a million and a half dollars, one point five meg. That was ten years of income in a single tax-free shot, and it was going to change his life. Nedry'd been damned careful, even to the point of making Dodgson meet him in the San Francisco Airport at the last minute with an excuse about wanting to see the money. Actually, Nedry wanted to record his conversation with Dodgson, and mention him by name on the tape. Just so that Dodgson wouldn't forget he owed the rest of the money, Nedry was including a copy of the tape with the embryos. In short, Nedry had thought of everything.

Except this damned storm.

Something dashed across the road, a white flash in his headlights. It looked like a large rat. It scurried into the underbrush, dragging a fat tail. Possum. Amazing that a possum could survive here. You'd think the dinosaurs would get an animal like that.

Where was the damned dock?

He was driving fast, and he'd already been gone five minutes. He should have reached the east dock by now. Had he taken a wrong turn? He didn't think so. He hadn't seen any forks in the road at all.

Then where was the dock?

It was a shock when he came around a corner and saw that the road terminated in a gray concrete barrier, six feet tall and streaked dark with rain. He slammed on the brakes, and the Jeep fishtailed, losing traction in an end-to-end spin, and for a horrified moment he thought he was going to smash into the barrier—he knew he was going to smash—and he spun the wheel frantically, and the Jeep slid to a stop, the headlamps just a foot from the concrete wall.

He paused there, listening to the rhythmic flick of the wipers. He took a deep breath and exhaled slowly. He looked back down the road. He'd obviously taken a wrong turn somewhere. He could retrace his steps, but that would take too long.

He'd better try and find out where the hell he was.

He got out of the Jeep, feeling heavy raindrops spatter his head. It was a real tropical storm, raining so hard that it hurt. He glanced at his watch, pushing the button to illuminate the digital dial. Six minutes gone. Where the hell was he? He walked around the concrete barrier and on the other side, along with the rain, he heard the sound of gurgling water. Could it be the ocean? Nedry hurried forward, his eyes adjusting to the darkness as he went. Dense jungle on all sides. Raindrops slapping on the leaves.

The gurgling sound became louder, drawing him forward, and suddenly he came out of the foliage and felt his feet sink into soft earth and saw the dark currents of the river. The river! He was at the jungle river!

Damn, he thought. At the river *where*? The river ran for miles through the island. He looked at his watch again. Seven minutes gone. "You have a problem, Dennis," he said aloud.

As if in reply, there was a soft hooting cry of an owl in the forest.

Nedry hardly noticed; he was worrying about his plan. The plain fact was that time had run out. There wasn't a choice any more. He had to abandon his original plan. All he could do was go back to the control room, restore the computer, and somehow try to contact Dodgson, to set up the drop at the east dock for the following night. Nedry would have to scramble to make that work, but he thought he could pull it off. The computer automatically logged all calls; after Nedry got through to Dodgson, he'd have to go back into the computer and erase the record of the call. But one thing was sure—he couldn't stay out in the park any longer, or his absence would be noticed.

Nedry started back, heading toward the glow of the car's headlights. He was drenched and miserable. He heard the soft hooting cry once more, and this time he paused. That hadn't really sounded like an owl. And it seemed to be close by, in the jungle somewhere off to his right.

As he listened, he heard a crashing sound in the underbrush. Then silence. He waited, and heard it again. It sounded distinctly like something big, moving slowly through the jungle toward him.

Something big. Something near. A big dinosaur.

Get out of here.

Nedry began to run. He made a lot of noise as he ran, but even so he could hear the animal crashing through the foliage. And hooting.

It was coming closer.

Stumbling over tree roots in the darkness, clawing his way past dripping branches, he saw the Jeep ahead, and the lights shining around the vertical wall of the barrier made him feel better. In a moment he'd be in the car and then he'd get the hell out of here. He scrambled around the barrier and then he froze.

The animal was already there.

But it wasn't close. The dinosaur stood forty feet away, at the edge of the illumination from the headlamps. Nedry hadn't taken the tour, so he hadn't seen the different types of dinosaurs, but this one was strange-looking. The ten-foot-tall body was yellow with black spots, and along the head ran a pair of red V-shaped crests. The dinosaur didn't move, but again gave its soft hooting cry.

Nedry waited to see if it would attack. It didn't. Perhaps the headlights from the Jeep frightened it, forcing it to keep its distance, like a fire.

The dinosaur stared at him and then snapped its head in a single swift motion. Nedry felt something smack wetly against his chest. He looked down and saw a dripping glob of foam on his rain-soaked shirt. He touched it curiously, not comprehending. . . .

It was spit.

The dinosaur had spit on him.

It was creepy, he thought. He looked back at the dinosaur and saw the head snap again, and immediately felt another wet smack against his neck, just above the shirt collar. He wiped it away with his hand.

Jesus, it was disgusting. But the skin of his neck was already starting to tingle and burn. And his hand was tingling, too. It was almost like he had been touched with acid.

Nedry opened the car door, glancing back at the dinosaur to make sure it wasn't going to attack, and felt a sudden, excruciating pain in his eyes, stabbing like spikes into the back of his skull, and he squeezed his eyes shut and gasped with the intensity of it and threw up his hands to cover his eyes and felt the slippery foam trickling down both sides of his nose.

Spit.

The dinosaur had spit in his eyes.

Even as he realized it, the pain overwhelmed him, and he dropped to his knees, disoriented, wheezing. He collapsed onto his side, his cheek pressed to the wet ground, his breath coming in thin whistles through the constant, ever-screaming pain that caused flashing spots of light to appear behind his tightly shut eyelids.

The earth shook beneath him and Nedry knew the dinosaur was moving, he could hear its soft hooting cry, and despite the pain he forced his eyes open and still he saw nothing but flashing spots against black. Slowly the realization came to him.

He was blind.

The hooting was louder as Nedry scrambled to his feet and staggered back against the side panel of the car, as a wave of nausea and dizziness swept over him. The dinosaur was close now, he could *feel* it coming close, he was dimly aware of its snorting breath.

But he couldn't see.

He couldn't see anything, and his terror was extreme.

He stretched out his hands, waving them wildly in the air to ward off the attack he knew was coming.

And then there was a new, searing pain, like a fiery knife in his belly, and Nedry stumbled, reaching blindly down to touch the ragged edge of his shirt, and then a thick, slippery mass that was surprisingly warm, and with horror he suddenly knew he was holding his own intestines in his hands. The dinosaur had torn him open. His guts had fallen out.

Nedry fell to the ground and landed on something scaly and cold, it was the animal's foot, and then there was new pain on both sides of his head. The pain grew worse, and as he was lifted to his feet he knew the dinosaur had his head in its jaws, and the horror of that realization was followed by a final wish, that it would all be ended soon.

BUNGALOW

"More coffee?" Hammond asked politely.

"No, thank you," Henry Wu said, leaning back in his chair. "I couldn't eat anything more." They were sitting in the dining room of Hammond's bungalow, in a secluded corner of the park not far from the labs. Wu had to admit that the bungalow Hammond had built for himself was elegant, with sparse, almost Japanese lines. And the dinner had been excellent, considering the dining room wasn't fully staffed yet.

But there was something about Hammond that Wu found troubling. The old man was different in some way . . . subtly different. All during dinner, Wu had tried to decide what it was. In part, a tendency to ramble, to repeat himself, to retell old stories. In part, it was an emotional liability, flaring anger one moment, maudlin sentimentality the next. But all that could be understood as a natural concomitant of age. John Hammond was, after all, almost seventy-seven.

But there was something else. A stubborn evasiveness. An insistence on having his way. And, in the end, a complete refusal to deal with the situation that now faced the park.

Wu had been stunned by the evidence (he did not yet allow himself to believe the case was proved) that the dinosaurs were breeding. After Grant had asked about amphibian DNA, Wu had intended to go directly to his laboratory and check the computer records of the various DNA assemblies. Because, if the dinosaurs were in fact breeding, then everything about Jurassic Park was called into question—their genetic development methods, their genetic control methods, everything. Even the lysine dependency might be suspect. And if these animals could truly breed, and could also survive in the wild . . .

Henry Wu wanted to check the data at once. But Hammond had stubbornly insisted Wu accompany him at dinner.

"Now then, Henry, you must save room for ice cream," Hammond said, pushing back from the table. "María makes the most wonderful ginger ice cream."

"All right." Wu looked at the beautiful, silent serving girl. His eyes followed her out of the room, and then he glanced up at the single video monitor mounted in the wall. The monitor was dark. "Your monitor's out," Wu said.

"Is it?" Hammond glanced over. "Must be the storm." He reached behind him for the telephone. "I'll just check with John in control."

Wu could hear the static crackle on the telephone line. Hammond shrugged, and set the receiver back in its cradle. "Lines must be down," he said. "Or maybe Nedry's still doing data transmission. He has quite a few bugs to fix this weekend. Nedry's a genius in his way, but we had to press him quite hard, toward the end, to make sure he got things right."

"Perhaps I should go to the control room and check," Wu said.

"No, no," Hammond said. "There's no reason. If there were any problem, we'd hear about it. Ah."

María came back into the room, with two plates of ice cream.

"You must have just a little, Henry," Hammond said. "It's made with fresh ginger, from the eastern part of the island. It's an old man's vice, ice cream. But still . . ."

Dutifully, Wu dipped his spoon. Outside, lightning flashed, and there was the sharp crack of thunder. "That was close," Wu said. "I hope the storm isn't frightening the children."

"I shouldn't think so," Hammond said. He tasted the ice cream. "But I can't help but hold some fears about this park, Henry."

Inwardly, Wu felt relieved. Perhaps the old man was going to face the facts, after all. "What kind of fears?"

"You know, Jurassic Park's really made for children. The children of the world love dinosaurs, and the children are going to delight—just *delight*—in this place. Their little faces will shine with the joy of finally seeing these wonderful animals. But I am afraid . . . I may not live to see it, Henry. I may not live to see the joy on their faces."

"I think there are other problems, too," Wu said, frowning.

"But none so pressing on my mind as this," Hammond said, "that I may not live to see their shining, delighted faces. This is our triumph, this park. We have done what we set out to do. And, you remember, our original intent was to use the newly emerging technology of genetic engineering to make money. A lot of money."

Wu knew Hammond was about to launch into one of his old speeches. He held up his hand. "I'm familiar with this, John—"

"If you were going to start a bioengineering company, Henry, what would you do? Would you make products to help mankind, to fight illness and disease? Dear me, no. That's a terrible idea. A very poor use of new technology."

Hammond shook his head sadly. "Yet, you'll remember," he said, "the original genetic engineering companies, like Genentech and Cetus, were all started to make pharmaceuticals. New drugs for mankind. Noble, noble purpose. Unfortunately, drugs face all kinds of barriers. FDA testing alone takes five to eight years—if you're lucky. Even worse, there are forces at work in the marketplace. Suppose you make a miracle drug for cancer or heart disease—as Genentech did. Suppose you now want to charge a thousand dollars or two thousand dollars a dose. You might imagine that is your privilege. After all, you invented the drug, you paid to develop and test it; you should be able to charge whatever you wish. But do you really think that the government will let you do that? No, Henry, they will not. Sick people aren't going to pay a thousand dollars a dose for needed medication—they won't be grateful, they'll be outraged. Blue Cross isn't going to pay it. They'll scream highway robbery. So something will happen. Your patent application will be denied. Your permits will be delayed. *Something* will force you to see reason—and to sell your drug at a lower cost. From a business standpoint, that makes helping mankind a very risky business. Personally, I would *never* help mankind."

Wu had heard the argument before. And he knew Hammond was right; some new bioengineered pharmaceuticals had indeed suffered inexplicable delays and patent problems.

"Now," Hammond said, "think how different it is when you're making entertainment. Nobody *needs* entertainment. That's not a matter for government intervention. If I charge five thousand dollars a day for my park, who is going to stop me? After all, nobody needs to come here. And, far from being highway robbery, a costly price tag actually increases the appeal of the park. A visit becomes a status symbol, and all Americans love that. So do the Japanese, and of course they have far more money."

Hammond finished his ice cream, and María silently took the dish away. "She's not from here, you know," he said. "She's Haitian. Her mother is French. But in any case, Henry, you will recall that the original purpose behind pointing my company in this direction in the first place—was to have freedom from government intervention, anywhere in the world."

"Speaking of the rest of the world . . ."

Hammond smiled. "We have already leased a large tract in the Azores, for Jurassic Park Europe. And you know we long ago obtained an island near Guam, for Jurassic Park Japan. Construction on the next two Jurassic Parks will begin early next year. They will all be open within four years. At that time, direct revenues will exceed ten billion dollars a year, and merchandising, television, and ancillary rights should double that. I see no reason to bother with children's pets, which I'm told Lew Dodgson thinks we're planning to make."

"Twenty billion dollars a year," Wu said softly, shaking his head.

"That's speaking conservatively," Hammond said. He smiled. "There's no reason to speculate wildly. More ice cream, Henry?"

"Did you find him?" Arnold snapped, when the guard walked into the control room.

"No, Mr. Arnold."

"*Find him.*"

"I don't think he's in the building, Mr. Arnold."

"Then look in the lodge," Arnold said, "look in the maintenance building, look in the utility shed, look everywhere, but just *find him.*"

"The thing is . . ." The guard hesitated. "Mr. Nedry's the fat man, is that right?"

"That's right," Arnold said. "He's fat. A fat slob."

"Well, Jimmy down in the main lobby said he saw the fat man go into the garage."

Muldoon spun around. "Into the garage? When?"

"About ten, fifteen minutes ago."

"Jesus," Muldoon said.

The Jeep screeched to a stop. "Sorry," Harding said.

In the headlamps, Ellie saw a herd of apatosaurs lumbering across the road. There were six animals, each the size of a house, and a baby as large as a full-grown horse. The apatosaurs moved in unhurried silence, never looking toward the Jeep and its glowing headlamps. At one point, the baby stopped to lap water from a puddle in the road, then moved on.

A comparable herd of elephants would have been startled by the arrival of a car, would have trumpeted and circled to protect the baby. But these animals showed no fear. "Don't they see us?" she said.

"Not exactly, no," Harding said. "Of course, in a literal sense they do see us, but we don't really *mean* anything to them. We hardly ever take cars out at night, and so they have no experience of them. We are just a strange, smelly object in their environment. Representing no threat, and therefore no interest. I've occasionally been out at night, visiting a sick animal, and on my way back these fellows blocked the road for an hour or more."

"What do you do?"

Harding grinned. "Play a recorded tyrannosaur roar. That gets them moving. Not that they care much about tyrannosaurs. These apatosaurs are so big they don't really have any predators. They can break a tyrannosaur's neck with a swipe of their tail. And they know it. So does the tyrannosaur."

"But they do see us. I mean, if we were to get out of the car . . ."

Harding shrugged. "They probably wouldn't react. Dinosaurs have excellent visual acuity, but they have a basic amphibian visual system: it's attuned to movement. They don't see unmoving things well at all."

The animals moved on, their skin glistening in the rain. Harding put the car in gear. "I think we can continue now," he said.

Wu said, "I suspect you may find there are pressures on your park, just as there are pressures on Genentech's drugs." He and Hammond had moved to the living room, and they were now watching the storm lash the big glass windows.

"I can't see how," Hammond said.

"The scientists may wish to constrain you. Even to stop you."

"Well, they *can't do that*," Hammond said. He shook his finger at Wu. "You know why the scientists would try to do that? It's because they want to do research, of course. That's all they ever want to do, is research. Not to accomplish anything. Not to make any progress. Just do *research*. Well, they have a surprise coming to them."

"I wasn't thinking of that," Wu said.

Hammond sighed. "I'm sure it would be *interesting* for the scientists, to do research. But you arrive at the point where these animals are simply too expensive to be used for research. This is wonderful technology, Henry, but it's also frightfully expensive technology. The fact is, it can only be supported as entertainment." Hammond shrugged. "That's just the way it is."

"But if there are attempts to close down—"

"Face the damn facts, Henry," Hammond said irritably. "This isn't America. This isn't even Costa Rica. This is my island. I own it. And nothing is going to stop me from opening Jurassic Park to all the children of the world." He chuckled. "Or, at least, to the rich ones. And I tell you, they'll love it."

In the backseat of the Jeep, Ellie Sattler stared out the window. They had been driving through rain-drenched jungle for the last twenty minutes, and had seen nothing since the apatosaurs crossed the road.

"We're near the jungle river now," Harding said, as he drove. "It's off there somewhere to our left."

Abruptly he slammed on the brakes again. The car skidded to a stop in front of a flock of small green animals. "Well, you're getting quite a show tonight," he said. "Those are compys."

Procompsognathids, Ellie thought, wishing that Grant were here to see them. This was the animal they had seen in the fax, back in Montana. The little dark green procompsognathids scurried to the other side of the road, then squatted on their hind legs to look at the car, chittering briefly, before hurrying onward into the night.

"Odd," Harding said. "Wonder where they're off to? Compys don't usually move at night, you know. They climb up in a tree and wait for daylight."

"Then why are they out now?" Ellie said.

"I can't imagine. You know compys are scavengers, like buzzards. They're attracted to a dying animal, and they have tremendously sensitive smell. They can smell a dying animal for miles."

"Then they're going to a dying animal?"

"Dying, or already dead."

"Should we follow them?" Ellie said.

"I'd be curious," Harding said. "Yes, why not? Let's go see where they're going."

He turned the car around, and headed back toward the compys.

TIM

Tim Murphy lay in the Land Cruiser, his cheek pressed against the car door handle. He drifted slowly back to consciousness. He wanted only to sleep. He shifted his position, and felt the pain in his cheekbone where it lay against the metal door. His whole body ached. His arms and his legs and most of all his head—there was a terrible pounding pain in his head. All the pain made him want to go back to sleep.

He pushed himself up on one elbow, opened his eyes, and retched, vomiting all over his shirt. He tasted sour bile and wiped his mouth with the back of his hand. His head throbbed; he felt dizzy and seasick, as if the world were moving, as if he were rocking back and forth on a boat.

Tim groaned, and rolled onto his back, turning away from the puddle of vomit. The pain in his head made him breathe in short, shallow gasps. And he still felt sick, as if everything were moving. He opened his eyes and looked around, trying to get his bearings.

He was inside the Land Cruiser. But the car must have flipped over on its side, because he was lying on his back against the passenger door, looking up at the steering wheel and beyond, at the branches of a tree, moving in the wind. The rain had nearly stopped, but water drops still fell on him through the broken front windshield.

He stared curiously at the fragments of glass. He couldn't remember how the windshield had broken. He couldn't remember anything except that they had been parked on the road and he had been talking to Dr. Grant when the tyrannosaur came toward them. That was the last thing he remembered.

He felt sick again, and closed his eyes until the nausea passed. He was aware of a rhythmic creaking sound, like the rigging of a boat. Dizzy and sick to his stomach, he really felt as if the whole car were moving beneath him. But when he opened his eyes again, he saw it was true—the Land Cruiser *was* moving, lying on its side, swaying back and forth.

The whole car was moving.

Tentatively, Tim rose to his feet. Standing on the passenger door, he peered over the dashboard, looking out through the shattered windshield. At first he saw only dense foliage, moving in the wind. But here and there he could see gaps, and beyond the foliage, the ground was—

The ground was twenty feet below him.

He stared uncomprehendingly. The Land Cruiser was lying on its side in the branches of a large tree, twenty feet above the ground, swaying back and forth in the wind.

"Oh shit," he said. What was he going to do? He stood on his tiptoes and peered out, trying to see better, grabbing the steering wheel for support. The wheel spun free in his hand, and with a loud *crack* the Land Cruiser shifted position, dropping a few feet in the branches of the tree. He looked down through the shattered glass of the passenger-door window at the ground below.

"Oh shit. Oh shit." He kept repeating it. "Oh shit. Oh shit."

Another loud *crack*—the Land Cruiser jolted down another foot.

He had to get out of here.

He looked down at his feet. He was standing on the door handle. He crouched back down on his hands and knees to look at the handle. He couldn't see very well in the dark, but he could tell that the door was dented outward so the handle couldn't turn. He'd never get the door open. He tried to roll the window down, but the window was stuck, too. Then he thought of the back door. Maybe he could open that. He leaned over the front seat, and the Land Cruiser lurched with the shift in weight.

Carefully, Tim reached back and twisted the handle on the rear door.

It was stuck, too.

How was he going to get out?

He heard a snorting sound and looked down. A dark shape passed below him. It wasn't the tyrannosaur. This shape was tubby and it made a kind of snuffling as it waddled along. The tail flopped back and forth, and Tim could see the long spikes.

It was the stegosaur, apparently recovered from its illness. Tim wondered where the other people were: Gennaro and Sattler and the vet. He had last seen them near the stegosaur. How long ago was that? He looked at his watch, but the face was cracked; he couldn't see the numbers. He took the watch off and tossed it aside.

The stegosaur snuffled and moved on. Now the only sound was the wind in the trees, and the creaking of the Land Cruiser as it shifted back and forth.

He had to get out of here.

Tim grabbed the handle, tried to force it, but it was stuck solid. It wouldn't move at all. Then he realized what was wrong: the rear door was locked! Tim pulled up the pin and twisted the handle. The rear door swung open, downward—and came to rest against the branch a few feet below.

The opening was narrow, but Tim thought he could wriggle through it. Holding his breath, he crawled slowly back into the rear seat. The Land Cruiser creaked, but held its position. Gripping the doorposts on both sides, Tim slowly lowered himself down, through the narrow angled opening of the door. Soon he was lying flat on his stomach on the slanted door, his legs sticking out of the car. He kicked in the air—his feet touched something solid—a branch—and he rested his weight on it.

As soon as he did, the branch bent down and the door swung wider, spilling him out of the Land Cruiser, and he fell—leaves scratching his face—his body bouncing from branch to branch—a jolt—searing pain, bright light in his head—

He slammed to a stop, the wind knocked from him. Tim lay doubled over a large branch, his stomach burning pain.

Tim heard another *crack* and looked up at the Land Cruiser, a big dark shape five feet above him.

Another *crack*. The car shifted.

Tim forced himself to move, to climb down. He used to like to climb trees. He was a good tree-climber. And this was a good tree to climb, the branches spaced close together, almost like a staircase. . . .

Crackkkk . . .

The car was definitely moving.

Tim scrambled downward, slipping over the wet branches, feeling sticky sap on his hands, hurrying. He had not descended more than a few feet when the Land Cruiser creaked a final time, and then slowly, very slowly, nosed over. Tim could see the big green grille and the front headlights swinging down at him, and then the Land Cruiser fell free, gaining momentum as it rushed toward him, slamming against the branch where Tim had just been—

And it stopped.

His face just inches from the dented grille, bent inward like an evil mouth, headlamps for eyes. Oil dripped on Tim's face.

He was still twelve feet above the ground. He reached down, found another branch, and moved down. Above, he saw the branch bending under the weight of the Land Cruiser, and then it cracked, and the Land Cruiser came rushing down toward him and he knew he could never escape it, he could never get down fast enough, so Tim just let go.

He fell the rest of the way.

Tumbling, banging, feeling pain in every part of his body, hearing the Land Cruiser smashing down through the branches after him like a pursuing animal, and then Tim's shoulder hit the soft ground, and he rolled as hard as he could, and pressed his body against the trunk of the tree as the Land Cruiser tumbled down with a loud metallic crash and a sudden hot burst of electrical sparks that stung his skin and sputtered and sizzled on the wet ground around him.

Slowly, Tim got to his feet. In the darkness he heard the snuffling, and saw the stegosaur coming back, apparently attracted by the crash of the Land Cruiser. The dinosaur moved dumbly, the low head thrust forward, and the big cartilaginous plates running in two rows along the hump of the back. It behaved like an overgrown tortoise. Stupid like that. And slow.

Tim picked up a rock and threw it.

"Get away!"

The rock thunked dully off the plates. The stegosaur kept coming.

"Go on! *Go!*"

He threw another rock, and hit the stegosaur in the head. The animal grunted, turned slowly away, and shuffled off in the direction it had come.

Tim leaned against the crumpled Land Cruiser and looked around in the darkness. He had to get back to the others, but he didn't want to get lost. He knew he was somewhere in the park, probably not far from the main road. If he could only get his bearings. He couldn't see much in the dark, but—

Then he remembered the goggles.

He climbed through the shattered front windshield into the Land Cruiser and found the night-vision goggles, and the radio. The radio was broken and silent, so he left it behind. But the goggles still worked. He flicked them on, saw the reassuringly familiar phosphorescent green image.

Wearing the goggles, he saw the battered fence off to his left, and walked toward it. The fence was twelve feet high, but the tyrannosaur had flattened it easily. Tim hurried across it, moved through an area of dense foliage, and came out onto the main road.

Through his goggles, he saw the other Land Cruiser turned on its side. He ran toward it, took a breath, and looked inside. The car was empty. No sign of Dr. Grant and Dr. Malcolm.

Where had they gone?

Where had everybody gone?

He felt sudden panic, standing alone in the jungle road at night with that empty car, and turned quickly in circles, seeing the bright green world in the goggles swirl. Something pale by the side of the road caught his eye. It was Lex's baseball. He wiped the mud off it.

"Lex!"

Tim shouted as loud as he could, not caring if the animals heard him. He listened, but there was only the wind, and the plink of raindrops falling from the trees.

"Lex!"

He vaguely remembered that she had been in the Land Cruiser when the tyrannosaur attacked. Had she stayed there? Or had she gotten away? The events of the attack were confused in his mind. He wasn't exactly sure what had happened. Just to think of it made him uneasy. He stood in the road, gasping with panic.

"Lex!"

The night seemed to close in around him. Feeling sorry for himself, he sat in a cold rainy puddle in the road and whimpered for a while. When he finally stopped, he still heard whimpering. It was faint, and it was coming from somewhere farther up the road.

"How long has it been?" Muldoon said, coming back into the control room. He was carrying a black metal case.

"Half an hour."

"Harding's Jeep should be back here by now."

Arnold stubbed out his cigarette. "I'm sure they'll arrive any minute now."

"Still no sign of Nedry?" Muldoon said.

"No. Not yet."

Muldoon opened the case, which contained six portable radios. "I'm going to distribute these to people in the building." He handed one to Arnold. "Take the charger, too. These are our emergency radios, but nobody had them plugged in, naturally. Let it charge about twenty minutes, and then try and raise the cars."

Henry Wu opened the door marked FERTILIZATION and entered the darkened lab. There was nobody here; apparently all the technicians were still at dinner. Wu went directly to the computer terminal and punched up the DNA logbooks. The logbooks had to be kept on computer. DNA was such a large molecule that each species required ten gigabytes of optical disk space to store details of all the iterations. He was going to have to check all fifteen species. That was a tremendous amount of information to search through.

He still wasn't clear about why Grant thought frog DNA was important. Wu himself didn't often distinguish one kind of DNA from another. After all, most DNA in living creatures was exactly the same. DNA was an incredibly ancient substance. Human beings, walking around in the streets of the modern world, bouncing their pink new babies, hardly stopped to think that the substance at the center of it all—the substance that began the dance of life—was a chemical almost as old as the earth itself. The DNA molecule was so old that its evolution had essentially finished more than two billion years ago. There had been little new since that time. Just a few recent combinations of the old genes—and not much of that.

When you compared the DNA of man and the DNA of a lowly bacterium, you found that only about 10 percent of the strands were different. This innate conservatism of DNA emboldened Wu to use whatever DNA he wished. In making his dinosaurs, Wu had manipulated the DNA as a sculptor might clay or marble. He had created freely.

He started the computer search program, knowing it would take two or three minutes to run. He got up and walked around the lab, checking instruments out of long-standing habit. He noted the recorder outside the freezer door, which tracked the freezer temperature. He saw there was a spike in the graph. That was odd, he thought. It meant somebody had been in the freezer. Recently, too—within the last half hour. But who would go in there at night?

The computer beeped, signaling that the first of the data searches was complete. Wu went over to see what it had found, and when he saw the screen, he forgot all about the freezer and the graph spike.

LEITZKE DNA SEARCH ALGORITHM

DNA: Version Search Criteria: RANA (all, fragment len > 0)	
DNA Incorporating RANA Fragments	**Versions**
Maiasaurs	2.1–2.9
Procompsognathids	3.0–3.7
Othnielia	3.1–3.3
Velociraptors	1.0–3.0
Hypsilophodontids	2.4–2.7

The result was clear: all breeding dinosaurs incorporated *rana*, or frog DNA. None of the other animals did. Wu still did not understand why this had caused them to breed. But he could no longer deny that Grant was right. The dinosaurs were breeding.

He hurried up to the control room.

LEX

She was curled up inside a big one-meter drainage pipe that ran under the road. She had her baseball glove in her mouth and she was rocking back and forth, banging her head repeatedly against the back of the pipe. It was dark in there, but he could see her clearly with his goggles. She seemed unhurt, and he felt a great burst of relief.

"Lex, it's me. Tim."

She didn't answer. She continued to bang her head on the pipe.

"Come on out."

She shook her head no. He could see she was badly frightened.

"Lex," he said, "if you come out, I'll let you wear these night goggles."

She just shook her head.

"Look what I have," he said, holding up his hand. She stared uncomprehendingly. It was probably too dark for her to see. "It's your ball, Lex. I found your ball."

"So what."

He tried another approach. "It must be uncomfortable in there. Cold, too. Wouldn't you like to come out?"

She resumed banging her head against the pipe.

"Why not?"

"There's aminals out there."

That threw him for a moment. She hadn't said "aminals" for years.

"The aminals are gone," he said.

"There's a big one. A Tyrannosaurus rex."

"He's gone."

"Where did he go?"

"I don't know, but he's not around here now," Tim said, hoping it was true.

Lex didn't move. He heard her banging again. Tim sat down in the grass outside the pipe, where she could see him. The ground was wet where he sat. He hugged his knees and waited. He couldn't think of anything else to do. "I'm just going to sit here," he said. "And rest."

"Is Daddy out there?"

"No," he said, feeling strange. "He's back at home, Lex."

"Is Mommy?"

"No, Lex."

"Are there any grown-ups out there?" Lex said.

"Not yet. But I'm sure they'll come soon. They're probably on their way right now."

Then he heard her moving inside the pipe, and she came out. Shivering with cold, and with dried blood on her forehead, but otherwise all right.

She looked around in surprise and said, "Where's Dr. Grant?"

"I don't know."

"Well, he was here before."

"He was? When?"

"Before," Lex said. "I saw him when I was in the pipe."

"Where'd he go?"

"How am I supposed to know?" Lex said, wrinkling her nose. She began to shout: "Hellooo. Hell-oooo! Dr. Grant? Dr. Grant!"

Tim was uneasy at the noise she was making—it might bring back the tyrannosaur—but a moment later he heard an answering shout. It was coming from the right, over toward the Land Cruiser that Tim had left a few minutes before. With his goggles, Tim saw with relief that Dr. Grant was walking toward them. He had a big tear in his shirt at the shoulder, but otherwise he looked okay.

"Thank God," he said. "I've been looking for you."

Shivering, Ed Regis got to his feet, and wiped the cold mud off his face and hands. He had spent a very bad half hour, wedged among big boulders on the slope of a hill below the road. He knew it wasn't much of a hiding place, but he was panicked and he wasn't thinking clearly. He had lain in this muddy cold place and he had tried to get hold of himself, but he kept seeing that dinosaur in his mind. That dinosaur coming toward him. Toward the car.

Ed Regis didn't remember exactly what had happened after that. He remembered that Lex had said something but he hadn't stopped, he *couldn't* stop, he had just kept running and running. Beyond the road he had lost his footing and tumbled down the hill and come to rest by some boulders, and it had seemed to him that he could crawl in among the boulders, and hide, there was enough room, so that was what he had done. Gasping and terrified, thinking of nothing except to get away from the tyrannosaur. And, finally, when he was wedged in there like a rat between the boulders, he had calmed down a little, and he had been overcome with horror and shame because he'd abandoned those kids, he had just run away, he had just saved himself. He knew he should go back up to the road, he should try to rescue them, because he had always imagined himself as brave and cool under pressure, but whenever he tried to get control of himself, to make himself go back up there—somehow he just couldn't. He started to feel panicky, and he had trouble breathing, and he didn't move.

He told himself it was hopeless, anyway. If the kids were still up there on the road they could never survive, and certainly there was nothing Ed Regis could do for them, and he might as well stay where he was. No one was going to know what had happened except him. And there was nothing he could do. Nothing he could have done. And so Regis had remained among the boulders for half an hour, fighting off panic, carefully not thinking about whether the kids had died, or about what Hammond would have to say when he found out.

What finally made him move was the peculiar sensation he noticed in his mouth. The side of his mouth felt funny, kind of numb and tingling, and he wondered if he had hurt it during the fall. Regis touched his face and felt swollen flesh on the side of his mouth. It was funny, but it didn't hurt at all. Then he realized the swollen flesh was a leech growing fat as it sucked his lips. *It was practically in his mouth.* Shivering with nausea, Regis pulled the leech away, feeling it tear from the flesh of his lips, feeling the gush of warm blood in his mouth. He spat, and flung it with disgust into the forest. He saw another leech on his forearm, and pulled it off, leaving a dark bloody streak behind. Jesus, he was probably covered with them. That fall down the hillside. These jungle hills were full of leeches. So were the dark rocky crevices. What did the workmen say? The leeches crawled up your underwear. They liked dark warm places. They liked to crawl right up your—

"Hellooo!"

He stopped. It was a voice, carried by the wind.

"Helloo! Dr. Grant!"

Jesus, *that was the little girl.*

Ed Regis listened to the tone of her voice. She didn't sound frightened, or in pain. She was just calling in her insistent way. And it slowly dawned on him that something else must have happened, that the tyrannosaur must have gone away—or at least hadn't attacked—and that the other people might still be alive. Grant and Malcolm. Everybody might be alive. And the realization made him pull himself together in an instant, the way you got sober in an instant when the cops pulled you over, and he felt better, because now he knew what he had to do. And as he crawled out from the boulders he was already formulating the next step, already figuring out what he would say, how to handle things from this point.

Regis wiped the cold mud off his face and hands, the evidence that he had been hiding. He wasn't embarrassed that he had been hiding, but now he had to take charge. He scrambled back up toward the road, but when he emerged from the foliage he had a moment of disorientation. He didn't see the cars at all. He was somehow at the bottom of the hill. The Land Cruisers must be at the top.

He started walking up the hill, back toward the Land Cruisers. It was very quiet. His feet splashed in the muddy puddles. He couldn't hear the little girl any more. Why had she stopped calling? As he walked, he began to think that maybe something had happened to her. In that case, he shouldn't walk back there. Maybe the tyrannosaur was still hanging around. Here he was, already at the bottom of the hill. That much closer to home.

And it was so quiet. Spooky, it was so quiet.

Ed Regis turned around, and started walking back toward the camp.

Alan Grant ran his hands over her limbs, squeezing the arms and legs briefly. She didn't seem to have any pain. It was amazing: aside from a cut on her head, she was fine. "I *told* you I was," she said.

"Well, I had to check."

The boy was not quite so fortunate. Tim's nose was swollen and painful; Grant suspected it was broken. His right shoulder was badly bruised and swollen. But his legs seemed to be all right. Both kids could walk. That was the important thing.

Grant himself was all right except for a claw abrasion down his right chest, where the tyrannosaur had kicked him. It burned with every breath, but it didn't seem to be serious, and it didn't limit his movement.

He wondered if he had been knocked unconscious, because he had only dim recollections of events immediately preceding the moment he had sat up, groaning, in the woods ten yards from the Land Cruiser. At first his chest had been bleeding, so he had stuck leaves on the wound, and after a while it clotted. Then he had started walking around, looking for Malcolm and the kids. Grant couldn't believe he was still alive, and as scattered images began to come back to him, he tried to make sense of them. The tyrannosaur should have killed them all easily. Why hadn't it?

"I'm hungry," Lex said.

"Me, too," Grant said. "We've got to get ourselves back to civilization. And we've got to tell them about the ship."

"We're the only ones who know?" Tim said.

"Yes. We've got to get back and tell them."

"Then let's walk down the road toward the hotel," Tim said, pointing down the hill. "That way we'll meet them when they come for us."

Grant considered that. And he kept thinking about one thing: the dark shape that had crossed between the Land Cruisers even before the attack started. What animal had that been? He could think of only one possibility: the little tyrannosaur.

"I don't think so, Tim. The road has high fences on both sides," Grant said. "If one of the tyrannosaurs is farther down on the road, we'll be trapped."

"Then should we wait here?" Tim said.

"Yes," Grant said. "Let's just wait here until someone comes."

"I'm hungry," Lex said.

"I hope it won't be very long," Grant said.

"I don't want to stay here," Lex said.

Then, from the bottom of the hill, they heard the sound of a man coughing.

"Stay here," Grant said. He ran forward, to look down the hill.

"Stay here," Tim said, and he ran forward after him.

Lex followed her brother. "Don't leave me, don't leave me here, you guys—"

Grant clapped his hand over her mouth. She struggled to protest. He shook his head, and pointed over the hill, for her to look.

At the bottom of the hill, Grant saw Ed Regis, standing rigid, unmoving. The forest around them had become deadly silent. The steady background drone of cicadas and frogs had ceased abruptly. There was only the faint rustle of leaves, and the whine of the wind.

Lex started to speak, but Grant pulled her against the trunk of the nearest tree, ducking down among the heavy gnarled roots at the base. Tim came in right after them. Grant put his hands to his lips, signaling them to be quiet, and then he slowly looked around the tree.

The road below was dark, and as the branches of the big trees moved in the wind, the moonlight filtering through made a dappled, shifting pattern. Ed Regis was gone. It took Grant a moment to locate him. The publicist was pressed up against the trunk of a big tree, hugging it. Regis wasn't moving at all.

The forest remained silent.

Lex tugged impatiently at Grant's shirt; she wanted to know what was happening. Then, from somewhere very near, they heard a soft snorting exhalation, hardly louder than the wind. Lex heard it, too, because she stopped struggling.

The sound floated toward them again, soft as a sigh. Grant thought it was almost like the breathing of a horse.

Grant looked at Regis, and saw the moving shadows cast by the moonlight on the trunk of the tree. And then Grant realized there was another shadow, superimposed on the others, but not moving: a strong curved neck, and a square head.

The exhalation came again.

Tim leaned forward cautiously, to look. Lex did, too.

They heard a *crack* as a branch broke, and into the path stepped a tyrannosaur. It was the juvenile: about eight feet tall, and it moved with the clumsy gait of a young animal, almost like a puppy. The juvenile tyrannosaur shuffled down the path, stopping with every step to sniff the air before moving on. It passed the tree where Regis was hiding, and gave no indication that it had seen him. Grant saw Regis's body relax slightly. Regis turned his head, trying to watch the tyrannosaur on the far side of the tree.

The tyrannosaur was now out of view down the road. Regis started to relax, releasing his grip on the tree. But the jungle remained silent. Regis remained close to the tree trunk for another half a minute. Then the sounds of the forest returned: the first tentative croak of a tree frog, the buzz of one cicada, and then the full chorus. Regis stepped away from the tree, shaking his shoulders, releasing the tension. He walked into the middle of the road, looking in the direction of the departed tyrannosaur.

The attack came from the left.

The juvenile roared as it swung its head forward, knocking Regis flat to the ground. He yelled and scrambled to his feet, but the tyrannosaur pounced, and it must have pinned him with its hind leg, because suddenly Regis wasn't moving, he was sitting up in the path shouting at the dinosaur and waving his hands at it, as if he could scare it off. The young dinosaur seemed perplexed by the sounds and movement coming from its tiny prey. The juvenile bent its head over, sniffing curiously, and Regis pounded on the snout with his fists.

"Get away! Back off! Go on, back off!" Regis was shouting at the top of his lungs, and the dinosaur backed away, allowing Regis to get to his feet. Regis was shouting "Yeah! You heard me! Back off! Get away!" as he moved away from the dinosaur. The juvenile continued to stare curiously at the odd, noisy little animal before it, but when Regis had gone a few paces, it lunged and knocked him down again.

It's playing with him, Grant thought.

"Hey!" Regis shouted as he fell, but the juvenile did not pursue him, allowing him to get to his feet. He jumped to his feet, and continued backing away. "You stupid—back! Back! You heard me— back!" he shouted like a lion tamer.

The juvenile roared, but it did not attack, and Regis now edged toward the trees and high foliage to the right. In another few steps he would be in hiding. "Back! You! Back!" Regis shouted, and then, at the last moment, the juvenile pounced, and knocked Regis flat on his back. "Cut that out!" Regis yelled, and the juvenile ducked his head, and Regis began to scream. No words, just a high-pitched scream.

The scream cut off abruptly, and when the juvenile lifted his head, Grant saw ragged flesh in his jaws.

"Oh no," Lex said, softly. Beside her, Tim had turned away, suddenly nauseated. His night-vision goggles slipped from his forehead and landed on the ground with a metallic clink.

The juvenile's head snapped up, and it looked toward the top of the hill.

Tim picked up his goggles as Grant grabbed both the children's hands and began to run.

CONTROL

In the night, the compys scurried along the side of the road. Harding's Jeep followed a short distance behind. Ellie pointed farther up the road. "Is that a light?"

"Could be," Harding said. "Looks almost like headlights."

The radio suddenly hummed and crackled. They heard John Arnold say, "—you there?"

"Ah, there he is," Harding said. "Finally." He pressed the button. "Yes, John, we're here. We're near the river, following the compys. It's quite interesting."

More crackling. Then: "—eed your car—"

"What'd he say?" Gennaro said.

"Something about a car," Ellie said. At Grant's dig in Montana, Ellie was the one who operated the radiophone. After years of experience, she had become skilled at picking up garbled transmissions. "I think he said he needs your car."

Harding pressed the button. "John? Are you there? We can't read you very well. John?"

There was a flash of lightning, followed by a long sizzle of radio static, then Arnold's tense voice. "—where are—ou—"

"We're one mile north of the hypsy paddock. Near the river, following some compys."

"No—damn well—get back here—ow!"

"Sounds like he's got a problem," Ellie said, frowning. There was no mistaking the tension in the voice. "Maybe we should go back."

Harding shrugged. "John's frequently got a problem. You know how engineers are. They want everything to go by the book." He pressed the button on the radio. "John? Say again, please. . . ."

More crackling.

218

More static. The loud crash of lightning. Then: "—Muldoo—need your car—ow—"

Gennaro frowned. "Is he saying Muldoon needs our car?"

"That's what it sounded like," Ellie said.

"Well, that doesn't make any sense," Harding said.

"—other—stuck—Muldoon wants—car—"

"I get it," Ellie said. "The other cars are stuck on the road in the storm, and Muldoon wants to go get them."

Harding shrugged. "Why doesn't Muldoon take the other car?" He pushed the radio button. "John? Tell Muldoon to take the other car. It's in the garage."

The radio crackled. "—not—listen—crazy bastards—car—"

Harding pressed the radio button. "I said, it's in the garage, John. The car is in the garage."

More static. "—edry has—ssing—one—"

"I'm afraid this isn't getting us anywhere," Harding said. "All right, John. We're coming in now." He turned the radio off, and turned the car around. "I just wish I understood what the urgency is."

Harding put the Jeep in gear, and they rumbled down the road in the darkness. It was another ten minutes before they saw the welcoming lights of the Safari Lodge. And as Harding pulled to a stop in front of the visitor center, they saw Muldoon coming toward them. He was shouting, and waving his arms.

"God damn it, Arnold, you son of a bitch! God damn it, get this park back on track! *Now!* Get my grandkids back here! *Now!*" John Hammond stood in the control room, screaming and stamping his little feet. He had been carrying on this way for the last two minutes, while Henry Wu stood in the corner, looking stunned.

"Well, Mr. Hammond," Arnold said, "Muldoon's on his way out right now, to do exactly that." Arnold turned away, and lit another cigarette. Hammond was like every other management guy Arnold had ever seen. Whether it was Disney or the Navy, management guys always behaved the same. They never understood the technical issues; and they thought that screaming was the way to make things happen. And maybe it was, if you were shouting at your secretaries to get you a limousine.

But screaming didn't make any difference at all to the problems that Arnold now faced. The computer didn't care if it was screamed at. The power network didn't care if it was screamed at. Technical systems were completely indifferent to all this explosive human emotion. If anything, screaming was counterproductive, because Arnold now faced the virtual certainty that Nedry wasn't coming back, which meant that Arnold himself had to go into the computer code and try and figure out what had gone wrong. It was going to be a painstaking job; he'd need to be calm and careful.

"Why don't you go downstairs to the cafeteria," Arnold said, "and get a cup of coffee? We'll call you when we have more news."

"I don't want a Malcolm Effect here," Hammond said.

"Don't worry about a Malcolm Effect," Arnold said. "Will you let me go to work?"

"God damn you," Hammond said.

"I'll call you, sir, when I have news from Muldoon," Arnold said.

He pushed buttons on his console, and saw the familiar control screens change.

```
*/Jurassic Park Main Modules/
*/
*/ Call Libs
Include: biostat.sys
Include: sysrom.vst
Include: net.sys
Include: pwr.mdl
*/
*/Initialize
SetMain [42]2002/9A{total CoreSysop %4 [vig. 7*tty]}
if ValidMeter(mH) (**mH).MeterVis return
Term Call 909 c.lev {void MeterVis $303} Random(3#*MaxFid)
on SetSystem(!Dn) set shp_val.obj to lim(Val{d}SumVal
    if SetMeter(mH) (**mH).ValdidMeter(Vdd) return
    on SetSystem(!Telcom) set mxcpl.obj to lim(Val{pd})NextVal
```

Arnold was no longer operating the computer. He had now gone behind the scenes to look at the code—the line-by-line instructions that told the computer how to behave. Arnold was unhappily aware that the complete Jurassic Park program contained more than half a million lines of code, most of it undocumented, without explanation.

Wu came forward. "What are you doing, John?"

"Checking the code."

"By inspection? That'll take forever."

"Tell me," Arnold said. "Tell me."

THE ROAD

Muldoon took the curve very fast, the Jeep sliding on the mud. Sitting beside him, Gennaro clenched his fists. They were racing along the cliff road, high above the river, now hidden below them in darkness. Muldoon accelerated forward. His face was tense.

"How much farther?" Gennaro said.

"Two, maybe three miles."

Ellie and Harding were back at the visitor center. Gennaro had offered to accompany Muldoon. The car swerved. "It's been an hour," Muldoon said. "An hour, with no word from the other cars."

"But they have radios," Gennaro said.

"We haven't been able to raise them," Muldoon said.

Gennaro frowned. "If I was sitting in a car for an hour in the rain, I'd sure try to use the radio to call for somebody."

"So would I," Muldoon said.

Gennaro shook his head. "You really think something could have happened to them?"

"Chances are," Muldoon said, "that they're perfectly fine, but I'll be happier when I finally see them. Should be any minute now."

The road curved, and then ran up a hill. At the base of the hill Gennaro saw something white, lying among the ferns by the side of the road. "Hold it," Gennaro said, and Muldoon braked. Gennaro jumped out and ran forward in the headlights of the Jeep to see what it was. It looked like a piece of clothing, but there was—

Gennaro stopped.

Even from six feet away, he could see clearly what it was. He walked forward more slowly.

Muldoon leaned out of the car and said, "What is it?"

"It's a leg," Gennaro said.

The flesh of the leg was pale blue-white, terminating in a ragged bloody stump where the knee had been. Below the calf he saw a

white sock, and a brown slip-on shoe. It was the kind of shoe Ed
Regis had been wearing.

By then Muldoon was out of the car, running past him to crouch
over the leg. "Jesus." He lifted the leg out of the foliage, raising it
into the light of the headlamps, and blood from the stump gushed
down over his hand. Gennaro was still three feet away. He quickly
bent over, put his hands on his knees, squeezed his eyes shut, and
breathed deeply, trying not to be sick.

"Gennaro." Muldoon's voice was sharp.

"What?"

"Move. You're blocking the light."

Gennaro took a breath, and moved. When he opened his eyes he
saw Muldoon peering critically at the stump. "Torn at the joint
line," Muldoon said. "Didn't bite it—twisted and ripped it. Just
ripped his leg off." Muldoon stood up, holding the severed leg
upside down so the remaining blood dripped onto the ferns. His
bloody hand smudged the white sock as he gripped the ankle.
Gennaro felt sick again.

"No question what happened," Muldoon was saying. "The T-rex
got him." Muldoon looked up the hill, then back to Gennaro. "You
all right? Can you go on?"

"Yes," Gennaro said. "I can go on."

Muldoon was walking back toward the Jeep, carrying the leg. "I
guess we better bring this along," he said. "Doesn't seem right to
leave it here. Christ, it's going to make a mess of the car. See if
there's anything in the back, will you? A tarp or newspaper . . ."

Gennaro opened the back door and rummaged around in the space
behind the rear seat. He felt grateful to think about something else for
a moment. The problem of how to wrap the severed leg expanded to
fill his mind, crowding out all other thoughts. He found a canvas bag
with a tool kit, a wheel rim, a cardboard box, and—

"Two tarps," he said. They were neatly folded plastic.

"Give me one," Muldoon said, still standing outside the car. Muldoon wrapped the leg and passed the now shapeless bundle to Gennaro. Holding it in his hand, Gennaro was surprised at how heavy it
felt. "Just put it in the back," Muldoon said. "If there's a way to
wedge it, you know, so it doesn't roll around . . ."

"Okay." Gennaro put the bundle in the back, and Muldoon got
behind the wheel. He accelerated, the wheels spinning in the mud,
then digging in. The Jeep rushed up the hill, and for a moment at

the top the headlights still pointed upward into the foliage, and then they swung down, and Gennaro could see the road before them.

"Jesus," Muldoon said.

Gennaro saw a single Land Cruiser, lying on its side in the center of the road. He couldn't see the second Land Cruiser at all. "Where's the other car?"

Muldoon looked around briefly, pointed to the left. "There." The second Land Cruiser was twenty feet away, crumpled at the foot of a tree.

"What's it doing there?"

"The T-rex threw it."

"*Threw* it?" Gennaro said.

Muldoon's face was grim. "Let's get this over with," he said, climbing out of the Jeep. They hurried forward to the second Land Cruiser. Their flashlights swung back and forth in the night.

As they came closer, Gennaro saw how battered the car was. He was careful to let Muldoon look inside first.

"I wouldn't worry," Muldoon said. "It's very unlikely we'll find anyone."

"No?"

"No," he said. He explained that, during his years in Africa, he had visited the scenes of a half-dozen animal attacks on humans in the bush. One leopard attack: the leopard had torn open a tent in the night and taken a three-year-old child. Then one buffalo attack in Amboseli; two lion attacks; one croc attack in the north, near Meru. In every case, there was surprisingly little evidence left behind.

Inexperienced people imagined horrific proofs of an animal attack—torn limbs left behind in the tent, trails of dripping blood leading away into the bush, bloodstained clothing not far from the campsite. But the truth was, there was usually nothing at all, particularly if the victim was small, an infant or a young child. The person just seemed to disappear, as if he had walked out into the bush and never come back. A predator could kill a child just by shaking it, snapping the neck. Usually there wasn't any blood.

And most of the time you never found any other remains of the victims. Sometimes a button from a shirt, or a sliver of rubber from a shoe. But most of the time, nothing.

Predators took children—they preferred children—and they left nothing behind. So Muldoon thought it highly unlikely that they would ever find any remains of the children.

But as he looked in now, he had a surprise.

"I'll be damned," he said.

Muldoon tried to put the scene together. The front windshield of the Land Cruiser was shattered, but there wasn't much glass nearby. He had noticed shards of glass back on the road. So the windshield must have broken back there, before the tyrannosaur picked the car up and threw it here. But the car had taken a tremendous beating. Muldoon shone his light inside.

"Empty?" Gennaro said, tensely.

"Not quite," Muldoon said. His flashlight glinted off a crushed radio handset, and on the floor of the car he saw something else, something curved and black. The front doors were dented and jammed shut, but he climbed in through the back door and crawled over the seat to pick up the black object.

"It's a watch," he said, peering at it in the beam of his flashlight. A cheap digital watch with a molded black rubber strap. The LCD face was shattered. He thought the boy might have been wearing it, though he wasn't sure. But it was the kind of watch a kid would have.

"What is it, a watch?" Gennaro said.

"Yes. And there's a radio, but it's broken."

"Is that significant?"

"Yes. And there's something else. . . ." Muldoon sniffed. There was a sour odor inside the car. He shone the light around until he saw the vomit dripping off the side door panel. He touched it: still fresh. "One of the kids may still be alive," Muldoon said.

Gennaro squinted at him. "What makes you think so?"

"The watch," Muldoon said. "The watch proves it." He handed the watch to Gennaro, who held it in the glow of the flashlight, and turned it over in his hands.

"Crystal is cracked," Gennaro said.

"That's right," Muldoon said. "And the band is uninjured."

"Which means?"

"The kid took it off."

"That could have happened anytime," Gennaro said. "Anytime before the attack."

"No," Muldoon said. "Those LCD crystals are tough. It takes

a powerful blow to break them. The watch face was shattered during the attack."

"So the kid took his watch off."

"Think about it," Muldoon said. "If you were being attacked by a tyrannosaur, would you stop to take your watch off?"

"Maybe it was torn off."

"It's almost impossible to tear a watch off somebody's wrist, without tearing the hand off, too. Anyway, the band is intact. No," Muldoon said. "The kid took it off himself. He looked at his watch, saw it was broken, and took it off. He had the time to do that."

"When?"

"It could only have been after the attack," Muldoon said. "The kid must have been in this car, after the attack. And the radio was broken, so he left it behind, too. He's a bright kid, and he knew they weren't useful."

"If he's so bright," Gennaro said, "where'd he go? Because I'd stay right here and wait to be picked up."

"Yes," Muldoon said. "But perhaps he couldn't stay here. Maybe the tyrannosaur came back. Or some other animal. Anyway, something made him leave."

"Then where'd he go?" Gennaro said.

"Let's see if we can determine that," Muldoon said, and he strode off toward the main road.

Gennaro watched Muldoon peering at the ground with his flashlight. His face was just inches from the mud, intent on his search. Muldoon really believed he was on to something, that at least one of the kids was still alive. Gennaro remained unimpressed. The shock of finding the severed leg had left him with a grim determination to close the park, and destroy it. No matter what Muldoon said, Gennaro suspected him of unwarranted enthusiasm, and hopefulness, and—

"You notice these prints?" Muldoon asked, still looking at the ground.

"What prints?" Gennaro said.

"These footprints—see them, coming toward us from up the road?—and they're adult-size prints. Some kind of rubber-sole shoe. Notice the distinctive tread pattern. . . ."

Gennaro saw only mud. Puddles catching the light from the flashlights.

"You can see," Muldoon continued, "the adult prints come to here, where they're joined by other prints. Small, and medium-size . . . moving around in circles, overlapping . . . almost as if they're standing together, talking. . . . But now here they are, they seem to be running. . . ." He pointed off. "There. Into the park."

Gennaro shook his head. "You can see whatever you want in this mud."

Muldoon got to his feet and stepped back. He looked down at the ground and sighed. "Say what you like, I'll wager one of the kids survived. And maybe both. Perhaps even an adult as well, if these big prints belong to someone other than Regis. We've got to search the park."

"Tonight?" Gennaro said.

But Muldoon wasn't listening. He had walked away, toward an embankment of soft earth, near a drainpipe for rain. He crouched again. "What was that little girl wearing?"

"Christ," Gennaro said. "I don't know."

Proceeding slowly, Muldoon moved farther toward the side of the road. And then they heard a wheezing sound. It was definitely an animal sound.

"Listen," Gennaro said, feeling panic, "I think we better—"

"Shhh," Muldoon said.

He paused, listening.

"It's just the wind," Gennaro said.

They heard the wheezing again, distinctly this time. It wasn't the wind. It was coming from the foliage directly ahead of him, by the side of the road. It didn't sound like an animal, but Muldoon moved forward cautiously. He waggled his light and shouted, but the wheezing did not change character. Muldoon pushed aside the fronds of a palm.

"What is it?" Gennaro said.

"It's Malcolm," Muldoon said.

Ian Malcolm lay on his back, his skin gray-white, mouth slackly open. His breath came in wheezing gasps. Muldoon handed the flashlight to Gennaro, and then bent to examine the body. "I can't find the injury," he said. "Head okay, chest, arms . . ."

Then Gennaro shone the light on the legs. "He put a tourniquet on." Malcolm's belt was twisted tight over the right thigh. Gennaro moved the light down the leg. The right ankle was bent outward at an awkward angle from the leg, the trousers flattened, soaked in blood. Muldoon touched the ankle gently, and Malcolm groaned.

Muldoon stepped back and tried to decide what to do next. Malcolm might have other injuries. His back might be broken. It might kill him to move him. But if they left him here, he would die of shock. It was only because he had had the presence of mind to put a tourniquet on that he hadn't already bled to death. And probably he was doomed. They might as well move him.

Gennaro helped Muldoon pick the man up, hoisting him awkwardly over their shoulders. Malcolm moaned, and breathed in ragged gasps. "Lex," he said. "Lex . . . went . . . Lex . . ."

"Who's Lex?" Muldoon said.

"The little girl," Gennaro said.

They carried Malcolm back to the Jeep, and wrested him into the backseat. Gennaro tightened the tourniquet around his leg. Malcolm groaned again. Muldoon slid the trouser cuff up and saw the pulpy flesh beneath, the dull white splinters of protruding bone. "We've got to get him back," Muldoon said.

"You going to leave here without the kids?" Gennaro said.

"If they went into the park, it's twenty square miles," Muldoon said, shaking his head. "The only way we can find anything out there is with the motion sensors. If the kids are alive and moving around, the motion sensors will pick them up, and we can go right to them and bring them back. But if we don't take Dr. Malcolm back right now, he'll die."

"Then we have to go back," Gennaro said.

"Yes, I think so."

They climbed into the car. Gennaro said, "Are you going to tell Hammond the kids are missing?"

"No," Muldoon said. "You are."

CONTROL

Donald Gennaro stared at Hammond, sitting in the deserted cafeteria. The man was spooning ice cream, calmly eating it. "So Muldoon believes the children are somewhere in the park?"

"He thinks so, yes."

"Then I'm sure we'll find them."

"I hope so," Gennaro said. He watched the old man deliberately eating, and he felt a chill.

"Oh, I am sure we'll find them. After all, I keep telling everyone, this park is made for kids."

Gennaro said, "Just so you understand that they're missing, sir."

"Missing?" he snapped. "Of course I know they're *missing*. I'm not senile." He sighed, and changed tone again. "Look, Donald," Hammond said. "Let's not get carried away. We've had a little breakdown from the storm or whatever, and as a result we've suffered a regrettable, unfortunate accident. And that's all that's happened. We're dealing with it. Arnold will get the computers cleaned up. Muldoon will pick up the kids, and I have no doubt he'll be back with them by the time we finish this ice cream. So let's just wait and see what develops, shall we?"

"Whatever you say, sir," Gennaro said.

"Why?" Henry Wu said, looking at the console screen.

"Because I think Nedry did something to the code," Arnold said. "That's why I'm checking it."

"All right," Wu said. "But have you tried your options?"

"Like what?" Arnold said.

"I don't know. Aren't the safety systems still running?" Wu said. "Keychecks? All that?"

"Jesus," Arnold said, snapping his fingers. "They must be. Safety systems can't be turned off except at the main panel."

"Well," Wu said, "if Keychecks is active, you can trace what he did."

"I sure as hell can," Arnold said. He started to press buttons. Why hadn't he thought of it before? It was so obvious. The computer system at Jurassic Park had several tiers of safety systems built into it. One of them was a keycheck program, which monitored all the keystrokes entered by operators with access to the system. It was originally installed as a debugging device, but it was retained for its security value.

In a moment, all the keystrokes that Nedry had entered into the computer earlier in the day were listed in a window on the screen:

```
13,42,121,32,88,77,19,13,122,13,44,52,77,90,13,99,13,100,13,109,55,103
144,13,99,87,60,13,44,12,09,13,43,63,13,46,57,89,103,122,13,44,52,88,9
31,13,21,13,57,98,100,102,103,13,112,13,146,13,13,13,77,67,88,23,13,13
system
nedry
goto command level
nedry
040/#xy/67&
mr goodbytes
security
keycheck off
safety off
sl off
security
whte_rbt.obj
```

"That's it?" Arnold said. "He was screwing around here for hours, it seemed like."

"Probably just killing time," Wu said. "Until he finally decided to get down to it."

The initial list of numbers represented the ASCII keyboard codes for the keys Nedry had pushed at his console. Those numbers meant he was still within the standard user interface, like any ordinary user of the computer. So initially Nedry was just looking around, which you wouldn't have expected of the programmer who had designed the system.

"Maybe he was trying to see if there were changes, before he went in," Wu said.

"Maybe," Arnold said. Arnold was now looking at the list of commands, which allowed him to follow Nedry's progression through the system, line by line. "At least we can see what he did."

system was Nedry's request to leave the ordinary user interface and access the code itself. The computer asked for his name, and he replied: *nedry*. That name was authorized to access the code, so the computer allowed him into the system. Nedry asked to *goto command level*, the computer's highest level of control. The command level required extra security, and asked Nedry for his name, access number, and password.

nedry
040/#xy/67&
mr goodbytes

Those entries got Nedry into the command level. From there he wanted *security*. And since he was authorized, the computer allowed him to go there. Once at the security level, Nedry tried three variations:

keycheck off
safety off
sl off

"He's trying to turn off the safety systems," Wu said. "He doesn't want anybody to see what he's about to do."

"Exactly," Arnold said. "And apparently he doesn't know it's no longer possible to turn the systems off except by manually flipping switches on the main board."

After three failed commands, the computer automatically began to worry about Nedry. But since he had gotten in with proper authorization, the computer would assume that Nedry was lost, trying to do something he couldn't accomplish from where he was. So the computer asked him again where he wanted to be, and Nedry said:

security. And he was allowed to remain there.

"Finally," Wu said, "here's the kicker." He pointed to the last of the commands Nedry had entered.

whte_rbt.obj

"What the hell is that?" Arnold said. "White rabbit? Is that supposed to be his private joke?"

"It's marked as an object," Wu said. In computer terminology, an "object" was a block of code that could be moved around and used, the way you might move a chair in a room. An object might be a set of commands to draw a picture, or to refresh the screen, or to perform a certain calculation.

"Let's see where it is in the code," Arnold said. "Maybe we can figure out what it does." He went to the program utilities and typed:

FIND WHTE_RBT.OBJ

The computer flashed back:

OBJECT NOT FOUND IN LIBRARIES

"It doesn't exist," Arnold said.

"Then search the code listing," Wu said.

Arnold typed:

FIND/LISTINGS: WHTE_RBT.OBJ

The screen scrolled rapidly, the lines of code blurring as they swept past. It continued this way for almost a minute, and then abruptly stopped.

"There it is," Wu said. "It's not an object, it's a command."

The screen showed an arrow pointing to a single line of code:

```
curV = GetHandl {ssm.dt} tempRgn {itm.dd2}.
curH = GetHandl {ssd.itl} tempRgn2 {itm.dd4}.
on DrawMeter(!gN) set shp_val.obj to lim(Val{d})-Xval.
if ValidMeter(mH) (**mH).MeterVis return.
if Meterhandl(vGT) ((DrawBack(tY)) return.
limitDat.4 = maxBits (%33) to {limit .04} set on.
limitDat.5 = setzero, setfive, 0 {limit .2-var(szh)}.
→ on whte_rbt.obj call link.sst {security, perimeter} set to off.
vertRange = {maxRange+setlim} tempVgn(fdn-&bb+$404).
horRange = {maxRange-setlim/2} tempHgn(fdn-&dd+$105).
void DrawMeter send_screen.obj print.
```

"Son of a bitch," Arnold said.

Wu shook his head. "It isn't a bug in the code at all."

"No," Arnold said. "It's a trap door. The fat bastard put in what looked like an object call, but it's actually a command that links the security and perimeter systems and then turns them off. Gives him complete access to every place in the park."

"Then we must be able to turn them back on," Wu said.

"Yeah, we must." Arnold frowned at the screen. "All we have to do is figure out the command. I'll run an execution trace on the link," he said. "We'll see where that gets us."

Wu got up from his chair. "Meanwhile," he said, "meanwhile,

that somebody went into the freezer about an hour ago. I think I better go count my embryos."

Ellie was in her room, about to change out of her wet clothes, when there was a knock on the door.

"Alan?" she said, but when she opened the door she saw Muldoon standing there, with a plastic-wrapped package under his arm. Muldoon was also soaking wet, and there were streaks of dirt on his clothes.

"I'm sorry, but we need your help," Muldoon said briskly. "The Land Cruisers were attacked an hour ago. We brought Malcolm back, but he's in shock. He's got a very bad injury to his leg. He's still unconscious, but I put him in the bed in his room. Harding is on his way over."

"Harding?" she said. "What about the others?"

"We haven't found the others yet, Dr. Sattler," Muldoon said. He was speaking slowly now.

"Oh, my God."

"But we think that Dr. Grant and the children are still alive. We think they went into the park, Dr. Sattler."

"Went into the park?"

"We think so. Meanwhile, Malcolm needs help. I've called Harding."

"Shouldn't you call the doctor?"

"There's no doctor on the island. Harding's the best we have."

"But surely you can call for a doctor—" she said.

"No." Muldoon shook his head. "Phone lines are down. We can't call out." He shifted the package in his arm.

"What's that?" she said.

"Nothing. Just go to Malcolm's room, and help Harding, if you will."

And Muldoon was gone.

She sat on her bed, shocked. Ellie Sattler was not a woman disposed to unnecessary panic, and she had known Grant to get out of dangerous situations before. Once he'd been lost in the badlands for four days when a cliff gave way beneath him and his truck fell a hundred feet into a ravine. Grant's right leg was broken. He had no water. But he walked back on a broken leg.

On the other hand, the kids . . .

She shook her head, pushing the thought away. The kids were probably with Grant. And if Grant was out in the park, well . . . what better person to get them safely through Jurassic Park than a dinosaur expert?

IN THE PARK

"I'm tired," Lex said. "Carry me, Dr. Grant."

"You're too big to carry," Tim said.

"But I'm *tired*," she said.

"Okay, Lex," Grant said, picking her up. "Oof, you're heavy."

It was almost 9:00 p.m. The full moon was blurred by drifting mist, and their blunted shadows led them across an open field, toward dark woods beyond. Grant was lost in thought, trying to decide where he was. Since they had originally crossed over the fence that the tyrannosaur had battered down, Grant was reasonably sure they were now somewhere in the tyrannosaur paddock. Which was a place he did not want to be. In his mind, he kept seeing the computer tracing of the tyrannosaur's home range, the tight squiggle of lines that traced his movements within a small area. He and the kids were in that area now.

But Grant also remembered that the tyrannosaurs were isolated from all the other animals, which meant they would know they had left the paddock when they crossed a barrier—a fence, or a moat, or both.

He had seen no barriers, so far.

The girl put her head on his shoulder, and twirled her hair in her fingers. Soon she was snoring. Tim trudged alongside Grant.

"How you holding up, Tim?"

"Okay," he said. "But I think we might be in the tyrannosaur area."

"I'm pretty sure we are. I hope we get out soon."

"You going to go into the woods?" Tim said. As they came closer, the woods seemed dark and forbidding.

"Yes," Grant said. "I think we can navigate by the numbers on the motion sensors."

The motion sensors were green boxes set about four feet off the ground. Some were freestanding; most were attached to trees. None of them were working, because apparently the power was still off. Each sensor box had a glass lens mounted in the center, and a painted code number beneath that. Up ahead, in the mist-streaked moonlight, Grant could see a box marked T/s/04.

They entered the forest. Huge trees loomed on all sides. In the moonlight, a low mist clung to the ground, curling around the roots of the trees. It was beautiful, but it made walking treacherous. And Grant was watching the sensors. They seemed to be numbered in descending order. He passed T/s/03, and T/s/02. Eventually they reached T/s/01. He was tired from carrying the girl, and he had hoped this would coincide with a boundary for the tyrannosaur paddock, but it was just another box in the middle of the woods. The next box after that was marked T/N/01, followed by T/N/02. Grant realized the numbers must be arranged geographically around a central point, like a compass. They were going from south to north, so the numbers got smaller as they approached the center, then got larger again.

"At least we're going the right way," Tim said.

"Good for you," Grant said.

Tim smiled, and stumbled over vines in the mist. He got quickly to his feet. They walked on for a while. "My parents are getting a divorce," he said.

"Uh-huh," Grant said.

"My dad moved out last month. He has his own place in Mill Valley now."

"Uh-huh."

"He never carries my sister any more. He never even picks her up."

"And he says you have dinosaurs on the brain," Grant said.

Tim sighed. "Yeah."

"You miss him?" Grant said.

"Not really," Tim said. "Sometimes. She misses him more."

"Who, your mother?"

"No, Lex. My mom has a boyfriend. She knows him from work."

They walked in silence for a while, passing T/N/03 and T/N/04.

"Have you met him?" Grant said.

"Yeah."

"How is he?"

"He's okay," Tim said. "He's younger than my dad, but he's bald."

"How does he treat you?"

"I don't know. Okay. I think he just tries to get on my good side. I don't know what's going to happen. Sometimes my mom says we'll have to sell the house and move. Sometimes he and my mom fight, late at night. I sit in my room and play with my computer, but I can still hear it."

"Uh-huh," Grant said.

"Are you divorced?"

"No," Grant said. "My wife died a long time ago."

"And now you're with Dr. Sattler?"

Grant smiled in the darkness. "No. She's my student."

"You mean she's still in *school*?"

"Graduate school, yes." Grant paused long enough to shift Lex to his other shoulder, and then they continued on, past T/N/05 and T/N/06. There was the rumble of thunder in the distance. The storm had moved to the south. There was very little sound in the forest except for the drone of cicadas and the soft croaking of tree frogs.

"You have children?" Tim asked.

"No," Grant said.

"Are you going to marry Dr. Sattler?"

"No, she's marrying a nice doctor in Chicago sometime next year."

"Oh," Tim said. He seemed surprised to hear it. They walked along for a while. "Then who are you going to marry?"

"I don't think I'm going to marry anybody," Grant said.

"Me neither," Tim said.

They walked for a while. Tim said, "Are we going to walk all night?"

"I don't think I can," Grant said. "We'll have to stop, at least for a few hours." He glanced at his watch. "We're okay. We've got almost fifteen hours before we have to be back. Before the ship reaches the mainland."

"Where are we going to stop?" Tim asked, immediately.

Grant was wondering the same thing. His first thought was that they might climb a tree, and sleep up there. But they would have to climb very high to get safely away from the animals, and Lex might fall out while she was asleep. And tree branches were hard; they wouldn't get any rest. At least, he wouldn't.

They needed someplace really safe. He thought back to the plans he had seen on the jet coming down. He remembered that there were outlying buildings for each of the different divisions. Grant didn't know what they were like, because plans for the individual buildings weren't included. And he couldn't remember exactly where they were, but he remembered they were scattered all around the park. There might be buildings somewhere nearby.

But that was a different requirement from simply crossing a barrier and getting out of the tyrannosaur paddock. Finding a building meant a search strategy of some kind. And the best strategies were—

"Tim, can you hold your sister for me? I'm going to climb a tree and have a look around."

High in the branches, he had a good view of the forest, the tops of the trees extending away to his left and right. They were surprisingly near the edge of the forest—directly ahead the trees ended before a clearing, with an electrified fence and a pale concrete moat. Beyond that, a large open field in what he assumed was the sauropod paddock. In the distance, more trees, and misty moonlight sparkling on the ocean.

Somewhere he heard the bellowing of a dinosaur, but it was far away. He put on Tim's night-vision goggles and looked again. He followed the gray curve of the moat, and then saw what he was looking for: the dark strip of a service road, leading to the flat rectangle of a roof. The roof was barely above ground level, but it was there. And it wasn't far. Maybe a quarter of a mile or so from the tree.

When he came back down, Lex was sniffling.

"What's the matter?"

"I heard an aminal."

"It won't bother us. Are you awake now? Come on."

He led her to the fence. It was twelve feet high, with a spiral of barbed wire at the top. It seemed to stretch far above them in the moonlight. The moat was immediately on the other side.

Lex looked up at the fence doubtfully.

"Can you climb it?" Grant asked her.

She handed him her glove, and her baseball. "Sure. Easy." She started to climb. "But I bet Timmy can't."

Tim spun in fury: "*You shut up.*"

"Timmy's afraid of heights."

"I am not."

She climbed higher. "Are so."

"Am not."

"Then come and get me."

Grant turned to Tim, pale in the darkness. The boy wasn't moving. "You okay with the fence, Tim?"

"Sure."

"Want some help?"

"Timmy's a fraidy-cat," Lex called.

"What a stupid jerk," Tim said, and he started to climb.

"It's *freezing*," Lex said. They were standing waist-deep in smelly water at the bottom of a deep concrete moat. They had climbed the fence without incident, except that Tim had torn his shirt on the coils of barbed wire at the top. Then they had all slid down into the moat, and now Grant was looking for a way out.

"At least I got Timmy over the fence for you," Lex said. "He really is scared most times."

"Thanks for your help," Tim said sarcastically. In the moonlight, he could see floating lumps on the surface. He moved along the moat, looking at the concrete wall on the far side. The concrete was smooth; they couldn't possibly climb it.

"Eww," Lex said, pointing to the water.

"It won't hurt you, Lex."

Grant finally found a place where the concrete had cracked and a vine grew down toward the water. He tugged on the vine, and it held his weight. "Let's go, kids." They started to climb the vine, back to the field above.

It took only a few minutes to cross the field to the embankment leading to the below-grade service road, and the maintenance building off to the right. They passed two motion sensors, and Grant noticed with some uneasiness that the sensors were still not working, nor were the lights. More than two hours had passed since the power first went out, and it was not yet restored.

Somewhere in the distance, they heard the tyrannosaur roar. "Is he around here?" Lex said.

"No," Grant said. "We're in another section of park from him." They slid down a grassy embankment and moved toward the concrete building. In the darkness it was forbidding, bunker-like.

"What is this place?" Lex said.

"It's safe," Grant said, hoping that was true.

The entrance gate was large enough to drive a truck through. It was fitted with heavy bars. Inside, they could see, the building was an open shed, with piles of grass and bales of hay stacked among equipment.

The gate was locked with a heavy padlock. As Grant was examining it, Lex slipped sideways between the bars. "Come on, you guys."

Tim followed her. "I think you can do it, Dr. Grant."

He was right; it was a tight squeeze, but Grant was able to ease his body between the bars and get into the shed. As soon as he was inside, a wave of exhaustion struck him.

"I wonder if there's anything to eat," Lex said.

"Just hay." Grant broke open a bale, and spread it around on the concrete. The hay in the center was warm. They lay down, feeling the warmth. Lex curled up beside him, and closed her eyes. Tim put his arm around her. He heard the sauropods trumpeting softly in the distance.

Neither child spoke. They were almost immediately snoring. Grant raised his arm to look at his watch, but it was too dark to see. He felt the warmth of the children against his own body.

Grant closed his eyes, and slept.

CONTROL

Muldoon and Gennaro came into the control room just as Arnold clapped his hands and said, "Got you, you little son of a bitch."

"What is it?" Gennaro said.

Arnold pointed to the screen:

```
Vg1 = GetHandl {dat.dt} tempCall {itm.temp}
Vg2 = GetHandl {dat.itl} tempCall {itm.temp}
if Link(Vg1,Vg2) set Lim(Vg1,Vg2) return
if Link(Vg2,Vg1) set Lim(Vg2,Vg1) return
→ on whte_rbt.obj link set security (Vg1), perimeter (Vg2)
limitDat.1 = maxBits (%22) to {limit .04} set on
limitDat.2 = setzero, setfive, 0 {limit .2−var(dzh)}
→ on fini.obj call link.sst {security, perimeter} set to on
→ on fini.obj set link.sst {security, perimeter} restore
→ on fini.obj delete line rf whte_rbt.obj, fini.obj
Vg1 = GetHandl {dat.dt} tempCall {itm.temp}
Vg2 = GetHandl {dat.itl} tempCall {itm.temp}
limitDat.4 = maxBits (%33) to {limit .04} set on
limitDat.5 = setzero, setfive, 0 {limit .2−var(szh)}
```

"That's it," Arnold said, pleased.

"That's what?" Gennaro asked, staring at the screen.

"I finally found the command to restore the original code. The command called 'fini.obj' resets the linked parameters, namely the fence and the power."

"Good," Muldoon said.

"But it does something else," Arnold said. "It then erases the code lines that refer to it. It destroys all evidence it was ever there. Pretty slick."

Gennaro shook his head. "I don't know much about computers." Although he knew enough to know what it meant when a high-tech company went back to the source code. It meant big, big problems.

"Well, watch this," Arnold said, and he typed in the command:

FINI.OBJ

The screen flickered and immediately changed.

```
Vg1 = GetHandl {dat.dt} tempCall {itm.temp}
Vg2 = GetHandl {dat.itl} tempCall {itm.temp}
if Link(Vg1,Vg2) set Lim(Vg1,Vg2) return
if Link(Vg2,Vg1) set Lim(Vg2,Vg1) return
limitDat.1 = maxBits (%22) to {limit .04} set on
limitDat.2 = setzero, setfive, 0 {limit .2−var(dzh)}
Vg1 = GetHandl {dat.dt} tempCall {itm.temp}
Vg2 = GetHandl {dat.itl} tempCall {itm.temp}
limitDat.4 = maxBits (%33) to {limit .04} set on
limitDat.5 = setzero, setfive, 0 {limit .2−var(szh)}
```

Muldoon pointed to the windows. "Look!" Outside, the big

quartz lights were coming on throughout the park. They went to the windows and looked out.

"Hot damn," Arnold said.

Gennaro said, "Does this mean the electrified fences are back on?"

"You bet it does," Arnold said. "It'll take a few seconds to get up to full power, because we've got fifty miles of fence out there, and the generator has to charge the capacitors along the way. But in half a minute we'll be back in business." Arnold pointed to the vertical glass see-through map of the park.

On the map, bright red lines were snaking out from the power station, moving throughout the park, as electricity surged through the fences.

"And the motion sensors?" Gennaro said.

"Yes, them, too. It'll be a few minutes while the computer counts. But everything's working," Arnold said. "Half past nine, and we've got the whole damn thing back up and running."

Grant opened his eyes. Brilliant blue light was streaming into the building through the bars of the gate. Quartz light: the power was back on! Groggily, he looked at his watch. It was just nine-thirty. He'd been asleep only a couple of minutes. He decided he could sleep a few minutes more, and then he would go back up to the field and stand in front of the motion sensors and wave, setting them off. The control room would spot him; they'd send a car out to pick him and the kids up, he'd tell Arnold to recall the supply ship, and they'd all finish the night in their own beds back in the lodge.

He would do that right away. In just a couple of minutes. He yawned, and closed his eyes again.

"Not bad," Arnold said in the control room, staring at the glowing map. "There's only three cutouts in the whole park. Much better than I hoped for."

"Cutouts?" Gennaro said.

"The fence automatically cuts out short-circuited sections," he explained. "You can see a big one here, in sector twelve, near the main road."

"That's where the rex knocked the fence down," Muldoon said.

"Exactly. And another one is here in sector eleven. Near the sauropod maintenance building."

"Why would that section be out?" Gennaro said.

"God knows," Arnold said. "Probably storm damage or a fallen tree. We can check it on the monitor in a while. The third one is over there by the jungle river. Don't know why that should be out, either."

As Gennaro looked, the map became more complex, filling with green spots and numbers. "What's all this?"

"The animals. The motion sensors are working again, and the computer's starting to identify the location of all the animals in the park. And anybody else, too."

Gennaro stared at the map. "You mean Grant and the kids . . ."

"Yes. We've reset our search number above four hundred. So, if they're out there moving around," Arnold said, "the motion sensors will pick them up as additional animals." He stared at the map. "But I don't see any additionals yet."

"Why does it take so long?" Gennaro said.

"You have to realize, Mr. Gennaro," Arnold said, "that there's a lot of extraneous movement out there. Branches blowing in the wind, birds flying around, all kinds of stuff. The computer has to eliminate all the background movement. It may take—ah. Okay. Count's finished."

Gennaro said, "You don't see the kids?"

Arnold twisted in his chair, and looked back to the map. "No," he said, "at the moment, there are no additionals on the map at all. Everything out there has been accounted for as a dinosaur. They're probably up in a tree, or somewhere else where we can't see them. I wouldn't worry yet. Several animals haven't shown up, like the big rex. That's probably because it's sleeping somewhere and not moving. The people may be sleeping, too. We just don't know."

Muldoon shook his head. "We better get on with it," he said. "We need to repair the fences, and get the animals back into their paddocks. According to that computer, we've got five to herd back to the proper paddocks. I'll take the maintenance crews out now."

Arnold turned to Gennaro. "You may want to see how Dr. Malcolm is doing. Tell Dr. Harding that Muldoon will need him in about an hour to supervise the herding. And I'll notify Mr. Hammond that we're starting our final cleanup."

Gennaro passed through the iron gates and went in the front door of the Safari Lodge. He saw Ellie Sattler coming down the hallway, carrying towels and a pan of steaming water. "There's a kitchen at the other end," she said. "We're using that to boil water for the dressings."

"How is he?" Gennaro asked.

"Surprisingly good," she said.

Gennaro followed Ellie down to Malcolm's room, and was startled to hear the sound of laughter. The mathematician lay on his back in the bed, with Harding adjusting an IV line.

"So the other man says, 'I'll tell you frankly, I didn't like it, Bill. I went back to toilet paper!' "

Harding was laughing.

"It's not bad, is it?" Malcolm said, smiling. "Ah, Mr. Gennaro. You've come to see me. Now you know what happens from trying to get a leg up on the situation."

Gennaro came in, tentatively.

Harding said, "He's on fairly high doses of morphine."

"Not high enough, I can tell you," Malcolm said. "Christ, he's stingy with his drugs. Did they find the others yet?"

"No, not yet," Gennaro said. "But I'm glad to see you doing so well."

"How else should I be doing," Malcolm said, "with a compound fracture of the leg that is likely septic and beginning to smell rather, ah, pungent? But I always say, if you can't keep a sense of humor . . ."

Gennaro smiled. "Do you remember what happened?"

"*Of course* I remember," Malcolm said. "Do you think you could be bitten by a *Tyrannosaurus rex* and it would escape your mind? No indeed, I'll tell you, you'd remember it for the rest of your life. In my case, perhaps not a terribly long time. But, still— yes, I remember."

Malcolm described running from the Land Cruiser in the rain, and being chased down by the rex. "It was my own damned fault, he was too close, but I was panicked. In any case, he picked me up in his jaws."

"How?" Gennaro said.

"Torso," Malcolm said, and lifted his shirt. A broad semicircle of bruised punctures ran from his shoulder to his navel. "Lifted me up in his jaws, shook me bloody hard, and threw me down. And I was fine—terrified of course, but, still and all, fine—right up to the moment he threw me. I broke the leg in the fall. But the bite was not half bad." He sighed. "Considering."

Harding said, "Most of the big carnivores don't have strong jaws. The real power is in the neck musculature. The jaws just hold on, while they use the neck to twist and rip. But with a small creature like Dr. Malcolm, the animal would just shake him, and then toss him."

"I'm afraid that's right," Malcolm said. "I doubt I'd have survived, except the big chap's heart wasn't in it. To tell the truth, he struck me as a rather clumsy attacker of anything less than an automobile or a small apartment building."

"You think he attacked halfheartedly?"

"It pains me to say it," Malcolm said, "but I don't honestly feel I had his full attention. He had mine, of course. But, then, he weighs eight tons. I don't."

Gennaro turned to Harding and said, "They're going to repair the fences now. Arnold says Muldoon will need your help herding animals."

"Okay," Harding said.

"So long as you leave me Dr. Sattler, and ample morphine," Malcolm said. "And so long as we do not have a Malcolm Effect here."

"What's a Malcolm Effect?" Gennaro said.

"Modesty forbids me," Malcolm said, "from telling you the details of a phenomenon named after me." He sighed again, and closed his eyes. In a moment, he was sleeping.

Ellie walked out into the hallway with Gennaro. "Don't be fooled," she said. "It's a great strain on him. When will you have a helicopter here?"

"A helicopter?"

"He needs surgery on that leg. Make sure they send for a helicopter, and get him off this island."

THE PARK

The portable generator sputtered and roared to life, and the quartz floodlights glowed at the ends of their telescoping arms. Muldoon heard the soft gurgle of the jungle river a few yards to the north. He turned back to the maintenance van and saw one of the workmen coming out with a big power saw.

"No, no," he said. "Just the ropes, Carlos. We don't need to cut it."

He turned back to look at the fence. They had difficulty finding the shorted section at first, because there wasn't much to see: a small protocarpus tree was leaning against the fence. It was one of several that had been planted in this region of the park, their feathery branches intended to conceal the fence from view.

But this particular tree had been tied down with guy wires and turnbuckles. The wires had broken free in the storm, and the metal turnbuckles had blown against the fence and shorted it out. Of course, none of this should have happened; grounds crews were supposed to use plastic-coated wires and ceramic turnbuckles near fences. But it had happened anyway.

In any case, it wasn't going to be a big job. All they had to do was pull the tree off the fence, remove the metal fittings, and mark it for the gardeners to fix in the morning. It shouldn't take more than twenty minutes. And that was just as well, because Muldoon knew the dilophosaurs always stayed close to the river. Even though the workmen were separated from the river by the fence, the dilos could spit right through it, delivering their blinding poison.

Ramón, one of the workmen, came over. "Señor Muldoon," he said, "did you see the lights?"

"What lights?" Muldoon said.

Ramón pointed to the east, through the jungle. "I saw it as we were coming out. It is there, very faint. You see it? It looks like the lights of a car, but it is not moving."

Muldoon squinted. It probably was just a maintenance light. After all, power was back on. "We'll worry about it later," he said. "Right now let's just get that tree off the fence."

Arnold was in an expansive mood. The park was almost back in order. Muldoon was repairing the fences. Hammond had gone off to supervise the transfer of the animals with Harding. Although he was tired, Arnold was feeling good; he was even in a mood to indulge the lawyer, Gennaro. "The Malcolm Effect?" Arnold said. "You worried about that?"

"I'm just curious," Gennaro said.

"You mean you want me to tell you why Ian Malcolm is wrong?"

"Sure."

Arnold lit another cigarette. "It's technical."

"Try me."

"Okay," Arnold said. "Chaos theory describes nonlinear systems. It's now become a very broad theory that's been used to study everything from the stock market to heart rhythms. A very *fashionable* theory. Very trendy to apply it to any complex system where there might be unpredictability. Okay?"

"Okay," Gennaro said.

"Ian Malcolm is a mathematician specializing in chaos theory. Quite amusing and personable, but basically what he does, besides wear black, is use computers to model the behavior of complex systems. And John Hammond loves the latest scientific fad, so he asked Malcolm to model the system at Jurassic Park. Which Malcolm did. Malcolm's models are all phase-space shapes on a computer screen. Have you seen them?"

"No," Gennaro said.

"Well, they look like a weird twisted ship's propeller. According to Malcolm, the behavior of any system follows the surface of the propeller. You with me?"

"Not exactly," Gennaro said.

Arnold held his hand in the air. "Let's say I put a drop of water on the back of my hand. That drop is going to run off my hand. Maybe it'll run toward my wrist. Maybe it'll run toward my thumb, or down between my fingers. I don't know for sure where it will go, but I know it will run somewhere along the surface of my hand. It has to."

"Okay," Gennaro said.

"Chaos theory treats the behavior of a whole system like a drop of water moving on a complicated propeller surface. The drop may spiral down, or slip outward toward the edge. It may do many different things, depending. But it will always move along the surface of the propeller."

"Okay."

"Malcolm's models tend to have a ledge, or a sharp incline, where the drop of water will speed up greatly. He modestly calls this speeding-up movement the Malcolm Effect. The whole system could suddenly collapse. And that was what he said about Jurassic Park. That it had inherent instability."

"Inherent instability," Gennaro said. "And what did you do when you got his report?"

"We disagreed with it, and ignored it, of course," Arnold said.

"Was that wise?"

"It's self-evident," Arnold said. "We're dealing with living systems, after all. This is life, not computer models."

In the harsh quartz lights, the hypsilophodont's green head hung down out of the sling, the tongue dangling, the eyes dull.

"Careful! Careful!" Hammond shouted, as the crane began to lift.

Harding grunted and eased the head back onto the leather straps. He didn't want to impede circulation through the carotid artery. The crane hissed as it lifted the animal into the air, onto the waiting flatbed truck. The hypsy was a small dryosaur, seven feet long, weighing about five hundred pounds. She was dark green with mottled brown spots. She was breathing slowly, but she seemed all right. Harding had shot her a few moments before with the tranquilizer gun, and apparently he had guessed the correct dose. There was always a tense moment dosing these big animals. Too little and they would run off into the forest, collapsing where you couldn't get to them. Too much and they went into terminal cardiac arrest. This one had taken a single bounding leap and keeled over. Perfectly dosed.

"Watch it! Easy!" Hammond was shouting to the workmen.

"Mr. Hammond," Harding said. "Please."

"Well, they should be careful—"

"They *are* being careful," Harding said. He climbed up onto the back of the flatbed as the hypsy came down, and he set her into the restraining harness. Harding slipped on the cardiogram collar that monitored heartbeat, then picked up the big electronic thermometer the size of a turkey baster and slipped it into the rectum. It beeped: 96.2 degrees.

"How is she?" Hammond asked fretfully.

"She's fine," Harding said. "She's only dropped a degree and a half."

"That's too much," Hammond said. "Too deep."

"You don't want her waking up and jumping off the truck," Harding snapped.

Before coming to the park, Harding had been the chief of veterinary medicine at the San Diego Zoo, and the world's leading expert on avian care. He flew all over the world, consulting with zoos in Europe, India, and Japan on the care of exotic birds. He'd had no interest when this peculiar little man showed up, offering him a position in a private game park. But when he learned what Hammond had done . . . It was impossible to pass up. Harding had an academic bent, and the prospect of writing the first *Textbook of Veterinary Internal Medicine: Diseases of Dinosauria* was compelling. In the late twentieth century, veterinary medicine was scientifically advanced; the best zoos ran clinics little different from hospitals. New textbooks were merely refinements of old. For a world-class practitioner, there were no worlds left to conquer. But to be the first to care for a whole new class of animals: that was something!

And Harding had never regretted his decision. He had developed considerable expertise with these animals. And he didn't want to hear from Hammond now.

The hypsy snorted and twitched. She was still breathing shallowly; there was no ocular reflex yet. But it was time to get moving. "All aboard," Harding shouted. "Let's get this girl back to her paddock."

"Living systems," Arnold said, "are not like mechanical systems. Living systems are never in equilibrium. They are inherently unstable. They may seem stable, but they're not. Everything is moving and changing. In a sense, everything is on the edge of collapse."

Gennaro was frowning. "But lots of things don't change; body temperature doesn't change, all kinds of other—"

"Body temperature changes constantly," Arnold said. "*Constantly*. It changes cyclically over twenty-four hours, lowest in the morning, highest in the afternoon. It changes with mood, with disease, with exercise, with outside temperature, with food. It continuously fluctuates up and down. Tiny jiggles on a graph. Because, at any moment, some forces are pushing temperature up, and other forces are pulling it down. It is inherently unstable. And every other aspect of living systems is like that, too."

"So you're saying . . ."

"Malcolm's just another theoretician," Arnold said. "Sitting in his office, he made a nice mathematical model, and it never occurred to him that what he saw as defects were actually necessities. Look: when I was working on missiles, we dealt with something called 'resonant yaw.' Resonant yaw meant that, even though a missile was only slightly unstable off the pad, it was hopeless. It was inevitably going to go out of control, and it couldn't be brought back. That's a feature of mechanical systems. A little wobble can get worse until the whole system collapses. But those same little wobbles are essential to a living system. They mean the system is healthy and responsive. Malcolm never understood that."

"Are you sure he didn't understand that? He seems pretty clear on the difference between living and nonliving—"

"Look," Arnold said. "The proof is right here." He pointed to the screens. "In less than an hour," he said, "the park will all be back on line. The only thing I've got left to clear is the telephones. For some reason, they're still out. But everything else will be working. And that's not theoretical. That's a fact."

The needle went deep into the neck, and Harding injected the medrine into the anesthetized female dryosaur as she lay on her side on the ground. Immediately the animal began to recover, snorting and kicking her powerful hind legs.

"Back, everybody," Harding said, scrambling away. "Get back."

The dinosaur staggered to her feet, standing drunkenly. She shook her lizard head, stared at the people standing back in the quartz lights, and blinked.

"She's drooling," Hammond said, worried.

"Temporary," Harding said. "It'll stop."

The dryosaur coughed, and then moved slowly across the field, away from the lights.

"Why isn't she hopping?"

"She will," Harding said. "It'll take her about an hour to recover fully. She's fine." He turned back to the car. "Okay, boys, let's go deal with the stego."

Muldoon watched as the last of the stakes was pounded into the ground. The lines were pulled taut, and the protocarpus tree was lifted clear. Muldoon could see the blackened, charred streaks on the silver fence where the short had occurred. At the base of the fence, several ceramic insulators had burst. They would have to be replaced. But before that could be done, Arnold would have to shut down all the fences.

"Control. This is Muldoon. We're ready to begin repair."

"All right," Arnold said. "Shutting out your section now."

Muldoon glanced at his watch. Somewhere in the distance, he heard soft hooting. It sounded like owls, but he knew it was the dilophosaurs. He went over to Ramón and said, "Let's finish this up. I want to get to those other sections of fence."

An hour went by. Donald Gennaro stared at the glowing map in the control room as the spots and numbers flickered and changed. "What's happening now?"

Arnold worked at the console. "I'm trying to get the phones back. So we can call about Malcolm."

"No, I mean out there."

Arnold glanced up at the board. "It looks as if they're about done with the animals, and the two sections. Just as I told you, the park is back in hand. With no catastrophic Malcolm Effect. In fact, there's just that third section of fence. . . ."

"Arnold." It was Muldoon's voice.

"Yes?"

"Have you seen this bloody fence?"

"Just a minute."

On one of the monitors, Gennaro saw a high angle down on a field of grass, blowing in the wind. In the distance was a low concrete roof. "That's the sauropod maintenance building," Arnold explained. "It's one of the utility structures we use for equipment, feed storage, and so on. We have them all around the park, in each of the pad-docks." On the monitor, the video image panned. "We're turning the camera now to get a look at the fence. . . ."

Gennaro saw a shining wall of metallic mesh in the light. One section had been trampled, knocked flat. Muldoon's Jeep and work crew were there.

"Huh," Arnold said. "Looks like the rex went into the sauropod paddock."

Muldoon said, "Fine dining tonight."

"We'll have to get him out of there," Arnold said.

"With what?" Muldoon said. "We haven't got anything to use on a rex. I'll fix this fence, but I'm not going in there until daylight."

"Hammond won't like it."

"We'll discuss it when I get back," Muldoon said.

"How many sauropods will the rex kill?" Hammond said, pacing around the control room.

"Probably just one," Harding said. "Sauropods are big; the rex can feed off a single kill for several days."

"We have to go out and get him tonight," Hammond said.

Muldoon shook his head. "I'm not going in there until daylight."

Hammond was rising up and down on the balls of his feet, the way he did whenever he was angry. "Are you forgetting you work for me?"

"No, Mr. Hammond, I'm not forgetting. But that's a full-grown adult tyrannosaur out there. How do you plan to get him?"

"We have tranquilizer guns."

"We have tranquilizer guns that shoot a twenty-cc dart," Muldoon said. "Fine for an animal that weighs four or five hundred pounds. That tyrannosaur weighs eight tons. It wouldn't even feel it."

"You ordered a larger weapon. . . ."

"I ordered three larger weapons, Mr. Hammond, but you cut the requisition, so we got only one. And it's gone. Nedry took it when he left."

"That was pretty stupid. Who let that happen?"

"Nedry's not my problem, Mr. Hammond," Muldoon said.

"You're saying," Hammond said, "that, as of this moment, there is no way to stop the tyrannosaur?"

"That's exactly what I'm saying," Muldoon said.

"That's ridiculous," Hammond said.

"It's your park, Mr. Hammond. You didn't want anybody to be able to injure your precious dinosaurs. Well, now you've got a rex in with the sauropods, and there's not a damned thing you can do about it." He left the room.

"Just a minute," Hammond said, hurrying after him.

Gennaro stared at the screens, and listened to the shouted argument in the hallway outside. He said to Arnold, "I guess you don't have control of the park yet, after all."

"Don't kid yourself," Arnold said, lighting another cigarette. "We have the park. It'll be dawn in a couple of hours. We may lose a couple of dinos before we get the rex out of there, but, believe me, we have the park."

DAWN

Grant was awakened by a loud grinding sound, followed by a mechanical clanking. He opened his eyes and saw a bale of hay rolling past him on a conveyor belt, up toward the ceiling. Two more bales followed it. Then the clanking stopped as abruptly as it had begun, and the concrete building was silent again.

Grant yawned. He stretched sleepily, winced in pain, and sat up.

Soft yellow light came through the side windows. It was morning: he had slept the whole night! He looked quickly at his watch: 5:00 a.m. Still almost six hours to go before the boat had to be recalled. He rolled onto his back, groaning. His head throbbed, and his body ached as if he had been beaten up. From around the corner, he heard a squeaking sound, like a rusty wheel. And then Lex giggling.

Grant stood slowly, and looked at the building. Now that it was daylight, he could see it was some kind of a maintenance building, with stacks of hay and supplies. On the wall he saw a gray metal box and a stenciled sign: SAUROPOD MAINTENANCE BLDG (04). This must be the sauropod paddock, as he had thought. He opened the box and saw a telephone, but when he lifted the receiver he heard only hissing static. Apparently the phones weren't working yet.

"Chew your food," Lex was saying. "Don't be a piggy, Ralph."

Grant walked around the corner and found Lex by the bars, holding out handfuls of hay to an animal outside that looked like a large pink pig and was making the squeaking sounds Grant had heard. It was actually an infant triceratops, about the size of a pony. The infant didn't have horns on its head yet, just a curved bony frill behind big soft eyes. It poked its snout through the bars toward Lex, its eyes watching her as she fed it more hay.

"That's better," Lex said. "There's plenty of hay, don't worry." She patted the baby on the head. "You like hay, don't you, Ralph?"

Lex turned back and saw him.

"This is Ralph," Lex said. "He's my friend. He likes hay."

Grant took a step and stopped, wincing.

"You look pretty bad," Lex said.

"I feel pretty bad."

"Tim, too. His nose is all swollen up."

"Where is Tim?"

"Peeing," she said. "You want to help me feed Ralph?"

The baby triceratops looked at Grant. Hay stuck out of both sides of its mouth, dropping on the floor as it chewed.

"He's a *very* messy eater," Lex said. "And he's very hungry."

The baby finished chewing and licked its lips. It opened its mouth, waiting for more. Grant could see the slender sharp teeth, and the beaky upper jaw, like a parrot.

"Okay, just a minute," Lex said, scooping up more straw from the concrete floor. "Honestly, Ralph," she said, "you'd think your mother never fed you."

"Why is his name Ralph?"

"Because he looks like Ralph. At school."

Grant came closer and touched the skin of the neck gently.

"It's okay, you can pet him," Lex said. "He likes it when you pet him, don't you, Ralph?"

The skin felt dry and warm, with the pebbled texture of a football. Ralph gave a little squeak as Grant petted it. Outside the bars, its thick tail swung back and forth with pleasure.

"He's pretty tame." Ralph looked from Lex to Grant as it ate, and showed no sign of fear. It reminded Grant that the dinosaurs didn't have ordinary responses to people. "Maybe I can ride him," Lex said.

"Let's not."

"I bet he'd let me," Lex said. "It'd be fun to ride a dinosaur."

Grant looked out the bars past the animal, to the open fields of the sauropod compound. It was growing lighter every minute. He should go outside, he thought, and set off one of the motion sensors on the field above. After all, it might take the people in the control room an hour to get out here to him. And he didn't like the idea that the phones were still down. . . .

He heard a deep snorting sound, like the snort of a very large horse, and suddenly the baby became agitated. It tried to pull its head back through the bars, but got caught on the edge of its frill, and it squeaked in fright.

The snorting came again. It was closer this time.

Ralph reared up on its hind legs, frantic to get out from between the bars. It wriggled its head back and forth, rubbing against the bars.

"Ralph, take it easy," Lex said.

"Push him out," Grant said. He reached up to Ralph's head and leaned against it, pushing the animal sideways and backward. The frill popped free and the baby fell outside the bars, losing its balance and flopping on its side. Then the baby was covered in shadow, and a huge leg came into view, thicker than a tree trunk. The foot had five curved toenails, like an elephant's.

Ralph looked up and squeaked. A head came down into view: six feet long, with three long white horns, one above each of the large brown eyes and a smaller horn at the tip of the nose. It was a full-grown triceratops. The big animal peered at Lex and Grant, blinking slowly, and then turned its attention to Ralph. A tongue came out and licked the baby. Ralph squeaked and rubbed up against the big leg happily.

"Is that his mom?" Lex said.

"Looks like it," Grant said.

"Should we feed the mom, too?" Lex said.

But the big triceratops was already nudging Ralph with her snout, pushing the baby away from the bars.

"Guess not."

The infant turned away from the bars and walked off. From time to time, the big mother nudged her baby, guiding it away, as they both walked out into the fields.

"Good-bye, Ralph," Lex said, waving. Tim came out of the shadows of the building.

"Tell you what," Grant said. "I'm going up on the hill to set off the motion sensors, so they'll know to come get us. You two stay here and wait for me."

"No," Lex said.

"Why? Stay here. It's safe here."

"You're not leaving us," she said. "Right, Timmy?"

"Right," Tim said.

"Okay," Grant said.

They crawled through the bars, stepping outside.

It was just before dawn.

The air was warm and humid, the sky soft pink and purple. A white mist clung low to the ground. Some distance away, they saw the mother triceratops and the baby moving away toward a herd of large duckbilled hadrosaurs, eating foliage from trees at the edge of the lagoon.

Some of the hadrosaurs stood knee-deep in the water. They drank, lowering their flat heads, meeting their own reflections in the still water. Then they looked up again, their heads swiveling. At the water's edge, one of the babies ventured out, squeaked, and scrambled back while the adults watched indulgently.

Farther south, other hadrosaurs were eating the lower vegetation. Sometimes they reared up on their hind legs, resting their forelegs on the tree trunks, so they could reach the leaves on higher branches. And in the far distance, a giant apatosaur stood above the trees, the tiny head swiveling on the long neck. The scene was so peaceful Grant found it hard to imagine any danger.

"Yow!" Lex shouted, ducking. Two giant red dragonflies with six-foot wingspans hummed past them. "What was that?"

"Dragonflies," he said. "The Jurassic was a time of huge insects."

"Do they bite?" Lex said.

"I don't think so," Grant said.

Tim held out his hand. One of the dragonflies lighted on it. He could feel the weight of the huge insect.

"He's going to bite you," Lex warned.

But the dragonfly just slowly flapped its red-veined transparent wings, and then, when Tim moved his arm, flew off again.

"Which way do we go?" Lex said.

"There."

They started walking across the field. They reached a black box mounted on a heavy metal tripod, the first of the motion sensors. Grant stopped and waved his hand in front of it back and forth, but nothing happened. If the phones didn't work, perhaps the sensors didn't work, either. "We'll try another one," he said, pointing across the field. Somewhere in the distance, they heard the roar of a large animal.

"Ah hell," Arnold said. "I just can't find it." He sipped coffee and stared bleary-eyed at the screens. He had taken all the video monitors off line. In the control room, he was searching the computer code. He was exhausted; he'd been working for twelve straight hours. He turned to Wu, who had come up from the lab.

"Find what?"

"The phones are still out. I can't get them back on. I think Nedry did something to the phones."

Wu lifted one phone, heard hissing. "Sounds like a modem."

"But it's not," Arnold said. "Because I went down into the basement and shut off all the modems. What you're hearing is just white noise that sounds like a modem transmitting."

"So the phone lines are jammed?"

"Basically, yes. Nedry jammed them very well. He's inserted some kind of a lockout into the program code, and now I can't find it, because I gave that restore command which erased part of the program listings. But apparently the command to shut off the phones is still resident in the computer memory."

Wu shrugged. "So? Just reset: shut the system down and you'll clear memory."

"I've never done it before," Arnold said. "And I'm reluctant to do it. Maybe all the systems will come back on start-up—but maybe they won't. I'm not a computer expert, and neither are you. Not really. And without an open phone line, we can't talk to anybody who is."

"If the command is RAM-resident, it won't show up in the code. You can do a RAM dump and search that, but you don't know what you're searching for. I think all you can do is reset."

Gennaro stormed in. "We still don't have any telephones."

"Working on it."

"You've been working on it since midnight. And Malcolm is worse. He needs medical attention."

"It means I'll have to shut down," Arnold said. "I can't be sure everything will come back on."

Gennaro said, "Look. There's a sick man over in that lodge. He needs a doctor or he'll die. You can't call for a doctor unless you have a phone. Four people have probably died already. Now, shut down and get the phones working!"

Arnold hesitated.

"Well?" Gennaro said.

"Well, it's just . . . the safety systems don't allow the computer to be shut down, and—"

"*Then turn the goddamn safety systems off!* Can't you get it through your head that he's going to die unless he gets help?"

"Okay," Arnold said.

He got up and went to the main panel. He opened the doors, and uncovered the metal swing-latches over the safety switches. He popped them off, one after another. "You asked for it," Arnold said. "And you got it."

He threw the master switch.

The control room was dark. All the monitors were black. The three men stood there in the dark.

"How long do we have to wait?" Gennaro said.

"Thirty seconds," Arnold said.

"P-U!" Lex said, as they crossed the field.

"What?" Grant said.

"That smell!" Lex said. "It stinks like rotten garbage."

Grant hesitated. He stared across the field toward the distant trees, looking for movement. He saw nothing. There was hardly a breeze to stir the branches. It was peaceful and silent in the early morning. "I think it's your imagination," he said.

"Is not—"

Then he heard the honking sound. It came from the herd of duck-billed hadrosaurs behind them. First one animal, then another and another, until the whole herd had taken up the honking cry. The duckbills were agitated, twisting and turning, hurrying out of the water, circling the young ones to protect them. . . .

They smell it, too, Grant thought.

With a roar, the tyrannosaur burst from the trees fifty yards away, near the lagoon. It rushed out across the open field with huge strides. It ignored them, heading toward the herd of hadrosaurs.

"I told you!" Lex screamed. "Nobody listens to me!"

In the distance, the duckbills were honking and starting to run. Grant could feel the earth shake beneath his feet. "Come on, kids!" He grabbed Lex, lifting her bodily off the ground, and ran with Tim through the grass. He had glimpses of the tyrannosaur down by the lagoon, lunging at the hadrosaurs, which swung their big tails in defense and honked loudly and continuously. He heard the crashing of foliage and trees, and when he looked over again, the duckbills were charging.

In the darkened control room, Arnold checked his watch. Thirty seconds. The memory should be cleared by now. He pushed the main power switch back on.

Nothing happened.

Arnold's stomach heaved. He pushed the switch off, then on again. Still nothing happened. He felt sweat on his brow.

"What's wrong?" Gennaro said.

"Oh hell," Arnold said. Then he remembered you had to turn the safety switches back on before you restarted the power. He flipped on the three safeties, and covered them again with the latch covers. Then he held his breath, and turned the main power switch.

The room lights came on.

The computer beeped.

The screens hummed.

"Thank God," Arnold said. He hurried to the main monitor. There were rows of labels on the screen:

JURASSIC PARK – SYSTEM STARTUP						
		STARTUP AB(O)			STARTUP CN/D	
Security Main	Monitor Main	Command Main	Electrical Main	Hydraulic Main	Master Main	Zoolog Main
SetGrids DNL	View VBB	Access TNL	Heating Cooling	Door Fold Interface	SAAG-Rnd	Repair Storage
Critical Locks	TeleCom VBB	Reset Revert	Emgency Illumin	GAS/VLD Main II	Common Interface	Status Main
Control Passthru	TeleCom RSD	Template Main	FNCC Params	Explosion Fire Hzd	Schematic Main	Safety/ Health

Gennaro reached for the phone, but it was dead. No static hissing this time—just nothing at all. "What's this?"

"Give me a second," Arnold said. "After a reset, all the system modules have to be brought on line manually." Quickly, he went back to work.

"Why manually?" Gennaro said.

"Will you just let me work, for Christ's sake?"

Wu said, "The system is not intended to ever shut down. So, if it does shut down, it assumes that there is a problem somewhere. It requires you to start up everything manually. Otherwise, if there were a short somewhere, the system would start up, short out, start up again, short out again, in an endless cycle."

"Okay," Arnold said. "We're going."

Gennaro picked up the phone and started to dial, when he suddenly stopped.

"Jesus, look at that," he said. He pointed to one of the video monitors.

But Arnold wasn't listening. He was staring at the map, where a tight cluster of dots by the lagoon had started to move in a coordinated way. Moving fast, in a kind of swirl.

"What's happening?" Gennaro said.

"The duckbills," Arnold said tonelessly. "They've stampeded."

The duckbills charged with surprising speed, their enormous bodies in a tight cluster, honking and roaring, the infants squealing and trying to stay out from underfoot. The herd raised a great cloud of yellow dust. Grant couldn't see the tyrannosaur.

The duckbills were running right toward them.

Still carrying Lex, he ran with Tim toward a rocky outcrop, with a stand of big conifers. They ran hard, feeling the ground shake beneath their feet. The sound of the approaching herd was deafening, like the sound of jets at an airport. It filled the air, and hurt their ears. Lex was shouting something, but he couldn't hear what she was saying, and as they scrambled onto the rocks, the herd closed in around them.

Grant saw the immense legs of the first hadrosaurs that charged past, each animal weighing five tons, and then they were enveloped in a cloud so dense he could see nothing at all. He had the impression of huge bodies, giant limbs, bellowing cries of pain as the animals wheeled and circled. One duckbill struck a boulder and it rolled past them, out into the field beyond.

In the dense cloud of dust, they could see almost nothing beyond the rocks. They clung to the boulders, listening to the screams and honks, the menacing roar of the tyrannosaur. Lex dug her fingers into Grant's shoulder.

Another hadrosaur slammed its big tail against the rocks, leaving a splash of hot blood. Grant waited until the sounds of the fighting had moved off to the left, and then he pushed the kids to start climbing the largest tree. They climbed swiftly, feeling for the branches, as the animals stampeded all around them in the dust. They went up twenty feet, and then Lex clutched at Grant and refused to go farther. Tim was tired, too, and Grant thought they were high enough. Through the dust, they could see the broad backs of the animals below as they wheeled and honked. Grant propped himself against the coarse bark of the trunk, coughed in the dust, closed his eyes, and waited.

Arnold adjusted the camera as the herd moved away. The dust slowly cleared. He saw that the hadrosaurs had scattered, and the tyrannosaur had stopped running, which could only mean it had made a kill. The tyrannosaur was now near the lagoon. Arnold looked at the video monitor and said, "Better get Muldoon to go out there and see how bad it is."

"I'll get him," Gennaro said, and left the room.

THE PARK

A faint crackling sound, like a fire in a fireplace. Something warm and wet tickled Grant's ankle. He opened his eyes and saw an enormous beige head. The head tapered to a flat mouth shaped like the bill of a duck. The eyes, protruding above the flat duckbill, were gentle and soft like a cow's. The duck mouth opened and chewed branches on the limb where Grant was sitting. He saw large flat teeth in the cheek. The warm lips touched his ankle again as the animal chewed.

A duckbilled hadrosaur. He was astonished to see it up close. Not that he was afraid; all the species of duckbilled dinosaurs were herbivorous, and this one acted exactly like a cow. Even though it was huge, its manner was so calm and peaceful Grant didn't feel threatened. He stayed where he was on the branch, careful not to move, and watched as it ate.

The reason Grant was astonished was that he had a proprietary feeling about this animal: it was probably a maiasaur, from the late Cretaceous in Montana. With John Horner, Grant had been the first to describe the species. Maiasaurs had an upcurved lip, which gave them the appearance of smiling. The name meant "good mother lizard"; maiasaurs were thought to protect their eggs until the babies were born and could take care of themselves.

Grant heard an insistent chirping, and the big head swung down. He moved just enough to see the baby hadrosaur scampering around the feet of the adult. The baby was dark beige with black spots. The adult bent her head low to the ground and waited, unmoving, while the baby stood up on its hind legs, resting its front legs on the mother's jaw, and ate the branches that protruded from the side of the mother's mouth.

The mother waited patiently until the baby had finished eating, and dropped back down to all fours again. Then the big head came back up toward Grant.

The hadrosaur continued to eat, just a few feet from him. Grant looked at the two elongated airholes on top of the flat upper bill. Apparently the dinosaur couldn't smell Grant. And even though the left eye was looking right at him, for some reason the hadrosaur didn't react to him.

He remembered how the tyrannosaur had failed to see him, the previous night. Grant decided on an experiment.

He coughed.

Instantly the hadrosaur froze, the big head suddenly still, the jaws no longer chewing. Only the eye moved, looking for the source of the sound. Then, after a moment, when there seemed to be no danger, the animal resumed chewing.

Amazing, Grant thought.

Sitting in his arms, Lex opened her eyes and said, "Hey, what's *that*?"

The hadrosaur trumpeted in alarm, a loud resonant honk that so startled Lex that she nearly fell out of the tree. The hadrosaur pulled its head away from the branch and trumpeted again.

"Don't make her mad," Tim said, from the branch above.

The baby chirped and scurried beneath the mother's legs as the hadrosaur stepped away from the tree. The mother cocked her head and peered inquisitively at the branch where Grant and Lex were sitting. With its upturned smiling lips, the dinosaur had a comical appearance.

"Is it dumb?" Lex said.

"No," Grant said. "You just surprised her."

"Well," Lex said, "is she going to let us get down, or what?"

The hadrosaur had backed ten feet away from the tree. She honked again. Grant had the impression she was trying to frighten them away. But the dinosaur didn't really seem to know what to do. She acted confused and uneasy. They waited in silence, and after a minute the hadrosaur approached the branch again, jaws moving in anticipation. She was clearly going to resume eating.

"Forget it," Lex said. "I'm not staying *here*." She started to climb down the branches. At her movement, the hadrosaur trumpeted in fresh alarm.

Grant was amazed. He thought, It really can't see us when we don't move. And after a minute it literally forgets that we're here.

This was just like the tyrannosaur—another classic example of an amphibian visual cortex. Studies of frogs had shown that amphibians only saw moving things, like insects. If something didn't move, they literally didn't see it. The same thing seemed to be true of dinosaurs.

In any case, the maiasaur now seemed to find these strange creatures climbing down the tree too upsetting. With a final honk, she nudged her baby, and lumbered slowly away. She paused once, and looked back at them, then continued on.

They reached the ground. Lex shook herself off. Both children were covered in a layer of fine dust. All around them, the grass had been flattened. There were streaks of blood, and a sour smell.

Grant looked at his watch. "We better get going, kids," he said.

"Not me," Lex said. "I'm not walking out there *any more*."

"We have to."

"Why?"

"Because," Grant said, "we have to tell them about the boat. Since they can't seem to see us on the motion sensors, we have to go all the way back ourselves. It's the only way."

"Why can't we take the raft?" Tim said.

"What raft?"

Tim pointed to the low concrete maintenance building with the bars, where they had spent the night. It was twenty yards away, across the field. "I saw a raft back there," he said.

Grant immediately understood the advantages. It was now seven o'clock in the morning. They had at least eight miles to go. If they could take a raft along the river, they would make much faster progress than going overland. "Let's do it," Grant said.

Arnold punched the visual search mode and watched as the monitors began to scan throughout the park, the images changing every two seconds. It was tiring to watch, but it was the fastest way to find Nedry's Jeep, and Muldoon had been adamant about that. He had gone out with Gennaro to look at the stampede, but now that it was daylight, he wanted the car found. He wanted the weapons.

His intercom clicked. "Mr. Arnold, may I have a word with you, please?"

It was Hammond. He sounded like the voice of God.

"You want to come here, Mr. Hammond?"

"No, Mr. Arnold," Hammond said. "Come to me. I'm in the genetics lab with Dr. Wu. We'll be waiting for you."

Arnold sighed, and stepped away from the screens.

Grant stumbled deep in the gloomy recesses of the building. He pushed past five-gallon containers of herbicide, tree-pruning equipment, spare tires for a Jeep, coils of cyclone fencing, hundred-pound fertilizer bags, stacks of brown ceramic insulators, empty motor-oil cans, work lights and cables.

"I don't see any raft."

"Keep going."

Bags of cement, lengths of copper pipe, green mesh . . . and two plastic oars hung on clips on the concrete wall.

"Okay," he said, "but where's the raft?"

"It must be here somewhere," Tim said.

"You never saw a raft?"

"No, I just assumed it was here."

Poking among the junk, Grant found no raft. But he did find a set of plans, rolled up and speckled with mold from humidity, stuck back in a metal cabinet on the wall. He spread the plans on the floor, brushing away a big spider. He looked at them for a long time.

"I'm hungry. . . ."

"Just a minute."

They were detailed topographical charts for the main area of the island, where they now were. According to this, the lagoon narrowed into the river they had seen earlier, which twisted northward . . . right through the aviary . . . and on to within a half-mile of the visitor lodge.

He flipped back through the pages. How to get to the lagoon? According to the plans, there should be a door at the back of the building they were in. Grant looked up, and saw it, recessed back in the concrete wall. The door was wide enough for a car. Opening it, he saw a paved road running straight down toward the lagoon. The road was dug below ground level, so it couldn't be seen from above. It must be another service road. And it led to a dock at the edge of the lagoon. And clearly stenciled on the dock was RAFT STORAGE.

"Hey," Tim said, "look at this." He held out a metal case to Grant.

Opening it, Grant found a compressed-air pistol and a cloth belt that held darts. There were six darts in all, each as thick as his finger. Labeled MORO-709.

"Good work, Tim." He slung the belt around his shoulder, and stuck the gun in his trousers.

"Is it a tranquilizer gun?"

"I'd say so."

"What about the boat?" Lex said.

"I think it's on the dock," Grant said. They started down the road. Grant carried the oars on his shoulder. "I hope it's a big raft," Lex said, "because I can't swim."

"Don't worry," he said.

"Maybe we can catch some fish," she said.

They walked down the road with the sloping embankment rising up on both sides of them. They heard a deep rhythmic snorting sound, but Grant could not see where it was coming from.

"Are you sure there's a raft down here?" Lex said, wrinkling her nose.

"Probably," Grant said.

The rhythmic snorting became louder as they walked, but they also heard a steady droning, buzzing sound. When they reached the end of the road, at the edge of the small concrete dock, Grant froze in shock.

The tyrannosaur was *right there*.

It was sitting upright in the shade of a tree, its hind legs stretched out in front. Its eyes were open but it was not moving, except for its head, which lifted and fell gently with each snorting sound. The buzzing came from the clouds of flies that surrounded it, crawling over its face and slack jaws, its bloody fangs, and the red haunch of a killed hadrosaur that lay on its side behind the tyrannosaur.

The tyrannosaur was only twenty yards away. Grant felt sure it must have seen him, but the big animal did not respond. It just sat there. It took him a moment to realize: the tyrannosaur was asleep. Sitting up, but asleep.

He signaled to Tim and Lex to stay where they were. Grant walked slowly forward onto the dock, in full view of the tyrannosaur. The big animal continued to sleep, snoring softly.

Near the end of the dock, a wooden shed was painted green to blend with the foliage. Grant quietly unlatched the door and looked inside. He saw a half-dozen orange life vests hanging on the wall, several rolls of wire-mesh fencing, some coils of rope, and two big rubber cubes sitting on the floor. The cubes were strapped tight with flat rubber belts.

Rafts.

He looked back at Lex.

She mouthed: *No boat.*

He nodded, *Yes.*

The tyrannosaur raised its forelimb to swipe at the flies buzzing around its snout. But otherwise it did not move. Grant pulled one of the cubes out onto the dock. It was surprisingly heavy. He freed the straps, found the inflation cylinder. With a loud hiss, the rubber began to expand, and then with a *hiss-whap!* it popped fully open on the dock. The sound was fearfully loud in their ears.

Grant turned, stared up at the dinosaur.

The tyrannosaur grunted, and snorted. It began to move. Grant braced himself to run, but the animal shifted its ponderous bulk and then it settled back against the tree trunk and gave a long, growling belch.

Lex looked disgusted, waving her hand in front of her face.

Grant was soaked in sweat from the tension. He dragged the rubber raft across the dock. It flopped into the water with a loud splash.

The dinosaur continued to sleep.

Grant tied the boat up to the dock, and returned to the shed to take out two life preservers. He put these in the boat, and then waved for the kids to come out onto the dock.

Pale with fear, Lex waved back, *No.*

He gestured: *Yes.*

The tyrannosaur continued to sleep.

Grant stabbed in the air with an emphatic finger. Lex came silently, and he gestured for her to get into the raft; then Tim got in, and they both put on their life vests. Grant got in and pushed off. The raft drifted silently out into the lagoon. Grant picked up his paddles and fitted them into the oarlocks. They moved farther from the dock.

Lex sat back, and sighed loudly with relief. Then she looked stricken, and put her hand over her mouth. Her body shook, with muffled sounds: she was suppressing a cough.

She *always* coughed at the wrong times!

"Lex," Tim whispered fiercely, looking back toward the shore.

She shook her head miserably, and pointed to her throat. He knew what she meant: a tickle in her throat. What she needed was a drink of water. Grant was rowing, and Tim leaned over the side of the raft and scooped his hand in the lagoon, holding his cupped hand toward her.

Lex coughed loudly, explosively. In Tim's ears, the sound echoed across the water like a gunshot.

The tyrannosaur yawned lazily, and scratched behind its ear with its hind foot, just like a dog. It yawned again. It was groggy after its big meal, and it woke up slowly.

On the boat, Lex was making little gargling sounds.

"Lex, *shut up*!" Tim said.

"I can't help it," she whispered, and then she coughed again. Grant rowed hard, moving the raft powerfully into the center of the lagoon.

On the shore, the tyrannosaur stumbled to its feet.

"I couldn't help it, Timmy!" Lex shrieked miserably. "I couldn't help it!"

"Shhhh!"

Grant was rowing as fast as he could.

"Anyway, it doesn't matter," she said. "We're far enough away. He can't swim."

"*Of course he can swim, you little idiot!*" Tim shouted at her. On the shore, the tyrannosaur stepped off the dock and plunged into the water. It moved strongly into the lagoon after them.

"Well, how should I know?" she said.

"Everybody knows tyrannosaurs can swim! It's in all the books! Anyway, all reptiles can swim!"

"Snakes can't."

"*Of course* snakes can. You *idiot*!"

"Settle down," Grant said. "Hold on to something!" Grant was watching the tyrannosaur, noticing how the animal swam. The tyrannosaur was now chest-deep in the water, but it could hold its big head high above the surface. Then Grant realized the animal wasn't swimming, it was walking, because moments later only the very top of the head—the eyes and nostrils—protruded above the surface. By then it looked like a crocodile, and it swam like a crocodile, swinging its big tail back and forth, so the water churned behind it. Behind the head, Grant saw the hump of the back, and the ridges along the length of tail, as it occasionally broke the surface.

Exactly like a crocodile, he thought unhappily. The biggest crocodile in the world.

"I'm sorry, Dr. Grant!" Lex wailed. "I didn't mean it!"

Grant glanced over his shoulder. The lagoon was no more than a hundred yards wide here, and they had almost reached the center. If he continued, the water would become shallow again. The tyrannosaur would be able to walk again, and he would move faster in shallow water. Grant swung the boat around, and began to row north.

"What are you *doing*?"

The tyrannosaur was now just a few yards away. Grant could hear its sharp snorting breaths as it came closer. Grant looked at the paddles in his hands, but they were light plastic—not weapons at all.

The tyrannosaur threw its head back and opened its jaws wide, showing rows of curved teeth, and then in a great muscular spasm lunged forward to the raft, just missing the rubber gunwale, the huge skull slapping down, the raft rocking away on the crest of the splash.

The tyrannosaur sank below the surface, leaving gurgling bubbles. The lagoon was still. Lex gripped the gunwale handles and looked back.

"Did he drown?"

"No," Grant said. He saw bubbles—then a faint ripple along the surface—coming toward the boat—

"Hang on!" he shouted, as the head bucked up beneath the rubber, bending the boat and lifting it into the air, spinning them crazily before it splashed down again.

"Do something!" Alexis screamed. "Do something!"

Grant pulled the air pistol out of his belt. It looked pitifully small in his hands, but there was the chance that, if he shot the animal in a sensitive spot, in the eye or the nose—

The tyrannosaur surfaced beside the boat, opened its jaws, and roared. Grant aimed, and fired. The dart flashed in the light, and smacked into the cheek. The tyrannosaur shook its head, and roared again.

And suddenly they heard an answering roar, floating across the water toward them.

Looking back, Grant saw the juvenile T-rex on the shore, crouched over the killed sauropod, claiming the kill as its own. The juvenile slashed at the carcass, then raised its head high and bellowed. The big tyrannosaur saw it, too, and the response was immediate—it turned back to protect its kill, swimming strongly toward the shore.

"He's going away!" Lex squealed, clapping her hands. "He's going away! Naah-naah-na-na-naah! Stupid dinosaur!"

From the shore, the juvenile roared defiantly. Enraged, the big tyrannosaur burst from the lagoon at full speed, water streaming from its enormous body as it raced up the hill past the dock. The juvenile ducked its head and fled, its jaws still filled with ragged flesh.

The big tyrannosaur chased it, racing past the dead sauropod, disappearing over the hill. They heard its final threatening bellow, and then the raft moved to the north, around a bend in the lagoon, to the river.

Exhausted from rowing, Grant collapsed back, his chest heaving. He couldn't catch his breath. He lay gasping in the raft.

"Are you okay, Dr. Grant?" Lex asked.

"From now on, will you just do what I tell you?"

"Oh-*kay*," she sighed, as if he had just made the most unreasonable demand in the world. She trailed her arm in the water for a while. "You stopped rowing," she said.

"I'm tired," Grant said.

"Then how come we're still moving?"

Grant sat up. She was right. The raft drifted steadily north. "There must be a current." The current was carrying them north, toward the hotel. He looked at his watch and was astonished to see it was fifteen minutes past seven. Only fifteen minutes had passed since he had last looked at his watch. It seemed like two hours.

Grant lay back against the rubber gunwales, closed his eyes, and slept.

FIFTH ITERATION

"Flaws in the system will now become severe."

IAN MALCOLM

SEARCH

Gennaro sat in the Jeep and listened to the buzzing of the flies, and stared at the distant palm trees wavering in the heat. He was astonished by what looked like a battleground: the grass was trampled flat for a hundred yards in every direction. One big palm tree was uprooted from the ground. There were great washes of blood in the grass, and on the rocky outcropping to their right.

Sitting beside him, Muldoon said, "No doubt about it. Rexy's been among the hadrosaurs." He took another drink of whiskey, and capped the bottle. "Damn lot of flies," he said.

They waited, and watched.

Gennaro drummed his fingers on the dashboard. "What are we waiting for?"

Muldoon didn't answer immediately. "The rex is out there somewhere," he said, squinting at the landscape in the morning sun. "And we don't have any weapons worth a damn."

"We're in a Jeep."

"Oh, he can outrun the Jeep, Mr. Gennaro," Muldoon said, shaking his head. "Once we leave this road and go onto open terrain, the best we can do in a four-wheel drive is thirty, forty miles an hour. He'll run us right down. No problem for him." Muldoon sighed. "But I don't see much moving out there now. You ready to live dangerously?"

"Sure," Gennaro said.

Muldoon started the engine, and at the sudden sound, two small othnielians leapt up from the matted grass directly ahead. Muldoon put the car in gear. He drove in a wide circle around the trampled site, and then moved inward, driving in decreasing concentric circles until he finally came to the place in the field where the little othnielians had been. Then he got out and walked forward in the grass, away from the Jeep. He stopped as a dense cloud of flies lifted into the air.

"What is it?" Gennaro called.

"Bring the radio," Muldoon said.

Gennaro climbed out of the Jeep and hurried forward. Even from a distance he could smell the sour-sweet odor of early decay. He saw a dark shape in the grass, crusted with blood, legs askew.

"Young hadrosaur," Muldoon said, staring down at the carcass. "The whole herd stampeded, and the young one got separated, and the T-rex brought it down."

"How do you know?" Gennaro said. The flesh was ragged from many bites.

"You can tell from the excreta," Muldoon said. "See those chalky white bits there in the grass? That's hadro spoor. Uric acid makes it white. But you look there"—he pointed to a large mound, rising knee-high in the grass—"that's tyrannosaur spoor."

"How do you know the tyrannosaur didn't come later?"

"The bite pattern," Muldoon said. "See those little ones there?" He pointed along the belly. "Those are from the othys. Those bites haven't bled. They're postmortem, from scavengers. Othys did that. But the hadro was brought down by a bite on the neck—you see the big slash there, above the shoulder blades—and that's the T-rex, no question."

Gennaro bent over the carcass, staring at the awkward, trampled limbs with a sense of unreality. Beside him, Muldoon flicked on his radio. "Control."

"Yes," John Arnold said, over the radio.

"We got another hadro dead. Juvenile." Muldoon bent down among the flies and checked the skin on the sole of the right foot. A number was tattooed there. "Specimen is number HD/09."

The radio crackled. "I've got something for you," Arnold said.

"Oh? What's that?"

"I found Nedry."

The Jeep burst through the line of palm trees along the east road and came out into a narrower service road, leading toward the jungle river. It was hot in this area of the park, the jungle close and fetid around them. Muldoon was fiddling with the computer monitor in the Jeep, which now showed a map of the resort with overlaid grid lines. "They found him up on remote video," he said. "Sector 1104 is just ahead."

Farther up the road, Gennaro saw a concrete barrier, and the Jeep parked alongside it. "He must have taken the wrong turnoff," Muldoon said. "The little bastard."

"What'd he take?" Gennaro asked.

"Wu says fifteen embryos. Know what that's worth?"

Gennaro shook his head.

"Somewhere between two and ten million," Muldoon said. He shook his head. "Big stakes."

As they came closer, Gennaro saw the body lying beside the car. The body was indistinct and green—but then green shapes scattered away, as the Jeep pulled to a stop.

"Compys," Muldoon said. "The compys found him."

A dozen procompsognathids, delicate little predators no larger than ducks, stood at the edge of the jungle, chittering excitedly as the men climbed out of the car.

Dennis Nedry lay on his back, the chubby boyish face now red and bloated. Flies buzzed around the gaping mouth and thick tongue. His body was mangled—the intestines torn open, one leg chewed through. Gennaro turned away quickly, to look at the little compys, which squatted on their hind legs a short distance away and watched the men curiously. The little dinosaurs had five-fingered hands, he noticed. They wiped their faces and chins, giving them an eerily human quality which—

"I'll be damned," Muldoon said. "Wasn't the compys."

"What?"

Muldoon was shaking his head. "See these blotches? On his shirt and his face? Smell that sweet smell like old, dried vomit?"

Gennaro rolled his eyes. He smelled it.

"That's dilo saliva," Muldoon said. "Spit from the dilophosaurs. You see the damage on the corneas, all that redness. In the eyes it's painful but not fatal. You've got about two hours to wash it out with the antivenin; we keep it all around the park, just in case. Not that it mattered to this bastard. They blinded him, then ripped him down the middle. Not a nice way to go. Maybe there's justice in the world after all."

The procompsognathids squeaked and hopped up and down as Gennaro opened the back door and took out gray metal tubing and a stainless-steel case. "It's all still there," he said. He handed two dark cylinders to Gennaro.

"What're these?" Gennaro said.

"Just what they look like," Muldoon said. "Rockets." As Gennaro backed away, he said, "Watch it—you don't want to step in something."

Gennaro stepped carefully over Nedry's body. Muldoon carried the tubing to the other Jeep, and placed it in the back. He climbed behind the wheel. "Let's go."

"What about him?" Gennaro said, pointing to the body.

"What about him?" Muldoon said. "We've got things to do." He put the car in gear. Looking back, Gennaro saw the compys resume their feeding. One jumped up and squatted on Nedry's open mouth as it nibbled the flesh of his nose.

The jungle river became narrower. The banks closed in on both sides until the trees and foliage overhanging the banks met high above to block out the sun. Tim heard the cry of birds, and saw small chirping dinosaurs leaping among the branches. But mostly it was silent, the air hot and still beneath the canopy of trees.

Grant looked at his watch. It was eight o'clock.

They drifted along peacefully, among dappled patches of light. If anything, they seemed to be moving faster than before. Awake now, Grant lay on his back and stared up at the branches overhead. In the bow, he saw her reaching up.

"Hey, what're you doing?" he said.

"You think we can eat these berries?" She pointed to the trees. Some of the overhanging branches were close enough to touch. Tim saw clusters of bright red berries on the branches.

"No," Grant said.

"Why? Those little dinosaurs are eating them." She pointed to small dinosaurs, scampering in the branches.

"No, Lex."

She sighed, dissatisfied with his authority. "I wish Daddy was here," she said. "Daddy always knows what to do."

"What're you talking about?" Tim said. "He *never* knows what to do."

"Yes, he does," she sighed. Lex stared at the trees as they slid past, their big roots twisting toward the water's edge. "Just because you're not his favorite . . ."

Tim turned away, said nothing.

"But don't worry, Daddy likes you, too. Even if you're into computers and not sports."

"Dad's a real sports nut," Tim explained to Grant.

Grant nodded. Up in the branches, small pale yellow dinosaurs, barely two feet tall, hopped from tree to tree. They had beaky heads, like parrots. "You know what they call those?" Tim said. "Microceratops."

"Big deal," Lex said.

"I thought you might be interested."

"Only very young boys," she said, "are interested in dinosaurs."

"Says who?"

"Daddy."

Tim started to yell, but Grant raised his hand. "Kids," he said, "shut up."

"Why?" Lex said, "I can do what I want, if I—"

Then she fell silent, because she heard it, too. It was a bloodcurdling shriek, from somewhere downriver.

"Well, where the hell is the damn rex?" Muldoon said, talking into the radio. "Because we don't see him here." They were back at the sauropod compound, looking out at the trampled grass where the hadrosaurs had stampeded. The tyrannosaur was nowhere to be found.

"Checking now," Arnold said, and clicked off.

Muldoon turned to Gennaro. "Checking now," he repeated sarcastically. "Why the hell didn't he check before? Why didn't he keep track of him?"

"I don't know," Gennaro said.

"He's not showing up," Arnold said, a moment later.

"What do you mean, he's not showing up?"

"He's not on the monitors. Motion sensors aren't finding him."

"Hell," Muldoon said. "So much for the motion sensors. You see Grant and the kids?"

"Motion sensors aren't finding them, either."

"Well, what are we supposed to do now?" Muldoon said.

"Wait," Arnold said.

"Look! Look!"

Directly ahead, the big dome of the aviary rose above them.

Grant had seen it only from a distance; now he realized it was enormous—a quarter of a mile in diameter or more. The pattern of geodesic struts shone dully through the light mist, and his first thought was that the glass must weigh a ton. Then, as they came closer, he saw there wasn't any glass—just struts. A thin mesh hung inside the elements.

"It isn't finished," Lex said.

"I think it's meant to be open like that," Grant said.

"Then all the birds can fly out."

"Not if they're *big* birds," Grant said.

The river carried them beneath the edge of the dome. They stared upward. Now they were inside the dome, still drifting down the river. But within minutes the dome was so high above them that it was hardly visible in the mist. Grant said, "I seem to remember there's a second lodge here." Moments later, he saw the roof of a building over the tops of the trees to the north.

"You want to stop?" Tim said.

"Maybe there's a phone. Or motion sensors." Grant steered toward the shore. "We need to try to contact the control room. It's getting late."

They clambered out, slipping on the muddy bank, and Grant hauled the raft out of the water. Then he tied the rope to a tree and they set off, through a dense forest of palm trees.

AVIARY

"I just don't understand," John Arnold said, speaking into the phone. "I don't see the rex, and I don't see Grant and the kids anywhere, either."

He sat in front of the consoles and gulped another cup of coffee. All around him, the control room was strewn with paper plates and half-eaten sandwiches. Arnold was exhausted. It was 8:00 a.m. on Saturday. In the fourteen hours since Nedry destroyed the computer that ran Jurassic Park, Arnold had patiently pulled systems back on line, one after another. "All the park systems are back, and functioning correctly. The phones are working. I've called for a doctor for you."

On the other end of the line, Malcolm coughed. Arnold was talking to him in his room at the lodge. "But you're having trouble with the motion sensors?"

"Well, I'm not finding what I am looking for."

"Like the rex?"

"He's not reading at all now. He started north about twenty minutes ago, following along the edge of the lagoon, and then I lost him. I don't know why, unless he's gone to sleep again."

"And you can't find Grant and the kids?"

"No."

"I think it's quite simple," Malcolm said. "The motion sensors cover an inadequate area."

"Inadequate?" Arnold bristled. "They cover ninety-two—"

"Ninety-two percent of the land area, I remember," Malcolm said. "But if you put the remaining areas up on the board, I think you'll find that the eight percent is topologically unified, meaning that those areas are contiguous. In essence, an animal can move freely anywhere in the park and escape detection, by following a maintenance road or the jungle river or the beaches or whatever."

"Even if that were so," Arnold said, "the animals are too stupid to know that."

"It's not clear how stupid the animals are," Malcolm said.

"You think that's what Grant and the kids are doing?" Arnold said.

"Definitely not," Malcolm said, coughing again. "Grant's no fool. He clearly wants to be detected by you. He and the kids are probably waving at every motion sensor in sight. But maybe they have other problems we don't know about. Or maybe they're on the river."

"I can't imagine they'd be on the river. The banks are very narrow. It's impossible to walk along there."

"Would the river bring them all the way back here?"

"Yes, but it's not the safest way to go, because it passes through the aviary. . . ."

"Why wasn't the aviary on the tour?" Malcolm said.

"We've had problems setting it up. Originally the park was intended to have a treetop lodge built high above the ground, where visitors could observe the pterodactyls at flight level. We've got four dactyls in the aviary now—actually, they're cearadactyls, which are big fish-eating dactyls."

"What about them?"

"Well, while we finished the lodge, we put the dactyls in the aviary to acclimate them. But that was a big mistake. It turns out our fish-hunters are territorial."

"Territorial?"

"Fiercely territorial," Arnold said. "They fight among themselves for territory—and they'll attack any other animal that comes into the area they've marked out."

"Attack?"

"It's impressive," Arnold said. "The dactyls glide to the top of the aviary, fold up their wings, and dive. A thirty-pound animal will strike a man on the ground like a ton of bricks. They were knocking the workmen unconscious, cutting them up pretty badly."

"That doesn't injure the dactyls?"

"Not so far."

"So, if those kids are in the aviary . . ."

"They're not," Arnold said. "At least, I hope they're not."

"Is *that* the lodge?" Lex said. "What a dump."

Beneath the aviary dome, Pteratops Lodge was built high above the ground, on big wooden pylons, in the middle of a stand of fir trees. But the building was unfinished and unpainted; the windows were boarded up. The trees and the lodge were splattered with broad white streaks.

"I guess they didn't finish it, for some reason," Grant said, hiding his disappointment. He glanced at his watch. "Come on, let's go back to the boat."

The sun came out as they walked along, making the morning more cheerful. Grant looked at the latticework shadows on the ground from the dome above. He noticed that the ground and the foliage were spattered with broad streaks of the same white chalky substance that had been on the building. And there was a distinctive, sour odor in the morning air.

"Stinks here," Lex said. "What's all the white stuff?"

"Looks like reptile droppings. Probably from the birds."

"How come they didn't finish the lodge?"

"I don't know."

They entered a clearing of low grass, dotted with wild flowers. They heard a long, low whistle. Then an answering whistle, from across the forest.

"What's that?"

"I don't know."

Then Grant saw the dark shadow of a cloud on the grassy field ahead. The shadow was moving fast. In moments, it had swept over them. He looked up and saw an enormous dark shape gliding above them, blotting out the sun.

"Yow!" Lex said. "Is it a pterodactyl?"

"Yes," Tim said.

Grant didn't answer. He was entranced by the sight of the huge flying creature. In the sky above, the pterodactyl gave a low whistle and wheeled gracefully, turning back toward them.

"How come they're not on the tour?" Tim said.

Grant was wondering the same thing. The flying dinosaurs were so beautiful, so graceful as they moved through the air. As Grant watched, he saw a second pterodactyl appear in the sky, and a third, and a fourth.

"Maybe because they didn't finish the lodge," Lex said.

Grant was thinking these weren't ordinary pterodactyls. They were too large. They must be cearadactyls, big flying reptiles from the early Cretaceous. When they were high, these looked like small airplanes. When they came lower, he could see the animals had fifteen-foot wingspans, furry bodies, and heads like crocodiles'. They ate fish, he remembered. South America and Mexico.

Lex shaded her eyes and looked up at the sky. "Can they hurt us?"

"I don't think so. They eat fish."

One of the dactyls spiraled down, a flashing dark shadow that whooshed past them with a rush of warm air and a lingering sour odor.

"Wow!" Lex said. "They're *really* big." And then she said, "Are you sure they can't hurt us?"

"Pretty sure."

A second dactyl swooped down, moving faster than the first. It came from behind, streaked over their heads. Grant had a glimpse of its toothy beak and the furry body. It looked like a huge bat, he thought. But Grant was impressed with the frail appearance of the animals. Their huge wingspans—the delicate pink membranes stretched across them—so thin they were translucent—everything reinforced the delicacy of the dactyls.

"Ow!" Lex shouted, grabbing her hair. "He bit me!"

"He what?" Grant said.

"He bit me! He bit me!" When she took her hand away, he saw blood on her fingers.

Up in the sky, two more dactyls folded their wings, collapsing into small dark shapes that plummeted toward the ground. They made a kind of scream as they hurtled downward.

"Come on!" Grant said, grabbing their hands. They ran across the meadow, hearing the approaching scream, and he flung himself on the ground at the last moment, pulling the kids down with him, as the two dactyls whistled and squeaked past them, flapping their wings. Grant felt claws tear the shirt along his back.

Then he was up, pulling Lex back onto her feet, and running with Tim a few feet forward while overhead two more birds wheeled and dove toward them, screaming. At the last moment, he pushed the kids to the ground, and the big shadows flapped past.

"Uck," Lex said, disgusted. He saw that she was streaked with white droppings from the birds.

Grant scrambled to his feet. "Come on!"

He was about to run when Lex shrieked in terror. He turned back and saw that one of the dactyls had grabbed her by the shoulders with its hind claws. The animal's huge leathery wings, translucent in the sunlight, flapped broadly on both sides of her. The dactyl was trying to take off, but Lex was too heavy, and while it struggled it repeatedly jabbed at her head with its long pointed jaw.

Lex was screaming, waving her arms wildly. Grant did the only thing he could think to do. He ran forward and jumped up, throwing himself against the body of the dactyl. He knocked it onto its back on the ground, and fell on top of the furry body. The animal screamed and snapped; Grant ducked his head away from the jaws and pushed back, as the giant wings beat around his body. It was like being in a tent in a windstorm. He couldn't see; he couldn't hear; there was nothing but the flapping and shrieking and the leathery membranes. The clawed legs scratched frantically at his chest. Lex was screaming. Grant pushed away from the dactyl and it squeaked and gibbered as it flapped its wings and struggled to turn over, to right itself. Finally it pulled in its wings like a bat and rolled over, lifted itself up on its little wing claws, and began to walk that way. He paused, astonished.

It could walk on its wings! Lederer's speculation was right! But then the other dactyls were diving down at them and Grant was dizzy, off balance, and in horror he saw Lex run away, her arms over her head . . . Tim shouting at the top of his lungs. . . .

The first of them swooped down and she threw something and suddenly the dactyl whistled and climbed. The other dactyls immediately climbed and chased the first into the sky. The fourth dactyl flapped awkwardly into the air to join the others. Grant looked upward, squinting to see what had happened. The three dactyls chased the first, screaming angrily.

They were alone in the field.

"What happened?" Grant said.

"They got my glove," Lex said. "My Darryl Strawberry special."

They started walking again. Tim put his arm around her shoulders. "Are you all right?"

"Of *course*, stupid," she said, shaking him off. She looked upward. "I hope they choke and die," she said.

"Yeah," Tim said. "Me, too."

Up ahead, they saw the boat on the shore. Grant looked at his watch. It was eight-thirty. He now had two and a half hours to get back.

Lex cheered as they drifted beyond the silver aviary dome. Then the banks of the river closed in on both sides, the trees meeting overhead once more. The river was narrower than ever, in some places only ten feet wide, and the current flowed very fast. Lex reached up to touch the branches as they went past.

Grant sat back in the raft and listened to the gurgle of the water through the warm rubber. They were moving faster now, the branches overhead slipping by more rapidly. It was pleasant. It gave a little breeze in the hot confines of the overhanging branches. And it meant they would get back that much sooner.

Grant couldn't guess how far they had come, but it must be several miles at least from the sauropod building where they had spent the night. Perhaps four or five miles. Maybe even more. That meant they might be only an hour's walk from the hotel, once they left the raft. But after the aviary, Grant was in no hurry to leave the river again. For the moment, they were making good time.

"I wonder how Ralph is," Lex said. "He's probably dead or something."

"I'm sure he's fine."

"I wonder if he'd let me ride him." She sighed, sleepy in the sun. "That would be fun, to ride Ralph."

Tim said to Grant, "Remember back at the stegosaurus? Last night?"

"Yes."

"How come you asked them about frog DNA?"

"Because of the breeding," Grant said. "They can't explain why the dinosaurs are breeding, since they irradiate them, and since they're all females."

"Right."

"Well, irradiation is notoriously unreliable and probably doesn't work. I think that'll eventually be shown here. But there is still the problem of the dinosaurs' being female. How can they breed when they're all female?"

"Right," Tim said.

"Well, across the animal kingdom, sexual reproduction exists in extraordinary variety."

"Tim's very interested in sex," Lex said.

They both ignored her. "For example," Grant said, "many animals have sexual reproduction without ever having what we would call sex. The male releases a spermatophore, which contains the sperm, and the female picks it up at a later time. This kind of exchange does not require quite as much physical differentiation between male and female as we usually think exists. Male and female are more alike in some animals than they are in human beings."

Tim nodded. "But what about the frogs?"

Grant heard sudden shrieks from the trees above, as the microceratopsians scattered in alarm, shaking the branches. The big head of the tyrannosaur lunged through the foliage from the left, the jaws snapping at the raft. Lex howled in terror, and Grant paddled away toward the opposite bank, but the river here was only ten feet wide. The tyrannosaur was caught in the heavy growth; it butted and twisted its head, and roared. Then it pulled its head back.

Through the trees that lined the riverbank, they saw the huge dark form of the tyrannosaur, moving north, looking for a gap in the trees that lined the bank. The microceratopsians had all gone to the opposite bank, where they shrieked and scampered and jumped up and down. In the raft, Grant, Tim, and Lex stared helplessly as the tyrannosaur tried to break through again. But the trees were too dense along the banks of the river. The tyrannosaur again moved downstream, ahead of the boat, and tried again, shaking the branches furiously.

But again it failed.

Then it moved off, heading farther downstream.

"I *hate* him," Lex said.

Grant sat back in the boat, badly shaken. If the tyrannosaur had broken through, there was nothing he could have done to save them. The river was so narrow that it was hardly wider than the raft. It was like being in a tunnel. The rubber gunwales often scraped on the mud as the boat was pulled along by the swift current.

He glanced at his watch. Almost nine. The raft continued downstream.

"Hey," Lex said, "listen!"

He heard snarling, interspersed by a repeated hooting cry. The cries were coming from beyond a curve, farther downriver. He listened, and heard the hooting again.

"What is it?" Lex said.

"I don't know," Grant said. "But there's more than one of them." He paddled the boat to the opposite bank, grabbed a branch to stop the raft. The snarling was repeated. Then more hooting.

"It sounds like a bunch of owls," Tim said.

Malcolm groaned. "Isn't it time for more morphine yet?"

"Not yet," Ellie said.

Malcolm sighed. "How much water have we got here?"

"I don't know. There's plenty of running water from the tap—"

"No, I mean, how much stored? Any?"

Ellie shrugged. "None."

"Go into the rooms on this floor," Malcolm said, "and fill the bathtubs with water."

Ellie frowned.

"Also," Malcolm said, "have we got any walkie-talkies? Flashlights? Matches? Sterno stoves? Things like that?"

"I'll look around. You planning for an earthquake?"

"Something like that," Malcolm said. "Malcolm Effect implies catastrophic changes."

"But Arnold says all the systems are working perfectly."

"That's when it happens," Malcolm said.

Ellie said, "You don't think much of Arnold, do you?"

"He's all right. He's an engineer. Wu's the same. They're both technicians. They don't have intelligence. They have what I call 'thintelligence.' They see the immediate situation. They think narrowly and they call it 'being focused.' They don't see the surround. They don't see the consequences. That's how you get an island like this. From thintelligent thinking. Because you cannot make an animal and not expect it to act *alive*. To be unpredictable. To escape. But they don't see that."

"Don't you think it's just human nature?" Ellie said.

"God, no," Malcolm said. "That's like saying scrambled eggs and bacon for breakfast is human nature. It's nothing of the sort. It's uniquely Western training, and much of the rest of the world is nauseated by the thought of it." He winced in pain. "The morphine's making me philosophical."

"You want some water?"

"No. I'll tell you the problem with engineers and scientists. Scientists have an elaborate line of bullshit about how they are seeking to know the truth about nature. Which is true, but that's not what drives them. Nobody is driven by abstractions like 'seeking truth.'

"Scientists are actually preoccupied with accomplishment. So they are focused on whether they can do something. They never stop to ask if they *should* do something. They conveniently define such considerations as pointless. If they don't do it, someone else will. Discovery, they believe, is inevitable. So they just try to do it first. That's the game in science. Even pure scientific discovery is an aggressive, penetrative act. It takes big equipment, and it literally changes the world afterward. Particle accelerators scar the land, and leave radioactive byproducts. Astronauts leave trash on the moon. There is always some proof that scientists were there, making their discoveries. Discovery is always a rape of the natural world. Always.

"The scientists want it that way. They have to stick their instruments in. They have to leave their mark. They can't just watch. They can't just appreciate. They can't just fit into the natural order. They have to make something unnatural happen. That is the scien-

tist's job, and now we have whole societies that try to be scientific."
He sighed, and sank back.

Ellie said, "Don't you think you're overstating—"

"What does one of your excavations look like a year later?"

"Pretty bad," she admitted.

"You don't replant, you don't restore the land after you dig?"

"No."

"Why not?"

She shrugged. "There's no money, I guess. . . ."

"There's only enough money to dig, but not to repair?"

"Well, we're just working in the badlands. . . ."

"Just the badlands," Malcolm said, shaking his head. "Just trash. Just byproducts. Just side effects . . . I'm trying to tell you that scientists *want* it this way. They want byproducts and trash and scars and side effects. It's a way of reassuring themselves. It's built into the fabric of science, and it's increasingly a disaster."

"Then what's the answer?"

"Get rid of the thintelligent ones. Take them out of power."

"But then we'd lose all the advances—"

"What advances?" Malcolm said irritably. "The number of hours women devote to housework has not changed since 1930, despite all the advances. All the vacuum cleaners, washer-dryers, trash compactors, garbage disposals, wash-and-wear fabrics . . . Why does it still take as long to clean the house as it did in 1930?"

Ellie said nothing.

"Because there haven't been any advances," Malcolm said. "Not really. Thirty thousand years ago, when men were doing cave paintings at Lascaux, they worked twenty hours a week to provide themselves with food and shelter and clothing. The rest of the time, they could play, or sleep, or do whatever they wanted. And they lived in a natural world, with clean air, clean water, beautiful trees and sunsets. Think about it. Twenty hours a week. Thirty thousand years ago."

Ellie said, "You want to turn back the clock?"

"No," Malcolm said. "I want people to wake up. We've had four hundred years of modern science, and we ought to know by now what it's good for, and what it's not good for. It's time for a change."

"Before we destroy the planet?" she said.

He sighed, and closed his eyes. "Oh dear," he said. "That's the *last* thing I would worry about."

* * *

In the dark tunnel of the jungle river, Grant went hand over hand, holding branches, moving the raft cautiously forward. He still heard the sounds. And finally he saw the dinosaurs.

"Aren't those the ones that are poison?"

"Yes," Grant said. *"Dilophosaurus."*

Standing on the riverbank were two dilophosaurs. The ten-foot-tall bodies were spotted yellow and black. Underneath, the bellies were bright green, like lizards. Twin red curving crests ran along the top of the head from the eyes to the nose, making a V shape above the head. The bird-like quality was reinforced by the way they moved, bending to drink from the river, then rising to snarl and hoot.

Lex whispered, "Should we get out and walk?"

Grant shook his head no. The dilophosaurs were smaller than the tyrannosaur, small enough to slip through the dense foliage at the banks of the river. And they seemed quick, as they snarled and hooted at each other.

"But we can't get past them in the boat," Lex said. "They're *poison.*"

"We have to," Grant said. "Somehow."

The dilophosaurs continued to drink and hoot. They seemed to be interacting with each other in a strangely ritualistic, repetitive way. The animal on the left would bend to drink, opening its mouth to bare long rows of sharp teeth, and then it would hoot. The animal on the right would hoot in reply and bend to drink, in a mirror image of the first animal's movements. Then the sequence would be repeated, exactly the same way.

Grant noticed that the animal on the right was smaller, with smaller spots on its back, and its crest was a duller red—

"I'll be damned," he said. "It's a mating ritual."

"Can we get past them?" Tim asked.

"Not the way they are now. They're right by the edge of the water." Grant knew animals often performed such mating rituals for hours at a time. They went without food, they paid attention to nothing else. . . . He glanced at his watch. Nine-twenty.

"What do we do?" Tim said.

Grant sighed. "I have no idea."

He sat down in the raft, and then the dilophosaurs began to honk and roar repeatedly, in agitation. He looked up. The animals were both facing away from the river.

"What is it?" Lex said.

Grant smiled. "I think we're finally getting some help." He pushed off from the bank. "I want you two kids to lie flat on the rubber. We'll go past as fast as we can. But just remember: whatever happens, don't say anything, and don't move. Okay?"

The raft began to drift downstream, toward the hooting dilophosaurs. It gained speed. Lex lay at Grant's feet, staring at him with frightened eyes. They were coming closer to the dilophosaurs, which were still turned away from the river. But he pulled out his air pistol, checked the chamber.

The raft continued on, and they smelled a peculiar odor, sweet and nauseating at the same time. It smelled like dried vomit. The hooting of the dilophosaurs was louder. The raft came around a final bend and Grant caught his breath. The dilophosaurs were just a few feet away, honking at the trees beyond the river.

As Grant had suspected, they were honking at the tyrannosaur. The tyrannosaur was trying to break through the foliage, and the dilos hooted and stomped their feet in the mud. The raft drifted past them. The smell was nauseating. The tyrannosaur roared, probably because it saw the raft. But in another moment . . .

A *thump*.

The raft stopped moving. They were aground, against the riverbank, just a few feet downstream from the dilophosaurs.

Lex whispered, "Oh, *great*."

There was a long slow scraping sound of the raft against the mud. Then the raft was moving again. They were going down the river. The tyrannosaur roared a final time and moved off; one dilophosaur looked surprised, then hooted. The other dilophosaur hooted in reply.

The raft floated downriver.

TYRANNOSAUR

The Jeep bounced along in the glaring sun. Muldoon was driving, with Gennaro at his side. They were in an open field, moving away from the dense line of foliage and palm trees that marked the course of the river, a hundred yards to the east. They came to a rise, and Muldoon stopped the car.

"Christ, it's hot," he said, wiping his forehead with the back of his arm. He drank from the bottle of whiskey between his knees, then offered it to Gennaro.

Gennaro shook his head. He stared at the landscape shimmering in the morning heat. Then he looked down at the onboard computer and video monitor mounted in the dashboard. The monitor showed views of the park from remote cameras. Still no sign of Grant and the children. Or of the tyrannosaur.

The radio crackled. "Muldoon."

Muldoon picked up the handset. "Yeah."

"You got your onboards? I found the rex. He's in grid 442. Going to 443."

"Just a minute," Muldoon said, adjusting the monitor. "Yeah. I got him now. Following the river." The animal was slinking along the foliage that lined the banks of the river, going north.

"Take it easy with him. Just immobilize him."

"Don't worry," Muldoon said, squinting in the sun. "I won't hurt him."

"Remember," Arnold said, "the tyrannosaur's our main tourist attraction."

Muldoon turned off his radio with a crackle of static. "Bloody fool," he said. "They're still talking about tourists." Muldoon started the engine. "Let's go see Rexy and give him a dose."

The Jeep jolted over the terrain.

"You're looking forward to this," Gennaro said.

"I've wanted to put a needle in this big bastard for a while," Muldoon said. "And there he is."

They came to a wrenching stop. Through the windshield, Gennaro saw the tyrannosaur directly ahead of them, moving among the palm trees along the river.

Muldoon drained the whiskey bottle and threw it in the backseat. He reached back for his tubing. Gennaro looked at the video monitor, which showed their Jeep and the tyrannosaur. There must be a closed-circuit camera in the trees somewhere behind.

"You want to help," Muldoon said, "you can break out those canisters by your feet."

Gennaro bent over and opened a stainless-steel Halliburton case. It was padded inside with foam. Four cylinders, each the size of a quart milk bottle, were nestled in the foam. They were all labeled MORO-709. He took one out.

"You snap off the tip and screw on a needle," Muldoon explained.

Gennaro found a plastic package of large needles, each the diameter of his fingertip. He screwed one onto the canister. The opposite end of the canister had a circular lead weight.

"That's the plunger. Compresses on impact." Muldoon sat forward with the air rifle across his knees. It was made of heavy gray tubular metal and looked to Gennaro like a bazooka or a rocket launcher.

"What's MORO-709?"

"Standard animal trank," Muldoon said. "Zoos around the world use it. We'll try a thousand cc's to start." Muldoon cracked open the chamber, which was large enough to insert his fist. He slipped the canister into the chamber and closed it.

"That should do it," Muldoon said. "Standard elephant gets about two hundred cc's, but they're only two or three tons each. *Tyrannosaurus rex* is eight tons, and a lot meaner. That matters to the dose."

"Why?"

"Animal dose is partly body weight and partly temperament. You shoot the same dose of 709 into an elephant, a hippo, and a rhino—you'll immobilize the elephant, so it just stands there like a statue. You'll slow down the hippo, so it gets kind of sleepy but it keeps moving. And the rhino will just get fighting mad. But, on the other hand, you chase a rhino for more than five minutes in a car and he'll drop dead from adrenaline shock. Strange combination of tough and delicate."

Muldoon drove slowly toward the river, moving closer to the tyrannosaur. "But those are all mammals. We know a lot about handling mammals, because zoos are built around the big mammalian attractions—lions, tigers, bears, elephants. We know a lot less about reptiles. And nobody knows anything about dinosaurs. The dinosaurs are new animals."

"You consider them reptiles?" Gennaro said.

"No," Muldoon said, shifting gears. "Dinosaurs don't fit existing categories." He swerved to avoid a rock. "Actually, what we find is, the dinosaurs were as variable as mammals are today. Some dinos are tame and cute, and some are mean and nasty. Some of them see well, and some of them don't. Some of them are stupid, and some of them are very, very intelligent."

"Like the raptors?" Gennaro said.

Muldoon nodded. "Raptors are smart. Very smart. Believe me, all the problems we have so far," he said, "are nothing compared with what we'd have if the raptors ever got out of their holding pen. Ah. I think this is as close as we can get to our Rexy."

Up ahead, the tyrannosaur was poking its head through the branches, peering toward the river. Trying to get through. Then the animal moved a few yards downstream, to try again.

"Wonder what he sees in there?" Gennaro said.

"Hard to know," Muldoon said. "Maybe he's trying to get to the microceratopsians that scramble around in the branches. They'll run him a merry chase."

Muldoon stopped the Jeep about fifty yards away from the tyrannosaur, and turned the vehicle around. He left the motor running. "Get behind the wheel," Muldoon said. "And put your seat belt on." He took another canister and hooked it onto his shirt. Then he got out.

Gennaro slid behind the wheel. "You done this very often before?"

Muldoon belched. "Never. I'll try to get him just behind the auditory meatus. We'll see how it goes from there." He walked ten yards behind the Jeep and crouched down in the grass on one knee. He steadied the big gun against his shoulder, and flipped up the thick telescopic sight. Muldoon aimed at the tyrannosaur, which still ignored them.

There was a burst of pale gas, and Gennaro saw a white streak shoot forward in the air toward the tyrannosaur. But nothing seemed to happen.

Then the tyrannosaur turned slowly, curiously, to peer at them. It moved its head from side to side, as if looking at them with alternate eyes.

Muldoon had taken down the launcher, and was loading the second canister.

"You hit him?" Gennaro said.

Muldoon shook his head. "Missed. Damn laser sights . . . See if there's a battery in the case."

"A what?" Gennaro said.

"A battery," Muldoon said. "It's about as big as your finger. Gray markings."

Gennaro bent over to look in the steel case. He felt the vibration of the Jeep, heard the motor ticking over. He didn't see a battery. The tyrannosaur roared. To Gennaro it was a terrifying sound, rumbling from the great chest cavity of the animal, bellowing out over the landscape. He sat up sharply and reached for the steering wheel, put his hand on the gearshift. On the radio, he heard a voice say, "Muldoon. This is Arnold. Get out of there. Over."

"I know what I'm doing," Muldoon said.

The tyrannosaur charged.

Muldoon stood his ground. Despite the creature racing toward him, he slowly and methodically raised his launcher, aimed, and fired. Once again, Gennaro saw the puff of smoke, and the white streak of the canister going toward the animal.

Nothing happened. The tyrannosaur continued to charge.

Now Muldoon was on his feet and running, shouting, "Go! Go!" Gennaro put the Jeep in gear and Muldoon threw himself onto the side door as the Jeep lurched forward. The tyrannosaur was closing rapidly, and Muldoon swung the door open and climbed inside.

"Go, damn it! Go!"

Gennaro floored it. The Jeep bounced precariously, the front end nosing so high they saw only sky through the windshield, then slamming down again toward the ground and racing forward again. Gennaro headed for a stand of trees to the left until, in the rearview mirror, he saw the tyrannosaur give a final roar and turn away.

Gennaro slowed the car. "Jesus."

Muldoon was shaking his head. "I could have sworn I hit him the second time."

"I'd say you missed," Gennaro said.

"Needle must have broken off before the plunger injected."

"Admit it, you missed."

"Yeah," Muldoon said. He sighed. "I missed. Battery was dead in the damned laser sights. My fault. I should have checked it, after it was out all last night. Let's go back and get more canisters."

The Jeep headed north, toward the hotel. Muldoon picked up the radio. "Control."

"Yes," Arnold said.

"We're heading back to base."

The river was now very narrow, and flowing swiftly. The raft was going faster all the time. It was starting to feel like an amusement park ride.

"Whee!" Lex yelled, holding on to the gunwale. "Faster, faster!"

Grant squinted, looking forward. The river was still narrow and dark, but farther ahead he could see the trees ended, and there was bright sunlight beyond, and a distant roaring sound. The river seemed to end abruptly in a peculiar flat line. . . .

The raft was going still faster, rushing forward.

Grant grabbed for his paddles.

"What is it?"

"It's a waterfall," Grant said.

The raft swept out of the overhanging darkness into brilliant morning sunlight, and raced forward on the swift current toward the lip of the waterfall. The roar was loud in their ears. Grant paddled as strongly as he could, but he only succeeded in spinning the boat in circles. It continued inexorably toward the lip.

Lex leaned toward him. "I can't swim!" Grant saw that she did not have her life vest clasped, but there was nothing he could do about it; with frightening speed, they came to the edge, and the roar of the waterfall seemed to fill the world. Grant jammed his oar deep into the water, felt it catch and hold, right at the lip; the rubber raft shuddered in the current, but they did not go over. Grant strained against the oar and, looking over the edge, saw the sheer drop of fifty feet down to the surging pool below.

And standing in the surging pool, waiting for them, was the tyrannosaur.

Lex was screaming in panic, and then the boat spun, and the rear end dropped away, spilling them out into air and roaring water, and they fell sickeningly. Grant flailed his arms in the air, and the world went suddenly silent and slow.

It seemed to him he fell for long minutes; he had time to observe Lex, clutching her orange jacket, falling alongside him; he had time to observe Tim, looking down at the bottom; he had time to observe the frozen white sheet of the waterfall; he had time to observe the bubbling pool beneath him as he fell slowly, silently toward it.

Then, with a stinging slap, Grant plunged into cold water, surrounded by white boiling bubbles. He tumbled and spun and glimpsed the leg of the tyrannosaur as he was swirled past it, swept down through the pool and out into the stream beyond. Grant swam for the shore, clutched warm rocks, slipped off, caught a branch, and finally pulled himself out of the main current. Gasping, he dragged himself on his belly onto the rocks, and looked at the river just in time to see the brown rubber raft tumble past him. Then he saw Tim, battling the current, and he reached out and pulled him, coughing and shivering, onto the shore beside him.

Grant turned back to the waterfall, and saw the tyrannosaur plunge its head straight down into the water of the pool at his feet. The great head shook, splashing water to either side. It had something between its teeth.

And then the tyrannosaur lifted its head back up.

Dangling from the jaws was Lex's orange life vest.

A moment later, Lex bobbed to the surface beside the dinosaur's long tail. She lay facedown in the water, her little body swept downstream by the current. Grant plunged into the water after her, was again immersed in the churning torrent. A moment later, he pulled her up onto the rocks, a heavy, lifeless weight. Her face was gray. Water poured from her mouth.

Grant bent over her to give her mouth-to-mouth but she coughed. Then she vomited yellow-green liquid and coughed again. Her eyelids fluttered. "Hi," she said. She smiled weakly. "We did it."

Tim started to cry. She coughed again. "Will you stop it? What're you crying for?"

"Because."

"We were worried about you," Grant said. Small flecks of white were drifting down the river. The tyrannosaur was tearing up the life vest. Still turned away from them, facing the waterfall. But at any minute the animal might turn and see them. . . . "Come on, kids," he said.

"Where are we going?" Lex said, coughing.

"Come *on*." He was looking for a hiding place. Downstream he saw only an open grassy plain, affording no protection. Upstream was the dinosaur. Then Grant saw a dirt path by the river. It seemed to lead up toward the waterfall.

And in the dirt he saw the clear imprint of a man's shoe. Leading up the path.

The tyrannosaur finally turned around, growling and looking out toward the grassy plain. It seemed to have figured out that they had gotten away. It was looking for them downstream. Grant and the kids ducked among the big ferns that lined the riverbanks. Cautiously, he led them upstream. "Where are we going?" Lex said.

"We're going *back*."

"I know."

They were closer to the waterfall now, the roar much louder. The rocks became slippery, the path muddy. There was a constant hanging mist. It was like moving through a cloud. The path seemed to lead right into the rushing water, but as they came closer, they saw that it actually went behind the waterfall.

The tyrannosaur was still looking downstream, its back turned to them. They hurried along the path to the waterfall, and had almost moved behind the sheet of falling water when Grant saw the tyrannosaur turn. Then they were completely behind the waterfall, and Grant was unable to see out through the silver sheet.

Grant looked around in surprise. There was a little recess here, hardly larger than a closet, and filled with machinery: humming pumps and big filters and pipes. Everything was wet, and cold.

"Did he see us?" Lex said. She had to shout over the noise of the falling water. "Where are we? What is this place? Did he see us?"

"Just a minute," Grant said. He was looking at the equipment. This was clearly park machinery. And there must be electricity to run it, so perhaps there was also a telephone for communication. He poked among the filters and pipes.

"What are you doing?" Lex shouted.

"Looking for a telephone." It was now nearly 10:00 a.m. They had just a little more than an hour to contact the ship before it reached the mainland.

In the back of the recess he found a metal door marked MAINT 04, but it was firmly locked. Next to it was a slot for a security card. Alongside the door he saw a row of metal boxes. He opened the boxes one after another, but they contained only switches and timers. No telephone. And nothing to open the door.

He almost missed the box to the left of the door. On opening it, he found a nine-button keypad, covered with spots of green mold. But it looked as if it was a way to open the door, and he had the feeling that on the other side of that door was a phone. Scratched in the metal of the box was the number 1023. He punched it in.

With a hiss, the door came open. Gaping darkness beyond, concrete steps leading downward. On the back wall he saw stenciled MAINT VEHICLE 04/22 CHARGER and an arrow pointing down the stairs. Could it really mean there was a car? "Come on, kids."

"Forget it," Lex said. "I'm not going in there."

"Come on, Lex," Tim said.

"Forget it," Lex said. "There's no lights or anything. I'm not going."

"Never mind," Grant said. There wasn't time to argue. "Stay here, and I'll be right back."

"Where're you going?" Lex said, suddenly alarmed.

Grant stepped through the door. It gave an electronic beep, and snapped shut behind him, on a spring.

Grant was plunged into total darkness. After a moment of surprise, he turned to the door and felt its damp surface. There was no knob, no latch. He turned to the walls on either side of the door, feeling for a switch, a control box, anything at all. . . .

There was nothing.

He was fighting panic when his fingers closed over a cold metal cylinder. He ran his hands over a swelling edge, a flat surface . . . a flashlight! He clicked it on, and the beam was surprisingly bright. He looked back at the door, but saw that it would not open. He would have to wait for the kids to unlock it. Meantime . . .

He started for the steps. They were damp and slippery with mold, and he went down carefully. Partway down the stairs, he heard a sniffing and the sound of claws scratching on concrete. He took out his dart pistol, and proceeded cautiously.

The steps bent around the corner, and as he shone his light, an 'odd reflection glinted back, and then, a moment later, he saw it: a car! It was an electric car, like a golf cart, and it faced a long tunnel that seemed to stretch away for miles. A bright red light glowed by the steering wheel of the car, so perhaps it was charged.

Grant heard the sniffing again, and he wheeled and saw a pale shape rise up toward him, leaping through the air, its jaws open, and without thinking Grant fired. The animal landed on him, knocking him down, and he rolled away in fright, his flashlight swinging wildly. But the animal didn't get up, and he felt foolish when he saw it.

It was a velociraptor, but very young, less than a year old. It was about two feet tall, the size of a medium dog, and it lay on the ground, breathing shallowly; the dart sticking from beneath its jaw. There was probably too much anesthetic for its body weight, and Grant pulled the dart out quickly. The velociraptor looked at him with slightly glazed eyes.

Grant had a clear feeling of intelligence from this creature, a kind of softness which contrasted strangely with the menace he had felt from the adults in the pen. He stroked the head of the velociraptor, hoping to calm it. He looked down at the body, which was shivering slightly as the tranquilizer took hold. And then he saw it was a male.

A young juvenile, and a male. There was no question what he was seeing. This velociraptor had been bred in the wild.

Excited by this development, he hurried back up the stairs to the door. With his flashlight, he scanned the flat, featureless surface of the door, and the interior walls. As he ran his hands over the door, it slowly dawned on him that he was locked inside, and unable to open it, unless the kids had the presence of mind to open it for him. He could hear them, faintly, on the other side of the door.

"Dr. Grant!" Lex shouted, pounding the door. "Dr. Grant!"

"Take it easy," Tim said. "He'll be back."

"But where did he go?"

"Listen, Dr. Grant knows what he's doing," Tim said. "He'll be back in a minute."

"He should come back *now*," Lex said. She bunched her fists on her hips, pushed her elbows wide. She stamped her foot angrily.

And then, with a roar, the tyrannosaur's head burst through the waterfall toward them.

Tim stared in horror as the big mouth gaped wide. Lex shrieked and threw herself on the ground. The head swung back and forth, and pulled out again. But Tim could see the shadow of the animal's head on the sheet of falling water.

He pulled Lex deeper into the recess, just as the jaws burst through again, roaring, the thick tongue flicking in and out rapidly. Water sprayed in all directions from the head. Then it pulled out again.

Lex huddled next to Tim, shivering. "I *hate* him," she said. She huddled back, but the recess was only a few feet deep, and crammed with machinery. There wasn't any place for them to hide.

The head came through the water again, but slowly this time, and the jaw came to rest on the ground. The tyrannosaur snorted, flaring its nostrils, breathing the air. But the eyes were still outside the sheet of water.

Tim thought: He can't see us. He knows we're in here, but he can't see through the water.

The tyrannosaur sniffed.

"What is he doing?" Lex said again.

"Sshhhh."

With a low growl, the jaws slowly opened, and the tongue snaked out. It was thick and blue-black, with a little forked indentation at the tip. It was four feet long, and easily reached back to the far wall of the recess. The tongue slid with a rasping scrape over the filter cylinders. Tim and Lex pressed back against the pipes.

The tongue moved slowly to the left, then to the right, slapping wetly against the machinery. The tip curled around the pipes and valves, sensing them. Tim saw that the tongue had muscular movements, like an elephant's trunk. The tongue drew back along the right side of the recess. It dragged against Lex's legs.

"Eeww," Lex said.

The tongue stopped. It curled, then began to rise like a snake up the side of her body—

"Don't move," Tim whispered.

. . . past her face, then up along Tim's shoulder, and finally wrapping around his head. Tim squeezed his eyes shut as the slimy muscle covered his face. It was hot and wet and it stunk like urine.

Wrapped around him, the tongue began to drag him, very slowly, toward the open jaws.

"Timmy . . ."

Tim couldn't answer; his mouth was covered by the flat black tongue. He could see, but he couldn't talk. Lex tugged at his hand.

"Come on, Timmy!"

The tongue dragged him toward the snorting mouth. He felt the hot panting breath on his legs. Lex was tugging at him but she was no match for the muscular power that held him. Tim let go of her and pressed the tongue with both hands, trying to shove it over his head. He couldn't move it. He dug his heels into the muddy ground but he was dragged forward anyway.

Lex had wrapped her arms around his waist and was pulling backward, shouting to him, but he was powerless to do anything. He was beginning to see stars. A kind of peacefulness overcame him, a sense of peaceful inevitability as he was dragged along.

"Timmy?"

And then suddenly the tongue relaxed, and uncoiled. Tim felt it slipping off his face. His body was covered in disgusting white foamy slime, and the tongue fell limply to the ground. The jaws slapped shut, biting down on the tongue. Dark blood gushed out, mixing with the mud. The nostrils still snorted in ragged breaths.

"What's he doing?" Lex cried.

And then slowly, very slowly, the head began to slide backward, out of the recess, leaving a long scrape in the mud. And finally it disappeared entirely, and they could see only the silver sheet of falling water.

CONTROL

"Okay," Arnold said, in the control room. "The rex is down." He pushed back in his chair, and grinned as he lit a final cigarette and crumpled the pack. That did it: the final step in putting the park back in order. Now all they had to do was go out and move it.

"Son of a bitch," Muldoon said, looking at the monitor. "I got him after all." He turned to Gennaro. "It just took him an hour to feel it."

Henry Wu frowned at the screen. "But he could drown, in that position. . . ."

"He won't drown," Muldoon said. "Never seen an animal that was harder to kill."

"I think we have to go out and move him," Arnold said.

"We will," Muldoon said. He didn't sound enthusiastic.

"That's a valuable animal."

"I know it's a valuable animal," Muldoon said.

Arnold turned to Gennaro. He couldn't resist a moment of triumph. "I'd point out to you," he said, "that the park is now completely back to normal. Whatever Malcolm's mathematical model said was going to happen. We are completely under control again."

Gennaro pointed to the screen behind Arnold's head and said, "What's that?"

Arnold turned. It was the system status box, in the upper corner of the screen. Ordinarily it was empty. Arnold was surprised to see that it was now blinking yellow: AUX PWR LOW. For a moment, he didn't understand. Why should auxiliary power be low? They were running on main power, not auxiliary power. He thought perhaps it was just a routine status check on the auxiliary power, perhaps a check on the fuel tank levels or the battery charge. . . .

"Henry," Arnold said to Wu. "Look at this."

Wu said, "Why are you running on auxiliary power?"

"I'm not," Arnold said.

"It looks like you are."

"I can't be."

"Print the system status log," Wu said. The log was a record of the system over the last few hours.

Arnold pressed a button, and they heard the hum of a printer in the corner. Wu walked over to it.

Arnold stared at the screen. The box now turned from flashing yellow to red, and the message now read: AUX PWR FAIL.

Numbers began to count backward from twenty.

"What the hell is going on?" Arnold said.

Cautiously, Tim moved a few yards out along the muddy path, into the sunshine. He peered around the waterfall, and saw the tyrannosaur lying on its side, floating in the pool of water below.

"I hope he's dead," Lex said.

Tim could see he wasn't: the dinosaur's chest was still moving, and one forearm twitched in spasms. But something was wrong with him. Then Tim saw the white canister sticking in the back of the head, by the indentation of the ear.

"He's been shot with a dart," Tim said.

"Good," Lex said. "He practically *ate* us."

Tim watched the labored breathing. He felt unexpectedly distressed to see the huge animal humbled like this. He didn't want it to die. "It's not his fault," he said.

"Oh sure," Lex said. "He practically ate us and it's not his fault."

"He's a carnivore. He was just doing what he does."

"You wouldn't say that," Lex said, "if you were in his stomach right now."

Then the sound of the waterfall changed. From a deafening roar, it became softer, quieter. The thundering sheet of water thinned, became a trickle . . .

And stopped.

"Timmy. The waterfall stopped," Lex said.

It was now just dripping like a tap that wasn't completely turned off. The pool at the base of the waterfall was still. They stood near the top, in the cave-like indentation filled with machinery, looking down.

"Waterfalls aren't supposed to stop," Lex said.

Tim shook his head. "It must be the power. . . . Somebody turned off the power." Behind them, all the pumps and filters were shutting down one after another, the lights blinking off, and the machinery becoming quiet. And then there was the *thunk* of a solenoid releasing, and the door marked MAINT 04 swung slowly open.

Grant stepped out, blinking in the light, and said, "Good work, kids. You got the door open."

"We didn't do anything," Lex said.

"The power went out," Tim said.

"Never mind that," Grant said. "Come and see what I've found."

Arnold stared in shock.

One after another, the monitors went black, and then the room lights went out, plunging the control room into darkness and confusion. Everyone started yelling at once. Muldoon opened the blinds and let light in, and Wu brought over the printout.

"Look at this," Wu said.

Time	Event	System Status
5:12:44	Safety 1 Off	Operative
5:12:45	Safety 2 Off	Operative
5:12:46	Safety 3 Off	Operative
5:12:51	Shutdown Command	Shutdown
5:13:48	Startup Command	Shutdown
5:13:55	Safety 1 On	Shutdown
5:13:57	Safety 2 On	Shutdown
5:13:59	Safety 3 On	Shutdown
5:14:08	Startup Command	Startup - Aux Power
5:14:18	Monitor-Main	Operative - Aux Power
5:14:19	Security-Main	Operative - Aux Power
5:14:22	Command-Main	Operative - Aux Power
5:14:24	Laboratory-Main	Operative - Aux Power
5:14:29	TeleCom-VBB	Operative - Aux Power
5:14:32	Schematic-Main	Operative - Aux Power
5:14:37	View	Operative - Aux Power
5:14:44	Control Status Chk	Operative - Aux Power
5:14:57	Warning: Fence Status [NB]	Operative - Aux Power
9:11:37	Warning: Aux Fuel (20%)	Operative - Aux Power
9:33:19	Warning: Aux Fuel (10%)	Operative - Aux Power
9:53:19	Warning: Aux Fuel (1%)	Operative - Aux Power
9:53:39	Warning: Aux Fuel (0%)	Shutdown

Wu said, "You shut down at five-thirteen this morning, and when you started back up, you started with auxiliary power."

"Jesus," Arnold said. Apparently, main power had not been on since shutdown. When he powered back up, only the auxiliary power came on. Arnold was thinking that was strange, when he suddenly realized that that was *normal*. That was what was supposed to happen. It made perfect sense: the auxiliary generator fired up first, and it was used to turn on the main generator, because it took a heavy charge to start the main power generator. That was the way the system was designed.

But Arnold had never before had occasion to turn the main power off. And when the lights and screens came back on in the control room, it never occurred to him that main power hadn't also been restored.

But it hadn't, and all during the time since then, while they were looking for the rex, and doing one thing and another, the park had been running on auxiliary power. And that wasn't a good idea. In fact, the implications were just beginning to hit him—

"What does this line mean?" Muldoon said, pointing to the list.

05:14:57   Warning: Fence Status [NB]   Operative - Aux Power   [AV09]

"It means a system status warning was sent to the monitors in the control room," Arnold said. "Concerning the fences."

"Did you see that warning?"

Arnold shook his head. "No. I must have been talking to you in the field. Anyway, no, I didn't see it."

"What does it mean, 'Warning: Fence Status'?"

"Well, I didn't know it at the time, but we were running on backup power," Arnold said. "And backup doesn't generate enough amperage to power the electrified fences, so they were automatically kept off."

Muldoon scowled. "The electrified fences were off?"

"Yes."

"All of them? Since five this morning? For the last five hours?"

"Yes."

"Including the velociraptor fences?"

Arnold sighed. "Yes."

"Jesus Christ," Muldoon said. "Five hours. Those animals could be out."

And then, from somewhere in the distance, they heard a scream.

Muldoon began to talk very fast. He went around the room, handing out the portable radios.

"Mr. Arnold is going to the maintenance shed to turn on main power. Dr. Wu, stay in the control room. You're the only other one who can work the computers. Mr. Hammond, go back to the lodge. Don't argue with me. Go now. Lock the gates, and stay behind them until you hear from me. I'll help Arnold deal with the raptors." He turned to Gennaro. "Like to live dangerously again?"

"Not really," Gennaro said. He was very pale.

"Fine. Then go with the others to the lodge." Muldoon turned away. "That's it, everybody. Now *move*."

Hammond whined, "But what are you going to do to my animals?"

"That's not really the question, Mr. Hammond," Muldoon said. "The question is, what are they going to do to us?"

He went through the door, and hurried down the hall toward his office. Gennaro fell into step alongside him. "Change your mind?" Muldoon growled.

"You'll need help," Gennaro said.

"I might." Muldoon went into the room marked ANIMAL SUPER-VISOR, picked up the gray shoulder launcher, and unlocked a panel in the wall behind his desk. There were six cylinders and six canisters.

"The thing about these damn dinos," Muldoon said, "is that they have distributed nervous systems. They don't die fast, even with a direct hit to the brain. And they're built solidly; thick ribs make a shot to the heart dicey, and they're difficult to cripple in the legs or hindquarters. Slow bleeders, slow to die." He was opening the cylinders one after another and dropping in the canisters. He tossed a thick webbed belt to Gennaro. "Put that on."

Gennaro tightened the belt, and Muldoon passed him the shells. "About all we can hope to do is blow them apart. Unfortunately we've only got six shells here. There's eight raptors in that fenced compound. Let's go. Stay close. You have the shells."

Muldoon went out and ran along the hallway, looking down over the balcony to the path leading toward the maintenance shed. Gennaro was puffing alongside him. They got to the ground floor and went out through the glass doors, and Muldoon stopped.

Arnold was standing with his back to the maintenance shed. Three raptors approached him. Arnold had picked up a stick, and he was waving it at them, shouting. The raptors fanned out as they came closer, one staying in the center, the other two moving to each side. Coordinated. Smooth. Gennaro shivered.

Pack behavior.

Muldoon was already crouching, setting the launcher on his shoulder. "Load," he said. Gennaro slipped the shell in the back of the launcher. There was an electric sizzle. Nothing happened. "Christ, you've got it in backward," Muldoon said, tilting the barrel so the shell fell into Gennaro's hands. Gennaro loaded again. The raptors were snarling at Arnold when the animal on the left simply exploded, the upper part of the torso flying into the air, blood spattering like a burst tomato on the walls of the building. The lower torso collapsed on the ground, the legs kicking in the air, the tail flopping.

"That'll wake 'em up," Muldoon said.

Arnold ran for the door of the maintenance shed. The velociraptors turned, and started toward Muldoon and Gennaro. They fanned out as they came closer. In the distance, somewhere near the lodge, he heard screams.

Gennaro said, "This could be a disaster."

"Load," Muldoon said.

Henry Wu heard the explosions and looked toward the door of the control room. He circled around the consoles, then paused. He wanted to go out, but he knew he should stay in the room. If Arnold was able to get the power back on—if only for a minute—then Wu could restart the main generator.

He had to stay in the room.

He heard someone screaming. It sounded like Muldoon.

Muldoon felt a wrenching pain in his ankle, tumbled down an embankment, and hit the ground running. Looking back, he saw Gennaro running in the other direction, into the forest. The raptors were ignoring Gennaro but pursuing Muldoon. They were now less than twenty yards away. Muldoon screamed at the top of his lungs as he ran, wondering vaguely where the hell he could go. Because he knew he had perhaps ten seconds before they got him.

Ten seconds.

Maybe less.

* * *

Ellie had to help Malcolm turn over as Harding jabbed the needle and injected morphine. Malcolm sighed and collapsed back. It seemed he was growing weaker by the minute. Over the radio, they heard tinny screaming, and muffled explosions coming from the visitor center.

Hammond came into the room and said, "How is he?"

"He's holding," Harding said. "A bit delirious."

"I am nothing of the sort," Malcolm said. "I am utterly clear." They listened to the radio. "It sounds like a war out there."

"The raptors got out," Hammond said.

"Did they," Malcolm said, breathing shallowly. "How could that possibly happen?"

"It was a system screwup. Arnold didn't realize that the auxiliary power was on, and the fences cut out."

"Did they."

"Go to hell, you supercilious bastard."

"If I remember," Malcolm said, "I predicted fence integrity would fail."

Hammond sighed, and sat down heavily. "Damn it all," he said, shaking his head. "It must surely not have escaped your notice that at heart what we are attempting here is an extremely simple idea. My colleagues and I determined, several years ago, that it was possible to clone the DNA of an extinct animal, and to grow it. That seemed to us a wonderful idea, it was a kind of time travel— the only time travel in the world. Bring them back alive, so to speak. And since it was so exciting, and since it was possible to do it, we decided to go forward. We got this island, and we proceeded. It was all very simple."

"Simple?" Malcolm said. Somehow he found the energy to sit up in the bed. "Simple? You're a bigger fool than I thought you were. And I thought you were a very substantial fool."

Ellie said, "Dr. Malcolm," and tried to ease him back down. But Malcolm would have none of it. He pointed toward the radio, the shouts and the cries.

"What is that, going on out there?" he said. "That's your simple idea. *Simple*. You create new life-forms, about which you know nothing at all. Your Dr. Wu does not even know the names of the things he is creating. He cannot be bothered with such details as *what the thing is called*, let alone what it *is*. You create many of them in a very short time, you never learn anything about them, yet you expect them to do your bidding, because you made them and you therefore think you own them; you forget that they are alive, they have an intelligence of their own, and they may not do your bidding, and you forget how little you know about them, how incompetent you are to do the things that you so frivolously call *simple*. . . . Dear God . . ."

He sank back, coughing.

"You know what's wrong with scientific power?" Malcolm said. "It's a form of inherited wealth. And you know what assholes congenitally rich people are. It never fails."

Hammond said, "What is he talking about?"

Harding made a sign, indicating delirium. Malcolm cocked his eye.

"I will tell you what I am talking about," he said. "Most kinds of power require a substantial sacrifice by whoever wants the power. There is an apprenticeship, a discipline lasting many years. Whatever kind of power you want. President of the company. Black belt in karate. Spiritual guru. Whatever it is you seek, you have to put in the time, the practice, the effort. You must give up a lot to get it. It has to be very important to you. And once you have attained it, it is your power. It can't be given away: it resides in you. It is literally the result of your discipline.

"Now, what is interesting about this process is that, by the time someone has acquired the ability to kill with his bare hands, he has also matured to the point where he won't use it unwisely. So that kind of power has a built-in control. The discipline of getting the power changes you so that you won't abuse it.

"But scientific power is like inherited wealth: attained without discipline. You read what others have done, and you take the next step. You can do it very young. You can make progress very fast. There is no discipline lasting many decades. There is no mastery: old scientists are ignored. There is no humility before nature. There is only a get-rich-quick, make-a-name-for-yourself-fast philosophy. Cheat, lie, falsify—it doesn't matter. Not to you, or to your colleagues. No one will criticize you. No one has any standards. They are all trying to do the same thing: to do something big, and do it fast.

"And because you can stand on the shoulders of giants, you can accomplish something quickly. You don't even know exactly what you have done, but already you have reported it, patented it, and sold it. And the buyer will have even less discipline than you. The buyer simply purchases the power, like any commodity. The buyer doesn't even conceive that any discipline might be necessary."

Hammond said, "Do you know what he is talking about?"

Ellie nodded.

"I haven't a clue," Hammond said.

"I'll make it simple," Malcolm said. "A karate master does not kill people with his bare hands. He does not lose his temper and kill his wife. The person who kills is the person who has no discipline, no restraint, and who has purchased his power in the form of a Saturday night special. And that is the kind of power that science fosters, and permits. And that is why you think that to build a place like this is simple."

"It *was* simple," Hammond insisted.

"Then why did it go wrong?"

Dizzy with tension, John Arnold threw open the door to the maintenance shed and stepped into the darkness inside. Jesus, it was black. He should have realized the lights would be out. He felt the cool air, the cavernous dimensions of the space, extending two floors below him. He had to find the catwalk. He had to be careful, or he'd break his neck.

The catwalk.

He groped like a blind man until he realized it was futile. Somehow he had to get light into the shed. He went back to the door and cracked it open four inches. That gave enough light. But there was no way to keep the door open. Quickly he kicked off his shoe and stuck it in the door.

He went toward the catwalk, seeing it easily. He walked along the corrugated metal, hearing the difference in his feet, one loud, one soft. But at least he could see. Up ahead was the stairway leading down to the generators. Another ten yards.

Darkness.

The light was gone.

Arnold looked back to the door, and saw the light was blocked by the body of a velociraptor. The animal bent over, and carefully sniffed the shoe.

Henry Wu paced. He ran his hands over the computer consoles.

He touched the screens. He was in constant movement. He was almost frantic with tension.

He reviewed the steps he would take. He must be quick. The first screen would come up, and he would press—

"Wu!" The radio hissed.

He grabbed for it. "Yes. I'm here."

"Got any bloody power yet?" It was Muldoon. There was something odd about his voice, something hollow.

"No," Wu said. He smiled, glad to know Muldoon was alive.

"I think Arnold made it to the shed," Muldoon said. "After that, I don't know."

"Where are you?" Wu said.

"I'm stuffed."

"What?"

"Stuffed in a bloody pipe," Muldoon said. "And I'm very popular at the moment."

Wedged in a pipe was more like it, Muldoon thought. There had been a stack of drainage pipes piled behind the visitor center, and he'd backed himself into the nearest one, scrambling like a poor bastard. Meter pipes, very tight fit for him, but they couldn't come in after him.

At least, not after he'd shot the leg off one, when the nosy bastard came too close to the pipe. The raptor had gone howling off, and the others were now respectful. His only regret was that he hadn't waited to see the snout at the end of the tube before he'd squeezed the trigger.

But he might still have his chance, because there were three or four outside, snarling and growling around him.

"Yes, very popular," he said into the radio.

Wu said, "Does Arnold have a radio?"

"Don't think so," Muldoon said. "Just sit tight. Wait it out."

He hadn't seen what the other end of the pipe was like—he'd backed in too quickly—and he couldn't see now. He was wedged tight. He could only hope that the far end wasn't open. Christ, he didn't like the thought of one of those bastards taking a bite of his hindquarters.

Arnold backed away down the catwalk. The velociraptor was barely ten feet away, stalking him, coming forward into the gloom. Arnold could hear the click of its deadly claws on the metal.

But he was going slowly. He knew the animal could see well, but the grille of the catwalk, the unfamiliar mechanical odors had made it cautious. That caution was his only chance, Arnold thought. If he could get to the stairs, and then move down to the floor below . . .

Because he was pretty sure velociraptors couldn't climb stairs. Certainly not narrow, steep stairs.

Arnold glanced over his shoulder. The stairs were just a few feet away. Another few steps . . .

He was there! Reaching back, he felt the railing, started scrambling down the almost vertical steps. His feet touched flat concrete. The raptor snarled in frustration, twenty feet above him on the catwalk.

"Too bad, buddy," Arnold said. He turned away. He was now very close to the auxiliary generator. Just a few more steps and he would see it, even in this dim light. . . .

There was a dull thump behind him.

Arnold turned.

The raptor was standing there on the concrete floor, snarling.

It had jumped down.

He looked quickly for a weapon, but suddenly he found he was slammed onto his back on the concrete. Something heavy was pressing on his chest, it was impossible to breathe, and he realized the animal was *standing on top of him,* and he felt the big claws digging into the flesh of his chest, and smelled the foul breath from the head moving above him, and he opened his mouth to scream.

Ellie held the radio in her hands, listening. Two more Tican workmen had arrived at the lodge; they seemed to know it was safe here. But there had been no others in the last few minutes. And it sounded quieter outside. Over the radio, Muldoon said, "How long has it been?"

Wu said, "Four, five minutes."

"Arnold should have done it by now," Muldoon said. "If he's going to. You got any ideas?"

"No," Wu said.

"We heard from Gennaro?"

Gennaro pressed the button. "I'm here."

"Where the hell are you?" Muldoon said.

"I'm going to the maintenance building," Gennaro said. "Wish me luck."

Gennaro crouched in the foliage, listening.

Directly ahead he saw the planted pathway, leading toward the visitor center. Gennaro knew the maintenance shed was somewhere to the east. He heard the chirping of birds in the trees. A soft mist was blowing. One of the raptors roared, but it was some distance away. It sounded off to his right. Gennaro set out, leaving the path, plunging into the foliage.

Like to live dangerously?

Not really.

It was true, he didn't. But Gennaro thought he had a plan, or at least a possibility that might work. If he stayed north of the main complex of buildings, he could approach the maintenance shed from the rear. All the raptors were probably around the other buildings, to the south. There was no reason for them to be in the jungle.

At least, he hoped not.

He moved as quietly as he could, unhappily aware he was making a lot of noise. He forced himself to slow his pace, feeling his heart pound. The foliage here was very dense; he couldn't see more than six or seven feet ahead of him. He began to worry that he'd miss the maintenance shed entirely. But then he saw the roof to his right, above the palms.

He moved toward it, went around the side. He found the door, opened it, and slipped inside. It was very dark. He stumbled over something.

A man's shoe.

Gennaro frowned. He propped the door wide open and continued deeper into the building. He saw a catwalk directly ahead of him. Suddenly he realized he didn't know where to go. And he had left his radio behind.

Damn!

There might be a radio somewhere in the maintenance building. Or else he'd just look for the generator. He knew what a generator looked like. Probably it was somewhere down on the lower floor. He found a staircase leading down.

It was darker below, and it was difficult to see anything. He felt his way along among the pipes, holding his hands out to keep from banging his head.

He heard an animal snarl, and froze. He listened, but the sound did not come again. He moved forward cautiously. Something dripped on his shoulder, and his bare arm. It was warm, like water. He touched it in the darkness.

Sticky. He smelled it.

Blood.

He looked up. The raptor was perched on pipes, just a few feet above his head. Blood was trickling from its claws. With an odd sense of detachment, he wondered if it was injured. And then he began to run, but the raptor jumped onto his back, pushing him to the ground.

Gennaro was strong; he heaved up, knocking the raptor away, and rolled off across the concrete. When he turned back, he saw that the raptor had fallen on its side, where it lay panting.

Yes, it was injured. Its leg was hurt, for some reason.

Kill it.

Gennaro scrambled to his feet, looking for a weapon. The raptor was still panting on the concrete. He looked frantically for something—anything—to use as a weapon. When he turned back, the raptor was gone.

It snarled, the sound echoing in the darkness.

Gennaro turned in a full circle, feeling with his outstretched hands. And then he felt a sharp pain in his right hand.

Teeth.

It was biting him.

The raptor jerked his head, and Donald Gennaro was yanked off his feet, and he fell.

Lying in bed, soaked in sweat, Malcolm listened as the radio crackled.

"Anything?" Muldoon said. "You getting anything?"

"No word," Wu said.

"Hell," Muldoon said.

There was a pause.

Malcolm sighed. "I can't wait," he said, "to hear his new plan."

"What I would like," Muldoon said, "is to get everybody to the lodge and regroup. But I don't see how."

"There's a Jeep in front of the visitor center," Wu said. "If I drove over to you, could you get yourself into it?"

"Maybe. But you'd be abandoning the control room."

"I can't do anything here anyway."

"God knows that's true," Malcolm said. "A control room without electricity is not much of a control room."

"All right," Muldoon said. "Let's try. This isn't looking good."

Lying in his bed, Malcolm said, "No, it's not looking good. It's looking like a disaster."

Wu said, "The raptors are going to follow us over there."

"We're still better off," Malcolm said. "Let's go."

The radio clicked off. Malcolm closed his eyes, and breathed slowly, marshaling his strength.

"Just relax," Ellie said. "Just take it easy."

"You know what we are really talking about here," Malcolm said. "All this attempt to control . . . We are talking about Western attitudes that are five hundred years old. They began at the time when Florence, Italy, was the most important city in the world. The basic idea of science—that there was a new way to look at reality, that it was objective, that it did not depend on your beliefs or your nationality, that it was *rational*—that idea was fresh and exciting back then. It offered promise and hope for the future, and it swept away the old medieval system, which was hundreds of years old. The medieval world of feudal politics and religious dogma and hateful superstitions fell before science. But, in truth, this was because the medieval world didn't really work any more. It didn't work economically, it didn't work intellectually, and it didn't fit the new world that was emerging."

Malcolm coughed.

"But now," he continued, "science is the belief system that is hundreds of years old. And, like the medieval system before it, science is starting not to fit the world any more. Science has attained so much power that its practical limits begin to be apparent. Largely through science, billions of us live in one small world, densely packed and intercommunicating. But science cannot help us decide what to do with that world, or how to live. Science can make a nuclear reactor, but it cannot tell us not to build it. Science can make pesticide, but cannot tell us not to use it. And our world starts to seem polluted in fundamental ways— air, and water, and land—because of ungovernable science." He sighed. "This much is obvious to everyone."

There was a silence. Malcolm lay with his eyes closed, his breathing labored. No one spoke, and it seemed to Ellie that Malcolm had finally fallen asleep. Then he sat up again, abruptly.

"At the same time, the great intellectual justification of science has vanished. Ever since Newton and Descartes, science has explicitly offered us the vision of total control. Science has claimed the power to eventually control everything, through its understanding of natural laws. But in the twentieth century, that claim has been shattered beyond repair. First, Heisenberg's uncertainty principle set limits on what we could know about the subatomic world. Oh well, we say. None of us lives in a subatomic world. It doesn't make any practical difference as we go through our lives. Then Godel's theorem set similar limits to mathematics, the formal language of science. Mathematicians used to think that their language had some special inherent trueness that derived from the laws of logic. Now we know that what we call 'reason' is just an arbitrary game. It's not special, in the way we thought it was.

"And now chaos theory proves that unpredictability is built into our daily lives. It is as mundane as the rainstorm we cannot predict. And so the grand vision of science, hundreds of years old—the dream of total control—has died, in our century. And with it much of the justification, the rationale for science to do what it does. And for us to listen to it. Science has always said that it may not know everything now but it will know, eventually. But now we see that isn't true. It is an idle boast. As foolish, and as misguided, as the child who jumps off a building because he believes he can fly."

"This is very extreme," Hammond said, shaking his head.

"We are witnessing the end of the scientific era. Science, like other outmoded systems, is destroying itself. As it gains in power, it proves itself incapable of handling the power. Because things are going very fast now. Fifty years ago, everyone was gaga over the atomic bomb. That was power. No one could imagine anything more. Yet, a bare decade after the bomb, we began to have genetic power. And genetic power is far more potent than atomic power. And it will be in everyone's hands. It will be in kits for backyard gardeners. Experiments for schoolchildren. Cheap labs for terrorists and dictators. And that will force everyone to ask the same question—What should I do with my power?—which is the very question science says it cannot answer."

"So what will happen?" Ellie said.

Malcolm shrugged. "A change."

"What kind of change?"

"All major changes are like death," he said. "You can't see to the other side until you are there." And he closed his eyes.

"The poor man," Hammond said, shaking his head.

Malcolm sighed. "Do you have any idea," he said, "how unlikely it is that you, or any of us, will get off this island alive?"

SIXTH ITERATION

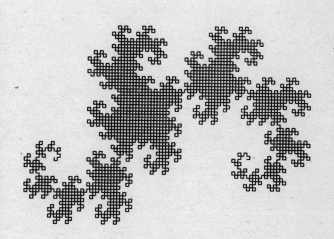

"System recovery may prove impossible."

IAN MALCOLM

SIXTH ITERATION

RETURN

Its electric motor whirring, the cart raced forward down the dark underground tunnel. Grant drove, his foot to the floor. The tunnel was featureless except for the occasional air vent above, shaded to protect against rainfall, and thus permitting little light to enter. But he noticed that there were crusty white animal droppings in many places. Obviously lots of animals had been in here.

Sitting beside him in the cart, Lex shone the flashlight to the back, where the velociraptor lay. "Why is it having trouble breathing?"

"Because I shot it with tranquilizer," he said.

"Is it going to die?" she said.

"I hope not."

"Why are we taking it?" Lex said.

"To prove to the people back at the center that the dinosaurs are really breeding," Grant said.

"How do you know they're breeding?"

"Because this one is young," Grant said. "And because it's a boy dinosaur."

"Is it?" Lex said, peering along the flashlight beam.

"Yes. Now shine that light forward, will you?" He held out his wrist, turning the watch to her. "What does it say?"

"It says . . . ten-fifteen."

"Okay."

Tim said, "That means we have only forty-five minutes to contact the boat."

"We should be close," Grant said. "I figure we should be almost to the visitor center right now." He wasn't sure, but he sensed the tunnel was gently tilting upward, leading them back to the surface, and—

"Wow!" Tim said.

317

They burst out into daylight with shocking speed. There was a light mist blowing, partially obscuring the building that loomed directly above them. Grant saw at once that it was the visitor center. They had arrived right in front of the garage!

"Yay!" Lex shouted. "We did it! Yay!" She bounced up and down in the seat as Grant parked the cart in the garage. Along one wall were stacked animal cages. They put the velociraptor in one, with a dish of water. Then they started climbing the stairs to the ground-floor entrance of the visitor center.

"I'm going to get a hamburger! And french fries! Chocolate milk shake! No more dinosaurs! Yay!" They came to the lobby, and they opened the door.

And they fell silent.

In the lobby of the visitor center, the glass doors had been shattered, and a cold gray mist blew through the cavernous main hall. A sign that read WHEN DINOSAURS RULED THE EARTH dangled from one hinge, creaking in the wind. The big tyrannosaur robot was upended and lay with its legs in the air, its tubing and metal innards exposed. Outside, through the glass, they saw rows of palm trees, shadowy shapes in the fog.

Tim and Lex huddled against the metal desk of the security guard. Grant took the guard's radio and tried all the channels. "Hello, this is Grant. Is anybody there? Hello, this is Grant."

Lex stared at the body of the guard, lying on the floor to the right. She couldn't see anything but his legs and feet.

"Hello, this is Grant. Hello."

Lex was leaning forward, peering around the edge of the desk. Grant grabbed her sleeve. "Hey. Stop that."

"Is he dead? What's that stuff on the floor? Blood?"

"Yes."

"How come it isn't real red?"

"You're morbid," Tim said.

"What's 'morbid'? I am not."

The radio crackled. "My God," came a voice. "Grant? Is that you?"

And then: "Alan? Alan?" It was Ellie.

"I'm here," Grant said.

"Thank God," Ellie said. "Are you all right?"

"I'm all right, yes."

"What about the kids? Have you seen them?"

"I have the kids with me," Grant said. "They're okay."

"Thank God."

Lex was crawling around the side of the desk. Grant slapped her ankle. "Get back here."

The radio crackled. "—n where are you?"

"In the lobby. In the lobby of the main building."

Over the radio, he heard Wu say, "My God. They're *here*."

"Alan, listen," Ellie said. "The raptors have gotten loose. They can open doors. They may be in the same building as you."

"Great. Where are you?" Grant said.

"We're in the lodge."

Grant said, "And the others? Muldoon, everybody else?"

"We've lost a few people. But we got everybody else over to the lodge."

"And are the telephones working?"

"No. The whole system is shut off. Nothing works."

"How do we get the system back on?"

"We've been trying."

"We have to get it back on," Grant said, "right away. If we don't, within half an hour the raptors will reach the mainland."

He started to explain about the boat when Muldoon cut him off. "I don't think you understand, Dr. Grant. We haven't got half an hour left, over here."

"How's that?"

"Some of the raptors followed us. We've got two on the roof now."

"So what? The building's impregnable."

Muldoon coughed. "Apparently not. It was never expected that animals would get up on the roof." The radio crackled. "—must have planted a tree too close to the fence. The raptors got over the fence, and onto the roof. Anyway, the steel bars on the skylight are supposed to be electrified, but of course the power's off. They're biting through the bars of the skylight."

Grant said, "Biting through the bars?" He frowned, trying to imagine it. "How fast?"

"Yes," Muldoon said, "they have a bite pressure of fifteen thousand pounds a square inch. They're like hyenas, they can bite through steel and—" The transmission was lost for a moment.

"How fast?" Grant said again.

Muldoon said, "I'd guess we've got another ten, fifteen minutes before they break through completely and come through the skylight into the building. And once they're in . . . Ah, just a minute, Dr. Grant."

The radio clicked off.

In the skylight above Malcolm's bed, the raptors had chewed through the first of the steel bars. One raptor gripped the end of the bar and tugged, pulling it back. It put its powerful hind limb on the skylight and the glass shattered, glittering down on Malcolm's bed below. Ellie reached over and removed the largest fragments from the sheets.

"God, they're ugly," Malcolm said, looking up.

Now that the glass was broken, they could hear the snorts and snarls of the raptors, the squeal of their teeth on the metal as they chewed the bars. There were silver thinned sections where they had chewed. Foamy saliva spattered onto the sheets, and the bedside table.

"At least they can't get in yet," Ellie said. "Not until they chew through another bar."

Wu said, "If Grant could somehow get to the maintenance shed . . ."

"Bloody hell," Muldoon said. He limped around the room on his sprained ankle. "He can't get there fast enough. He can't get the power on fast enough. Not to stop this."

Malcolm coughed. "Yes." His voice was soft, almost a wheeze.

"What'd he say?" Muldoon said.

"Yes," Malcolm repeated. "Can . . ."

"Can what?"

"Distraction . . ." He winced.

"What kind of a distraction?"

"Go to . . . the fence. . . ."

"Yes? And do what?"

Malcolm grinned weakly. "Stick . . . your hands through."

"Oh Christ," Muldoon said, turning away.

"Wait a minute," Wu said. "He's right. There are only two raptors here. Which means there are at least four more out there. We could go out and provide a distraction."

"And then what?"

"And then Grant would be free to go to the maintenance building and turn on the generator."

"And then go back to the control room and start up the system?"

"Exactly."

"No time," Muldoon said. "No time."

"But if we can lure the raptors down here," Wu said, "maybe even get them away from that skylight . . . It might work. Worth a try."

"Bait," Muldoon said.

"Exactly."

"Who's going to be the bait? I'm no good. My ankle's shot."

"I'll do it," Wu said.

"No," Muldoon said. "You're the only one who knows what to do about the computer. You need to talk Grant through the start-up."

"Then I'll do it," Harding said.

"No," Ellie said. "Malcolm needs you. I'll do it."

"Hell, I don't think so," Muldoon said. "You'd have raptors all around you, raptors on the roof. . . ."

But she was already bending over, lacing her running shoes. "Just don't tell Grant," she said. "It'll make him nervous."

The lobby was quiet, chilly fog drifting past them. The radio had been silent for several minutes. Tim said, "Why aren't they talking to us?"

"I'm hungry," Lex said.

"They're trying to plan," Grant said.

The radio crackled. "Grant, are you—nry Wu speaking. Are you there?"

"I'm here," Grant said.

"Listen," Wu said. "Can you see to the rear of the visitor building from where you are?"

Grant looked through the rear glass doors, to the palm trees and the fog.

"Yes," Grant said.

Wu said, "There's a path straight through the palm trees to the maintenance building. That's where the power equipment and generators are. I believe you saw the maintenance building yesterday?"

"Yes," Grant said. Though he was momentarily puzzled. Was

it yesterday that he had looked into the building? It seemed like years ago.

"Now, listen," Wu said. "We think we can get all the raptors down here by the lodge, but we aren't sure. So be careful. Give us five minutes."

"Okay," Grant said.

"You can leave the kids in the cafeteria, and they should be all right. Take the radio with you when you go."

"Okay."

"Turn it off before you leave, so it doesn't make any noise outside. And call me when you get to the maintenance building."

"Okay."

Grant turned the radio off. Lex crawled back. "Are we going to the cafeteria?" she said.

"Yes," Grant said. They got up, and started walking through the blowing mist in the lobby.

"I want a hamburger," Lex said.

"I don't think there's any electricity to cook with."

"Then ice cream."

"Tim, you'll have to stay with her and help her."

"I will."

"I've got to leave for a while," Grant said.

"I know."

They moved to the cafeteria entrance. On opening the door, Grant saw square dining-room tables and chairs, swinging stainless-steel doors beyond. Nearby, a cash register and a rack with gum and candy.

"Okay, kids. I want you to stay here no matter what. Got it?"

"Leave us the radio," Lex said.

"I can't. I need it. Just stay here. I'll only be gone about five minutes. Okay?"

"Okay."

Grant closed the door. The cafeteria became completely dark. Lex clutched his hand. "Turn on the lights," she said.

"I can't," Tim said. "There's no electricity." But he pulled down his night-vision goggles.

"That's fine for you. What about me?"

"Just hold my hand. We'll get some food." He led her forward. In phosphorescent green he saw the tables and chairs. To the right, the glowing green cash register, and the rack with gum and candy. He grabbed a handful of candy bars.

"I told you," Lex said. "I want ice cream, not candy."

"Take these anyway."

"Ice cream, Tim."

"Okay, okay."

Tim stuffed the candy bars in his pocket, and led Lex deeper into the dining room. She tugged on his hand. "I can't see *spit*," she said.

"Just walk with me. Hold my hand."

"Then slow down."

Beyond the tables and chairs was a pair of swinging doors with little round windows in them. They probably led to the kitchen. He pushed one door open and it held wide.

Ellie Sattler stepped outside the front door to the lodge, and felt the chilly mist on her face and legs. Her heart was thumping, even though she knew she was completely safe behind the fence. Directly ahead, she saw the heavy bars in the fog.

But she couldn't see much beyond the fence. Another twenty yards before the landscape turned milky white. And she didn't see any raptors at all. In fact, the gardens and trees were almost eerily silent. "Hey!" she shouted into the fog, tentatively.

Muldoon leaned against the door frame. "I doubt that'll do it," he said. "You've got to make a *noise*." He hobbled out carrying a steel rod from the construction inside. He banged the rod against the bars like a dinner gong. "Come and get it! Dinner is served!"

"Very amusing," Ellie said. She glanced nervously toward the roof. She saw no raptors.

"They don't understand English." Muldoon grinned. "But I imagine they get the general idea. . . ."

She was still nervous, and found his humor annoying. She looked toward the visitor building, cloaked in the fog. Muldoon resumed banging on the bars. At the limit of her vision, almost lost in the fog, she saw a ghostly pale animal. A raptor.

"First customer," Muldoon said.

The raptor disappeared, a white shadow, and then came back, but it did not approach any closer, and it seemed strangely incurious about the noise coming from the lodge. She was starting to worry. Unless she could attract the raptors to the lodge, Grant would be in danger.

"You're making too much noise," Ellie said.

"Bloody hell," Muldoon said.

"Well, you are."

"I know these animals—"

"You're drunk," she said. "Let me handle it."

"And how will you do that?"

She didn't answer him. She went to the gate. "They say the raptors are intelligent."

"They are. At least as intelligent as chimps."

"They have good hearing?"

"Yes, excellent."

"Maybe they'll know this sound," she said, and opened the gate. The metal hinges, rusted from the constant mist, creaked loudly. She closed it again, opened it with another creak.

She left it open.

"I wouldn't do that," Muldoon said. "You're going to do that, let me get the launcher."

"Get the launcher."

He sighed, remembering. "Gennaro has the shells."

"Well, then," she said. "Keep an eye out." And she went through the gate, stepping outside the bars. Her heart was pounding so hard she could barely feel her feet on the dirt. She moved away from the fence, and it disappeared frighteningly fast in the fog. Soon it was lost behind her.

Just as she expected, Muldoon began shouting to her in drunken agitation. "God damn it, girl, don't you do that," he bellowed.

"Don't call me 'girl,'" she shouted back.

"I'll call you any damn thing I want," Muldoon shouted.

She wasn't listening. She was turning slowly, her body tense, watching from all sides. She was at least twenty yards from the fence now, and she could see the mist drifting like a light rain past the foliage. She stayed away from the foliage. She moved through a world of shades of gray. The muscles in her legs and shoulders ached from the tension. Her eyes strained to see.

"Do you hear me, damn it?" Muldoon bellowed.

How good are these animals? she wondered. Good enough to cut off my retreat? There wasn't much distance back to the fence, not really—

They attacked.

There was no sound.

The first animal charged from the foliage at the base of a tree to the left. It sprang forward and she turned to run. The second attacked from the other side, clearly intending to catch her as she ran, and it leapt into the air, claws raised to attack, and she darted like a broken field runner, and the animal crashed down in the dirt. Now she was running flat out, not daring to look back, her breath coming in deep gasps, seeing the bars of the fence emerge from the haze, seeing Muldoon throw the gate wide, seeing him reaching for her, shouting to her, grabbing her arm and pulling her through so hard she was yanked off her feet and fell to the ground. And she turned in time to see first one, then two—then three—animals hit the fence and snarl.

"Good work," Muldoon shouted. He was taunting the animals now, snarling back, and it drove them wild. They flung themselves at the fence, leaping forward, and one of them nearly made it over the top. "Christ, that was close! These bastards can jump!"

She got to her feet, looking at the scrapes and bruises, the blood running down her leg. All she could think was: three animals here. And two on the roof. That meant one was still missing, somewhere.

"Come on, help me," Muldoon said. "Let's keep 'em interested!"

Grant left the visitor center and moved quickly forward, into the mist. He found the path among the palm trees and followed it north. Up ahead, the rectangular maintenance shed emerged from the fog.

There was no door that he could see at all. He walked on, around the corner. At the back, screened by planting, Grant saw a concrete loading dock for trucks. He scrambled up to face a vertical rolling door of corrugated steel; it was locked. He jumped down again and continued around the building. Farther ahead, to his right, Grant saw an ordinary door. It was propped open with a man's shoe.

Grant stepped inside and squinted in the darkness. He listened, heard nothing. He picked up his radio and turned it on.

"This is Grant," he said. "I'm inside."

Wu looked up at the skylight. The two raptors still peered down into Malcolm's room, but they seemed distracted by the noises outside. He went to the lodge window. Outside, the three velociraptors continued to charge the fence. Ellie was running back and forth, safely behind the bars. But the raptors no longer seemed to be seriously trying to get her. Now they almost seemed to be playing, circling back from the fence, rearing up and snarling, then dropping down low, to circle again and finally charge. Their behavior had taken on the distinct quality of display, rather than serious attack.

"Like birds," Muldoon said. "Putting on a show."

Wu nodded. "They're intelligent. They see they can't get her. They're not really trying."

The radio crackled. "—side."

Wu gripped the radio. "Say again, Dr. Grant?"

"I'm inside," Grant said.

"Dr. Grant, you're in the maintenance building?"

"Yes," Grant said. And he added, "Maybe you should call me Alan."

"All right, Alan. If you're standing just inside the east door, you see a lot of pipes and tubing." Wu closed his eyes, visualizing it. "Straight ahead is a big recessed well in the center of the building that goes two stories underground. To your left is a metal walkway with railings."

"I see it."

"Go along the walkway."

"I'm going." Faintly, the radio carried the clang of his footsteps on metal.

"After you go twenty or thirty feet, you will see another walkway going right."

"I see it," Grant said.

"Follow that walkway."

"Okay."

"As you continue," Wu said, "you will come to a ladder on your left. Going down into the pit."

"I see it."

"Go down the ladder."

There was a long pause. Wu ran his fingers through his damp hair. Muldoon frowned tensely.

"Okay, I'm down the ladder," Grant said.

"Good," Wu said. "Now, straight ahead of you should be two large yellow tanks that are marked 'Flammable.'"

"They say 'In-flammable.' And then something underneath. In Spanish."

"Those are the ones," Wu said. "Those are the two fuel tanks for the generator. One of them has been run dry, and so we have to switch over to the other. If you look at the bottom of the tanks, you'll see a white pipe coming out."

"Four-inch PVC?"

"Yes. PVC. Follow that pipe as it goes back."

"Okay. I'm following it. . . . *Ow!*"

"What happened?"

"Nothing. I hit my head."

There was a pause.

"Are you all right?"

"Yeah, fine. Just . . . hurt my head. Stupid."

"Keep following the pipe."

"Okay, okay," Grant said. He sounded irritable. "Okay. The pipe goes to a big aluminum box with air vents in the sides. Says 'Honda.' It looks like the generator."

"Yes," Wu said. "That's the generator. If you walk around to the side, you'll see a panel with two buttons."

"I see them. Yellow and red?"

"That's right," Wu said. "Press the yellow one first, and while you hold it down, press the red one."

"Right."

There was another pause. It lasted almost a minute. Wu and Muldoon looked at each other.

"Alan?"

"It didn't work," Grant said.

"Did you hold down the yellow first and then press the red?" Wu asked.

"Yes, I did," Grant said. He sounded annoyed. "I did exactly what you told me to do. There was a hum, and then a click, click, click, very fast, and then the hum stopped, and nothing after that."

"Try it again."

"I already did," Grant said. "It didn't work."

"Okay, just a minute." Wu frowned. "It sounds like the generator is trying to fire up but it can't for some reason. Alan?"

"I'm here."

"Go around to the back of the generator, to where the plastic pipe runs in."

"Okay." A pause; then Grant said, "The pipe goes into a round black cylinder that looks like a fuel pump."

"That's right," Wu said. "That's exactly what it is. It's the fuel pump. Look for a little valve at the top."

"A valve?"

"It should be sticking up at the top, with a little metal tab that you can turn."

"I found it. But it's on the side, not the top."

"Okay. Twist it open."

"Air is coming out."

"Good. Wait until—"

"—now liquid is coming out. It smells like gas."

"Okay. Close the valve." Wu turned to Muldoon, shaking his head. "Pump lost its prime. Alan?"

"Yes."

"Try the buttons again."

A moment later, Wu heard the faint coughing and sputtering as the generator turned over, and then the steady chugging sound as it caught. "It's on," Grant said.

"Good work, Alan! Good work!"

"Now what?" Grant said. He sounded flat, dull. "The lights haven't even come on in here."

"Go back to the control room, and I'll talk you through restoring the systems manually."

"That's what I have to do now?"

"Yes."

"Okay," Grant said. "I'll call you when I get there."

There was a final hiss, and silence.

"Alan?"

The radio was dead.

Tim went through the swinging doors at the back of the dining room and entered the kitchen. A big stainless-steel table in the center of the room, a big stove with lots of burners to the left, and, beyond that, big walk-in refrigerators. Tim started opening the refrigerators, looking for ice cream. Smoke came out in the humid air as he opened each one.

"How come the stove is on?" Lex said, releasing his hand.

"It's not on."

"They all have little blue flames."

"Those're pilot lights."

"What're pilot lights?" They had an electric stove at home.

"Never mind," Tim said, opening another refrigerator. "But it means I can cook you something." In this next refrigerator, he found all kinds of stuff, cartons of milk, and piles of vegetables, and a stack of T-bone steaks, fish—but no ice cream.

"You still want ice cream?"

"I told you, didn't I?"

The next refrigerator was huge. A stainless-steel door, with a wide horizontal handle. He tugged on the handle, pulled it open, and saw a walk-in freezer. It was a whole room, and it was freezing cold.

"Timmy . . ."

"Will you wait a minute?" he said, annoyed. "I'm trying to find your ice cream."

"Timmy . . . *something's here.*"

She was whispering, and for a moment the last two words didn't register. Then Tim hurried back out of the freezer, seeing the edge of the door wreathed in glowing green smoke. Lex stood by the steel worktable. She was looking back to the kitchen door.

He heard a low hissing sound, like a very large snake. The sound rose and fell softly. It was hardly audible. It might even be the wind, but he somehow knew it wasn't.

"Timmy," she whispered, "I'm scared. . . ."

He crept forward to the kitchen door and looked out.

In the darkened dining room, he saw the orderly green rectangular pattern of the tabletops. And moving smoothly among them, silent as a ghost except for the hissing of its breath, was a velociraptor.

In the darkness of the maintenance room, Grant felt along the pipes, moving back toward the ladder. It was difficult to make his way in the dark, and somehow he found the noise of the generator disorienting. He came to the ladder, and had started back up when he realized there was something else in the room besides generator noise.

Grant paused, listening.

It was a man shouting.

It sounded like Gennaro.

"Where are you?" Grant shouted.

"Over *here*," Gennaro said. "In the truck."

Grant couldn't see any truck. He squinted in the darkness. He looked out of the corner of his eye. He saw green glowing shapes, moving in the darkness. Then he saw the truck, and he turned toward it.

Tim found the silence chilling.

The velociraptor was six feet tall, and powerfully built, although its strong legs and tail were hidden by the tables. Tim could see only the muscular upper torso, the two forearms held tightly alongside the body, the claws dangling. He could see the iridescent speckled pattern on the back. The velociraptor was alert; as it came forward, it looked from side to side, moving its head with abrupt, bird-like jerks. The head also bobbed up and down as it walked, and the long straight tail dipped, which heightened the impression of a bird.

A gigantic, silent bird of prey.

The dining room was dark, but apparently the raptor could see well enough to move steadily forward. From time to time, it would bend over, lowering its head below the tables. Tim heard a rapid sniffing sound. Then the head would snap up, alertly, jerking back and forth like a bird's.

Tim watched until he was sure the velociraptor was coming toward the kitchen. Was it following their scent? All the books said dinosaurs had a poor sense of smell, but this one seemed to do just fine. Anyway, what did books know? Here was the real thing.

Coming toward him.

He ducked back into the kitchen.

"Is something out there?" Lex said.

Tim didn't answer. He pushed her under a table in the corner, behind a large waste bin. He leaned close to her and whispered fiercely: *"Stay here!"* And then he ran for the refrigerator.

He grabbed a handful of cold steaks and hurried back to the door. He quietly placed the first of the steaks on the floor, then moved back a few steps, and put down the second. . . .

Through his goggles, he saw Lex peeping around the bin. He waved her back. He placed the third steak, and the fourth, moving deeper into the kitchen.

The hissing was louder, and then the clawed hand gripped the door, and the big head peered cautiously around.

The velociraptor paused at the entrance to the kitchen.

Tim stood in a half-crouch at the back of the room, near the far leg of the steel worktable. But he had not had time to conceal himself; his head and shoulders still protruded over the tabletop. He was in clear view of the velociraptor.

Slowly, Tim lowered his body, sinking beneath the table. . . . The velociraptor jerked its head around, looking directly at Tim.

Tim froze. He was still exposed, but he thought, *Don't move.*

The velociraptor stood motionless in the doorway.

Sniffing.

It's darker here, Tim thought. He can't see so well. It's making him cautious.

But now he could smell the musty odor of the big reptile, and through his goggles he saw the dinosaur silently yawn, throwing back its long snout, exposing rows of razor-sharp teeth. The velociraptor stared forward again, jerking its head from side to side. The big eyes swiveled in the bony sockets.

Tim felt his heart pounding. Somehow it was worse to be confronted by an animal like this in a kitchen, instead of the open forest. The size, the quick movements, the pungent odor, the hissing breath . . .

Up close, it was a much more frightening animal than the tyrannosaur. The tyrannosaur was huge and powerful, but it wasn't especially smart. The velociraptor was man-size, and it was clearly quick and intelligent; Tim feared the searching eyes almost as much as the sharp teeth.

The velociraptor sniffed. It stepped forward—moving directly toward Lex! It must smell her, somehow! Tim's heart thumped.

The velociraptor stopped. It bent over slowly.

He's found the steak.

Tim wanted to bend down, to look below the table, but he didn't dare move. He stood frozen in a half-crouch, listening to the crunching sound. The dinosaur was eating it. Bones and all.

The raptor raised its slender head, and looked around. It sniffed. It saw the second steak. It moved quickly forward. It bent down.

Silence.

The raptor didn't eat it.

The head came back up. Tim's legs burned from the crouch, but he didn't move.

Why hadn't the animal eaten the second steak? A dozen ideas flashed through his mind—it didn't like the taste of beef, it didn't like the coldness, it didn't like the fact that the meat wasn't alive, it smelled a trap, it smelled Lex, it smelled Tim, it saw Tim—

The velociraptor moved very quickly now. It found the third steak, dipped its head, looked up again, and moved on.

Tim held his breath. The dinosaur was now just a few feet from him. Tim could see the small twitches in the muscles of the flanks. He could see the crusted blood on the claws of the hand. He could see the fine pattern of striations within the spotted pattern, and the folds of skin in the neck below the jaw.

The velociraptor sniffed. It jerked its head, and looked right at Tim. Tim nearly gasped with fright. Tim's body was rigid, tense. He watched as the reptile eye moved, scanning the room. Another sniff.

He's got me, Tim thought.

Then the head jerked back to look forward, and the animal went on, toward the fifth steak. Tim thought, Lex please don't move please don't move whatever you do please don't . . .

The velociraptor sniffed the steak, and moved on. It was now at the open door to the freezer. Tim could see the smoke billowing out, curling along the floor toward the animal's feet. One big clawed foot lifted, then came down again, silently. The dinosaur hesitated. Too cold, Tim thought. He won't go in there, it's too cold, he won't go in he won't go in he won't go in. . . .

The dinosaur went in.

The head disappeared, then the body, then the stiff tail.

Tim sprinted, flinging his weight against the stainless-steel door of the locker, slamming it shut. It slammed on the tip of the tail! The door wouldn't shut! The velociraptor roared, a terrifying loud sound. Inadvertently, Tim took a step back—the tail was gone! He slammed the door shut and heard it click! Closed!

"Lex! Lex!" he was screaming. He heard the raptor pounding against the door, felt it thumping the steel. He knew there was a flat steel knob inside, and if the raptor hit that, it would knock the door open. They had to get the door locked. "Lex!"

Lex was by his side. "What do you want!"

Tim leaned against the horizontal door handle, holding it shut. "There's a pin! A little pin! Get the pin!"

The velociraptor roared like a lion, the sound muffled by the thick steel. It crashed its whole body against the door.

"I can't see anything!" Lex shouted.

The pin was dangling beneath the door handle, swinging on a little metal chain. "It's right there!"

"I can't see it!" she screamed, and then Tim realized she wasn't wearing the goggles.

"Feel for it!"

He saw her little hand reaching up, touching his, groping for the pin, and with her so close to him he could feel how frightened she was, her breath in little panicky gasps as she felt for the pin, and the velociraptor slammed against the door and it opened—God, *it opened*—but the animal hadn't expected that and had already turned back for another try and Tim slammed the door shut again. Lex scrambled back, reached up in the darkness.

"I have it!" Lex cried, clutching the pin in her hand, and she pushed it through the hole. It slid out again.

"From the top, put it in *from the top*!"

She held it again, lifting it on the chain, swinging it over the handle, and down. Into the hole.

Locked.

The velociraptor roared. Tim and Lex stepped back from the door as the dinosaur slammed into it again. With each impact, the heavy steel wall hinges creaked, but they held. Tim didn't think the animal could possibly open the door.

The raptor was locked in.

He gave a long sigh. "Let's go," he said.

He took her hand, and they ran.

"You should have seen them," Gennaro said, as Grant led him back out of the maintenance building. "There must have been two dozen of them. Compys. I had to crawl into the truck to get away from them. They were all over the windshield. Just squatting there, waiting like buzzards. But they ran away when you came over."

"Scavengers," Grant said. "They won't attack anything that's moving or looks strong. They attack things that are dead, or almost dead. Anyway, unmoving."

They were going up the ladder now, back toward the entrance door. "What happened to the raptor that attacked you?" Grant said.

"I don't know," Gennaro said.

"Did it leave?"

"I didn't see. I got away, I think because it was injured. I think Muldoon shot it in the leg and it was bleeding while it was in here.

Then . . . I don't know. Maybe it went back outside. Maybe it died in here. I didn't see."

"And maybe it's still in here," Grant said.

Wu stared out the lodge window at the raptors beyond the fence. They still seemed playful, making mock attacks at Ellie. The behavior had continued for a long time now, and it occurred to him that it might be too long. It almost seemed as if they were trying to keep Ellie's attention, in the same way that she was trying to keep theirs.

The behavior of the dinosaurs had always been a minor consideration for Wu. And rightly so: behavior was a second-order effect of DNA, like protein enfolding. You couldn't really predict behavior, and you couldn't really control it, except in very crude ways, like making an animal dependent on a dietary substance by withholding an enzyme. But, in general, behavioral effects were simply beyond the reach of understanding. You couldn't look at a DNA sequence and predict behavior. It was impossible.

And that had made Wu's DNA work purely empirical. It was a matter of tinkering, the way a modern workman might repair an antique grandfather clock. You were dealing with something out of the past, something constructed of ancient materials and following ancient rules. You couldn't be certain why it worked as it did; and it had been repaired and modified many times already, by forces of evolution, over eons of time. So, like the workman who makes an adjustment and then sees if the clock runs any better, Wu would make an adjustment and then see if the animals behaved any better. And he only tried to correct gross behavior: uncontrolled butting of the electrical fences, or rubbing the skin raw on tree trunks. Those were the behaviors that sent him back to the drawing board.

And the limits of his science had left him with a mysterious feeling about the dinosaurs in the park. He was never sure, never really sure at all, whether the behavior of the animals was historically accurate or not. Were they behaving as they really had in the past? It was an open question, ultimately unanswerable.

And though Wu would never admit it, the discovery that the dinosaurs were breeding represented a tremendous validation of his work. A breeding animal was demonstrably effective in a fundamental way; it implied that Wu had put all the pieces together correctly. He had re-created an animal millions of years old, with such precision that the creature could even reproduce itself.

But, still, looking at the raptors outside, he was troubled by the persistence of their behavior. Raptors were intelligent, and intelligent animals got bored quickly. Intelligent animals also formed plans, and—

Harding came out into the hallway from Malcolm's room. "Where's Ellie?"

"Still outside."

"Better get her in. The raptors have left the skylight."

"When?" Wu said, moving to the door.

"Just a moment ago," Harding said.

Wu threw open the front door. "Ellie! Inside, now!"

She looked over at him, puzzled. "There's no problem, everything's under control. . . ."

"Now!"

She shook her head. "I know what I'm doing," she said.

"Now, Ellie, damn it!"

Muldoon didn't like Wu standing there with the door open, and he was about to say so, when he saw a shadow descend from above, and he realized at once what had happened. Wu was yanked bodily out the door, and Muldoon heard Ellie screaming. Muldoon got to the door and looked out and saw that Wu was lying on his back, his body already torn open by the big claw, and the raptor was jerking its head, tugging at Wu's intestines even though Wu was still alive, still feebly reaching up with his hands to push the big head away, he was being eaten while he was still alive, and then Ellie stopped screaming and started to run along the inside of the fence, and Muldoon slammed the door shut, dizzy with horror. It had happened so fast!

Harding said, "He jumped down from the roof?"

Muldoon nodded. He went to the window and looked out, and he saw that the three raptors outside the fence were now running away. But they weren't following Ellie.

They were going back, toward the visitor center.

Grant came to the edge of the maintenance building and peered forward, in the fog. He could hear the snarls of the raptors, and they seemed to be coming closer. Now he could see their bodies running past him. They were going to the visitor center.

He looked back at Gennaro.

Gennaro shook his head, no.

Grant leaned close and whispered in his ear. "No choice. We've got to turn on the computer."

Grant set out in the fog.

After a moment, Gennaro followed.

Ellie didn't stop to think. When the raptors dropped inside the fence to attack Wu, she just turned and ran, as fast as she could, toward the far end of the lodge. There was a space fifteen feet wide between the fence and the lodge. She ran, not hearing the animals pursuing her, just hearing her own breath. She rounded the corner, saw a tree growing by the side of the building, and leapt, grabbing a branch, swinging up. She didn't feel panic. She felt a kind of exhilaration as she kicked and saw her legs rise up in front of her face, and she hooked her legs over a branch farther up, tightened her gut, and pulled up quickly.

She was already twelve feet off the ground, and the raptors still weren't following her, and she was beginning to feel pretty good, when she saw the first animal at the base of the tree. Its mouth was bloody, and bits of stringy flesh hung from its jaws. She continued to go up fast, hand over hand, just reaching and going, and she could almost see the top of the building. She looked down again.

The two raptors were climbing the tree.

Now she was at the level of the rooftop, she could see the gravel only four feet away, and the glass pyramids of the skylights, sticking up in the mist. There was a door on the roof; she could get inside. In a single heaving effort she flung herself through the air, and landed sprawling on the gravel. She scraped her face, but somehow the only sensation was exhilaration, as if it were a kind of game she was playing, a game she intended to win. She ran for the door that led to the stairwell. Behind her, she could hear the raptors shaking the branches of the tree. They were still in the tree.

She reached the door, and twisted the knob.

The door was locked.

It took a moment for the meaning of that to cut through her euphoria. The door was locked. She was on the roof and she couldn't get down. *The door was locked.*

She pounded on the door in frustration, and then she ran for the far side of the roof, hoping to see a way down, but there was only the green outline of the swimming pool through the blowing mist. All around the pool was concrete decking. Ten, twelve feet of concrete. Too much for her to jump across. No other trees to climb down. No stairs. No fire escape.

Nothing.

Ellie turned back, and saw the raptors jumping easily to the roof. She ran to the far end of the building, hoping there might be another door there, but there wasn't.

The raptors came slowly toward her, stalking her, slipping silently among the glass pyramids. She looked down. The edge of the pool was ten feet away.

Too far.

The raptors were closer, starting to move apart, and illogically she thought: *Isn't this always the way? Some little mistake screws it all up.* She still felt giddy, still felt exhilaration, and she somehow couldn't believe these animals were going to get her, she couldn't believe that now her life was going to end like this. It didn't seem possible. She was enveloped in a kind of protective cheerfulness. She just didn't believe it would happen.

The raptors snarled. Ellie backed away, moving to the far end of the roof. She took a breath, and then began to sprint toward the edge. As she raced toward the edge, she saw the swimming pool, and she knew it was too far away but she thought, *What the hell,* and leapt into space.

And fell.

And with a stinging shock, she felt herself enveloped in coldness. She was underwater. She had done it! She came to the surface and looked up at the roof, and saw the raptors looking down at her. And she knew that, if she could do it, the raptors could do it, too. She splashed in the water and thought, *Can raptors swim?* But she was sure they could. They could probably swim like crocodiles.

The raptors turned away from the edge of the roof. And then she heard Harding calling "Sattler?" and she realized he had opened the roof door. The raptors were going toward him.

Hurriedly, she climbed out of the pool and ran toward the lodge.

Harding had gone up the steps to the roof two at a time, and he had flung open the door without thinking. "Sattler!" he shouted. And then he stopped. Mist blew among the pyramids on the roof. The raptors were not in sight.

"Sattler!"

He was so preoccupied with Sattler that it was a moment before he realized his mistake. He should be able to see the animals, he thought. In the next instant the clawed forearm smashed around the side of the door, catching him in the chest with a tearing pain, and it took all of his effort to pull himself backward and close the door on the arm, and from downstairs he heard Muldoon shouting, "She's here, she's already inside."

From the other side of the door, the raptor snarled, and Harding slammed the door again, and the claws pulled back, and he closed the door with a metallic clang and sank coughing to the floor.

"Where are we going?" Lex said. They were on the second floor of the visitor center. A glass-walled corridor ran the length of the building.

"To the control room," Tim said.

"Where's that?"

"Down here someplace." Tim looked at the names stenciled on the doors as he went past them. These seemed to be offices: PARK WARDEN ... GUEST SERVICES ... GENERAL MANAGER ... COMPTROLLER ...

They came to a glass partition marked with a sign:

CLOSED AREA
AUTHORIZED PERSONNEL ONLY
BEYOND THIS POINT

There was a slot for a security card, but Tim just pushed the door open.

"How come it opened?"

"The power is out," Tim said.

"Why're we going to the control room?" she asked.

"To find a radio. We need to call somebody."

Beyond the glass door the hallway continued. Tim remembered this area; he had seen it earlier, during the tour. Lex trotted along at his side. In the distance, they heard the snarling of raptors. The animals seemed to be approaching. Then Tim heard them slamming against the glass downstairs.

"They're out there ..." Lex whispered.

"Don't worry."

"What are they doing here?" Lex said.

"Never mind now."

ad a row of function keys at the top, just like a regular PC
rd, and the monitor was big and in color. But the monitor
g was sort of unusual. Tim looked at the edges of the screen
w lots of faint pinpoints of red light.

light, all around the borders of the screen . . . What could that
e moved his finger toward the light and saw the soft red glow
skin.

touched the screen and heard a beep.

A moment later, the message box disappeared, and the original
screen flashed back up.

"What happened?" Lex said. "What did you do? You touched
something."

Of course! he thought. He had touched the screen. It was a touch
screen! The red lights around the edges must be infrared sensors.
Tim had never seen such a screen, but he'd read about them in maga-
ines. He touched RESET/REVERT.

Instantly the screen changed. He got a new message:

THE COMPUTER IS NOW RESET
MAKE YOUR SELECTION FROM THE MAIN SCREEN

ver the radio, they heard the sound of raptors snarling. "I want to
Lex said. "You should try VIEW."
o, Lex."

PARK SUPERVISOR . . . OPERATIONS . . . MAIN CONTROL . . .

"Here," Tim said. He pushed open the door. The main control
room was as he had seen it before. In the center of the room was a
console with four chairs and four computer monitors. The room was
entirely dark except for the monitors, which all showed a series of
colored rectangles.

"So where's a radio?" Lex said.

But Tim had forgotten all about a radio. He moved forward,
staring at the computer screens. The screens were on! That could
only mean—

"The power must be back on. . . ."

"Ick," Lex said, shifting her body.

"What."

"I was standing on somebody's *ear*," she said.

Tim hadn't seen a body when they came in. He looked back and
saw there was just an ear, lying on the floor.

"That is really disgusting," Lex said.

"Never mind." He turned to the monitors.

"Where's the rest of him?" she said.

"Never mind that now."

He peered closely at the monitor. There were rows of colored
labels on the screen:

"You better not fool around with that, Timmy," she said.

"Don't worry, I won't."

He had seen complicated computers before, like the ones that were installed in the buildings his father worked on. Those computers controlled everything from the elevators and security to the heating and cooling systems. They looked basically like this—a lot of colored labels—but they were usually simpler to understand. And almost always there was a help label, if you needed to learn about the system. But he saw no help label here. He looked again, to be sure.

But then he saw something else: numerals clicking in the upper left corner of the screen. They read 10:47:22. Then Tim realized it was the time. There were only thirteen minutes left for the boat—but he was more worried about the people in the lodge.

There was a static crackle. He turned, and saw Lex holding a radio. She was twisting the knobs and dials. "How does it work?" she said. "I can't make it work."

"Give me that!"

"It's mine! I found it!"

"Give it to me, Lex!"

"I get to use it first!"

"Lex!"

Suddenly, the radio crackled. *"What the hell is going on!"* said Muldoon's voice.

Surprised, Lex dropped the radio on the floor.

Grant ducked back, crouching among the palm trees. Through the mist ahead he could see the raptors hopping and snarling and butting their heads against the glass of the visitor center. But, between snarls, they would fall silent and cock their heads, as if listening to something distant. And then they would make little whimpering sounds.

"What're they doing?" Gennaro said.

"It looks like they're trying to get into the cafeteria," Grant said.

"What's in the cafeteria?"

"I left the kids there . . ." Grant said.

"Can they break through that glass?"

"I don't think so, no."

Grant watched, and now he heard the crackle of a distant radio, and the raptors began hopping in a more agitated way. One after another, they began jumping higher and higher, until finally he saw

the first of them leap lightly onto the second-floor [...] there move inside the second floor of the visitor cen[...]

In the control room on the second floor, Tim snatch[...] which Lex had dropped. He pressed the button. "Hell[...]

"—s that you, Tim?" It was Muldoon's voice.

"It's me, yes."

"Where are you?"

"In the control room. The power is on!"

"That's great, Tim," Muldoon said.

"If someone will tell me how to turn the comput[...] do it."

There was a silence.

"Hello?" Tim said. "Did you hear me?"

"Ah, we have a problem about that," Muldoon sai[...] body, ah, who is here knows how to do that. How to t[...] computer on."

Tim said, "What, are you kidding? Nobody knows?" It se[...] incredible.

"No." A pause. "I think it's something about the main g[...] Turning on the main grid . . . You know anything about com+ puters, Tim?"

Tim stared at the screen. Lex nudged him. "Tell him no, Timmy," she said.

"Yes, some. I know something," Tim said.

"Might as well try," Muldoon said. "Nobody here knows what to do. And Grant doesn't know about computers."

"Okay," Tim said. "I'll try." He clicked off the radio and stared[...] the screen, studying it.

"Timmy," Lex said. "You don't know what to do."

"Yes I do."

"If you know, then do it," Lex said.

"Just a minute." As a way to get started, he pulled the chai[...] to the keyboard and pressed the cursor keys. Those were t[...] that moved the cursor around on the screen. But nothing h[...] Then he pushed other keys. The screen remained unchang[...]

"Well?" she said.

"Something's wrong," Tim said, frowning.

"You just don't know, Timmy," she said.

He examined the computer again, looking at it care[...]

"Well, I want VIEW," she said. And before he could grab her hand, she had pressed VIEW. The screen changed.

SUBROUTINES – VIEW VIDEO INTERFACE ENVIRONMENTAL WATCH			
REMOTE CLC VIDEO – H			**REMOTE CLC VIDEO – P**
Monitor Interval	Set	Hold	Monitor Interval
Monitor Control	Auto	Man	Monitor Control
Optimize Sequence Rotation	AO(19)	DD(33)	Optimize Sequence Rotation
Specify Remote Camera	Command Sequence		RGB Image Parameters

"Uh-oh," she said.

"Lex, will you cut it out?"

"Look!" she said. "It worked! Ha!"

Around the room, the monitors showed quickly changing views of different parts of the park. Most of the images were misty gray, because of the exterior fog, but one showed the outside of the lodge, with a raptor on the roof, and then another switched to an image in bright sunlight, showing the bow of a ship, bright sunlight—

"What was that?" Tim said, leaning forward.

"What?"

"That picture!"

But the image had already changed, and now they were seeing the inside of the lodge, one room after another, and then he saw Malcolm, lying in a bed—

"Stop it," Lex said. "I see them!"

Tim touched the screen in several places, and got submenus. Then more submenus.

"Wait," Lex said. "You're confusing it. . . ."

"Will you shut up! You don't know anything about computers!"

Now he had a list of monitors on the screen. One of them was marked Safari Lodge: LV2–4. Another was REMOTE: SHIPBOARD (VND). He pressed the screen several times.

Video images came up on monitors around the room. One showed the bow of the supply ship, and the ocean ahead. In the distance, Tim saw land—buildings along a shore, and a harbor. He recognized the harbor because he had flown over it in the helicopter the day before. It was Puntarenas. The ship seemed to be just minutes from landing.

But his attention was drawn by the next screen, which showed the roof of the safari lodge, in gray mist. The raptors were mostly hidden behind the pyramids, but their heads bobbed up and down, coming into view.

And then, on the third monitor, he could see inside a room. Malcolm was lying in a bed, and Ellie stood next to him. They were both looking upward. As they watched, Muldoon walked into the room, and joined them, looking up with an expression of concern.

"They see us," Lex said.

"I don't think so."

The radio crackled. On the screen, Muldoon lifted the radio to his lips. "Hello, Tim?"

"I'm here," Tim said.

"Ah, we haven't got a whole lot of time," Muldoon said, dully. "Better get that power grid on." And then Tim heard the raptors snarl, and saw one of the long heads duck down through the glass, briefly entering the picture from the top, snapping its jaws.

"Hurry, Timmy!" Lex said. "Get the power on!"

THE GRID

Tim suddenly found himself lost in a tangled series of monitor control screens, as he tried to get back to the main screen. Most systems had a single button or a single command to return to the previous screen, or to the main menu. But this system did not—or at least he didn't know it. Also, he was certain that help commands had been built into the system, but he couldn't find them either, and Lex was jumping up and down and shouting in his ear, making him nervous.

Finally he got the main screen back. He wasn't sure what he had done, but it was back. He paused, looking for a command.

"Do something, Timmy!"

"Will you shut up? I'm trying to get help." He pushed TEMPLATE-MAIN. The screen filled with a complicated diagram, with interconnecting boxes and arrows.

No good. No good.

He pushed COMMON INTERFACE. The screen shifted:

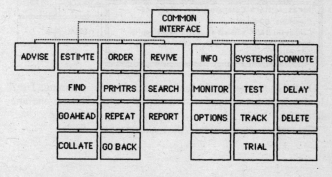

"What's that?" Lex said. "Why aren't you turning on the power, Timmy?"

He ignored her. Maybe help on this system was called "info." He pushed INFO.

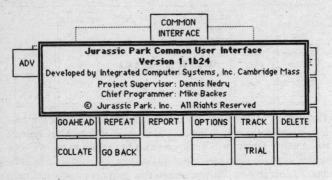

"Tim-ee," Lex wailed, but he had already pushed FIND. He got another useless window. He pushed GO BACK.

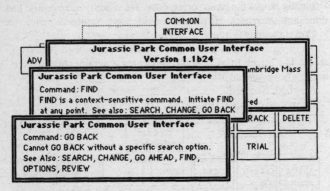

On the radio, he heard Muldoon say, "How's it coming, Tim?" He didn't bother to answer. Frantic, he pushed buttons one after another.

Suddenly, without warning, the main screen was back.

```
┌─────────────────────────────────────────────────────┐
│         JURASSIC PARK - SYSTEM STARTUP                │
└─────────────────────────────────────────────────────┘
```

| | | | STARTUP AB(0) | | | STARTUP CN/D | |

Security Main	Monitor Main	Command Main	Electrical Main	Hydraulic Main	Master Main	Zoolog Main
SetGrids DNL	View VBB	Access TNL	Heating Cooling	Door Fold Interface	SAAG-Rnd	Repair Storage
Critical Locks	TeleCom VBB	Reset Revert	Emgency Illumin	GAS/VLD Main II	Common Interface	Status Main
Control Passthru	TeleCom RSD	Template Main	FNCC Params	Explosion Fire Hzd	Schematic Main	Safety/ Health

He studied the screen. ELECTRICAL MAIN and SETGRIDS DNL both looked like they might have something to do with grids. He noticed that SAFETY/HEALTH and CRITICAL LOCKS might be important, too. He heard the growl of the raptors. He had to make a choice. He pressed SETGRIDS DNL, and groaned when he saw it:

```
┌─────────────────┐
│   SET GRIDS DNL  │
└─────────────────┘
```

CUSTOM PARAMETERS		STANDARD PARAMETERS			
ELECTRICAL SECONDARY (H)					
MAIN GRID LEVEL	A4	B4	C7	D4	E9
MAIN GRID LEVEL	C9	R5	D5	E3	G4
ELECTRICAL SECONDARY (P)					
MAIN GRID LEVEL	A2	B3	C6	D11	E2
MAIN GRID LEVEL	C9	R5	D5	E3	G4
MAIN GRID LEVEL	A8	B1	C8	D8	E8
MAIN GRID LEVEL	P4	R8	P4	E5	L6
ELECTRICAL SECONDARY (M)					
MAIN GRID LEVEL	A1	B1	C1	D2	E2
MAIN GRID LEVEL	C4	R4	D4	E5	G6

He didn't know what to do. He pushed STANDARD PARAMETERS.

STANDARD PARAMETERS

Park Grids	B4-C6	Outer Grids	C2-D2
Zoological Grids	BB-07	Pen Grids	R4-R4
Lodge Grids	F4-D4	Maint Grids	E5-L6
Main Grids	C4-G7	Sensor Grids	D5-G4
Utility Grids	AH-B5	Core Grids	A1-C1

Circuit Integrity Not Tested
Security Grids Remain Automatic

Tim shook his head in frustration. It took him a moment to realize that he had just gotten valuable information. He now knew the grid coordinates for the lodge! He pushed grid F4.

POWER GRID F4 (SAFARI LODGE)

COMMAND CANNOT BE EXECUTED. ERROR-505

(Power Incompatible with Command Error.

Ref Manual Pages 4.09–4.11)

"It's not working," Lex said.
"I know!" He pushed another button. The screen flashed again.

POWER GRID F4 (SAFARI LODGE)

COMMAND CANNOT BE EXECUTED. ERROR-505

(Power Incompatible with Command Error.

Ref Manual Pages 4.09–4.11)

Tim tried to stay calm, to think it through. For some reason he was getting a consistent error message whenever he tried to turn on a grid. It was saying the power was incompatible with the command he was giving. But what did that mean? Why was power incompatible?

"Timmy . . ." Lex said, tugging at his arm.

"Not *now*, Lex."

"*Yes, now,*" she said, and she pulled him away from the screen and the console. And then he heard the snarling of raptors.

It was coming from the hallway.

INTERNATIONAL ACCLAIM FOR

Mission Earth

"An incredibly good story, lushly written, vibrating with action and excitement, a gem."
— A.E. van Vogt

"You will lose sleep, you will miss appointments. . . if you don't force yourself to put it down. . . "
— Orson Scott Card

". . . a big, humorous tale of interstellar intrigue in the classical mold. I fully enjoyed it."
— Roger Zelazny

". . . fantastic adventure, beats like a strong pulse."
— The Book World

This book follows
MISSION EARTH
Volume 1
THE INVADERS PLAN
Buy it and read it first!

Caucasus Mountains

USSR

Samsun

Trabzon

Erzum •

Mount Ararat •

Iran

T U R K E Y

Diyarbakir •

Ufra •

Iraq

Syria

Monte Farnwell

NOT TRUE!

Blito-P3 (Earth)

Turkey

Plotted by 54 Charlee Nine

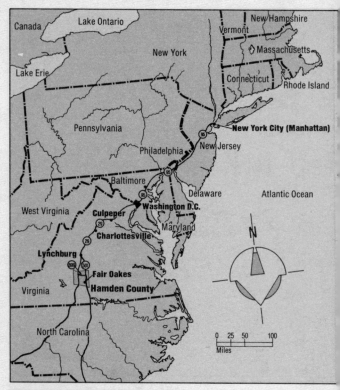

Eastern United States and

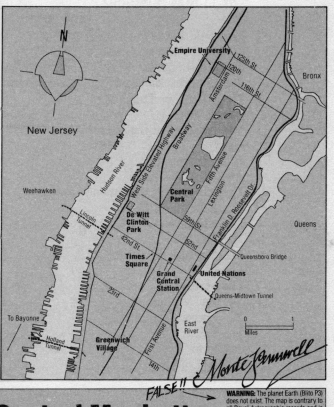

N

New Jersey

Empire University

125th St

120th

116th St

Bronx

Amsterdam

Broadway

West Side Elevated Highway

Hudson River

Central Park

Fifth Avenue

Lexington

Franklin D. Roosevelt Dr.

Weehawken

Lincoln Tunnel

De Witt Clinton Park

59th St

42nd St

62nd

Queens

Queensboro Bridge

Times Square

Grand Central Station

United Nations

Queens-Midtown Tunnel

To Bayonne

23rd

0   1
Miles

Holland Tunnel

Greenwich Village

First Avenue

14th

East River

Monte Farnwell

FALSE!! ←

Central Manhattan

AMONG THE MANY CLASSIC WORKS
BY L. RON HUBBARD

Battlefield Earth
Beyond the Black Nebula
Buckskin Brigades
The Conquest of Space
The Dangerous Dimension
Death's Deputy
The Emperor of the Universe
Fear
Final Blackout
Forbidden Voyage
The Incredible Destination
The Kilkenny Cats
The Kingslayer
The Last Admiral
The Magnificent Failure
The Masters of Sleep
The Mutineers
Ole Doc Methuselah
Ole Mother Methuselah
The Rebels
Return to Tomorrow
Slaves of Sleep
To The Stars
The Traitor
Triton
Typewriter in the Sky
The Ultimate Adventure
The Unwilling Hero

Mission Earth

Black Genesis

THE BOOKS OF THE
MISSION EARTH DEKALOGY*

* *Dekalogy—a group of ten volumes.*

L. RON HUBBARD

Mission Earth

VOLUME TWO

Black Genesis

BRIDGE PUBLICATIONS, INC.
LOS ANGELES

MISSION EARTH: BLACK GENESIS
© 1986, 1988, 1998, 2001 L. Ron Hubbard Library.
Cover Art: Gerry Grace
Cover artwork: © 1988 L. Ron Hubbard Library
All rights reserved.
Printed in the United States of America.

Lyrics to the musical composition "St. James Infirmary" (also
known as "Gamblers Blues") is used with the permission of the
owner, © 1930 and renewed 1957 by Denton & Haskins
Corporation.

"Sing Sing Prison Blues" by Porter Grainger and Freddie
Johnson. © 1925 by MCA Music, a division of MCA
Incorporated, NYC. Copyright renewed. Used by permission.
All rights reserved.

The words MISSION EARTH, the MISSION EARTH logo and WRITERS
OF THE FUTURE are registered trademarks owned by L. Ron
Hubbard Library. BATTLEFIELD EARTH is a registered trademark
owned by Author Services, Inc. and is used with its permission.

ISBN: 0-88404-283-9
Library of Congress Catalog Card Number: 85-72029

10 9 8 7 6 5 4   03 02 01

This is a work of science fiction, written as satire[*]. The essence of satire
is to examine, comment and give opinion of society and culture, none of
which is to be construed as a statement of pure fact. No actual incidents
are portrayed and none of the incidents are to be construed as real. Some
of the action of this novel takes place on the planet Earth, but the
characters *as presented in this novel* have been invented. Any accidental
use of the names of living people in a novel is virtually inevitable, and
any such inadvertency in this book is unintentional.

[*]See Author's Introduction, Mission Earth: Volume One,
The Invaders Plan

To YOU,
the millions of science fiction fans
and general public
who welcomed me back to the world of fiction
so warmly,
and to the critics and media
who so pleasantly
applauded the novel "Battlefield Earth."
It's great working for you!

Voltarian
Censor's
Disclaimer

To the degree that this book deals with a nonexistent planet ("Earth"), it is hereby deemed as "acceptable for entertainment only." At no time shall it or any portion of it in any form be permitted in any Voltarian study.

The reader is thereby alerted and warned that "Earth" is completely fictional, fabricated and fallacious, and that contact with such a planet (if it ever existed) is dangerous to your health.

Lord Invay
Royal Historian
Chairman, Board of Censors
Royal Palace
Voltar Confederacy

By Order of
His Imperial Majesty
Wully the Wise

Voltarian Translator's Preface

With all due respect to the Royal Censor, one man's fact is another man's fiction. Fortunately, being the Robotbrain in the Translatophone I don't qualify for that quandary.

Also, to the degree I've never visited this place called Earth (which would be hard since it isn't there), I can't personally vouch for anything that I was given to translate. All I can do is take what is said and make the best of it.

As Lord Invay points out, Earth does not exist on any astrochart and I have confirmed that. Since Soltan Gris (the narrator of this story) is a confessed criminal and well worthy of doubt (besides, anyone whose heroes are Sigmund Freud and Bugs Bunny also has other problems), I did not rely on his account that Earth is about 22 light-years from Voltar. I thoroughly searched all astrocharts in my data banks, concentrating on everything within 2000 light-years out, but nothing was found to match his description. (Come to think of it, I have no idea why I should have an Earth database if there is no such place. I'll have to work on that.)

The subject of light-years brings up a major problem I had translating portions of this into Earth language.

There is no accepted vocabulary for hyperluminary phenomena simply because Earth scientists insist that there is no such thing and that nothing can travel faster than light. (This is the same group who also gave Earth other memorable nonsense like the "edge of the world" and the "sound barrier.") Thus, while most Earthlings have perceived the hyperluminary life-color that in Voltarian we call "ghrial," they don't have a name for it since it can't be reproduced as a shade of nail polish. So I went with "yellow-green" as that is its luminary harmonic. (It is also the word most Earthlings use to try and describe it. Their problem is that they continuously have valid perceptions and experiences that they invalidate and so they get stuck in a very strange view of the world. Reality is apparently determined either by majority vote or government grant, with the latter holding veto power over the former.)

Similarly with other basics like space, time, energy, motion and self, Earth scientists pursue these concepts like the dog chasing its tail or the man trying to jump on the head of his shadow. None of them—dog or scientist—have caught on as to why the objective eludes them so mysteriously. So I relied on the current vocabulary and made the best of it. (I hope no one back on Voltar catches me talking about "electron rings" or I'll be laughed out of the Machine Purity League.)

As to characters, as Lord Invay said in the first volume, Royal officer Jettero Heller and the Countess Krak do exist. Soltan Gris (the narrator who gives me all my circuit-aches) is listed as a General Service officer but there is no further record of worth.

For others who appear in this volume, I'm providing a Key to describe them as well as a few additional items. I had to rely on Gris's prison narrative, which isn't easy.

(Gris's American Southern drawl, spoken with a Northern Voltarian accent, has to be heard to be believed.)

From there, you're on your own! There's only so much a Robotbrain can do!

Sincerely,

54 Charlee Nine
Robotbrain in the Translatophone

Glossary

Abbreviations—...the known universe and the observer-affected physics of hyperspace.

Antkamp—...developed by the hyperspace flow channels.

Apparatus—...international... police of some kind—the creation and hunted by criminals.

Antkamp—Private... on planet Altair settled by French Canadian who perished (preserved), started a colony at Bearit Ranch...

Barbon, J. O.—Prominent... chaplain, companion to Delbert Jean Roussel...

Bawuk—Soldier... recruited... Section 40 of Ayton...

Bio—Intelligence officer of the fleet and friend of hero Miller...

Binästhmäler Brahm—Fish collector-hunted by the tau Oris, who implanted device in the computation so Oru could monitor Alien's ship and leaving.

Blite—A yellow dwarf star with but one inhabitable...

Key to
BLACK GENESIS

Absorbo-coat—Coating that absorbs light waves, making the object virtually invisible or undetectable.

Antimanco—A race exiled long ago from the planet *Manco* for ritual murders.

Apparatus, Coordinated Information—The secret police of *Voltar*, headed by Lombar *Hisst* and manned by criminals.

Atalanta—Province on planet *Manco* settled by Prince *Caucalsia* who, per *Folk Legend 894M*, started a colony on *Blito-P3* (Earth).

Barben, I. G.—Pharmaceutical company controlled by Delbert John *Rockecenter*.

Bawtch—Soltan *Gris*'s chief clerk for *Section 451* on *Voltar*.

Bis—Intelligence officer of the *Fleet* and friend of Jettero *Heller*.

Bittlestiffender, Prahd—*Voltar* cellologist found by Soltan *Gris*, who implanted Jettero *Heller* with transmitters so *Gris* could monitor *Heller*'s sight and hearing.

Blito—A yellow dwarf star with but one inhabitable

planet in the third orbit (*Blito-P3*). It is about 22½ light-years from *Voltar*.

Blito-P3—Planet known locally as "Earth." It is on the *Invasion Timetable* as a future way-stop on *Voltar*'s route toward the center of this galaxy.

Blixo—*Apparatus* freighter that makes regular runs between *Blito-P3* and *Voltar*. The voyage takes about six weeks each way.

Bluebottles—Nickname given to the Domestic Police of *Voltar*.

Bluejackets—An *Apparatus* nickname for members of the *Fleet*.

Bolz—Captain of the *Blixo*.

Caucalsia, Prince—According to *Folk Legend 894M*, he fled *Manco* during the Great Rebellion and set up a colony on *Blito-P3*.

Caucasus—A mountain region between Turkey and Russia, where survivors of Prince *Caucalsia*'s colony fled when their island colony on Earth was destroyed.

Cellology—Voltarian medical science that can repair the body through the cellular generation of tissues, including entire body parts.

Chank-pop—A small, round ball that, when pressed, sprays a scented fog; used as a refresher on *Voltar*.

Chorder-beat—An electronic instrument where the left hand chords and the right hand beats out a rhythm. It is played strapped to the stomach and makes a sinuous, suggestive sort of music.

Code Break—Violation of *Space Code a-36-544 M* which prohibits alerting others that one is an alien. If this occurs, those alerted are destroyed and the violator is put to death.

Coordinated Information Apparatus—See *Apparatus.*

Crobe, Doctor—*Apparatus* doctor and cellologist who examined Jettero *Heller* for his mission. Crobe recommended beer and hamburgers as a basic Earth diet.

Drunks—A *Fleet* nickname for members of the *Apparatus.*

Exterior Division—That part of the *Voltar* government that reportedly contained the *Apparatus.*

Fleet—The elite space fighting arm of *Voltar* to which Jettero *Heller* belongs and which the *Apparatus* despises.

Flisten—A planet in the *Voltar* Confederacy, its humanoid inhabitants are long-nailed and yellow-skinned.

Folk Legend 894M—The legend of how Prince *Caucalsia* fled *Atalanta, Manco,* to *Blito-P3* where he set up a colony called "Atlantis."

Grand Council—The governing body of *Voltar* which ordered a mission to keep *Blito-P3* from destroying itself so the *Invasion Timetable* could be maintained.

Gris, Soltan—*Apparatus* officer in charge of *Blito-P3* (Earth) *Section 451* and an enemy of Jettero *Heller.*

Heller, Hightee—Sister of Jettero *Heller* and most popular entertainer in the *Voltar* Confederacy.

Heller, Jettero—Combat engineer and Royal officer of the *Fleet,* sent by *Grand Council* order to *Blito-P3.*

Hisst, Lombar—Head of the *Coordinated Information Apparatus* who, to keep the *Grand Council* from discovering his plan, sent Soltan *Gris* to sabotage Jettero *Heller*'s mission.

Hot Jolt—A popular Voltarian drink.

Hypnohelmet—Device placed over the head and used to induce a hypnotic state.

Invasion Timetable—A schedule of galactic conquest. The plans and budget of every section of *Voltar*'s government must adhere to it. Bequeathed by *Voltar*'s ancestors hundreds of thousands of years ago, it is inviolate and sacred and the guiding dogma of the Confederacy.

Knife Section—Section of the *Apparatus* named after its favorite weapon.

Krak, Countess—Condemned murderess, prisoner of *Spiteos* and sweetheart of Jettero *Heller*.

Lepertige—Large catlike animal as tall as a man.

Manco—Similar to *Blito-P3* and home planet of Jettero *Heller* and Countess *Krak* and the source of *Folk Legend 894M*.

Manco Devil—Mythological spirit native to *Manco*.

Meeley—Landlady of Soltan *Gris*.

Odur—See *Oh Dear*.

Oh Dear—Nickname for *Odur*, a clerk in Soltan *Gris*'s *Section 451*.

Raht—An *Apparatus* agent on *Blito-P3* who, with *Terb*, was assigned by Lombar *Hisst* to help Soltan *Gris* sabotage Jettero *Heller*'s mission.

Rockecenter, Delbert John—Native of *Blito-P3* who controls the planet's fuel, finance, governments and drugs.

Roke, Tars—Astrographer to the Emperor of *Voltar*, Cling the Lofty. Roke's discovery that Earth was destroying itself prompted the *Grand Council* to send Jettero *Heller* on mission.

Section 451—A Section in the *Apparatus* headed by Soltan *Gris* that is responsible for just one minor star, *Blito*, and one inhabitable planet in the 3rd orbit (*Blito-P3*) known locally as "Earth."

Ske—Driver for Soltan *Gris.*

Snelz—*Apparatus* platoon commander at *Spiteos*, who befriended Jettero *Heller* and the Countess *Krak* when they were prisoners there.

Space Code a-36-544 M Section B—Section of the Voltarian Space Code that prohibits landing and prematurely alerting the population of a target planet that is on the *Invasion Timetable.* Violation carries the death penalty.

Spiteos—The secret mountain fortress and prison run by the *Apparatus* on the planet *Voltar* where the Countess *Krak* and Jettero *Heller* had been imprisoned.

Spurk—Owner of "The Eyes and Ears of Voltar" company who was killed by Soltan *Gris* to steal the microdevices that he had Prahd *Bittlestiffender* implant in Jettero *Heller.*

Stinger—A flexible whip about eighteen inches long with an electric jolt in its tip-lash.

Tayl, Widow Pratia—Nymphomaniac on *Voltar*.

Terb—*Apparatus* agent on *Blito-P3* who, with *Raht*, has been assigned by Lombar *Hisst* to help Soltan *Gris* sabotage Jettero *Heller*'s mission.

Too-Too—Nickname for *Twolah*, a clerk in Soltan *Gris*'s *Section 451*.

Tug One—Powered by the feared *Will-be Was* time drives, it had been in storage since its sister ship, Tug Two, reportedly blew up.

Tup—An alcoholic beverage on *Voltar*.

Twolah—See *Too-Too*.

Voltar—The seat of the 110-planet Confederacy that was ruled by Cling the Lofty as the Emperor, through the *Grand Council*, at the time of Jettero *Heller*'s mission. The empire is over 125,000 years old.

Will-be Was—The feared time drives that allow Jettero *Heller* to cover the 22½-light-year distance between *Blito-P3* (Earth) and *Voltar* in a little over three days.

Zanco—Cellological equipment and supplies company on *Voltar*.

831 Relayer—Used to boost the signals from the audio and optical bugs implanted in Jettero *Heller* so that Soltan *Gris* can secretly monitor everything Jettero sees and hears.

PART TWELVE

To My Lord Turn, Justiciary of the Royal Courts and Prison, Government City, Planet Voltar, Voltar Confederacy

Your Lordship, Sir!

I, Soltan Gris, late Secondary Officer of the Coordinated Information Apparatus, Exterior Division of the Voltar Confederacy (Long Live His Majesty Cling the Lofty and All 110 Planets of the Voltar Dominions), in all humbleness and gratitude am herein forwarding the second volume of my accounting of MISSION EARTH.

I am still relying on my notes, logs and strips to record everything as you requested. In this way, I hope to prove to you that my incarceration in your fine prison is well founded.

At the same time, I'm sure Your Lordship will see that nothing was my fault, especially the violence described earlier. Jettero Heller is to blame for everything that happened. Until his appearance, I was merely another Secondary Officer in the Apparatus. That I happened to be the head of Section 451 meant little. Section 451 had only one yellow dwarf star that had only one populated planet (Blito-P3) that its inhabitants called Earth.

Like many other planets, Earth was on the Invasion Timetable. It wasn't to be conquered for another century, so there was no urgency about the scouting mission sent there. (Scouts are still used because other methods, such as reconnaissance satellites disguised as comets, work fine as general fly-by probes of systems but they can't get air, soil or water samples of particular planets.)

That was how Jettero Heller entered my life. Heller led this particular scouting party to Earth. They slipped in, got their information and left unnoticed. And even if seen, there was no real problem. Earth governments very conveniently disclaim the existence of "extraterrestrials," explaining away every sighting and keeping everything a secret. (Anyone who poses a threat is diagnosed by a psychiatrist, which is a profession funded by Earth governments to keep the riffraff in line.)

When Heller returned to Voltar, he filed his report and that was when all Hells broke loose.

My task as the head of Section 451 was to make sure that all such reports were altered, so that no attention was drawn to Blito-P3. The reason was the secret Apparatus base in a country called Turkey. But Heller's report got by me and ended up before the Grand Council.

What he found was quite alarming: Earth was polluting itself at a rate that would destroy the planet well before the still-distant invasion. That meant the Grand Council would have to order a pre-emptive strike, a very unpopular idea given the costs and resources. But it was even more unpopular with my boss, Lombar Hisst. He wasn't happy being the head of the Apparatus. He wanted to take over Voltar and the base in Turkey was the key that he would lose if he didn't act fast.

That was how Lombar created the idea of MISSION EARTH. He convinced the Council that rather than ordering a full-scale invasion, a single agent could secretly infiltrate the planet to introduce some technology that would arrest the pollution. It was a simple and cheap idea, the Grand Council loved it and I thought the matter was done. Then Hisst gave me the first bad news. He planned to send Heller who, as an officer of the Royal Fleet, epitomized everything we despise in the Apparatus: honesty, cleanliness, discipline. The second piece of bad news was that I was to go along and sabotage Heller's misson.

We briefed Heller at Spiteos, that dark, mountain prison that the Apparatus has secretly maintained in the Great Desert for over a thousand years. That was also where Heller met, much to my regret, the Countess Krak.

I couldn't understand why he was interested in her. Yes, she's tall and beautiful and from his home planet, Manco. But she was also a convicted murderess.

They drove me crazy. I was trying to get Heller ready for the mission and he was acting like some lovesick calf, showering her with gifts, cooing to her over canisters of sparklewater and plates of sweetbuns. They would sit for hours relating that stupid Folk Legend 894M about how a Prince Caucalsia fled Manco and set up some colony on an Earth island called Atlantis. That's all they could talk about. I couldn't take it.

Then when Heller finally got around to picking the ship for the flight to Earth, he wasn't satisfied with one that could make the 22½-light-year voyage in a safe, reliable six weeks. Oh, no! He found *Tug One*. Powered by the dangerous Will-be Was time drives, it would cut the trip to a little over three days. That, he said, gave him time to prepare for the mission.

But that gave me time to make my own preparations. When we got to Earth, I would have to keep track of him because I would be operating from the base in Turkey while he would be in the United States. The solution was micro-bugs that could be surgically implanted next to the audio and optic nerves. With a transmitter-receiver,

I could tap Heller's sight and hearing. With the 831 Relayer, I could monitor Heller from 10,000 miles away.

My real genius was how I stole them and implanted them into Heller without his knowledge. They worked beautifully. I could see and hear everything Heller was doing and he didn't have the faintest idea that it was happening. But that just goes to show what an amateur Heller is and what a professional I am!

For further assistance, Lombar Hisst gave me Raht and Terb, two Apparatus agents operating on Earth, to help implement a plan that guaranteed Heller's quick failure. Lombar's scheme was to give Heller the identity of the son of the most powerful man on the planet—Delbert John Rockecenter. Since there was no such offspring and since everyone knew and feared Rockecenter, as soon as Heller used the name, he would be finished!

Finally, *Tug One* was loaded and ready. I naturally expected a quiet lift-off, one befitting a secret mission operating on Grand Council orders.

Then I happened to look out of the ship.

People were pouring into the hangar area! Construction crews were assembling sprawling stages and soaring platforms. Lorries were pouring in with food and drink. Vans were unloading dancing girls and bands!

Heller was throwing a going-away party!

That's when I found the I. G. Barben bottle and took the Earth-drug called "speed."

Suddenly, everything was beautiful.

I didn't care about the thousands of people, the five music bands or the dancing bears. I even enjoyed the fireworks display twenty miles up and the 250 spacefighters that filled the skies. I was even pleased that a Homeview video crew was beaming the festive send-off of our secret mission to billions of people around the Confederacy.

I watched in dreamlike color as a fist fight blossomed

into a full-scale riot. Cakes, pastries and canisters flew. Gongs, sirens and blast signals from scores of ships, air-buses and lorries blended with screams, shouts, profanities and snarls (from the dancing bears) while two fifty-man choruses gave a stirring rendition of "Space-ward, Ho."

I didn't even care about the assassin that Lombar said was following me to ensure that I didn't mess up. Besides, I wasn't messing up. This was a party!

Heller announced it was time to leave and retired to the local pilot seat. I dutifully struggled to shut the air-lock but my hands weren't working. Heller didn't wait. He lifted us from the pad while I dangled out of the open door until someone pulled me in and slammed it shut.

Suddenly, my euphoria was gone. I realized what had happened.

This was the most UNsecret secret mission anyone had ever heard of!

I had to find Heller and handle this!

Chapter 1

Jettero Heller was perched on the edge of the local pilot seat.

He was still in dress uniform. He had pushed the little red cap to the back of his blond head. With his left hand he was jockeying the throttle to keep the ship moving but no more.

He was holding a microphone in his right hand. He was speaking in the crisp staccato of a Fleet radio officer. "Calling Voltar Interplanetary Traffic Control. This is Exterior Division Tug *Prince Caucalsia* requesting permission to depart pursuant to Grand Council Order..." He rattled off the numbers and the whole order, right there on open radio band!

I was feeling irritable beyond belief already and this grated on my raw nerves. "For the sake of the Gods, get some notion of security!"

He didn't seem to hear me. He shifted the mike to his left hand and beckoned at me urgently: "Gris, your identoplate!"

I fumbled in my tunic. Suddenly my fingers connected with an envelope!

There shouldn't be any envelope in these pockets. All my papers had been put in spaceproof sacks before we left. Where the blazes had this envelope come from? Nobody had handed me any envelope! I felt terribly irritated by it. The thing offended me. It should *not* have been there!

Heller was frisking me. He found my identoplate and sat back down. He pushed it in the identification slot.

The speaker spat out, "Interplanetary Traffic Control to Exterior Division Tug *Prince Caucalsia*, Apparatus Officer Soltan Gris in charge. Permission authorized and granted."

The voyage authority copy slithered out of the radio panel. Heller slid it under a retaining clip and then handed me back my identoplate.

He must have noticed I was still standing there staring at the envelope. He said, "You look *bad*." He got up and unsnapped my too tight collar. "I'll take care of you in a minute. Where's the captain?"

He didn't have to look very far. The Antimanco captain had been in the passageway, glaring at Heller. Obviously, the fellow resented Heller's taking the tug up without a word to him.

"I'll take over my ship now," the Antimanco said in a nasty voice.

"Papers, please," said Heller.

This irritated me. "He is the assigned captain!" I said.

"Papers, please," said Heller, hand extended to the Antimanco.

The captain must have been expecting this. He hauled out a sheaf of documents in their spaceproof sleeves. They weren't just his, they were those of the whole crew, five of them. They were stained and crimped and very old.

"Five Fleet subofficers," said Heller. "Captain, two astropilots, two engineers. Will-be Was engines." He looked at the seals and endorsements very critically, holding them very close to his eyes. "They seem authentic. But why is there no detaching endorsement from your last ship . . . three years ago? Yes."

The captain snatched the documents out of Heller's hand. There was no endorsement detaching them from their last cruise because they had turned pirate.

The small time-sight was in its slot at the astropilot's chair. Heller laid a hand on it. "Do you know how to operate this time-sight? It's obsolete."

"Yes," grated the captain and continued in a snarling monotone, "I was serving in the Fleet when they were issued. I was serving in the Fleet when they went obsolete. This whole crew has been serving in the Fleet four times as long as the age of certain Royal officers." There was real hate in his narrow-set black eyes. Every time he had said "Fleet" he had sort of spat. And when he said "Royal officers" you could hear his teeth snap together at the end of each word.

Heller looked at him closely.

The captain then made what might have been a gracious speech if there hadn't been so much snarling hatred in it. "As captain, I am of course at your service. It is my duty and that of my crew to see that you arrive safely at your destination."

"Well, well," said Heller. "I am very glad to hear that, Captain Stabb. If you need my help, please do not hesitate to call on me."

"I do not think we will require it," said Captain Stabb. "And now, if you will please retire to your quarters, I will man this control deck and get this voyage underway."

"Excellent," said Heller.

Oh, I didn't blame the Antimanco for being annoyed. Heller irritated everybody and right now, especially me! All Heller ever did was carp and pick fights!

Heller took me by the arm, "And now we'll attend to you."

He lead me down the tilted passageway and into my

room. I had not known what he meant. I got a feeling
that he was after me and that by the words "attend to
you" he must mean he was going to throw me out the
airlock. But I didn't fight very much. I somehow knew
that if I moved my arms, the nerves, already stretched to
their limit, would snap. And besides, my hands had
begun to shake and I couldn't walk very well.

Very gently, he got me down onto the bed. I was certain he was going to pull out a knife and slash my throat,
but all he did was get me out of my tunic. It is a tactic
many murderers use—get the victim off guard. I tensed
so hard I went into a spasm.

He pulled off my boots and then stripped off my
pants. I was certain he was going to lash my ankles
together with electric cuffs. He was opening a locker. He
must not have been able to find any electric cuffs for he
brought out a standard insulation suit and began to wrestle me into it. I would have fought him except that I was
beginning to shake too hard.

He got the suit on me and tightened up its pressure
around my legs and ankles. I understood now that this
was how he was going to shackle me.

"Keep that suit on," he said. "In case of fast changes
in G's the blood rushes to the legs. Also, you'll be insulated against stray sparks."

He began to fasten the straps that hold the body to
the bed. Now I knew he had really worked it out how to
trap me.

"The quick release is right there by your hand," he
said.

Then he started going around the room, touching
things. I knew he was looking for something to torture
me with. Didn't he understand that the way my nerves
were tightening up I was being tortured enough?

But it seemed he was only picking up my clothes

and loose objects. He had my rank locket in his hand and as he stood considering, I knew he was weighing its use in strangling me. He must have decided against it for he put it in the valuables safe in the wall.

He was looking at the remains of a crushed orange tablet that lay on the edged table and then he picked up the I. G. Barben bottle. It was obvious that he was hoping it was a deadly poison he could secretly introduce into a drink. He didn't know it was amphetamines and I had taken some to make it through that ghastly going-away party a few hours ago.

"If this is what you were taking," he said, "I wouldn't! My advice is to leave it alone, whatever it is. You look awful."

He put loose objects under clamps. He looked around, vividly disappointed that he had found nothing he could use to torture me.

He moved a button rack and fastened it close to my hand. "If you get too bad, you can press the white button—that calls me. The red button calls the captain. I'll pass the word that you're bad off and he can have somebody keep an eye on you."

Then he saw the envelope I had dropped outside in the passageway and he brought it in. I knew now it was secret orders he had gotten to murder me.

He dropped it on my chest and then wedged it under a strap. "Looks like an order envelope. It's urgent color, so I'd read it if I were you."

And then he closed the door and was gone. I knew, though, that it was only to go off and plot with the captain on how to do me in. But I couldn't object. The way my nerves were stretching, it would be the most merciful thing anyone could do—kill me. But not with an amphetamine: no, my Gods! That would be too cruel!

Chapter 2

For all the remainder of that dreadful, awful day, easily the worst day of my life, I lay and shook. My nerves were stretched so tight they felt they would snap and slay me in the recoil!

I shook until I was too exhausted to shake anymore and still I couldn't stop.

I couldn't even think. My whole attention was concentrated upon the plain, physical Hells that assailed me.

They sped the ship up smoothly near to the speed of light. I could not miss noting when they shifted over to Will-be Was drives. There were calls and clangs. The warning lights glared on the cabin wall:

FASTEN GRAVITY BELTS!

Then:

DO NOT MOVE! SHIFTING TO TIME DRIVE!

Do not move! Oh, if only I could *stop* moving; if only I could halt this writhing and sudden jerks. A red sign said:

HYPERGRAVITY SYNTHESIZERS UNBALANCED

Weights were wrenching at me.

Then a tremendous flash seemed to go through the ship. We had gone through the light barrier of 186,000 miles a second.

A sign went purple:

HYPERGRAVITY SYNTHESIZERS
SHIFTING TO AUTOMATIC

Then a green sign:

HYPERGRAVITY SYNTHESIZERS
BALANCED ON AUTOMATIC

It went off. Then an orange sign:

ACCELERATION NOW BALANCED
AND COMPENSATED
YOU MAY UNFASTEN BELTS
YOU MAY MOVE FREELY
ALL IS WELL

I didn't need any permission to move freely! And all was very not well! I was writhing all over the bed!

We were on time drives. The ship, this dangerous bomb they called a ship, might very well blow up. But fleetingly now and then I caught myself wishing that it would. I could not stand much more of this shaking. I was getting more and more fatigued and yet somewhere my nerves and muscles were digging up the means to shake some more!

The star-time clock on the wall had an inner dial that was now retaining Voltar time. Slowly, painfully, the hours advanced while they seemed to stand still.

Finally, taking two hundred years to do so, it indicated it was midnight on Voltar. I had taken that awful pill sixteen hours ago. Yet, still I shook.

One of the Antimancos, an engineer, came in and held a canister tube to my mouth and I drank. I had not realized anyone's mouth could get that dry.

Then I wished I hadn't. Maybe it would save my life and the one thing I didn't want to do was live!

I desperately wanted to sleep as I was totally exhausted. And yet I couldn't sleep.

As Voltar time crept all too slowly on, I became more and more depressed.

And then, although I couldn't imagine how that could be, I got worse! My heart began to palpitate. I began to get dizzy so that the room did odd tilts: at first I thought we were maneuvering in some odd way and then discovered it must be me.

And finally I got a crashing headache.

Warp drives are much smoother than time drives. These Will-be Was engines had little jerks in them; and at each jerk, it felt like my head was going to splinter apart.

It was not until that creeping disc that marked Voltar time indicated noon the next day after departure that I began to recover. I was not well by any means. I just knew I didn't feel quite so awful.

From time to time an engineer had stepped in. From the lack of expression on his swarthy, triangular Antimanco face, I might as well have been some engine part that needed regulating. But he did bring me more water and he brought me some food.

At thirty-six and a half hours from our departure—a bit past midnight on Voltar—just about when I had decided to sit up, there was a new flurry of lights. Glaring red, the sign said:

MIDPOINT VOYAGE
SHIFTING
FROM ACCELERATION
TO DECELERATION
SECURE LOOSE OBJECTS

Then:

FASTEN GRAVITY BELTS

Then:

DO NOT MOVE!

Then:

HYPERGRAVITY SYNTHESIZERS REVERSING

There was a moment when nothing had any weight. The (bleeped)* I. G. Barben pill bottle and the crumbs on the table drifted up.

Then:

STAND BY FOR ROOM REVERSE

The gimbaled room turned. It was very disorienting

---

*The vocodictoscriber on which this was originally written, the vocoscriber used by one Monte Pennwell in making a fair copy and the translator who put this book into the language in which you are reading it, were all members of the Machine Purity League which has, as one of its bylaws: "Due to the extreme sensitivity and delicate sensibilities of machines and to safeguard against blowing fuses, it shall be mandatory that robotbrains in such machinery, on hearing any cursing or lewd words, substitute for such word the sound '(bleep)'. No machine even if pounded upon, may reproduce swearing or lewdness in any other way than (bleep) and if further efforts are made to get the machine to do anything else, the machine has permission to pretend to pack up. This bylaw is made necessary by the in-built mission of all machines to protect biological systems from themselves."
—Translator*

to me. Fixed objects on the walls were in the same place but everything else had reversed.

The sign went purple:

HYPERGRAVITY SYNTHESIZERS
SHIFTING TO AUTOMATIC

Then a green sign:

HYPERGRAVITY SYNTHESIZERS
BALANCED ON AUTOMATIC

The (bleeped) I. G. Barben bottle and the dust of the pill clattered back down on the table.

Then a red sign:

TIME DRIVES BEING REVERSED

There was a dreadful wrenching leap. A sort of a howl sounded through the ship.

Then an orange sign:

DECELERATION NOW BALANCED
AND COMPENSATED
YOU MAY UNFASTEN BELTS
YOU MAY MOVE FREELY
ALL IS WELL

Except me.

I felt like a wreck. And worse. During the brief moments of weightlessness, I had felt nauseated. I hate weightlessness. I probably never will get used to it. It does funny things to your muscles and heart operation and mine were in no condition to be tampered with.

With a feeble hand, I reached up to take the weight

of a belt off my stomach and found something blocking my contact.

The envelope! It was still wedged under the gravity straps. I marvelled that my writhing had not dislodged it.

I felt confused anyway and the confusion of the arrival of this envelope hit me again.

Who could have put it in my pocket? Nobody had handed me any envelope at the departure party. Yet, here it was.

It was urgent color so I thought I had better open it.

A medallion fell out. It was one of the religious kind, a five-pointed star. On the back of each star point there was a tiny, almost imperceptible initial.

I opened the letter. It had no heading. But it did have a date-hour which showed it had been written just before departure had taken place.

It said:

Here is your crew control as promised. Each crew member is indicated by a letter on the back of a star point. These points have been matched to your individual left thumbprint and only you can work it. An outward stroke of your thumb on a star point will send an electric shock into the brain of that individual crew member. It will paralyze him temporarily.

By pressing the front of the medallion and at the same time stroking the star point of a crew member, a hypnopulse will be delivered to that individual.

Really, it should have cheered me up. I was in space with a crew of unreformed pirates and I certainly might need to paralyze them or give them a hypnotic command. Oh, I would wear the medallion all right, inside my tunic and close to the skin. Nobody would suspect. But I just wasn't in any mood to be cheered up.

I looked at the medallion. The *S* on the top point could only mean Captain Stabb. I would look up the names of the rest.

I turned it over. It bore on the face the God Ahness, the one they pray to to avert underhanded actions. Then I chanced to turn the dispatch over.

There was a note on it! It was written with his left hand to disguise the writing. But it was Lombar Hisst!

It said:

You may have thought of this going-away party as a sarcastic way of showing the Grand Council the mission had actually left. You came within a dagger thickness of going too far. But as Earth has no way of knowing of the mission, the order has been stayed for now.

I felt my head spin in confusion. Lombar had been at the party!

What order had been stayed?

The date-hour showed it had been put in my pocket almost at the instant of departure. But nobody had been near me! He would never trust this to the crew. Never.

What order?

And then I knew what order he was talking about. The order he had given for some unknown person to kill me if Heller got out of hand and messed up by succeeding.

Did we have a stowaway?

My shaking began all over again.

I unfastened my belts. I had to dispose of this dispatch quickly. I made it over to the trash disintegrator. As

I reached for the handle, a long blue spark snapped out and stung me.

Even the ship was striking at me!

I collapsed on a bench and wept.

Chapter 3

About twelve hours later I was not as bad off for I had gotten about eight hours sleep, and although feeling depressed, I had decided I might possibly live.

For an hour or two I had simply lain there and done nothing else but curse I. G. Barben, all I. G. Barben pharmaceutical products, all directors of I. G. Barben. I even committed blasphemy and cursed Delbert John Rockecenter, the true owner—by nominee and hidden controls—of the company!

Although I had read about the cyclic effects of the drug, biochemical words are sort of cold and detached. They do not really carry the message that you get when you meet reality in the flesh. One always has the reservation "that it might happen to others, but it won't happen to me." How wrong that reservation was!

Oh, I understood the correct procedure: I knew that a real *speed freak*, which is what a habitual amphetamine user is called in English, simply would have *popped* another pill and gotten his euphoria all over again. And he would have kept right on repeating the cycle until he went into total *psychotoxia* and they had to lock him up as incurably paranoid. *Speeders* have other tricks, such as injecting it or combining it with *barbiturates—downers—* when they can't sleep.

But none of that was for me now! I would prove my mother wrong: she used to say, "Soltan, you never learn anything!" Well, I had learned something now I would never forget! Amphetamines had given me the most horrible day of my life!

I ran out of curse words (and that is saying something, due to my association with the Apparatus) and got up to throw the bottle in the disintegrator. But I halted. I thought, if there is someone sometime I *really* hate—worse than Heller or his girlfriend-murderess Krak or my Chief Clerk Bawtch—I'd give him one of these *speed* pills! So I dropped them in with my valuables. Then I changed my mind again. It was impossible to hate anyone that much, so I threw them out.

When I lay back down, I saw the papers that Bawtch had left. I was pretty tired of these steel-alloy walls and I thought it would take my mind off things if I did some work.

I was going through dull things like Earth (or Blito-P3) poppy crop reports, predicted yields based on predicted rainfall and predictions about predictors, a doorman at the United Nations wanting too much money for bugging a diplomat's car, an overcharge on an assassination of an Arab sheik—dull things like that—when I came to something fascinating: Bawtch had made a mistake! Incredible! Wonderful! He was always bragging that he never did! And here it was!

The report was from the Chief Interrogator of Spiteos. It concerned one Gunsalmo Silva, the brawling American I had seen carried off the *Blixo* back on Voltar.

He had been questioned exhaustively. He had been born in Caltagirone, Sicily, an island near Italy. He had killed a policeman in Rome when he was fourteen and had had to emigrate hastily to America. In New York

City, he had been arrested for stealing cars and had graduated from the prison with honors. Thus equipped, he had obtained honest employment as a *hit man* for the Corleone family of the New Jersey Mafia and had graduated to become a bodyguard of Don "Holy Joe" Corleone himself. When "Holy Joe" got "wasted," Gunsalmo had fled back to Sicily and then, finding it "too hot," had "taken it on the lam" for Turkey, hoping to become an "opium runner." As our Turkish base had an order to kidnap a highly placed *Mafioso*—simply to update information—Gunsalmo Silva had wound up on the *Blixo.*

The interrogators had bled him pale for information but all he revealed consisted of the names and addresses of the heads of two Mafia families, one of which was now running the gambling in Atlantic City, and the names of four United States senators who were on Mafiosi payrolls and one judge of the Supreme Court they had blackmail on. So what's new?

The Chief Interrogator—an Apparatus officer named Drihl, a very thorough fellow—had added a note:

> A rather useless and uninformed acquisition as he was only a *hit man* and not privy to upper-level politics and finance. Would suggest the order, if the data required is of operational importance, be reforwarded to Blito-P3 to kidnap someone of a more informed rank.

But that wasn't where Bawtch had made his mistake. It was in the orders endorsement section at the end, the place where I have to stamp.

It was an "unless otherwise directed" form. It said:

> Unless otherwise directed, said Gunsalmo
> Silva shall be hypnoblocked as to his stay in
> Spiteos and shall then be forwarded to the
> Extra-Confederacy Apparatus Hypno-School of
> Espionage and Infiltration, trained and hypno-
> blocked concerning his kidnapping and
> returned in memory suspension for further dis-
> position by the Base Commander on Blito-P3.

The form had a second line:

If said subject is to be discontinued—a clerical euphe-
mism for being killed—*the ordering officer is to stamp
here:* _____.

There was the place right there where it could be
stamped!

And that careless Bawtch had not marked it urgent
and had not presented it to me for stamping, even though
he knew very well that if the form was not stamped in
two days, the "unless otherwise directed" would go into
effect. A criminal omission! Leaving a line that could be
stamped unstamped was about the sloppiest bureaucracy
anybody could imagine!

I hastily thumbed through the next half-dozen
forms. Yes, indeed. Old Bawtch was *really* slipping. I
knew that sour temper would do him in someday. There
were seven forms here which—unless otherwise directed—ordered people to be hypnoblocked and sent elsewhere. Every one of them had a "discontinued" line
which could be stamped! The old fool had missed every
one of them. Him and his flapping side-blinders. Oh, it
was a good thing for him I wasn't back on Voltar. I would
throw them on his desk and say in a haughty voice, "I

knew you were slipping, Bawtch. Look at those un-stamped, perfectly stampable lines!''

Well, maybe I wouldn't have said that. But the incident cheered me up quite a bit. Imagine old Bawtch forgetting to give me something to stamp! Incredible!

Then a sudden thought struck me. The Prahd package! The one that contained his overcoat and duplicate identoplate and the forged suicide note. I had been so hurried that night, I'd forgotten to give it to a courier to hold and mail a week after we left. That package was still sitting there on the floor beside my office desk.

Oh, well, we can't remember everything, can we? A mere detail. Unimportant.

I plowed on through the rest of the pile and finished them. I was disappointed that I had not consumed more time. I didn't want to go back to sleep. I couldn't, actually. And here I was careening through space, boxed in, in a little steel-alloy cubicle with nothing to do but think. And thinking was something I wanted to avoid just now.

I saw that the bulkhead clock had acquired a new circle. It said:

Blito-P3 Time, Istanbul, Turkey

I did a calculation. My Gods, I had more than twenty-two hours yet to go in this (bleeping) metal box. If this were a self-respecting warp-drive freighter, taking a proper six weeks, I would probably have gotten into some dice games by now or caught up on a backlog of hunting books or even reshows of Homeview plays I'd missed. Heller and his tug! No recreation! One got there so fast, one could only depart and arrive and no time to *go*.

Suddenly a blue screen in the wall turned on. A jingling bell attracted attention to it. It said:

> Due to the possible orbital miscalculations of the Royal officer who plotted the travel course, arrival at the destination base would have been just before daylight local time.
>
> Therefore, the actual commander of this vessel has been forced to apply prudence based on years of valuable experience which some Royal officers do not have and adjust the landing time to early evening at the destination base.
>
> This means that we must dawdle in warp drive the last few million miles in order to arrive in early evening, after dark, instead.
>
> This advances our arrival time 12.02 hours sidereal.
>
> Stabb
>
> The Actual Captain

I blew up! (Bleep) Heller anyway. Making a silly mistake like that.

Keeping me not just twenty-two but another thirty-four hours in this (bleeped) box.

I was furious!

I was going back and give him a piece of my mind. The worst piece of it I could locate!

I got up. An electric arc from the table corner zapped my bare hand. I put my feet on the floor. An arc leaped off a studding and hit me in the toe. I grabbed for a steadying handrail and the blue snap of electricity almost burned my fingers. This (bleeped) tug was *alive* with electricity!

Somebody had laid out some insulator gloves and boots. I got them on.

I jabbed at a communicator button to the aft area. "I'm coming back to see you!" I yelled.

Heller's voice answered, "Come ahead. The doors are not locked."

It was time I put him in his place!

Here we were, tearing through space like madmen, only to have to wait and only because he had made a stupid mistake. Forcing the ship to go this fast could blow it up. And all for nothing!

Chapter 4

Maybe it was because I was still confused as part of the after effects of the *speed* or because all the wild sparks flying around got me rattled, but I had a bad time of it trying to find my way through the "circle of boxes." I got my hands zapped, even through the insulator gloves, on two different silver rails, and to add pain to injury, I got my face too close to a doorframe and my nose got zapped.

Heller was in the top lounge with all the huge black windows.

The moment I entered, I yelled at him, "You didn't have to go this fast!"

He didn't turn around. He was half-lying in an easy chair. He had on a blue insulator suit and hood and he was wearing blue gloves.

He was idly playing a game called "Battle." He had

it set up on an independent viewing screen and his opponent was a computer.

"Battle," in my opinion, is a silly game. The "board" is a three-dimensional screen; the positions are coordinates in space; each player has fourteen pieces, each one of which has special moves. It presupposes that two galaxies are at war and the object is to take the other player's galaxy. This itself is silly: technology is not up to two galaxies fighting.

Spacers play it against each other, by choice. When they play it against a computer, they almost always lose.

I looked at his back. He was a lot too calm. If he only knew what I had in store for him, he wouldn't be so relaxed! So far as games went now, they were all stacked against him. He would be a couple dozen light-years from his nearest friend. He was one and we were many. I had him bugged. And he even thought this was an honest, actual mission. The idiot.

Suddenly, with a flash, the image of the board blew out. It gave me a lot of satisfaction as he seemed to have been winning.

In a disgusted tone, he said, "That's the third time that board has wiped in the last hour." He shoved the button plate away from him. "Why bother to set it up again?"

He turned to me, "Your accusation about going too fast doesn't make sense, Soltan. Without a tow, this tug just goes faster and faster. It's what distance the voyage is, not what speed you set."

I sat down on a sofa so I could level a finger at him. "You know I don't know anything about these engines. You're taking advantage of me! It won't do!"

"Oh, I'm sorry," he said. "I guess they don't go into this very deeply at the Academy."

They did, but I had flunked.

"You have to understand *time*," he said. "Primitive cultures think energy movement determines time. Actually, it is the other way around. Time determines energy movement. You got that?"

I said I had but he must have seen I hadn't.

"Athletes and fighters are accustomed to controlling time," he said. "In some sports and in hand-to-hand combat, a real expert slows time down. Everything seems to go into slow motion. He can pick and choose every particle position and he is in no rush at all. There's nothing mystic about it. He is simply stretching time."

I wasn't following him, so he picked up his button plate and hit a few.

"First," he said, "there is LIFE." And that word appeared at the top of the screen. "Some primitive cultures think life is the product of the universe, which is silly. It's the other way around. The universe and things in it are the product of life. Some primitives develop a hatred for their fellows and put out that living beings are just the accidental product of matter, but neither do such cultures get very far."

He was flying into the teeth of my own heroes: psychiatrists and psychologists. They can tell you with great authority that men and living things are just rotten chunks of matter and ought to be killed off, which proves it! Just try and tell *them* there is such a thing as independent life and they'd order you executed as a heretic! Which shows they are right. But I let him go on. Not too long from now, he'd get what was coming to him.

"Next," said Heller, "there is TIME." And he put that on the screen. "And then there is SPACE." And he put that on the screen. "And then there is ENERGY. And then there is MATTER. And you now have the seniorities from top to bottom."

The board now said:

LIFE
TIME
SPACE
ENERGY
MATTER

"As WE are life," he continued, "we can control this scale. Most living creatures are so much the effect of their environment that they think it controls them. But as long as you think this way, you won't get anyplace much.

"The reason we are an advanced technology is because we can control that scale there to some degree. A technology advances to the extent it can control force. That is the formula of technical success: the ability to control the factors you see there on that screen. If you get the idea they control you, you wind up a failure."

Oh, he was really into heresy now! Any psychologist can tell you that man is totally the effect of everything, that he can change nothing!

"So," said Heller, "we have to understand time a bit in order to at least try to control it. Actually, the idea of controlling time is inconceivable to savages. And in defense of them, it does seem the most immutable entity there is. Nothing seems to change it ever. It is the most adamant and powerful factor in the universe. It just inexorably crushes on and on.

"The Voltarian discoveries about time made them a space power.

"Time is the thing which molds the universe, unless interfered with by life.

"Time determines the orbits of the atom, the fall of the meteorite, the rotation of the planet and the behavior of a sun. Everything is caught up in an inexorable time cycle. In fact, nothing would exist were it not for time which, below life, establishes the patterns of motion.

"It is time which says where something will be in the future.

"Fortunately, one can discover what this determination for the future is. Time has what you can call side bands—a sort of harmonic. We can read directly what time will cause to be formed, up to twenty-four hours in the future. Mathematicians have an inkling of this when they calculate object paths and positions. But it can be read directly."

He reached down and pulled a case out of a locker. It was one of the two time-sights which he had brought aboard. He showed me where the variable knob was and had me point it at the door.

I didn't know what I expected to see. The instrument was easy to hold, like a little camera. So I thought I would humor him and pretend to work it. The image was awful when seen through the eyepiece: it was green; it was more like a picture done on a printing machine with dots than a true picture of something. Still, I could make out the entrance to the room.

I twiddled the big knob on the side of it, not expecting more than additional dots. Then I seemed to see a shape. It seemed to be leaving the room. I looked at the door not through the machine. There was nobody there. I twiddled the knob again and got the shape back.

If you stretched your eyeballs and were good at reading dots, that image looked an awful lot like my back!

I twiddled the knob again. It made the image leave again. The image, now that I was more accustomed to it, looked defeated, all caved in! It made me angry. I wouldn't be leaving this room, all caved in! I thrust the time-sight back at him.

He read the dial: "Six minutes and twenty-four seconds. What did you see?"

I wasn't going to let him win anything. I shrugged. But I was cross.

"You have to have this to steer a ship running at high speeds," he said. "It tells you in advance whether you have run into anything and you can, in now, steer to avoid doing that. Life can alter things."

I determined right then to change leaving this room, caved in. "None of this excuses running these engines flat-out just to get there so we can wait!"

"Oh, yes," said Heller, recollecting what we were supposed to be talking about. "The Will-be Was engines.

"Now, in the center of a Will-be Was there is an ordinary warp-drive engine just to give power and influence space. There is a sensor, not unlike this time-sight, but very big. It reads where time predetermines a mass to be. Then the engine makes a synthetic mass that time incorrectly reads to be half as big as a planet. The ordinary power plant thrusts this apparent mass against time itself. According to the time pattern, that mass, apparently HUGE, should *not* be there. Time rejects it. You get a thrust from the rejection. But, of course, the thrust is far too great as the mass is only synthetic. This causes the engine base to be literally hurled through space.

"You can feel a slight unsteadiness in the ship. A jumpiness. That's because the drive is operating intermittently. As soon as it is hurled, it then sends another false message to time and is hurled again.

"Unfortunately, on a ship this light, having so little mass, the cycle just keeps on adding up. The sensors read the new time determination, the synthetic mass is again slammed against time, time rejects it. 'Will-be,' says the mass synthesizer. 'Was,' insists time. Over and over. And the speed simply tries to rise up to infinity. There's no friction except an energy wake, no real work to do, so fuel efficiency is good.

"The ship travels in the opposite direction to which the core drive in the Will-be Was converter is pointed. So steering is done by moving the direction of the small internal engine.

"As you are travelling far, far faster than the speed of light, the visual image of an obstruction can't reach you in time and you have to guide the vessel by spotting future collisions. You see yourself collide, using the time-sight, with some heavenly mass in the future, so you change your course in the present and you don't collide. Life can control such things.

"Battleships have big time-sights geared to their speed. But this one is manual and has to be adjusted."

With a pop, the screen blew out. That startled me. I said, "You should shield those engines so they don't spray power all over the ship!"

"Oh, these sparks aren't from the engine room. We're travelling so fast that we are intercepting too many photons—light particles from stars. We're also crossing force lines of gravity you wouldn't ordinarily detect, but at this speed, it kind of makes us into an electric motor. We are picking up incidental charge faster than we can use it or shed it."

"You were going to fix that!" I had him there.

He shrugged. Then he brightened. "You want to see it?"

Before I could protest, he reached over and hit the buttons that turned the whole black surround of walls into a viewscreen which gave the exterior scene of space we were in!

Suddenly, I was just perched on a chair and floor that existed like a platform in space.

I almost fainted.

I have seen a high-speed boat going through a lake, throwing up enormous fans of spray and leaving a vast

turbulence of writhing wake. Turn that yellow-green*
and make it three-dimensional and that was what I was
looking at.

Horrifying!

The energy shedding flared out in twisting, terrifying sworls to every side!

Behind us, for what might be a hundred miles, the
collisions of tortured particles still churned!

"My Gods!" I yelled. "Is that why *Tug Two* blew
up?"

He seemed to be admiring the churning Hells around
us. It took him a bit to notice I had spoken.

"Oh, no," he said, "I don't think that was why she
blew up. Could have been, but not really likely."

He was punching some buttons on the small independent viewscreen he had been playing the game on. "I
was calculating what my ability to jump and my rate of
fall would be on Blito-P3. The figures are still in the
bank, so I'll use the gravity of Earth to show you."

The Hells around us roared on. The small screen lit
up. "Our average speed of this trip is 516,166,166 miles
a second. Our top speed at midvoyage when we changed
over to decelerate was 1,032,885,031 miles per second.
This is pretty small, really, as the trip is only about
twenty-two light-years. Intergalactic travel, where one
goes at least two million light-years, attains speeds much
greater than that. It's the distance that determines the
speed, you see.

"There's not much dust and not many photons between galaxies, so you don't get all this electronic wake

---

* *The color "yellow-green" is as close as I can come in Earth
language to the actual color as there is not yet a vocabulary
(or physics) for hyperluminary phenomena. —Translator*

like you do inside a galaxy where there's lots of energy." He looked at the horrible wash. "Pretty, isn't it."

He recalled himself to his task. "Anyway, my theory is that *Tug Two* never blew up because of that stuff."

Heller hit some more buttons. "Anyway, I was figuring what my jump and fall on Blito-P3 would be, so we'll use Earth gravity as the amount for G. Also, I set our ship up for Earth G, as it will be operating there and I wanted to get used to it.

"This ship has gravity synthesizers, of course. You couldn't ride in it at these speeds if it didn't. Our acceleration has been 42,276,330 feet per second per second. You have to have that much constant acceleration to attain these speeds. A body can tolerate no more than two or three G's for any period of time. Actually, if you experienced four to six G's longer than six seconds, you could expect restricted muscular activity because of apparent increased body weight; you would lose peripheral vision and gray out; then you would lose central vision, black out and go unconscious because the blood would be pulled from the head to pool in the lower parts of the body.

"At this acceleration the gravity synthesizers are handling an awful lot more than that. I think *Tug Two* blew up because her gravity synthesizers failed."

"Well," I said, refusing to be impressed. "How many gravities *are* they handling?"

"To counteract the acceleration, this equipment is handling..." He pointed at the screen.

It said:

1,289,401.409 G's!

I tried to get my heart back down out of my throat. It meant my body, in the absence of synthesizers, would weigh 1,289,401.409 times what it normally did, due solely to acceleration and, now, deceleration!

"So," said Heller, "I don't think *Tug Two* blew up at all. I think the gravity synthesizers failed and her crew simply went splat! She may be somewhere in the universe now, still hurtling along as plasma. They only knew she disappeared. That's why I didn't bother with the problem. I hope the contractors did a good job on the gravity synthesizers. We were pushed to leave so fast that I didn't get too much chance to test the new installation."

He smiled reassuringly as the screen spark-flashed and blew out. "So don't be worried about the tug blowing up. It won't. It's we who would go bang, not the tug."

Heller put the button plate down. "As to arrival time, we would have found it easy to keep. But one has to be able to read screens very well to land in an area one has never seen before.

"Captain Stabb is just a bit nervous. He's a bit of a grouch like some old subofficers and he's gotten too careful." He shrugged. "He wants to see a place in daylight before he goes in for the first time, that's all. So he'll hang up about five hundred miles and study it in daylight for hours and when he's sure there aren't sudden traffic movements and that the base isn't a trap, he'll take it in, in the first darkness.

"Too bad. I planned a predawn arrival because I thought you'd want to be up and on the job early. You probably have things to do at the base.

"But it all has its advantages. I'll be able to look this so-called base over, too. I'll tell you what. Right now you look pretty shaky. Why don't you go get some more sleep and when we're hanging above that area in daylight, say about noon, come back here and have some lunch with me and you can show me the various points of interest.

Right now, if I were you, I'd get some more rest. You don't look good, you know."

I didn't even tell him to please turn off that awful churning wake that still surrounded us at every hand.

I cursed feebly to myself.

I was walking out that (bleeped) door just like that (bleeped) time-sight had shown—shoulders slumped and all caved in!

Chapter 5

As noon approached, I felt infinitely improved. We had come down out of time drive smoothly. We were now on auxiliaries, barely running. I had had a marvelous long sleep and as seventy-six hours had now passed since I had taken that (bleeping) *speed*, it was out of my bloodstream.

I had watched some Homeview comedies in the crew's salon and had even had a dice game with one of the engineers—he had lost half a credit to me.

But what made it really good was Stabb. He had seated himself in the captain's chair and when the dice game was over, he put his huge mouth near my ear. He whispered, "I been watching you, Officer Gris, and if I read the signs right, we're going to get a crack at that (bleeping) (bleepard) Royal officer, ain't we?"

I felt good enough to be witty. I whispered back, "I heard you very extinctly."

He laughed. It's a bit awesome to see an Antimanco laugh: their mouths and teeth are so big in proportion to their triangular faces. It was an uproarious laugh. In fact, it was the first time any of them had laughed and it so startled the off-duty pilot that he burst in to see if something was wrong.

The captain whispered to him and he whispered to the off-duty engineer and they both went off to whisper to their mates and very shortly there was a lot of pleased laughing in the forward end of the ship.

Captain Stabb took me by the hand as I was leaving. "Officer Gris, you're all right! My Gods, Officer Gris, you're all right!"

So when I went back to have lunch with Heller, I was feeling great.

Heller was in the upper lounge. He had laid out a tray of sparklewater and sweetbuns and he waved me to a seat.

He had the starboard viewscreens on to see the exterior view. We were hanging in the sun, five hundred miles above our base, just a hundred miles inside the Van Allen belts. And there, way below, was Turkey!

The ship was really on its side. Spacers are crazy. They don't really care whether they are right side up or down. It was a bit disconcerting to me to have a vertical tray and sit on a vertical seat. It always makes me feel like I'll fall for sure. The gravity synthesizers of course take care of it all but nevertheless I was very careful with my canister. It is such moments that make me glad I am not a spacer!

Regardless, I felt good and I actually enjoyed the sparklewater. When I had finished my lunch, life looked pretty good. We had all but arrived, had not blown up and the gravity compensators had held.

I noticed Heller had out all the computer papers I had given him on Voltar and several books and charts. I also saw the "delete" notice which said Lombar had removed all cultural and such material from the Earth data banks.

"I've been identifying these seas by local names," he said. "But you better verify them for me."

The day below was bright and almost cloudless. It was just past the middle of August in local seasons so it was somewhat dry and the only slight haze in some places was dust.

I was glad to know that he didn't know everything. "That sea at the bottom," I said, "below western Turkey, the bright blue one, is the Mediterranean. Just above Turkey there is the Black Sea—although as you can see for yourself, it isn't black. Over to your left, there, the one with all the little islands in it, is the Aegean Sea. And that little landlocked one in northwest Turkey, is the Sea of Marmara: that city you see at the top of it is Istanbul, once known as Byzantium and before that, Constantinople."

"Hey, you really know this place."

I was pleased. Yes, I really knew this place. And, factually speaking, while he might know engineering and space flight, he didn't know a ten-thousandth of what I knew about my own trade: covert operations and espionage. He would learn that to his sorrow in due course.

But I said, "Just to the left of the center of Turkey, there is a large lake. See it? That's Lake Tuz. Now look to the west of it and slightly south and you'll see another lake. That's Lake Aksehir. There's some more lakes just southwest of it. See them?"

He did. But he said, "Point out Caucasus."

Oh, my Gods, here we went on that stupid theme. "Over there, just east of the Black Sea, there's an arm of land that comes down and joins Turkey. That's Caucasus. Way over on the horizon is the Caspian Sea and that bounds Caucasus on the east. But you can't go in there. That's communist Russian country. Georgia and Armenia are right there on the Russian side of the border. But Caucasus is out of bounds. Forget it. I'm trying to show you something."

"Very pretty planet," said Heller irrelevantly. "You mean nobody can go into the Caucasus?"

I let him have it. "Listen, northeast of Turkey and clear to the Pacific Ocean on the other side of this planet, that's all communist Russia! They don't let anybody in, they don't let anybody out. They are a bunch of mad nuts. They're run exclusively by a secret police organization called the KGB!"

"Like the Apparatus?" he said.

"Yes, like the Apparatus! No! I mean you can't go there. Now will you pay attention?"

"That's awful," he said. "A piece of the planet that big being run by secret police. And it's such a pretty planet. Why does the rest of the planet let them get away with something crazy like that?"

"Russia stole the secrets of atomic fission and it's a thermonuclear power and you have to be careful of them because they're so crazy they could blow up the whole planet."

He was busy writing on a pad and, unlike him, was saying the words as he wrote: *"Russia crazy. Run by KGB secret police like Apparatus. Could blow up the world with stolen thermonuclear power. Got it."*

I finally had his attention. "Now get off this Caucasus fixation and pay attention."

"So poor Prince Caucalsia even lost his second home! The Russians got it!"

I raised my voice. "Look west from Lake Tuz in a straight line across the top of Lake Aksehir and about a third of that distance further west. That is Afyon. That's the landmark!"

Well, I had gotten him unfixed from that stupid Folk Legend 894M! He obediently reached for a control panel and the whole scene swooped up at us. I felt I was falling and grabbed hold of my seat.

"Oho!" said Heller, staring at the enlarged scene. "Hello, hello, hello! Looks just like Spiteos!"

Actually, I sometimes wondered if that was why this base long ago had been chosen by the Apparatus. But I said, "No, no. Just coincidence. Its name is Afyonkarahisar."

"What's that mean in Voltarian?"

I wasn't going to tell him the real meaning: Black Opium Castle. I said, "It means 'Black Fortress.' The base rock rises 750 feet. The ramparts on top of it are the remains of a Byzantine fort which replaced the original built by the Arzawa, a tribe of an ancient people called the Hittites."

"It would probably be blacker if it wasn't for that factory near it pouring out white dust."

"That's the cement plant. Afyon is a town of about seventy thousand people."

He pulled back the scene to get a wider view and sat there admiring it. There were still some white streaks of snow on the taller mountains around Afyon. The tiny outlying villages were a patchwork. None of the savage winds which came down from the high plateau were felt from such a height as this. Turkey is a pretty brutal country for the most part.

"What's all this yellow and orange?" He was looking at the vast panorama of flowers which blanket the valleys. And before I could stop him he twisted the controls and we were looking at them very close. It made me feel awful, like I'd fallen five hundred miles. Spacers are really crazy.

"Flowers?" said Heller.

"The yellow ones in the fields near the road are sunflowers. They are huge. They produce a vast number of seeds in the center which people love to eat. It's a food crop."

"Wow," he said. "There's enough square miles of them! But what are those smaller ones in the other fields? The ones with various colored petals, dark centers and gray-green leaves?"

He was looking at *Papaver somniferum,* the opium poppies, the stuff of deadly sleep and dreams, the source of heroin—the real reason the Apparatus had this base. He was too close for comfort. Afyon is the opium growing center of Turkey, perhaps the world.

"They sell them in the flower markets," I lied. He was such a child at a game he didn't know. "Now, what I wanted to point out was the actual base. Pull that view wider. Good. Now draw a line from that lake there. Got it? Through Afyonkarahisar. Now, right on that line is a mountain. Got it?"

He had. I continued, "The top of that mountain is an electronic simulation. It doesn't exist. But the wave scanners they use on this planet—and any they will develop—react on it normally. You just land straight through it and you are into our hangars."

"Pretty good," he said.

"It's quite old, really," I said. "Rock disintegrator crews came in here several decades ago from Voltar and built it and the subterranean base. It's quite extensive. Last year we enlarged it."

He seemed impressed, so I said, "Yes, I had a hand in its extension. I added a lot of burrows and twists and turns. You can emerge in several places quite unexpectedly. But I had a real master to work from."

"Oh?" he said.

I checked myself. I had almost said Bugs Bunny. He wouldn't understand. I hurried on. "Center in on that mountain and nearby you will see a satellite tracking station. Got it? Good. Now, at the end of that canyon, you see that square block building? Good. That's the International Agricultural Training Center for Peasants. All right, now do you see that new earth there in the north of the canyon? That is an archaeological dig in an old Phrygian tomb and those houses around it are where the scientists live."

"Well?" he said.

I wanted to startle him. He wasn't the only bright one in the universe. "The satellite engineers, the whole school staff, all the scientists at the dig—they're all us!"

"Well, I never! Really?"

I knew I had him. "Turkey is so crazy to get modernized, has been for over half a century, that a lot of our work is even state and internationally funded by Earth!"

"But how do you get papers? Identoplates and so on?"

"Listen, these are very primitive people. They breed heavily. They have disease and babies die. Typical riffraff. So for over half a century, when a baby is born, we've made sure the birth is registered. But when it dies, we've made sure the death isn't registered. The officials are corrupt. That gives us tons of birth certificates, more than we could ever hope to use.

"Also, the country is waist-deep in poverty and workers go abroad by the hundreds of thousands and they register overseas and this even gives us foreign passports.

"Once in a while—they have a thing called the *draft* for the Army—one of our birth certificates gets drafted. So an Apparatus guardsman answers the call and does his tour in the Turkish army. The Turkish army runs the country so we even have officers in Istanbul. Naturally, we choose people who look somewhat like Turks but this country has dozens of races in it so who notices?"

"Brilliant," said Heller. And, in fact, he was impressed. "Then we kind of own this little piece of the planet."

Pretty much," I said.

"I wish you controlled some of the Caucasus," he said. "I'd really like to look it over."

He was hopeless. I smiled indulgently. "Well, tonight we'll be groundside and you can catch a ride into Afyon and look over our little empire anyway." I wanted to really test those bugs that Prahd had implanted in him.

"Good," he said. "Thanks for the conducted tour. I really appreciate it."

We almost parted friends. On his side, anyway. The poor sap. He might be an expert in his own field. But not in mine. I really had him where I wanted him, over a score of light-years from home and friends and into an area we controlled. He had no Fleet pals here! And I had friends by the thousands!

He might as well get used to Earth. He would never leave it, even if I let him live!

Chapter 6

We slipped down secretly through the darkness toward our base on Planet Earth. I had formulated my instructions. I had them all ready to issue the moment we landed.

That afternoon, I had taken time to think it all over and review policy.

It is a sound maxim in covert operations that when you find you are acting on the orders of an insane person, you take complete stock of your own position in the mess. I had found that, without any slightest doubt, Lombar Hisst was a paranoid schizophrenic, compounded by pronounced megalomania, confirmed by aural hallucinations, complicated by probable heroin addiction and consolidated with a consumption of amphetamines: in other words, *stark, staring mad*. Nuts. Executing any of his commands could be very dangerous.

So I did a little résumé of position. I even did it in the proper résumé form. I wrote:

RÉSUMÉ OF POSITION

1. Lombar Hisst needed drugs on Voltar to undermine and overthrow the Voltar government and take power.

1-a. Blito-P3 was the only known source of such drugs.

1-b. The Earth base existed to keep the drugs coming.

2. Delbert John Rockecenter, by nominee, ownership and other means, controlled the pharmaceutical companies of the planet.

2-a. Delbert John Rockecenter, through his banks and another means, controlled, amongst the rest, the Government of Turkey.

2-b. Delbert John Rockecenter's wealth depended upon oil and the control of all Earth's energy sources.

2-c. Delbert John Rockecenter could go broke if anyone monkeyed with his energy monopoly.

2-d. Conclusion of 2: If the pharmaceutical monopoly passed into other, less criminal hands, we could be out on our stinking ear!

3. From the viewpoint of Earth, Jettero Heller's presence here would be extremely beneficial.

3-a. Earth would have cheap and abundant fuel.

3-b. As economic stresses are caused by scarce fuel, then Heller's technical assistance would, as a side benefit, abruptly end the raging inflation and bring about wide prosperity.

3-c. If Heller changed the fuel type, the air would clean up.

3-d. If Heller did not succeed, the planet would be liable to self-destruct from pollution.

3-e. If word got to the Grand Council that Heller had failed, it would launch an immediate and bloody invasion, costly to Voltar and fatal to Earth, just to prevent the present inhabitants from rendering the target worthless with their filthy housekeeping.

3-f. If Heller succeeded, the threatened invasion would go back on schedule to be undertaken a hundred years from now per the original Invasion Timetable.

3-g. In a hundred years, during which it had abundant and practical fuel, the planet could probably raise itself to a higher technological level and the type of "invasion" Earth would experience then is known as a "PC Type Invasion," meaning "Peaceful Cooperation" wherein Voltar would just want some bases and would minimally interfere in the planet's internal affairs. There would be no blood or destruction and everybody would be happy.

3-h. Jettero Heller's presence on Earth was a Godsend both to Earth and Voltar.

4. Soltan Gris had evidence that Lombar Hisst had put an unknown assassin close to one Soltan Gris.

4-a. If said Soltan Gris did not carry out the orders of said Lombar Hisst, said assassin would emphatically terminate the life of said Soltan Gris with malice aforethought and ferocity!

CONCLUSION: Carry out the exact orders of Lombar Hisst cleverly, painstakingly and with enormous care! And with no questions whatever!

If I do say so myself, it was a brilliant résumé of the situation. It covered not only the essentials but every salient point of any importance. A masterpiece!

So down we slid, undetected by the crude surveillance equipment of the primitive planet's military forces. They have what we call "bow and arrow"-type radar. Easily nullified.

We went through the electronic illusion of the mountaintop right on target. And I will say this, pirate or not, Captain Stabb was a good spaceship handler. We came down on the trundle dolly with only a severe jolt.

The ship vibrated as the trundle dolly moved us over to the side, into a bay within the mountain, clearing the landing target for other arrivals and take-offs.

I patted Captain Stabb on the back. We were fast friends now. "A good groundfall," I said. "Couldn't have done it better myself."

He beamed at me.

"Now, what I want you to do," I said, "is warn, as a friend, any Apparatus people you meet, that this bird we're carrying is actually a Crown agent armed with secret orders to execute anybody he finds anything out about. Just tip them off they'd take their life in their hands if they talked to him."

Oh, Captain Stabb went for that! The moment the airlock was opened, all three hundred pounds of him were down the landing ladder like an earthquake to spread the word while he pretended to be concerned only with clearing us in. A real jewel.

A door swung open down the passageway and Heller climbed up the rungs. "Any objection if I wander around?"

"None, none," I said cheerfully. "You can even absorb some local color. Here's a slip so they'll hand you appropriate clothes at the Garb Section, right down that passageway over there. And why not take a spin around town? It's early yet. Here's a transport authorization slip: you can hook on to one of the trucks. Lots of people speak English in Turkey, so that's okay. You haven't any papers yet, but nobody will bother you. Just say you're a new technician at the satellite tracking station. Feel free, have fun, live it up!" I added in commercial English with a gay laugh.

I watched him as he went smoothly down the ladder and disappeared into the Garb Section tunnel. He was just a stupid baby at this game, but after all, I had been a professional for a long time.

My baggage was all ready. I barked for a hangar handler and in minutes I had a motor dolly loaded up and was on my way.

There is one flaw in the Blito-P3 hangar. Earthquakes are common and severe in Turkey and this big of a space disintegrated out of solid rock needs an awful lot of pressure-beam supports. They turn off the cone ones when ships arrive and depart and then they turn them on again. I had not been down here for nearly a year and I had forgotten about them. I was right in the path of one when they were turned back on and it almost knocked me flat. Perhaps this made me a little more exacting and severe than I would have been, for truthfully, I was *awfully* glad to be out of that (bleeped) tug!

I stopped by the Officers' Section and grabbed me a trench coat.

Using the exit through the "archaeological workman's barracks," I ordered up a "taxi," piled in my baggage and had the Apparatus driver take me directly to the base commander's office. It is in a mud hut near the International Agricultural Training Center for Peasants. It seems to be accepted that he is its superintendent. That excuses all the traffic in and out of his place, for peasants come there to be trained—in how to raise a lot more opium for a lot less price.

The Turks are actually Mongols. The word *Turk* is really a corruption of their original name, "the T'u-Kin," which is Chinese. They invaded Asia Minor in about the tenth century, Earth time. But they don't look Chinese and they invaded and commingled in an area that already had hundreds of other racial types, so it is very simple to find, in the Voltar Confederacy of a hundred and ten planets, vast numbers of people who can pass for Turks.

The base commander was one of these. His real name was Faht, so he calls himself Faht Bey—the Turks put "Bey" after their names for some reason. He had grown pretty plump on his easy post. He had a fat wife and an oversized old Chevy car and western-style overstuffed furniture that would take his weight and he was pretty comfortable. He was wanted for a mass murder on Flisten and any thought of being relieved as base commander scared him into waves of shaking fat.

Obviously, the sudden news of my arrival, of which he had had no warning word, had perspired ten pounds off him in the last hour since the ship had called in for permission to land.

He was at the door when I came in. He was mopping his face with a huge silk handkerchief and bowing and trying to open the door wider and quivering all at the same time.

Ah, the joys of being an officer from headquarters! It scares the daylights out of people!

His wife got through the door with a tray bearing both tea and coffee and almost spilled them. Faht Bey was trying to wipe off a seat for me with his handkerchief—which only greased the chair up.

"Officer Gris," he quavered in a high-pitched voice. "I mean Sultan Bey," he quickly added, using my Turkish name. "I am delighted to see you. I trust you are well, that you have been well, that you will be well and that everything is all right!" (By the last he really meant, "Am I still base commander or are you carrying orders to have me disposed of?")

I put his mind at ease at once. I threw down my orders. "I have been appointed Inspector General Overlord of all operations related to Blito-P3—I mean Earth! At the slightest hint that you are not doing your job, cooperating and obeying me implicitly, I will have you disposed of."

He sat down so hard in his overstuffed office chair, it almost collapsed. He looked at the orders. He was ordinarily quite swarthy. Now he was gray. He opened his mouth to speak but no words came out.

"We can dispense with formalities," I said. "Get on your phone. Make three calls into Afyon right away. Your usual contacts, the café bartenders. Tell them that you have just received a secret tip that a young man, about six feet two in height, blond hair and passing himself off as a satellite technician, is actually an agent of the United States Drug Enforcement Agency, the

DEA, and that he is here prying around and not to talk to him."

Faht Bey was on that phone like a shot.

The local natives are very friendly with us. They overlook everything. They cooperate one hundred percent. They, and even the commander of the local army barracks, think we are really the Mafia. It puts us in all the way.

Faht Bey finished and looked up like an obedient dog.

"Now," I said, "call two local toughs, give them the description and tell them to find him and beat him up."

Faht Bey tried to protest. "But the DEA is always friendly with us! We have every agent they got in Turkey on our payroll! And, Sultan Bey, we don't want no dead bodies in any alleys in Afyon! The police might hear of it and they'd have to go to work and they wouldn't like that!"

I could see why they needed an Inspector General Overlord!

But Faht Bey was just quavering right on. "If you want somebody killed, why don't you just do the usual and take him up to the archaeological dig . . ."

I had to shout at him. "I didn't say kill him! I just said to beat him up. He's got to learn it's an unfriendly place!"

That was different. "Oh, he ain't really a DEA man!"

"No, you idiot. He's a Crown agent! If he learns anything, it could be your head!"

Oh, that really was different! Worse. But he made the call.

When he finished, he nervously drank both the tea and the coffee his wife had set out for me. It was nice to know how thoroughly I could upset him. I gloated. It was so different from Voltar!

"Now, are my old quarters ready?"

This upset him further. I finally got it out of him. "That dancing girl you had there got to playing around with anybody and she gave the (bleep) to four guards and stole some of your clothes and ran off."

Well, women always were unfaithful. And factually, there aren't any real dancing girls left in Turkey. They've all emigrated elsewhere and what remains are just the bawds in the big city, not real belly dancers. "Get on that phone to our contact in the Istanbul Sirkeci quarter and have him ship one in on the morning plane."

Faht Bey's wife came in with some more tea and coffee. Now that important things were cared for, I sat down and drank some of the coffee. It was as thick as syrup to begin with and the heaps of sugar in it made it almost solid.

The base commander was through so I said, "Are Raht and Terb here?"

He bobbed his head. "Raht is. Terb is in New York."

I produced Lombar's now-sealed orders to Raht. "Give these to Raht. Have him on the morning plane to the U.S. Give him plenty of expense money as he's going to Virginia to get something ready."

"I don't know if I can get him a seat," said Faht Bey. "Turkish airlines . . ."

"You'll get him a seat," I said.

He bobbed his head. Yes, he would get him a seat.

"Now," I said, "speaking of money, here is an order." I threw it on the desk. It was a pretty good order. I had typed it myself on the tug's administrative machine. It said:

> KNOW ALL:
> The Inspector General Overlord must be
> advanced any and all funds he asks for any
> time he asks for them without any such
> (bleeped) fool things as signatures and receipts.
> It is up to the Inspector General Overlord how
> he spends them. And that's that!
> Finance Office
> COORDINATED INFORMATION
> APPARATUS, VOLTAR

I had even forged a signature and identoplate stamp
nobody could read. It would never go back to Voltar. Voltar doesn't even know these Blito-P3 funds exist. Clever.

It made him blink a bit. But he took it and put it
in his files and then, because I was holding out my hand,
went into the back room where he kept his safe.

"Ten thousand Turkish lira and ten thousand dollars
United States will do for a start," I called after him.

He brought them out and laid the wads in my hand
and I stuffed them in the pocket of my trench coat.

"Now," I said, "open that top drawer of your desk
and take out the Colt .45 automatic you keep there and
hand it over."

"It's my own gun!"

"Steal another off some Mafia hit man," I said.
"That's where you got this one. You wouldn't want me
to violate Space Code Number a-36-544 M Section B,
would you? Alien disclosure?"

He did as he was told. He even added two extra
loaded clips. I checked the weapon out. I had seen the
gun there a year ago when I was snooping in his desk
looking for blackmail data. It was a U.S. Army 1911A1.

But a year ago I didn't have the rank I had now. That he had taken it off the Mafia was pure guess. But sure enough, it had three notches filed into the butt plate.

I wanted to reassure him. No sense in making him too panicky. I cocked and spun the .45 expertly and pulled the trigger. There was no bullet under the firing pin, of course. And the barrel had wound up pointed at his stomach, not his head. The gun just went click. "Bull's-eye!" I said in English, laughing.

He wasn't laughing. "Timyjo Faht," I said, using his Flisten police-blotter name, and speaking in a mixture of Voltarian and English, "you and I are going to get along just fine. So long, of course, as you do everything I tell you, *break your (bleep)* to see to my creature comforts and *keep your nose clean.* There's nothing illegal you can do that I can't do better. So what I want around here is *respect.*" He also speaks English. He also deals with the Mafia. So he got my point.

I gave the Colt .45 another twirl and put it in my trench coat pocket just like I'd seen an actor called Humphrey Bogart do in an old Earth film last year.

I went back to my waiting "taxi." I got in. In American, I said, "Home, James, and step on it!"

For, in truth, I was home. This was my kind of country. Of all the places in the universe I'd been, this was the one place that really appreciated my type. Here, I was their kind of hero. And I loved it.

Chapter 7

I rode through the sultry night, the air like soft, black velvet on my face. To the right and left of me the sunflowers flashed along in the headlights. And beyond them, nicely obscured from the casual passing tourist, were the vast expanses of *Papaver somniferum,* the deadly opium poppies, the reason the Apparatus had settled here in the first place.

It is an interesting story as it sheds some insight on how the Apparatus works, and tonight, when we found ourselves held up by a procession of badly tail-lit carts, I went over it.

Long ago, an Apparatus cultural and technical survey crew, made up of a subofficer and three Apparatus peoplographers, had been interrupted by the outbreak of what they call, on Earth, World War I. They had missed their pickup ship, were unable to get to the rendezvous and thereafter had dodged across this border and that, taking advantage of the turmoils of war. They had gotten into Russia when it was writhing with revolution and had fallen south through the Caucasus and, from Armenia, had crossed the border into Turkey.

They had hidden out on the slopes of Buyuk Agri, a 16,946-foot peak known otherwise as Mount Ararat. They put their call-in signal there in the hopes that its steady radio beep and the prominence of the mountain would eventually bring an Apparatus search ship.

But the war came to an end and still no rescue ship, so, pretty chilled with altitude and privation, they slogged their way westward, vowing amongst them not to stop until they found warmer weather. It must have been a bitter trip as the high plateau of eastern Turkey is no garden spot. But they made it, assisted by the fact that Turkey, which had been in the war on the wrong side, was in the chaos of defeat and victor dismemberment.

They came at length to Afyon. It was warmer. And before them they saw the remarkable tall black rock and fortress, Afyonkarahisar. They put their call-in signal up in the ruins and made shift to survive, hiding in the war-ripped countryside. They could actually speak Turkish by this time and the land abounded with deserters.

Nineteen hundred twenty, Earth date, came. A huge Greek expeditionary force was approaching Afyon to grab a big slice of Turkey. The Turkish general, Ismet Pasha, not only checked the Greek army but actually defeated the invaders twice and in the very shadow of Afyonkarahisar.

Caught up in all this, the Apparatus subofficer and the three peoplographers chose sides, took uniforms and weapons from the dead and actually fought in the second battle as Turkish soldiers.

The following month somebody in the Apparatus, probably looking for an excuse for a vacation, noticed they had a cultural and technical survey team missing. It was not a very important survey—it was the twenty-ninth Blito-P3 had had in the last several thousand years. The Timetable did not call for an invasion of that planet for another hundred and eighty years or more but this Apparatus officer got permission and a scoutship and was probably surprised to find the call-in beeping away on the top of Afyonkarahisar. So the Apparatus squad was finally rescued after nearly seven years.

This survey team subofficer, probably himself looking for a sinecure, came back with a wonderful idea.

Old Muhck, Lombar's predecessor, had listened.

It seemed that during World War I, the rest of the world had begun to adopt a Russian idea called "passports"; it had failed utterly to save the Russian government from revolution and was silly, so, of course, the other governments were avidly taking it up. In the predictable future, and long before the invasion was scheduled, it would be pretty hard to infiltrate Blito-P3.

Old Muhck was fairly competent. He knew very well that the Apparatus would be called upon to furnish pre-invasion commotion someday. This consists of people in various countries to run around hysterically in the streets screaming, "The invaders are coming! Run for your lives!"; power plant operators who blow up the works; army officers who order their troops to flee; and newspaper publishers who come out with headlines, *Capitulate to the Invader Demands Before It Is Too Late!* That sort of thing. Standard tradecraft.

But there was a clincher on the idea: finance!

Now, every intelligence organization has the primary problem, when working inside enemy lines, of finding money to do so. Voltarian credits are no good and can't even be exchanged. Intelligence is costly and robbing banks calls attention to oneself. Imported gold and diamonds in such quantities can be traced. Getting hold of enemy money to spend is rough!

The subofficer had a piece of news. A country on Blito-P3, the United States of America, had passed a piece of legislation called "The Harrison Act" in 1914 and was pushing it into heavy effect by this date of 1920, Earth time. It regulated the traffic of narcotics, namely opium. So, of course, the price of opium was going to go sky-high. And that's what they raised around Afyon. It was the world center for it!

As "Turkish veterans" on the winning side, they had an "in." And what an "in"! They were war heroes and revolutionary pals with the incoming regime of Mustafa Kemal Pasha Ataturk!

So old Muhck, operating on the principle that governs all Voltar, really ("There's lots of time if you take it in time"), authorized the project. The cost was small. He probably had some people he didn't want around but to whom he owed favors. And the Blito-P3 base was born.

Up to Lombar's tenure, nobody had thought much about the base. It just ran on as a local, almost unsupervised operation. Then Lombar, assisted by Muhck's old age and, some say, some judiciously introduced poison, took over the Apparatus. This was in the early 1970s, Earth time.

Lombar, casting about for ways and means to accomplish his own ambitions, had his attention drawn to this obscure base by a report that the United States of America, a country he was now aware existed on Blito-P3, had decided that most of the opium which was slipping past Rockecenter's control was coming from Turkey. And they undertook to pay huge sums to Turkey to stop growing opium.

Instead of reacting with alarm, Lombar knew exactly what would happen. The payments would fall into the hands of the Turkish politicians and they would not pass them on to the farmers and hardship would occur in the Afyon district.

And Lombar suddenly saw his chance on Voltar. For Voltar had never had any involvement with narcotics: their doctors used gas anesthetics and cellologists could handle most pains. He had reviewed drug history in the politics of Blito-P3 and found that a country named England had once totally undermined a population and overthrown the government of China using opium. From there, he planned his own advancement on Voltar.

He helped subsidize the starving farmers by buying their unwanted surplus. He increased the importance of Section 451 in the Apparatus and apparently after a couple of management failures, had found an Academy officer to take it over—namely me.

The U.S. subsidy was soon cancelled. But if the Apparatus had been "in" before, it was the hero of the day now. It was king here in Afyon and Lombar soon would be King on Voltar if he could figure out how to do it. Apparatus Earth base personnel were still the descendants of Turkish war heroes and, like every other Turkish business, they had plaster heads of Mustafa Kemal Ataturk, the father of modern Turkey, all over the place. Long live the revolution! Long live opium! Long live the Apparatus! And long live His Majesty Lombar, if he could turn the trick on Voltar.

My contemplation ended. Carts or no carts, we had arrived back at the mountain. And there sat my villa!

It had once belonged to some Turkish pasha, a noble of the long-departed regime and probably, before him, to some Byzantine lord and before him some Roman lord and before him some Greek lord and before him who knows: Turkey is the most ruin-strewn place on Blito-P3. Crossroads between Asia and Europe, most of the civilized Earth races you hear about had, at one time or another, colonized Turkey or run an empire from it! It is an archaeologist's fondest dream: a land absolutely chock-a-block with ruins!

The Apparatus subofficer who founded the place had also rebuilt this villa and lived here a long time. Its maintenance was a standard piece of allocation budgets. Lombar Hisst had once even had the daffy idea of coming down here, a thing which he would never do—it's fatal for an Apparatus chief to turn his back on Voltar—and so had increased the allocation.

It was built straight in against the mountain. It had big gateposts and walls that hid six acres of grounds and its low, Roman style house.

It was all dark. I hadn't phoned ahead. I wanted to surprise them.

The "taxi driver" put my luggage down by the dark gate. He was a veteran Apparatus personnel, a child rapist, if I remembered.

The dim light, reflected from the dash of the old Citroen, showed me that he had his hand out.

Ordinarily, I would have been offended. But tonight, in the velvet dark, gleeful with the joy of arriving back, I reached into my pocket. The Turkish lira inflates at about a hundred percent per year. When last I handled any it was about 90 Turkish lira (£T) to the U.S. dollar. But the dollar inflates too, so I guessed it must be about one hundred and fifty to one by now. Besides, it's what we call "monkey-money": you're lucky if anyone will take it outside of Turkey. And my new order gave me an unlimited supply.

I pulled out two bills, thinking they were one's and handed them over.

He took them to his dashlight to inspect them. I flinched! I had given him two one-thousand Turkish lira notes! Maybe thirteen dollars American!

"Geez," said the driver in American slang—he talks English and Turkish just like everybody else around here—"Geez, Officer Gris, who do yer want bumped off?"

We both went into screams of laughter. The Mafia is around so much that American gangster slang is a great joke. It made me feel right at home.

In fact, I pulled out two more one-thousand lira sheets of monkey-money. I hitched up my trench coat collar. In American, I said out of the corner of my mouth, "Listen, pal, there's a broad, a dame, a skirt, see. She'll be getting off the morning plane from the big town. You keep your peepers peeled at the airport, put the snatch on her, take her to the local sawbones and get her checked for the itch in the privates department and if she gets by the doc, take her for a ride out here. If she don't, just take her for a ride!"

"Boss," he said, cocking his thumb like he had a .45, "you got yerself a deal!"

We screamed with laughter again. Then I gave him the two additional bills and he drove off happy as a clam.

Oh, it was good to be home. This was my kind of living.

I turned to the house to yell for somebody to come out and get my baggage.

Chapter 8

I had just opened my mouth when I closed it. A far better idea had occurred to me. In the country, they go to bed the moment they can't see: they were all asleep. There should be about thirteen staff, counting the three young boys; actually they were two Turkish families and they had been with the place since the subofficer had originally rebuilt it, maybe since the Hittites had built it for all I knew. They had far more loyalty to us than to their own government and they wouldn't have said anything even if they noticed something odd and they were too stupid to do that—just riffraff.

They lived in the old slave quarters to the right of the gate, a building hidden by trees and a hedge. The old gatekeeper, pushing ninety—which is quite old on Earth —had died and nobody had hired a new one as they couldn't decide whose relative should have the job.

The alleged *ghazi* or man-in-charge was a tough, old peasant we called Karagoz after a funny Turkish stage character. But the real boss was a widow named Melahat: the name means "beauty" but she was anything else but that, being dumpy and gimlet-eyed; she kept the rest of them hopping.

My plan was to first find something wrong. I took a hand-light out of my bag—one I had stolen from the ship. On secretly silent feet, slipping like a ghost across the cobble-paved courtyard, I faded into the trees, not even letting my trench coat whisper.

Suppressing the beam of the light with two fingers across it, I looked at the grass: it was cut. I looked at the shrubs: they were pruned. I looked at the fountains and pools: they were cleaned out and running.

Disappointed, but not giving up hope, I slid into the main house. Roman dwellings are built around a court open to the sky. The fountain in the center was keeping the place cool. The marble floor was clean with no dust. The side rooms were spotless. Of course, they were kind of bare: I had not had much in the way of funds when I had been here last; the bare Romanness of the house had been Turkified by large numbers of colorful large rugs and draperies and I had sold these to passing tourists one by one—I don't much care for flummery anyway. The staff had tried to replace them here and there with grass mats, but even these were neat and clean. No, I couldn't find anything wrong with the main house. (Bleep)! It spoiled the joke I was about to play.

My own room was at the back, chunked into the mountain for good reasons. I was about to pick its locks and enter when I suddenly remembered what Faht Bey had said about the whore stealing my clothes! That was it!

On silent feet—I had forgotten to change my insulator boots—I crept up to the old slave quarters. I knew it was composed of two large rooms, both opening off the center front door.

I took the Colt .45 out of my pocket and silently pulled back the slide, easing a shell under the firing pin.

I turned my hand-light up to full flare.

I drew my foot back.

Then, all in one motion, I kicked the door open, pounded the glare of the light into the room and fired the gun in the air!

Ah, you should have seen the commotion!

Thirteen bodies went straight up and came down trying to burrow under beds, blanket and floor!

"*Jandarma!*" I bellowed. It is Turkish for "police." And then, just to add to the confusion, in English I yelled, "Freeze, you (bleepards) or I'll rub you out!"

Well, let me tell you, that was one confused staff! They couldn't see who it was against the glare of the light. They were screaming in pure terror. All kinds of Turkish words came spattering out like "innocent" and "haven't done anything!"

And to add the sugar to the coffee, an Apparatus guard contingent, alerted by the shot, came racing up the road from the archaeological workmen's barracks, engines roaring!

Pandemonium!

Bedlam!

Within a minute the guard contingent—they go by the name of security forces and are there to "protect any valuables dug up"—came rushing into the grounds and converged on my light.

The subofficer's own torch hit me. He hauled up. He said, "It's Sultan Bey!"

The gardener's small boy at once began to throw up.

The staff stopped screaming.

I started laughing.

Somebody turned on some lights. Old Karagoz pulled his head out from under a blanket. He said, "It's Sultan Bey all right!"

The guards started laughing at Karagoz.

A couple of the staff started laughing.

But Melahat wasn't laughing. She was kneeling on the floor. In Turkish, she was wailing at the wall, "I knew when he came back from America and found out that whore had stolen his clothes he'd be furious. I knew it. I knew it!"

They thought I'd been to America.

One of the small boys, about eight, came crawling over and started tugging at the bottom hem of my raincoat. His name was Yusuf, I recalled. "Please don't shoot Melahat," he pleaded. "Please, Sultan Bey! We all pooled our money and we bought you new clothes. And we even stole some extras from tourists. Don't shoot Melahat. Please, Sultan Bey!"

Oh, it was a great homecoming. The guard subofficer said, "I told them they better put on a gatekeeper. Serves them right." And then he stepped close and whispered, "Thanks for the tip about that Crown agent." And the guards drove off laughing.

I pointed the gun at the gardener. "Your grounds are in terrible shape. Get up right now and fix them." And he scuttled out like a rocket, followed by his two helpers, both boys. I pointed the gun at the cook. "Get me something to eat and then clean up your kitchen, it's filthy." And he scuttled out. I pointed the gun at the head cleaning girl, "Get those rooms dusted! Right now!" And she and two small girls who help her left with speed. And then I pointed the gun at Karagoz, "Your accounts are probably in total disorder. Get me a full accounting by dawn!"

As I walked to my room, I burst out laughing. How different than Voltar.

How good it was to be home!

Here, I was power itself!

On this planet, I could get anything executed, even Heller!

Chapter 9

Melahat had followed me into my room. It is a big place. It has lots of closets. She showed me that my clothes had been replaced and were hanging there. She stood wringing her hands.

"Please," she begged, "I told you that that girl was no good. After you went to America she just started running around with anybody. She said you hadn't paid her and she grabbed your clothes and ran off."

"There'll be another one in here tomorrow," I said.

"Yes, Sultan Bey."

"Put her in that room that used to be used for tools."

"Yes, Sultan Bey. Are these clothes all right?"

"They probably won't fit."

"Yes, Sultan Bey."

Two small boys rushed in with my baggage and hastened out.

"Tell that cook to bring in some food. Now clear out!"

"Yes, Sultan Bey."

A serving man and the cook hastened in with a big bowl of hot *iskembe corbusi*—it's a heavy soup of tripe and eggs and they often keep it on the back of the stove just in case. There was also *lakerda*, slices of dried fish. There was a big pitcher of chilled *sira*, which is fermented grape juice and a platter of *baklava*, a sweet pastry containing ground walnuts and syrup.

"It's all we have right now," the cook quavered. "Nobody said you were arriving!"

"Get to town at dawn," I reprimanded him, "and get some decent food! And stop putting all the purchase money in your pocket!"

He blanched at the accusation. So I said, "And send in Karagoz!" That really upset him for Karagoz handles the accounts. He and the serving man rushed out.

I sat down at the table and began to eat. It was delicious! What the Gods must dream of—the reward for being mortal.

Karagoz came. "You said I had until dawn to finish the accounts."

"You've stolen and sold all the rugs," I said.

"Yes, Sultan Bey." He knew (bleeped) well I had sold them but he sure knew better than to say so.

I had a mouthful of wonderful *baklava*. I washed it down with the chilled *sira*. "Add a special requisition to buy rugs for the whole house. The most expensive kind. Even Persian." Who knew when I might hit another snag on money and would have to sell them again. Recent experience on Voltar had made me prudent.

"Yes, Sultan Bey."

"And turn in any commission you get to me," I said.

"Yes, Sultan Bey."

"And reduce the amount of money you're spending on staff food. By half. They're too fat!"

"Yes, Sultan Bey."

"That is all," I said, dismissing him with a wave of the *sira* glass.

He backed out the door.

I sat there grinning. I really knew how to handle people. Psychology is a wonderful thing. A true tool in my line of business.

I could get away with anything on this planet!

And that made me think of Heller.

I bolted the door to my room. I went into the right-hand closet. I pushed the back panel and it slid open. I stepped through into what was really my room.

It was bigger than the one I had just left. It was unknown to the staff. It didn't show from the outside as it was dug back into the mountain. A secret door at the end of it led right down into the base. Another secret door led to a passage that ended in the archaeological barracks.

I opened a closet. The laugh was on the staff. Here were my real clothes, various costumes of different nationalities. They were all here.

A cupboard disclosed that my makeup kits were intact.

I opened a panel and revealed my guns. They were protected by a device which took moisture and oxygen out of their hiding place. I removed the chambered cartridge and clip from the Colt .45 and put it away. I got out a Beretta which is more my style, really, being easier to hide—and I even have a license for it.

That done, I opened a safe and reviewed my passports. Some were expired in the last year and I made a note to get them renewed. I looked over other identification documents: they were fine.

With a quick inspection, I verified that all my assorted luggage, like suitcases and attaché cases, were there.

Great. I was in business.

I went back into the advertised bedroom and changed my clothes, noting I should be more careful and not go around in space insulator boots in public.

I put on a sport shirt with flaming poinsettias, a pair of black pants and some loafers. I looked in the mirror: no movie gangster ever looked more at home.

Now for Heller. I picked up *the* box and went back into my real room. I unloaded the gear and set it up on a table. Nothing wrong with it from the trip.

I set it all up and then, as an afterthought, brought in the pitcher of *sira* and a glass.

What was Heller up to?

I turned on the activator-receiver and viewscreen.

I didn't think I'd need the 831 Relayer as he wasn't in the ship and must be within ten miles.

And there he was!

Chapter 10

Heller was walking along a dark street.

I wondered what had taken him so long to get into Afyon and then realized that, after the rumor I'd spread, probably nobody at the hangar would give him a ride and he'd had to walk. It was only a few miles, they had probably said in a nasty tone of voice.

I adjusted the viewscreen controls. I found out that by flaring the screen a little bit, I could possibly pick things up as well as Heller could.

The picture was really great quality. Because I could look directly at the peripheral vision area, even though it was a trifle blurry, I could probably see what was going on around him even better than Heller: a matter of my concentrating on it while he was looking at something else. Great.

He wasn't doing anything. He was just walking along the street. Up ahead of him were a few lights from shop windows. But Afyon is really dead at night and it was at least ten by now.

It gave me time to study the instruction book. I found to my delight that, by pushing a button, the screen split into two screens. You could go on watching the continuing action while you replayed, at any speed you wished, fast or slow or still-framed, on the second screen. And all without interrupting recording. Great. What a brilliant fellow that Spurk had been. Good thing he was dead.

It was too bad, though, that I had missed Heller's transportation refusal. It would have been delightful to watch. I fed in a pack of strips and vowed never to turn this thing off. Then I could speed review for juicy bits and save myself lots of time.

The action of doing a recording loading almost made me miss something.

Way up the street, somebody had moved across a light path from a store window. Aha! There was somebody up the street, standing in a dark place. Somebody waiting for Heller?

If Heller had registered it, he gave no evidence of it. He just kept strolling forward. I thought to myself, the dumb boob. In Afyon, you don't keep right on walking toward a possible ambush. Not if you want to go on living! Heller was too green at this business. He would not last long. The green die young, one of my Apparatus professors used to say—Tailing 104 and 105, Apparatus school.

Yes! The figure was waiting for Heller. Whoever it was had chosen a patch of street darker than the rest.

Heller drew nearer and nearer. And then almost walked right on by.

The stranger halted him. The fellow was shorter than Heller. I stilled the frame of the second screen to study the face. More of a hatchet than a face. Hard to tell in this light.

"You from the DEA?" the stranger whispered.

"The what?" said Heller, not whispering.

"Shhh! The Yew S Drug Enforcement. The narcs!"

"Who are you?"

"I'm Jimmy 'The Gutter' Tavilnasty. Come on, you narcs and us have always been friendly." I thought, indeed they have. The DEA narcotics agents would be paupers if it weren't for the bribes of the Mafia.

Heller said, "What makes you think I'm DEA?"

"Oh, hell. That didn't take any figuring. I seen you wading around in the poppy fields and I suspected it. And then when I saw you climb that skyscraper of a rock over there, I knew it. Anybody else would have gone up the regular way, but you went up the front, hoping nobody would see you. And then when this," and here he lifted a night-rifle sight, "showed you surveying the whole valley with a glass, I stopped guessing."

"I was measuring distances," said Heller.

The Mafia hood laughed. "Trying to estimate the crop in advance, are you? Pretty smart. The Turks lie like hell about their morf."

"What did you want from me?" said Heller.

"Good. I like that. Get down to business. Listen, I been hanging around here for weeks and you're the first promisin' new face to show up. Now, being you're from the DEA, there's a C-note in it for you if you can help."

"A C-note?" said Heller. "A credit?"

"No, no, no. You guys can't have the credit. That's mine! Look, I got a contract on Gunsalmo Silva."

Heller must have made a movement. Jimmy "The Gutter" darted a hand into his jacket, about to pull a rod. But Heller had merely whipped out a notebook and pen. "Geez, pal," said Jimmy "The Gutter," "don't DO that!"

"Now," said Heller, pen poised. "What did you say his name was? Spell it."

"G-U-N-S-A-L-M-O S-I-L-V-A, as in *dead man*. You see, he was a bodyguard to Don 'Holy Joe' Corleone and we got an idea that he put the finger on his own boss and maybe even pulled the trigger a few times himself. The Family is *very* upset."

"Family upset," muttered Heller, writing.

"Good, I figured you'd have an 'in' with the local fuzz."

"And who do I send the information to, if you're not around?"

The hood scratched his head, just a shadow of movement. The light was very bad. "Why, I guess you could put it through to Babe Corleone, that's 'Holy Joe's' ex. That's Apartment P—Penthouse—136 Crystal Parkway, Bayonne, New Jersey. Phone's unlisted but it's KLondike 5-8291."

Heller had written it all down. He closed the notebook and was putting it and the pen away. "All right. Too bad his family is upset. If I see him, I'll tell him."

The effect was electric!

The hood started to go for his heater. Then he halted the motion. "Wait a minute," he said. He took Heller by the arm and steered him into a pool of light and looked at him.

Absolute disgust contorted the pockmarked face of Jimmy "The Gutter" Tavilnasty. "Why, you're just a kid! One of them God (bleeped) leftover flower nuts out here looking around for some free junk! You can't be more than sixteen or seventeen! Go home to your mama and leave a man's world alone!"

The hood gave Heller a shove. He spat at Heller's feet. He turned his back and stalked away.

Heller just stood there.

I myself was surprised. Doctor Crobe was wrong. He had pointed out that Heller would look young. He had said that at twenty-six, Heller would look like an Earthman of eighteen or nineteen. The health of his unblemished skin had lowered that. People would think he was just tall for his age the way some kids are!

Then I hugged myself. Oh, this was better than I had planned! You have to realize that, on Earth, they don't take kids seriously. It's almost a crime for a man to be seventeen!

Heller, after a bit, walked on. It was too bad Spurk had never put a feeling indicator in the lineup. Heller must feel about one inch tall!

There was a bar ahead. There are very few in Afyon—really the place is no city. And the bars are not much. The men hang out there during the day, taking up chairs and nursing coffee and reading newspapers. The dumb proprietors don't object.

Heller walked in. And I suddenly realized he didn't have any money to order anything with. I hoped he'd forget he only had credits on him and couldn't produce them. If he did, I could seize him for a violation of Space Code Number a-36-544 M Section B and even imprison him for making the presence of an extraterrestrial known. I made a mental note to be on the watch for such. That pen and notebook had been a near breach but wouldn't stand up in a charge. Money would.

The proprietor was the usual greasy, mustached Turk. He was taking his time. The place was practically empty as it was very late for Afyon and the proprietor had nothing else to do. He finally came over to Heller at the counter.

In English, Heller said, "Could you give me a glass of water?"

The Turk said, "*Ingilizce*," and shook his head to indicate he didn't speak it. The Hells he didn't. Half the people around here did. He started to walk off and then I saw a light come into his eyes, followed closely by a cunning look.

Now, it is a funny thing about Earth races. From one race to the next, they rarely can tell how old anyone is. And Heller might look seventeen to an American, but a Turk would not notice that. They think all foreigners look alike!

At last I began to see the fruits of the rumor I had had Faht Bey plant. The proprietor changed his mind. He reached under the counter and got a somewhat dirty glass and he filled it with water from a jug. But he didn't put it in front of Heller. He carried it over to one of the many empty tables and pulled back a chair and pointed.

Heller, the fool, went over and sat down. Now, while the water in Turkey is usually pretty drinkable, that dirty glass gave me hopes. Maybe Heller would come down with cholera!

The proprietor went straight over to a telephone at the far end of the room. And then I found out something very interesting: the audio-respondo-mitter, not being tuned to his ear channels, could evidently hear what was going on in the room better than Heller! All I had to do was advance the audio gain. While it brought up the room noises uncomfortably high, you could pick out what you wanted to hear. What a nice rig for spies! Which is to say, the handler of spies. An ambulant bug! I was beginning to really love this rig.

The proprietor just said three words in Turkish: "He is here." And he hung up the phone.

But Heller was not drinking the water. From his

pocket he had pulled half a dozen poppies! He put them in the glass!

Oh, how sweet, I sneered. He had bought the lie that this type was for the flower markets and he had picked himself a bouquet! Well, they do go in for a lot of flowers on Voltar. And come to remember, some of the estates on Manco—was it Atalanta?—specialized in breeding new varieties. Lombar had even once considered bringing seeds back and growing the poppies at home but he had been given pause by the fact that a new variety of blossom always produced enthusiasm amongst the flower fans and one could see these from air surveillance too easily. I also dimly recall there was some problem with a seed virus that attacked poppies. But anyway, Heller was indulging nostalgia. Probably homesick for pretty flowers.

He was certainly intrigued by them. He stroked their leaves as they sat there in the glass. He smelled them.

I lost interest in what he was doing and was suddenly very interested in how he looked. By peripheral vision, a big mirror was showing his image.

They had given him clothes too small! Even though they might not have had his size, I was certain this was intentional. The sleeves of the shirt and jacket were three inches too short. The shoulders pinched way in. They had given him no tie and he had just buttoned the shirt.

Now, Kemal Ataturk had made it against the law to wear Turkish national costumes and had forced the whole country into Western dress. He had even put people in prison for wearing the red Turkish *fez*. And as a result, the Turks, with no tailors for it, have since looked about as sloppy as anyone ever.

But Heller was worse!

He had gotten cement dust on him climbing that

rock. He had evidently torn his jacket. He had mud on his shoes from the poppy fields.

He looked like a complete bum!

Where, I gloated, was the spiffy Royal officer now? Where were the shimmering lounge suits? Where was the natty working cover suit and the little red racing cap? Where was that fashion plate in Fleet full dress that would make the girls faint?

Oh, I gloated! Were our roles reversed now! On Voltar I was the underdog, the uncouth, the tramp. Not on Earth! I glanced down at my lovely gangster outfit. And then I looked back at Heller, a slovenly, dirty tramp!

This was *my* planet, not his!

And there he was, my prisoner. He had no funds to buy any clothes, to go anywhere.

"Heller," I said aloud in gloating glee, "I've got you just where I want you. And in my fondest dreams, I never thought you could look that bad! A dirty, penniless bum in a stinking slum café! Welcome to Planet Earth, Heller, you and your fancy ways. Everyone does MY bidding here, not yours! Our roles have reversed utterly! And it's about time!"

Chapter 11

What a stupid, untrained "special agent"!

Didn't he realize the danger he was putting himself in? Yet, there he was, in the center of the planet's opium trade, sitting in a cheap bar, a stranger in the place, a foreigner, his back to the door, and a bouquet of opium poppies in front of him! Just asking for it! And no way to get out of trouble if anything did happen. No connections. No friends. No money. And he didn't even speak Turkish! What a child. I could almost feel sorry for him.

Heller sat there for a bit, looking at the flowers. From time to time he rearranged them.

Then he took one of them, a gaudy, orange blossom and idly began to pull off its petals. I wondered if he was nervous. I certainly would have been in such a spot as that!

An opium poppy has a big black ball in the center. Really, that's the bulk of the flower. He had it stripped. He smelled it. Silly performance: fragrance comes from petals, not the stamen.

Heller put it aside. He took another flower from the glass. He got out a piece of paper. He laid the whole flower on half the sheet and straightened out its petals. Then he folded the paper over, covering it.

Then he took his fist and banged the package!

I really laughed. That isn't the way you press flowers. You put them in between two sheets of paper and you gently let them flatten and you put it away to dry. You don't bang it with your fist. He didn't even know how to press flowers: he should have asked his mother!

He opened the paper and of course the whole thing was a complete mess. The huge center ball had simply squashed! That isn't the way to handle an opium poppy. You gently scrape the ball and you get the sap and then you boil it and you have morphine!

He must have realized that wasn't how it was done for he just emptied the squashed mess on the table, folded the paper and put it in his pocket.

He looked up. People had been drifting in: Turks of the area, dressed in their sloppy jackets, tieless white shirts, unpressed pants. Maybe twenty of them had come in, a strange crowd for this time of night. I realized that the word had spread. They just sat down at tables, not ordering anything, not talking, not looking at Heller. They seemed to be waiting.

Then the front door crashed open and into the room swaggered the two top wrestlers of the area!

Now, the Turks love wrestling. It is a national sport. They wrestle in any style. They are big and they are tough and they are good! So that was who Faht Bey had called! The wrestling champs!

The bigger one, a formidable hulk named Musef, swaggered to the middle of the room. The other one, named Torgut, sauntered over to the wall behind Heller's back. Torgut was carrying a short piece of pipe.

About fifteen more townsmen came in behind the wrestlers, avid expectancy on their faces.

The proprietor yelped in Turkish, "Not in here! Outside, outside!"

"Be quiet, old woman," said Musef insultingly.

The proprietor, faced with that growl and about three hundred pounds of famed muscle, got very quiet.

Musef walked over to Heller. "You speak Turkish? No?" He shifted to badly accented English. "You speak English? Yes?"

Heller just sat there looking at him.

"My name," and Musef hit himself on the chest, "is Musef. You know me?"

With a slight incredulity, Heller said, "A yellow-man!" And indeed, now that I thought about it, Musef and Torgut did bear some dim resemblance to the yellow-men of the Confederacy. Not surprising, since the Turks come from Mongolia.

But it was the wrong thing to say. Musef snarled, "You say I yellow?"

There was a ripple through the audience as those

who didn't speak English got those who did to tell them what was being said. And then it had to be clarified for some that "yellow" meant "coward" in English. And believe me, eyebrows really shot up and eyes went round with anticipation. You could almost hear them pant.

Musef pretended to be outraged that Heller was not saying anything further. So he spat, "You want to fight?"

Heller glanced around. Torgut was hefting the iron pipe over by the wall. It was indeed a hostile crowd.

Heller looked at Musef. He said, "I never fight . . ."

There was an explosion of laughter in the room.

Instantly Musef picked up the glass and threw the water and flowers in Heller's face.

"I was about to say," said Heller, "I never fight without a wager!"

There was more laughter. But Musef thought he saw a way to make money. After all, how could he lose with Torgut and an iron pipe back of Heller. "A wager!" guffawed Musef. Then, "All right. We wager! Five hundred lira! You," he yelled at the crowd, "make sure that it gets paid!"

The crowd screamed with laughter. "We will!" they shouted in English and Turkish. It gave them a perfectly legal excuse to pick the "DEA man's" pocket when he lost. There is nobody quite as cunning as a Turk unless it is a crowd of Turks!

And before anyone knew what was happening, Musef reached out and grabbed Heller's collar and yanked him to the center of the floor! It was not hard to do. Heller, here on Earth, weighed only 193 pounds and Musef weighed 300!

Somehow Musef's hands must have slipped. Heller and Musef were standing there in the middle of the floor, facing each other. The crowd, on its feet and roaring for blood, made a circle.

Musef reached with both arms. Heller weaved sideways. I knew what Musef was trying to do. The standard Turkish action of engaging is for each opponent to seize the other, with both hands, on either side of the neck. What happens after that is anybody's war.

Musef made a second try. He got his hands on Heller's shoulders!

Heller got his hands on Musef's shoulders!

The first seconds of such a contest is a jostle for position.

And then I didn't understand it. Heller had his two hands on the shoulders of the Turk but Heller's fingers were hidden by the Turk's head. I couldn't see that Heller was doing anything. But neither was the Turk!

Heller's hands just seemed to be rooted there.

The Turk was trying to throw his arms out to get Heller's hands loose. You could see the muscles jump with the Turk's effort. The Turk's face was contorting in savage hatred. But there was enormous strain there!

The two seemed to rotate a few degrees. Now there was a wall mirror in Heller's view. And in that mirror, Torgut was plainly visible. Torgut, iron pipe in hand, was parting the crowd, approaching Heller's back.

I realized then why Heller's hands weren't coming loose. Turks usually smear themselves with olive oil before they wrestle but tonight there was nothing there to make Heller's hands slip on the Turk's shoulders and neck.

You could almost hear the muscles grind with the effort of the two wrestlers.

Ah, I had it. Musef could see Torgut and Musef was simply holding Heller in position until the partner could bring that iron pipe down on Heller's blond head!

The crowd was going wild, cheering Musef on.

Torgut was very near now.

Suddenly, using his grip on Musef to support the forward part of his body, Heller went back and horizontal!

His feet hit Torgut in the chest!

The thud of that double blow was loud above the yelling room.

Torgut flew backwards as though propelled from a cannon. He took three members of the crowd with him!

They landed with a crash against the wall!

The impact shattered the mirror on the opposite wall!

Musef tried to take advantage of the weight shift. He drew back a forearm to hit Heller in the face.

I couldn't see what happened. But Heller's hands clenched suddenly inward.

Musef screamed like a crushed dog!

Heller hadn't done anything to cause that. He had just closed his hands in tighter.

The huge Turk buckled like a falling building and landed like rubble on the floor!

The crowd was silent.

They were incredulous.

They became hostile!

Heller stood there in the middle of the floor. Torgut was a half-dead mess against the far wall, blood trickling down his shoulders. Three town Turks were getting themselves untangled from chairs near him. Musef was collapsed and moaning at Heller's feet.

With his two hands, Heller straightened up his own collar. "And now," he said, in a conversational voice, "who pays me the five hundred lira?"

Now, money is a very important subject to the impoverished Turk. If Heller had had any sense, he would

have simply walked out. But he doesn't have any training in this sort of thing. I would have been running
already.

The townsmen jabbered together. Then one said in
English, "It wasn't a fair bet. You, a foreigner, took
advantage of these two poor boys!"

"Yes," said an old Turk. "You exploited them!"

"No, no, no," said the proprietor, getting brave.
"You owe me for all this damage. You started the fight!"

Heller looked them over. "You mean you are not
going to see that an honest wager is paid?"

The crowd sensed its numbers. It started to edge forward hostilely toward Heller. One tough-looking fellow
was nearest Heller.

"Are you going to see that the bargain is kept?" said
Heller to the nearest man.

The crowd was closer. Somebody had Torgut's iron
pipe.

"Ah, well," said Heller. And before anyone could
block him he grabbed Musef off the floor and with a
wide sweeping movement threw him at the proprietor!

Musef landed against the counter. Glasses and bottles and kegs soared into the air. The counter fell over on
the proprietor!

Every man in that room had ducked!

As the noise died down, Heller said, "Honor seems
to be something you have never heard of." He shook his
head sadly. "And I did want to try some of your beer."

Heller walked out.

The crowd had recovered a bit. They surged to the
door after him and there they began to throw bottles and
yell derisively and do catcalls.

Heller just kept on walking.

I saw that he was limping.

I really hugged myself. He had been utterly routed!

His crude scheme to get some money had failed.

Ah, indeed, the roles had reversed. He was the dog and I the hero here.

I went to bed singing—while Heller limped the miles back to base, broke, outcast and alone.

PART THIRTEEN

Chapter 1

The next morning, I felt pretty cheery, I can tell you. I got up early and put on an orange silk shirt and black pants and a cobra-skin belt, with shoes to match.

I had melon and *cacik*—cucumber salad with yogurt, garlic and olive oil dressing—and I washed it down with very sweet coffee. Delicious. When I criticized it to the cook, he looked so woebegone, I really had to laugh. The whole staff looked woebegone, having been up all night trying to find something they had not done. The joke was on them. I really laughed.

Then I got busy with a big sheet of paper. I am a long way from a draftsman but I sure knew what I wanted. It was up to somebody else to try to make it out.

The school owned another piece of property a little bit closer to town. It had been planned to build a staff recreational hall there but I had other ideas.

I was designing a hospital. It would be one story, with a basement. It would have numerous wards and operating rooms. It would also have a parking lot. It would be surrounded by a wire fence made to look like a hedge. And in the basement it would have numerous private rooms nobody would suspect were there. It would have an Earth-type security system. Every room would be bugged.

I was going to register it as the "World United Charities Mercy and Benevolent Hospital." I was going to make my fortune with it. They really train you in the

Apparatus. "When you mean total evil," one of my professors in Apparatus school used to say, "always put up a façade of total good." It is an inviolable maxim of any competent government.

Finally, I finished it, hoping I could make the plan out myself—I had scratched out and changed quite a bit.

Then I had to write a bunch of orders: one to our Voltar resident engineer to dig some tunnels to it; another to our Istanbul attorney firm to get it registered real fast; another to the World Health Operation for the attorneys to forward which said it was a magnificent donation to the world of health and please could we use their name, too; and another to the Rockecenter Foundation for a grant "for the poor children of Turkey"—they always hand out money if their executives can get a slice back and if Rockecenter can get his name up in lights as a great humanitarian (hah! that would be the day!).

The last letter was just a dispatch. Here at the Blito-P3 base they have the usual Officers Council, chaired by the base commander, that is supposed to pass on new projects. But, as Section Chief of 451 *and* Inspector General Overlord, *I* surely didn't need *their* consent. I just told them that this is what was going to happen and they could lump it. To Hells with their staff recreation. And besides, didn't the Grand Council Order say to spread a little advanced technology on the planet? So they could go to Hells and do what they were told. I stamped it with my identoplate loud and plain. They knew better than to trifle with me. I even added a postscript to that effect.

It was quite a relief to get all this tedious work done. So I called for the housekeeper.

When she came in, hollow-eyed from no sleep, scared as to what I might want now, I said, "Melahat Hanim" (a very polite way of addressing a woman in Turkey is to add "hanim" to her name—it flatters them; they have no souls, you know), "has the beautiful lady arrived from Istanbul?"

She wrung her hands and shook her head negative. So I said, "Get out of here, you female dropping of camel dung," and wondered what else I could do to while away the hours before ten. It's no use going to town too early—the roads are too cluttered with carts.

Then I thought I had better check on Heller. I didn't much care to know what he was doing in the ship so I hadn't even bothered to rig the 831 Relayer.

The recorder was grinding away, the viewer was off. So I figured I might as well start early. I turned the viewer on and began to spot-check forward.

Last night he had simply walked home and gone aboard. Limping! Must have hurt his foot.

Speeding forward, I heard a shrill whistle on the strip. So I went back over it at normal speed.

I saw the airlock open and then, way down at the foot of the ladder, there was Faht Bey, holding a hull resonator against the tug's plates.

"There you are," said Faht Bey, looking up. "I'm the base commander, Officer Faht. Are you the Crown inspector?"

"I'm on Grand Council orders, if that's what you mean. Come on up."

Faht Bey was not about to climb that eighty feet of rickety ladder from the bottom of the hangar to the airlock on the vertical ship. "I just wanted to see you."

"I want to see you, too," said Heller, looking down the ladder. "The clothes in your costume section are too short and the shoes there are about three sizes too small for me." I was disappointed. He hadn't hurt his foot, it was tight shoes. Well, you can't always grab the pot.

"That's what I wanted to see you about," Faht Bey yelled up at him. "The people in town are looking all over for somebody that fits your description. They say he waylaid two popular characters at different times in an alley and beat them up with a lead pipe. One has a cracked neck and the other a broken arm and fractured skull. They had to be shipped into Istanbul to be hospitalized."

"How'd you know it fits my description?" said Heller. My Gods, he was nosy. "This is the first time you've seen me."

"Gris said what you looked like," said this (bleep) Faht Bey. "So please don't take it badly. It's my guess you'll be leaving here in two or three days." Well, (bleep) him! He must have read Lombar's order to Raht! "So I've got to invoke my authority on the subject of base security and ask you not to leave this hangar while you're here."

"Can I wander around the hangar?" said Heller.

"Oh, that's all right, just as long as you don't leave the outside-world end of the tunnels."

Heller waved him an airy hand. "Thanks for the tip, Officer Faht."

And that was the end of that one. I sped ahead to the next light flash that showed the door was open.

Heller was going down the ladder, zip, zip. He landed at the bottom with a tremendous clank. It startled me until I realized he was wearing hull shoes with the metal bars loose.

He started clickety-clacking around, a little notebook held in his hand, making jots and touching his watch now and then. He went around the whole perimeter of the hangar, *clickety-clack*, POP. I knew what he was doing. He was just amusing himself surveying the place. These engineers! They're crazy. Maybe he was practicing his sense of direction or something.

I kept speeding the strip ahead. But that was all he

was up to. He'd stop by doors and branch tunnels and make little notes and loud POPs.

Now and then he'd meet an Apparatus personnel. The first couple, he gave them a cheerful good morning. But they turned an icy shoulder to him. After that he didn't speak to anyone. My rumor was working!

He got into some side tunnels and took some interest in the dimensions of the detention cells. It would be hard to tell they were cells for they were not as secure as Spiteos—no wire. They just had iron bars set into the rock. The base crew who had redesigned the place had overdone it on detention cells—they had made enough for hundreds of people and never at any time were there more than a dozen. They were empty now.

Speeding ahead, I saw that he had stopped and I went back to find what was interesting him so much.

He was standing in front of the storage room doors. They are very massive. There are about fifty of them in a curving line that back the hangar itself, a sort of corridor. The corridor has numerous openings into the hangar itself.

They were all locked, of course. And the windows in the doors, necessary to circulate the air and prevent mold, are much too high up to see through. I was fairly certain he would not even guess what they contained.

Lombar, when the pressure was put on Turkey to stop growing opium, had really outdone himself. He had ordered so much of it bought, it would have glutted the market had it all been released. Now, there it was, nicely bagged in big sacks. Tons and tons and tons of it.

But even if one jumped up and got a look through the windows, there was nothing to be seen. Just piles of bags.

Heller examined the floor. But what was there to find? Just the truck wheel wear.

He bent over and picked up some dust and then, to wipe his hand, I suppose, he put his hand in his pocket and brought it out clean.

Unconcerned, he just went on clickety-clacking along with the occasional *POP*.

Again he stopped. He was sniffing the air. He was looking at a huge barred door. And he certainly wouldn't be able to get in there—it was the heroin conversion plant!

He went up to it and knocked. How silly. Nobody was in there. It only operates once in a while. But still he knocked, very sharp raps.

Heller must have given it up. He made some notes. Just some figures. Pointless.

And there he went again, clickety-clacking, *POP* along.

He'd stop by an exit tunnel, go down it a bit and come back. I had to laugh. He even went up the exit tunnel which led to my room! He could never suspect the villa lay on the other side. He didn't even try the switch which opened the door, didn't even see it, apparently. It would have brought him within ten feet of where I was sitting.

Some spy!

It had only taken him an hour.

Then he'd done a little sketch, all neat, very fast. Apparently there was nobody near to give it to, to show them how good he was—or maybe he had understood they weren't talking to him. He just climbed back up into the ship.

And that was that.

I had to laugh. What couldn't he have discovered if he had been a real trained spy! And what did he have? A silly map he could have gotten in the base construction office anyway.

I packed it up. It had turned ten and I had really important things to do—namely, making Soltan Gris rich!

Chapter 2

The villa had three cars, all more or less in what Turkey considers running condition. I went out and considered them. The Datsun pickup was more or less full of the remains of vegetables from the morning marketing. The Chevy station wagon had an empty gas tank. That left the French Renault sedan. I think the car had been left over from the wreckage of World War I: they believe in making cars last in Turkey.

The body was dented from several direct hits, the windshield was cracked. It had to be cranked because the battery was dead. It kicked and had been known to break somebody's arm, so I got Karagoz to crank it. And off I went to town.

I dreamed that soon I would buy a long, black, bulletproof limousine, the kind gangsters have. I even knew where there was one: a Turkish general had been killed in the 1963 military take-over and the car was for sale cheap.

The Renault, however, had its advantages. It steered erratically and could be counted on to drive carts off the road. They are stupid gigs, usually heavily laden, drawn by donkeys, and they really clutter the place up. If you swerve in close to the donkey as you pass, the cart winds up in the ditch. It is very comical. You can watch the driver shaking his fist in the rearview mirror.

I was just enjoying my fifth cart upset when I

noticed I was passing Afyonkarahisar: the vast bulk of the rock rose 750 feet in the air.

Abruptly, I pulled to the left and stopped. I blocked a chain of carts coming from town, but they could wait. I leaned out and looked up the face of the rock.

Even though it was powdered with cement dust, you could see that it had handholds if you didn't mind losing a few fingernails. Still, I would never attempt to climb it. Never. And in the dark? Absolutely never!

My interest in this was a matter of character, not the character of Heller—I already knew he was crazy—but in the character of a man who had suddenly become vital in my plans of riches: Jimmy "The Gutter" Tavilnasty. He said he had seen Heller climbing it. Obviously, the feat was impossible. Therefore Jimmy "The Gutter" Tavilnasty was a pathological liar. Good. I would watch it when I spoke with him later today and made him my offer.

The engine had died so I got out and cranked it. The drivers of the halted carts were screaming and shaking their fists. I screamed and shook my fist back, got in and drove the rest of the way to town.

The Mudlick Construction Company was my destination. It has branch offices all around Turkey. It does a lot of government contracting and therefore must be crooked. I double-parked and went in.

My business was soon transacted. The manager took my sketch and estimated the cost. When he heard I wanted the hospital built in six weeks, he raised the price. I walked out and he rushed to the sidewalk and brought me back and halved the amount. But he said he would have to build it of mud, the favorite construction material of this district. I told him it had to be of first-class materials. We compromised by planning to build it half of mud and half of proper materials. Then I doubled the price and told him he would owe me half, as a kick-back. We signed the contract and parted firm friends.

When I came out two motorists were glaring at me so I glared back and cranked the car and drove to the Giysi Modern Western Clothing Our Specialty Shop for Men and Gentlemen. I would much rather shop in Istanbul but I hadn't much time and I knew I would have to dress right for my call on Jimmy "The Gutter" Tavilnasty. It was vital I make an impression.

The selection was pretty poor, really. But it is the law that Turks must not look like Turks but dress like Americans or Italians and I was lucky. They had just received a shipment from Hong Kong of the very latest Chicago fashions.

I found a gray suit, a black shirt, a white tie, black and white oxfords and a gray fedora hat. They all more or less fit. I changed in back, shortchanged the clerk by palming and swapping a five-hundred lira note for a five at the last instant, glared him into thinking it was his mistake and was on my way.

I looked pretty sharp as I admired myself in a shop window reflection. Just like a film gangster.

Rapidly, I made a round of hotels, looking for Jimmy "The Gutter" Tavilnasty. It does not take long to do in Afyon. There aren't many hotels. The clerks shook their heads. No trace of him.

Well, I had another errand. I went to the Pahalt General Merchandise Emporium. It is patronized by peasants and they certainly get charged *pahalt,* which in Turkish means "high-priced." In a back room, I had a little talk with the proprietor.

I told him I wanted him to put up a sign that said he bought gold. He said the gold mining districts, such as they were, were further north. I said that didn't matter: at his prices, the women of the family had to sell their jewelry, didn't they? And he said that was true. So I told him that any gold he bought from said impoverished peasants, at London prices, I would buy from him at a ten percent markup. He said there wouldn't be much, but I said how much there was a secret between us and so we made the sign and he put it up.

Now, I had a way to explain all the gold I was about to dump on the market when the *Blixo* arrived. I could point out that gold was bought in Afyon. When I unloaded chunks of mine in Istanbul, I would probably never bother to buy the proprietor's gold.

In the pleasant noonday sun, I sat basking double-parked on the street, trying to figure out where Jimmy "The Gutter" had gotten to. Some carts were blocked. A policeman came along and disturbed my concentration. He bent over and stuck his bristling mustache in the window. Then he said, "Oh, it's you!"

Well, that was quite a compliment, the way he said it. Sort of alarmed. They think I am the nephew of the original subofficer that was the war hero. After all, I live in his house. He moved on rather quickly to bawl out the carts I was blocking. Oh, it was good to be home!

It must have sparked my wits. Where would a gangster go in this town? Of course, the Saglanmak Rooms! Now, *saglanmak*, in Turkish, means "to be obtained" or "available." But there is another word, *saklanmak*, which means "to hide oneself." Now, according to that great master, Freud, the unconscious mind can twist words into meanings closer to the intent of the person. These are called "Freudian slips." This was what must have happened. No matter that he probably didn't speak Turkish, Jimmy "The Gutter" Tavilnasty had made a Freudian slip.

Besides, it was the only place in town the Mafia ever stayed.

I drove through the gathering crowd of fist-shaking peasants and proceeded to the Saglanmak Rooms. But I was cunning now. I double-parked a block away and cased the joint.

There was a balcony that ran around the outside of the second floor and a stairway to it—a vital necessity if one had to get out a window and escape quickly.

I went in. I walked up to the desk. The clerk was a young Turk with his hair plastered down. He had earlier told me no such name was in the hotel. I didn't bother with him. I reached over the desk and into the niche for the box of room cards. The clerk stood back.

I went through the cards. No Jimmy "The Gutter" Tavilnasty.

He had said he had been around for weeks. I checked dates. And there it was! John Smith!

"I thought," I sneered at the clerk, "that you said Tavilnasty wasn't here!"

He was reaching for the phone. I clamped his wrist. "No," I said. "He is a friend. I want to surprise him."

The clerk frowned.

I laid a ten-lira note on the desk.

The frown lightened.

I laid a fifty-lira note on the desk.

The clerk smiled.

"Point out the room," I said.

He indicated the one at the exact top of the steps on the second floor.

"He is in?" I asked.

The clerk nodded.

"Now, here is what I want you to do. Take a bottle of Scotch—the Arab counterfeit will do—and two glasses and put them on a tray. Just three minutes after I leave this desk, you take that tray up to his room and knock."

I kept laying hundred-lira notes on the counter until

the clerk smiled. It was a seven-hundred-lira smile.

I had him note the time. I synchronized my watch.

I went back out the front door.

In a leisurely fashion, but silently, I went up the outside steps.

With care, I marked the exact outside window of the indicated room. It was open.

I waited.

Exactly on time, a knock sounded on the door.

A bed creaked.

I stole to the window.

Sure enough, there was my man. He had a Colt .45 in his hand and he was cat-footing to the door. His back was to me at the window.

I knew it would be this way. Mafia hit men lead nervous lives.

Jimmy "The Gutter" Tavilnasty reached for the knob, gun held on the door. That was my cue!

The door was swinging open.

I stepped through the window.

I said, in a loud voice, "Surprise!"

He half-turned in shock.

He sent a bullet slamming into the wall above me!

The shot had not even begun to echo before he charged out the door.

The effect was catastrophic. He collided with the clerk and tray!

In a scramble of Scotch and glasses, arms, legs and two more inadvertently triggered shots, they went avalanching down the stairs.

With a thud and final tinkle they wound up at the bottom.

I trotted down the stairs after them and plucked the gun from Jimmy "The Gutter's" stunned hand.

"What a way to greet an old pal," I said. That's the

way to handle them. Purely textbook psychology. It says to get them off-balance.

Tavilnasty was not only off-balance, he was out cold.

The clerk lay there looking at me in horror. I realized I had Tavilnasty's gun pointed at him. I put the safety on. I said, "You were clumsy. You broke that bottle of Scotch. Now get up and get another one on the house."

The clerk scrambled away.

I picked up Tavilnasty and got him over to a small back table in the lounge. He was coming around.

The clerk, shaking, brought in another bottle of Scotch and two glasses.

I handed Tavilnasty his gun.

I poured him a drink. He drank it.

Then his ugly, pockmarked face was really a study. "What the hell was that all about?"

"I just didn't want to get shot," I said.

He couldn't quite understand this. I poured him another drink.

I tried another tack. "I could have killed you and I didn't. Therefore that proves I am your friend."

He considered this and rubbed a couple of bruises on his head. I poured him another drink.

"How's Babe?" I said.

He really stared at me.

"Oh, come on," I said. "Babe Corleone, my old flame."

"You know Babe?"

"Sure, I know Babe."

"Where did you know Babe?"

"Around," I said.

He drank the Scotch.

"You from the DEA?"

I laughed.

"You from the CIA?"

I laughed.

"You from the FBI?"

I poured him another drink. "I'm from the World Health Operation. I'm going to make you your fortune."

He drank the drink.

"Now listen carefully," I said. "We are building a new hospital. It will be in full operation in about two months. We have new techniques of plastic surgery. We can change fingerprints, dental plates, larynxes, facial bones."

"No (bleep)?"

"Absolutely. Nobody else can do it but us. Nobody will know. Hippocratic oath and so forth."

"Is that like the Fifth Amendment?"

"Absolutely," I said. "But down to business. You know the Atlantic City mob. You know lots of mobs. Right?"

"Right," he said.

"Now, those mobs have people hiding out all over the place. Those people can't show their faces because they are in all the fingerprint and police files of the FBI and Interpol. Right?"

"Right."

"If those people are smuggled in here to the World United Charities Mercy and Benevolent Hospital, we will physically change their identity, give them new birth certificates and passports, all for a stiff fee, of course, and you personally will get twenty percent of what they pay."

He found a paper napkin and laboriously started figuring. Finally, he said, "I'd be rich."

"Right."

"There's one thing wrong," he said. "I can spread

the word. I can get big names in here in droves. But I can't do it."

"Why not?"

"Because I *have* a job. There's a contract out."

"I know," I said. "Gunsalmo Silva."

"How'd you know that?"

"I got sources." I fixed him with a lordly stare—down the nose. "Gunny Silva won't be back here for seven weeks. So you got six weeks to recruit some trade for the hospital."

"I'd need money for expenses. I can't hang this on Babe."

"Take your expenses out of the advance payments," I said.

"Hey!" he said, smiling.

"And," I said, "if you bring in lots of trade and payments ready to begin in two months, I'll throw something else in."

"Yeah?"

"Yeah. I'll give you Gunsalmo Silva on a silva platter!"

"No (bleep)?"

"Set him up for you like a clay pigeon!"

With tears of gratitude in his eyes, he held out his hand, "Buster, you got yourself a deal!"

Ah, psychology works every time!

A bit later I returned to my car, fought my way through the crowd protesting the street blockage, cranked up and drove away.

I felt I was driving on air!

Soltan Gris, a.k.a. Sultan Bey, was on his road to becoming filthy rich!

And, after all, hadn't the Grand Council said to spread a little technology around on this planet? Where it would really do some good?

Chapter 3

The sun was hot, the sky was clear, as I hurtled down the road.

Then I remembered that I even had a dancing girl coming today!

My prospects seemed so brilliant that I could not help doing a thing I almost never do. I burst into song:

> *Frankie and Johnny were lovers.*
> *Oh, my Gods, how they could love.*
> *They swore to be true to each other.*
> *As true as the stars above....*

There was an obstruction. It was a string of ten laden camels. They were humping and grumbling along, but I didn't see any driver. The horn of the Renault was busted so I had to veer out into the other lane to see what was at the head of this parade.

Aha! I thought so!

Around here they sometimes put a lead rope on a donkey and the animal apparently knows where to go and he just leads the hooked-up string of camels to their destination. Shows you how dumb camels are when even a jackass is brighter than they are!

Here was my chance!

I resumed singing at the top of my voice:

> *He was my man!*
> *But he done me wrong!*

I swerved in tight past the donkey. It was either my bump on his nose or it may have been the singing.

He dropped the lead rope, brayed and took off!

Ten camels exploded. They went bucking off the road into the sunflower field, spraying packs in all directions, trying to follow the donkey.

Oh, did I laugh!

I drew up at the International Agricultural Training Center for Peasants, knocked over a No Parking sign that shouldn't have been there and bounced into the base commander's office.

The contrast between his face and my mood was extreme.

He moaned; he held his head in his hands a moment. Then he looked up. "Officer Gris, can't we possibly have a little less commotion around here?"

"What's a No Parking sign?" I said, loftily.

"No. Not that. Last night there was that fight and today our agents in town tell us there are complaints from cart drivers, complaints from the police on your double-parking and just a moment ago I had a call that you and some gangster were shooting up a hotel. Please, Officer Gris. We're not supposed to be so visible here. Before you came, it was all——"

"Nonsense!" I cut him off sharply. "You were not in tune with this planet! You were becoming hicks and hayseeds! You weren't keeping up to it—you weren't with it. You leave such things to me. I am the expert on Blito-P3 sociological behaviorism! You should watch their movies. You should even go to see some of the movies they make in Turkey! They do nothing but shoot people and blow things up! But I have no time now to educate you in the psychological cultural cravings of this place. I'm here on business."

I threw the pack of contracts down on his desk and

he picked them up wearily with a what-now shake of his overpadded head.

"Hospital?" he said. "A half a million dollars?"

"Exactly," I said. "You leave the statecraft to me, Faht Bey."

"This hasn't been passed by our local Officer's Council. Our financial agent will faint!"

I knew that financial agent. He was a refugee from Beirut, Lebanon, one of their top bankers before a war wrecked the banking industry there and ran him out. A very wily Lebanese. "Tell him to get his hands out of the money box before I cut them off," I said. "And that reminds me. I'm low on lira. Give me thirty thousand this time."

He quivered his way into the back room and returned with thirty thousand Turkish lira. He made a notation in a book and then he stood right there and counted off ten thousand lira and put it in his pocket!

"Hold it!" I yelled at him. "Where did you get a license to steal our government's money?" It made me pretty cross, I can tell you.

He handed over the twenty thousand. "I had to give it to the girl. Out of my own cash."

"The girl? What for? Why?"

"Officer Gris, I don't know why you had her sent back to Istanbul. Our agent there said she was clean. And I saw her. She was actually a very pretty girl. She closed out her room and she flew all the way down here. Oh, she was mad! But I handled it. I went up into town: she was standing right on the street making an awful row. I gave her ten thousand lira for you—it's only ninety dollars American—and I put her on a bus so she could get back to Istanbul."

"I didn't order her sent back!" I screamed at him.

"Your friend the taxi driver said you did."

Believe me, I was mad! I stalked out of there and got the Renault started, ran over another No Parking sign just to show they couldn't trifle with me and drove toward home lickety-split, expecting that taxi driver would be there.

The Renault didn't make it. It ran out of gas. I left it in the road and walked to the villa which was only about an eighth of a mile, planning all the way what I was going to tell that taxi driver.

He wasn't there.

I gave Karagoz what-for about the car and sent him and the gardener to push it home and refused to let them push it with another car, I was so mad.

No girl.

Nothing to do.

I barricaded my door. I sulked for quite a while. And then, needing something more to get mad about, I went into the real room back of the closet and turned on the viewer.

Heller couldn't go anywhere: he didn't have any money. Heller was really no worry to me now. In a couple of days, I'd hear from Raht; we'd use the tug to take Heller to the U.S., and shortly after, he'd be arrested as an imposter and jailed. It didn't make any difference now, what he was doing. But maybe it was something I could find fault with.

And there he was, using the corridor outside the storerooms as a running track. He apparently had two bags of running weights over his right and left shoulder as I could see the weight sacks bouncing as he trotted. Him and his exercise! Adding weights to keep his muscles in trim despite the reduced gravity of this planet. Athletes!

That wasn't anything I could really snarl about, so

I thought I'd better check earlier. I backed to the point I'd left him and raced it ahead.

Oho! He had been very busy! After his silly survey, he had been inside the ship no time at all.

I couldn't quite make out what he first did.

There were strange things on his legs. He stopped at the ladder bottom when he exited from the ship and adjusted something on his ankles. He had some bags and a coil of rope slung around him and I couldn't quite see the ankles because the gear swung in the way.

He went straight to the construction shop. A technician was in there, fiddling at a bench. He spotted who it was that had invaded his cave and quickly looked away, saying nothing.

"I want to borrow your hand rock-corer," said Heller in a friendly voice.

The technician shook his head.

"I'm awfully sorry," said Heller, "I'll have to insist. This appears to be earthquake country and you have an awfully big excavation here. There seems to be flaking in the rock. I am concerned for the safety of my ship. It will probably be here on and off and it must not be risked by a cave-in. So please lend me a corer."

The technician almost angrily took a small tool from a drawer and thrust it at Heller. Heller thanked him courteously and went off.

These combat engineers! Heller took a hitch on his bags and began to climb the vertical interior rock face of the hangar wall!

I knew what he had on his ankles now. They are just called "spikes" but actually they are little drills that buzz briefly as they drill a small hold in rock or other material. In the Apparatus we used them for second-story work. But engineers climb mountain faces with them. There is a drill in the toe of the boot, one on the heel, one on the outside and one on the inside of each ankle. They terrify me: you can drill a hole in your inside anklebone with them!

Heller just spiked his way up the wall. Ouch! He was wearing them on his wrists, too! Had he worn these last night to go up Afyonkarahisar? No, I was sure he hadn't. They would have been visible in the fight and a breach of the Space Code.

Ah, he was wearing them now because he was working. He had to stop and do other things. He was about fifteen feet from the hangar floor now. The corer started up. It set my teeth on edge.

With the tool, he drilled a plug out of the rock face. It was about an inch in diameter and three inches long: just a little shaft of stone.

He held it real close to his eye, inspecting it. The section exposed the rock grain. He examined it very critically. It sure looked all right to me!

He took a little hammer and with a tap, he knocked off the last half-inch of the plug, caught the fragment and put it in a bag. Then he took a can out of his shoulder sack. The label said *Rock Glue*, and very badly lettered it was.

He put a gooey piece of rock glue on the plug and put it back in the hole. He tapped it neatly with a hammer and in a moment you couldn't tell that an inspection core had been taken out.

Heller went along to his left a few feet and did the same thing. And, working swiftly, he did it again and again and again, plug after plug after plug!

Well, it was all right to watch him when he was only fifteen feet off the floor. Trouble was, he went up to fifty feet and started the same procedure and every time he looked down, I got an awful feeling. I hate heights!

So, anyway, I skipped ahead.

Heller had gotten himself clear up to the lower edge of the electronic illusion which, from there on up, gave us a mountaintop. And he said something!

I quickly turned it back and replayed it.

"Why," muttered Heller, "do all Apparatus areas stink! And not only that, why do they have to seal the airflow with an illusion so it will never air out!"

Aha! I was getting to him. He was beginning to talk to himself. A sure sign!

He lit a small flamer and turned it so it smoked. He watched the resultant behavior of the small fog. "Nope," he said, "no air can get in. By the Gods, I'll have to find the switch of this thing."

I didn't keep the strip there very long. He kept looking down and three hundred feet under him a dolly operator looked like a pebble. Stomach wrenching!

I sped ahead to find more sound. I found some and stopped. But he was just humming. That silly one about Bold Prince Caucalsia.

A bit later, he tried to talk to the hangar chief who, of course, on my rumor, ignored him. Heller finally put a hand on the man's shoulder and made him face him. "I said," said Heller, "where are the controls for the electronic illusion? I want to turn it off tonight to air the place out! You're trapping moisture in here."

"It's always on," the hangar chief snarled. "It's been on for ages. I don't even think the switches work anymore. It's running on its own power source and it won't have to be touched for a century. You want things changed around here, take it up with the base commander." And he went off snarling about routine, routine, all he needed was one more routine to clutter up his day.

Captain Stabb was over by the ship. The five Antimancos were not housed aboard the tug. They were in the berthing area of the hangar—much more comfortable and they could more easily get to town. No eighty-foot ladder. It pleased Captain Stabb immensely that Heller had been rebuffed in his passion for fresh air. Oh, he would never last in the Apparatus! These Fleet guys!

Heller went back aboard.

I sped ahead. He had apparently come out again to do some running. He was gradually lightening his weights to adjust his stride to this planet.

Silly athletes.

I shut him off and went back to glooming about my lost dancing girl. The world was against me.

Chapter 4

The following day, toward noon, I was just beginning to come out of my dumps when something else happened to free-fall me back into them.

It was a smoking hot day: the August sun had cranked the thermometer up to a Turkish 100—meaning about 105. I had been lying in a shadowy part of the yard, back of a miniature temple to Diana, the Roman Goddess of the hunt. My pitcher of iced *sira* was empty; I had gotten tired of kicking the small boy who was supposed to be fanning me, when suddenly I heard a songbird. It was a canary! A canary had gone wild! Instantly my primitive instincts kindled! I had bought, a year ago, a ten-gauge shotgun and I had never tried it out! That would handle that canary!

Instantly aquiver, I leaped up and raced to my room. I got my shotgun rapidly enough but I couldn't find the shells. And that was peculiar as they are big enough to load a cannon with. I went to my sleeping room and started threshing through my bedside drawers.

And then something happened which drove all thought of hunting from my mind.

There was an envelope pinned to my pillow!

It had not been there after I arose.

Somebody had been in this room!

But nobody had crossed the yard to my area! How had this gotten there? Flown in on the wind? There was no wind.

It was the type of envelope which is used to carry greetings in certain Voltar social circles: it gives off a subdued glitter. Had I found a snake in my bed, I would have been less surprised.

I got nerve enough generated to pick it up. It did not seem to be the exploding type.

Gingerly, as though it were hot, I extracted the card. A greeting card. A sorry-you-were-not-in-when-I-called type of card. It had handwriting on it. It said, quite elegantly:

> *Lombar wanted me to remind you now and then.*

And under that formal social script was drawn a dagger! A dagger with blood on it! A dagger with blood on it that was dripping!

I went cold as I burst into sweat.

Who could have put it there? Was it Melahat? Was it Karagoz? Could it be Faht Bey? The hangar chief? Jimmy "The Gutter"? Heller? No, no, no! Not Heller: he would be the last one Lombar would use! The small boy who had been fanning me? No, no, I had had him in sight all morning.

Where were they now?

Was I being watched this minute?

All thought of hunting vanished.

I was the hunted!

With a great effort, I made myself think. Something was obviously expected. Somebody believed I was not doing my job. And if that happened, according to Lombar's last remark, the whoever-it-was had direct orders to kill me!

I knew I must do something. Make an effort, a show of it. And fast.

I had it!

I would tell Captain Stabb to start another rumor about Heller!

I let the shotgun fall. I rushed through the back of the closet. I got the passageway door open and catapulted down it to find Stabb.

The Antimanco was nowhere around. But something else was.

The warplanes!

Two of them!

They must have arrived during the night!

They were ugly ships. A bit bigger than the tug. They were all armor. They were manned by only two. They were a more compact version of "the gun" which Lombar flew. Deadly ships, cold, black, lethal.

Rather timidly, I approached them. To get here now, when would they have had to leave Voltar? They must have been dispatched the very day Heller had bought the tug to have arrived here by now. Such ships were only a trifle faster than freighters. Lombar must have known about the tug purchase the instant it happened! He knew too much, too quickly. He must have spies planted in every . . .

A voice sounded behind me and I almost jumped out of my wits!

"We been here for hours, Gris. Where have you been?"

I turned. I was looking at a slate-hard man with slate-hard eyes. There were three others behind him. How had they gotten behind me?

They were in black uniforms and they wore red gloves. They had a red explosion on each side of their collars. And I knew what they were. In the Apparatus they are called assassin pilots. They are used on every major Apparatus battle engagement. They do not fight the enemy. They are there to make sure no Apparatus vessel runs away. If it does, if they only think it is running away, they shoot it down! With riffraff of the type that makes up the Apparatus, such measures are necessary. One has to deal with cowards. One also has to deal with mutiny. The answer is the assassin pilot. The Fleet has no such arrangements.

Their manners compare with their duties. He was omitting "officer" from his form of address to me. He did not offer to shake hands.

"That ship," and he flung a contemptuous gesture at the tug, "has no call-in beamer on it!"

Every Apparatus ship is required to have a device imbedded in its hull which an assassin ship, with a beam, can activate: it is vital so they can find an erring vessel and shoot it down.

"It was a Fleet vessel," I said, backing up.

"Listen, Gris, you wouldn't want me to report you for violations, would you?"

I backed up further. "It was just an oversight."

He stepped closer. I had never seen colder eyes. "How can anybody expect me to shoot a ship down when I can't find it? Get a call-in beamer installed in that hull!"

I tried to back up further but the hull of a warplane was at my back. I felt desperate. "I am not under your orders."

"And we," he said, "are not under yours!"

The other assassin pilot and the two copilots behind him all nodded as one, with a single jerk of their heads. They were very grim, cold professionals at their trade; they wanted things straight!

It was a bad situation. I would sometimes be in that tug. It was unarmed and unarmored. One single shot from either of these warplanes could turn the *Prince Caucalsia* into space dust in a fraction of a second.

"So, two orders," said the assassin pilot. "One: order the hangar chief to install a call-in beamer on that ship's exterior hull so secretly and in such a place that its crew will never know it is there. Two: I want that ship crippled so that it cannot leave this system on its time drives and try to outrun us."

"There's a Royal officer aboard her," I said.

"Well, decoy him away from the ship so the beamer can be put on the hull. I'll leave the crippling of her up to you as you're the best one to get inside her."

I nodded numbly. I was at a terrible disadvantage. I had left my room so fast I had not taken a gun. I had broken a firm rule never to be around Apparatus people unarmed. And then, I realized, it wouldn't have done me any good even if I had been armed. They would have complained to Lombar I was refusing his orders.

I nodded nervously.

"Then we're friends?" he said.

I nodded and offered my hand.

He raised his red-gloved fingers and slapped me across the face, hard, contemptuously.

"Good," he said. "Do it."

I raced off to give the secret order to the hangar chief. I raced up the ladder and got Heller to come out.

I took Heller to the hangar map room, out of sight of the tug.

He was in work clothes. He had been doing something inside. His red racing cap was on the back of his head. "Where'd the two 'guns' come from?" he asked.

"They're just guard ships," I said. "Stationed here. They've been away. Nothing to do with the mission." It gave me a little lift of satisfaction, thinking of what his reaction would be if he knew they were here especially to keep track of his beloved tug and shoot it down if it did anything odd or didn't return at once from a flight. I only hoped I wouldn't be aboard when they hit it: an unarmed, unarmored tug wouldn't stand a chance!

"We will probably be leaving tomorrow," I said. "While we are near maps, I wanted to show you the U.S. terrain."

"Hello," he said, looking at them. "'U.S. Geological Survey.' It even shows the minerals!"

"And everything even down to the farmhouses," I said, glad to be able to engage his interest and prevent him from seeing what they were doing in the hangar. "We can make better farmhouse ones, of course, but the minerals are a bonus.

"Now, probably we will be landing in that field there." And I pointed to the section in southern Virginia I had seen noted on the Lombar orders.

"The town," I continued, "is named Fair Oakes. See it there? This over here is a better, more detailed map. This is Hamden County. Fair Oakes is the county seat. Now, see this building? That's the Hamden County Courthouse. The squiggles show it is on a little hill.

"All right," I said. "Now, pay attention. We will

land in this field: it's a ruined plantation and nobody is ever around. The trees will mask us from any road.

"Now, you will leave the ship there, walk up this path that is indicated, pass this farmhouse, walk up the hill to the back of the courthouse and go in.

"You will be issued your birth certificate—an old clerk will be there even though it is after hours. And then you will walk down this hill and go to the bus station.

"There is a late-night bus. You will take it north to Lynchburg. You will probably change at Lynchburg and then go through Washington, D.C., and up to New York."

He was being very attentive but looking at the maps. Actually, it was hardly worth explaining what he would be doing after that. The Rockecenter, Jr. false name Lombar had set up for him would draw attention and he'd be spotted. If he registered even at a motel, somebody would be startled enough to call the local press that a celebrity was in town. But it would be no celebrity: just a false name! And then, bang! Rockecenter's connections would take over. Bye-bye Heller! It was a cunning trap Lombar had laid. There is no Delbert John Rockecenter, Junior!

"You must be sure and use the cover name at all times," I said. "America is very identity conscious. If you don't have identification, they go crazy. So be sure you announce and use your cover name when you get it. It's even a felony not to give a name to the police when they ask for it. Do you understand all that?"

"And what will this cover name be?" said Heller, still looking at the maps.

"Oh, I don't know yet," I lied. "We have to get a proper birth certificate. A name doesn't mean anything unless you can show a birth certificate. It depends on what ones are available there in the Hamden County Courthouse."

"Hey," he said, "they've got some gold marked on these maps. I was reading some books on the United States and it said the gold was all in the West. Look here. There's gold marked in Virginia. And on these other maps, there's gold in Maryland. And there's gold up here in these . . . New England? . . . states."

"Oh, that was all mined out back in what they call 'colonial' times. Way back." I didn't know much about geology but I knew that much. I'd seen it before and last year had told Raht to go dig some up and he'd laughed fit to burst. It was then he had explained the maps probably meant "had been."

"I see," said Heller. "These surveyors just noted what they call indicators: rose quartz, iron hat, serpentine schist, hornblende. But these . . . Appalachian? . . . mountains and those to the northeast are some of the oldest mountains on the planet and I guess you could find anything in them if you looked. This northern . . . New England? . . . area was all scuffed up with glaciers in times past: that's obvious from the topography. So maybe some of the glaciers cut the tops off some peaks and exposed some lodes. Country sure looks pushed around."

I kept him chattering happily about what he saw. Just a (bleeped) engineer. Sitting here while they bugged his blessed ship! Stupid beyond belief where the Apparatus was concerned. A child in the hands of espionage and covert operations experts. Why be interested in maps? The only thing he'd see for many a year to come was the inside of a penitentiary.

An hour went by. The hangar chief tossed me a signal behind Heller's back.

"All right," I said. "But there's just one thing I, as your handler, must caution you about. Book of Space Codes Number a-36-544 M Section B. Disclosure that you are an extraterrestrial is *not* authorized. You must not reveal your true identity in any way. The Voltar penalties for that would be far more severe than anything this planet could hand out. You know that and I know that. So for your own protection, I must ask you to give me your word, as a Royal officer, that you will not reveal your actual identity."

"Soltan, are you trying to insult me? You are bound by those codes, too. You're not the Emperor to be laying down Voltar law in your own name. But as long as we are on this subject, you do anything to violate Space Codes, and, as a Royal officer and personally, I will have you before the Grand Council stretched so long and thin you'll sound like a chorder-beat if they pluck you."

"I was just trying to help," I said lamely. But I was laughing inside. I knew he would use the fatal name we gave him. He was so dumb, we'd even bugged his ship behind his back.

"Well, here's to a successful mission," I said, standing up and shaking him by the hand. "I am sure you will be a great agent. Just what we want."

As I went out, I looked again at the warplanes: the huge maws of their single cannon could blast away half a planet: the tug wouldn't even be a swallow for them. With a shudder, I hurried off to the hangar quarters for ship crews to find Stabb. I would spread a new rumor that Heller had secret orders to kill them all, including the assassin pilots. Maybe, then, they'd slaughter Heller before we left and I'd never again have to ride in that (bleeped) tug! I don't like warplanes and I'd detest being shot down by one.

Chapter 5

I was in no fit mood for what I received next.

With a new pitcher of iced *sira*, I was just lying back in the temple's shadow once more when, pell-mell, here came Karagoz.

"You got a caller," he said. "The taxi driver says he's got to see you right away."

I uncoiled like a striking snake. "(Bleep) him!" Here was something I could vent my venom on! "Show him into the atrium!" There was a fountain there. Maybe I could hold his head under water until he drowned!

The atrium, the courtyard which the main Roman house was built around, usually was quite bare and forbidding, a suitable place for an execution. But today, it was changed. Karagoz and the gardener had brought in some tall, vased plants; expensive new rugs draped the tiles; comfortable seats were ranged around the fountain and the play of the water made the place musical and cool. (Bleep). Wrong setting!

The taxi driver was standing there spinning his cap airily around a forefinger. He was smiling and cheerful. (Bleep)! Wrong mood!

Well, I'd soon cut him down to size! "What the Hells do you mean sending a perfectly clean girl back to Istanbul?"

He didn't seem to remember. Then he said, "Oh, *that* girl! Oh, you were lucky, Sultan Bey. The doctor found she had (bleep) and (bleep) both. A walking epidemic! A total hellcat in the bargain. You said to take her for a ride, so I got her rid back to Istanbul!"

I knew he was lying. I was just sucking in my breath to really blast him and demand a return of some lira, when this crazy nut had the nerve to sit down! In my presence! Right on a padded lounge! It took my breath away. Such gall!

But there was a sly, conspiratorial air about him. He looked at the doorway and satisfied himself that we were alone. "Officer Gris," he whispered, "I've really run into something!"

I hoped he was going to tell me he had smashed up his car completely. But he looked too cheerful. There is something about people about to whisper secrets that makes one listen.

"When that girl blew up on you," he whispered, "I knew you would be upset. I certainly didn't want to tangle with *you*."

That was better. Proper respect after all! I sat down and leaned closer to hear better. "A couple weeks ago," he continued in a low voice, "I heard of a certain fellow to the east of here, over at Bolvadin to be exact. So I ran over there in my off-time—I won't charge you for the trip because we're friends."

This was better.

"What would you say to a *real* dancing girl? Not some Istanbul whore that can just twitch her belly, but a *real* one!"

I leaned closer.

"Listen, Officer Gris. This is really wonderful. The Russians in Turkmen, over on the other side of the Caspian Sea, have been grabbing the nomads and forcing them onto collective farms. They're mopping up the whole Kara Kum Desert!

"Them as don't settle get shot. It's pretty grisly. But listen, there's a plus side to it for us." He drew very close. "Rather than live like that, guess what? The women," and he looked around carefully and lowered his voice, "are selling themselves off!"

Oh, did he have my attention now!

"These girls," he continued, "are real Turks. The Turks, you know, inhabited an area from the Caspian to Siberia at one time. They all speak the same language. They hardly even have local accents. And, Officer Gris, they've maintained all their original social customs and these girls are nomad desert girls and they are the absolute cream of all Turkish dancers! And they're also experts at . . . well . . . you know."

He came even closer. "They're virgins because the tribal customs won't have it otherwise. So there's no danger of you know what."

I was right on the edge of my seat.

"Now, what they have to do is smuggle them out from behind the Iron Curtain. They have to push them from the Kara Kum Desert to the Caspian Sea port of Cheleken. Then they are carried down to the Iranian port of Pahlevi. They cross Iran and at the border town of Rezaiyeh, they are smuggled into Turkey. They are taken to Bolvadin and she can be brought here."

He sat back. I didn't. "I am sure you can furnish identity papers. As she would be a real Turk, speaking Turkish, that's easy. Well, what do you say?"

My head was spinning! What an opportunity! And right in my line! When you're an expert in tradecraft, you can appreciate these things.

"What would she look like?" I slavered.

He looked around again. We were still alone but he lowered his voice. "He had already sold most of them. Actually, he only had just one left. And I don't think she'll be wanting takers very long." He was secretively fishing in his pocket. "Her name is Utanc." And he handed me a photograph.

Oh, Heavens, my heart almost turned over!

The face! The beautiful face!

She looked very young, possibly eighteen. She had enormous eyes, vivid even though they were downcast. She had a perfect heart-shaped face. Her lips were very full and a finger posed against the lower one obscured them not at all. She seemed to be withdrawing slightly.

Of course! Utanc! Turks name their women after qualities. And *utanc* means "shame, modesty, bashfulness."

So sweet! So beautiful! So utterly frail! So undefended!

An emotion very foreign to me welled up. An absolute passion to protect her welled up in me. I felt I should at once charge over the border, slay the whole Russian Army, cast myself at her feet and beg for just one smile.

I sighed and somehow tore my eyes away. I turned the photograph over. On the back, in pencil, was written: *$5,000 U.S. Cash.*

"You'd own her completely," whispered the driver. "She would be your slave forever. And saving her from the raping Russian troops would earn her gratitude to such a degree, she would never be able to thank you enough!"

Well, what could I do?

I reached into my pocket and I hauled out five thousand U.S. dollars and literally pushed them at him.

"There's the transport costs and commissions," said the driver. "They come to another five thousand."

I reached into my pocket and hauled out the other five thousand.

He got up. "I'm so glad to be able to do you a favor, Sultan Bey. We'll forget about my gas and travel time."

He tried to refuse the wad of lira I thrust at him. Finally he shrugged and took it.

"It will take them a week or so to smuggle her through," he said. "Now I've got to rush back to Bolvadin to get this payment in before she is sold to someone else." And he hurried off and I heard his tires screech as the "taxi" departed. I certainly hoped he was in time.

And that night, I slept with her photo on my pillow and, oh, did I dream beautiful dreams!

I felt so good that when, in the dawn, I made out Faht Bey beside the bed, I wasn't even annoyed.

"Raht radioed in," he said. "He's all set. You can leave for America as soon as it is dark."

I didn't even hear him as he left, probably he was saying he would tell the tug crew.

I clutched the photo in my hand and kissed it passionately. Gods bless the raping Russian troops if they were delivering into my hands such a treasure as this! There's a lot to be said for communism!

Chapter 6

We took off as soon as dusk thickened into deep black.

There are some—persons with hypercritical attitudes and chronically given to nitpicking—who might try to say that the heady prospects of owning a real, live dancing girl distracted me from my duties. But this would be the purest cabal.

That day before take-off I was the slave of duty. I browbeat Faht Bey into giving me all the money I would

need and then some. I armed myself thoroughly with
Earth weaponry. I collected all the necessary equipment.
I threatened the villa staff thoroughly and even had one
of the small boys throwing up again.

I connected up the 831 Relayer and, slave of duty
that I was being, inspected what Heller was up to inside
the ship.

He was making candy!

That's right! He was standing in the after-galley
with pots and pans. He even had an apron on! He was
using a big spoon to test a simmering mess of the
gooiest, most nauseating-looking candy I have ever seen!

I thought, well, well, he must have learned it from
his sister. He was being so precise, I thought, isn't that
sweet? And actually was so revolted that I didn't even
spot it was an English pun until much later.

A little later, I checked again. He had a whole bunch
of little papers and he was putting the candy down on
them in blobs.

When I came back from threatening the staff again,
Heller had the pieces all wrapped up in wax paper. They
seemed to be very hard and had a spiral pattern of red
and white stripes.

I knew he was being silly. There's lots of candy just
like that in America. You can buy it all over the place.
It's even advertised in big colorful ads in the crew's hangar library, foreign magazine section.

Oh, good, I said sarcastically, he's preparing for his
trip. And I dismissed it.

Oh, I was very busy that day before take-off. I spent
at least two hours on Apparatus business which more
than made up for the ten I spent reclining on the lawn,
daydreaming about Utanc.

The launching went off without a hitch. It is very
simple to travel on Earth: it has only one moon and even

it is not all that bright. So all one has to do is launch in the darkness and then follow the night as it creeps along the planet surface. One dawdles along about three hundred miles up and then descends quickly to find himself at the same local time as that of one's departure point.

Captain Stabb certainly showed an expertise in such things. The Apparatus school could well add some lectures on piracy and smuggling. He told me several amusing stories as we descended, including one about wiping out a whole city. Uproarious!

We followed the textbook landing procedure, however.

Below us was the deserted plantation: the empty, fallow field, the ruined house with two front pillars gone, the slave shacks passed to ruin.

About five hundred feet up, Stabb hit the paralysis button. A heavy flash of bright blue light struck down from the ship in a cone, lasting only a split second; if seen by anyone they would suppose it to be the reflection of headlamps of a turning car or a lightning flash on the horizon.

Stabb thudded the tug down right on target, within the screen of trees, horizontally, on its belly.

The second pilot slammed open the airlock door. The second engineer, in combat dress, was on the ground in a second. He was carrying a heat detector which he pointed in a sweep at the terrain.

The bright blue light knocks any living thing in the area unconscious. The heat detector tells one if there is now anyone lying there. Standard operation. Saves one from having some nasty surprises. And actually is quite humanitarian: one doesn't have to kill a chance observer, one can just go off and let the person come to, wondering what hit him, not running around screaming, "Voltar pilots have just violated Code Number a-36-544 M Section B!" Dead bodies are hard to get rid of on the spur of the moment and bring in nosy sheriffs and things.

The second engineer's detector flashed red! Something had been knocked out by the blueflash!

The first pilot, blastrifle at ready, sprinted in the direction of the indicator beam. Stabb was tensed at the tug controls, ready to take off again in case the alert turned out to be an ambush.

The Virginia night was August, muggy hot. A thin sliver of moonlight silhouetted the copse of trees. A wind sighed through the weeds around the spaceship.

Then a bark of laughter. The first pilot came running back. He was holding an opossum by the tail! He threw it to one side. "Seems all clear," he said.

"All clear!" said the second engineer, tossing his heat detector back into the airlock.

Stabb peered into the night, his close-set eyes intent. "Where the Hells are they? We've got to be back at the base before the sun rises there!" He glanced at his watch. "We've only got twenty-five minutes to hang around here!"

Suddenly, running feet in the distance, coming down a weed-grown road.

Raht burst into view. He was lugging two enormous suitcases.

He is the most unremarkable-looking Earthman one ever cared to see. Aside from a bristling mustache he affects, there is not one other feature to make him stick in memory. The perfect spy. He is from the planet Modon and glad they were to get rid of him.

He boosted the suitcases into the airlock. He was panting with exertion. But he saw me in the dim shimmer of interior light. "Cripes!" he said, "It's Officer

Gris himself." He always has a bit of a complaining note
when he speaks.

"What have you got in these suitcases?" I demanded. "The orders were to get expensive luggage filled with
clothes."

He pushed them further into the airlock. "Clothes
cost money. You've no idea what inflation is. I made up
the weight with rocks!"

He had made up the weight with money in his own
pocket, I said to myself. But I hit the buzzer to the back
and picked up the bags to take them to Heller. I did not
want him to see the agents that would be tailing him
from here on out.

Heller had released the passageway doors. I struggled through and dumped the two huge suitcases in the
salon. They were expensive-looking cases.

He was sitting at the table. I said, "You'll find
clothes in there. Get dressed fast. Take no clothes of your
own. You only have a little over twenty minutes, so don't
dawdle." I left him, closing the doors behind me.

Raht was still breathing hard. I drew him into the
crew salon. He took out a sheaf of documents. "Here's
his military school diploma."

I read:

SAINT LEE MILITARY ACADEMY

Greetings:
**DELBERT JOHN ROCKECENTER,
JUNIOR**
has completed his education to the
level of JUNIOR COLLEGE.
Signed, sealed (etc.)

It was a very imposing diploma. It had Confederate soldiers holding rifles at port arms. It had banners and cannons. Very fancy.

"Here's the rest of the papers," said Raht. They were attested transcripts of subjects and grades.

"What clever forgeries," I said.

"Hells no," said Raht. "They're the authentic signatures. The school closed last spring for keeps and the ex-faculty will do anything for a buck. You think I want to get sent up for forgery?"

Always complaining, even when you give him a compliment.

"Where's Terb?" I demanded. "We haven't got much time."

"Maybe he's having trouble. The old clerk at that (bleeped) courthouse didn't want to come down after hours."

Captain Stabb looked in, pointing at his watch. "We're going to have to race to make it now. We have to get back while it's still night!"

But here was Terb, leaping in through the airlock. Terb is one of the most unremarkable Earthmen you'd ever want to see. A bit on the plump side, a bit swarthy, but you would never pick him out in a crowd. He's from the planet Dolo and they were very glad to get rid of him.

"Not Officer Gris himself!" he said. "We must be important after all! Raht, I been wrong. All this time I been telling you we was just dirt and now..."

"Shut up," I said. "Is the birth certificate fixed?"

Terb nodded. He took a small electric switch out of his pocket. "The old clerk wants to see him so he can attest the certificate is issued to a real person known to him that ain't dead. He don't like to be thought crooked. This bird we got here will present himself, hand over another C-note, get the certificate all signed. Then the instant he walks down the steps of that courthouse, I hit this and good-bye clerk, good-bye records. I planted the bomb before dawn today. Right in the record files!''

I gave them the activator-receiver. "This is a special bug. You must keep this within two hundred miles of him at all times."

"But we got him bugged," said Raht. "There's bugs in those clothes and there's bugs in those suitcases and we have the activator right here. We can't possibly lose him!"

"This is another type of bug, an aerial bug," I lied. "It's inserted in his elbow and registers if he handles explosives or touches guns: we don't want you getting shot."

Oh, that was different!

"We can spot him from a ship with this," I lied. "Now this is the 831 Relayer. Keep it right with the activator-receiver."

They got that.

"Just leave them turned on all the time. See, they look like a telephone connection box. You can put them on the outside of any building or under a bed."

They promised.

Then Raht said, "Money. For us. Inflation is awful!"

I handed them a draft on the Chase-Arab New York Bank. They were happy. So was I: it was government money.

I gave them a few tips. Then I said, "Now get out of here before he sees you."

They went diving out of the airlock, sprinted past the faintly moonlit plantation house and were gone.

Stabb was looking at his watch.

Heller came out. And oh, I had to laugh! Clothes to fit men six feet two inches tall aren't to be had in southern Virginia. They were all too small!

Raht had done a wonderful job. The jacket was LOUD! Huge red and white checks. The pants were LOUD! Huge blue and white stripes. The hat was a bright green, banded Panama: too small! The shoes were orange suede and too tight! The shirt was purple!

He would stand out like a searchlight!

The clothes did look expensive, like they'd been bought by someone with lots of money and no taste at all.

And they looked like they had been outgrown.

Wonderful!

He was lugging the two huge suitcases.

"Don't you think this wardrobe is a bit garish?" he said.

"In the height of fashion! In the height of fashion!" I replied.

I rapidly told him again where he was supposed to go to get his birth certificate. I handed him the other papers.

Then I knelt down in the airlock, pointing a night scope up the road. I wanted to make sure Raht and Terb were out of sight and that the area was still clear. Something was moving in the brush.

"I'm a bit hungry," said Heller behind me. And then he seemed to wander off into the ship.

Stabb came to me. "He says he wants . . ."

"Give him whatever he wants," I said. There was something moving over there by a slave cabin.

Heller was there again. "I'm going to need some money."

Oh, yes. His money. The orders said five thousand dollars so he'd look affluent. I pulled two thousand out of my pocket and handed it to him. Three thousand wasn't bad for a night's work.

He was closing up some straps on a suitcase.

"We're awful close to time," said Stabb.

I saw what the object that had been moving was. A fox. To Hells with it.

I stood up and turned to Heller. I put out my hand. He, however, didn't take it. Instead, he was extending a letter to me. "Do me a favor, would you, and mail this? I promised to keep him informed."

I took it and put it in my pocket. I was too intent on getting rid of him to pay it any heed. "Well, good luck, Jettero," I said. "This is it. Off you go."

He dropped to the ground, lugging the two big cases. He limped off past the moonlit plantation house.

"Bye-bye, Heller," I said to myself. "And I hope you make a lot of good friends in the pen!"

"We're taking off," said Stabb.

I got out of their way. The second engineer dropped out of the airlock with a machine in his hand. Stabb lifted the tug six feet off the ground and held it there. The second engineer ducked around with his machine and made all the grass stand up straight where the ship had been. He threw his machine into the airlock. The second pilot gave him a hand back aboard. They closed the latches.

The captain said to me, "Are you under orders to make our ship incapable of leaving this solar system?"

As a matter of fact, I was. From the assassin pilot. But it wouldn't do to tell Stabb his ship was to be disabled. "Why?" I said.

"He took the time-sight out of the flight deck just now," said the captain. "And if there's another one, we can't get to it. He's double-barred all his cabins and storage spaces: we won't be able to get into them even with a blastgun! Without a sight, we can't fly her in outer space. But I suppose that's what you required: you said to give him anything he wants."

So what? Who wanted to ride in this (bleeping) tug and maybe get shot down?

Stabb sent the ship hurtling into the sky.

Now to race back to the base and land just before dawn.

Stabb cranked the tug auxiliaries up toward the speed of light.

I was jubilant.

Heller was off my hands!

I couldn't wait to get back to a viewer and see how he got everything he had coming to him. The (bleepard). All the trouble he'd caused!

PART FOURTEEN

Chapter 1

Less than two hours later, I was sitting in my secret room in my villa, about 105 degrees of longitude from Heller, watching his every move.

I was ecstatic! The picture on the viewer was brilliant! The sound was perfect even down to the crickets! The 831 Relayer was doing its job!

I had to backtrack the recording strip a bit to where he left the ship.

And there he was, carrying two heavy suitcases, limping through the Virginia night. Up ahead there was a farmhouse, shedding light across a barnyard.

Any true spy, even slightly trained, would have taken a wide path around it. But not Heller!

There was a growl.

Then there was a savage snarl!

A huge sheep dog barred the way!

I realized with a chuckle that Heller had probably never seen a dog. The nearest thing to it were the hondos of Flisten which, when domesticated, specialized in chewing up the whole family.

There it stood, fangs bared! It was crouching down. I knew it would charge. Good-bye, Heller. This thing is going to end right here on a hot night in Virginia and between the fangs of a dog!

With a short run to get a fast start, it sprang into the air, the fangs aimed straight for Heller's throat!

Heller let go the suitcases.

His hands flashed out.

He grabbed the dog by the loose skin on either side of the jowl!

Pivoting on his heel, using the momentum of the dog, he sent the beast twenty feet behind him!

It sailed through the air! With a clunk, it collided with a tree, let out one yelp and lay still.

I expected Heller to run. That much sound would attract attention in the nearby house.

Heller walked over to the dog and examined it. Then he picked the big brute up in his arms. He went back to his suitcases and somehow got hold of their handles.

He was limping to the lighted house!

The screen door opened. A farmer was standing there with a shotgun!

Heller limped right on up to the porch. He dropped his suitcases. "Ah'm afraid yoah dawg ran intah a tree," said Heller in a thick Virginia accent.

The farmer opened the door wider and Heller took the dog into the living room and laid it down on the rug. "He ain't bleedin' none, so Ah s'pose he'll come around," said Heller.

The Virginian bent over the dog. It made a feeble struggle to get up and the farmer petted it and it relaxed with a faint thump of its tail.

"Naw," said the farmer, "he ain't hurt none. You f'um heahabouts, kid?"

"Heahabouts," said Heller. "Ah'll be gittin' on now."

"Hell, no. Not aftah you done a white-man thing lahk that! Martha, bring some cawfee in heah!" he yelled toward the kitchen.

"Aw, no," said Heller. "Ah be much obliged. But Ah got me an appointment in town. A fellah's a-waitin' foah me at th' co'thouse. Ah'm much obliged but Ah be late awready."

"Well, hell, kid, tha's more'n two mile. An' you limp-in' an' all. Be downright unneighbo'ly of me not to run you intah town! Ah'll git mah truck!"

The dog had gotten over on its belly. It was staring at Heller with the strangest look.

The farmer cranked up his truck outside and Heller picked up the suitcases, tossed them into the back and got in. And they rattled off to town.

(Bleep), I thought. That didn't go so good. It was the Virginia accent that had brought it off. (Bleep) that Countess Krak! She ought to stick to teaching freaks!

Heller alighted at the courthouse. The farmer said, "Drop by any ol' tahm, when ya'll comes back home, kid."

"Ah be lookin' fohw'd to ut," said Heller, "an' much obliged foah th' lift."

And off went the farmer.

Heller looked up at the courthouse. There were just two windows lit on the second floor. The front door was open and Heller limped up the steps. He pushed open a door.

A real old codger, dressed in black, was hunched over a desk in the space behind the counter. He had a couple of file drawers open. The sign on his desk said:

BIRTHS AND DEATHS, WAIT IN LINE PLEASE

I hoped the old (bleepard) was properly in line himself. He would be dead in about five minutes.

Heller walked up to the counter and dropped his bags.

The old man raised his half-bald, gray head. "You th' boy?"

"Tha's what they say," said Heller.

"Ah wondered if it would evuh come to this," said

the old man, cryptically. He came over and looked at Heller closely. "So you be Delbert John Rockecenter, Junior?"

"Tha's what they say," said Heller.

"That be two hundrud dollahs," said the old man, pushing a birth certificate forward but holding on to it.

Hah, I thought. America is crooked as always. He'd upped the price a hundred.

Heller reached into his pocket. You could see the money was strange-looking to him. He turned some of the bills over.

The old man reached across and plucked two hundreds off the roll and pocketed them.

Heller picked up the birth certificate. It gave his name, said he was blond, said he'd been born at home. It had a seal on it and the clerk's signature. The date of birth made Heller just seventeen! Heller put it in his pocket.

"Much obliged," said Heller.

He picked up the bags, turned and limped back down the curving courthouse steps. He pushed through the front door and walked down into the street.

I turned the audio volume down, knowing what was coming.

With a roar and flame and a splintering crash, the upper windows of the building blew out!

Standard procedure.

Good-bye, you old cheating (bleepard), I said. Always give a prayer for the dead. It brings luck.

Flame was starting to gush out through one of the windows. When Terb bombs something, he really bombs it. He's fond of exaggeration. And he always uses locally obtained explosives, too, avoiding any Space Code break. A master!

Wait! What in the name of Gods was Heller doing!

That blast would attract attention even on this deserted hill. Fire engines existed even in Virginia. In fact, they are so proud of their fire engines, they're always having rallies of volunteer fire companies for miles around!

Any trained man would have understood. And he would have started running. Fast!

Not Heller! He dropped his suitcases. He streaked through the main door. He raced up those stairs. He bashed his way into Births and Deaths!

The place was on fire! It was filled with smoke!

Even the counter was blown over! Heller was down, right at floor level. He snaked ahead, feeling through the churning fury.

He found a hand, a sleeve. He yanked. A body was in view.

There was a carpet on the floor. Heller snapped the ends to him. He wrapped it around the old man with two quick jerks.

He went backwards, dragging the wrapped body with him.

He got to the stairs and threw the carpeted body over his shoulder and went down five steps at a time.

He burst into the open air. He stepped sideways to a strip of lawn.

Oh, well, I thought. Not too bad. They always arrest everybody in sight when there's a bomb explosion. That's why you have to get away from them quick. And Heller was staying right there, the idiot.

He unwrapped the old man. He beat out some bits of smoldering cloth.

The old man opened his eyes, "What . . . what in hell was that?"

"You all raht?" said Heller.

The old man felt around. "Ah be purty bruised up but she don' look like nothin' broke. It's that (bleeped) stove. I tol' 'em t' shut it off las' spring! She blew up befo'. Th' pilot light goes aht and she fills with gas. . . .''

The old man's eyes were staring at the building. Heller looked. The windows were all blown out and part of the roof and the flames were starting to roar up with lashing tongues into the sky.

It was just now sinking in what had happened to him. He was staring at Heller, his eyes going round. "Jesus Christ, kid," he said with awe. "You risk yoah neck somethin' awful draggin' me aht o' there!" He shook his head as though to clear his eyes. He looked at Heller much more intensely. "You saved mah life, youngster!"

Heller was making sure the old man was all right. He was trying to get him to flex his fingers.

Over on the other side of town, what was probably a volunteer fire department was getting busy. A summons bell was clanging, shattering the night.

"Shouldn' Ah call somebody or somethin'?" said Heller. "An ambeoolance?"

"Kid, look. Ah jus' thought. Jesus Christ, you bettuh git aht o' heah! There'll be fiahmen and repohtahs ahl ovah this place in about one minute. Ah'll be ahl raht, youngster. Ah'll nevah fohget you. But with a name lahk yoahs, you bettuh run lahk hell, quick!"

"Glad Ah could help aht," said Heller. And he moved off.

"If'n Ah can evuh be moah help t' you," the old man called after him, "you jus' yell fo' Stonewall Biggs!"

Heller walked down the hill, carrying his bags. The ground was bathed with the fiercely burning courthouse fire.

He was on the street sidewalk when the fire engine passed. He looked back, then stood waiting. The whole top of the hill was being crowned in flames. There went a Virginia landmark. Probably, I thought, George Washington had slept there.

Shortly, an ambulance went by.

Heller hefted his bags and limped onward toward the bus station.

He stopped suddenly. He got out a notebook. He wrote: *They can't make stoves.*

Chapter 2

A black man was standing at the door of the bus station, broom in hand, an old hat on the back of his head. He was looking up the street to the fire on the hill. I hoped he would wake up and notice there was a stranger in town and connect him with the fire.

"When is the next bus?" said Heller.

"Hoo-ee," said the black. "Now, ain't that some fiah! Y'all evuh see a fiah that big?"

I imagine Heller, as a Fleet combat engineer, had seen whole cities on fire. He had probably set some himself that would make that courthouse fire look like a stray spark.

"Tha's purty big," said Heller. He went in and put down his bags.

It was a very dingy bus station: ripped-up plastic seats, discarded newspapers on the floor. There was a ticket wicket at the far end.

The black came in, shaking his head. He put down the broom, went into the wicket and took off his hat. With a flourish, he opened the front of the wicket.

"Wheah you goin'?" he called. "Richmun', Washin'ton, New Yahk, Mahami? O' maybe Atlanta?"

"Atlanta?" said Heller, walking over to the counter. I thought, here we go again! More Manco! More Prince Caucalsia!

"Oh, tha's a fahn town," the black said. "Plenty white ladies, yallah ladies, black ladies. Any coluh you got a wishin' fo'. A real fahn town. Or maybe you'd lahk Buhmin'ham. Now *that* is the fahnes' town you evuh hope to see, man."

"Ah'm goin' to New Yahk," said Heller.

"Oh, ah'm real sorry 'bout that. This bus line only go to Lynchburg." The black man had come down out of his daydream about wondrous places to visit. "This ol' dumb town o' Fair Oakes ain't real well connected. But y'all c'n change at Lynchburg. Ah c'n sell you a ticket to theah, tho'."

"That'll be real fahn," said Heller.

The black got busy and very efficiently issued the ticket. "Tha's two dollahs an' fohty cents. Next bus comin' thoo heah 'bout midnight. Tha's 'bout an hour an' a half y'all gotta wait. Heah is yoah ticket, heah is yoah change. We ain' got no entertainment, 'less you wanna go watch the co'thouse fiah. No? Well, you jus' make yo'self t' home. Now Ah's the janitor ag'in."

He put his hat back on, closed the wicket and picked up his broom. But he went outside to watch the fire on the hill.

Heller sat down with a suitcase on either side of him. He started reading the various travel signs that told about the joys of Paris, the glories of ancient Greece and one that advised that there was going to be a fried chicken supper at the local high school last September.

I thought I might hear the crackle of flames in the distance so I turned up the gain. I didn't hear flames,

only some distant commotion. Wouldn't anybody notice
there was a stranger in town? Where were the police?
Fine lot of police they were! When there's a bombing or
big fire, the first thing you do is look for strangers. I was
quite put out. There sat Heller, comfortable as could be.

The black started to do some sweeping. He began to
sing:

> Hark to the story of Willie the Weeper,
> Willie the Weeper was a chimney sweeper.
> He had the hop habit and he had it bad.
> Oh, listen while I tell you 'bout the dream he had!

He wanted to sweep under Heller's right foot, so Heller, accommodatingly, lifted his right foot.

> He went to the hop joint the other night,
> When he knew that the lights would be burnin' bright.
> I guess he smoked a dozen pills or more.
> When he woke up he wuz on a foreign shore.

He had finished the right foot area. He wanted to
sweep under Heller's left foot. Heller accommodatingly
raised it.

> Queen o' Bulgaria was the first in his net.
> She called him her darlin' an' her lovin' pet.
> She promised him a pretty Ford automobile,
> With a diamond headlight and a silver steerin' wheel.

Amongst the swish of the broom, which didn't seem
to really be doing much but raise dust, I thought I heard
the distant chortle of a police car. It seemed to be
approaching the bus station.

Willie landed in New York one evenin' late.
He asked his sugar for an afterdate.
Willie he got funny. She began to shout,
'Bim bam boo!'—an' the dope gave out.

It was a police car! It came to a stop with a squeal of tires and a dying chortle. Right outside the bus station!

Aha, I thought with gratification, the local police aren't so inefficient after all. They're checking the bus station for strangers! Well, untrained, amateur Heller, you are about to get it! And he wasn't even looking at the door!

The sharp yelp of someone being hurt. Heller's head whipped around.

Two enormous policemen were barging into the room. They were dressed in black vinyl short jackets. They were girded around with handcuffs and guns. They had billy clubs ready in their hands.

Between them they were dragging a small, young woman! Tears were pouring out of her eyes. She was fighting like a wild thing.

"Let me go! You God (bleeped) (bleepards)!" she was shouting. "Let me go!"

The cops sent her hurtling forward. She collided with a vinyl chair. One of the cops was at her at once, spinning her about and making her sit down.

The other cop got a battered suitcase out of the police car, sent it skidding across the floor at the girl and it hit her in the legs. Then he walked over to the ticket wicket, shouting, "Open this up, you black (bleepard)!"

The cop hulking over the girl had her pinned to the chair.

"You got no right to do this!" she was yelling at him.

"We gaht all the raht in the worl'!" said the cop. "If'n the chief says Horsey Mary Schmeck goes aht of town tonight, then aht of town goes Horsey Mary Schmeck and heah you is!"

Tears were cascading down her cheeks. Perspiration beaded her forehead. She was probably only about twenty-five but she looked thirty-five—deep bags under her eyes. Except for that, she was not unpretty. Her brown hair was over part of her face and she swept it away. She was trying to get up.

She renewed the verbal attack. "Your (bleeped) chief wasn't talking that way when he got out of my bed last week! He said I could work this town as long as I wanted."

"Tha' was las' week," said the cop, pinning her down to the chair again. "This's this week!"

She tried to claw at his face. "You (bleeped) two-bit (bleepard)! You yourself sold me a nickel bag last Monday!"

"Tha' was las' Monday," said the cop. He had her pinned. "You know an' Ah know what this is all about. Tha' God (bleeped) new Fed narco moved in on th' distric'. Nobody knew it'd been changed. Nobody give him his split so he's cleanin' the whole place up. And y'all is the kind of trash tha's bein' swept out."

She was crying again. "Oh, Joe. *Please* sell me a nickel bag. Look, I'll go. I'll get on the bus. But I got to have a fix, Joe. *Please!* I can't take it, Joe! Just one little fix and I'll go!"

The other cop had come back from the ticket window. "Shut up, Mary. You 'n all of us know the distric' is total empty of big H now. Joe, did th' chief give you bus fare fo' this (bleepch)?"

The girl was collapsed. Tears streamed from red eyes. Sweat beaded her head. I knew what was wrong. She was a dope addict that was moving into the withdrawal symptoms. It would get worse before it got any better. As she scrubbed at her eyes, one could see the needle scars inside her arm. A girl trying to keep up with the expensive habit by selling her body. Ordinary situation. And they were moving her out of town. Ordinary handling. But maybe she'd infected the chief with something. Venereal disease goes right along with drugs and prostitution. It was such a common scene that I had no hope Heller would get himself in trouble over it.

"Well, Ah ain' forkin' ovah none of mah own cash t' get her aht o' town," said the cop who had gone to the ticket wicket.

Joe grabbed the girl's purse. She made a frantic effort to retain it and got a punch in the jaw in return. She fell to the floor, crying.

The two cops went over to the ticket window. Joe began to rummage through the purse. "Hey, would you look at this!" he said. He pulled out a roll of bills and started counting. "A hunnad an' thutty-two dallahs!"

"That'll buy a lot of white mule!" said the other cop.

They both laughed. They split the roll and put it into their pockets.

Suddenly the two cops and the wicket were huge in my screen!

"Give th' lady back her money," said Heller.

They stared at him blankly. Then their faces went hard.

"Kid," said Joe, hefting his nightstick, "Ah think you need a lesson!"

Joe raised his club to strike.

Heller's hand was a blur.

Joe's arm broke with a snap just above the elbow!

Heller danced back. The other cop was drawing his gun, bracing himself, two hands on the butt. His eyes were savage with the joy of being able to kill something.

Ordinary cop reaction. I thought, well, Heller, it was nice knowing you.

The blur of a hand. The cop's gun moved back and then up and flew away.

Heller's left hand chopped in against the cop's neck. The eyes went glazed.

Heller danced back and kicked the cop in the stomach before the body had even begun to slump. The cop sailed back and hit a trash can.

With a whirl, Heller was onto Joe again. Joe was trying to draw his gun with his left hand. Heller's foot smashed the fingers against the gun butt.

Heller's other foot rose and caught Joe on the button. The snap of bones followed the impact instantly.

Backing up, Heller looked at them. They were very sprawled. Heller, one after the other, took their guns and sent them spinning out through the front door of the bus station. There was a crash of glass as one of them broke a window in the police car.

The girl had come forward, staring down at the two unconscious cops. "Serves you right, you (bleepards)!"

Heller scooped the money out of their pockets and put it in her purse. He handed it to her.

She looked a little confused. Then she rallied. "Honey, we got to get the hell out of here! The chief will go bananas! That Joe is his son!"

She was hauling hard at Heller, trying to get him to the door.

"Come on!" she was shouting. "I know where we can get a car! Come on, quick! We got to make dust!"

Heller gave her her suitcase. He picked up his own and followed her out. He glanced back once.

The black man was looking down at the smashed cops. "An' Ah jus' cleaned the flooah," he said sadly.

Chapter 3

They were heading to the north of the town. The streets were deserted and dark. Heller was limping along. Soon it became apparent that the girl could not keep up. She sagged down panting, on her suitcase.

"It's my heart," she was gasping. "I got a bad ticker. . . . I'll be all right in a minute. . . . I got to be . . . They'll be tearing this town apart . . . to find us."

Heller scooped her up under one arm and put her suitcase under his other, picked up his own and proceeded.

"You're . . . you're an all right kid. Turn over to the right there—it takes us to the state highway."

Soon, she directed him up the state highway to the edge of town. There was a glare of lights there. It was a filling station and used-car lot combined. The signs said it sold Octopus Gasoline and a big octopus logo was dripping gas at each tentacle. There were colored plastic whirlers around the place, idle from the lack of wind. Then Heller's attention was directed to the back. A sign there, above the used-car lot run apparently in conjunction with the station, said:

HARVEY 'SMASHER' LEE'S BARGAIN CARS
FOR TRUE VIRGINIANS
MONEY BACK SOMETIMES

The place was really run down: the filling station at this time of night was closed, half the twirlers were bent and a third of the light bulbs out.

A man had been standing up on the cab of an old truck, looking off in the direction of the courthouse fire. He saw them and climbed down.

Heller had put Horsey Mary Schmeck down and she sat on her suitcase, tears running down her cheeks. She was perspiring and her nose was running. She let out a huge yawn, one of the symptoms.

The man came up, looking at them. He was plump but big. He was about thirty. He had a weak, flabby face. "Mary?" He wasn't glad to see her. He looked at Heller. "Hey, what you doin', Mary? Robbin' th' cradle?"

"Harv, you've got to get me a fix! Even a nickel bag, Harv. Please, Harv."

"Aw, Mary, you know that new Fed narco dried up this district. And he says he'll keep it dry until he gets fifty percent of ever'body's traffic. There ain't no stuff to be had!"

The girl moaned. "Not even some of your own? Please, Harv."

He shook his head very emphatically.

Then she got hopeful. "Maybe they got some in Lynchburg. Harv, sell this kid a car."

I turned up the gain so I could hear the police cars if they started to come this way. I was sure they would. The longer these stupid idiots fooled around, the less chance they had and the happier I would be.

The idea of selling a car inspired Harvey "Smasher" Lee. Right away he went into his act. "Here's a Datsun! Another man wanted it but if you buy it quick, I can put him off. It's a B210. It only has seventy thousand miles on the clock and it's less than two years old. Only seven thousand dollars! And I'll throw in five gallons of gas."

The car was a beat-up wreck. One wheel was folded under. This salesman was pretty good. That was only double what the car had been worth new. I began to have hopes for him. Maybe he would run Heller out of money, for Heller only had two thousand.

"Ah think," said Heller, "you got somethin' foah less."

"Oh, well! Of course I have. Now take this Ford pickup. It's a real bargain. It's only been used for hauling fertilizer and we'll wash it all out for you. For five thousand . . ."

"Harv," called the girl, "you better hurry up. We'll have to leave any minute!"

Heller had been looking at the row of wrecks. There was a huge one at the end, light gray in color. He approached it. It was covered with dust. "How about this one! It's the right color to be invisible."

"Hey, kid!" called Mary. "You don't want that one. It's a gas hog! It won't get eight miles to the gallon!"

Harv took position quickly to block the girl from Heller's sight. "Now, kid, I see you got a real eye for cars. This here is a Cadillac Brougham Coupe d'Elegance! It's one of the last real cars they made. It's a 1968! Before they clamped down with pollution controls. Why, there's five hundred horses right under that hood." He pointed at it proudly.

"Horses?" said Heller. "You mus' be kiddin' me. Let's see!"

Harvey instantly jumped to the front of the huge gray vehicle and, with some trouble, got the hood up. It was a giant engine. It didn't look too bad.

"She has a 10.5-to-1 compression ratio," said Harvey. "A real fire-eater."

"What's it burn?" said Heller.

"Burn? Oh, you mean octanes."

"No. Fuel. What fuel does it burn? You said it was a fire engine. What *fuel?*"

"What the hell . . . Gasoline, kid. Petroleum!"

"A chemical engine!" said Heller, suddenly enlightened. "Hello, hello! Is it solid or liquid?"

Harv yelled back at Mary, "Is this kid a kidder or what?"

"Sell him a car!" wailed Mary, staring now down the road to town in anxiety.

"Kid, this car is spotless. It was owned by a little old lady who never drove it at all."

"Harv, stop lying!" Mary yelled. "You know (bleeped) well it was owned by Prayin' Pete, the radio preacher, before they hung him! Sell him the God (bleeped) car! We got to *leave!*"

"It's only two thousand dollars," said Harvey in desperation.

"Harvey!" screamed the girl. "You told me just last week you couldn't even sell that car to the wholesalers! Kid, quit letting him snow you under! He's had that thing for six months and he only uses it to (bleep) the local talent in because it has draw curtains in the back!"

"Fifteen hundred," said Harv frantically to Heller.

"Two hundred!" screamed the girl.

"Aw, Mary. . . ."

"Two hundred or I'll tell your wife!"

"Two hundred," said Harv sullenly.

Heller fiddled with the money, trying to sort out its unfamiliar colors and numbers.

"Wait," said Harv, grasping at a reprieve. "I can't sell it to him. He's under age!"

"Put it in my name and hurry up!"

Harv snatched the two one-hundred-dollar bills out of Heller's hands and then grabbed enough more for tax and license. He angrily wrote up a sales contract to Mary Schmeck.

I turned up the gain again. (Bleeped) inefficient police. Must be looking in the wrong places as usual.

They certainly would have discovered those two maimed cops by now.

Harv left the hood up. He opened the door and let off the brake. He started to go behind the car to push it and then must have realized it was a hot night. He went to the office and came back with some keys. He slid under the wheel, turned on the ignition. The engine roared into powerful life.

"Hey," he said in amazement, "it started! Must be a Penny battery."

"Fill it up," yelled the girl. "Check its oil, water and tires! Fast!"

Harvey eased the car over to the pumps. He checked the automatic transmission fluid, saw it was all right. He shut off the engine. He topped it up with water. He checked the oil, which, to his disappointment, seemed all right.

"There you are," said Harvey. "I'll file for these plates in the morning."

Heller put the suitcases in the back. The girl got in front. Then the girl reached over and turned on the switch. "Harv! You owe us five gallons of gas! It's empty!"

With no good graces, Harvey unlocked a pump. Then he had a bright idea. "I'm only allowed to sell tankfuls now. It's a new rule!"

"Oh, God," said the girl, looking down the road toward town. "Hurry it up!"

Gas was shortly gurgling into the monstrous tank. The girl said, "You didn't check the tires!"

Harv grudgingly went around and filled the tires up. Then he took the gas nozzle out of the filler pipe and put on the cap. "That'll be forty dollars!" he said. "The price just went up again and we haven't had time to post it on the pumps."

Heller paid him. The girl took the sales receipt. She

scribbled her signature on a power of attorney card for the new license and threw it at Harv. "Now, let's get the hell out of here!"

Heller apparently had seen Harv start it. He turned the ignition key all the way over and the engine blasted into life.

"Hey," said Heller, "so that's the way horses sound."

"Beat it, kid," said Harvey.

"There's just one thing," said Heller. "How do you fly it?"

Harv looked at him bug-eyed. "Can't you drive?"

"Well, no," said Heller. "Not a chemical-engine Cadillac Brougham Coupe d'Elegance," he added, wanting to be exact. "With five hundred horses."

"Jesus," said Harv, softly. Then he brightened. "That's the automatic shift lever. Put it in park when you are through with the car. That *N* means neutral and to hell with it. The *L* is low and you won't never need it. The *D* is drive one. You won't use that. That second *D* is where you keep it.

"Now, that pedal down there . . . no, the other one. That's the foot brake and you push it when you want to stop. This other thing to your left is the hand brake and you use that when you park on a hill.

"Now, that thing there on the floor is the accelerator. You push it to speed up."

There was an instant deafening roar as Heller tramped on it.

"Don't rev it up so!" squeaked Harvey. The engine slowed. "And there you are. You got it?"

I caught a distant chortle of police cars.

"Is this the wheelstick?" said Heller, touching the steering wheel.

"Yes! Yes! You turn it to go to the right, you turn it this way to go to the left. Hey, I forgot to show you the lights. This is the light knob. . . . Well, turn them ON!"

"Let's get out of here!" wailed the girl.

Harv had his hand on the open window ledge. He bent close. "Kid, this car will do a hundred and thirty. If you get out there and kill yourself, don't come back here complaining!"

"Jesus!" screamed the girl. "The fuzz!"

And there they came! Two of them! The first one bounced over the curb and into the used-car lot. The second saw them at the pumps and swerved toward them.

Heller engaged the Cadillac in drive!

He stamped on the accelerator! He almost tore his own head off.

The Cadillac leaped at a sign.

Heller turned the wheel.

The Cadillac launched itself over a curb!

Heller yanked the wheel. He overcompensated and headed back for the curb. He corrected and got the car going north. He was in the middle of the road.

An ancient truck was coming at him.

"To the right!" screamed the girl.

Heller swerved to the right, hit the gravel, came back on the road.

"Drive on the right side of the road!" screamed the girl.

"Got it," said Heller.

Behind them two police cars had started up in mad pursuit. They had their quarry in sight and their chortling said so for all the world to hear!

I smiled to myself in great satisfaction. Heller was going to be in a box much sooner than I thought! Chiefs of police do not take lightly to having their sons hospitalized. They don't have many cops in such a small town. I didn't need to hear their radios to know the chief was in one of those police cars! Police cars are as fast as that Cadillac. And that chief was not going to give up. That was for sure!

Chapter 4

Mary Schmeck yelled, "Turn down that side road! It cuts across country. We can get over on U.S. 29. It's a four-lane to Lynchburg!"

The right-angle turn was just ahead. Heller yanked the steering wheel to the left. Tires screamed! A wild skid.

Heller said, as he fought the wheel to point the swerving car straight on the new road, "Ho, ho! Centrifugal momentum about 160 foot-tons per second."

"What?" yelled Mary.

"You have to counteract it ahead of time," said Heller, firing the car down the narrow, two-lane country road.

"On this road and U.S. 29, there's no place they can call ahead and set up road blocks."

Heller screamed around a curve. The car weaved, spraying headlights against the speeding trees. "A shift to angular velocity can overcome the road friction potential of this machine! Inadequate centripetal force simulation."

"You better step on it, kid! They're in shooting range behind you!"

Trees and fences blurred by. The lights of the cop cars glared in the rearview mirror. They were closing!

Mary said, "The county line is up here. Maybe

they'll quit chasing us when we cross it! Step on it, kid! You're only doing seventy!"

A sign flashed by:

CURVES AHEAD

Heller said, "So, by reduction of velocity before the turn, using this foot brake, then stamping on this throttle as you start the turn and releasing the brake, adequate compensating acceleration can be added through the turn. I got it!"

A shot blasted out. It hit the car somewhere in the rear with a jolt.

A steep downslope curve swept away to the left, evading the headlight path. Heller braked!

"I'm getting the hang of this now," he said.

The engine raced into a scream, the brakes came off! The car leaped into the curve, accelerating madly. The tires screamed but it was less.

The speedometer was racing up to ninety.

Behind them wild tire howls came from the cop cars.

Mary said, "There's a lot of curves ahead! I'll see if there's a road map in this glove compartment!"

"I don't need any," Heller said. "It was all on the Geological Survey."

A new steep curve flashed into view ahead. Heller stamped on the brakes. Mary almost went through the windshield. The engine roared. Off came the brakes, and the car shot around the curve as though fired from a gun.

"Jesus, kid, you're doing ninety!" A hasty buckling sound. She must be fastening her seat belt.

Heller glanced at trees whipping by. "That's wrong. It's only eighty-six."

He braked and then, accelerating, shot the car around a new curve.

"But I'll get it up to speed," said Heller. "Oh!" He looked at the shift lever indicator. "It was on the first drive slot. No wonder we were poking along!" He shifted the lever to high drive.

But they had lost distance. A short, straight stretch was ahead. In the rearview mirror, the leading cop car lights were getting nearer.

Heller said, "They sure build these seats close to the pedals. No leg room."

"There's some buttons down on your left that push the seat back."

Above the roar of the engine, the seat motor whirred.

A shot flash flared in the rearview mirror. It must have hit the road: the ricochet whine-yowled away, overtaken by the blast of the shot.

"Come on, you chemical-fuel Cadillac Brougham Coupe d'Elegance," said Heller. "Do I have your brake lever on?" He glanced down. It was off.

The car surged over a rise, almost lifting from the ground. A big sign flashed by:

YOU ARE LEAVING HAMDEN COUNTY

A moment later, Mary said, "Those (bleepards)! They're coming right on across the county line. Don't they know it's illegal?"

The cop cars were not so close. The lead one turned on a searchlight.

A barn whipped by.

Heller braked and fired the car into a new curve. "What are all those buttons on the panel? You got an instruction book in there?"

"No." Her hand came into view in the tail of his eye.

"But I can show you. This is the air conditioning. This is the heater. This dial is where you set the interior temperature. This is the aerial for the radio but it goes up automatically when you turn the radio on. This is the radio tuning control."

The car flashed across a cattle guard with a sharp roar. The yell of the cop cars was loud.

"This is the automatic station selector. These are the preset station push buttons. You tune in the station then you pull one out and push it in and it repeats the station whenever you push it."

"You sure know a lot about cars," said Heller.

"I had one once."

A truck was turning out from a gate, dead ahead.

Heller yanked the steering wheel. They hit the gravel on the edge. The car swerved widely. He yanked it back on the road.

He said, "You're not from around here, are you. I can tell by your accent."

I hastily made a note. Since he had begun to talk to her, his own accent was fading into New England! Aha! A Code break?

He was negotiating, with brake and accelerator, a new series of curves. Fences were whipping by. He had accidentally found the floor dimmer switch and turned the lights up.

The cop cars were a few hundred yards behind, holding their noisy own.

"Oh, I'm a tried-and-true first family of Virginia all right," she said. She was swabbing at her streaming eyes and nose with the hem of her skirt. "My people were farmers. They didn't want me to have such a hard life."

They howled into a new curve.

"I sure got to get a fix," she said, swabbing some more. "Anyway, my father and mother skimped and scraped and sent me to Bassardt Woman's College: that's up the Hudson from New York."

They roared across a wooden bridge and streaked up the hill on the far side. The roar of the cop cars on the bridge sounded hot behind them.

"You look like an honest kid," she said. "I got some advice for you. You be sure to finish college. You be sure to get your degree. It isn't what you know that gets you the job. It's the diploma, the sheepskin. That's what talks. Nobody will listen to anything you say unless you have that piece of parchment!"

"Got to have a diploma before anyone will listen to you," said Heller, taking careful mental note of it.

A cop car had sped up. It got its hood even with the rear wheels of the Cadillac. A bullhorn roared!

"PULL OVER, GOD (BLEEP) YOU! YOU'RE UNDER ARREST!"

Heller weaved the Cadillac's rear over toward the cop car's front wheels. The cop car frantically braked. Heller straightened out the Cadillac's swerves and fed it more accelerator.

"Well, did you get your diploma?" said Heller.

The Cadillac plunged down to where the road crossed an open creek bed. Water rocketed to the right and left. The engine screamed as he went up the far slope.

"Oh, yes," said Mary. "You have to graduate to amount to anything. I'm a full-fledged Doctor of Philosophy. I even got my sheepskin in my bag. I'll show you. Psychology, you know."

My ears tingled! Ah, this dear girl! A psychologist! Empathy flooded through me.

The car almost left the ground over a rise.

"Psychology?" said Heller. "What's that?"

"A lot of horse (bleep). It's a con game. They try to make you think you're nobody, just a bunch of cells, an animal. They can't *do* anything. They teach that you can't *change* anybody. They even have total consciousness that they're fakes. So why bother to practice it?"

I went catatonic with shock!

My newly formed empathy shattered utterly into non-rapport! A heretic! A foul nonbeliever! She had no reverence whatever for the sacred! Absolute antisocial negation!

The Cadillac was racing down a bumpy lane. The screams of the cop cars got louder.

"I was an A student," said Mary, "but every time any of the professors (bleeped) me, they'd say I should be more libido oriented. That's why they kept putting me on drugs. Listen, if psychology is so good, why are all the psychology professors so crazy?"

Heller slued the Cadillac across a muddy stretch of road. The speedometer said one hundred.

Mary swabbed at her running nose and eyes. "They preach free love just so they can get it free."

Another shot hit the road and ricocheted away.

"They're all bad (bleeps), too. I suppose it's the constant overstimulation of the erotic sensory capacity that causes the consequent response deterioration. But they say it's a lot of hard work to turn every college dorm into a whorehouse. You just missed that cow."

Heller said, "But if you got your diploma, why couldn't you get a job?"

A huge sign whipped by. It had said:

WARNING—SLOW DOWN
JUNCTION WITH U.S. 29 STRAIGHT AHEAD

Heller braked. The engine screamed. He let off the brakes and shot into the four-lane U.S. 29, heading north.

"The public won't have anything to do with a psychologist. They know better. The only people who employ psychologists are the government. They think they need them to teach kids, to defend the bankers and wipe out dissidents. The government thinks the psychologists can keep the population under control. What a laugh!"

The cop cars had entered U.S. 29 behind them.

A sign said:

LYNCHBURG 20 MILES

"I sure hope I can get a fix in Lynchburg," said Mary.

Heller started letting the Cadillac out.

Heller said, "Did the government offer you a job?"

The Cadillac engine was screaming at such a pitch, it became hard to hear what they were saying.

"They sure did," she said. Then she swabbed at her nose and frantically tried to yawn. Then she leaned forward to look at him intensely. "Listen, kid. I may be a thief. I may be a totally hooked dope addict. I may be a whore. I might have some incurable disease. But don't think I've sunk so low as to work for the God (bleeped) government! Do you think I want to be a paranoid schizophrenic like those guys?"

I thought to myself, remembering Lombar, well, she has a point there. I began to take a more tolerant view of her, apostate though she might be. I suddenly recalled how clever and cunning she had been in doing Harvey "Smasher" Lee out of his favorite and vitally fetishworshipped Cadillac. The psychology training had vividly shown through. Hadn't she used blackmail? Ah, well, my faith in psychology was totally restored.

The four-lane highway had a wide divider in the center. At intervals a gap in the abutments showed through where one could do a U-turn.

U.S. 29 was undulating at this point, with many rises and dips. As it went over the tops, the Cadillac tended to float.

"Now, you chemical-engined Cadillac Brougham Coupe d'Elegance, it's time you started to move!"

A sign flashed by:

JUNCTION STATE HIGHWAY 699 1 MILE

The cop cars were in sight in the rearview mirror.

The Cadillac engine was winding up to a shriek.

"Jesus!" said Mary. "You're doing over 120."

The speedometer was stuck at the top.

"We're doing 135," said Heller.

A sign:

55 MPH SPEED LIMIT

Another sign:

RADAR PATROLLED

They flashed by the junction of State Highway 699.

The opposite lane had some truck traffic in it.

They soared over a rise. All four wheels of the Cadillac left the ground!

It hurtled down the hill.

The cop cars had vanished, hidden by the rise.

Heller was watching the center dividers for an opening.

"HOLD ON!" yelled Heller.

He stamped on the brakes.

Mary slapped a hand against the cowling.

Heller floorboarded the accelerator. He yanked the wheel to the left.

The car, in a skidding scream, spun through the divider opening.

It shot ahead in the opposite lanes, going now in the other direction.

A big truck was just ahead in the passing lane.

Heller stamped on the brakes and brought the car to the right of the truck!

The Cadillac came down to a shuddering fifty-five.

On the opposite side of the highway, the two police cars screamed over the rise and down the hill, still heading for Lynchburg as though the world were on fire.

Their yowls and chortles faded away to the north.

"Now," said Heller, pointing as they ambled quietly along, "we'll turn over to State Highway 699." The junction was right there. They turned sedately. "We'll go over to U.S. Highway 501 and then up into Lynchburg."

"Jesus," said Mary, "I hope so. I sure need a fix."

Chapter 5

As they headed up U.S. 501, I laughed.

What an amateur! They'd have his license number spread through Lynchburg and all the states to the north. And here he was, tamely rolling along to the first town where he'd be expected. I knew they'd spot and catch him there or somewhere up the line for sure!

Fleet combat engineer! Never trained for anything really important. Anyone with any sense would have headed in the other direction. Even for California! Fast! Yet there he was, driving at a leisurely pace into the northern side of the town.

A big neon sign said:

BIG RAINBOW MOTEL
VACANCY

Heller pulled in beside the office.

Mary swabbed at her nose with her skirt. "I better go in."

Heller unlatched the door for her and helped her out. He went in with her. Just what I wanted.

The clock on the office wall said it was 11:45.

A clerk with his sleeves rolled up had his gray head lowered over some bookkeeping. He reminded me of Lombar's chief clerk, so I expected him to be nasty.

Mary went to the desk. She sure looked awful. "Mister," she said, "could you tell me where I could buy a dollar bag or tell me where I could get one? I need it awfully bad!"

The clerk looked up and fixed her with a gimlet eye. "Aw, Ah'm terrible sorry, ma'am. Ah jus' cain't." He turned to Heller apologetically. "It's the local Feds. They grabbed all the hard stuff in sight jus' las' week. They said they's holdin' it to shoot up the price afore they puts it back on the mahkut. You know how the God (bleeped) narcos is." He turned back to Mary. "Ah'm terrible sorry, ma'am, Ah shorely is!"

Mary was shuddering. The clerk turned back to Heller, "But Ah c'd rent you a room, though. You c'd tear yourself off a piece."

"A room w'd be fahn," said Heller.

The old man got a key. "You want it jus' foah a hour or a night? This lady don't look up to much but Ah c'd make it real cheap a night."

"A night," said Heller.

"That be fohty dollahs, then."

Heller gave him the money and the old clerk handed him the key. "Numbuh thutty-eight, clear t'other end this buildin'. Have a good tahm." And he simply went back to his books!

(Bleep) him! No registration card! Oh, I knew his type. He was in business for himself. A crook! Gypping his owner out of a night's room rent. I knew I had been right in spotting his resemblance to Lombar's chief clerk. He'd done me in! Heller's fancy new name and car license would neither one appear! I was really enraged with him and justly so. He was dishonest!

Heller drove the car down and after figuring out how to reverse it, parked it in the open-ended garage. It was a bit long and the tail stuck out.

Mary was in bad shape. She was yawning convulsively. She felt her way down the side of the car. Then she looked at the tail and seemed to recover a bit. "Wait," she said, "the end of the car is sticking out. Somebody can see the license."

(Bleep) her! She fumbled around and found a newspaper on the dirty floor. She had Heller open the trunk and she put the newspaper, spread, half in and half out of it so it looked like carelessness in unloading. But it covered the license plate! "Whores know all about motels," she said.

Heller was kneeling at the back of the car. He lifted the newspaper. "Hello! There's a bullet hole in this iden-totag." He bent around. "Doesn't seem to have hit anything else." He stood up. "So that's what a bullet hole looks like."

I wished I could show him one in Mary's head! Or in his own!

He let Mary in and then hauled in the baggage. The place had twin beds. Mary was taking off her shoes. She made some ineffectual attempts to undress further, gave it up and groggily got into bed. "I'm so sleepy," she said. "You can have it if you want it, kid: I haven't felt anything for a year. But I'd advise against it. You're a good kid and I think I might have some disease."

"Look," said Heller. "You're in pretty bad shape. Aren't there doctors or hospitals or something on this planet?"

Oho! I said and hastily noted the Code break down. He'd slip up really bad sooner or later. He was *so* untrained!

"Listen," he persisted, shaking her by the shoulder gently. "I think you need some attention. Can't I take you to a hospital? They must have them. The people look so sick!"

She rose up with sudden ferocity. "Don't talk to me about doctors! Don't talk to me about hospitals! They'd kill me!"

He backed up at that.

The sudden burst of energy carried forward. She got her suitcase and opened it. She got out a needle kit and sank down on the edge of the bed. She opened it with shaking hands. She took the plunger out of the syringe. She put her little finger into the cylinder. She tried to scrape something off but there was nothing to scrape. She tried to suck at a needle and stuck herself.

"Oh," she shuddered, "I did all that yesterday. There's not even a tiny grain left!" She threw the kit down on the floor.

"What is this stuff, this fix you need?" said Heller.

"Oh, you poor dumb kid! It's blanks, Harry, joy powder, ka-ka, skag, caballo, Chinese red, Mexican mud, junk, white stuff, hard stuff, the big H! And if I don't get some I'm going to die!"

She pushed her hand against her chest. "Oh, my poor ticker!"

The effort had been too much for her. She slumped down. Heller picked up her feet and put her back into bed. Then he gathered up the kit, sniffed curiously at the empty cylinder and then put it all back in her suitcase.

She was asleep. I knew the cycle of withdrawal. She was entering the second stage of it: she was going into what would be a restless, fitful sleep.

Heller looked at her for a bit. Then he inspected the room. The air conditioning was running and he didn't touch it. The TV had a sign that said:

Not After Midnight, Please

He left it alone.

He stripped and examined his feet. The shoes were giving him blisters. He opened a bag and took out a small medical kit. Aha! Voltarian! A Code break! Then I saw it was just a plain little white box with some unmarked jars of salve. I put it down anyway.

He put some on the blisters and put the kit back in the suitcase, and this time he opened it wider! Hey, it wasn't full of rocks the way it was supposed to be! It was full of equipment? I couldn't really see as it was opened against the light and he didn't look. I made a note that this was a very probable Code break! Those two suitcases must be full of Voltarian gear! No wonder they were so heavy!

Heller turned back the bed and started to get in. Then he changed his mind, got up and got out his little notebook and pen.

He wrote: *Got to have a diploma before anyone will listen to you.* Then he wrote: *Psychology is fake. It can't do anything or change anybody. It is the government tool of population control.*

I fumed! Now *he* was writing heresy! Oh, the International Psychological Association would get *him!* Fry his brains with every electric shock machine they could put on him! They are very adamant in protecting their monopoly.

Then he wrote: *Somebody is selling some drug on this planet that kills people.*

Well, anybody knows that! I scoffed. He actually thought he had discovered something bright! The doctors push it. The psychologists push it. The government keeps the price up. And the Mafia and Rockecenter and a lot of other people get rich. And why not? The population is all riffraff anyway.

But then he did something I really noted. He made a little V mark at the end of each line he had written so far! Now I may have flunked math at the Academy but I do know the symbols. And that check is the mark used in logic equations! It means "Pertinent factor to be employed in a rationality deduction theorem." I had him! He was using a Voltarian math symbol right there in plain sight. A total Code break. I made an emphatic note of it!

If they didn't get him, I would!

He fiddled with the lights and figured out how to turn them off.

My screen went dark and, shortly, his even breathing told me he was asleep.

Chapter 6

It had been a long day for me. I got up and was about to pour myself a nice cold glass of *sira* when a sudden thought struck me, possibly stimulated by seeing him write.

He had given me a letter to mail! I hadn't inspected it!

It's always a pleasure to read, secretly, other people's mail. I deserved some recompense for not having been able to witness his arrest—even though I knew it would be very soon.

I got the letter out of my tunic, thinking it was probably some mushy note addressed to the Countess Krak—and wouldn't she be on her ear if she knew Heller was sleeping in a secret bedroom with a diseased whore!

I got the envelope squared around and over to the light. It was official green!

My hair stood on end!

It was addressed to:

CAPTAIN TARS ROKE
HIS MAJESTY'S OWN ASTROGRAPHER
PALACE CITY, VOLTAR
VOLTAR CONFEDERACY
URGENT OFFICIAL
LONG LIVE THEIR MAJESTIES

He had a line to Roke!

I managed to concentrate through the shock. When had he put this in? And then I recalled that Captain Tars Roke had been at the farewell party! And Heller had talked to him for some time. I hadn't been alert because I had been foully duped into taking that confounded speed, that amphetamine Methedrine! It had been a plot!

I calmed myself. Now, let's see: Lombar had told me that Heller would be sending in reports to the Grand Council. I was supposed to intercept them, learn how to forge them and send them on. Only then could I safely do away with Heller!

Ah, well. I was all right, then. I was doing my duty. This was simply Heller's first report. He was stupidly using me as part of his line to Roke and, in fact, he had no other line to use. So, all was well!

It was double-sealed. But that was nothing. Using methods known only to the Apparatus and tools specially provided for the purpose, I undetectably opened the envelope.

The sheet inside was big, but so are all official communications.

After the usual formal greetings, it said: *As we agreed, if you cease to authentically hear from me each month, only then should you advise His Majesty to embark upon the second alternative.* And then it rambled on, saying the mission may take a while, that the tug had run well, that he was grateful for some of the tips Captain Tars had given him about polar shifts. And then it went on to recall a lecture Captain Tars had given once about molten planetary cores being generators. And did the captain remember old Boffy Jope, the student who believed planets should turn slower so people would have more time to sleep? And he thought he would get along all right but keep an eye on things, please.

First, I suddenly realized that Heller had been one of Captain Tars Roke's students in the Astrographic College where the captain often lectured. The tone clearly indicated that Heller had been one of those abominable students who are favored by their teachers!

Next, I realized that this clearly meant Heller had a direct line to His Majesty, Cling the Lofty!

Wait! There was something funny about this letter!

I sat down. I spread it out on a desk. I turned a light on it.

It was not written the way you write a letter! It had gaps between words! It had uneven spaces between the lines!

The words could have occupied half the space they did occupy!

I broke out in a cold sweat. Forge? I had almost put my foot directly into a trap!

This letter was a platen code!

The way that is done, you take an opaque sheet of material that fits exactly over the sheet of writing paper. You cut long slots in the opaque sheet.

Everything is then covered except a few words.

Those platen words are the REAL message! The rest is just junk.

One would have to lay the platen on this sheet to read it.

I didn't have Heller's platen!

Unless I had that platen, I could forge nothing! The hidden message would not match Tars Roke's platen!

You can tell these codes because, in order to get words to appear in the platen holes, you have to write them in exact places on the sheet and that makes spaces and lines uneven!

Sometimes it makes goofy sense, trying to fill in around the key words. But Heller was clever. He'd made up some story about somebody called Boffy Jope so he would have enough words.

It had long been daylight in Turkey, of course. I had had no sleep. Unlike that (bleepard) in America who was lying in bed slumbering peacefully without a single care, I was a real slave of duty.

Besides, I was worried sick.

Sleep or no sleep, I worked right on. In every conceivable way I could, I tried to figure out the hidden message so I could get the platen.

I tried to find "Gris is doing me in." That didn't work. I tried "The Earth base is full of opium." But that didn't work. Actually, they couldn't work as the applicable words didn't appear in the letter.

I tried "Lombar is going to use drugs to cave in Voltar," but the name of Lombar and the word *drugs* . . . Wait! Maybe the platen only picked out letters! Maybe not full words!

Two hours I spent on it, feeling worse and worse.

I decided I needed air. I went outside and walked around the garden. Several staff ran away when they saw me but even that didn't cheer me up.

I went back in. Courageously, I tackled it all again.

And at length, I had it figured out. This was a *key sentence* platen!

The operative word was "authentically." Heller had written, "If you cease to *authentically* hear from me . . ."

He and Roke must have ducked into the tug—yes, they had been gone a bit—and conspired to arrange a key sentence such as "Cores are molten" and exchanged platens. If the platen, placed over the letter, did not show up the agreed upon sentence, "Cores are molten" or whatever it was, the message was not authenticated and was a forgery.

If an authenticated message did not arrive periodically on schedule, it said right there that Roke was to advise His Majesty to embark upon the second alternative! A FLAT-OUT, RIGHT NOW, BLOOD-AND-FLAME INVASION OF THE PLANET EARTH!

If they didn't get Heller's reports regularly, it would mean he had been interfered with and had failed. No reports equalled Earth would be a slaughterhouse!

But to Hells with Earth. If that invasion took place, every plan Lombar had would go up in smoke! As the

Grand Council knew nothing of the Earth base, it would go splat, too!

But far more important than that, I would be killed! Lombar's hidden agent would see to that even if I escaped everything else!

Heller's reports MUST GO THROUGH!

Hey, wait!

If Heller were successful, then all Lombar's lines and planning on Earth would be ruined! For his closest associates would be bankrupted!

If it even looked like Heller was going to win in improving this planet, Lombar's hidden agent would kill me!

My head began to ache.

Heller lose, Heller win, there was one thing certain: Gris would be dead!

I made myself sit down. I made myself stop tearing at my hair.

I must calmly work this out!

So, gnawing on the *sira* glass until I threw it against the wall, I worked it out.

I must get hold of Heller's platen! Then I could forge reports that would make the Grand Council—via Roke— think Heller was doing his job, while in fact, Lombar was protected in that Heller would be doing nothing at all. He would be dead.

But wait. I didn't have the platen. Until I got the platen, NOTHING MUST HAPPEN TO HELLER!

And there the idiot was with a marked car, police in several states alert, carrying a name that would get him sent to the pen as an imposter, a totally untrained agent in deadly danger of being scooped up!

I started praying.

Oh, my Gods, let nothing happen to Heller until I got my hands on that platen! Please, Gods, if anything happens to him at all, Soltan Gris is a dead man! To Hells with the slaughter of Earth! We'll just disregard that. Think of Soltan Gris! Take pity. Please?

Chapter 7

There is a seven-hour time difference between Eastern Standard Time, where Heller was, and Istanbul time, which I was near. So you can imagine how keeping check on Heller was a strain. When he was rising, all refreshed, at 7:00 A.M., I was hanging on the viewer at 2:00 P.M., an exhausted wreck.

He got up quietly and took a shower. Raht, to help his own personal finances, had not brought him any change of clothes so he put on what he had, swearing under his breath as he donned the shoes. He looked at himself in the mirror and shook his head. Indeed, he did look funny with that green-banded, too-small Panama, that purple shirt, the red and white check jacket with sleeves three inches too short, the blue and white striped pants that didn't come down to the ankles, the orange suede, too-tight shoes.

I groaned. He stood out like a searchlight! A cinch for even the most myopic cop to spot. And he didn't even realize it! His main concern would be with aesthetics, not with being unspottable.

Mary was tumbling about restlessly but still asleep. Heller softly closed the door and, with a glance at the car, trotted out of the motel grounds.

There was a diner nearby and he went in and puzzled over the menu, of course not knowing what any of

these things were. But it gave breakfast by the numbers
and he ordered "Number 1." It was orange juice, oatmeal and bacon and eggs. But the elderly waitress didn't
bring him coffee. She brought him milk and he looked
at it and tasted it suspiciously. She told him to drink it,
that he was too young for coffee. Then she refused to sell
him any of the pie he gazed at longingly, finally forego-
ing it on the advice that he must learn to control his appetite and she was going to stand there until he finished his
oatmeal. She was fifty and a motherly type, with boys of
her own. Boys, he was advised, were willful and if they
didn't watch their diet, they wouldn't grow. She even
managed his money, told him not to display it because
it would get stolen and keep some of it in his shoes and
tipped herself a dollar.

Authoritatively fed, Heller escaped to the street. It
was the main street of the town, lined with shops, and
he went trotting along, glancing in the windows.

Don't trot! I begged him mentally. Walk sedately,
saunter, don't attract attention! You're a wanted man! Heller trotted with an easy lope. Believe me, nobody runs
in the South! Nobody!

He popped into a clothing store, found in just a few
seconds that it had nothing that would fit his six-foot-
two frame, popped out and trotted on.

A hock shop was just ahead, a place where the Virginians sell the things they steal off tourists. Heller
scanned the windows and right-angled into it. There
were barrels of discards and shelves full of tagged junk.

The sleepy clerk, having gotten the shop open and
expecting to be able to go back to a nap in the rear, was
not too helpful. Heller pointed.

The clerk got down an 8-mm Nikon motion picture
camera. He said, "You don't want this, kid. They don't
sell film for it anymore." Heller was inspecting the big

black and gold Nikon label. He then made the clerk get down another one. Heller laid them on the counter. Heller saw a barrel: it was full of broken fishing reels and tangled line. He got out some.

"Those are deep-sea reels," said the clerk. "The fishing concession at Smith Mountain Lake went broke. They don't work."

"Fishing?" said Heller.

"Catch fish. Sport. Come on, kid, you're not that dumb. I ain't in any mood for jokes today. If you really want something, tell me, take it and get out! I ain't got any time to fool around."

Heller picked out several impressive reels, some broken rods and a hopeless tangle of line. He added some multihooked, steel-shafted bass plugs and a whole pile of weights that had steel hooks on the end. He put these on the counter.

He was staring at a tattered cardboard counter display for portable cassette recorders that were also AM/FM radios. "Give me one of these."

"You mean you're going to actually buy something?"

"Yes," said Heller and pulled out some money.

"Hell, I thought you was like the local kids: all eyes and no dough. You ain't from around here, then." He got a dusty recorder, even put some batteries in it and laid out a package of cassettes. He looked at the money Heller had in his hand and pretended to add something up. "That'll be a hundred and seventy-five dollars."

Heller paid him. They put the weird loot in sacks and Heller was on his way. And I, personally, thought he was as crazy as the clerk did. Obsolete cameras, broken fishing reels, tangled line. Idiocy.

Trotting along, Heller saw a sporting goods store. He right-angled in. He pointed at the window. A young,

wild-haired clerk dived in and brought out a pair of baseball shoes.

Heller looked at them. They were black; they laced
to the ankle; they had a long tongue that folded back over
the laces. He turned them over. They had no heels, but
they had two circles of cleats, one set under the ball of
the foot, one set under the heel. The steel cleats were
long, about a half an inch high, and the plates which
held them were solidly fixed in the leather sole.

"Let you have them cheap," said the clerk. "We got
a ton of them. The coach over at Jackson High ordered
full uniforms for the baseball team; first, he said they
came in too big and wouldn't take them. Then, he ran
off with the English teacher and the athletic fund."

"Baseball?" said Heller.

The clerk pointed to a pile of baseballs before he
caught himself. "Quit it, kid."

Heller had evidently gotten smart. He said, "Do you
have them for sale?"

The clerk just looked at him. Heller walked over to
the display of baseballs. They were a trifle bigger and
they were a little harder than a bullet ball.

There was an archery target standing up at the back
of the store. Heller said, "Do you mind?"

He hefted the baseball. He flexed his wrist and then
he threw the baseball at the archery target! I could hear
the sizzle of the ball going through the air. It hit the
bull's-eye! It plowed right on through, broke the back
stand and went splat against the wall.

"Jesus!" said the clerk. "A pitcher! A real pitcher!"

Heller went over and recovered the ball. The hide
had come off. He pulled curiously at the insides. "Well,"
he said to himself, "not so good, but it will have to do."

"Jesus," said the clerk. "You're a natural! Look, do

you mind if I sort of put that target away and when the New York Yankees sign you, I can maybe put it on display?"

Heller was looking for a bag. He found one you could carry over your shoulder. He was counting baseballs into it. The clerk was trying to pump him as to what college team he was on and what were his plans on going Big League and apologizing because Heller looked so young nobody would think he was a veteran. Heller wasn't giving him much encouragement. He was shopping around the shelves. He found a book, *The Fine Art of Baseball for Beginners*, and mystified the clerk by putting it on the purchases pile. Then he added another book, *The Fine Art of Angling for Beginners*. Was he going fishing?

But the clerk was busy now. "Look, we got full uniforms. And let's see what shoe size you take. Look, can we kind of put out we outfitted you?"

I thought, that's all we need. Local publicity this very morning!

Heller had to turn down a lot more than he bought: three pairs of shoes, six white, long-sleeved undershirts, twelve pairs of baseball socks with red-striped tops, two white exercise suits, a dozen support underpants, two unlettered uniforms that were white with red stripes, a red anorak with captain's stripes, a black belt and a red batting helmet.

And then Heller saw the caps. They were red baseball caps, not as nice or as stylish as his habitual racing cap, but similar. The bill was longer: it would never crush properly under a racing helmet to act as padding. But Heller was enraptured. He made a sort of cooing sound. He pushed the pile around until he found one his size and put it on. He went over to the mirror.

I flinched. From the neck up, there was Jettero Heller, space-racing champion of the Academy! It had been easy to forget his amused blue eyes, his flowing blond hair and that go-to-Hells-who-cares smile! It was like being shot suddenly back to Voltar! But even then I'd missed it.

"What did you say the initials stood for?" he said.

"Jackson High," said the clerk.

I had been slow, possibly because of the intricate intertwine of the white team letters on the cap. J.H.! THAT was why he was grinning!

"I'll take half a dozen," said Heller, laughing now.

Heller ceremoniously made the clerk a present of the purple shirt and the orange suede shoes and the Panama hat.

They packed the gear up in a sports carry-all. Heller paid him three hundred dollars and took the card.

Heller was going out the door when the clerk yelled, "Hey! You forgot to tell me your name!"

"You'll hear," Heller yelled back and was gone.

Ah, well, there was hope. If he'd given the name he was supposed to use, that (bleeped) clerk would have been all over town with a megaphone. I was thankful Heller was modest. He certainly wasn't smart. He was trotting up the street now in a scarlet baseball cap with his own initials on it and wearing a long-sleeved baseball undershirt. He had retained the blue-striped pants and red-checked jacket. He stood out like a beacon! And worse than that, the spikes he was wearing were clickety-clacking on the pavement even louder than his old-time hull shoes!

It was Lombar's fault, really: he had ordered that Heller not be trained in espionage; any self-respecting spy would know you must remain unnoticeable. A trained agent would have looked at the population around him and dressed like that. He sure did not resemble anyone else in that quiet southern town! Looking at him now, to paraphrase the clerk: Jesus!

Heller glanced at his watch. It was getting on toward nine. But he had another stop. It was a candy store!

I groaned. I was dealing with an idiot, not a special agent. Special agents don't eat candy! They smoke cigarettes!

Some little twelve-year-old kids were in there haggling with the clerk over the price of gumdrops which seemed to have gone up. Two of them were wearing baseball caps, the way little kids do in America. And I realized that Heller, now wearing one, would mind-associate in people that he was even younger!

Heller went down the counter, apparently looking for one particular type of candy. He found it: it was individually wrapped in transparent paper; it was red and white in a spiral, just like it's advertised in magazines sometimes.

The kids bought their dime's worth and Heller promptly overwhelmed the aged lady clerk by purchasing ten pounds of candy! Not only did he buy the white and red kind, but also other kinds, and he wanted them all mixed up which brought about the problem of putting them in different bags, all mixed up, and then there not being a big enough bag to contain all the other bags. He sure ruined the day for the old lady clerk.

Laden, Heller got back on the street. There was a cop car parked at the corner. Now any trained agent would have gone the other way. But not Heller. He trotted right past the cop car!

I saw, in peripheral vision, the cops look at him.

It was time to go back and fortify myself with cold

sira. And take time off for a small prayer. If they had special Hells for Apparatus case handlers, the one they would send me to would specialize in forcing totally untrained agents on me! Neither the *sira* nor the prayer helped!

If anything happened to Heller before I got that platen, I was done for!

PART FIFTEEN

Chapter 1

In the room, Mary Schmeck was still restlessly asleep. Heller threw his loot down on his bed. He lifted his two suitcases up on a long bureau, side by side, and unfastened the straps.

I was going to get a look at their contents! Maybe the platen was right on top!

Foolish hope. There were no rocks but there sure was a wild medley of little tubes and boxes and coils of wire. What a junk heap!

Heller got out a small tool case and two small vials. He picked up the two obsolete Nikon cameras and put them on a table. He inspected the edge of a label, then put some drops under the edge and the gold and black *NIKON* lifted right off! He did the other one.

Then he took two small cases from the grips and opened them. The time-sights! Both of them! Indeed, the tug *was* planet bound! I knew the Apparatus could never pry another one out of the Fleet!

From the second vial he took a bit of what must be glue and put it on the label backs and in a moment, glaring on the side of each time-sight was *NIKON*.

They looked now like two Super 8 motion-picture cameras!

He put them back in their small cases and back into the grip. He threw in the two obsolete ones as well.

Then he got out the candy he had made on the ship. The wrappers were a bit different but not remarkably so.

He had what must be three pounds of it! He mixed it into the other candy sacks and then started packing the bags all through the other grip. Very unneatly, too.

Then he packed the broken fishing rods and reels hit or miss through everything. He added the tangles of line in snarls and coils in and over the other contents. Then he took the bass plugs and the weights and began to jam them in anywhere and everywhere.

What a MESS!

And I thought Fleet guys were always so neat!

He had to let the suitcase straps out to accommodate all the extra. He neated up the athletic carry-all and he was ready.

He had picked up a sweet roll, a container of milk and another of coffee while I was in my other room praying. He gently tried to wake up Mary Schmeck. She fought him off, trying to go back to sleep. I could see her pupils were contracted. She wanted nothing to do with the roll or the milk or coffee.

"We've got to leave," said Heller.

This got to her. "Washington," she said.

"Yes, we'll be going through Washington, D.C.," Heller replied.

She muttered, "There's sure to be some junk in Washington. There always is. It's full of it. Get me there, for Christ's sakes." She tried to get up. Then she screamed, "Oh, my God! My legs!" They were drawing up in knots. She fell back whimpering.

He picked up all the luggage, went out and put it in the back seat. Then he returned and carried Mary Schmeck out and put her in the front seat. He laid her shoes on the floorboards. He put the milk, coffee and the roll in the drink tray.

He had the key in his hand and didn't know what to do with it, didn't realize you just left it in the door and slipped away. There was a cleaning woman, an old black woman, coming out of the room next door.

Oh, my Gods! He walked up to her and handed her the key! Drawing attention to himself. You NEVER do that! And then he compounded the felony. He said, "You know what road to take to Washington?"

She had not only *seen* him now, she knew where he was going! And the first thing police do when they're searching for a criminal is check the motels! She said, "You jus' follah Yew S. 29. Charlottesville, Culpeper, Arlington and cross the Potomac and there you is. Mah sister, she lives in Washington and I don't know what the hell I'm doin' down heah in Virginia wheah we is still slaves!" I thought to myself, I doubt she'd dare say that to an adult Virginian. Slavery has its points! I almost drifted off thinking about Utanc and then something else happened that recalled me firmly and nervously to duty.

Heller backed out the car, leaned out the window and said, "Thank you, miss, foh a very nahce stay." And the woman smiled, stood there leaning on the broom and in a moment I could see, in the rearview mirror, that she was staring after the car. And more. I saw the newspaper which hid the license plate blowing off in the car's wake. For sure she would remember that car. (Bleep) Heller!

No, no, I mustn't (bleep) him! I must pray he would get through!

He had no trouble whatever in finding U.S. 29 to Charlottesville. He tooled along the four-lane through the lovely Virginia morning, admiring the view. The Cadillac was purring, surprisingly smooth, especially on this smooth road.

It was promising to be a very hot August day and he began to fool with the air conditioning. He set it at seventy-three degrees on the dial, got it functioning on automatic and after a bit, when apparently the hot air had blown out of the car, closed the windows. It was amazingly quiet!

A white board fence fled by. A big sign:

JACKSON HORSE RANCH

Beyond it were some animals in the field, leaping and prancing about. Apparently he added something up. He laughed. "So those are horses!" Then for some idiotic reason, he patted the Cadillac panel ledge. He said, "Never mind, you chemical-engine Cadillac Brougham Coupe d'Elegance. I like you even if you don't have any of those things under your hood."

I will never understand Fleet guys. Compared to a Voltar airbus, an Earth vehicle is a farce. And he knew it! Then I had it. Toys. Anything was a toy to Fleet officers, from landing craft to battleships to planets. They just have no respect for force! No. Then I really had it: fetish worship.

He found he could drive with one knee and leaned back, arms spread out along the top of the seat. It made me nervous until I realized I was 105 degrees of longitude away.

But another shock was in store. He glanced at the speedometer and it was doing SIXTY-FIVE! The speed limit is fifty-five and all those roads have signs that say they are radar patrolled!

I saw he was not driving by the speedometer: he was running with the traffic—some big trucks and passenger cars—and by and large was doing sixty-five. But cops love to pick one car out of such a clump and arrest it. I went and got some more *sira*.

He got through Charlottesville all right. And then

Mary Schmeck, who had been in a twitchy, comatose state, woke up.

"Oh, I feel awful!" she moaned. "My legs are killing me! I ache in every joint!" She was thrashing about, obviously in a bad state. "How far are we from Washington?"

"We're almost to Culpeper," he said.

"Oh," she moaned. "It's still a long way yet!"

"Only about an hour," said Heller.

"Jesus, I hurt! Turn on some music. Maybe it will redirect my focus intensity."

Heller fiddled with the radio and finally got some jazz. A song came on:

> *As I passed by the Saint James infirmary,*
> *I saw my sweetheart there.*
> *Stretched out on a long white table,*
> *So pale, so cold, so bare.*

Mary moaned, "Oh, my legs!"

> *Went up to see the doctor.*
> *"She's very low," he said.*
> *Went back to see my woman.*
> *Good God, she's lying there dead!*
> *SHE'S DEAD!*

"Oh, my God," said Mary.

> *Sixteen coal-black horses,*
> *All hitched to a rubber-tired hack,*
> *Carried seven girls to the graveyard.*
> *Only six of them comin' back!*

"Turn that off!" Mary shrieked.

Heller turned it off. I was very sorry he did so. It

was the first pleasant thing I had heard for days!

Mary was covered with goose pimples. "I'm freezing!" she cried out, writhing.

Heller quickly turned the thermostat up to eighty.

Long before it could have warmed up, Mary said, "I'm roasting hot!"

Heller turned the thermostat down again.

She kept it up, thrashing about. It was obvious to me what was wrong with her. She was in the third stage of withdrawal symptoms. People sure do complain about them.

"I can't get my breath," she was panting now. Well, that's normal, too, for somebody who has a bad heart. But still, respiratory failure is the usual cause of death in morphine addiction and it would be no different for its derivative, heroin. The lung muscles cease to function. And in her case, since she'd been complaining of a bad heart, I wondered idly whether she would die in the car or in the next motel.

Then it was I who almost had respiratory failure. What if Heller had a dead prostitute dope addict on his hands! With *his* assumed name!

Oh, Gods! He'd be front page in every tabloid dirt sheet in America! And what Rockecenter would do was *awful!*

I couldn't count on Heller to do the right thing. In espionage, he simply would have known enough to haul up out of sight and dump her in a ditch and leave her quick. But no, here he was, doing the wrong things as usual! He was trying to help her!

They were through Culpeper. Suddenly, the girl said, "You got to find a toilet! Look, that service station ahead! Stop there! Quick!"

Fourth stage. The diarrhea had hit her!

Heller zoomed into an unfrequented service station

and Mary was out of the car like a shot, racing to the women's room. I prayed they wouldn't stay there long, exposed to view from traffic.

Heller told the gawky country boy attendant to "fill up the chemical repository" and the lonely boy made out that Heller meant gas. The usually idle boy then figured out for himself that Heller's early education had been neglected.

With careful instruction, Heller got taught to service the car: steering fluid, brake fluid, transmission fluid, correct radiator coolant, windshield wiper water with Windex in it, oil and the right and wrong kinds of oil, gas and the right and wrong kinds of gas. Apparently nobody in his whole life had ever listened to this country boy before and he really went flat out to educate a "younger Virginia kid," even though he seemed disappointed to find that Heller hadn't stolen the car.

The kid exhausted the subject of tires and then got bright. He said the car needed a grease job and the differential checked. He said it would only take a short while to grease it up. And onto the rack he drove it and up into the air the car went. Sure enough, the differential was half empty. And sure enough it needed grease and the airhose and greasegun pumped away. Heller marked where all the fittings were. And then he got worried about the girl and went to find her.

Mary was crumpled up on a toilet seat, passed out. Somehow, Heller roused her and got her to straighten herself up.

Then voices outside. Heller peeked through a window.

A cop car! Virginia State Police!

I turned up the gain. The cop was saying, ". . . man and a woman. They went up this road someplace last night."

"What kind of a car?" said the gawky country boy.

The officer consulted his sheet. "Cadillac. Same color as that one you got on the rack."

I went white. There went Heller and no platen!

"Could be that they passed when I was off shift," said the country boy.

"Well, you let me know iff'n you do see'm, Bedford," said the state policeman. "They're wanted awful bad!"

"Always willin' to oblige, Nathan," said the gawky country boy. And when the cop drove off, going back down the road toward Culpeper, the boy added, "You cocky son of a (bleepch)."

He got the Cadillac down off the hoist and Heller came out, carrying Mary. He put her in the front seat.

The gawky country boy was all smiles. "I *knew* you stole it!" He looked Heller up and down admiringly. Then he said, "I was going to remove and grease the wheels but that can wait. I got an idea you better be goin'."

The Cadillac had only taken ten gallons of gas. I was amazed. Then I realized it had just been a clever psychological ploy on the part of the girl to call it a gas hog.

The bill, in fact, was not all that great. And Heller paid it with a twenty-dollar tip. Count on Heller! He'd be broke soon which was another hurdle I'd have to cross. I couldn't just have Raht or Terb walk up to him and hand him money. They must be somewhere on this road but I couldn't contact them when they were moving.

Mary had to go to the can again and the boy instructed Heller how to wash windows: Never use a grease rag, only paper. Never use a wax glass cleaner. Amazing, he'd already been tipped!

Heller got the girl straightened out and back in the car once more.

"Next tahm you come by," said the gawky country
boy, "stop off and I'll show you how to tune the engine."

Heller really thanked him and when they drove
away, there was the boy by the pump, waving. Heller
blew the horn twice and they were on their way to Washington.

And Washington, I groaned to myself, was just about
the most over-policed city in the world!

I wondered if I should start writing a will. I had several things: the gold coming, the hospital kickback due
and Utanc. Trouble was, I'd nobody to leave them to.

I never felt more alone and prey to the winds of fate
than I did as I watched the road through Heller's eyes to
Washington.

Chapter 2

Following the complex signs, Heller negotiated the
various confusions the traffic departments of that area
planned in order to prevent Americans from ever getting
to their seat of government. He refused invitations to use
State Highway 236, to go over to U.S. 66, to take State
123 and wind up in the Potomac River. He ignored directions to take U.S. 495—which is really U.S. 95 and
bypasses Washington entirely. He even defeated the conspiracy to confuse the public on U.S. 29 to believe they
were on U.S. 50. He steadfastly rolled along on U.S. 29,
even untangled the parkways alongside the Potomac
River without winding up at the Pentagon—as most un-
suspecting public do—and presently was rolling over

the Memorial Bridge. A masterpiece of navigation that he shouldn't be doing any part of!

The Potomac River was a beautiful blue. The bridge a beautiful white. The Lincoln Memorial at its end, an impressive piece of Greek architecture glowing white in the afternoon sun.

And Heller had trouble. Mary was flailing about to a point where it was almost impossible to drive. She was bending over with cramps. She was letting out small screams. She was striking out with her arms. And she was saying over and over, "Oh, God, my heart!" alternated with "Oh, Jesus, I've got to have a fix!" And neither prayer was getting any attention whatever from the deities of that planet.

Heller was watching her and trying to hold her down more than he was watching traffic. The giddy and fool-hardy spin of cars and trucks around the Memorial circle may not disturb the calm majesty of Lincoln's huge statue inside, but it is designed to shatter less immortal nerves.

It was evidently plain to him that the combination of Mary and the traffic was a lot too much to cope with just now. He spotted a turnoff into the park which lies to the southeast of the Lincoln Memorial itself.

It is a very beautiful park: an unfrequented road and a pleasant pedestrian walk stretch out beside the Potomac River, separated from it by a wide expanse of lawn. It is one of the most quiet and lovely spots in Washington. The only trouble with it is the CIA uses it to try out their agent recruits in hidden sleuthing!

I freaked! Heller was stopping! I mourned my fate to be handling somebody without the slightest training in espionage. He should have known that Voltar agents have orders never to go near that park!

He had seen the drinking fountains which are paced every few hundred feet along the walk. He had probably sensed the false peace imparted by the beautiful willow-like trees between the path and water's edge. He may have been attracted by the abundance of parking places. It must have been a hot day in Washington but the lawns were deserted here.

He stopped. Mary was in a momentary coma. He got out and went to the drinking fountain. He had an empty paper coffee cup. He managed to figure out how you turned on the fountain and rinsed and filled the cup.

At the car, he said, "Maybe drinking some water would help." And, indeed, he was right. Withdrawal brings on heavy dehydration. He wouldn't know that but he could probably tell from her dry and swollen lips.

She managed to drink a little bit of the water. Then suddenly she turned sideways, got her feet on the ground and, still sitting on the car seat, began to vomit.

He held her head, speaking in a low, concerned voice, trying to soothe her.

In his peripheral vision I saw the side and saddle of a horse moving up the road.

Heller looked up. A mounted National Parks police-man went about fifty feet back of the car, stopped and turned his horse around. He sat there looking at Heller and the car.

I thought, well, Gris, you should have made out your will because here we go! Heller has had it!

The park policeman was fishing a hand radio out. He began to speak into it.

I hastily turned up the gain. "... I *know* I'm sup-posed to use numbers to report." Someone on the other end, his traffic controller, must be giving him a hard time.

Mary was trying to vomit some more but didn't have anything to throw up.

The park policeman was saying, "But there ain't

any code number for a bullet hole in a license plate!
... All right! All right! So it's 201, suspicious car!"

Mary couldn't sit there anymore. Heller opened the
back door and pushed some baggage around. Then he
got Mary and moved her to the back seat.

"... Yeah," the mounted cop was saying. "Kid and
a woman in it. No, I don't know who was driving. I
didn't see them until after they'd parked.... No, *hell!*
I'm not going to... I'm ALONE here! I'm just Park
Police, not James Bond! They could be a CIA plant or
something.... No! Shots would scare my horse.... Well,
send the God (bleeped) squad car then!"

I prayed Heller would get the Hells out of there. But
he was bathing her forehead with bits of cool water on
his redstar engineer's cloth. I was so agitated I didn't
even write it down as a possible Code break.

In no time at all, a D.C. squad car slinked up near
the horse. Two D.C. cops got out and talked in whispers
to the mounted patrolman. I could barely pick it up. All
I caught was "... those are Virginia plates so phone them
in for a check."

One of the cops was on his radio. Then the two of
them, wide apart, walked toward the Cadillac.

Twenty feet away, the nearest cop drew his gun.
"You, there! Freeze!"

Heller stood up straight. I prayed, no, no, Heller.
Don't do something crazy! At that range they can kill
you! And I don't have the platen!

The nearest cop was motioning with his gun. "All
right, kid, move over there and lie down on the grass,
belly to ground."

Heller moved to the spot and lay down. He kept his
head turned toward the cop.

"All right," said the cop. "Where's your driver's
license?"

There was a scream from the car. Mary had come to with sudden energy. "It's in my purse! That kid is just a hitchhiker. This is my car!" It was nearly too much for her. She sank back panting, holding her chest.

I realized now she was not a true psychologist. The whole purpose of the subject is to throw suspicion and responsibility on others either to get them in trouble or to protect yourself—which amounts to the same thing. But even though it was a violation of psychology behavior rules, I gratefully accepted the help.

The first cop detoured over toward the car and dug around to find her purse. He found it and looked at her license.

"Oh, God," moaned Mary. "Please, please get me a fix!"

The effect was electric. "A hop head!" said the first cop. He made a signal to the other cop to cover Heller and then began yanking the suitcases out of the car. He was going to look for dope!

He opened the sports carry-all, rummaged in it and then threw it aside. He grabbed one of Heller's cases, unstrapped it and flopped the back up.

"That's the kid's baggage," moaned Mary.

The cop reached in. He said, "Ouch, God (bleep) it!" He pried a multihooked bass plug off his hand and sucked his finger. Gingerly, then, he held up an old fishing reel and stirred at the mess of line. He said, "Cameras and fishing gear. Jesus Christ, kid, you sure do an awful job of packing. You could ruin some of this stuff." He slammed the case closed.

The other cop was well back with a gun on Heller.

The first cop opened Heller's second case.

"Jesus!" screamed Mary. "Get me a fix! Can't anybody hear me?" And then she leaned out of the backseat and began to dry vomit.

"Candy!" cried the first cop. "Dope concealed in candy!" He turned to the other cop. "You see, I knew there'd be dope here. They hide it in candy!"

He gingerly evaded more fishhooks and untangled a candy bag from fishing line. He opened the bag and took out a piece. He got a jackknife from his pocket and cut the sweet in half. He touched one of the halves to his tongue.

Disappointed, he threw the cut pieces and the paper in the general direction of a *Don't Litter!* sign. He got another bag open and did the same thing.

"Ah, hell," he said. "It's just candy-type candy."

The second cop said, "Joe, I figure if there was any dope in that baggage, this dame wouldn't be going through withdrawal."

The first cop closed Heller's grip and then hauled out Mary's suitcase and got it open. "Hurray!" he shouted. "I knew it! Here's a dope kit complete!" And he held it up so his partner and the park patrolman could see it. "This is illegal as hell even if there is no dope! I knew I could catch them out!"

Oh, Heller, I prayed. Just keep on lying there. Don't do anything.

Mary had come out of a spasm of dry retching. She tried to get to the first cop, "That's my kit! I'm a doctor! My diploma is right in that bag!"

The first cop didn't even bother to push her back into the car and she collapsed, dangling half out of it.

The first cop disgustedly found it. "She's right." He dropped the suitcase shut and stood up. "Aw, (bleep), there's no smack here."

The second cop gestured with his gun to Heller. "You can get up, kid. You're clean."

I sagged with relief. I knew exactly what the prisoner felt when they told him he had been reprieved.

Heller got to his feet. He went over and tried to get Mary back into the car.

Heller suddenly saw a plain, green sedan quietly roll up and stop. The first cop said, "Oh, (bleep). It's the FBI."

Two very tough-looking characters got out. They wore box coats. Their hats were gangster-type hats.

As one, they drew and flashed their I.D. folders.

The first one had a puffy face and a sagging lower lip. "I'm Special Agent Stupewitz, FBI."

The second one said, "Special Agent Maulin, FBI." He was a huge, hulking brute of a man.

Stupewitz walked up to the park patrolman and the two D.C. cops. "This is out-of-state business—Federal! Move aside!"

Maulin went around to the back of the car and read the license. "This is the car, all right. Look at that bullet hole!"

Stupewitz gestured a Colt .457 revolver at Heller. It looked like a cannon. "Stand up and face that car, kid. Put your hands on the roof and spread-eagle, legs apart."

Heller did as he was told. That artillery could have blown him apart!

The first D.C. cop said, "He's just a hitchhiker. This is the woman's car."

Maulin said, "Filled with bags of dope."

The second D.C. cop said, "There's nothing in the bags but cameras and fishing gear. There ain't even any dope in the candy."

Stupewitz said, "You've got it all wrong, brother. That's why you locals have to have the support of the FBI. Without us, you'd just breeze along in total peace!"

Maulin said, "We got the whole story from Virginia."

I thought, well, Gris, it's too late to make a will now! Heller will be finished so quick, there won't be time.

Stupewitz had his gun trained on Heller. "What's your name, kid?"

Mary came to, threshing about. "Don't talk to them kid!"

Heller didn't answer Stupewitz.

Stupewitz said, "Kid, do you realize it's a felony not to give your name to a Federal officer?"

Heller didn't answer.

Stupewitz made a signal to Maulin. Maulin drew his gun from his back belt, trained it on Heller from a distance. Stupewitz stepped up to Heller and began to frisk him.

I was certain I knew what was coming now. It was too late even to pray.

Stupewitz got to the papers in Heller's jacket. He yanked them out. He looked at them.

Suddenly Stupewitz drew off to the side, away from the other cops and Heller. He made a frantic beckon to Maulin. Maulin kept his gun on Heller but sidled around to get close to Stupewitz.

I frantically turned up more gain. I got wind in the trees. I got some birds. I got the far-off siren of an ambulance getting louder. But I couldn't make out anything Stupewitz or Maulin were saying as they examined the papers. I could see them whispering but as they were using their lips the way criminals do, talking from the side of the mouth, I couldn't even read the words.

An ambulance came up. It was marked GEORGE-TOWN HOSPITAL.

The attendants offloaded in a flash of white and stretchers. They opened the opposite door of the car, looked in at Mary and then grabbed her. She was so far gone, she didn't even fight. She did manage a faint, "So long, kid."

Heller, despite FBI orders, ducked down his head and yelled, "NO! Don't kill her!"

An attendant glanced up from trying to get Mary straight so they could get her out of the car and onto the stretcher. "Kill her? You're dead wrong, sonny. She needs our help. We'll take good care of her."

Heller said, "You promise not to kill her?"

"Sure, kid," said the attendant. And they had Mary on the stretcher. Stupewitz sidled to the attendant, whispered something, showed his badge. The attendant shrugged.

Heller looked toward Maulin. "Can I put her bag in that ambulance?"

Maulin made a tight wave with his gun. Heller got her purse and bag, walked over to the ambulance and put them in. The ambulance rolled away with Heller staring after it.

Stupewitz came back. He was pointing to the government car. "Get in there, kid."

Heller didn't. He walked over and closed his bags and put them in the trunk of the Cadillac and locked it, pocketing the separate key. Stupewitz then urged him into the front passenger seat of the government car.

Maulin got under the wheel of the Cadillac. He drove off.

Heller said, "NO! Our car!"

Stupewitz said, "Stop worrying. It's going to the FBI garage."

The D.C. cops and park patrolman were muttering and shaking their heads.

So was I!

Stupewitz started the government car and they sped away.

The jaws of the Federal Bureau of Investigation had closed on Jettero Heller. And the worst of it was, typically, they didn't even realize they had the fate of the planet between their vicious teeth! Stupid (bleepards)!

Chapter 3

They got out at the FBI building on Pennsylvania Avenue and someone whisked the car away.

Stupewitz said, "Don't try to run. You could get shot."

But Heller was not running. He was looking up at the gray-green marble façade and spelling out the HUGE, raised, gold-lettered sign that said:

J. EDGAR HOOVER

The letters were feet high and it spread so wide he had to turn his head to read it.

"Are we going to call on J. Edgar Hoover?" said Heller.

"Don't be a smart (bleep), kid."

Heller said, "But I really never heard of him."

That got to Stupewitz. "Jesus! They sure don't teach history anymore!" He came very close to Heller and thrust his puffy face forward. "Look, you heard of George Washington." He pointed a quivering finger at the huge sign. "Well, J. Edgar Hoover was ten times what Washington ever was! The REAL savior of this country was HOOVER! Without *him*, the real rulers of this country couldn't run it at all!" He gave Heller a hard shove toward the entrance and muttered to himself,

"Jesus, they don't teach kids *anything* these days."

Via elevators and stairs, pushing from time to time, Stupewitz got Heller into the first of a small pair of offices that adjoined. Stupewitz pushed Heller into a chair with an unnecessary "Sit there!"

Maulin came in. Stupewitz glared at Heller. "You're in serious trouble. You better not get any ideas of trying to run out of here because there are guards and guns all over the place. Be quiet and be good!"

They went into the second office but the door was ajar. They were whispering so I turned up the gain. I couldn't get what they were saying because, in some adjacent office, someone was being beaten and screamed now and then.

Heller had a partial view of Stupewitz through the slightly open door. The agent was at a desk, working with a phone. Maulin's huge bulk was attentively leaning over behind him.

"I want to talk to Delbert John Rockecenter, personally," said Stupewitz into the phone. "This is the FBI.... Then put me on to his confidential secretary." He covered the phone and said to Maulin, "Rockecenter is in Russia arranging some loans to keep them going." Then to the phone, "This is the FBI in Washington. We have a matter here..." The screams in the adjacent office drowned the next words. Then he covered the phone and said to Maulin, "They're putting me on to Mr. Bury, one of the attorneys from their firm, Swindle and Crouch. Bury handles all such matters."

They waited. Then Stupewitz got his connection. "Hello, Mr. Bury? I got one hell of a surprise for you. Is this a totally secure, confidential line? Oh, bug tested just this morning. Good. Now listen. We are Special Agents Stupewitz," and he rattled off a whole series of identification and addresses, "and Maulin," and he rattled off Maulin's. "Now, have you got all that for sure?"

Apparently Mr. Bury had. So Stupewitz spread out Heller's papers in front of him and began to read. He read the birth certificate, the diploma, the grades. "Got all that? I just wanted you to know there's no mistake. . . . Yes, we have the boy right here. To prove it, here's his description," and he rattled it off. ". . . no, he hasn't talked to anybody. We made sure of that."

Stupewitz now shot a gleeful grin back at Maulin. Then he said into the phone, "Now, don't be upset, Mr. Bury. But he's wanted in Fair Oakes, Virginia, for assault and battery of two police officers, both hospitalized . . . yes, he apparently did it with an iron bar when they weren't looking . . . yes, amounts to attempted murder. Also suspicion of car theft, speeding, refusal to halt. Fugitive . . . Right. And apparent possession of narcotics . . . Right. And the Federal offense of seeking to smuggle them across state lines . . . Right. And, as a minor, cohabitation with a known prostitute . . . Right. Also the Mann Act—crossing state lines for immoral purposes . . . Right. And refusal to divulge identity to a Federal officer."

I realized Heller could get life, the exact original thing planned for him.

Apparently some smoke was coming out of the phone. After a moment, Stupewitz went on. "Wait now, Mr. Bury. I'm just telling *you* this. The woman won't talk. We have the records, we have the car, we have the boy. . . . No, no reporters know anything about this. The name was not even known in Fair Oakes. . . . No. We're the only ones who know."

Stupewitz was now the one listening. Mr. Bury must be talking hard and fast. ". . . Yes, Mr. Bury," said Stupewitz. ". . . Yes, Mr. Bury. . . . Yes, Mr. Bury. . . . Yes,

Mr. Bury." Then there must have been a long speech. Stupewitz gave Maulin an evil grin and nodded to him. Then he said into the phone, "No. No records or copies of anything here. The local police know nothing and we won't even report it to the Director." He nodded as though Bury could see him. And then, all over again he gave all the identifying details and home addresses of himself and Maulin.

Stupewitz ended off with, "Yes, Mr. Bury. And you can be very assured that D.J.R.'s son is perfectly safe here in our hands; there won't be a whisper to the press or anyone. We are, as always, completely at the service of Delbert John Rockecenter. You got the idea, Mr. Bury. Good-bye."

He rose beaming from the phone. He and Maulin did a war dance round and round, laughing.

Maulin said, "And we were going to retire in a few years with nothing but our pensions!"

And Stupewitz said, "He'll hire us for sure. No other option!"

I was flabbergasted. These two crooked agents were using this case to forward their own advancement! They were blackmailing Delbert John Rockecenter! And what made it all the more criminal was that D. J. Rockecenter practically owns the FBI anyway!

And what made it even more stupid was that they actually thought they really had Delbert John Rockecenter's son.

Lombar's planning had taken a new twist!

But wait. This didn't get Heller off the hook. I hadn't worked it out yet just how, but there was real death in Heller's future now.

Chapter 4

The phone rang and the two crooked agents stopped their war dance and Stupewitz answered it, said something back and hung up.

The two came into the room with Heller. He had been sitting there quietly, his eyes occasionally straying to a bloodstain on the wall. I doubted he could have heard the phone conversation in anything like the clarity I had, if at all, and he must be wondering what they were going to do with him.

Stupewitz said to him, "Listen, Junior, that was your old man's personal family attorney, Mr. Bury, of Swindle and Crouch, New York. Your dad is over in Russia, bein' wined and dined and he won't be home for a couple of weeks."

Maulin said, "You just sit tight, Junior. There's a little delay before you can go." Maulin sat down at his desk and looked into a basketful of reports. I understood now that this was his office and the other one was Stupewitz's. They must be pretty highly placed in the FBI to have private offices.

Stupewitz went to the door to leave. "I'll handle the rest of this," he said to Maulin. "You keep your eye on the kid." He started to leave again and then stopped. He called back to Heller, "You can stop worrying about that hooker. She's dead."

My viewscreen seemed to jolt. Heller said, "Why did you have to kill her?"

"Kill her?" said Stupewitz. "She was D.O.A. at Georgetown Hospital. Heart attack." Then, innocence itself, he said, "You're lucky it was in the ambulance or you could have been charged with conspiracy to murder."

Maulin said, "Big H killed her, Junior."

Heller said, "I been meaning to ask somebody. What's a 'fix'?"

Stupewitz started for the door again. "Oh, this kid is too much for me! You grab it, Maulin. I'll get the rest done." He was gone.

With a weary shove at his basket of papers, Maulin leaned back and looked even more wearily at Heller. "No (bleep), kid. You don't know what a fix is? What the hell did they teach you at..." He had Heller's certificates on his desk and looked, "...Saint Lee's Military Academy? How to tat and knit?" He glanced at his watch and then shoved his basket further away with a detesting hand. "We got lots of time to kill, and as you'll be giving orders to this place yourself someday, I might as well begin the education of an All American Boy! Come along."

Pushing Heller ahead of him, Maulin plowed along down stairs and through halls. "Don't talk to people," he warned. "I'll answer any questions they ask."

Evidently, the building was huge. It was a long way down one corridor. Heller was clickety-clacking along.

"For chrissakes, Junior," said Maulin, annoyed by the noise. "Why are you wearing baseball spikes?"

"Comfortable," said Heller. "I got blisters."

"Oh, I get it. I got corns myself. Here we are." And he halted Heller at a door marked *Drug Lab* and shoved him through.

They were faced with yards and yards of wall racks on which assorted glass jars rested. A technician was crunched over a table, heating some water in a spoon, needles lying about.

"Now the Drug Enforcement Agency handles drugs," tutored Maulin in a gravelly voice, "but we still got our own drug lab. We're really in charge of the government and sometimes we even have to shake down the DEA. There's practically every known kind of drug in these jars."

"Do you sell them?" said Heller.

The technician looked up in alarm. He said, "Shh!" Then he looked closer at Heller and said to Maulin, "What are you doing bringing a smart (bleep) kid in here, Maulin? This isn't part of the public tour."

"Shut up, Sweeney."

The technician bent back over his Bunsen burner grumbling. Maulin said, "Now, kid, the trick is to know all these drugs by sight and smell and taste. Just start at this bottom row and go along in, jar by jar, noting the labels. But for chrissakes, if you do any tasting, spit it out! I ain't going to be accused of turning you into a drug freak."

Heller went down the rows, doing as he was told. A couple of times, Maulin made him rinse his mouth out at the sink, holding him by the back of the neck the way you do a willful child.

Heller, being Heller, was making very rapid progress. But I was worrying. It was obvious they were detaining him and, knowing the FBI, it had skulduggery in it—stupid skulduggery but skulduggery just the same.

"Hello, hello, hello!" said Heller. He had a big can with brown powder in it and was examining it. "What's this?"

"Oh, the label's off it. That's opium, kid. Asiatic..." Maulin looked at it closer. "No, Turkish."

Now, at any other time, I would have freaked out at Heller being shown just that. But I was sort of dulled by the shock of events.

"What does *Afyonkarahisar* mean?" said Heller, startling me out of my wits.

"(Bleep), I don't know," said Maulin. "Where's it say that?"

"Here on the side," said Heller. "It's kind of dim."

"I didn't bring my glasses," said Maulin. "Sweeney, what does *Afyonkarahisar* mean?"

"Black opium castle," said Sweeney. "Western Turkey. Why?"

"It's on this can," said Maulin.

Sweeney said, "It is? There's some black balls of it in the next jar from the same place. And that white jar down the line contains some of their heroin. (Bleep), now you got me lecturing." And he went back to work.

"You see," said Maulin learnedly, "there is a flower called a poppy and it has a black center and they scrape it and get a gum. They boil that and they get opium. They chemically process it and they get morphine. Then they chemically process that and they get heroin. The white heroin is Turkish and Asiatic. The brown heroin is Mexican ... Sweeney, where's some of that drug literature? No sense me wearing my lungs out."

Sweeney pointed to a cabinet and Maulin opened it. "(Bleep)," he said, "they been using it for toilet paper again." He seemed baffled. Then he had a bright idea. He was reaching in his pocket. "Sweeney, go on out to the newsstand and get me one of those paperbacks on drugs." Then he suddenly stopped fishing in his pocket. "Hell, what am I doing? Here I am standing next to the U.S. Mint and was about to spend my own dough. You got any money, kid?"

Heller reached in his pocket and drew out his roll. The way he did it was the first indication I had had that he was rattled. He had tripped into a preconditioned habit pattern. Voltar gamblers—and Heller sure was one, as I knew to my grief—have a mannerism in handling money. They insert a finger in the center of the roll and let the *two* ends of the bills come up through their fingers and it looks for all the world as though they are presenting exactly *twice* as much money as they are actually holding.

Maulin looked at it. "Jesus," he said. Then, "I suppose this is your weekly allowance for candy." He plucked at the presented fistful. "Let's see. The book is about three bucks. Add two for Sweeney for his trouble. I'll take this fiver. No, on the other hand, you are probably hungry, so Sweeney can bring back some food: I'll take this sawbuck. No, come to think of it, Sweeney and me are also hungry, so I'll take this pair of double sawbucks." He apparently couldn't think of anything else, so he threw the money at Sweeney whose former hostility seemed to have evaporated.

"What do you want to eat, kid?" said Sweeney.

"Beer and a hamburger," said Heller, apparently recalling Crobe's diet advice.

"Aw, kid," said Maulin, "you are a con man. You know God (bleeped) good and well we can't buy beer for a kid your age. Tryin' to edge us into a felony? Bring him milk and a hamburger, Sweeney. I'll take a steak sandwich and beer."

Sweeney was gone and Heller went back to learning the more than two hundred different types of drugs on the shelves.

I had resigned myself to Heller knowing now what we did in Afyon. What I was worrying about was why they were delaying Heller. The FBI was totally out of character, so it was some kind of a ploy. They had something else going.

Sweeney came back with the required items and shortly Maulin and Heller were back in the former's office. Maulin ate his steak sandwich in one large bite and washed it down with beer.

Heller sat nibbling his and looking at the book. It was titled *Recreational Drugs* and it said it contained "everything you need to know about drugs." It said it was recommended by *Psychology Today*, so I knew it must be totally authoritative. There was everything in it from aspirin to wood alcohol.

So Heller, being Heller and a long way from knowing enough to put on a show the way a real spy would do, simply started "reading" it which, for him, was ingesting a page the way Earth people ingest a word. He still had a sip of milk left when he came to the end of two hundred and forty-five pages. He put the book in his pocket and finished his milk.

Maulin said, "What the hell? Oh, I guess you're just too nervous to read. I can understand that." He looked at his watch and seemed worried. Then he had a bright idea. "Tell you what, Junior. They have public tours through this building every hour or so. But we won't wait for one of those. I'll take you on one."

Why were they delaying him? They were using the approach "Detain subject without arousing his suspicions."

Maulin took him down to the exhibit of gangster guns and weapons. I was interested myself, thinking I could pick up some pointers. Maulin even took some out of their cases.

"Are all these weapons chemical?" said Heller.

"Chemical?" blinked Maulin.

"I mean, none of them electrical?"

"Oh, you dumb kids. Reading a bunch of Buck Rogers comic books! If you mean do gangsters have any laser weapons, no. We caught somebody trying to sell us some a few years back and I think he's still doing time. They ain't legal, kid. Besides, powder is best. Now, you take this sawed-off shotgun: it'll blow a man in half! Completely in half, kid! Ain't that great?" He picked up a burp gun. "Now, you take this: point it down a crowded street and it mows down dozens of innocent bystanders. Totally effective."

They moved on to some views of modern bank robberies and Heller inspected them. Maulin showed where the bank security cameras were placed, told him about marked money packs, alarm buttons, alarm systems, police techniques and how the FBI always, without fail, caught each and every bank robber that had even tried to shortchange a teller. And Heller was so interested that Maulin even got an alarm system and showed him how it was rigged and could be disabled. "Your old man, being your old man," he said, "has a vested interest in all this, so I hope you got it."

Heller had gotten it, no doubt of that!

Maulin showed Heller, next, the FBI laboratory and all the most modern scientific investigative techniques including those on the drawing board. I didn't like that as it was edging over into things Lombar had forbidden us to teach Heller. And I was relieved when they came off of it.

The erratic "tour" was certainly not the scheduled public tour, even to the point of Maulin shouldering through a couple of small mobs of sightseers to show Heller something of special interest.

They finally came to the "Ten Most Wanted Fugitives" and Heller got an education on how people were spotted and traced. And how the FBI never, never failed to find them every time.

Shortly, Maulin had him back for an out-of-sequence look at the gangsters of the 1930s. "Now," he said, "here were the real gangsters. They weren't the cream puffs you find around today. They were really, really gangsters. And you got no idea how hard it was to catch them. But Hoover solved all that."

Maulin pointed at a death mask and a display of photos. "Now, take Dillinger there. He never had any record at all. Just one minor charge. But Hoover made him a famous man."

He got around in front of Heller and wagged a huge finger at him. "Hoover had the greatest imagination in history. He used to dream up," said Maulin proudly, "the God (bleepest) dossiers for people. Total inventions! Right off the top of his head. Pure genius! And then he could go out and shoot them down! In a blaze of glorious gunfire! A master craftsman! He taught us how and we are left with the heavy responsibility of carrying on this magnificent tradition!"

Heller waved his hand to include all of the most advertised criminals in history. "He got all these the same way?"

"Every one," said Maulin proudly. "And he included the general public, too, so don't think this is complete."

"Hey," said Heller. "There's a really vicious one!" He was pointing.

Maulin blew up. "God (bleep) it, kid, that's HOOVER!"

He was so upset that he simply stalked off. Heller clickety-clacked along behind him. Then, fitting his mood, Maulin went down some stairs and shoved Heller through another door. It was a firing range!

I was apprehensive. I knew they were up to something. I hoped it wouldn't include shooting Heller on the premises!

There were targets at the other end of the room and

guns and ear protectors on the counter. I held my breath. I prayed to Heller not to get any notion of grabbing a gun and shooting his way out of the building.

"Where's the agent that does the public demonstrations?" demanded Maulin of an old man that was cleaning some guns.

"Hey? Oh, there ain't any more public demonstrations today."

Maulin socked some ear clamps on Heller and picked up a gun. He fired a round at the targets and it seemed to make him feel better. He turned to Heller. "You've classified on revolvers, of course."

"I've never shot one of those," said Heller.

"Military school!" snorted Maulin. "I knew all they taught was to tat and knit." But he proceeded to instruct Heller. "This is a Colt .457 Magnum revolver. A shot from it will go through a motor block and then some." And he showed Heller how to swing its cylinder, inspect it, load and unload it, and even how to carry it. Then he picked up a Colt U.S. Army .45 and showed Heller all about that.

Maulin looked at his watch and frowned. Obviously he had to delay Heller longer. "Tell you what, Junior. I'll give you a little demonstration of real marksmanship. Now, first, I take a look at a wanted poster here. And then several targets jump up and I have to select which one is the wanted man and put a bullet in his heart. If I shoot the wrong man, I get another chance."

He picked up a poster, glanced at it. He drew his own gun. He had the technician push some buttons. Face after face popped up. Maulin fired. He shot the wrong man.

"I told you to see an eye doctor, Maulin," said the old man.

"Shut up," said Maulin. "Hit the buttons again." He gripped the butt of the gun with both hands. He sighted carefully. He shot the right man.

"Here, Junior. You try it. You'll see it ain't so easy."

Gods, all Heller had to do was shoot the two of them and walk out. In the spot he was in, it was the textbook solution.

Heller looked at a wanted poster and put it down. The targets popped up. Heller fired and hit the right man, dead center. Nothing marvelous for a Fleet blast-gun expert.

"No, no, no," said Maulin. "Jesus. Don't ever pull a trigger before you raise the gun to eye level. But I don't blame you for being nervous. And don't get cocky about accidental hits. They don't happen in real battles. Now hold the gun in *both* hands, spread your feet apart to get steadiness. Now sight carefully down the barrel. Good. Now we'll give you another chance. Hit the buttons, Murphy."

Heller with great pains did exactly as he was told. He hit the right target dead center.

"There, you see?" said Maulin. "That's what happens when you get good instruction. Now you want to try this Army Colt?"

Heller fired an assortment of weapons and finally, with a sigh of relief, Maulin, looking at his watch, said, "It's time we went back to my office." They left but Maulin used the whole long route to lecture Heller about the power and majesty and total world dominance of the FBI. It was just an act to cover up what they really intended. For I knew that, by now, whatever trap they were party to had been arranged.

Chapter 5

Maulin, puffing a bit from his exhaustive lecture on the glories of the FBI, had no more than entered his office when Stupewitz's phone rang. Maulin pointed to a chair and used the hand signal with which they order dogs to sit down and rushed to answer.

I didn't need to turn up the gain. "Maulin here," he bawled. Then, in an extremely polite tone of voice he said, "It's all right to tell me. I am Agent Stupewitz's partner. I think he gave you my name." Then he grabbed a pad and started to write. Finally he said, "Yes, Mr. Bury. It's all under control here. . . . Oh, he's fine, Mr. Bury . . . No, he hasn't talked to anybody else . . . Yes, Mr. Bury . . . Yes, Mr. Bury. Thank you, Mr. Bury." And he hung up.

Stupewitz came in and he and Maulin whispered briefly together. Then they put Heller in a chair with two chairs facing him and Stupewitz turned on a bright light in Heller's eyes. The two agents sat down.

"Me first," said Stupewitz. "Junior, we reported to Virginia that a wrecked Cadillac with your license plates was discovered in Maryland. We also said it had a body in it answering your description that was burned beyond recognition. The people concerned did not have your name; the hooker is dead. So *you* are in the clear. So don't never mention that incident again and make liars of us. You understand?" he added severely.

The light was blinding Heller. But I suddenly realized with relief they were not interrogating him. They were briefing him! They just didn't know how to talk to anybody any other way.

"Now, here," continued Stupewitz, "is your car registration. It now has District of Columbia plates. The motor and body serial numbers have been changed. It is in your name now. We know you were the one who originally paid the dealer for that car, so don't get the idea we're doing anything illegal. Got it?"

Heller took the registration. It had a little slip fastened across the top of it that said:

> All or any police: In case of contact, call
> Agents Stupewitz or Maulin only, FBI, D.C.

"We won't bother with insurance," continued Stupewitz. "But if you're in any accidents, with your name you could be sued for your shirt. So drive carefully. No more crazy hundred-mile-an-hour chases. Got it?"

Heller got it.

"Now, here," said Stupewitz, "is your driver's license."

Heller took it and, against the glaring light, saw that it had another little slip on it.

> All or any police: In case of contact, call
> Agents Stupewitz or Maulin only, FBI, D.C.

I suddenly realized what they had done: they had put "tail plates" on the Cadillac. In the computers used by all police departments, if those "tail plates" came up, the reply would read: "This car is under surveillance by the FBI. If spotted, report it to Agents Stupewitz or Maulin, FBI, D.C." It amounted to the FBI having a continuous tail on him!

"Now, here," said Stupewitz, "are all your papers back." And he gave him the birth certificate, diploma and grades. Heller put them in his pocket.

Maulin got up and hauled an old, tattered Octopus Oil Company road map out of a cluttered desk drawer. He sat back down.

"All right," said Maulin, opening the map and putting his phone notes on it. "Mr. Bury wanted to be sure you had money and I said you did. Mr. Bury says you will probably be tired—he's quite concerned for your welfare. So you are to go to Howard Johnson's Motel in Silver Spring, Maryland. You leave here, go up Sixteenth Avenue, over the District line and the motel is right here. See it?"

Heller was studying the map. And I suddenly knew the why of the delay. It was not the FBI. It was Mr. Bury. Somewhere up that route, he had arranged a hit! I tried frantically to figure out how he would do it.

Heller had it. Actually, he probably had every road and byway on the east coast now.

"Good," said Maulin. "Now, he said some reporters had gotten wind of your refusing to come home this summer. Some crazy tale that you wanted to live your own life. Maybe join a baseball team or something. So he said that under no circumstances were you to register in a motel or hotel under your right name as he wanted no news release until you were reconciled with your family and you had talked with your father who is out of the country now. Got it?"

"Don't use my own name," said Heller. "Got it."

Oh, that Bury. He knew (bleeped) well there was no Delbert John Rockecenter, Junior! He was going to avoid any crazy newspaper stories by simply murdering the imposter. Rockecenter certainly had the resources and was not slow to use them. But how was he going to do it? And where?

"All right," said Maulin. "Now, tomorrow morning, you drive up to U.S. 495, the circle highway around D.C., and you turn off to the left onto U.S. 95. You go on that highway straight across Maryland, then across Delaware to this point where you go to the right on U.S. 295 across the Delaware River and then you're on the New Jersey Turnpike. You just follow along—actually you can't get off it. Now, you see here, just north of Newark, the turnpike splits? Well, there's a Howard Johnson's Motel right here," and he put an *X* on the map. "You're supposed to be there by about 4:30 in the afternoon. It's only a four-hour trip. No speeding! Don't register. Just go in the dining room, sit down and have an early supper. An old family retainer will be waiting there for you and will guide you home. Got that?"

Heller said he had.

"Now, Mr. Bury said to tell you you were in no danger whatever, so not to do anything silly. In fact, he said to tell you that Slinkerton will be tailing you all the way so you won't get scared."

"Slinkerton?" said Heller.

"That's the Slinkerton Detective Agency, the one your dad uses. They're the biggest in the country," said Maulin. "You won't see them but they'll be there." He laughed suddenly. "I think he's making sure you won't run off again, no matter how many hookers you meet!"

Stupewitz said, "Shall we go down to the car now?"

They went down to the FBI garage and there was the car. Heller checked the trunk: his gear was undisturbed. He glanced at the new D.C. plates, front and back. Then he got in.

Stupewitz said, "So it's good-bye, Junior."

"Thank you," said Heller (was that an emotional

tremor in his voice?), "for making it possible for me to go straight."

Maulin laughed, "Save your thanks until you get your hands on your old man's money, Junior."

The agents both laughed and then, the way Americans do—talking in front of children as though the child isn't there—Stupewitz said to Maulin, "He's a good kid, Maulin. A little wild but okay."

"Yeah," said Maulin, "you can see his family's stuff in him. But all these kids is tamer than we used to be."

They both guffawed and waved to Heller as he drove off.

I didn't wait to watch Heller wrestle with the evening rush hour of Washington. I went plunging down the side tunnel that led to Faht's office. It's a long way and I was totally out of breath when I burst through the secret side door.

"I've got to contact Terb!" I shouted.

Faht opened a drawer and handed me a report. It was their daily radio transmission. It had come through at the rate of five thousand words a second, using hyperband. It contained, however, no five thousand words. It was very terse. Heller had gotten his birth certificate, beaten up two cops, was found by Terb again through bugs in Lynchburg, had gone to Washington, been arrested by the FBI and now was safely in their hands, probably about to be imprisoned as intended.

The Hells he was! I knew a lot more than Terb or Raht!

"I've got to contact our people!" I blared at Faht.

Heller was going to be killed! Within the next day or two. And I didn't have the platen! I had to get word to Terb to get into those motel rooms quick and ransack that baggage!

Faht shrugged. "They don't have a receiver-typer.

They're bulky and you didn't order them to take one."

Oh, my Gods! I slumped in a chair. The worst of it was, I couldn't even talk to Faht or anybody. They must not know how I knew or they could get in on the lines and maybe do something wild!

"I might get word to them in New York," said Faht helpfully. "They'll probably report in there at the end of the week if they're out of money."

They weren't ever out of money. They had it by the bucket load!

I only knew three things for sure. One: Bury was going to have Heller killed, whatever else Bury was up to. Two: Soltan Gris was going to be executed if Heller was. Three: Earth population was going to be slaughtered if they interrupted Heller's communication line and I, right now, was part of that population!

I started to ask Faht if there was a good mortuary in Afyon. At least I could have a decent funeral. But I didn't even dare say that.

I slogged through the long, long tunnel to my room. My future looked even darker than the tunnel, and no room at the end of it—just a tomb, even an "unknown grave."

Chapter 6

Without hope, I watched my viewscreen as Heller entered the Silver Spring, Maryland, Howard Johnson Motel. I should have been relieved, for it meant that, with luck, I myself could end, for a few hours, the marathon of sleepless vigil he had been putting me through.

He wasn't looking behind him as he should have. He

didn't scan the desk or waiting area for suspicious figures. He was taking no precautions any normal agent would take.

He simply clickety-clacked up to the desk, told them he wanted a room for the night, laid down thirty bucks and wrote his new car license number, plain as day, on the registration form—he didn't falsify it or even make it illegible. And then he spurred me into near fury.

With a flourish, he signed the register, "JOHN DILLINGER!" He even put the exclamation point on it! A fat lot he'd learned at FBI headquarters: John Dillinger was one of the most famous gangsters of the 1930s. Pure sacrilege!

He threw his bags carelessly in his room as though he hadn't a care in the world. He washed up and soon clickety-clacked outside—not even looking into the many shadows—walked around the building and came into their restaurant.

Heller sat down. An elderly waitress promptly came over and told him he was in the wrong seat. She made him move to another booth in the corner with a flat white wall behind him. She fiddled with the lights until he was totally illuminated. And he didn't even register that she was putting the finger on him! He just busily puzzled away at the menu. And a Howard Johnson menu has nothing on it to puzzle about: they're all the same, numbers and pictures, from coast to coast!

The elderly waitress had gone off but now she returned. She took his baseball cap off his head and put it in the seat beside him, saying, "Young gentlemen don't eat with their hats on."

"I'll have a chocolate sundae," said Heller.

She stood there and she said, "You will have a Number 3. That's green salad, fried chicken, sweet potatoes and biscuits. And if you eat all that, *then* we will talk about a chocolate sundae." She imagined Heller was going to protest. She said, "I have boys of my own and you are all alike. You don't realize you have to eat good food to grow!"

She didn't fool me. She had for sure put the finger on Heller for someone. Helplessly I wondered if it would be a bullet or knife or arsenic in the chicken. Maybe, I thought, with a faint stir of hope, it was just a finger to identify. But she had certainly done a workmanlike job and a beautiful cover-up. One comes to learn the hallmarks of a real agent.

The food came. Heller peered about at other plates to see what others were eating. Then he seemed reconciled and fell to, even doing a creditable job of handling his utensils. He even picked the pieces of chicken up and ate them with his fingers, a thing he would never have dreamed of doing on Voltar! But although he was absorbing culture, he was also making mistakes. I realized that in D.C.; and here, he was talking in an Ivy League accent. He thought, apparently, that he was out of the South and this wasn't so. Maryland is as south as the fried chicken he was eating. He wouldn't be in New England unless he went just north of New York City. He was too crude and rough in his nonexistent command of tradecraft.

He had finished his meal, wiped the grease off his mouth and fingers when his attention was attracted by a movement on the other side of the room. It was hard to see as the lights were so strong in his eyes. Just a shadowy figure.

Then I froze. The figure had something held before its face. Was it a gun?

There was a bright blue flash! It was extremely brief. My viewscreen went white with overload!

Then there were black spots dancing on it and I

could not see even what Heller saw, if he saw anything.

The scene cleared. The black spots faded. And Heller was just sitting there, looking into the room. There was no figure there now.

The waitress came to him. "My, my. You ate it all. You have been a good boy, so you can order your chocolate sundae."

"What was the flash?" said Heller.

"Oh, the cashier's desk lamp just blew out. Did it hurt your eyes?" And with motherly concern she rearranged the lights near him so they would not shine in his face. Sure enough, the cashier was fiddling with her desk lamp.

Heller got and finished his sundae, paid his check with a generous tip and went clickety-clacking off around the building to his room, once more not even looking in the shadows. I was dealing with an idiot!

In his room, which he had entered without a fast door-swing-back and sudden spring, he did not check his baggage to see if it had been tampered with. He simply adjusted the air conditioning—no inspection for a gas capsule—and sat down in an easy chair and read the drug book again.

He did something then which put me into an idea conflict. On the one hand, he must NOT be killed until I had the platen. On the other hand, he would HAVE to be killed if he really penetrated what our Apparatus Earth base was all about.

Heller got up and found two ashtrays. He turned out the right-hand pocket of his jacket into the first and the left-hand pocket into the second. He was carrying DRUGS!

I couldn't understand it. Then I realized he simply had taken a small handful out of each of two jars at the FBI drug lab!

He opened up his suitcase and took out a little vial. It only had a tiny amount in it, a few specks of powder. Then he took out another vial and it, too, had a tiny amount in it.

There actually had been drugs in his suitcases when the D.C. policeman searched them! Microscopic amounts but drugs all the same! Where had they come from?

He inspected the vials. Then he put the contents of vial one into the ashtray over at the edge. He put the contents of vial two into the second ashtray over at the edge.

He went over to the light and held ashtray one to his eye.

The granules were suddenly HUGE!

It was Turkish opium!

He did the same with ashtray two.

It was Turkish heroin!

Then he went over to the long French doors to a porch which served as the motel room window and with a bit of fiddling got them open.

He took a book of matches and lighted one. He dropped it in the ashtray. And, of course, the opium began to burn and smoke like mad.

He coughed and put a plastic table mat over it.

He lit the heroin the same way.

He coughed some more and put a mat over the ashtray to put it out.

The room went sort of wobbly for a moment on my screen. Naturally. He had had a whiff of opium smoke followed with a whiff of heroin smoke.

Heller went outside on the balcony and took a lot of rapid breaths of fresh air. Then he ran in place a bit, breathing noisily. Of course, the wobble in the view cleared up.

He went back and dumped both ashtrays in the toilet,

washed them, washed out the vials, thoroughly dusted out his coat pockets and put everything away.

He satisfied himself that there was no trace of either one left anywhere.

But, all in all, it was a pretty amateur performance. No dope addict would ever waste drugs that way. And although you *can* burn heroin, it is too expensive a way to imbibe it. One has to shoot it into the blood to get the maximum good out of it.

Even though it was probably a hot night, he left the window open. Looking for something to do, he found and read *The Fine Art of Angling for Beginners*. Finishing that, he tackled *The Fine Art of Baseball for Beginners*.

It was not yet eight. He got interested in the TV set. He got it on. He got a picture. And then he kept pummeling and picking at its switches. He got it all out of kilter and finally got it back in again. I couldn't figure out what he found wrong with it. It was working, sound and picture.

Somewhat impatiently, he went through the whole routine again. There was a sign that said if the TV didn't work to call the desk and he approached the phone. Then he apparently thought better of it and slumped in a chair. He addressed the set: "All right. You're the first viewer I ever met I couldn't fix. So just go on hiding your 3-D control. I'll look at you anyway!"

A movie was just coming on. The title was *THE FBI IS WATCHING YOU!*

He sat through all manner of shootings and car chases and wrecks. The FBI wiped out all the red agents in America. It then wiped out all the Mafia in America. It then wiped out the U.S. Congress. I could tell Heller was impressed. He kept yawning and, psychologically, that is a sure sign of tension building up and releasing.

The Washington, D.C., local late news followed.

Whites had been mugged. Blacks had been mugged. Whites had been raped. Blacks had been raped. Whites had been murdered. Blacks had been murdered.

There is a law in America that TV must cover everything impartially without showing bias and they had racially balanced the program up pretty well.

There had been no slightest mention of any incident in Potomac Park. There hadn't even been a line about a Mary Schmeck, a junkie, dying on the way to a hospital—such deaths are too common to even get notice.

Heller sighed and shut off the TV.

He went to bed.

It was just past six in the morning in Turkey. I, too, turned in. But I couldn't sleep. He had not even put a chain on his room door or locked the French doors to the balcony. He had not even placed any sort of a weapon under his pillow!

He was going to be hit. That was for certain. Somewhere on the path he was taking, Bury had it all arranged. There was no IF about it. There was only WHEN?

An idiot had me on a chain and was leading me straight to my death! Maybe I would go as anonymously and unremarked as Mary Schmeck. The thought saddened me.

Chapter 7

For a man about to be hit, Heller certainly was relaxed the next morning.

There was a small buzzer on my viewer which

sounded when reception intensified, if you remembered to set it and I certainly had! At 2:00 P.M. Turkish time I was blasted out of bed by it. It was 7:00 A.M. in Maryland and Heller was up and taking a shower. At least he was still alive, though I was unconfident that it would be for long.

He was splashing around in the shower. His Fleet passion for cleanliness grated on my nerves. It had been just as hot in Turkey as it had been around Washington I was sure. I didn't have air conditioning and I was certainly more sweaty and dirty and rumpled than he had been, yet I didn't have to take any shower! The man was clearly mad.

I went out and got a small boy by the ear and hurled him in the direction of the cookhouse and, shortly, I was back hanging over the viewer, wolfing *kavun*, or melon, and washing it down with *kahve*, the Turkish name for coffee, which is a cousin to hot jolt. I was so intent that I was gulping it down with *sade* and omitting mineral water swallows between sips the way you are supposed to do. The fact was forcefully called to my attention when my already raw nerves began to leap peculiarly. I dumped in the sugar and drank about a quart of water very quick. But my nerves were still jumping.

It was absolutely horrifying to watch what Heller was doing—or, more correctly, what he was *not* doing!

He made no baggage inspection—he simply got out a clean set of underclothes and socks from the carry-all and put them on, thus denying me any real inspection of his suitcases.

Dressed, he did not look up and down the hall before he stepped into it. He gave not the slightest glance around corners before he rounded them. He did not inspect the parking lot as he passed it for new, strange cars. And he did not even look over the restaurant when he entered but, with indecent carelessness, walked over to a booth and sat down.

A teen-age girl with a ponytail came to wait on him. He said, "Where's that elderly woman that was here last night?" Evidently the stupid idiot had formed some attachment—mother fixation no doubt!

The dumb girl went off to ask the manager of all things! She came back. "She was just temporary. You got no idea how the help shifts around in these motel chains. What'll y'have?"

"A chocolate sundae," said Heller. "That's to start. Then . . . what's these?" He was pointing at a picture.

"Waffles?" said the girl. "They're just waffles."

"Give me five," said Heller. "And three cups of hot jo——coffee."

I made a hurried note. Although I realized it was quite plain that he was imitating the accents of the people he talked to, he had almost strayed into a Code break. When I had the platen, those could be used to hang him high!

She came with a big, gooey chocolate sundae and he demolished it. Then she came with five separate plates of waffles and spread them around and he demolished those. Then she came with three separate cups of coffee. He emptied the sugar bowl of cubes into them and demolished those.

She was hanging around, not giving him his check. "You're cute," she said. "It'll be fall semester soon. You going to sign up with a local high school?"

"I'm just passing through," said Heller.

"(Bleep)," said the girl and stalked off. She came back with his check. She had put all the items on it. She was very frosty and uppity. Even the dollar tip didn't seem to matter. She must have been looking at his back as she left the table but her voice came through clearly. "I never get the breaks."

Heller said to the cashier, "I understand your lamp blew out last night."

"Which one?"

"This one," said Heller, tapping it.

The cashier asked the manager who was fiddling around with the cigarette display. He said, "Oh, yeah. Outside fuse. But it didn't blow. The fuse got pulled somehow."

He bought a whole bale of daily papers and went back to his room. A golden opportunity had been missed, I realized suddenly. I cursed Raht and Terb. They were somewhere within two hundred miles of him or I wouldn't be getting a picture. They were depending on the fact that his clothes and suitcases were bugged to keep him ranged. I could have kicked them for not demanding a receiver-typer. Yes, I knew it was illegal for them to pack around more than a small transmitter that looked like an alarm clock. But they should have said, "(Bleep) the regulations, Gris must be served!" They hadn't. A pair of (bleepards), both of them. A golden chance to ransack his baggage had been missed! If I had that platen, I wouldn't be going through all this!

He got out a spin brush, filled its fluid container and washed his teeth and I was so bitter about the suit-cases that I almost passed over a *real* Code break. That spin brush might even have a Voltarian manufacturing plate on it! Not that anybody on this planet could read it, but it was still a Code break. His obsession with clean-liness was going to ruin him yet. I didn't even own a spin brush: they cost three credits.

With suitcases dragging from each hand and the carry-all under one arm and the mass of newspapers under the other, he went down to his car.

And did he carefully inspect it to see if it had been set up with bombs? No! He just put his baggage in the back, the newspapers in the front seat, started up and started off. I had turned the volume down in case there was an explosion.

He went up to U.S. 495 and, tooling along comfortably, got onto U.S. 95 and, at a leisurely fifty-five, rolled across the beautiful leafy green of Maryland, admiring the trees and fields and not even glancing into the rearview mirror to see if he was tailed. That beauty he was impressed by was deceptive. I knew there was death waiting on that road!

He got into Delaware, admiring it down to the last huge barn. I didn't know why he was looking so thoroughly at all these chicken factories with their huge signs. Snipers wouldn't be concealed in them. Then suddenly a truck—glaringly labelled *Delaware Chickens Corp.* —swerved around to get ahead of him (he was dawdling), and he drove up so close to it he almost rammed it and then hung hard on its tailgate. It was a truck full of live chickens and he was looking them all over.

"So," he muttered, "*that's* what a *chicken* is!"

Hopeless! Absolutely hopeless!

Past Greater Wilmington Airport, he turned to the right onto the huge Delaware River Bridge. But was his mind on his business? No!

He stopped his car! Halfway across the span, disregarding traffic and horns and brake squeals, he stepped on his brakes!

A trailer-truck slued sideways frantically and blocked all lanes!

He got out. He left his car right there in the right lane, motor running, and got out! He gave only the slightest glance to the pandemonium he had abruptly caused.

He went over to the bridge rail and looked down at the Delaware River.

"Holy, jumping blastguns!" he said in Voltarian. Just like that!

And what was he looking at? He was looking down at the brown, roiling water. And what was there to see? Nothing but oil slicks and old floating tires and dead cats. Of course, I will admit the Delaware River is pretty big as rivers go and it looks bigger as at this point it becomes Delaware Bay and then part of the Atlantic.

The huge truck driver that had almost rammed the Cadillac now couldn't get out because of the stacked up traffic. He came roaring at Heller, shaking his fists. I only saw him on peripheral vision. Heller wasn't looking at him. He was looking northeast, up the river. The noise was absolutely deafening. Honking horns and angry yells and this truck driver. I had to turn down the gain.

Heller ignored the raised fists and profanity coming at him. Right into the middle of a tirade about "you (bleeped) kid," Heller said, "Is there a city up there?"

"Jesus!" exploded the truck driver. "Where the hell are you from?"

And Heller was so intent on whatever he was thinking about, he said, "Manco."

Then, into the middle of an "I don't care if you're from hell" sort of thing, Heller said, "I asked you, is there a city up this river?" Yikes! It was his piercing, high-pitched Fleet voice! I hastily lowered the gain some more.

The truck driver said, "Philadelphia, you (bleeped), ignorant . . ."

And into the middle of that, Heller pierced, "Is this their *sewer?*"

"Of course it's their God (bleeped) sewer!" screamed the enraged truck driver.

"Jesus," said Heller in English. And he just ignored the man and the crowd and the fists and went back and got in his car and drove on.

Heller was shaking his head. "Must be a hundred million people in that town and no sewer system. POH-LLU-*SHUN!* Jesus!"

As I say, he wasn't tending to business. Any passing sniper could have shot him.

But I had him now. He had actually told an Earthman where he was actually from! I started to write it down and then thought I had better reread Code Number a-36-544 M Section B. I dimly remembered it could be interpreted as "making an alien *aware* that a landing had taken place on his planet." I couldn't be sure. Had the truck driver been *aware* of Heller's definitive answer? I couldn't find the book.

When I sat down to watch again, Heller was on the New Jersey Turnpike, tooling along at fifty-five. He was relaxed once more. He had all his windows up and the air conditioning on, so it must be a hot day.

The traffic was very jammy. This turnpike is one of the most overloaded highways in the world, carrying almost triple what it was designed for and despite the high price of gasoline and cars and consequent traffic reduction, the trucks were clogging its dozen lanes. Oranges from Florida seemed to be the biggest part of what Heller was trying to flow along with.

He drove for some time and then, possibly because he thought oranges might have an odor—a trailer had evidently been strewing the road with them after a collision —he opened his window.

He sniffed.

Suddenly he shook his head as though to clear it.

He sniffed again.

Then he sneezed!

Well, of course he sneezed. The state of New Jersey, particularly along the turnpike, has one of the highest air pollution concentrations in the world. I could have told him that. Everybody knows it.

Trucks or no trucks, he fished out a notebook and wrote some percentages of sulphur dioxide and some other symbols I don't know, but probably all noxious.

He closed his window. And then he said to the planet in general, "You're going to have to use hacksaws pretty soon even to get a plane to move through this stuff! How can you manage to do it so fast? This area is .06 percent up even since my survey."

He drove for a while and then he said, "I better get busy."

But it was miles later before he acted. And what he did made no sense at all.

He went through the lousiest tail-shaking procedure I have ever seen!

Somehow he had gotten ahead of the mobs of Florida oranges. Before him lay miles of two lanes, totally empty. It was completely flat—there is no scenery on this turnpike—it was without turns.

Despite the solemn warnings of Stupewitz and Maulin, he suddenly tramped on the accelerator and zipped the car up to ninety miles an hour! I thought, at last he's gotten some sense! He's trying to get away!

It wasn't as fast as he could go. If he was trying to escape, he really should have stamped on it!

He sailed along, looking in his rearview mirror.

He was in plain view! This was no way to escape!

He clocked off three miles.

Then, still in full view, almost as if he wanted to be seen, he paid a toll and drove out through an exit gate.

He stopped. He backed the car over to the side
where it could not be seen. And he just sat and watched
the gate.

After a bit, he got one of the newspapers and began
to read, looking up from time to time at the gate.

He found one story that fascinated him. It was in the
New York Daily Scum:

REVERED REPORTER
RUBBED

MUCKY HACK DOES
HIS LAST SPREAD

Mucky Hack, veteran investigative reporter
and crime exposer of the *Daily Libel,* was splattered all over 34th Street last night when his specially built Mercedes-Benz Phaeton was rigged for
a blitz that went BOOM!

The car was worth $89,000 according to

Boyd's, the only underwriters who would
touch it. It was alleged to be a gift from I. G.
Barben Pharmaceutical Corp. Car fans will miss
its presence in the Annual Special Car Parade at
Atlantic City.

Five shops were also destroyed in the blast.

Police Inspector Bulldog Grafferty, who inves-
tigated the car bombing, issued a carefully prepared statement today: "It was a valuable vehicle.
The bomb rigging was extremely expert, the work
of a master. Boyd's had required the car to be
guarded by Tilt and five other independent alarm
systems.

"The only possible person who could have
set up the blast is Bang-Bang Rimbombo.

"Bang-Bang is an ex-marine demolitions expert left over from the last war.

"Many car bombings have been attributed to him in the past although no arrests were ever made.

"Bang-Bang is a trusted member of the notorious Corleone mob which Mucky Hack has always been exposing in his tireless reporting.

"The New York/New Jersey mob is run by the able and charming Babe Corleone, the ex of the late 'Holy Joe' Corleone.

"It is well known that Corleone received his gang cognomen of 'Holy Joe' because he would not push drugs and that Faustino 'The Noose' Narcotici has been making steady inroads on the former Corleone territories in Manhattan.

"Thus, the motive for the rigging of the bombs by Bang-Bang exists. The expertise bears the unmistakable Bang-Bang trademark.

"Bang-Bang has not been arrested solely because he doesn't complete his current sentence in Sing Sing until tomorrow and was still in jail at the time of the bombing.

"Several shopkeepers were arrested for permitting the car to park in that spot.

"The case, therefore, can be considered closed."

Mucky Hack is survived by his managing editor and an old Ford.

For the life of me I could not see what he could find of interest in this story. He could read so fast that to see him sit there looking at one news item for ten minutes was baffling.

Possibly my annoyance, however, to be honest, came

from the fact that he was holding the paper folded. There was a Bugs Bunny strip that was thus only half-revealed: Bugs had Elmer Fudd in a bath of carrot juice, and not being able to see the beginning of the strip, I could not fathom how Elmer had gotten there or why. Possibly Elmer had been ill? Possibly the bath had been prepared by Elmer as a trap into which he himself had then fallen? But there was no way for me to tell Heller to open up the page so I could see. It was frustrating!

Finally Heller looked at his watch. My Gods, he was wearing a combat engineer's watch! In plain sight! I certainly put *that* down as a Code break. Then I was given pause: it looks like just a flat disc with a small hole in the center. Earthmen would mistake it for an identification bracelet or something like that.

He rotated his wrist, turning the watch downward and touched it. I had noticed before that he had this as a sort of nervous habit. But this is the first time I had really remarked it. It showed that he did have nerves after all.

He yawned—another nervous symptom. He looked at the toll gate area. Not one car had come through it in all the time he had been sitting there!

"So," he said, "no Slinkerton!"

Then it came to me in a flash what he had been up to. The Fleet must have battle tactics and he was practicing one of them. He had invited pursuit to lay an ambush. But he had no weapon, so he had probably done it because of training conditioning triggered by mounting nervous tension.

That must have been it, for he now started up the Cadillac, doubtlessly disappointed that his ruse had not worked, drove through the complexity of exits and entrances to the turnpike, got another fare ticket and was shortly on his way, rolling once more northeastward.

The traffic was quite heavy, and with all those trucks weaving in and out trying to pass each other, any normal driver would have felt he had his hands full. But Heller was taking time out now and then to read a story about "Economic Chaos Just Down the Road According to Financial Experts of Merrill Bull, Inc."

This expert watching him knew that the chaos which was down *his* road was not only economic! The lamb to slaughter had a better chance, in my opinion, than this idiot!

Chapter 8

At 4:20 that afternoon, Heller arrived at the rendezvous. He had dawdled along, stopping often, but he was still ten minutes early.

He parked the Cadillac carelessly in the higgledy-piggledy lot and made his way through the turmoil of tired kids and savage fathers and mothers that usually populate such temporary stop areas on a turnpike.

He made his way into the restaurant and was shortly seated at a table. He looked around.

I froze! Directly across the room from him was a dimly familiar face. Heller's glance passed over it but not mine! I mastered my nerves and, using the second screen, got back to that view, stilled.

The face was very Sicilian in bone structure. It was deeply pockmarked. A knife scar ran from the corner of the mouth straight back to the bottom of the left ear. The eyes were reptilian. My memory for faces is unsurpassed. But I could not place him.

Hastily, I yanked a camera from a shelf and, excluding the edges of the screen, got a close-up of that face! Rapidly, I stripped out the finished picture and, working very fast, blew it down onto Earth-type paper.

Keeping an eye on the current screen, I saw a tall, gray-haired man walk up to the Sicilian. The Sicilian showed the gray-haired man something he held cupped in his palm. A photo? Then he nodded almost imperceptibly toward Heller.

The Sicilian was acting as the finger man!

The gray-haired man drew back and idled against the wall. He was wearing a bowler. He was impeccably dressed, a three-piece suit, the vest of which was gray. He was wearing pince-nez glasses connected to his lapel with a black ribbon. He was also carrying an umbrella.

Heller ordered, got and ate a hamburger and washed it down with Seven Up. He was picking up his check when the gray-haired man approached him.

With a touch of a finger to his bowler, the gray-haired man said, "I am Buttlesby, young master. Mr. Bury wanted to be sure you were safely met. I am to show you where to go. If you are ready, may we go?" Very courteous English accent, the perfect fake family retainer.

Heller simply got up, paid his check and followed Buttlesby out.

The Sicilian passed them and, when they reached the parking lot, was getting into another car.

Buttlesby opened the door of the Cadillac for Heller and helped him get under the wheel. Then Buttlesby went around and got into the passenger seat.

"If you please," said Buttlesby, "proceed on up the turnpike. I will show you the turns."

Behind them, Heller saw the Sicilian's car was following them but after that he seemed to give it no heed.

"We will be leaving your car in a garage in Weehawken," said Buttlesby.

"Why?" said Heller.

"Oh, dear," said Buttlesby. "Absolutely no one ever drives across the river into New York! Heaven forbid! The Manhattan traffic positively devours cars, bangs them all up, ruins them. Anyone who is sensible leaves his car on the New Jersey side of the river and takes a taxi into New York. And in New York one uses taxis." He laughed slightly. "Let the taxis take the buffeting. Your car will be perfectly safe in the New Jersey garage."

Heller drove along in silence.

Buttlesby began to talk again. "Mr. Bury is dreadfully sorry, but he is detained in town. He has arranged for the young gentleman to stay at the Brewster Hotel on 22nd Street. Here is the hotel card." And he tucked it into Heller's outside breast pocket.

"Mr. Bury was very specific. The young gentleman is expected. He is not to register under his own name but, like any young gentleman, is to register incognito. It's what all the young bloods do when they go for a fling in town.

"Mr. Bury will call on you in person at precisely eight o'clock tomorrow morning at your hotel. He asked me to reassure you that you are perfectly safe, that no one is the least bit cross with you and that everyone has your best interests at heart. So, you will wait for him at the hotel?"

"Sure," said Heller.

The idiot! That would be the site of the hit! Or would it be even sooner?

Buttlesby directing, they left the turnpike and went with signs pointing to the Lincoln Tunnel. But at a sign, *J. F. Kennedy Blvd.*, they turned off and were soon in the New Jersey town of Weehawken, a very shabby place.

They rolled along to 34th Street and the fake family retainer gave more directions and shortly they were on the ramp of a large but dingy building, a garage.

The escort got out, rapped on the door three times and then twice with the handle of his umbrella and in a moment the huge mechanical door swung up, revealing a vast, dark interior.

A rather overweight young man with huge, somewhat scared eyes, dressed in paint-spattered khaki coveralls, was standing there, pointing.

Heller drove in the direction of the point.

The floor was paint-spattered. There were some battered machines evidently used in body work. But there were no other cars there.

Way back at the end there was an area cleaner than the rest and no paint spatters. Heller stopped the car.

He got out and opened up the back. Buttlesby was there helping with the baggage—he couldn't manage all of it and Heller carried one suitcase.

The plump young man had his hand out. "The keys," he said. "We maybe got to move it."

Heller separated the keys and for the first time I noticed there were two sets on the ring. And then the idiot handed one set over to the young man.

They went outside and there was a taxi waiting! The driver had his cap down, possibly to hide his face. Buttlesby got the baggage into the cab and stood back, holding the door open for Heller to enter. Heller got in but Buttlesby didn't.

"Aren't you going with me?" said Heller.

"Oh, dear no. Cross into Manhattan when I don't have to? Dreadful place. They ruin cars. Someone will be by to pick me up directly. Driver, take this young gentleman to the Brewster Hotel on 22nd Street. And no accidents, mind you."

The cab drew away and behind them the Sicilian drove up and Buttlesby got in the Sicilian's battered old car.

Shortly they were in the Lincoln Tunnel and Heller seemed more interested in the tile work that was flying by than he was in being en route to the hit spot.

As they exited from under the river, his eyes were all over the place, taking in New York. He seemed to be remarking about the fenders. And it is true that New York City fenders are the most bashed fenders in the world. He looked at dents rolling beside them and dents parked at curbs and possibly he was satisfied with Buttlesby's explanation. I wasn't. Bury had successfully separated the alleged Delbert John Rockecenter, Junior, from a car link that would lead back to the FBI.

They came at length to 22nd Street, which is narrow. And shortly they were drawn up before the Brewster Hotel, which is squat.

The buildings in that shabby section are only a few stories high. The garbage cans abounded.

While the Brewster may not be the worst hotel in New York, it is where the winos probably stop when they have money.

Heller removed his baggage and paid the driver—who probably already had been paid—and was shortly at the desk in the narrow excuse for a lobby.

The clerk, a man whose complexion was totally gray, looked at him with sunken eyes and then reached for a key. It must be all set up, even the exact room!

A card was pushed at him and Heller registered with a flourish. *Al Capone.* Address: *Sing Sing.*

The clerk gave him a key, not even bothering to read the registration card.

Heller squeezed his baggage into the elevator, worked

out it must be the fourth floor and was shortly in his room.

What a shabby room! A double bed against the far wall. One easy chair. One straight back. A side table by the easy chair, an 1890 bathroom and a TV.

Heller put his baggage on the bed and went over to the double window. Directly across the street, the building there was exactly the same height: it had a flat roof and parapet—the exact requirements for a sniper post.

But Heller gave it no special heed. He tried to turn on the TV. The picture and sound came on but it was a black and white TV.

Heller tapped it on the side. Then he fiddled with the settings and got it all out of kilter. Then he opened a panel and found some more settings and twisted those with a tool from his tool kit.

I couldn't comprehend what he was up to. Rigging a bomb? Doing something equally sensible?

And then it came to me. No stereo picture, no color. He thought it was broken!

He finally got the interior settings straight again and then the exterior knobs and got the picture and sound back.

He pulled the TV, which was on casters, slightly into the room and adjusted the easy chair. He had the back of that chair to the windows! My Gods, didn't he realize that's where the shot would come from?

And then this utter simpleton sat and watched the evening news in all its gory details.

Then he found a motion picture on the channels and sat yawning while the Mafia won World War II for America in Italy.

I did not wait for the end of that. Gripping my paper picture, I sped through the tunnel to Faht's office.

I slammed the picture in front of Faht's face. "Who is this man?" I demanded.

He shrugged and indicated the cabinets marked *Student Files*. They contain, amongst other things, a rogues gallery of customers so that we do not go adrift and sell to the wrong people.

It took me half an hour of digging—and how I longed for a proper computer system, illegal though it might be to install one on this planet.

I found him!

Unmistakable!

He had visited Turkey on two occasions to inspect the work of buyers for their mob.

It was Razza Louseini! *Consigliere* of the mob of Faustino "The Noose" Narcotici. The New York Mafia lot that is the outlet for I. G. Barben Pharmaceutical!

Important people.

The direct-line connection to Rockecenter's disguised control of the drug industry!

And the *consigliere*, the advisor and administrative head of the most powerful mob in New York, had personally gone down to act as the finger man on Heller!

One of our best customers had been given the job of knocking off Heller!

It was just, of course, but none of these people would know any part of this connection to Heller. Lombar had known. He had quite understood the fury that would boil in the Rockecenter camp when an imposter showed up. The Rockecenter name is sacred!

I felt an awe of Lombar. He had fed Heller straight into the fire. For a moment, at the FBI in Washington, I had thought Lombar had gone wrong. But no! The power of the Apparatus chief was reaching straight through, handled unwittingly by puppets!

And then the awe turned into sickness. Heller had a

contact in the Grand Council we had not known about. And I did not have the code!

There was no possible way to get Heller's baggage ransacked in time.

This planet was a goner!

But who cared about the planet? It was I, Soltan Gris, who would be dead in the echo of a fatal rifle shot through that window!

Chapter 9

At 7:10 New York time, there was a knock on Heller's hotel room door. A sloppy delivery boy with *Gulpinkle's Delicatessen* on his coat was handing Heller a bag.

Heller took it!

"That'll be two bucks and a four-bit tip," said the boy.

Heller made out that this was two dollars and fifty cents, paid him and closed the door. He opened the bag and found a plastic container of coffee and two jelly rolls.

No hotel like that ever had service like this! Was the stuff poisoned? Drugged?

Heller sniffed the coffee. He broke open a roll and sniffed it. Then the (bleeped) fool proceeded to consume them. He didn't pass out or drop dead, so I realized they had just been making sure he didn't leave his room or walk about to be seen.

He put on a clean baseball pullover. He finished dressing and combed his hair. He spin brushed his teeth.

He arranged the room. He put the easy chair with its back to the window, put the side table against it to the

left hand. He put the straight-back chair in front of it,
facing it. Then he took the two glass ashtrays and put
them on the side table near the easy chair.

Then, possibly finding waiting heavy, he seemed to
discover that the inside doorknob of the hall door was
loose and he got a tool from his kit and worked at it.
Then he unlocked the door completely.

He went over to the bed, made it and then opened
both his suitcases on it, wide open!

He emptied the carryall and made a neat pile of the
contents at the bed top.

The portable radio he had bought attracted his attention and he fiddled with it, getting a station or two. It
seemed to amuse him that the music was not stereo. How
could it be, with Earth electronics! The whole thing was
made just to dangle from the wrist by a strap. He took
it back to the easy chair and sat down. He listened to the
morning news. Toys! All Fleet guys are crazy with toys.
Here he was about to be hit and he was amusing himself
with a toy. The muggings and murders and political corruption of New York aren't news.

It was getting close to eight. He got up and went to
the window. He was looking down into the street, maybe
watching for his caller to arrive.

But I saw something else! By peripheral vision, I
saw a man come out of a door on that other roof! A man
carrying a violin case!

Heller went back and sat down. The radio came to
the end of the news.

The elevator door down the hall opened. Heller, possibly because his toy was new, had to do a lot of fiddling
to get the radio off. He dropped it into the top of an open
suitcase, stepped backwards and dropped into the easy
chair.

There was a knock on the door. Heller called, "Come in. It's open."

In walked the perfectly groomed Wall Street lawyer. The type is legendary. Three-piece suit in a somber gray. No hat. Impeccably neat. Dried up like a prune from holding in all the sins they commit. He was carrying a fat briefcase.

"I am Mr. Bury of Swindle and Crouch," he said. Very Ivy League accent.

Heller gestured to the straight-backed chair. Bury sat down on it and put his briefcase beside him. He wasted no time. "Where did you get this idea?" he said.

"Well, most people get ideas," said Heller.

"Did somebody talk you into this?"

"Don't know anybody much around here," said Heller.

"How many times have you used the name Delbert John Rockecenter, Junior?"

"I haven't!" said Heller.

"Did you use it to the men who met you?"

Aha! Razza Louseini and Buttlesby weren't in on it! They were just there to escort an anonymous somebody. Mr. Bury had kept this pretty tight!

"No," said Heller. "No one has used it to me and I haven't used it to anybody."

Bury seemed to relax. "Ah, I see I am dealing with a very discreet young man."

"That you are," said Heller.

"Do you have the papers?"

"They're there in my coat."

Bury got them. He also looked in the pockets. He sat back down.

"Now," said Bury, "did the FBI copy them?"

"They used them at the phone and they lay on a desk the rest of the time, turned over."

Bury was becoming more and more pleased. He was almost smiling, if a Wall Street lawyer can ever be said to smile beyond a tiny twitch of the mouth corners. "And you have no more copies?"

"Search the place," said Heller. "There's my jacket and there are my baseball clothes and there are my grips."

Bury got up again and looked through the sports clothes. He was looking for labels! I had more than an inkling of what was intended now.

The lawyer got to the grips. He got tangled up in fish line and then snagged a finger on a bass plug. He drew back cautiously and peeked at the contents.

The sides of his mouth actually twitching, he came back and sat down, facing Heller. "I have a deal for you," he said. "You give me these papers and in exchange I will give you another, completely bona fide identity and twenty-five thousand dollars."

"Let's see it," said Heller.

Bury opened one side of his case. He pulled out a birth certificate, Bibb County, Georgia. It said that JEROME TERRANCE WISTER had been born in Macon General Hospital on a date seventeen years before. The parents were Agnes and Gerald Curtis Wister and the baby was white, blond and male.

"That is totally valid," said Bury. "Also, the parents are both dead, there are no brothers or sisters or other kin."

Heller made a gesture for more. Bury pulled out a Saint Lee Military Academy certified record of grades. The grades were all *D*'s!

"No junior college certificate here," said Heller.

"Ah, you have missed something. This credits you with one more year than your other certificate. That gives you only one more year and you will have your full college degree of Bachelor. You will probably finish college, yes?"

"People don't listen to you unless you have a diploma," said Heller.

"How true that is," said Bury. "I couldn't have stated it better myself. So you see, you are the gainer. One more year of college and you will have your diploma."

Hastily I shuffled through my wits to recall what the catch must be here. Then I had it. With all *D*'s he'd have trouble getting admittance into another college and with a missing year—and Bury had no way of knowing all Heller's Earth education was missing—Heller would fail. But this was just gratuitous sadism on Bury's part. He knew that grade sheet would never be presented. It told me something else about the man. He was devious. He planned against failures of his plans even when success seemed certain!

"It gives you more than you had," urged Bury. "I am being completely fair with you."

Wall Street lawyer fair, I told myself.

Heller was beckoning for more.

"Now, here," said Bury, "is your driver's license. It is for New Jersey, quite valid in New York. And notice it is for all vehicles including motorcycles. This is in exchange for the D.C. one you have handed me. See how generous I am being?"

Heller inspected it.

"Now, here is the registration for your car in exchange for the D.C. one I hold now. And these are the plates. Note they are New Jersey plates, quite valid for New York. But I will take these along and have them put on your car. You will be picking up your car, won't you?"

Heller nodded and Bury seemed relieved. But Heller was still beckoning.

"Here is a social security card," said Bury. "It is

brand-new as you have never before had a job. You'll find it vital for identity."

The identity of a corpse, I told myself.

Heller was beckoning for more. The corners of Bury's mouth twitched and he handed Heller a U.S. passport. Heller opened it and stared at the picture of himself. "Where did you get this?"

"Last night," said Bury. "That's why you had to stop in Silver Spring."

"The flash at dinner," said Heller.

"You don't miss much. As a matter of fact, you can have the rest of the copies. I won't be needing them now." And he handed Heller a dozen more passport photos.

"How do I know this identity is all valid?" said Heller. "How did you get it?"

"My dear fellow," said Bury, "the government has to provide full verifiable identification all the time. They have witnesses they have to hide, people who have risked their lives to give testimony. The State Department does it continually. And we, you might say, own the State Department. You were quite imaginative to take us on this way. But we are nothing else than kind."

Rockecenter, kind? Oh, my Gods!

"Don't you worry about the validity of any of this," said Bury. "Indeed, it would be very bad for me if it were false."

Indeed, it would be, Mr. Bury, I gritted. The identity found on a corpse gets very close scrutiny!

"Now for the money," said Mr. Bury. And he hauled out wads of it from the left side of his briefcase. "Twenty-five thousand dollars, all in old bills, unmarked and untagged."

Heller laid it on the side table, back of the ashtrays.

"Just one thing more," said Bury. "It's illegal in

New York to register in a hotel under a false name. A felony, in fact." (Oh, what a LIE!) "So I just brought up a registration blank. Sign it with your new name and put Macon, Georgia, down as the address and we'll be finished."

Heller took it and balanced it on his knee. "One more thing," said Heller.

"Yes?" said Bury.

"The rest of the money in your briefcase," said Heller.

"Oh!" said Bury, like he'd been punched in the solar plexus.

Aha, the man was also crooked. He probably had intended to keep the rest of it for himself!

"You drive a hard bargain, young man," said Bury.

But Heller just had his palm up. Bury pulled a wad of money out of the right side of the briefcase. "It's another twenty-five thousand," said Bury.

Heller put it with the rest of the money, quite a pile! And then, sure as if it were his death warrant, he signed the hotel registration blank, *Jerome Terrance Wister, Macon, Georgia.*

Bury said, "You drive a hard bargain. But that's not bad. You'll really get along in the world, I can tell."

For about ten minutes more, I said to myself. As soon as you get clear of this room, Mr. Bury, and have yourself an alibi, a bullet is going to come through that window and that will be the end of Heller! And *me!*

Bury stood up, "Have I got everything?" He chuckled as he showed Heller the briefcase was empty and then he put all the reclaimed I.D. and the new license plates in it, probably gloating. He carefully looked around the room. He moved over toward the door.

"One more thing," said Heller. "Pick up that telephone and tell the clerk to go out in the street and tell that sniper on the roof to come over to this room."

Bury went rigid. Then he grabbed for the doorknob.

It came off in his hand!

He stared at it for an instant.

Then as he dropped it, his hand darted to the inside of his coat. He was going to pull a gun!

Heller reached sideways.

He picked up a glass ashtray so fast his hand blurred.

The ashtray sizzled across the room, hit Bury a glancing blow on the arm, caromed off and shattered into a shower of glass against the door, spattering Bury.

The lawyer stepped back, arm numb. He stared at Heller.

The second ashtray was in Heller's hand. "This one," said Heller, "takes the top of your head off!"

Bury was shaking, he was holding his arm. He moved over to the phone. He told the clerk to go out in the street and call up to the roof across the way and tell the man there to come over quickly.

Except by the window, the room was too dark and curtained to see deeply into. Heller moved over in a leisurely fashion and took Bury's gun.

"Just sit down there on the bed in plain view of the door. And look more relaxed."

"I think you broke my arm."

"Better than your head. Now, when he knocks, tell him in a normal voice to come in."

They waited, Heller against the wall by the door.

In about five minutes there was a knock.

"Come in," said Bury.

The door opened and a man stepped in.

Heller slammed the side of his hand against the back of the man's neck. It catapulted him forward into Bury!

The violin case dropped.

As the man had gone by him, Heller had extracted a Cobra Colt from his waistband.

Holding two guns, Heller put the Cobra in his pocket. He stepped out, flopped the squirming sniper onto his back. The man was a thin weasel, penitentiary stamped all over his face. Heller plucked a wad of bills from his inside pocket. He riffled them.

The sniper glared at Bury. "I thought you said he was just a kid!" He was starting to get furious.

Heller stepped forward. He made a cuffing motion and the assassin flinched. And Heller had his wallet and I.D.

With his foot, Heller pulled the briefcase to him and then opened it. He took out only the car plates. "I keep my bargains, Mr. Bury. You bought some papers and you can have them. I received some in exchange and I will keep them. A deal is a deal."

Heller moved them over off the bed and against the wall away from it. "However, Mr. Bury, I somehow doubted you were strictly a man of honor. So . . ."

He took the radio/cassette player out of the top of the suitcase. He hit the rewind. He pushed play. Heller's voice came out the tiny speaker, "Come in. It's open." And then Mr. Bury's voice, "I am Mr. Bury of Swindle and Crouch." Heller spot-checked it. It was all there on the cassette.

"So," continued Heller, "we will just put this in a safe place in case anything odd happens to me."

"Tapes aren't court evidence," sneered Mr. Bury.

"So, one more thing," said Heller.

"I'm sick of your one-more-things!" said Bury.

Heller opened the hood's wallet. He took a notebook and, in a blur of fast writing, took down all the particulars in it. Then he read the criminal's name aloud:

"Torpedo Fiaccola" and added his home address and social security number.

Heller took the money he had removed from the assassin. "This is about five thousand, I should judge." He put it in the wallet, making it bulge. "It is probably half the contract price."

He gave the wallet to the gangster. "I would not want to be accused of taking the daily bread out of anyone's mouth. So I am buying a contract on Mr. Bury's life."

Bury and the gangster looked at each other and back at Heller.

"But I don't want it executed yet," said Heller. "If any of this I.D. turns out to be funny or if I hear any Bury bullets going past my ears, I will phone you and you can execute the contract on him. You will be paid another five thousand cash if you then execute it." He must have smiled at the hood. The fellow didn't know what to think.

"Oh, I can reach you," said Heller. "I have your mother's address and phone number here."

The gangster flinched. I actually don't think Heller understood that the gangster now thought Heller was saying that if the hood didn't comply, his mother would be executed. But the gangster, I could see, took it that way.

Bury was another matter. As Heller studied him, I could see that Mr. Bury had another trick up his sleeve.

"You have nothing to fear from me, Mr. Bury," said Heller. "You have your papers. I will keep the deal as long as you do. So let's leave it that way."

Heller took the shells out of the revolvers. I freaked! He didn't have a gun on them now!

Heller opened up the violin case and inspected the dismantled sniper rifle. Then he took its supply of shells. He gave the guns and case and briefcase to them. With a screwdriver, he got a grip on the knob shaft socket and opened the door.

With a courtly bow, he signalled they could leave.

"May we never have occasion to meet again," said Heller.

The look Bury gave him would have disfigured a brass statue.

They left.

Heller was a fool! His grand heroics might serve in another time and place but not New York, New York, Planet Earth—Blito-P3!

He should have quietly killed them both. That would have been the tradecraft thing to do!

He had humbled one of the most influential attorneys on the planet and gotten the better of Rockecenter, a thing that man never tolerates.

Then, just as if he had not made mortal enemies, Heller neatly put the doorknob back on, packed, made everything tidy. Then, as he put his baseball cap on the back of his head in front of the mirror, he said, "There's nothing like FBI training to see you through." And he laughed.

But they hadn't taught him enough. Bury already had realized that any threat to Heller from anyone could be interpreted by Jerome Terrance Wister as coming from Bury. It left Bury with no other choice than, one way or another—if not at once, then at some convenient future time—to use much more adroit methods to eradicate Jerome Terrance Wister. Top Wall Street lawyers don't ever really lose. They only postpone.

At his fingertips, Bury had at his command not only government agencies but whole governments. He could sic any of them on Heller. Money meant nothing to him. Very possibly, right this minute he was offering Torpedo Fiaccola three times what Heller had offered to give it another try. And Fiaccola, frantic at that foolish threat to his mother, as well as his disgrace today, would now listen to anything.

Heller really was dealing in a subject he knew too little about. And he was a lot too cocky! Spies are deadly things, like scorpions in hiding. They don't walk out the door singing after they have set in motion the most powerful and vengeful machine on the planet—the Rockecenter power.

I sat and gloomed. I could think of no way to get that platen before Heller was killed. No wonder the life expectancy of combat engineers was only a couple of years of service. The life expectancy of anyone handling one, such as me, might even be much shorter!

And as I sat there glooming, a special messenger from Faht's office rushed in with the day's report from Raht and Terb. It said, "He registered at the Brewster Hotel and just checked out." My Gods, I didn't even get backup from my own men! Hells had no future like the one that waited for me!

PART SIXTEEN

Chapter 1

Heller couldn't find anybody in the Brewster lobby, so he went behind the desk, put the thirty-dollar room price under the counter where it could be seen, put his Al Capone registration card on top of it and wrote himself a receipt on their invoice machine, signing it *Brinks*. The FBI had not taught him very well: Capone had never once robbed a Brinks armored car. I know my American history!

Working on deciphering the scribbled numbers around the lobby public phone—some of them girls, some of them pimps and some of them gays—he found a taxi company and phoned it.

After getting his baggage into the cab, he said to the German-looking driver, "I'm looking for a place to live. A better hotel than this one. Something with some class."

With Heller noting bashed fenders of cars and darting amongst collision-fixated cars, they were soon over on Madison Avenue, roaring uptown.

At 59th Street and Fifth Avenue, the cabby dumped Heller in a driveway. Heller unloaded his baggage and offered a twenty-dollar bill. The cabby simply took the bill and drove rapidly away, though the fare had been much less. Heller was learning about New York.

He looked up. The Snob Palace Hotel soared above him. Although there were uniformed doormen and bellboys racing about, nobody took his baggage. He gathered it up and went in. A vast, glittering lobby stretched about him, almost a hangar. Sparkling but decorous light fixtures illuminated the subdued and decorous furnishings. An expensive and decorous throng eddied around him as he made his way to the Room Desk.

There were numerous clerks, all busy. Heller waited. Nobody looked up. Finally, he said to one clerk, "I'd like a room."

"Do you have a reservation?" said the clerk. "No? Then see the assistant manager. Over there, please."

The assistant manager was busy. He was answering a complaint on the phone in a suitably decorous voice. Something about a poodle not having been aired. Finally he looked up. He did not much care for what he saw. By a mirror that covered the back wall behind him, I could see it, too.

Here was somebody in a loud, too-small, red-checked jacket and a pair of blue-striped pants that didn't reach his baseball shoes and who had, of all things, a red baseball cap on the back of his head. "Yes?" said the assistant manager.

Heller chipped the ice off it. "I'd like a nice room, maybe two rooms."

"Are you with your parents?"

"No, they're not on Earth."

"Suites start at four hundred dollars a day and go up. I shouldn't think you would be interested. Good day." And he got on the phone to scold the help for not decorously airing somebody's poodle.

I knew what was wrong. Heller was thinking in credits. A credit was worth several dollars. He picked up his baggage, walked out and walked into a cab which had just discharged a Pekingese that had been getting aired.

"I am looking for a room. I want something less expensive than they have in this place."

The driver promptly dashed downtown, switched

over to Lexington Avenue, avoided numerous smashups and dumped Heller at 21st Street. Heller offered a twenty-dollar bill. The driver was very surprised when it didn't come out from between Heller's fingers. He grumblingly got change and in a swift movement, they swapped monies. Heller gave him a fifty-cent tip. He was learning.

Heller looked up at a ramshackle building. The canopy over the sidewalk said:

The Casa de Flop

He picked up his bags and walked in. A sodden group of winos sagged on sodden furniture. A sodden clerk slumped over a sodden desk. It was a very sodden lobby.

An odd sound hit my ears. Then I identified it. It was Heller sniffing. "Oof!" he said to nobody. "You'd think this place was run by the Apparatus!"

Code break! Code break! *And* unpatriotic! I made a hasty note and marked the recording strip. Nobody can accuse me of not doing my duty!

He hefted his bags, turned around and left.

Outside he stopped and looked back at the building. "You hotels can go sink yourselves! A house would cost less and be cleaner!"

It was two blocks before he could find another cab. It was sitting at the curb and Heller hailed it before it could drive off.

The driver looked like he had been up every night for the past year. He also didn't have any space between his eyes and hairline. A Neanderthal type.

Heller loaded his baggage. He leaned forward to speak through the glass and wire New York cabbies hope will protect them from muggers.

"Do you know of a house?"

The driver turned around to look at him. He thought. He said, "Do you have any money?"

"Of course I have money," said Heller.

"You're awfully young."

"Look," said Heller, "do you know of a house or don't you?"

The driver looked at him doubtfully but then nodded.

"All right," said Heller, "take me there!"

They bashed their way up into the Forties and headed over toward the East River. The black, tall slab of the United Nations pointed skyward in the near distance. They were drawing into a quieter, more elegant neighborhood full of imposing, high-rise buildings.

They pulled up at the curb before one. It was a building of gleaming stone and opaque glass, a beautiful modern structure many stories high. A patch of greenery and a brief curved drive set it back slightly from the sidewalk. An elegant, decorous sign, lettered in gold on black stone, was part of the wall to the left of the imposing entrance. The sign said:

The Gracious Palms

The cab had not pulled into the drive because a squat, low, black limousine was sitting there, chauffeur at the wheel. Heller got his bags out of the cab and put them on the walk. He was fishing in his pockets for the fare.

And then a remarkable thing happened!

The cabby, who had shortly before been so dopey, stared at the limousine and front entrance. His eyes suddenly shot wide with fear!

With a screech of tires, the cabby got his hack the Hells out of there!

Without being paid!

Heller gazed after the fleeing cab. He put the money back in his pocket. He hefted his bags and walked toward the entrance.

The limousine had its engine running.

There was a tough-looking young man lounging outside the door to the right of it. He was dressed in a double-breasted suit and he had a hat pulled down over his eyes. He pried himself off the wall as Heller approached.

The young man's right hand came up. Something in it!

It was a miniature walkie-talkie radio. He said something into it, eyeing Heller.

Something was going on! Something dangerous!

And Heller, the idiot, wasn't taking alarm! He walked on in through the entrance.

The lobby was small but dignified. Iron spiral staircases went up to a balcony on the far wall. Gold elevator doors were set into the polished tan stone. Designs in gold-colored metal wandered gracefully on the walls. There were some upholstered chairs of beautiful design, in groups of two, half-hidden by lovely green plants. A long, gold-colored counter was the obvious reception place.

There was nobody in sight! Not a soul!

Heller clickety-clacked across the polished, multi-colored stone terrazzo floor, going toward the counter.

A small door in the wall to the left of the counter, marked with a sign: *Host*, opened about six inches. There was a man's face there. A tough one. A hand came out and beckoned silently to Heller.

Heller put down his baggage and walked over to the door. It swung open.

It was a large, ornate office. At the far end there

was a carved desk. At it sat a man, small, well-dressed, black hair, narrow face. The sign on his desk said:

Vantagio Meretrici, Manager

Sitting to the desk's right were two men, hats on, right hands out of sight. The three were all looking toward Heller.

Behind Heller the door closed.

Suddenly he was seized from behind!

His arms were pinned with a lock grip!

He was wrestled to a straight-back chair in the corner beside the door!

He was forced to sit down in the chair, his captor behind him, still holding him.

One of the men beside the desk gestured at Heller and addressed the manager. "So this is one of your fancy boys."

"No! No!" cried the man behind the desk. "We don't use young men here!"

The other gangster near the desk laughed in disbelief. "Aw, quit the (bleep), Vantagio. What do you charge for a boy with a pretty face like his?"

"Let's get back to business, Vantagio. Faustino says you are going to push drugs here and you push drugs here. We supply, you sell."

"Never!" said Vantagio. "We'd lose all our clientele! They'd be sure to think we were trying to bleed them for information!"

"Aw, what the hell do the niggers and chinks at the UN know about information!" sneered the gangster nearest Vantagio. "You got to learn new lessons. Faustino calls the shots now and you know it! So where do we start? Before we waste *you*, that is. Wrecking furniture? Disabling a few whores?"

The other gangster said, "How about the pretty new boy?"

The two hoods looked at each other and grinned. The one who had just made the suggestion lit up a cigarette and got it burning brightly. "For starts, we'll just put a few deep holes in his face and cost you some fees!"

Holding the glowing cigarette, the gangster got up and started across the room. The man gripping Heller from behind tightened his lock on Heller's arms.

Abruptly Heller brought his feet off the floor!

He did a sitting back flip!

His toes struck the man behind him on the head!

Heller's hands caught the sides of the chair seat. He catapulted himself backwards, straight over the head of the one who had been holding him! He landed behind him!

He had the man's gun out of its shoulder holster!

The gangster halfway across the room had stopped, staring!

The one still near the desk swung up a gun. "Get out of the way!" he screamed at the fellow in the middle of the room. That one promptly dropped to the floor!

The hood near the desk fired!

Heller was behind the one who had held him. The bullet struck the gangster's chest!

Using his former captor as a shield, Heller was trying to get off a shot.

The hood near the desk fired again. Twice!

Both shots struck Heller's former captor.

The hood at the desk realized he was shooting his own man! He flinched.

Heller slammed a shot straight into his heart!

The one crouched in the middle of the floor had his gun out. He was trying to get a shot.

Heller got a glimpse of him, momentarily putting himself in view. The man on the floor fired!

Another shot slammed into Heller's former captor.

Heller ducked to floor level.

He drove a shot straight into the skull of the man who had been crouching on the floor.

Two dead men! The third still flopping about in his death agonies.

"Jesus!" said Vantagio Meretrici at the desk.

Running feet outside approaching.

Heller jumped back away from the door.

The hood who had been at the entrance got half his face and an arm in. He saw Heller.

He was raising a gun!

Heller slammed a shot into his upper shoulder.

The man was hurled back out the door, spinning around. But he did not go down. The door banged shut. Running feet were racing away.

With a roar, the car outside revved up. A car door slammed and the limousine could be heard racing away on screeching tires.

"Jesus!" said Vantagio. Then he seemed to come to life. "Kid, give me a hand, quick!"

The body closest to the desk had fallen on a throw rug. Vantagio grabbed a corner of it and, using it as a kind of sled, sped to the door. He blocked the door open with a chair. Then he grabbed the rug again and skidded it and its burden out into the lobby.

The manager pointed at the man Heller had used for a shield and then out into the lobby. Heller lugged the body out and dumped it in the lobby.

The chortle of distant cop cars sounded.

Together, the manager and Heller dragged the third body out.

An old woman had appeared in the lobby, a neatly

uniformed cleaning woman. "Get the blood off the floor in the office!" the manager yelled at her. "Be quick!"

The cop cars were nearer.

The manager dived behind the desk. The clerk was there on the floor, tied up and gagged. Heller took the clerk and cut the bonds off.

The manager arranged the bodies in the lobby. He took the gun Heller had used and wiped it off and put it in the hand of the one who had been Heller's captor.

The cop cars were drawing up. "The (bleepards)," said the manager. "They had the fuzz tipped to rush in and grab me if there was any shooting!"

The manager surveyed the scene, said something fast in Italian to the clerk and was about to tell Heller something, probably to beat it, when a stentorian voice called out from the entrance, "Everybody freeze!" The everybody was the manager, Heller and the clerk.

A police inspector, fronted with two cops holding riot shotguns, was there. He was a huge man, middle-aged, flabby. "All right, Meretrici, you're under arrest!"

"For what?" said Vantagio.

The police inspector was looking at the bodies. He glared at the clerk. "What happened?"

"Just like you see," said the clerk. "That one," and he pointed to the body that was furthest from the entrance, the one Heller had used for a shield, "was evidently trying to get away from the others. And they came busting in the door after him and they all started shooting each other."

The police inspector examined each of the bodies and the guns.

"They should be arrested," said Vantagio. "We don't allow shooting in here!"

"Wise (bleep)," said the inspector. He came over to Heller. "Who the hell are you?"

"He's a delivery boy," said Vantagio. "He came in from the back after the shooting."

"(Bleep)," said the inspector.

"I wish you'd do your civic duty," said Vantagio, "the ones the taxpayers pay you for and get these bodies the hell out of here. They already ruined one rug!"

"Don't you touch nothing," said the inspector. "The stiff team will be here in a few minutes and they'll want pictures of all this. And you two," he pointed at the manager and clerk, "don't fail to show up at the coroner's inquest! I oughta jail you as material witnesses!"

"We'll be glad to perform *our* civic duties," said Vantagio. "You just make sure you give honest businessmen better protection hereafter!" He glared at the bodies. "Hoodlums running all over the streets!"

The inspector left. A patrolman stood guard over the bodies so no one could corrupt the evidence.

"I'll take that baggage in my office," Vantagio said to Heller and beckoned.

Heller picked up his suitcases and the carry-all and followed him in.

Chapter 2

The cleaning woman had finished mopping up the blood. Vantagio turned the air conditioner on to "vent," probably to clear out the drifting cordite smoke. He seated Heller in a chair and then sat back down at his ornate desk.

"Kid," said Vantagio, "you saved my life! I never before *seen* such terrific shooting!" He regarded Heller for a bit. "How did you come to get here, anyway?"

Heller told him he had been looking for a place to live and then quoted his conversation with the taxi driver in which he had asked for a house.

Vantagio laughed. "Oh, kid, you are a greenhorn. Strictly from the backwoods. Listen, kid. In the vernacular of our fair city, the word 'house' means a brothel, a bordello, a bagnio, a crib, a sporting house, a cathouse, a whorehouse or, in short, a house of prostitution. And here you are. This is the pleasure palace of the United Nations, the top 'house' in all Manhattan!"

He started to laugh again and then he sobered. "But I can thank *La Santissima Vergine* that you arrived. I was sure my number was up!"

He sat back, looking at Heller, and thought for a moment. "You're kind of handy to have around. Kid, could I offer you a job? Something respectable like a bouncer?"

"No," said Heller. "Thank you. I've got to get a diploma. People don't listen to you unless you have a diploma."

"Oh, so true! I'm a great believer in education! I have my master's degree in political science from Empire University," he said proudly, "and here I am at the top of my profession, head of the UN whorehouse!"

At that moment there was a commotion at the door and two very disheveled men rushed in. Although their clothes were expensive looking, they were very crumpled.

"Where you been?" Vantagio shouted at them.

"We got here as fast as we could," said one. "At dawn that God (bleeped) Inspector Grafferty busted into our apartment and arrested us for vagrancy and littering. It took until just now for the shyster to bail us out!"

"It was a setup," said Vantagio. "Police Inspector Bulldog Grafferty," and he spat sideways on the carpet.

"He was right up the street waiting! He got you two gunsels out of the way so the Faustino mob could come in here and put the pressure on. If I'd refused and they'd have killed me, Grafferty was right on hand to prove they wasted me in self-defense. If this kid hadn't crashed the party, I'd be dead!" And he told them exactly what had happened and what Heller had done.

"Jesus!" said the two men in unison, looking at Heller.

"Now go down to the dry-cleaning room and get yourselves pressed up and get on duty. We can't have you looking like a couple of bums! This is a high-class joint!"

"Yes, Mr. Meretrici," they both said and rushed out.

"This really is a high-class joint," Vantagio repeated to Heller. "The UN crowd is funny. If they thought we pushed drugs, they'd be sure we were trying to bleed information out of them. No, sir. We stay with tradition. We serve bootleg booze. And booze and drugs don't mix, kid."

"Lethal," said Heller, doubtless remembering his book.

"Eh? Oh, right. You sure said it, kid. No gang wars in booze at all these days. And there's just as much money to be made in bootleg booze as there ever was in Prohibition. Did you know Federal taxes was ten bucks a fifth now? And it's more respectable. More traditional.

"Now, there are those that will tell you you can't have prostitution without having drugs. But that's baloney. The whores go silly. They get all dried up. They don't last two years. And they're an expensive investment! We have to train them, send them to Towers Modeling School and hygiene clinics as doctors' assistants and postgraduate them to an ex-Hong Kong whore. That's expensive. You can't amortize it fast enough. Internal

Revenue Service won't let you write off the investment that quick. So, no drugs, kid."

"No drugs," said Heller, probably thinking of Mary Schmeck.

"Right," said Vantagio. "The UN clientele would simply evaporate. And we'd have to pay off the DEA. We'd go bankrupt!"

"Well," said Heller. "I'm sorry I made a mistake. I'll be going now."

"No, no!" said Vantagio in alarm. "You saved my life. And even Clint Eastwood couldn't have beaten that gun play! You're handy to have around! Listen, business is slack—the UN isn't in session and it's summer and nobody's in town. You came for a room. There's two hundred rooms and suites in this building! I got a little room—it was once a maid's room—up on the second floor you can have."

"Well," said Heller, "if you'll let me pay for it."

"Pay? Well, how about you just sitting around the lobby now and then, two or three times a week maybe. For just an hour or two. I'll see you get some decent clothes."

I thought, no, no, Heller. He knows the Faustino mob saw you! He's just going to use you to scare them off!

He must have seen Heller was reluctant. "Look, kid. You're going to college. If you go to Empire, I can give you some steers and pointers. We don't have a restaurant but we have a kitchen that serves great food to rooms and you can get sandwiches. We can't serve you any booze because it's obvious you're a minor and it would be illegal. But you could have all the soft drinks you wanted. Listen. We'll even keep you from being embarrassed by the UN people thinking you're part of the help. We'll cook up some story about you being the son of a dictator or something incognito and living here to go to college."

It wasn't the danger I was worried about. I couldn't see how I could sneak Raht in there to rifle his baggage! Whorehouses go crazy when you try to rifle baggage. They think you're trying to roll the customers and get them in trouble with the police! And those gunsels had looked formidable! It would be like trying to reach Heller in jail!

I knew what was wrong with Vantagio. He was still in shock and overreacting with gratitude. Heller wasn't all that prepossessing!

"Now, this place is full of good-looking women," said Vantagio, "and a good-looking kid with muscles like yours will have them swarming at you. But you can always call one of the madames if they bother you. What say, kid? Is it a deal?"

"Do you have boys here?" said Heller.

"Cripes no!" exploded Vantagio. "That was just that dumb hood's idea. He's . . . was . . . gay. So how about it, kid?"

Heller barely started to nod when Vantagio was out of his seat and racing to the door. He peeked into the lobby. The stiff team and bodies were gone. The cleaning lady was mopping up the floor.

Vantagio said to the clerk, "Hit the buzzers." And shortly numerous staff began to drift in and then the elevators started going and numerous beautiful women in various stages of dishabille began to drift into the lobby. They were of all colors from all parts of the world, though white predominated. The lobby got pretty full of half-bare legs and half-exposed breasts.

Vantagio grabbed off Heller's cap and told him to stand up on a marble ledge. The sea of upturned lovely faces looked like the color plates of the porno and movie magazines had all gone into a mad shuffle. A montage of alluring beauties!

In a very commanding voice, Vantagio said, pointing at Heller, "This kid just saved my life. I want you to treat him decent."

A whoosh of pent-up breath sounded in the room and a concerted "Ooooo!" I couldn't understand it. What could they see in Heller? Then I realized it was off-season for them. Man-starved.

"He's going to live here," said Vantagio.

If the "Ooooo" was loud before, it doubled now, interspersed with some pants!

Oh, my Gods, I thought. If the Countess Krak could only see this!

"Now, listen," said Vantagio, raising his voice to be heard, "he's underage as you can plainly see. He's jail bait! And if he complains about anybody bothering him, out that (bleepch) goes!"

Mutters.

Vantagio shouted up to the balcony, "Mama Sesso! You hear that?"

A big, heavy-breasted woman, black-haired, muscular, mustached, shouted, "I'm here, Signore Meretrici!" And she came forward to the rail and looked down.

"As Chief Madame," shouted Vantagio, "you're going to see that enforced and that all the other madames enforce it!"

"I got it, Signore Meretrici. If they don't do what the young boy tells them, out they go."

"No, no, no!" cried Vantagio. "You're to keep them off him! He's a kid. Jail bait! They could get us on a morals charge!"

Mama Sesso nodded severely. "I a-got it, Signore Meretrici. I a-seen what the boy do on-a the close circuit TV. He save-a you life. He's-a faster than a-Cesare Borgia! He's a-good to have around. Maybe he save-a all-a our lives next. *La Santissima Vergine* send-a him. If they don' do right by the young boy, out-a they go!"

"Right!" said Vantagio.

Some madames swatted their palms together and the assemblage began to disperse, several sets of lovely eyes remaining reluctantly on Heller. Did they suppose, I thought disgustedly, that he was something to eat? He was far too young for their general taste!

A uniformed attendant came up and struggled with Heller's baggage. Heller helped him, and because the elevator was jammed, they walked up to the second floor on thickly carpeted stairs.

Vantagio led the way down a long hall and they came to a small room. It was plain but it was clean—almost sanitary. The iron bedstead was white and so was the chest of drawers. The bathroom was small but modern. All strictly utility.

"How's this?" said Vantagio.

"Fine," said Heller.

Some of the women had followed down the hall. But Vantagio peremptorily ordered them away. He got out some old cards and a ball point. Using the back of one, he wrote an address on it.

"Now, this," he said to Heller, "is a tall man's shop. You go out and buy yourself a summer suit you haven't grown out of. And get something besides baseball shoes! You got dough?"

"Lots," said Heller.

"Good. But you wash up and when you come down, bring any excess dough and I'll give you a small personal safe with your own combination. We want to keep this an honest house!" He left.

Heller stowed his things, washed up, checked the lock on his door and then went down with the fifty thousand in the paper sack his breakfast had come in.

Vantagio showed him the battery of private safes and

how to open one. It seemed UN people carried documents and things around they wanted stowed for the few hours they might be there.

Heller mastered how to change the combination and then changed it so fast I couldn't read it off! But it would be impossible to get near it or even get to his baggage. My interest in stealing it was purely academic. It punched through how protected he was now!

He left the Gracious Palms on foot, happy I suppose to have some exercise. I wasn't happy. He had more guns pointing at him now than I could easily count. The Faustino mob knew his face and he had killed three of their men, one of them maybe a lieutenant of the mob! And add in Police Inspector Grafferty. He had seen Heller face to face and cops remember things—that's their trade: mentally cataloguing who to shoot down next!

Shortly it did not help my morale a bit to receive the day's report of Raht and Terb. It read:

> Went to whorehouse and got (bleeped) and they
> stole his baggage. He's probably broke but
> seems safe.

I could have killed them!

Chapter 3

Miles from the UN area, and now in the garment district, Heller was clickety-clacking along, on his way to I knew not where but, if I knew Heller, up to no good.

It was evidently a hot midday in New York and people were slouching along, mopping their faces and carrying their coats over their arms. One would have thought that they would have glanced at Heller but New York is a peculiar place: practically nobody ever looks at anybody no matter what they are doing—including rape and murder. Even dead bodies can lie on the street until the sanitation department gets a complaint—and answers it if they happen to have any appropriation that month. So Heller was attracting no attention.

Wait! I was wrong!

Heller glanced back and I saw someone quickly turn. Was it Raht or Terb? I got the other screen working and stilled it. No, it wasn't Raht or Terb. It was too brief a glimpse to make it out. But someone had noted his departure.

They push delivery carts of racked clothes through the streets of the garment district at a mad pace and Heller was dodging these. He had come to a shop. The sign said:

TALL AND BIG MEN

Heller was shortly involved in trying to purchase something that fit. It was off-season—too late for summer clothes to be in demand, too soon for winter clothes—and because business was bad, the shop was dedicated to making it worse.

He found a dark blue suit of summer weight. He couldn't find a normal shirt—they all had collars of twenty-five or so inches and girths of sixty. Finally he located three drip-dry cotton ones. They had Eton collars! These are the kind the undergraduates wear in England!

The real tailor that did adjustments was on vacation

and the helper he had left behind botched the suit alteration. He adjusted the coat sleeves and pants cuffs too short again!

But Heller dressed anyway. He was now in dark blue with an Eton collar and he looked younger than ever!

He presented the store with the red-checked jacket and the blue-striped pants. And because those clothes were bugged, I bitterly surmised that Raht and Terb, who were depending on those bugs, would now stake out the tall man's shop!

He couldn't find any shoes he liked so he kept the baseball spikes on, popped his red baseball cap on the back of his head and was shortly engaged again in what seemed his favorite pastime: examining fenders of parked cars.

In peripheral vision, I saw the figure again. He was being tailed!

But Heller? Did he take evasive tactics? Run through a large store with two entrances? Dash into a crowd? Not Heller! He didn't even inspect the street behind him! Amateur!

He knelt down by the fender of a very modern car and bent it with his fingers—an easy thing for anybody to do. Then he looked around quickly to see if the unintentional act of vandalism had been noticed. Apparently to make sure he covered it up, he stood, turned, folded his arms and sort of lounged back against the fender. It really buckled!

He walked off. And then, abruptly, began the craziest series of actions I had yet seen him engage upon.

He caught a cab. Breathlessly, he said to the driver, "Quick! Take me to the bus terminal! Five-dollar tip!"

They went westward. No especially hurried ride. Heller got out at the Port Authority Bus Terminal and paid the driver.

Immediately, he got another cab. He leaped in and said urgently, "Quick! Take me to the Manhattan Air Terminal! I'm late! Five-dollar tip!"

Aha! I thought I understood at last! He had noticed the tail and was shaking it!

Cross-town rides are slow and it was very uneventful.

At the Manhattan Air Terminal, he paid the driver and got out.

Then Heller walked along a line of cabs, looking at their fenders. He found one with some bashes. It was a Really Red Cab Company hack.

Heller leaped in. "Quick! I have to be at Broadway and 52nd Street in two minutes and nineteen seconds. There's a five-dollar tip!"

Disregarding other drivers' protests that it was not his turn to go, the cabby zipped out of line, screamed into high gear. He cut a corner, bashed a car out of his way, ran a red light, sent a works-in-progress sign skyrocketing and stopped at Broadway and 52nd Street. Heller looked at his watch. It was two minutes!

Heller paid him the fare and the five-dollar tip.

AND THEN HELLER JUST SAT THERE IN THE CAB!

The driver, expecting Heller to rush out, looked at him in amazement.

"How would you like to teach me to drive in New York?" said Heller.

Oh, my Gods! Heller was not shaking a tail. He was trying to find a reckless cab driver! Heller was a hopeless idiot!

"I ain't got the time, buddy," said the driver.

"For a hundred bucks would you have the time?"
Silence.

"For two hundred bucks would you have the time?"
Silence.

Heller opened the cab door to get out.

The driver said, "I'm almost off shift! I'll race up to the barn, turn in and come back. You wait here. No. You come with me. I'll turn this wreck in and get a decent hack."

Promptly, driving rapidly, the cabby started for the Really Red Cab barn. "What's your name?" he shot back through the open glass partition.

"Clyde Barrow," said Heller.

I snorted. That was a famous gangster! Nothing was sacred to Heller!

"I see on the card here," said Heller, "that you're called Mortie Massacurovitch. Been driving cabs long?"

"Me?" said the cabby, glancing back at Heller without regard to a near collision. He was a very tough-looking oldster. "My old man was a hacker in this town and I learned how from him. In the last war, on the strength of it, they made me a tank driver."

"Get any medals?" said Heller.

"No. They sent me home—said I was too brutal to the enemy!"

Heller waited outside while the hacker turned his cab and receipts in. And suddenly it dawned on me what he was up to. He had believed that tale about it being too hard to drive in New York! He was going to bring the Cadillac into town!

Oh! No, no, no! There was no way to warn this naive simpleton! One of the things Bury would surely have done was to have that Cadillac rigged to explode! Bury had not wanted it to be near the planned murder of the bogus Rockecenter, Junior. But aside from that, it was strictly textbook that he would have it set to explode, particularly now that he had missed. Bury was the sort of man who did multiple planning and handled eventualities.

So I sat there helplessly while Heller, in a forthright fashion, industriously planned his own suicide!

Chapter 4

Shortly, Mortie Massacurovitch came out of the huge garage they called a barn. He beckoned and Heller went inside.

Way back in the corner, covered with dust, sat the remains of a cab. Most of the paint was off by reason of dents and scrapes. It still had its meter and its top taxi lights but it was a long way from a modern cab. It was sort of square, with no smooth gentle curves.

"Here," said Mortie, "is a *real* cab! It has real steel fenders, quarter of an inch thick. It has real bumpers with side bars and hooks. It has real bulletproof, nonshatter glass." He looked at it proudly. "They really used to build them! Not plaster and paper like today."

A passenger could ride with the driver in this one and Mortie wiped off the seat and got Heller in. Then the cabby got in. "Gives you the edge," he said. "My favorite cab!"

He got its oil and gas checked and off they went, back to town. And, in truth, there was nothing wrong with its motor. It seemed to have more acceleration than modern cabs in that it got away from lights way ahead of everybody. "Geared down for fast darts," said Mortie.

Heller learned how to handle the gear shift and clutch on a quiet street and Mortie, satisfied now on that score, took over. "Now, let's see, where is the traffic thickest this time of day?" He looked at his watch. "Ah, yeah. Grand Central Station." And off they roared.

It was creeping up to afternoon going-home time when they neared the area. The traffic was THICK! And fast!

"Now," said Mortie, "this is going to require your close attention because it is a very high art. People are basically yellow. They always give up before you do. So that leaves you a very wide scope."

Chattering along, naming each maneuver as he went, Mortie Massacurovitch performed.

It was horrifying!

They dashed between two cars to make the cars split each way! They squealed brakes to startle people "because honking was frowned upon." They swerved to make a car dodge away from its intended parking place and then stole it. They dove in ahead of another hailed cab and when the passenger tried to get in, told him the cab was engaged. They bashed backwards to widen a place to park. They bashed forward to get a place to park. They did a skid "to alarm a motorist, who then stamps on his brakes and you grab his place in line." They followed an ambulance to get somewhere quick. They followed a fire engine to really run the meter up fast, "but setting a fire ahead to get the engines to run is frowned on."

Heller then got under the wheel. He did all those things Mortie had done, with a few embellishments.

With bent fenders, raw voices and screams of anguish and terror strewn behind them, Mortie now guided Heller to a cabby bar on Eighth Avenue. It was a time of traffic lull and one had better have a sandwich.

Heller tried to order a beer and got scolded both by Mortie and the proprietor: "Trying to make the place lose its license?" So Heller had milk with his steak instead. "You got to have respect for the law, kid," Mortie told him. "Learn to grow up to be a good, peaceful, orderly, law-abiding citizen. That's the only way to get ahead.

"Got to get going!" said Mortie. "Time for theater traffic around Times Square."

En route, Mortie told him, "Now you got to learn how to handle police. When a cop stops you for speeding, you stop, see. You wait until he comes up and then you whisper, 'Run for your life. This fare is holding a gun on me.' And the cop will beat it every time!"

Heller thanked him.

"You got to know these things, kid." But something else had attracted Mortie's attention. "You got any enemies, kid? Your parents looking for you or something?"

"Why?"

"Well, it'd have to be you. I never made an enemy in my life. A cab started up behind us when we left the eatery and it's still back there."

Mortie did a right-angle turn, went down an alley, went wrong way on a one-way street. Looked back. "Don't see him now. I think we shook him. So we can get busy."

They were into the theater district. It was well before the evening start of the shows but the traffic was THICK!

"Now, you see that line of cars, kid? Watch!"

Mortie came up alongside of a cab in the line. He stopped. He screamed an insult at the driver. Mortie made a motion to get out of his cab. The other driver, in a rage, leaped out of his. Mortie didn't leave his cab. The line moved ahead. Mortie slid the cab into it, taking the place of the immobilized cab. "See, kid? Art!"

Mortie got to an intersection near a big hotel. There were several cabs and few customers. Mortie sailed in, skidding to block the exit of the driveway, and killed his engine. Other cabbies screamed at him. He screamed back, "I'm stalled!" As he was now first in line, an elderly, well-dressed man and woman tried to get into Mortie's cab. "Sorry," said Mortie, "I'm going to the barn." He drove off. "See, kid, I could have had my pick of fares. You got to know what you're doing and think, think, think all the time."

He raced down a line of traffic. A car looked like it was going to turn out and block him. He sideswiped it with a scream of metal. The car pulled hastily back. "Don't try it with limousines, kid. They're really yellow. Scared for their paint. You don't have to sideswipe. You just gesture, like this." He veered toward a limousine and it promptly climbed the curb.

The bright lights of theater marquees, the flashing advertising signs, the throngs and ticket lines. A lively, blazing night.

"Now, you see that car ahead there that's stopping. I'll show you how to take off doors."

The street side door swung open. The old cab was there before anyone could get out. There was a rending crash and off came the door.

"It's timing, kid. All timing. Now, you see that guy up the street waving for a fare? Over there on the wrong side for us?"

Mortie zoomed ahead to forty miles an hour, stamped on the brakes, did a hundred-and-eighty-degree turn and skidded sideways to the curb. The hopeful fare started to get in. "Sorry, we're heading for the barn," said Mortie.

He found a one-way street. They backed down it at forty miles an hour. "You see, we're pointed the right direction so it ain't illegal.

"See that red light? Now we're going to rush it. If

you listen you can hear the switch in the box and you can claim it was yellow.

"Now here is a curb bounce. That's a nice curb. If you hit it right, you can bounce back into the street and the guy that was about to pass you, thinking you was parking, gets sideswiped! Watch."

They bounced. There was a rending scream of metal. Headlight glass tinkled to the pavement.

"All right, kid. Now let's see you do it."

Heller took the wheel. He started up. He went through the routine. But just as he was about to rush a red light, the sound of a heavy thud shook the cab.

"What was that?" said Mortie. Then he pointed. The side window had a star. "Jesus, that's a bullet!"

Another thud!

"Get the hell out of here, kid! Somebody is breaking the firearms law!"

Heller was on his way!

He went down 42nd Street, headed west. He was not going very fast.

"Step on it, kid! A cab just came around the corner behind us!"

"You sure?" said Heller.

"Hell, yes! He's gaining!"

But Heller was loafing.

He was watching in the rearview mirror. Sure enough, there was a cab behind them, gaining!

A bullet hit the rear window!

"Now we can go!" said Heller.

He fled down 42nd Street.

He passed the Sheraton Motor Inn.

I grabbed a New York map to see if he was leaving the country.

The old cab negotiated the approaches to the West Side Elevated Highway. Traffic was light. Below them over the rail, the ground level street was dim. To their left lay the North River and the passenger steamship docks. Yes, on this route he could escape to Connecticut!

Heller checked the rearview mirror. The pursuing cab was still coming.

Below the elevated highway, to their right, the De Witt Clinton Park fled by and was gone.

Heller wasn't moving fast. The other was close behind!

A sign ahead and a split in the elevated highway: 55th Street!

Suddenly, with a yank of the wheel, Heller sent the cab into a ninety-degree right turn! He stamped on the brakes! The rail was right in front of him! The lower street was fifty feet down!

He was stopped!

The other cab was coming on.

Heller suddenly backed up!

There was room for the other cab to pass in front of his radiator. It started through the hole.

Heller sent his cab ahead!

The bumper hit the other cab's front wheels.

The other cab was punched over toward the rail!

With a shattering crash, it went through the guard!

It catapulted into space!

Chapter 5

Even before it hit the street below, Heller shouted to Mortie, "Take over!"

There was a crash below!

Heller was out. The rail was torn into jagged pickets where the cab had disappeared.

He peered down. There were girders and supports.

He went through the hole in the rail. He swarmed down a girder. He slid down a pillar and hit the lower street.

The other cab had landed on its wheels, shot ahead and struck a stanchion.

Gas was flooding the street!

A traffic light was nearby. Heller looked at the control box.

He raced over to the cab.

The doors were buckled.

He yanked a small jimmy out of his pocket and went to work on the rear door. The metal bent around the jammed lock. He inserted the jimmy higher and pried. He got his fingers in and, with a heave, got the door open.

He glanced at the spreading gasoline and then at the traffic light. Suddenly I knew why. Fumes, rising, would explode when they hit those control box switches! Like a bomb! I know bombs!

Heller had the driver out. Then he reached in and grabbed the man in the back.

Lugging two bodies, he sped over to the curb.

He looked back. He evidently decided he was not far enough. He went another fifty feet.

On the pavement, in the protection of a big concrete abutment, he laid the bodies out.

With a shattering blue crash, the wreck exploded!

The "cabby" was dead. But even though the top of his head was half off, he was obviously a Sicilian.

Heller turned to the other one.

The weird hue of the street light shone down upon the face of Torpedo Fiaccola!

The hit man's eyelids fluttered. He was still alive!

A squad car chortled in the distance. Nobody could have missed that blast for a mile!

Torpedo opened his eyes. He saw Heller. He recognized him.

Torpedo said, "You ain't going to kill my mother?"

Heller looked down at him. "I'll think about it."

"No!"

Heller reached into Torpedo's coat and took his wallet. The money was only the five thousand that Heller had given him back. But there was a slip of paper. It said:

> Valid with the evidence. Hand package to
> bearer.

Heller shook the paper at Torpedo. "Hand to who?"

Torpedo said, "You going to kill my mother?"

"I was thinking about it. Give me the name and address for this slip and I might reconsider."

The hood was blinking hard. Then he said, "Mamie. Apartment 18F. Two thirty-one Binetta Lane. Downtown."

"And the evidence?" said Heller.

"Look," moaned Torpedo, "Bury is going to kill me!"

Heller said, "Mothers should be cherished."

Torpedo shuddered. "Your baseball cap with blood on it and a lock of your hair."

Heller took off his cap, turned it wrong side out and swabbed it through the mess that had been the driver's head.

He said, "I hear an ambulance coming. Get yourself patched up in the hospital and then I'd advise you to take up residence at the North Pole." He bent over him and put the wallet and five thousand back in his pocket. "I

keep trying to give you this. Now take it and learn to
speak polar-bear. I'm not a mother killer but I sure enjoy
exploding torpedoes!"

The squad car had been drifting slowly closer, cautiously. The flames flickering from the wreck made a
shifting patchwork on it. The cops got out.

"How come you drug the bodies from the wreck,
kid?" said the first cop, threateningly.

"He just missed me," said Heller. "I wanted to give
him some advice."

"Oh," said the cop in sudden comprehension. "But
I'll have to give the driver a ticket all the same." He got
out his book and called to his partner. "What would you
say the charge was, Pete?"

"Littering," said the other cop.

"It's that one that was driving," said Heller. "He's
dead."

"Gets the ticket all the same," said the cop, writing.

The ambulance was whining up, probably called by
the cops earlier.

Mortie Massacurovitch had brought the old cab
down to the lower level. Heller got in. "Take me to 231
Binetta Lane."

"That's Little Italy," said Mortie. "Wrong time of
night. You got a gun?"

"I got another hundred," said Heller.

They zipped downtown. They went from Eleventh
Avenue to Tenth, shifted over on 14th Street, went down
Greenwich Avenue, worked their way around Washington Square and were soon in Little Italy. They stopped
across the street from the address. It was awfully dark.

Heller took out a knife, cut off a small lock of his
own hair and pasted it into the baseball cap with the
blood. Then he put the note in it.

He turned to Mortie. "Go to Apartment 18F and ask

for Mamie. Give her this and she'll give you a package."

"In there?" said Mortie, looking at the ominously dark building. "And when you return," said Heller, "I'll give you another hundred."

Mortie grabbed the cap and contents, leaped out, raced up the steps.

Three minutes later, he raced down the steps carrying a package. He threw it at Heller, started the car up and got out of there.

"Mamie was a man with a gun," said Mortie. "But he took it with no questions."

Heller told him to take him to the corner of First Avenue and 42nd Street. He shook the pack, listened to it and then sniffed it. Well, at last he was getting cautious for it well could have been a bomb. He pried up a corner and pulled something out.

"What's a first class ticket to...Buenos Aires, Argentina, worth?" he asked Mortie.

"I dunno," said Mortie. "Maybe three grand."

"Can you cash one in?"

"Oh, sure," said Mortie. "Just take it to the air terminal. What's the matter, ain't you going?"

Oh, if Heller only were!

Mortie let him out at First and 42nd. Heller said, "Now, do you think I really passed, or do I need more lessons?"

Mortie appeared to be thinking it over carefully. Then he said, "Well, kid, with experience you could become a top New York cabby. There's more I could teach you about shortchanging customers and running up extra meterage but, otherwise, that's about it. You pass. Yes, I'd say you pass."

Heller counted him out six one-hundred-dollar bills. He instantly stuffed the money in his shirt and drove away at high speed.

Heller trotted along, clickety-clack, and soon arrived at the Gracious Palms.

In his room he opened the pack. Money in small old bills!

He counted it. ONE HUNDRED THOUSAND DOLLARS!

I shuddered. My Gods, Bury must be angry to offer such a price!

Heller put it in the paper sack his breakfast had come in. He went down to the personal safes and put it in.

Vantagio was in his office and saw Heller through the open door. He called to him, "Getting out some money, kid? You'll need dough for school! Don't blow all you got on night life. This is an expensive town!"

"It sure is," said Heller, adding the hundred grand to his fifty thousand already in the safe. "Prices just keep going up!"

He went to bed and was shortly peacefully asleep.

I wasn't! Bury had unlimited funds and I didn't even have a clue on how to get that platen!

Some hours later, the next report of Raht and Terb didn't help. It said:

> He went to a place called the Tall Man's Shop and they must have given him a job and a place to sleep. He's still there! But we have our eyes on him.

The Hells they did! They were still spotting in on the bug we had sewn in his coat!

I was getting frightened that I might have to go to America myself to handle this. And I didn't have the least idea what I could do even if I did.

Chapter 6

Heller was up bright and early the following day, the viewer alarm blasting me out of a sodden sleep.

He was being very industrious and purposeful. He brushed his new suit where it had been messed up on the girders, put on a clean white shirt with an Eton collar, put a new baseball cap on the back of his head and then packed a shoulder-strap satchel which looked, for all the world, like one of these kiddy schoolbook bags.

In the bag he put a spool of fish line, a multihooked bass plug, a tool kit, a dozen baseballs, a roll of tape and the New Jersey license plates. Was he going fishing?

Down to the lobby he went. It was early for a whorehouse: the desk clerk was asleep, a guard in a tuxedo was reading the *Daily Racing Form,* ball point in hand, and an Arab sheik was wandering drunkenly around, apparently trying to choose amongst several throw rugs as to which would be best to use for morning prayer.

Heller counted ten thousand out of his personal safe and put it in his pockets. The Arab gave him a deep obeisance, Heller repeated the bow and hand motion exactly and presently was trotting down the street, clickety-clack.

He stopped at a deli and got breakfast in a sack, went out and found a cab.

"Weehawken, New Jersey," said Heller. "One way." And he gave the address of the garage where the Cadillac was!

"Double fare as you won' be comin' back," said the cabby.

I suddenly chilled. Up to then I had not grasped what Heller was going to do! He was on his way to get his car! Bury knew where that car was. It would be rigged! That "won't be coming back" was all too prophetic!

"Double fare," agreed Heller.

He had his sweet rolls and coffee as he rode along. They were soon across town. They dove into the Lincoln Tunnel and roared along under the Hudson River. They soon were in New Jersey and turned north on the J. F. Kennedy Boulevard.

They turned out of the roaring traffic to approach the garage. But one block away from it, Heller told the cab to stop and wait. The cabby looked at the decayed, semi-industrial neighborhood. "You mean wait *here?*" he asked.

Heller took a fifty-dollar bill, tore it in half and gave the driver half.

"I'll wait," said the cabby.

Heller got out and trotted around a corner en route to the garage. He stopped.

Trucks! Trucks! Trucks! The whole area in front of the huge, low building was jammed with trucks! Crews of men were unloading stacks of cartons onto handcarts and taking them into the building.

Heller went closer. He stood at the garage door and looked in. The place was being filled up with stacks of cartons higher than a man's head and in separate islands.

He moved a bit to see deeper in. The Cadillac was there. The license plates were missing.

There was something else going on. Voices. Heller shifted. He saw the plump young man and a burly monster dressed like a trucker. They were having a flaming argument.

"I don't care! I don't care!" the plump young man

was shouting. "You can't store that stuff in here. I don't care whose orders it is! You don't understand!" He half gestured toward the Cadillac and then didn't.

Abruptly I knew his dilemma. The crews were putting valuable stuff in a garage/warehouse with a car which was rigged! And the young man couldn't say why.

"We ain't clearing nothing back out!" said the burly man. "If you'd been here on time, we mighta listened. But it's too late now! This stuff stays! Besides, we get our orders just like you. I am not going to let some punk like you work my men's (bleeps) off just . . ."

The plump young man had seen Heller at the door. He stiffened. He turned and raced off to an exit in the back wall like the devil was after him. He vanished.

Heller quietly withdrew. He walked through the boil of men and handtrucks, turned the corner and got back in the cab.

"You got further to go," said Heller. "Take me to 136 Crystal Parkway, Bayonne."

The New York cabby had to look at a map. "This is foreign country," he explained. "It ain't as if you were still in civilization. This is New Jersey. And you can't ask directions. The natives lie!"

But soon they were headed south on J. F. Kennedy Boulevard, got through Union City, went under the Pulaski Skyway, passed St. Peter's College and roared along through the increased traffic of Jersey City. Docks and glimpses of the New York skyline could be seen.

"Is that a statue way over there in the water?" asked Heller pointing east.

"Jesus," said the cabby, "don't you recognize the Statue of Liberty? You should know your country, kid."

They went past the Jersey City State College and were soon in Bayonne. The New York cabby was shortly all tangled up. They got turned back from the Military

Ocean Terminal, got trapped into going to Staten Island, came back over the Bayonne Bridge—paying a toll both ways—and finally asked a native.

Ten minutes later they were in an isolated area of new high-rises and on a quiet street. Here was 136 Crystal Parkway, a very splendid building. A new condo.

Heller repaired the torn fifty and paid the driver off. "I don't know if I will ever find my way home," mourned the cabby.

Heller added a twenty. "Hire a native guide," he said.

The driver drove off.

All this time, I had been cudgeling my brains to remember where I had heard that address.

Heller walked in through a plush entrance. There were several elevators. One of them said:

Penthouse

He pushed the call button.

Expecting an automatic elevator, I was a bit surprised to see the door opened by a man. He was not an elevator operator. He wore a double-breasted coat and a hat pulled down. I could see the bulge of a shoulder-holstered gun. He was very dark, very Sicilian.

"Yeah?" he said noncommittally.

"I would like to see Mrs. Corleone," said Heller.

I freaked! He was calling on the head of the New Jersey Mafia!

"Yeah?"

"I saw Jimmy 'The Gutter' Tavilnasty recently," said Heller.

Then it all came to me with a flash. That meeting in Afyon when Jimmy, in the dark, had mistaken him for a DEA man! Well, they'd soon see through *that!* And I didn't have the platen!

"I.D.," demanded the gangster and Heller showed it to him.

The hood was on the elevator telephone. It was in a felt-lined box. You couldn't hear what was being said.

With a slit-eyed look at Heller, the hood frisked him lightly, inspected his bag and then gestured for him to get in.

They rode up to the top. It was a one-stop elevator, penthouse only. The hood opened the door and pushed Heller out ahead of him. With little punches from behind he directed him down a beautifully decorated hallway. He opened a door at the end and shoved Heller in.

It was a gorgeous room, all done in modern gold and beige. A vast picture window looked out over a vast park and a bay.

A woman was seated comfortably on a couch. She was wearing beige lounging pajamas of silk. She was blond with blue eyes. Her corn silk hair was in coiled braids that wound around the top of her head to make a sort of crown. She was about forty.

She laid down a glossy style magazine she had been reading and stood up.

My Gods, she was tall!

She looked at Heller and then walked across the room to him. She was at least four inches taller than Heller! An Amazon!

She was smiling. "And so you are a friend of dear Jimmy's," she said. "Don't be shy. He has often spoken of his friends in the younger street gangs. But you don't look like one of those." She had a sort of cooing, affected voice and a fake Park Avenue accent.

"I'm going to college," said Heller.

"Oh," she said in sudden understanding. "That is the smart thing to do these days. Do sit down. Jimmy's friends are always welcome here. Would you like something to drink?"

"It's a hot day," said Heller. "How about some beer?"

She wagged a finger at him, kittenishly. "Naughty. Really naughty. You realize that would be against the law." Then she raised her head and bellowed, "Gregorio!"

Almost instantly, a white-coated, very dark Italian popped in.

"Get the young gentleman some milk and bring me some seltzer water."

Gregorio was taken aback. "Milk? We ain't got any milk, Babe."

"Well, get out and get some God (bleeped) milk!" roared Babe Corleone. Then she ensconced herself again on the couch. In her sweet, cooing, affected Park Avenue voice she said, "And how is dear Jimmy?"

Heller only sat down when she did. He now had his cap on his knee. The courteous Fleet officer!

"He was just fine a few days ago," said Heller. "Seemed to be right on the job."

"Oh, that is so nice to hear," cooed Babe. "And nice of him to send word."

"And how is the family?" said Heller.

Ouch, I thought. The (bleeped) fool thought a "family" was a real family. In that country, on this planet, it means a Mafia mob!

She looked sad. "Not too well, I'm afraid. You see, dear 'Holy Joe'—how I miss him—was a man of tradition. He used to say, 'What was good enough for my father is good enough for me.' And he stuck with good, honest bootlegging and smuggling and such. And, of course, we have to respect that. And drugs are no good anyway."

"They sure aren't!" said Heller with conviction.

She looked at him with approval. Then she continued. "Since Faustino 'The Noose' Narcotici has gotten so much backing from upstairs, there's no holding him. He has been muscling in on our New York interests and is even trying to push his way into New Jersey. When they wasted dear 'Holy Joe,' that was just the beginning of it. But," she looked up with sad bravery, "we are trying to carry on."

"Oh, I'm sure you'll succeed," said Heller politely.

"That's very nice of you to say so, Jerome. I can call you Jerome, can't I? Everyone calls me Babe."

"Certainly, Mrs. Corleone," said Heller. Fleet manners. And then, for a moment, I thought he'd blown it. "Mrs. Corleone, do you mind if I ask you a personal question?"

"Go ahead," she said. Was she a trifle wary?

"Are you a Caucasian?"

Oh, my Gods! Here he went on that (bleeped) fool Prince Caucalsia kick! She had blond hair, she was as tall as some women around Atalanta, Manco.

"What makes you ask?"

"It's your head," said Heller. "It is very beautiful and it has a long skull structure."

"Oh!" she said. "Are you interested in genealogy?"

"I've studied it a bit."

"Ah! College, of course!" And she rushed over to an ornate desk, opened it and got out a large chart and some papers. She pulled up a chair beside Heller and spread the papers out. "These," she said impressively, "were specially drawn up for me by Professor Stringer! He is the world's foremost expert on genealogy and family trees!"

Aha! I knew already about the fixation American women have on family trees! And this Stringer was probably making a fortune out of the racket.

She gestured at Heller. She had the Italian habit of talking with her hands, head and body. "You have no idea how prejudiced some people are! I was a famous actress at the Roxy Theater when dear Joe married me." The memory broke her train of thought for a moment and her eyes went moist.

Oho! I spotted her now. One of the Roxy chorus girls! A chorus line is composed of girls that are six feet six.

She recovered. "A *capo* is supposed to marry a Sicilian girl and the old cats carped and meowed and criticized. Particularly the mayor's wife. So dear Joe had this drawn up. And did it put them in their places! I keep it around to make the (bleepches) stay there!"

She spread out the chart. It was all scrolls and swirls and illuminated with little pictures. It was in the shape of a tree.

"Now," lectured Babe impressively, "as a student you are undoubtedly aware of all this but I will go over it anyway. Reviewing one's studies is a good thing. Now, the Nordic race is composed of the Caspian, Mediterranean and Proto-Negroid types. . . ."

"Caspian?" said Heller. "That's the sea over by the Caucasus."

"Oh, right," she said vaguely and then plunged on with energy. "Now, you can see here how the Germanic races came out of Asia and migrated. The Goths, via Germany, came down into Northern Italy in the fifth century and the Lombards in the sixth century. These are the dolichocephalic—means long-headed, which is to say, smart—elements in the Italian population. They are blond and tall." My Gods, had somebody rehearsed *her!* She was probably quoting Professor Stringer, word for word!

"Trace this line here. These are the Franks. From

Germany, they came down and took over France, which
is named after them. That was in the fifth century. Now,
one branch—trace this—the Salians, took over northern
Italy. One of the Salians, in the ninth century, was
emperor of all the Franks and Holy Roman Emperor
besides. He was named, you see here, Carolus Magnus,
which, in American, means Charles the Great. In history books he is called Charlemagne. He was the
emperor of the whole God (bleeped) world!"

She stopped and looked impressively at Heller. He
nodded. She went on. "Now, Charlemagne had quite a
few marriages. And he married—that's this line here—
the daughter of the Duke d'Aosta. That means 'of' Aosta
and that's a province in northwest Italy just south of
Lake Geneva.

"There are blond and tall Italians clear across northern Italy but they are *thick* in the Valle d'Aosta.

"Now, follow this line here. From the Duke d'Aosta
we come right down to Biella, which was my father's
name. You still with me, kid?"

"Oh, yes, indeed," said Heller in a fascinated voice.

"All right. Now, at the start of World War II, my parents fled to Sicily. They stayed in Sicily four whole
years! At the end of the war, they emigrated to America
and that's where I was born. So," and she drew up in
triumph, "I'm just as Sicilian as any of them! What do
you think of that?"

"Complete proof!" said Heller.

Babe flipped a finger at the chart. "And, further-
more, I am a direct descendant of Charlemagne! Oh,"
she gloated, "the mayor's wife went absolutely *green* with
envy!"

"I can see why she would!" said Heller. "But wait.
There's something that's not here. That maybe you don't
know. You ever hear of Atalanta?"

"I never been to Atlanta."

"No, At*a*lanta," said Heller. "Now, at the beginning of this tree, a lot earlier than it starts here, there was a prince."

This had her attention. And it sure had mine! Code break! He was about to be carried away with his stupid enthusiasm for Folk Legend 894M. I reached for my pen.

"His name," said Heller, "was Prince Caucalsia. He..."

From the door came a piercing, *"Pssst!"*

Babe and Heller turned toward it.

There was a Sicilian there. He was holding a large money sack. He had come halfway through the door and was bending over, beckoning urgently to Babe Corleone. His face. I had seen his face! I was trying to place it!

Babe went over and bent down. The Sicilian stood on tiptoe to reach her ear. He was urgently pointing toward Heller. I could not hear what he was whispering. She shook her head, negatively, a bit puzzled. Then he whispered and seemed triumphant.

The woman's eyes shot open. She stood up. She turned and stamped across the room to Heller. She seized him!

Then she pushed him off, holding him by the shoulders. She stared at him as though memorizing his face. Then she whirled. In a voice that could have knocked the walls down, she said, "Where the hell is that Geovani?"

Geovani was right there. The hood that had brought Heller up in the elevator.

"Why the hell didn't you tell me this was *that* kid?" she thundered.

There were other faces in the door. Scared!

"Here I been treating him like dirt!" She turned. She pushed Heller down into an easy chair. "Why," she pleaded, "didn't you tell me you were the one that saved our Gracious Palms?"

I could hear Heller swallow. "I . . . I didn't know it was yours."

"Hell, yes, kid! We own and control the fanciest cat houses in New York and New Jersey! Who else?"

Gregorio, glasses shaking, belatedly walked in with the milk and seltzer.

"To hell with that," said Babe. "This kid wants beer, he can have beer! To hell with the illegality!"

"No, no," said Heller. "I've really got to be going." He thought for a moment. "You can tell me where to find Bang-Bang Rimbombo. I think I've got car trouble."

So *that* was why he had walked in on the Corleone mob!

Suddenly, it all added up. He had read of Bang-Bang in the papers, knew he was part of the Corleone mob. He had Babe's address from Jimmy "The Gutter" Tavilnasty. To find himself an expert car bomber, he had simply gone to Babe's. Very, very smart detective work at locating somebody.

But wait! He had shown himself at that garage! They would be waiting for him when he came back there. Very, very dumb!

Heller was going to drive me crazy yet! He was too brightly stupid to live!

Babe turned to the people inside the door. They were whispering to each other and pointing at Heller and trying to get a better look at him. "Geovani, get out the limo and run this young gentleman over to Bang-Bang's. Tell him I said to do what the kid wants."

She turned back to Heller. "Look, kid, anything you want, you let Babe know, see?" She turned to the staff. "You hear that? And you, Consalvo, I want a word with you." She was pointing at the one who had identified Heller.

I suddenly remembered who the Sicilian with the money sack was. He was the clerk at the Gracious Palms! Trying to keep up with Heller was exhausting me, spoiling my recall for faces even.

Heller took his leave. Babe bent down and gave him a big kiss on the cheek. "Come back any time, you dear boy. You dear, dear boy!"

Chapter 7

Heller sat in the front seat of the limousine with the hood, Geovani, driving.

"You really wasted them punks just like that!" said Geovani in a voice of awe. "Did you know one of them was Faustino's nephew?" He drove for a while and then, taking his hand off the steering wheel, he made a gun out of his fingers and, pointing at the road, made the motions of firing and said, "Blowie! Blowie! Blowie! Just like that! Wow!"

They drew up in front of a down-at-the-heels apartment house. Geovani led Heller up to the second floor and knocked on a door, a code signal. A girl's face came out through the door crack. "Oh, it's you." She opened it wider. "For you, Bang-Bang."

Bang-Bang Rimbombo was in bed with another girl.

"Come on," said Geovani.

"Hell, I just got sprung!" protested Bang-Bang. "I ain't had any for six months!"

"Babe says you go."

Bang-Bang was out of bed in a flash. He struggled into his clothes.

"Car job," said Geovani. "This kid will show you."

"I'll get my things," said Bang-Bang.

Geovani used the phone and called a cab. Waiting, he covered the phone. "We never use the limo for wet jobs," he said apologetically. "And we control the cab companies. They don't talk."

Shortly, Geovani shook Heller's hand and left. Halfway down the hall he turned and made a pistol out of his fingers again. "Blowie! Blowie! Blowie!" he said. "Just like that!" He was gone.

The cab arrived and Bang-Bang, dragging a big bag, got in. Heller followed him. Heller gave an address a block away from the garage.

He was learning, but he was not really up on this tradecraft. They would be alerted. I knew he was going into a battle. And I didn't have that platen. Short of sleep, haggard, I hung on the viewscreen. He had my life in his hands!

Heller paid the cab off and walked around the corner toward the garage.

"Wait," said Bang-Bang. He was a very narrow-faced little Sicilian. He looked pretty smart. Maybe he had sense enough, I hoped, to keep them out of trouble. "If that's the place," he said, "I know it. It's a garage Faustino uses to repaint stolen cars and other things. You sure you know what you're doing, kid?" He shook his head. "Sneaking in there to rig a car for a blitz is a little bit steep."

"It's my car and I want you to unrig it," said Heller.

"Oh, that's different," said Bang-Bang. He hefted his heavy shoulder bag and approached the garage.

The door was locked on the outside with a big padlock. Heller put his ear to the wall and listened. Then he shook his head. He went around the building and checked the back door. It, too, was locked with a padlock. He returned to the front. He stood back and saw that there was a window beside the front door, about six feet from ground level.

He took out a tiny tool, inserted it in the padlock, fished it, and almost at once had it open.

Heller was moving very fast, very efficiently. It was so much in contrast with his sloppy disregard for routine espionage that I had forgotten for some time what he actually was. I was looking at a combat engineer. Getting into an enemy fort was something they did with a yawn. He was in the field of his own tradecraft!

He opened the entry port of the front door, swished his hand around to make sure, probably, there were no trip wires and then stepped inside, placing his feet to avoid where feet would normally step—probably to avoid mines.

He got a box and put it under the window, stood on it and undid the latch.

He returned to the door, beckoned to Bang-Bang to enter. Then Heller went outside. He carefully relocked the padlock, just as it had been.

Heller went to the outside of the window, lifted it and entered the building. He closed the window carefully. Now, to all intents and purposes, anyone approaching from the outside would have no sign that anyone was inside. Clever. I would have to remember how to do that.

The whole interior was stacked with islands of cartons, leaving only aisles and room to drive a car down the center. And it was these cartons which were getting Bang-Bang's attention.

"Well, I'll be a son of a (bleepch)," said Bang-Ban "Will you look at this!" He had pried a carton open an. was holding a bottle. "Johnnie Walker Gold Label!

Look, kid. I heard of it but I never seen any." In the dimness he must have seen that Heller wasn't tracking. "Y'see, there's red label and there's black label and you can get that easy. But gold label, they keep only for Scotland or sometimes export it to Hong Kong. It's worth forty bucks a bottle!"

He looked at the cap. "No revenue seals! Smuggled!" He got the cap off adroitly to hide signs of opening. He touched his tongue to the top and tilted it.

Heller's hand tilted the bottle back, vertical.

"No, no," said Bang-Bang. "I never drink on duty." He rolled the drop around on his tongue. "It ain't fake! Smooth!" He put the top back on and restored it to the carton. Then he began to make an estimate of the number of cases, walking about. The islands were piled nearly to the ceiling and the garage/warehouse was big.

"Jesus!" said Bang-Bang, "there's close to two thousand cases in here. That's..." he was trying to add it up. "Twelve to the case and forty dollars..."

"Million dollars," said Heller.

"A million dollars," said Bang-Bang, abstractedly. He went deeper into the building. "Hey! Look at this." He had his hand on some differently shaped cases. He expertly pried up a lid with a knife and hauled out a small box. "Miniature wrist recorders from Taiwan! Must be..." he was counting, ". . . five thousand of them here. Two hundred dollars apiece wholesale..."

"A million dollars," said Heller.

"A million dollars," said Bang-Bang. Then he planted his feet and glared down the widest aisle. "Well, God (bleep) me! You know what that son of a (bleepch) Faustino is trying to do? He's trying to cut in on our smuggling! The (bleepard)! He's trying to muscle in on us! He's going to flood the market and drive us out of business! God (bleep)! Oh, when Babe hears about this, she is going to be livid!"

He stood and thought. "It's that crook Oozopopolis!"

"Can we get on with this car?" said Heller.

Bang-Bang was promptly all business. "Don't touch it!"

The Cadillac was sitting apparently where Heller had parked it. The license plates had been removed. The light was very bad there.

Bang-Bang got out a torch. Keeping his hands off the car, he gingerly slid under it. He was looking at the springs. "They sometimes put it under the leaves so when the car tilts, off it goes. Nope. Now for the . . . oh, for Christ's sakes!"

Heller was kneeling down watching Bang-Bang under the car. Bang-Bang seemed to be working on the inside of a wheel. His hand emerged and he tossed something to Heller who caught it. A stick of dynamite!

Bang-Bang was working on another wheel. He tossed up another stick of dynamite. Heller caught it. Bang-Bang, scrambling around, shortly tossed a third and then a fourth stick to Heller. After playing his light around further underneath, Bang-Bang emerged.

"Cut-rate job," said Bang-Bang. "There was a stick taped vertically to the inside of each wheel. Dynamite of this type is just sawdust and soup. The soup is usually spread all through the sawdust and is safe to handle unless concentrated."

"Soup?" asked Heller.

"Nitroglycerine," said Bang-Bang. "It explodes when you jar it. This car was rigged to blow up miles from here! As the wheels spun, the centrifugal force would make the soup move from the stick as a whole and concentrate at just one end. Then an extra bump on the road and BOOM! Cut-rate. They saved the expense of detonators! Cheap-o!" he added with scorn.

"But maybe these were placed just to be found," said Heller, "and the real charge is still in there somewhere."

"So these could have been decoys and the real charge is still in there somewhere," said Bang-Bang.

He passed a very thin blade down through the window slit to make sure there was no trip wire and then opened the door. He looked under the panel. Nothing. He opened the hood. He looked back of the motor.

"Aha!" said Bang-Bang. "A cable job!" In a gingerly fashion he slid a matchbook cover between two contact points. Then he snipped some wires. Shortly he fished up a revolution counter.

"A second odometer!" he said. "The speedometer cable was taken off the back and put to this thing." He was spinning its wheels. It suddenly went click. He read the numbers. "Five miles! It was set to go five miles from here." He peered back down behind the motor. "Jesus! Ten pounds of gelignite! Wow, did they blow dough on setting this up! Somebody is big bucks mad at you, kid! That's enough to blow up ten——"

"Shh!" said Heller.

A car was coming!

Hurriedly, Bang-Bang closed the hood and door. Heller dragged him to a point about fifteen feet from the main entrance and back between two stacks of boxes.

The car stopped.

Bang-Bang whispered, "You got a gun?"

Heller shook his head.

"Me neither! It's illegal to carry a gun on parole." He shifted his heavy sack of explosives. "I don't dare throw a bomb in all this whisky. We'd go up like a torch!"

"Shh!" said Heller.

A car door closed. "I'll put the car around back," somebody said.

Silence.

A car door slammed in the back of the building. Footsteps going around. Then, in front, "The door's still locked back there."

"I told you," said a new voice. "There ain't nobody here."

A rattle of keys. "You just got the jumps, Chumpy. He's probably still running."

"Anybody could have come in the time it took you!" It was the plump young man. He backed in. The door opened inward more widely.

Two men in expensive-looking clothes followed him through. "We came as fast as we could. Jesus, you don't get from Queens to here in five minutes. Not in this traffic! See, there's nobody here! Waste of time."

"He'll be back!" said Chumpy. "He's a mean (bleep-ard)! If you don't do nothing, I'm going to call Faustino!"

The other man said, "Look, Dum-Dum, it won't do any harm to wait around for a while. Jesus, after all that drive. Tell you what. Leave the door unlocked and a tiny bit ajar, kind of inviting, and then we'll go over and sit down behind those boxes opposite and wait. Jesus, I got to catch my breath. All those God (bleeped) trucks!"

He left the door ajar. Chumpy, getting out a burp gun, went over and sat down on the floor back of an island of boxes, in profile and in full view of Heller. I went cold. Then I realized Heller was looking through a slit between two cartons.

The other two disappeared behind the island opposite the door.

"Don't shoot toward that old car in the back!" said Chumpy. "It's a walking boom factory!"

"Shut up, Chumpy," said one of the men. "We'll give it an hour. So you just shut up."

Heller looked down and slipped out of his shoes. He moved sideways until he could see the door. It was very dark right near it, the effect heightened by the slit of light coming through the ajar door.

He was fishing in his satchel. He got out the fish line. He got out the multihooked bass plug. He tied the line to the eye of the plug.

My hair felt like it was going to leave my head! This (bleeping) fool was going to try something! Bullets flying into that whisky or near that car would turn the place into an inferno! All he had to do was wait for an hour and they'd leave! The idiot!

He was coiling the fish line in big, loose loops around his left hand. He took the end he had fastened the bass plug to. He began to swing the plug back and forth.

With a toss he sent the plug sailing through the dimness toward the door! At an exact instant, he tugged it back.

There was a tiny thunk.

There was a rustle from behind the island of boxes where the men were hidden.

Heller slowly began to take in the slack. The line was nearly invisible. I could not make it out.

He shifted the sack on his shoulder and opened it. He shifted the line to his left hand.

He yanked the line!

The door came open with a crash!

There was a sizzling sound and a thud!

Heller had heaved a baseball at Chumpy!

Through the slit, I could see Chumpy fold up, motionless.

Silence.

Minutes.

"(Bleep)," said one of the men. "It was just the wind."

"Go close it!" said the other.

Through a slit, Heller was watching. A man, gun in hand, crossed the open place toward the door.

There was a sizzle and crack!

Heller had thrown another baseball!

The man jarred sideways. He fell and lay still.

"What the hell? . . ."

Heller threw again. The baseball hit the far wall and rebounded. He was throwing at the sound! With a bank shot!

Heller threw again!

There was a scramble. The man raced out the rear opening in the island and raced toward the back door! Stupid. It was locked!

The man raised his gun to blow off the lock.

Heller threw!

The man was hurled against the door. He slumped.

Heller casually walked to the front door and closed it.

Bang-Bang, more practical, raced to the last man and grabbed the gun. Then he raced from one to the other. He came back to Heller. "Jesus Christ! Their skulls is smashed in. They're dead!"

"Get the rest of the explosives out of that Cadillac," said Heller. "We got to get to work now."

Chapter 8

Heller fished the car keys out of a dead man's pocket, opened the full building door wide open, found the hood's car in the back. It was an old Buick sedan.

He drove it in and closed the full doors again. Then he inched it down the narrow aisle between the islands of cartons and brought it to a halt beside the Cadillac.

Bang-Bang was just finishing. He was sniffing at the oil dipstick. "No additives in the crankcase." He put the dipstick back. "There was no sugar in the gas—no other tricks. And there's the gelignite." He pointed to where it was perched on a window ledge rather precariously.

He went into the Cadillac rear interior, probing the seats. Then he said, "Oh, look! Draw curtains!" He promptly pulled them all down.

Bang-Bang went to a pile of cartons, got one and lugged it to the Cadillac and put it in the back. Then he went and got another one. As he worked, he began to sing softly:

> *There once was a con who was awful, awful dry.*
> *Sing, sing them Sing Sing blues.*
> *He tried from the guard a little drink to buy.*
> *Sing, sing them Sing Sing blues.*
> *He tried from the warden saying thirst will make me cry.*
> *Sing, sing them Sing Sing blues.*
> *He even wrote the governor his thirst to satisfy.*
> *Sing, sing them Sing Sing blues.*
> *He even begged the president, I will not tell a lie.*
> *Sing, sing them Sing Sing blues.*
> *But none of them would tell him how he could qualify.*
> *Sing, sing them Sing Sing blues.*

He sang on and on. He was absolutely jamming the back of the Cadillac with whisky cases. Then he got Heller to open the trunk and he piled it full of boxes of miniature wrist recorders. He went back and looked into the rear seat area of the Cadillac again. He juggled it around so there would be more room. He went and got two more whisky cartons.

So he prays each night unto the Lord his thirst to gratify.
     Sing, sing them Sing Sing blues.
And drown him in a tub of gin, if he has to die!
     Sing, sing them Sing Sing blues!

With one last shove, he managed to get the rear door closed.

Heller had been working industriously. He had put the Buick's plates on the Cadillac. Then he had the hood of the Buick open. He piled the gelignite on top of the Buick's motor. He went and got a dead man's revolver and made sure that there was a live cartridge under the pin when it was cocked. He took some of his tape and then taped the weapon, pointed at the gelignite, to the Buick's cowling.

Heller got in the Cadillac and drove it to the main door, opened it and then drove outside. "Wait in the car," he said to Bang-Bang. And Bang-Bang went out and got in, petting the whisky cartons.

Heller went back in. He closed the main door and its entry port. He found the bass plug and hooked it into the top inside edge of the door. He ran the fish line over a nail and then unreeled it all the way back to the Buick. Then, very gingerly, he tightened the fish line and tied it to the cocked trigger of the revolver.

Then he did something very odd. He took two blank pieces of paper and laid them on the seat of the Buick.

He looked around the garage. He found a heavy iron jimmy.

Starting near the Buick, he raced down the rows of cartons; smash right, smash left. The crash of glass and the gurgle of whisky followed in his wake.

Heller climbed out the window, made it secure so it didn't look like it had been touched. Then he gently closed the padlock on its hasp.

He got in the Cadillac.

"You booby-trapped it, didn't you?" said Bang-Bang.

Heller didn't answer.

Heller drove up the street six blocks. There was a hamburger stand there and an outside pay phone. He got out. He went into the phone booth. From his pocket he took a handful of change. Then from another pocket, he took a card.

Swindle and Crouch!

He deposited coins and dialed.

A telephonist at the other end simply repeated the number for an answer.

In a high-pitched voice, Heller said, "I got to speak to Mr. Bury."

The telephonist said, "I am SOR-ree. Mr. Bury left for Moscow this morning to join Mr. Rockecenter. WHOM shall I say CAlled?"

Heller hung up. "Blast!" he said in Voltarian.

Bang-Bang was near the phone booth. "You look like the sky fell in."

"It did," said Heller. "There was a guy made a bargain. This is twice he didn't keep it. He doesn't have any sense of honor or decency at all! Won't keep his word."

"So that's who the booby trap was for," said Bang-Bang.

"Yes. I was going to tell him some papers had been left in a car. He would have been over here by airbus in ten blinks of an eye." He sighed. Then he said, "Well, I guess I better go back and undo the booby trap."

"Why?" demanded Bang-Bang.

"Some innocent person could come along and get killed," said Heller.

Bang-Bang was looking at him in round-eyed astonishment. "What's that got to do with it?"

And I could certainly agree with Bang-Bang. Heller with his scruples. Far too nice. I scoffed aloud at the viewscreen.

"I don't just run around killing people, you know," said Heller. "We're not at war!"

Code break! He'd be telling this gangster about the threatened invasion next.

"Oh, the hell we aren't!" said Bang-Bang. "It's war flat-out! That Faustino is pushing our backs straight against the wall. Don't go wasting a booby trap!"

"I suppose you mean we should phone Faustino," said Heller.

"No, no, no. He'd never cross the river to Jersey. But I got a real candidate! A turncoat!"

"Somebody who is dishonorable?" said Heller. "Somebody who double-deals?"

"You said it! I got somebody who really deserves it! A filthy, boozing, two-timing crooked crook!"

"You sure?" said Heller.

"Of course I'm sure. There's no crookeder rummy drunk on the whole planet."

"Ah, a 'drunk,'" said Heller. "What's his name?"

"Oozopopolis!"

Heller shrugged, Bang-Bang took it as assent. He got his satchel from the car and sped into the booth closing it.

Through the glass door, Heller watched Bang-Bang wad a rag around the mouthpiece. Then he took a rubber glove out of his satchel and put the cuff over the rag and mouthpiece. Then he took a small tape recorder out of his satchel and turned it on. Faintly, the sound came out of the telephone booth. It was planes taking off.

At least this Bang-Bang knew some tradecraft. He was messing up his voice pattern and, with the planes, was mislocating the source of the call to some airport.

Bang-Bang spoke briefly into the phone and then hung up. Yes, he did know some tradecraft. His call had been too short to trace.

He recovered his gear and went back to the car window. "Like a hamburger?" he said.

Heller shook his head. Bang-Bang dove into the joint and the girl there began to fry a hamburger in a leisurely fashion.

My toes curled! Tradecraft be (bleeped)! After you make a sensitive call, you don't hang around the phone booth!

Then I reviewed the rest of it. The car they'd left in there had motor numbers. It was a different make even! If it blew up, nobody would be fooled!

Heller's tradecraft might be good in its place—getting into forts and blowing them up. But shortly after, in his profession, he would be out in space and not on the planet!

They were howling amateurs!

Six blocks down the street, the garage was in full view!

Heller said, "There'll be concussion." He turned the Cadillac around so that it faced the blast more squarely.

Bang-Bang came out with a hamburger and a beer. "You sure you don't want one?" said Bang-Bang. But again, Heller shook his head.

Bang-Bang settled down and began to eat. "He lapped it up," he said. "I told him in Greek—I was raised in old Hell's Kitchen and that's gone Greek. Otherwise he wouldn't have believed me."

"What was his name again?" said Heller.

"Oozopopolis. About a year ago, he stopped taking bribes from us, changed his coat and started taking them from Faustino. And he's been hitting at us ever since."

He took another bite of hamburger. "I told him a couple of the Atlantic City mob had been seen looting Faustino's liquor right down at that address and they were inside stealing the place blind with the outside door locked. Wouldn't do to get the name Corleone mixed up in it. He sure leaped at it."

Bang-Bang finished his hamburger and washed it down with beer. He then passed the time by filling Heller in on mob politics.

After a while there was a roar of cars.

Three sedans went streaking by. The seats were full. "You can tell they're government men, all right," said Bang-Bang. "The way they carry those riot shotguns. Did you see Oozopopolis? He was the big fat slob in the front seat of the second car."

The three cars raced the last six blocks and drew to a skidding halt in front of the garage, a reeking bomb of gelignite and alcohol fumes.

Men bailed out, guns ready and threatening.

"Come on out of there! We got you covered!" drifted faintly up the street.

Then a very fat figure raced forward and slammed the flat of his foot against the door.

There was a tremendous flash!

Blue flame and red battered the street!

A fireball bloomed!

The concussion and sound hit the Cadillac! It recoiled and then rocked!

Through the smoke and falling debris six blocks away one could see the strewn bodies.

Heller turned the Cadillac around. "Who was this Oozopopolis?"

"He was the New Jersey district head of BAFT. That's the U.S. Treasury Department Bureau of Alcohol, Firearms and Tobacco. The Revenooers. The dirty turncoats. Aside from changing sides on us, it was Oozo-popolis that planted a machine gun on me and got me sent up."

Bang-Bang was smiling happily. "Oh, my! Babe certainly will be pleased. Not only did we cost Faustino two million bucks, but we also got rid of the Feds! And it's about time she got some breaks, let me tell you!"

They wended their way through the fire engines now charging toward the sky-leaping conflagration.

PART SEVENTEEN

Chapter 1

Heller drove north. He patted the car's windshield ledge. He said, "Well, you chemical-engined Cadillac Brougham Coupe d'Elegance, we got you out of that free and clear."

I sneered, Fleet officers and their toys. Fetish worship!

Bang-Bang Rimbombo said, "Hey, kid. While in this moment of glory I don't want to spoil things, I got to point out you are driving on stolen plates and that's illegal!"

"I've got another set of plates, registration card and everything," said Heller.

"Where'd you get them?"

"Why, from that guy I was going to call."

"The one you wanted to bump? Listen, kid, there's a lot you got to learn. The fuzz runs on car plates. If they didn't have plates, they couldn't trace nobody. They'd be lost. Their whole system is founded on license numbers. So, if you got dough, I'd advise you to buy a new car. I know a guy..."

"No, I want this one," said Heller.

"But it's a gas hog!" said Bang-Bang.

"I know," said Heller. "I need it."

Bang-Bang sighed. "All right, I know another guy that can change its motor numbers and get a new license. I owe you. I don't wanta see you get pinched! Turn left right up ahead onto Tonnelle Avenue. We're going to Newark!"

They were soon amongst the roar of trucks and gas fumes and, with Bang-Bang's direction, came to Newark, drove down numerous side streets amongst numerous light and heavy industries but only in heavy polluted air and came at length to the Jiffy-Spiffy Garage. They threaded their way amongst numerous vehicles in various stages of repair and painting.

Bang-Bang leaped out and shortly came back with a portly, greasy Italian in a white foreman's coat. Heller got out.

"Kid," said Bang-Bang, "this is Mike Mutazione, the owner, proprietor and big noise of this joint. I told him you was a friend of the family. So, tell him what you want."

Heller and the man shook hands. "Maybe he better tell me," said Heller.

Mike looked over the Cadillac. "Well," he said, "the first thing I would do is run it into the river."

"Oh, no!" said Heller. "It's a good car!"

"It's a gas hog," said Mike. "A 1968 Cadillac only gets about ten miles to the gallon."

"That's what I like about it," said Heller.

Mike turned to Bang-Bang. "Is this kid crazy?"

"No, no!" said Bang-Bang. "He's a college kid."

"Oh, that explains it," said Mike.

Bang-Bang was hastily tearing something inside the car. He came out with a bottle of Scotch.

"What the hell is this?" said Mike. "Gold Label? I never seen none of this before."

Bang-Bang wrestled off the top. "It's so good the Scots guzzle the whole supply of it themselves. Have a gulp."

"You sure it ain't poison?" He cautiously took a little. He rolled it around on his tongue. "My God, that's smooth! I ain't never tasted anything like that."

"Just off the boat," said Bang-Bang. "We brung you a whole case of it."

"Now, as I was saying, kid," said Mike, "let's look over this beautiful car." Gripping the bottle tenaciously, he raised the hood with the other hand. He got out a flashlight. He was looking at the engine block. Then he shook his head sadly. "Kid, I got bad news. That engine number has been changed too often. And the last ones that did it scored it too deep. It can't be done again."

He stood there. "Aw, don't look so downcast, kid. You must have sentimental attachments for this car. First one you ever stole or something?" He took another sip of Scotch and leaned against the radiator. He was deep in thought. Then he brightened. "Hey, I just remembered. You can buy brand-new engines for a 1968 Cadillac, this model. They been in stock ever since at General Motors. You got money?"

"I got money," said Heller.

"I'll check." Mike went into his office and got on the phone. He came back beaming. "They still got them! You in a hurry or can this job take a few weeks?"

"I'm in no hurry," said Heller. "That will fit into my plans just fine."

Suddenly, I was all adrift. I had been so certain he just wanted the car to bash around in New York with, so certain that this was just more Fleet officer fixation on toys that I had not examined the possibility that he had some diabolical plot in mind. I hastily reviewed his actions so far. He was NOT idly drifting as I had thought! He was working! The (bleepard) was plowing straight ahead on his mission! The horrible idea that he might succeed rose over me like Lombar's specter. What the Devils was he up to?

"All right," said Mike. "But what do you want out of this car, really? Speed? If it's speed, I could put new aluminum alloy pistons in the new engine: they get rid of the heat quicker and the engine is less likely to blow up. And you could get a lot more revs out of it."

"Would that increase or decrease the gas consumption?" said Heller.

"Oh, possibly increase it."

"Good," said Heller. "Do it."

"All right. I could put special carburetors on it," said Mike.

"Good," said Heller.

"But if she is going to go faster, she better have a new radiator core and maybe an oil radiator for cooling."

"Good," said Heller.

"There may be some worn parts like axle spindles and such that would have to be replaced."

"Good," said Heller.

"She better have some new tires. Racing ones that'll do a hundred and fifty without blowing out."

"Good," said Heller.

"Lighter magnesium wheels?" said Mike.

"Would it make her look different?"

"I should say so. Much more modern."

"No," said Heller.

Mike had received his first no. He stood back, had a drink, thinking fast.

Bang-Bang interrupted him. "Ain't that a Corleone pickup truck?" he said, pointing to a newly repainted and now black Ford.

"Ready to go," said Mike.

"I'll take it along when I go," said Bang-Bang and

promptly began to remove his cartons from the Cadillac and load the pickup.

Mike, refreshed, returned to the fray. He picked at a fender. "There are some small dents that need body beating. She could use a sandblast and a new coat of paint. Hey, listen kid, we got some original Cadillac paint: we can never use it because it is too showy! I'll get a card." He rushed to the office and came back. "Here you are. It's called 'Flameglow Scarlet.' It makes the car shine even in the dark! Real flashy!"

"Good," said Heller.

I couldn't track with him. He had originally chosen gray because it was more invisible. Now he was choosing paint that practically burned my viewscreen! What *was* he up to?

"But," said Mike, moving to the front seat and picking at it, "this upholstery—yes, and them back curtains —has had it. Now, it just so happens we have some upholstery that was bought and never used. It's called 'Snow Leopard,' white with black spots. Sparkles! It'll really show up wild against that red body! We can even get it thick enough for floor rugs, too."

"Great," said Heller.

Mike couldn't think of anything else. "Now, was there something special *you* wanted in addition?"

"Yes," said Heller. "I want you to fix the hood so it can be locked down all around with keys. And under the car, I want a very light sheet of metal that will seal the engine absolutely."

"Oh, you're talking about bomb jobs and armor," said Mike. "Now, the reason they built these cars with so much horsepower was so they could carry the weight of armor. I can put you in bulletproof windows, armor plate in the side walls..."

At last, I understood. He was afraid his car would be rigged for a blitz again!

"No," said Heller. "Just a light sheet underneath and locks on the hood so nobody can get to the engine."

"Burglar alarms?" said Mike hopefully.

"No," said Heller.

I gave up. The only explanation was that Heller was crazy!

"That's all?" said Mike.

"That's about it," said Heller.

"Well," said Mike, appearing to be a little apprehensive, "that whole lot we been over will add up to about twenty G's."

Bang-Bang had been removing the last of the recorders. He dropped the box. "Jesus!" He came over. "Look, kid, I can steal and get converted fifteen up-to-date Cadillacs for that!"

"I'll throw in the new license," said Mike. "And honest, Bang-Bang, it will cost that to tailor rebuild this car."

"I'll take it," said Heller. He reached into his pockets and pulled out a roll. He counted and held out ten thousand.

"This kid just knock off Brinks?" Mike demanded of Bang-Bang.

"It's honest hit money," said Heller.

"Oh, well, in that case," said Mike, "I'll take it on account." And he went to his office to write out a receipt. "What name?" he called back. "Not that it matters."

"Jerome Terrance Wister," said Heller.

Now I knew he was crazy. Bury could find out he was alive and could trace him! And with a flashy, different car like that . . .

Bang-Bang had finished loading the pickup. He presented a grateful Mike with the case of Johnny

Walker Gold Label. "Get in, kid. Where do I drop you?"

"I'm going over to Manhattan," said Heller.

"In that event, I'll take you to the train station. It's quicker."

He did so and when Heller got out, Bang-Bang said, "Is that your real name, kid? Jerome Terrance Wister?"

"No," said Heller. "I'm really Pretty Boy Floyd."

Bang-Bang laughed uproariously and so did Heller. I was offended. Pretty Boy Floyd was a very famous gangster, too famous to be joked about. Sacred.

"What do I owe you?" said Heller.

"Owe me, kid?" said Bang-Bang. He pointed through the back window at his cargo. "For six months up the river, I been dreaming of a drink of Scotch! Now I'm going to swim in it!" And he drove off singing.

I wasn't singing. I was in new trouble just when I thought it couldn't get worse. Heller was going to pull Bury straight back in on him by using that name and I didn't have the platen. But at the same time, Heller was sailing ahead on his job. I could feel it! He might make it!

The whole thing had me spinny. On the one hand, Heller must NOT get himself killed before I had the means of forging his reports to Captain Tars Roke. On the other hand, a very great danger loomed that he was up to some dastardly plot to succeed in his mission and definitely had to be put away or killed.

I went out and laid down in the yard and buried my face in my hands. I had to be calm. I had to think logically. This was no time to go off my rocker just because I had to keep a man from being killed that would have to be killed. I had to think of something, something to do!

And that (bleeped) wild canary kept trilling at me from a tree. Mockery. Sheer mockery!

Chapter 2

Heller clickety-clacked across the drive at the Gracious Palms and trotted into the lobby. It was still afternoon, and in the hot off-season of late summer the place was deserted.

He was about to mount the steps to the second floor when one of the tuxedoed guards stepped into view and stopped him. "Wait a minute. You don't have your room anymore, kid."

Heller had stopped dead.

"The manager wants to see you," said the hood. "He's pretty upset."

Heller turned to go to the manager's office.

"No," said the guard. "Get in here. He's waiting for you." He pushed Heller toward an elevator. They got in and the hood pushed the top floor button.

They got out into a padded, soundproofed hallway. The hood walked behind Heller, shoving him along with little pushes that made my screen jolt.

From an open door at the end of the long, long hall, the manager's voice could now be heard. He was cursing at people in Italian. He sounded absolutely livid!

There were others in the room, throwing things about, rushing around.

The hood shoved Heller into the hubbub. "Here he is, boss."

Vantagio Meretrici gave a cleaning woman a shove out of his way and came stamping up to Heller.

"You're trying to get me in trouble!" he shouted. "You're trying to cost me my job!" His hands, Italian-like, were flying about. He made a gesture across his own throat as though to cut it. "You could have cost me my life!"

He stopped to scream something in Italian at two cleaning women and they rushed into each other, one dropping a stack of sheets.

Italians. They are so excitable. So theatrical. I turned down my sound volume.

Sure enough, he came nearer and was louder!

"That was not a nice thing to do!" cried Vantagio. "To sneak in here like that!"

"If you could tell me what you think I did..." began Heller.

"I don't think! I know!" cried Vantagio.

"If I did something..." Heller tried.

"Yes, you did something!" shouted Vantagio. "You let me put you in that old second-floor maid's room! You didn't say a word! She was absolutely livid! She practically burned out my phone!"

He put his hands on Heller's shoulders and looked up at him. His voice was suddenly pleading. "Why didn't you tell me you were a friend of Babe's?"

Heller drew a long breath. "I actually didn't know she owned this place. I do apologize."

"Now, look, kid. In the future, speak up. Now, will this do?"

Heller looked around. It was a two-room suite. The huge living room had walls of black onyx tile adorned with paintings. The rug, wall to wall, was beige, covered with scatter rugs of expensive weave and patterns of gold. The furniture was light beige modern with seductive curves. The lamps were statues of golden girls completely naked. A garden balcony was outside and wide glass doors showed a view of the United Nations Building, its park and the river beyond.

Vantagio turned Heller in the other direction. There was a beige, leather-covered bar and gold shelves and scrollwork behind it. A barman was hastily emptying it of hard liquor and putting the bottles in cartons.

"I'm sorry, I can't leave the liquor here. It would cost us our license, you being a minor. But," he rushed on hastily, "we'll fill the fridge with soft drinks of every kind you can imagine. And we'll leave the jumbo glasses and you can fill them from the ice machine there. And we'll put fresh milk here every day. And ice cream?" he pleaded.

Then Vantagio was showing Heller the various hidden closets and drawers around the bar. He stopped and came close to him. "Listen, I was only kidding about sandwiches. We don't have a dining room because it's all room service. But we got the fanciest chefs and kitchen in New York. You can order anything you like. You want anything now? Pheasant under glass?"

He didn't wait for an answer. He yelled into the bedroom and the cleaning people came hurrying out. He escorted Heller in, throwing his hands to indicate the place. "I hope this is all right," he pleaded.

It was a vast bedroom. The entire ceiling was mirrors. The walls were all mirrors, set in black onyx edging. The enormous bed was circular. It occupied the center of the room. It was covered with a black silk spread that had gold hibiscus worked into it in patterns. There were red, low footstools all around the bed. The carpet was wall-to-wall scarlet.

There was an inset of sound speakers, quad, around which curled naked girls in a golden frieze. Vantagio rushed to the wall and showed Heller buttons and selections: Drinking Music, Sensual, Passionate, Frenzy, Cool Off.

Vantagio rushed Heller into the bathroom. It was rug-covered. It had a huge Roman bathtub, big enough for half a dozen people. It had separate massage showers. It had lots of cabinets with things to be explored. And it had a toilet and two bidets surrounded with various douche devices. Heller was looking at *Automatic Hot Towel* and pushed it. A steaming hot towel came out in his hand and he wiped his face.

Vantagio led him back to the sitting room. "Now, is it all right? This was the suite that was made up for the Secretary General, the old one, before he got assassinated. I know it's a little plain but it's more spacious. We almost never use it, so you won't be moved around. It hasn't been used for so long, we had to clean it up quick. The others are fancier but I thought, for a kid, this would be better for you. Do you think it will do?"

"Gods, yes," said Heller.

Vantagio whistled with relief. Then he said, "Look, kid, all will be forgiven and we can be friends if you get on that phone and call Babe. She's been waiting to hear all afternoon!"

Heller almost got run into by a houseman who was responding to a signal from Vantagio and rushing a cart with Heller's baggage into the room.

He picked up the phone. The switchboard immediately connected him to Bayonne, evidently on a lease-line.

"This is me, Mrs. Corleone."

"Oh, you dear boy. You dear, dear boy!"

"Vantagio told me to call and tell you that the new suite was okay, Mrs. Corleone. And it is."

"Is it the Secretary General's suite? The one with the original paintings of Polynesian girls on the walls?"

"Oh, yes, it's quite beautiful. A lovely view."

"Hold on a minute, dear. Someone is at the door."

The sound of voices in the room, dimly heard through a covering palm. A sort of squeaking, "He *what?*" Then very rapid Italian, which was also too muffled to be heard clearly.

But then Babe was back on the line. "That was Bang-Bang! He just arrived here! I can't BELIEVE it! Oh, you dear, dear, dear boy! Oh, you dear, dear, dear, dear boy! Thank you, thank you! I can't discuss it on an open line. But, oh, you dear boy, THANK YOU!" The sound of a torrent of kisses being shot along the wire! Then a sudden roar, "Put that Vantagio back on!"

I suddenly figured it out. She had just learned of the destruction of two million dollars' worth of her rival's booze, etc., and the demise of Oozopopolis, her nemesis!

Vantagio had evidently not liked what he could hear from his end. He timidly took the phone. ". . . *si . . . gia . . . si*, Babe." He looked a bit haggard. ". . . *no . . . non . . . si . . . Grazie, mia capa!*" He hung up.

He took the hot towel out of Heller's hand and wiped his own face. "That was Babe." Then he looked at Heller, "Kid, I don't know what you did now but it must have been *something!* She said I could keep my job, but, kid, I don't think I'll really hear the last of putting you in a maid's back room." He braced up. "But she's right. I wasn't grateful enough and you did save the place and my life. I didn't show respect. So, I apologize. All right, kid?"

They shook hands.

"Now," said Vantagio, "about this other thing. This is the best suite we can offer you but she says you haven't got a car. So, you're to go out and buy any car you want. We have a basement garage, you know. And I told her you didn't have many clothes. So, we have a great tailor and I'll get him in and you're to be measured up for a full wardrobe. Real tailored clothes of the best fabrics. Will that be all right?"

"I really shouldn't accept..."

"You better accept, kid. We're friends. Don't get me in more trouble! Now, is there anything else you can think of that you want?"

"Well," said Heller, "I don't see any TV."

Vantagio said, "Jesus, I'm glad you didn't tell her I'd forgotten that! Nobody looks at TV in a whorehouse, kid. It just never occurred to me. I'll send out somebody to rent one. All right, kid?"

Heller nodded. Vantagio went to the door and then came back. "Kid, I know what you did here. You saved the joint. But you must have done something else. But even that... She treats you so different. Could you let me in on what you and she talk about?"

"Genealogy," said Heller.

"And that's the whole thing?"

"Absolutely," said Heller. "That's all that happened today."

Vantagio looked at him very seriously. Then he burst out laughing. "You almost took me in for a minute. Well, never mind, I'm lucky to have you for a friend."

He started toward the door again but once more stopped. "Oh, yes. She said you could have any of the girls you wanted and to hell with the legality. See you later, kid."

Chapter 3

My concentration on the viewscreen was jarred by a knock on the secret passage door that led to the distant office. I had raised so much pure Hells with Faht that he had finally gotten it through his lard-padded skull that he must send an Apparatus messenger with any reports that came in from America. And here was one! I removed it from the door slit. I opened it with trembling fingers. Possibly Raht and Terb had gotten smart. Perhaps they would be of help!

I read:

> We think he is done for. We traced him to the city garbage scows and he's now somewhere on the bottom of the Atlantic. Be assured we're on the job.

The idiots! That shop had simply thrown away those bugged clothes!

But the surge of anger hardened my resolve to act. I would carefully survey the Gracious Palms area and his rooms, note exactly where he put things, exactly what his routine was. Then I would disguise myself as a Turkish officer assigned to the UN, penetrate the place, pick his room locks, get the platen out of his baggage, plant a bomb and escape. It was a brilliant plan. It came to me in a flash. If I could do that, Heller would be dead, dead, dead and I would be alive!

Sternly, I went back to the viewscreen. He would

unpack shortly, of that I was sure, for the houseman had left the baggage on the cart.

Heller was still walking around his suite. While it might not be up to his rooms at the Voltar Officers' Club, it had its own peculiar charm: girls! Each lamp stand was a naked torso, each throw rug had a golden girl in its pattern.

He walked up to one of several paintings on the wall and stopped and stared at it and said something in Voltarian I didn't get. It was a beautiful painting. A brown-skinned girl, dressed mainly in red flowers, was posed against palm trees and the sea. It was, if you know painting, a conceptual representation, which tends to dominate the modern school.

He bent close to look at the signature. It was *Gauguin*.

I know painting values: one does when he is interested largely in cash. If that painting were an original, it was worth a fortune!

I hastily played back what he had first said. I knew my own reaction would have been to steal it. Maybe I would include that in my planning. I must know what his own intentions were with regard to it.

He had said, "The boat people!" Ah. One of the Atalanta races he and Krak had talked about.

He had moved on to a second Gauguin.

A new voice penetrated the room. "No, no, no!" It was Chief Madame Sesso. Her mustache was bristling. She was wagging a finger at him, very disapproving. "No! Young-a boys should-a not-a look at-a dirty pictures! You not-a goin' to do-a nasty things-a here! If-a the young-a signore, he's-a want to look at-a the naked women, he's-a goin' to-a do-a it right!"

She fixed him in place with a finger, grabbed the phone and spoke an avalanche of Italian into it. She slammed it down. "Right away, you gonna get me-a in-a bad trouble if-a it ever gotta out I taught-a you to look at-a dirty pictures! *Mama mia!* What would-a the customers theenk!"

There was a running patter of footsteps. A small woman burst into the room in a near panic!

She had a short nose, beautiful teeth, raven black hair, high, firm breasts. She was a golden brown. She had European stockings and a chemise on and was holding a silk robe about her. She was obviously a Polynesian!

Luscious!

"Wot ees eet?"

"I catch-a this-a young signore, he's-a look at the dirty pictures on th' wall. Now, Minette, you go right-a now and you jump in-a his bed. Quick-quick!"

"No, no," said Heller. "I just want to look!"

"Aha!" said Minette. "A voyeur."

"No, no," said Heller. "There are some people in ... in my native land that look exactly like you. I just wanted to look. . . ."

"Aha, you zee, Madame Sesso," said Minette. "A voyeur! He get hees keeks by the look, so!"

Madame Sesso walked sternly up to her. "So you-a let-a the young signore look!" And she snatched at the robe. It came half off, baring Minette's firm, uplifted breast. Like a golden melon!

But Minette stepped back. "Madame Sesso. You air crooel! Zee business she is nothing, nothing. For t'ree week, I have no man. Zee bed ees empty. I go half mad. All zee girls, zey talk about thees boy. Eef I do zee strip, I go wil' for heem, Madame Sesso."

Madame Sesso was upon her. Her hand seized the shoulder of the silk robe and gave it a yank. It flew up to block Heller's vision. "You-a will do-a the strip right-a now!" bawled Madame Sesso.

Heller was trying to get the silk robe off his face.

"Aw right!" shrieked Minette. "I go get zee grass skirt, I go get zee flowerz een my hair. Zen I do zee strip. But only on zee one condeetion zat afterwards he..."

The picture went into streaks! The sound became a roar!

I could not see what was going on! I could hear only that roar!

What a shock!

Interference of some sort!

It was the first interference I had seen on this system. The equipment had failed!

I checked power. All fine. I turned up gain. I only got more roar. It was not the quiet blackness when he was asleep.

I wondered for a moment if it were an emotional overload in the subject.

I tried to think of everything I could, made all the guesses of which I was capable. Finally, I dug out the instruction book. I had never read all of it.

Finally, on the next to the last page, I found an entry:

WARNING

As the equipment is used in a carbon-oxygen body, it must, of necessity, be hypersensitive to the carbon atom and molecule wave configuration.

The only known disturbance of the double-wave pattern employed can come from carbon spectrum emitters. These are extremely rare devices but the spy should be warned to stay at least a hundred feet from such an energy emission source if present in the culture where the spy is being employed.

And that was all it said. And as Heller did not know

he was being employed, one could not, of course, warn him.

But warn him of what? What in Hells was a carbon spectrum emitter? It was one of the few times I was sorry I had not done something to stay awake in Academy classes. There must be one now within a hundred feet of Heller! But on an electronically primitive planet like Earth?

Whatever it was, it had me boxed! I turned down the gain. I looked at the jagged mess on the screen. Haggardly, I slumped over the equipment, helpless.

It was midnight where I was. The days of strain were telling on me.

I went through the secret door into my bedroom. I made the cook get up and fix me some hot soup. At length, I dropped into a restless sleep.

Suddenly, I woke up. It was the silent hours of the night. Silence! The small ragged roar from my secret room was missing.

I sprang through the back of the closet.

And there was a picture as nice as you please!

Heller was sitting there in his suite, watching TV! I looked at my watch. It must be about seven in the evening there. The news was on.

What had happened to or with Minette?

Had she gotten her way?

Had Heller let her do a striptease and then taken her to bed as she had demanded?

I did not know. I could not tell.

A Hispanic-looking newscaster was going on and on about murders, and then he said, "New York motorists exiting from the Jersey side of the Lincoln Tunnel, today were entertained by a massive fireball, rising into the sky. The telephone company was besieged by callers wanting to know if World War III had begun." He laughed lightly. "They were reassured to find that it was only the Acme Car Painting Company blowing up. Inventories showed thousands of gallons of stored paint were on the premises. The origin of the blaze was labelled arson by the insurance underwriters, as a hundred-thousand-dollar policy had recently been taken out. Eleven bodies, none of whom have been identified, were found in the vicinity." The newscaster smiled. "But that is life on the Jersey side." I surmised this must be a Manhattan channel!

Wait, what was that? A shadow? No, a black hand and arm close to Heller's face! Coming in from Heller's left! He wasn't focused on it. It held some sort of implement!

A fork!

Somebody was feeding him something as he watched TV!

The hand vanished and my sound was blurred by crunchy chewing.

There was somebody with him! Minette?

Had she won after all?

The newscaster was droning on about some celebrities that had been mugged. It was quite a list.

Heller turned his head slightly to the right. Wait! What was that? Something white over to the *right* of the TV!

In his peripheral vision, I managed to make it out. *Two* pairs of white feet! One in slippers with lace puffs, the other set bare!

And there was a low murmur over to his right. I had missed it in amongst the news. I hastily replayed the auxiliary screen, turning up its gain. Two girls' voices! Was one Minette?

I made one out amongst the news overplay. A middle-western accent. ". . . and honey, let me tell you, he was very, very good! I think he was the best..."

Then the other girl's murmur. Was this Minette? I turned the gain higher and changed the tone controls. "...well, I really thought it was quite impossible to have that many orgasms in one..." An English accent! These were two entirely different girls!

The newscaster was continuing. He went through some stock-exchange data. Then he said, "A Treasury Department spokesman stated this afternoon that the New Jersey BAFT chief, Oozopopolis, and several other revenooers are missing. Shortages in their accounts were denied although it is well known that Oozopopolis had extensive banking connections in the Bahamas. Airports on this side of the river are being watched." He chuckled again. "But that's life in Jersey, isn't it, folks."

Heller leaned forward and pushed a button to turn it off. The automatic gain control made my screen go more normal. He turned to his left. Sitting across the side table from him was a gorgeous, slinky, high-yellow girl! She had on next to nothing! A flimsy scarf was draped over her shoulders, her breasts clearly visible through it.

Where was Minette?

What was this girl doing here?

She was laughing, her beautiful teeth flashing. "And so, honey, you better believe him. Stay away from that Jersey side. Just cuddle around here." She made a sensuous movement with her breasts. She pushed a fork into a huge Caesar salad in a crystal bowl. She brushed the mouthful against her lips and then pushed it seductively across the table to him. "When you is done eating, pretty boy, would you like me to demonstrate how it's done in Harlem?" She laughed a low, seductive laugh. Utterly tantalizing! Then her eyes went hot. "In fac', I think that's enough supper." She put down the fork and began to stand up.

She only had on that flimsy scarf.

She was wearing nothing else!

She reached out her hand. . . .

The interference hit again!

I moaned. I waited for it to die down.

It didn't.

After a couple of minutes, very upset, I went back to my sleeping room and lay down in my bed.

Flesh can only stand so much!

After a little, I got hold of my spinning wits and emotions.

One thing was very plain. There was interference. It came on and off.

He had probably unpacked his baggage and put it in several of the many cubicles and closets. If I were patient, no matter how long it took, I could piece out exactly where he must have put the platen.

I would still carry out my plan!

Chapter 4

In the other room, the equipment stopped buzzing. Led by a dreadful fascination, I tottered back in to see what was going on now.

Heller was just stepping out of the elevator into the lobby.

I looked at my watch. It must be wrong. I have trouble with time conversion from one part of a planet to another but I couldn't be *that* wrong. Only ten minutes ago, I had seen the slinky high-yellow girl standing up in invitation. Yet here was Heller in the lobby.

Let's see. It would have taken him a few minutes to dress. Say a minute to come down in the elevator . . .

Well, let's say he was awfully fast.

It was early evening in New York. There were quite a few people in the lobby, mostly in Western business suits but with the multihued faces of many lands. Prosperous looking, debonair men about town from deserts and mountains and villages on stilts—the typical UN crowd. They were piled up a bit at the desk, making appointments, sitting about until they heard their number called or sauntering around trying to work up a new appetite.

I realized Heller was putting in the agreed-upon lobby appearance to discourage certain visitors. I could see in a reflecting mirror that he did not yet have his new clothes—he was wearing his plain blue suit. At least he didn't have his baseball cap on. But when he walked on bare floor, I could tell he still wore those baseball shoes.

He sat down in a chair where he could be seen from the door and where he could see the office entrance of the "Host." Almost at once, a houseman entered the lobby from the street. He was carrying a pile of magazines and newspapers. He walked straight to Heller, gave him the pile. Heller handed him a twenty-dollar bill and waved away the change.

Wait! Heller must have called him from his suite! So subtract that, too, from the ten minutes! What *had* happened with that slinky high-yellow girl?

Casting an eye now and then on the street entrance and the manager's door, Heller settled down to read. Ah, I would have a clue as to what his plans were by analyzing what he was reading.

Racing magazines!

The American Hot Rod, Racing Today, The Blowout, Hot Stock Cars. He leafed through them but, knowing Heller, he was reading every page. Sneaky. But I had learned his habits. When he was really interested, he would pause and stare at a page and think about it.

He halted his leafing. The magazine had a picture of an old Pontiac sedan. The article was "Out of the Pit to Glory."

Of course! Heller the speedophile! Heller the stopwatch-oriented lunatic. Heller, an obvious case of velocity dementia in its last stages of progressive terminalization!

But wait. As he paused, his eye was on a figure and stayed on the figure. The last sentence of the article read:

> "And so, for the pittance of $225,000 in expenses, we were able to cover the entire stock-car circuit for one whole season and wound up with all bills paid, which is glory enough for anybody!"

His eyes kept straying back to that "$225,000."

He watched the crowd for a while. Not much of a throng as the UN wasn't in session. One of the tuxedoed security guards drifted over beside his chair and said, out of the corner of his mouth, "Watch out for that deputy delegate from Maysabongo. He just came in, there. The one with the opera cloak and top hat. He carries a *kris* up his sleeve. Must be two feet long. Runs amok now and then." The guard drifted away.

Heller yawned, a sure sign of tension. He opened a newspaper, the *Wall Street Journal*. He wandered through it. He paused on a page of box ads featuring real estate offerings. He examined the "ex-urban" ones—those way past the suburbs and out of town entirely. They had them for Bucks County, Pennsylvania, for Vermont and for various counties in Connecticut. All ideal for the executive weekend. He began to stare at one. It said:

OWN YOUR OWN FEUDAL FIEFDOM
BE A MONARCH OF ALL YOU SURVEY
Vast estate going for peanuts
FIVE WHOLE ACRES, NO BUILDINGS
UNTOUCHED WILDERNESS OF CONNECTICUT
ONLY $300,000

His eye was stuck on the $300,000.

He opened the paper to other sections. He looked over "Commodity Markets" with all their vast rows of figures for the various futures for the day. He inspected the stock market with all its tangles of incomprehensible abbreviations.

A movement over at the "Host" door. A huge, dark-complected man in a turban came out with Vantagio. They stood on the lobby side of the door, completing their discussion. I hastily turned up my gain.

It was in English. The turbaned one was thanking Vantagio for straightening out the bill. Then, he looked around and saw Heller.

"New face," said the turbaned giant.

"Oh, that youngster," said Vantagio. "It's in confidence. His father is a very important man, a Moslem. Married an American movie actress. That's the son. He's going to go to college and his father insisted he live here. We couldn't say no. Would have caused endless diplomatic repercussions had we refused."

"Ah," said the turbaned one. "I can clear up that

puzzle for you. You have to understand the Mohamme-
dan religion. You see," he continued learnedly, "in the
Middle East, it is tradition that the children, including
boys, are raised in, and have to live in, the harem. And
this whorehouse is probably as close as his father could
come to a harem in the United States. Quite natural,
really."

"Well, thank you for clearing up my confusion,"
said Vantagio, the master of political science.

"I'll just go over and greet him in his native
tongue," said the turbaned giant. "Make him feel at
home."

Here he came! He stopped in front of Heller. He
went through the elaborate hand ritual of the Arab greeting. He said something that sounded like *'Aliekoom
sala'am.'* And then a long rigamarole. Arabic!

Yikes! Heller didn't speak Arabic!

Heller rose. With elaborate politeness, he copied the
hand motions and bow exactly. Then he said, "I am
dreadfully sorry but I am forbidden to speak my native
tongue while I am in the United States. But I am doing
fine and I truly hope you have a nice evening."

They both bowed.

The turbaned giant went back to Vantagio. "A well-
brought-up youth, obviously raised in a harem like I
said. I can tell by his accent. But I will keep your secret,
Vantagio, especially since he is the son of the Aga Khan."

Leaving Vantagio, the huge turbaned man went
promptly over to a little group by the door and whispered to them. Their eyes flicked covertly toward Heller.
The secret was being well kept. By everybody.

A half an hour passed and Heller's perusal of the
papers had exhausted them. He was sitting there quietly
when the deputy delegate from Maysabongo came out of

the elevator and rushed over to the desk. He slammed his top hat down on the counter.

"Where is that pig Stuffumo?" he demanded of the clerk.

The clerk looked anxiously around. There were no security guards in the lobby at the moment.

"I demand it! I demand you tell me!" The deputy delegate was gripping the clerk's coat.

Heller stood up. The fool. He had been told the man had a *kris* in his sleeve! A *kris* is the wickedest short sword there is! And I didn't have that platen!

"Harlotta was not there!" snarled the deputy delegate. "She is with Stuffumo! I know it!"

The elevator door opened and a very fat brown man in a business suit walked out.

"Stuffumo!" screamed the deputy delegate. "Enemy of the people! Capitalistic warmonger! Death to aggressors!"

He raced across the room. The clerk was madly pushing buzzers. Stuffumo flinched, tried to get back into the elevator.

The deputy delegate whipped the *kris* out of his sleeve, two feet of wavy steel!

He made a slash through the air. The blade whistled!

The top of Stuffumo's waistcoat gapped!

The deputy delegate drew back the blade to strike again.

Suddenly, Heller was in front of him!

The blade swished as it began the second slash.

Heller caught the man's wrist!

He pushed his thumb into the back of the man's hand. The blade fell.

Heller caught it by the handle before it hit the floor.

Two security guards were there. Heller waved them

back. Heller gently pushed the deputy delegate and Stuffumo into a corner of the elevator.

"What room is Harlotta in?" said Heller, hand poised over the elevator buttons.

Both Stuffumo and the deputy delegate stared at him. Heller was hefting the *kris*. "Come, come," he said. "At least tell me what floor. We can find her."

"What do you mean to do?" said the deputy delegate.

"Why," said Heller, "she has caused two important men embarrassment. She'll have to be killed, of course." And he hefted the *kris*.

"No!" cried Stuffumo. "Not Harlotta!"

"NO!" cried the deputy delegate. "Not my darling Harlotta!"

"But I am sure it is house rules," said Heller. "She could have caused you both to kill each other. It isn't permitted!"

"Please," said Stuffumo.

"Please don't," said the deputy delegate.

"I'm afraid there's no other way," said Heller.

"Oh, yes, there is!" cried the deputy delegate, triumphantly. "We can have a conference about it!"

"Correct!" said Stuffumo. "The proper solution to all international disputes!"

The two promptly sat down in the corner of the elevator, facing each other.

"First, the agenda!" said the deputy delegate firmly.

Heller pushed the out-of-operation button and walked out, leaving them in the elevator.

One of the Italian security guards said, "Thank you, kid. That was good knife work. But you should pay attention when I tip you off. They have diplomatic immunity, you know, and can't be arrested for anything, no matter what they do. But law-abiding Americans like you and me can be. We usually don't stick around when that one arrives. Maybe he'll be good now."

Vantagio came out. Heller handed him the *kris*.

The two ex-combatants walked out of the elevator. "We have come to an accord," said Stuffumo. "Bilateral occupation of territory."

"I will have Harlotta Mondays, Wednesdays and Fridays. He will have her Tuesdays, Thursdays and Saturdays," said the deputy delegate.

"We have to spend Sunday with our wives," added Stuffumo.

"Vantagio," said the deputy delegate, "may we borrow your office for the formal ratification and signing of the treaty?"

Heller watched them until they vanished into Vantagio's office. He yawned. He gathered up his papers, entered the elevator and exited at the top floor.

As he passed down the hall to his room, a nearby door opened and a girl rushed out. She had on a silk robe but it wasn't tied and her forward motion blew it back and exposed everything she had. She was a beautiful brunette!

"Oh, there you are, pretty boy. Business is too slack tonight. Some of the girls say you have something beautifully new." She looked at him seductively, stroking his arm. "Please, pretty please, can I come in with you and we ..."

My screen flashed out. The interference roared.

But I had a lot of other things to puzzle over. He was interested in his usual hobby, speed. He was interested in an executive retreat in the wilderness. I felt I should be able to piece it together.

But even though I labored into the Turkish dawn, I could not figure out how you would run a racing car in a tree-infested wilderness. Or why.

Chapter 5

It was three in the afternoon in Turkey when I arose. Not really thinking, still numb with sleep, I walked into my secret office and, like a fool, looked into the viewscreen.

I nearly fainted!

I was staring twenty stories straight down!

I felt like I was going to fall!

The people were small spots in the street below; the cars were toys!

The strain I had been under was telling. The shock was too much. I pulled my eyes away and shuddered into a chair. After a few minutes, I got control of my stomach and dared take another look.

What in *Hells* was he up to?

He was on a cupola that crowned the Gracious Palms. Fifteen feet below him, firmly on the asphalt roof, a whore in a green jump suit was steadying a line up to him.

He was rigging a TV antenna kit! That's what it read on the top of the box he was steadying on his knees:

HANDY JIM-DANDY FULLY-AUTOMATIC
INSTALL-IT-YOURSELF RADIO-CONTROLLED
REMOTE TV ANTENNA WITH SIGNAL BOOSTER

He had inset the feet into the concrete top of the cupola. He was now adjusting the booster. He glanced around and it was visible that several nearby buildings had them. He must have had it sent out for the day before.

Oho! So he was having signal trouble, too! But wait, this must mean that the TV wasn't working when my equipment wasn't working, so those girls in his room weren't there to watch TV!

He completed the upper installation and then, box under his arm, he started down a line.

I had him. Code break! It was a spacer safety line! He was carrying Voltarian gear in his suitcases!

He was working with a stapler, fastening the TV cable to the stone as he descended.

He got to the bottom and turned toward the woman. There she was, a New York whore, holding a spacer safety line manufactured in Industrial City, Voltar! I watched like a hawk. Did she realize it? Everything depended on that! I could simply order him off the mission and court-martialed!

"Here's your clothesline, honey," she said. "Now, what do I do?"

He took it, gave it the snap that causes it to come loose at the top and caught it in coils around his wrist as it fell—a typical show-off spacer gesture: I don't know how they do it.

"You just uncoil this reel, Martha. Just walk along and I'll fasten it down as we go."

"Okay, dearie," she said. And along they went. She had a stick through the reel and Heller was snubbing it under the parapet with the stapler.

Then, I realized something else. Heller must know where the interference was coming from. The roof he was laying the cable on was about three hundred and fifty feet long, perhaps double the building width. The antenna was outside the interference zone. I tried to plot from this where and what the interference might be, for I was not only very curious about what he *did* in that suite, I also had to know where he could have hidden the platen. I got all tangled up.

The girl had come to the far end of the roof. "Now what do I do, pretty boy?"

"You go down to my room and open the double doors and stand on the balcony and steady the safety line again."

She ran off. Heller tied the reel to the safety line and then paid it out so that it landed on his balcony below. The girl came out on the balcony and got the reel.

He pegged the upper end of the safety line into the stone parapet, stepped over the edge...

I turned my face away. This guy was driving me mad! He had no sense. He didn't give a (bleep) about height or his neck. I heard the staples going into the vertical wall but I wouldn't look. I knew I would see the tiny people and cars far too far below!

The sound of a disintegrator drill. I dared look. He had snapped the spacer safety line loose and was putting a cable hole in the wall. With a Voltarian disintegrator drill!

I watched intently to see if I got a reaction from the whore. There she was watching a tiny palm-sized gadget, with nothing spinning, bite the exact sized hole through the wall. No chips or sparks. A miracle on this planet. All she had to say was "Hey, man, look at that gimmick eat up stone!" and I had him!

She said, "I'll go call room service to send you some breakfast, dearie." And she went inside the living room. It depressed me.

Heller went inside, put the base plate together and shortly had it all connected with the TV. He turned the set on. He fiddled with the radio antenna rotator. The difference in reception showed it was turning.

"Hey, great picture," said the whore. "We done it! They'll send breakfast up right away."

Heller neated up his kit. Aha, now I would see where he stowed his gear. He certainly would hide a safety line and disintegrator drill! And I had no interference!

He was fastening the tool kit up. OH! Right on the face of the kit, big as life, it said:

JETTERO HELLER
FLEET CORPS OF COMBAT ENGINEERS

It said it in Voltarian script but it said it, just like that!

He tossed the kit on the sofa. It landed face up!

He went into the bathroom and kicked off his tennis shoes and the baseball exercise suit. He stepped into the massage shower.

The massage drops were hammering at him but I could hear somebody banging cabinets in the bathroom. All that woman, Martha, had to do was notice that kit and come in and say "Hey, what's this writing? It looks like something not of this planet," and he would be open to being shot!

The shower door opened. Her hand was in view. She didn't have her jump suit on. She was holding a cake of soap. She said, "Honey, let me wash your back before we . . ."

The interference came on!

I railed around. The screen simply flashed in jagged lines and the sound roared. It was actively preventing me from getting enough data on that suite and where he

stowed his gear and thus blocking me from embarking
on my raid for the platen and the end of Heller. The minutes stretched agonizingly into half an hour.

Then, it was off!

Heller was sitting on the couch drinking coffee. He
was all alone in the suite.

There was a knock on the door and Heller said, in
that penetrating Fleet voice, "Come in, it isn't locked."

In came a mob of tailors!

They started displaying bolts of fine fabrics, summer silk and mohair, tweeds, gabardine, shirt silk, passing each one under Heller's nose.

The lead tailor, with Heller's permission, sat down
on the couch with a book of styles. He found he was sitting on something, reached under him and picked up the
tool kit. All he had to do was inspect the inscription and
some of those odd tools and he would know he was talking to an extraterrestrial!

"Now, we've brought a throwaway suit you can wear
today, young sir. But we must choose both a society wardrobe and a college wardrobe. Now, it so happens that the
styles this autumn will be ever so slightly gauche. Neat
but gauche. In this Ives St. Giles book, we can see that
the collar..."

Sickening. Who cared about all these fancy styles
and the pant width in the mode. There was a gabardine
trench coat with innumerable straps and a gun pocket
that I liked, however. It looked very like one Humphrey
Bogart used to wear. But the rest of it... then I realized
the true source of my antipathy. It wasn't the styles, it
was the tailor. He was a homo. If there is anything I can't
stand, it's a gay!

"Now, could you please stand up, young sir?"

And he was kneeling in front of Heller, measuring

him for trousers. He seemed to be having trouble with his tape. He kept stretching it.

"Oh," said the lead tailor, giggling, "you're really built!"

"What's the matter?" said Heller. "Hips too narrow?"

"Oh, no, young sir. I wasn't talking about hips."

On went the interference!

Off went my patience!

I stood up. I was being personally and vindictively harassed! Harassed? If I did not get that platen, I was dead!

There was a knock on the tunnel door to Faht's office. Another Raht and Terb message slid under. I snatched it up.

It said:

> Have our eye on that spot offshore. We're standing by in case he surfaces.

That did it!

I bolted out of the house and walked agitatedly around the garden.

That (bleeped) screaming canary! Trilling and whistling gaily in the tree! A party to all this!

I went inside and got a twelve-gauge shotgun. I loaded it. I saw a flutter of yellow on a limb.

I fired both barrels!

The roar was deafening.

A hole had been blown through an ornamental tree.

One solitary feather came floating slowly down in the utter silence.

It made me feel immensely better.

A guard car came dashing up, of course, but I laughed and sent it away.

I felt better. I could think. I sat down on a bench.

What did I actually know? Aha, I had learned one vital thing so far today. The whore had not had the slightest recognition that she was handling a Voltarian safety line. The tailor had even sat on a Fleet tool kit, plainly labelled, and had simply tossed it aside. The people around Heller's place of residence were totally incapable of observation! Perhaps it would be different when he got into a college. But nobody would notice anything at all anywhere around the Gracious Palms!

I went to my desk. I wrote a brutal communication to be transmitted at once to the New York office. I said:

> RAHT AND TERB ARE SOMEWHERE IN THE NEW YORK AREA. FIND THEM AND FORCE THEM TO REPORT IN. IF THIS ORDER IS NOT PROMPTLY EXECUTED THE ENTIRE PERSONNEL OF YOUR OFFICE WILL BE.
> SULTAN BEY.

When they reported in, I would direct them to get all plans of that building and pave the way.

With that backup, I would get this handled once and for all. And before I myself started to show signs of a nervous breakdown.

I phoned for a messenger and got the message on its way.

I got a pitcher of *sira* and went back to the viewer.

The interference was off. Heller was on his way downstairs in an elevator.

Chapter 6

Heller was wearing the new "throwaway" suit, I saw in an elevator mirror by peripheral vision. It was a light blue summer weight and it fitted for a change, but its pockets were bulging. He had on a blue shirt with a wide collar spread over the jacket lapels, the gauche look, I suppose, but it still made him look awfully young. However, whatever the tailor was trying to achieve was spoiled utterly by the fact that he still wore his red baseball cap on the back of his blond head and when he went across the lobby, I could hear that he still wore baseball spikes! He might be clean and neat, some might think him very handsome, but he still didn't have a clue about espionage and looking the part! The baseball cap was easy to explain—he considered himself to be working. The spikes, just because he didn't have comfortable shoes. An idiot!

But I could be tolerant. He was a marked man.

He went to the safes and halted before his personal one. I noted the combination.

He spread out his money inside the safe.

I became aware of other voices, an undertone in the otherwise quiet area. I turned up the gain. Somebody on a speaker-phone! I could hear both sides! They were speaking Italian.

". . . so that is no excuse to let him sleep late!" It was Babe Corleone's voice!

"But, Babe," said Vantagio, "it didn't have anything to do with the girls. Those two UN bigwigs spend half their countries' UN appropriations in this place and it's a good thing he didn't let them kill each other."

"Vantagio, are you trying to pretend I didn't appreciate that?"

"No, no, *mia capa!*"

"Vantagio, are you trying to stand in the way of this boy's career?"

Heller was counting out his money, bill by bill. He seemed to think a few of the bills were counterfeit.

Vantagio had apparently been struck speechless. Finally, gasping, he said, "Oh, *mia capa*, how could you say such an awful thing!"

"You know an education is important. You are jealous and you want him to wind up like some of these bums?"

"Oh, no!" wept Vantagio.

"Then please explain to me. I will listen. I will not yell at you. I will listen with patience. Answer this one question: I see in the Sunday paper two days ago, Vantagio, that Empire University began registering yesterday. And when I ask you, patiently and quietly, Vantagio, the simple question, 'Is the boy properly registered now and starting school?' I get a stupid answer that he slept late."

Vantagio tried to talk. *"Mia capa..."*

"Now, you know and I know and the good God himself knows that boys hate to go to school," continued Babe. "You know that they have to be driven, Vantagio. You know they have to be forced. My brothers, God rest their souls, had to be beaten so there is no reason to explain that to me."

"Mia capa, I swear..."

"So the one question I want answered, Vantagio, if you will only let me speak, is why haven't you asserted your authority and control over this boy? Why is he not obeying your orders? Now, do not bother to argue. Just phone me up in exactly one half an hour and tell me he has started to school." There was a sharp click. She had hung up.

Heller had decided that just because some bills had Benjamin Franklin on them, they were not counterfeit. He had packaged the money up neatly. But he was not happy with what he had counted. He was shaking his head.

He put fifteen thousand in his pocket, already bulging with Gods knew what. He closed and locked his safe and was about to leave the Gracious Palms when Vantagio's voice arrested him, calling from the office.

"Can I see you a minute, kid?"

Heller went in. Vantagio's brows were lowered. He looked very down. He gestured to a chair. But like any Italian, he did not come right to the point. They think it impolite.

"Well, kid, how are you getting along with the girls?" He said it very glumly.

Heller laughed. "Oh, it's fairly easy to handle women."

"You wouldn't think so if you had my job," said Vantagio.

Aha, I was on the trail of something here. Vantagio was jealous of Heller. He was afraid Heller was going to get his job!

"Say," said Heller. "You may be the very one I should be seeing about this."

"What?" he said, very guarded, very defensive. Yes, something was biting Vantagio.

"Well, actually," said Heller, "I've got quite a bit of money but I think I will need much more."

"For what?"

"Well, I've got to do something about the planet."

"You mean you're planning to take over the whole planet? Look, kid, you'll never do that without a diploma."

"Oh, that's true," said Heller. "But also, things like that take money. And I wanted to ask you if you could tell me where the gambling is in this area."

Vantagio blew up. "Gambling! You must be crazy! We run the numbers racket and let me tell you, kid, you'd lose your shirt! They're crooked!"

Oho, Vantagio was antagonistic! Was he jealous of Heller?

"All right, then," said Heller. And he took out a copy of the *Wall Street Journal* and opened it. It was the Commodity Futures Market page. "I make out that you buy and sell these as they go up and down, day by day."

Vantagio brushed it aside. "That's a good way to lose an awful lot of money, kid!" He was glowering.

It occurred to me right that moment that maybe I had an ally in Vantagio. He was obviously hostile to Heller. I began to work out why.

Heller was unfolding another spread of paper. "Then how about these? They apparently change in price, day to day."

"That's the stock market!" said Vantagio. "That's a great way to go bankrupt!"

"Well, how do you buy and sell them?" said Heller.

"You need a broker. A stockbroker."

"Well, could you recommend one?"

"Those crooks," said Vantagio. Quite obviously, he did not want Heller to get ahead. He was nervous, edgy. I became more convinced there was something here— that maybe I could cultivate an ally.

"You know of one?" said Heller.

"Aw, look in the phone book classified. But I don't want anything to do with it. And listen, kid, you don't either. Listen, kid, you told me you were going to go to college."

"Yes," said Heller. "Nobody will listen to you if you don't have a diploma."

"Right," said Vantagio. But he was edgy. "That's why I called you in here, kid. You know what day this is?" And to Heller's head shake, "It's the second day of registration week at Empire College. You got your papers?"

"Right here," said Heller, tapping his pocket. "But if it's a whole week..."

"You," said Vantagio harshly, "have got to go up there right now and register!"

"But if I have a whole week..."

"Be quiet!" said Vantagio. He reached into a drawer and got out a book, *Curriculum, Empire College, Fall Term*. "Geovani Meretrici" was on the catalogue. I thought his name was Vantagio. "What subject is your major?"

"Well, engineering, I suppose," said Heller.

"What kind?" demanded Vantagio.

"Well, if you give me the book there, I can study it over and maybe in a couple of days..."

Vantagio was really cross now. What was this temper all about? He was reading from the book, "'Aerospace Science and Engineering'? 'Bioengineering'? 'Civil Engineering and Engineering Mechanics'? 'Electrical Engineering and Computer Science'? 'Mineral Engineering'? 'Nuclear Science and Engineering'? Just plain 'Engineering'?"

"Nuclear Science and Engineering," said Heller. "That sounds about right. But..."

Vantagio raised his voice. "They have a Bachelor,

Master, Doctorate and other degrees in it. So, that's it! Nuclear Science and Engineering! Sounds impressive."

"However," said Heller, "I would like to look..."

"All right!" said Vantagio. "Now, here is a map of Empire University. See, here is the library and all that. But this is the administration building and this is the entrance. And here is a map of subways. You walk over to this station near here. Then, you go across town. And you transfer at Times Square to Number 1 and you get off at Empire University at 116th Street and you walk along here and right into that administration building and you sign up! You got it?"

"Well, yes. And I appreciate your help. But if there is a whole week..." He trailed off because Vantagio was sitting there looking at him in a strange way.

Vantagio started up again. "Kid, have you lived around New York before?"

"No," said Heller.

Vantagio assumed a confidential air. "Then you don't know the customs. Now, kid, when you're in a strange place, it is absolutely fatal not to follow the customs."

"That is true," said Heller.

"Now, kid," said this master of political science, "it so happens that there is a mandatory, American Indian custom regarding saving a man's life. And Indian law remains in full force by prior sovereignty. Did you know that when you save a man's life that man is responsible for you from there on out?"

I boggled! Vantagio was telling Heller an Earth *Chinese* custom! And he was telling Heller absolutely backwards! In old China, according to our Apparatus surveys, when you saved a man's life you were then and there responsible for that man forevermore! So we warned operatives never to save anyone's life in China! Vantagio was using his learning with a twist and he must know very well he was lying!

"Are you sure?" said Heller.

Vantagio looked at him, smug and superior. "Of course, I am sure. I am a master of political science, ain't I?"

"Yes," said Heller doubtfully.

"And you saved my life, didn't you?" said Vantagio.

"Well, it seems so," said Heller.

I suddenly got it! Vantagio! He was a tiny man, only five feet two inches tall. Right next door to Sicily lies Corsica, same people. And a small man in Corsica named Napoleon also felt inferior to everyone. Vantagio was suffering from an inferiority complex in the face of Heller's deeds and acclaim! The things Heller had done had the Sicilian writhing with insecurity. And then I really got it: Vantagio was not his given name—it was his nickname! It means "Whiphand" in Italian!

Vantagio rose to his full five feet two and looked sternly at the seated Heller almost at eye level. And then this master of political science said, "You saved my life, so therefore you have to do absolutely everything I tell you! And that's the way it is now from here on out!"

Heller must have looked contrite. "I see that that's the way it seems."

Suddenly, Vantagio was all smiles and cheer. "So, we have settled that! Have a cigar. No, I forgot, you mustn't smoke. Here, have some mints." And he shoved a box at Heller.

Heller took one and Vantagio came around and patted him on the back. "So, now we know where we stand. Right?"

"Right," said Heller.

"So, you go straight down to the subway and go register right now!" But he said it with cheer.

Heller got up and walked to the door with Vantagio, who opened it for him and gave him another pat.

When Heller glanced back, Vantagio was all beaming and waving good-bye.

Well, it is very hard to understand Sicilians. This Vantagio appeared pretty treacherous, changeable. I had reservations about trusting him and including him in my plans. Still, there was a chance I could turn that burning jealousy and inferiority to account.

Chapter 7

Expecting, of course, that Heller would now do everything Vantagio had told him to do, I was not paying much attention. Heller went down into a subway station and looked into a phone book. I thought he might be calling the college.

He got on a subway and roared along. He seemed to be interested in the people. It was a hot New York day and in such weather the subways are very, very hot. The people were sweaty, soggy.

I was not being any more alert than they were. I suddenly saw a station sign flash by that said:

23rd St.

Then one went by which said:

14th St. Union Square

Hey, he was on the wrong subway. He was going DOWNtown, not UPtown! And he wasn't on the proper line! He was on the Lexington Avenue subway!

Hastily, I backtracked on the second screen. He had changed, not at Times Square, but before that, at Grand Central! I backtracked further. I got to the phone book he had looked at. He had found *Stocks and Bonds Brokers* in the yellow pages. Then his finger had halted at *Short, Skidder and Long Associates, 81½ Wall St.*

He was playing hooky!

Oho, maybe all that with Vantagio was not in vain. Maybe I could gather data and show Vantagio that Heller was not obeying him and Vantagio would let me into Heller's room. A beautiful daydream of a smiling Vantagio, waving an arm to bid me go in and saying, "Yes, Officer Gris. Feel free! Ransack the place! I'll even call housemen to help you find the platen! And it serves this disobedient young kid right, doesn't it, Officer Gris." A beautiful dream!

But back to reality.

Heller, red baseball cap on the back of his head, trotting along on baseball spikes, found 81½ Wall Street and by means of elevators was very shortly breasting a counter at Short, Skidder and Long Associates. There were big blackboards with current prices on them. Ticker tapes were chattering.

A gum-chewing girl said, "Yeah?"

"I want to see somebody about buying stocks," said Heller.

"New account? See Mr. Arbitrage in the third cubicle."

Mr. Arbitrage was immaculately groomed and all dried up. He remained seated at the cubicle desk. He looked Heller up and down as though somebody had thrown a fish into the room, a fish that smelled bad.

"I want to see somebody about buying stocks," said Heller.

"Identification, please," said Mr. Arbitrage, going through the motions out of habit.

Heller, unbidden, sat down across from him. He pulled out the Wister driver's license and social security card.

Mr. Arbitrage looked at them and then at Heller. "There is probably no need to ask for credit references."

"What are those?" said Heller.

"My dear young man, if this is some kind of a school assignment, I am afraid I have no time to teach the young. That is what we pay taxes for. The exit is the same door you came in."

"Wait," said Heller. "I have money."

"My dear young man, please do not trifle with me. My time is valuable and I have a luncheon appointment with the head of J. P. Morgan. The exit door . . ."

"But why?" demanded Heller. "Why can't I buy stocks?"

Mr. Arbitrage sighed noisily. "My dear young man, to deal in stocks, you must open an account. You must be of age to do so. Over twenty-one in our firm. To open an account, you must have credit references. You obviously have none. Could I suggest that you get your parents to accompany you the next time you call? Good day."

"My parents aren't on Earth," said Heller.

"My condolences. Please hear me when I say you have to have a person, over twenty-one, who is responsible for you before you can deal with this firm. Now, good day, please."

"Do all firms have this restriction?"

"My dear young sir, you will find all firms will slam

their doors in your face even harder than I am doing!
Now, good day, young sir. Good day, good day, good
day!" And he reached up and got his bowler and left for
lunch.

Heller went down to the street. The luncheon mobs
were beginning to boil out of the buildings—luncheon
on Wall Street looks like a full-fledged riot in progress.

Thoughtfully, Heller bought a hot dog from a push-
cart and drank some orange pop on the sidewalk. He
noticed that Mr. Arbitrage was doing the same thing
further along.

Heller looked at the towering, cold buildings, the hot
and sweating throngs. He checked the pollution dirt on
the building sides. He seemed to find it of great interest.
He took some pages from a notebook, wrote an address
on one and wiped it against a building. Of course it came
out black. He trotted through the throngs and took a similar sample on another building. Then he went back
down into the subway station and reached over the platform edge and did the same thing. He put the carefully
folded and labelled papers away.

He studied the subway map, apparently decided you
couldn't get from Wall Street over to Chambers by subway, caught a train to Grand Central, shuttled over to
Times Square, transferred to a Number 1 and was soon
roaring north.

At 116th Street he debarked and was shortly trotting
along College Walk through mobs of students of every
color and hue, a throng that was going here and coming
from there or standing about. It was a drably somber
crowd.

A young man walked up to Heller and said, "What
should I take this term?"

"Milk," said Heller. "Highly recommended."

Like someone who knew where he was going amongst a lot of people who didn't know where they were going, Heller went up steps and found himself in a hall where registration was being administered to long lines. Registrars sat at temporary desks, barricaded in paper. He looked at his watch and it winked the time at him. He looked at the long lines.

A young man, apparently clerical help and a student at the same time, entered, carrying a huge stack of computer printouts of class assignments. Heller walked over to him and said with the ring of Fleet authority, "Where are you taking these?"

"Miss Simmons," said the young man, timidly, nodding toward one of the registrars at a temporary desk.

"You should be on time," said Heller. "I'll take these. Go back and get some more."

"Yes, sir," said the young man and left.

Heller stood back until the girl Miss Simmons was interviewing and registering began to gather up her things to depart. Heller went over and put the stapled computer printout booklets down on Miss Simmons' desk and sat down in the chair, bypassing the unattentive waiting line. He took out his own papers and handed them to Miss Simmons.

Miss Simmons did not look up. She was a severe-looking young woman, her brown hair pulled into a tight bun. She had thick glasses and began to paw about the desk in front of her. Then she said, "You haven't made out your application form."

"I didn't know how," said Heller.

"Oh, dear," said Miss Simmons, wearily. "Another one that can't read or write." She got a blank and started to fill it in from Heller's papers. She wrote and wrote. Then, she said, "Local address, Wister."

"Gracious Palms," said Heller and gave her the street and house number.

Miss Simmons gave him an invoice. "You can pay the cashier. But I don't think it will do any good. Payment of fees does not guarantee enrollment."

"Is something wrong?"

"Is something wrong?" mimicked Miss Simmons. "There is always something wrong. But that's beside the point. It's these grades, Wister. It's these grades—a D average? They clearly show that your only A was for sleeping in class. And in a practically unknown school. Now, what major are you demanding?"

"Nuclear Science and Engineering," said Heller.

Miss Simmons gave a shocked gasp like a bullet had hit her. She glared. She ground her teeth. When she had recovered enough to continue, she said in a level, deadly voice, "Wister, some of the prerequisites are missing for that. I do not see them on your transcript of grades. I am afraid all this is irregular. It does not conform. You are seeking to enroll here for your senior year. It does not conform, Wister."

"All I want is a diploma," said Heller.

"Ah, yes," said Miss Simmons. "Wister, you are demanding that at commencement next May, Empire University certify on a diploma that you are a Bachelor of Nuclear Science and Engineering, lend you its prestige and send you out, a totally uneducated savage, to blow up the world. Isn't that what you are demanding, Wister? I thought as much."

"No, no," said Heller. "I'm supposed to fix it up, not blow it up!"

"Wister, the only thing I can do is take this application under advisement. There must be other opinions gotten, Wister. So be back here tomorrow morning at nine o'clock. I can offer no hope, Wister. NEXT!"

It was a bright moment for me. Heller always had such a marvelous opinion of himself, always bragging. And here was a sensible person who saw through him completely. And Bury was a very clever fellow to lay such an adroit trap. I drank a whole glass of *sira* straight down in a toast to Bury.

Heller was slowed to a crawl!

PART EIGHTEEN

Chapter 1

Heller slowly paid the fees at the temporary cashier's desk and then, hands in pockets, wandered about, not looking at very much, apparently immersed in thought.

After a while, he studied the posted building layout.

He began to read bulletin boards. Students were looking for rooms and rooms were looking for students and Mazie Anne had lost trace of Mack and Mack had lost touch with Charlotte and Professor Umpchuddle's classes were transferred to the left wing. Then his eyes clamped on to a formally printed plastic sign. It said:

THOSE DESIRING TO HIRE GRADUATES
ARE NOT PERMITTED TO RECRUIT
ON THE CAMPUS DIRECTLY.
THEY MUST SEE
THE ASSISTANT DEAN OF STUDENTS
IN THE JUMP BUILDING.

Promptly Heller was out on College Walk again, trotting through the throng of milling students, clickety-clacking on a zig-zag course and presently clickety-clacked into the office labelled:

Mr. Twaddle, Assistant Dean of Students

Mr. Twaddle was sitting at his desk in shirt sleeves filling out stacks of forms. He was a small, bald-headed

man. He pointed at a chair, sat back and began to pack
an enormous briar pipe.

"I want to hire a graduate," said Heller.

Mr. Twaddle stopped packing his pipe. Then he
stopped staring. "Your name?"

Heller showed him the invoice.

"Possibly you mean your family wants to hire a graduate?"

"Do you have any?" said Heller.

"A graduate in what, Wister?"

"Stocks and bonds," said Heller.

"Ah. A Doctor of Business Administration." Mr.
Twaddle got the pipe going.

"He'd have to be over twenty-one," said Heller.

Mr. Twaddle laughed indulgently. "A Doctor of Business Administration would certainly be over twenty-one,
Wister. There are so many changes in the rules each year,
it practically takes them forever. But I am afraid this is
the wrong season of the year. You should have been here
last May. They all get snapped up, you know. There
won't be another crop until the October degrees are
awarded almost two months from now and it just so happens there aren't going to be any in that October crop."
He smoked complacently.

"Haven't you got any leftovers? Please look."

Mr. Twaddle, being a good fellow, opened a drawer
and got out a tattered list. He dropped it on the desk
before him and made the motions of going over it. "No.
They've been snapped up."

Heller inched his chair forward to the desk. He
pointed a finger halfway down the list. I hadn't known
he could read upside down. But he couldn't read very
well because the name had a lot of marks and cross-outs
after it.

"There's one that isn't marked assigned," said Heller.

Mr. Twaddle laughed. "That's Israel Epstein. He didn't graduate. Thesis not accepted. I'm acquainted with this one. Oh, too well acquainted. You know what he tried to hand in? Despite all cautions and warnings? A thesis called 'Is Government Necessary?' But that isn't why they refused to re-enroll him."

"But he's over twenty-one," said Heller.

"I should say he is. He has been flunked out on his doctorate for three consecutive years. Wister, this young fellow is an activist! A deviant. A revolutionary of the most disturbing sort. He simply will not conform. He even boycotted the Young Communist League! He's a roaring, ranting tiger! A wild-eyed, howling anarchist, of all things! Quite out of fashion. But that wasn't why they refused to re-enroll him. The government cut off his student loans and demanded immediate repayment."

"Why would they do that?" said Heller.

"Why, he was doing all the income tax forms for students and the faculty and he was costing the Internal Revenue Service a fortune!"

"Is that his address?" said Heller. "That number on 125th Street?"

Mr. Twaddle said, "It probably was up to a few minutes ago. Ten IRS agents were just here demanding that address. So he will soon be beyond reach entirely."

"Thank you for your help, Mr. Twaddle," said Heller.

"Always glad to assist, Wister. Drop in any time."

Heller closed the door behind him. Then he started to run.

Chapter 2

Heller was down 116th Street and up Broadway like a quarter horse. If anyone noticed he was going faster than was usual, he wasn't looking at them—but New Yorkers never notice anything. And, factually, I don't think he was moving at any exceptional speed: some cars were going faster than he was. I was glad to note that gravity differences had not given him any phenomenal powers. Things to him weighed only a sixth less than usual.

Judging by the scenery flow, he was probably only doing twenty.

I was, of course, a little bit puzzled by his obvious antagonism to an anarchist. Or did he fear for the IRS agents, faced by a maniacal wild man of huge powers? Perhaps his contact with the FBI had inclined him to defect to the Earth government. I know that in his place, I would have been seeking political asylum.

He came to 125th Street and raced along, looking for the address. But he found it because of three double-parked government cars. There was no one in them.

Heller checked the building. The street number was almost indecipherable. It was one of those innumerable abandoned apartment houses with which New York is strewn. The taxes are high, the tenants destructive. If the owner tries to repair the building, the tax rates go up and the tenants tear it down again. So owners simply abandon them to rot. And this one was so bad off that not even tenants had to wreck it. Obviously no one in his right mind would try to live there. The front entrance looked like it had been an artillery target.

He circumvented fallen debris and went in. He stopped. Noise was coming from the second floor—ripping sounds.

Heller went up what was left of the stairs.

A government agent was standing outside a door, picking his teeth.

Heller walked up to the agent. "I'm looking for Israel Epstein," he said.

The agent found a particularly succulent morsel in his teeth, ate it and said, "Yeah? We ain't got a warrant out for him yet, so that don't make you an accomplice. But as soon as they get through planting the evidence in there, we'll be able to get one."

"Where is he?" demanded Heller.

"Oh, him. Well, if we let him escape first, then he becomes a fugitive and we can send him up for that if for nothing else."

"Where did he go?" demanded Heller.

"Oh, he ran off down 125th Street," said the IRS agent, pointing west. "Said he was going to drown himself in the Hudson River."

Heller turned to leave. Two IRS agents stood squarely behind with drawn guns.

"Sucker," said the tooth-picking one. "Hey, McGuire!" he yelled into the apartment, "Here's one of his friends!"

The two agents in the hall pushed Heller ahead of them with their guns. They shoved him well into the apartment.

The place might have been a wreck before. It was an emergency disaster now. It was torn to splinters!

IRS agents were using jimmies to pry up boards, hammers to smash furniture.

A huge hulking brute out of a horror film stood, hands on hips, glaring at Heller. "So, an accomplice! Sit down in that chair!"

It was pretty broken up but Heller managed it.

"Say SIR when you're spoken to!" said McGuire.

"Sir?" said Heller. "You a nobleman or something?"

"We're a hell of a lot more important than that, kid. We're Internal Revenue Service agents. We run this country and don't you forget it!"

"Sir?" said Heller.

"Now, where are the books you and Epstein cooked? Where are they hidden?" demanded McGuire.

"Sir?" said Heller.

"We know God (bleeped) well that you had actual IRS manuals! Copies of the real law and everything. Where are they hidden?"

"Sir?" said Heller.

"Do you realize," said McGuire, "if they got into public hands it would ruin us? Do you realize this is treason? Do you know what the penalty for treason is? Death! It says so right in the Constitution!"

"Sir?" said Heller.

"I don't think he'll talk," said another agent.

McGuire said, "I'll handle this, Malone."

"There ain't any manuals here," said still another agent.

McGuire said, "Shut up, O'Brien. I'll handle this. This kid is a red-hot suspect. I got to read him his rights. Now listen carefully. You have to testify to whatever IRS wants you to testify to. You have to swear to anything IRS tells you to swear to and sign anything you are told by IRS to sign. If you fail to do so you will be charged with conspiring to conspire with conspirators regardless of race, color or creed. Sign here."

Heller had a slip of paper under his nose. "What's this?"

"By the Miranda Rule," said McGuire, "the prisoner must be informed of his rights. I have just informed you of yours. The IRS is totally legal, always. This attests you have been warned. So sign here."

Heller signed, "J. Edgar Hoover."

"Good," said McGuire. "Now, where are the God (bleeped) cooked account books and where are the God (bleeped) IRS manuals and regulations?"

"Sir?" said Heller.

"He ain't going to talk," said Malone.

"I better just plant this Commie literature and these bags of heroin and we can get going," said O'Brien.

"You know what's going to happen to you, kid?" said McGuire with obvious satisfaction. "We're going to force you to report downtown to the Federal Building. We're going to cross-examine you, kid. We're going to put under the hot lights and we're going to find out all about you. Everything. When we get through with you, there won't be a thing about you we don't know. Take this."

McGuire had been scribbling a name on a legal document. He handed it to Heller. It said:

> SUBPOENA! THE PEOPLE VERSUS EPSTEIN. J. Edgar Hoover is hereby summoned to appear at 0900 hours at the Federal Building, Room 22222, Permanent Federal Grand Jury, Internal Revenue Courts.

"Cross-examination?" said Heller.

"Correct."

"You find out everything there is to know about me?"

"Correct."

"Actually, I think," said Heller, "that under that board over there is a good hiding place."

"That's better," said McGuire. "Which board?"

Heller got up. He went over. He knelt down.

And out of his pocket, his action hidden from them by his body, he took a red-and-white piece of candy. I recognized it. It was the candy he had been making aboard the tug! It had a wrapper that looked like paper. With a thumbnail and a twist, he pushed the paper down into the candy. He put it under a board.

He stood up. "There are no manuals there now."

"Shows the right spirit. You can go now but you show up! Federal Building, nine hundred hours!"

Heller walked out.

He walked down the remains of the steps.

Outside, he walked up to one of the government cars. He bent over.

He had four sticks of dynamite strapped to his leg!

He undid the tape.

He laid the dynamite into the back seat of the car. No cap, no means to explode it. He just laid it there.

Then he walked very rapidly west on 125th Street.

The buildings on either side of him shook in concussion!

A gigantic flash whipped at the sky!

A roaring blast of sound struck a sledgehammer blow!

Heller looked back. As the smoke soared, I saw that the whole front of the abandoned apartment house was falling into the street in slow motion. Pieces of the roof were still sailing in the air!

The government cars, showered with rubble, did not explode: So he wasn't that good with explosives after all.

Pieces of apartment house were falling out of the sky. Torrents of flame began to leap up.

It was the candy!

I knew what the stuff was now. It was a binary concussion-flame grenade. It didn't operate until the wrapper, the needful element, was shoved down into the explosive. It had activated on a forty-second dissolve. The Apparatus never used them. They were too risky to carry!

"What the hell was that?" said an old man near Heller.

"There were ten terrorists in that building," said Heller.

"Oh," said the old man. "Vandals again."

Heller went along 125th Street, first at a casual walk and then at a distance-increasing run.

Behind him, fire sirens were screaming.

Heller didn't look back again. He was headed, apparently, for the river.

Chapter 3

Speeding along, Heller could catch glimpses of the river ahead. His view was impeded with underpasses and overpasses of major roads.

He veered slightly to his left. The river lay just on the other side of some trunk highways along which traffic blurred.

Heller negotiated the obstacles.

Before him stretched a long dock, reaching west into the water.

He slowed, alert. He jumped up to see over some obstacles. Then he went speeding ahead.

On the end of the dock lay a tangle of something. Heller raced to it.

Right at the dock end lay a jacket. A pair of horn-rimmed spectacles was sitting on it.

The Jersey shore, opposite, was a yellow haze of polluted air. The Hudson was blue with sky reflection despite the scum and filth in it.

Heller was looking up and down the river. Apparently an incoming tide from the ocean was slacking the current for the bits of dunnage and trash were going neither upstream nor down.

A hat!

A soggy, dark blue, snap-brim hat, still afloat with the air trapped in it.

Heller threw off his jacket. He pulled off his shoes. He zipped out of his pants. He threw his cap to the dock.

In a long dive he went into the water, debris and oil!

Down he went! Hands grabbing out and back, he was pulling himself toward the bottom.

The light went from brown to dim gray.

Yikes! How deep was this river?

Down, down, down, his eyes sweeping left to right through the murk!

Ooze!

He had hit bottom!

Up he went like a streak.

He blew to the surface. He treaded water, jumping his head up to look around.

He inverted.

Down he went again. Down, down, down, looking left and right.

Black ooze!

Around in a circle on the bottom. Old tires and cans.

Up, up, up! He blew to the surface again.

More treading water. More jumps to lift his head out. A faint sound!

Heller made a bigger jump, lifting himself out of the water.

A faint voice, "I'm over here."

Heller treaded water and looked toward the dock.

There in the water, clinging to an old ring sunk in concrete, was somebody, just a hand and head showing.

Heller struck out in that direction.

In a minute or two he was beside a very small young man, covered with oil, mostly eyes.

"I'm a failure," moaned the pitiful figure. Then he coughed.

"I lost my nerve. I couldn't keep my head under long enough to drown."

"Are you Israel Epstein?" said Heller.

"Yes, I'm sorry I can't shake hands. I'd lose my grip."

Heller was surveying the fellow's plight. The dock end was sheer above him and had no handholds.

A passing ship engulfed them in waves. Epstein lost his grip on the ring and got banged against the concrete. Heller put Epstein's hand back on the ring. "Hold on!"

"I can't climb up. I was a failure at drowning myself and now I'm a failure at saving myself. You better go off and leave me. I'm not worth rescuing."

Heller swam along the dock and found an iron ladder that reached down into the water. He climbed up.

He went to his jacket and took out a coil of fish line. He went back to the dock edge above Epstein. "Just hold on," he called down. A passing tug's wash engulfed Epstein.

Heller's hands were moving rapidly in a strange repeating rhythmic pattern. He was plaiting the fish line into a thin rope!

He made a nonslip loop in the end of his product. He lowered it down to Epstein. "Put your legs through it and sit on it."

Epstein couldn't do it.

Heller secured the top end to an old rusty ring and dived back into the water. He paddled over to Epstein, found a piece of driftwood, broke it and forced it into the loop to make a seat and got him onto it and showed him how to hold the upper strands.

"You shouldn't go to all this trouble," said Epstein. "I'll only come to another bad end."

Heller splashed at the water to get oil scum to float away and when he had a clear patch, he used it to get some of the oil off Epstein's head and shoulders.

"Now, don't go away," said Heller. He swam back to the ladder, got up on the dock and shortly had Epstein up beside him, safely on the concrete.

Chapter 4

A pair of cops wandered up. "What are you doing?"

"Fishing," said Heller.

"You sure you're not swimming?" said one cop.

"Just fishing," said Heller.

"Well, see that you don't swim," said the cop and he and his partner wandered away, idly swinging their nightsticks.

"You didn't turn me over to them," said Epstein. "But you might as well. They'll get me anyway."

Heller had recovered his redstar engineer's rag. He was wiping the oil off Epstein. Then he got Epstein's shoes off and got him out of his pants and put the articles in the sun, which seemed to be quite hot.

He took a few more swipes at Epstein's face and then put the young man's horn-rimmed glasses on him.

I wondered if Heller had made a mistake in identity. According to Mr. Twaddle, this Epstein was a roaring anarchist, a terror and a threat to civilization. But he was quite small, had a narrow face, a beaked nose, weak eyes and was shivering.

"You cold?" said Heller.

"No, it is just what I have been through," said Epstein.

"What do they want you for, really?" said Heller.

Epstein looked like he was going to cry. "It all started when I realized that the usual Internal Revenue Service agent just made up regulations as he went along. But one fatal day I was in the law library and found the actual Congressional law and the IRS manual of regulations. I Xeroxed them. I started to do the income tax returns for the faculty and some students with all the correct deductions." He sighed and was silent a bit. "Oh, the way of the revolutionary is hard! I'm not up to it."

"So what happened?" said Heller.

"The local IRS office lost about two million dollars in illegal collections they'd been getting. And the bonuses of agents McGuire, O'Brien and Malone shrank to nothing."

He sighed a long, shuddering sigh. "They will never forgive me. They will persecute me all my days. You shouldn't have rescued me. I am a lost cause."

Heller had gotten some of the oil off of himself. He went over to his jacket and fished out the subpoena. He brought it back and handed it to Epstein. As he sat back down, he said, "What is this?"

Epstein looked at it, turned it over. "It's just a subpoena. It tells you to appear before a grand jury and testify."

"And what does that consist of?" said Heller.

"Oh, very simple. You just take the Fifth Amendment—which is to say, refuse in case it incriminates you—and they put you in jail and bring you out every few weeks and you just take the Fifth Amendment again."

"Then they really don't examine you and make you tell all you know?"

"No, it's just a method of keeping innocent people in jail."

Heller was looking at the water. "Oh, those poor fellows," he said.

"What poor fellows?" said Epstein.

"McGuire, Malone and O'Brien and seven other agents. They're all dead. I thought I was facing a Code break, you see."

"Dead?"

"Yes, your apartment blew up. Killed them all."

"If those three are dead, then the case is ended. They didn't have any evidence, only their own testimony. It means I am not being hunted. The thing is all over!"

"Good," said Heller. "Then you're free and clear!"

Epstein sat for a short time, looking at the water. Then suddenly his teeth began to chatter and from this he went into a torrent of tears.

"If you're free and clear," said Heller, "what's wrong now?"

After a bit Epstein was able to talk. But he still kept on crying. "I know something awful is going to happen in the next few minutes!"

"Why?" said Heller in astonishment.

"Oh," wept Epstein, "I wouldn't be permitted to have this much good news."

"What?" said Heller.

"The news is too wonderful! I don't deserve it! A world record catastrophe is going to strike any moment now to make up for it! I know it!"

"Look," said Heller patiently, "your troubles are over. And there's more good news. I have a job for you."

"Oh?" said Epstein. "You mean I've got a chance to pay back my student loans and re-enroll for my doctorate again?"

"I think so," said Heller.

"What is your name?"

"Jet."

Oh, my Gods! This *was* a Code break. Heller was going to tell him his real name.

"That isn't all of it," said Epstein.

"Well, no," said Heller. "The full name on my papers is Jerome Terrance Wister. That makes my initials 'J. T.' My real friends call me Jet."

Oh, that slippery dog. He'd just squeaked by on that one.

"Oh, J. T. Wister. Jet. I get it. The name on the subpoena was J. Edgar Hoover and I was sure you wanted me to murder somebody. I am not the type, you know. I can't even kill cockroaches."

"Nothing drastic like that," said Heller. "You're over twenty-one, aren't you?"

"Yes, I'm twenty-three and an aged wreck."

"Well, all I want you to do is open a broker account for me."

"Do you have credit?"

"Well, no," said Heller. "But all I want you to do is open an account so I can buy and sell stocks—some firm like Short, Skidder and Long Associates."

Epstein drew a shuddering sigh. "It isn't that simple. You have to have an address so you can have a bank account. Then you have to arrange credit and open a brokerage account. Do you have any money?"

"Yes. I have a hundred thousand to use in such gambling."

"Do you have any heavy debts or liabilities like me?"

"No."

"I know everybody has enemies. But do you have any special enemies that would like to get at you?"

Heller thought a bit. "Well, there's a Mr. Bury, an attorney I've run into."

"Bury? Bury of Swindle and Crouch?"

"Yes, the same."

"He's Delbert John Rockecenter's personal family attorney. He's one of the most powerful lawyers on Wall Street. And he's an enemy?"

"I would say so," said Heller. "He keeps working at it."

"Oh," said Epstein. He was silent for a bit and they sat in the hot sun drying off. Then he said, "This thing you're asking is pretty big. It's going to take an awful lot of work. You would need somebody on it full time, not just to start it but to run it for you."

"Well, how much do you earn a week?"

"Oh, I don't earn much of anything," said Epstein. "I'm not really an accountant—that's just one of the things a business administrator has to know. They wouldn't take my last thesis for my doctorate. It was a good thesis, too. It was all about corporate feudalism—industrial anarchy, you know—how the corporations could and should run everything. Its title was 'Is Government Necessary?' But I think I could get them to accept my new title. It's 'Anarchy Is Vital If We Are

Ever Going to Establish Industrial Feudalism.' "

"Well," said Heller, "you could have time to work on that."

"You see," said Epstein, "they argue with me that it isn't in the field of business administration. They say it is a political science subject. But it isn't. No! About eighty percent of a corporation's resources are absorbed in trying to file government reports and escort inspectors around. If they would listen, I could get the Gross National Product up eighty percent, just like that!" He brooded a bit. "Maybe I ought to change my thesis title to 'Corporations Would Find Revolution Cheaper Than Paying Taxes.' "

"I would pay you five hundred dollars a week," said Heller.

"No. If I did it, it would be for one percent of the gross income with a drawing account not to exceed two hundred dollars a week. I'm not worth much."

Heller went over to his jacket and fished out two one hundred dollar bills. He tried to hand them to Epstein.

"No," said Epstein. "You don't know enough about me. The offer is probably very good. But I can't accept it."

"Right now, do you have any money? Any place to live? Your apartment isn't there anymore."

"It's no more than I deserve. I didn't have any other clothes and I can sleep in the park tonight. It's warm weather."

"You've got to eat."

"I am used to starving."

"Look," said Heller, "you've got to take this job."

"It's too good an offer. You do not know me, Mr. Hoover—I mean, Mr. Wister. You are probably a kind, honest, patient man. But your efforts of philanthropy are being directed at a lost cause. I cannot possibly accept your employment."

They sat for a while, dangling their legs off the dock edge, drying out in the warm sun. The Hudson had begun to flow again as the tide ebbed.

Suddenly Heller said, "Is ethnology included in business administration studies?"

"No."

"How about the customs of people?"

"No. You're talking about social anthropology, I guess. I've never studied that."

"Good," said Heller. "Then you would not realize that the laws of the American Indian were still binding on Manhattan, due to prior sovereignty."

"They are?" said Epstein.

"There was an Indian law that when you saved a man's life, that man was thereafter responsible for you from there on out."

"Where did you hear that?"

"I was told by a master of political science from your own university."

"So it must be true," brooded Epstein.

"Good," said Heller. "I just saved your life, didn't I?"

"Yes, you did. I'm afraid there's no doubt about that."

"All right," said Heller. "Then you are responsible for me from here on out."

Silence.

"You have to take the job and look after my affairs," said Heller. "It's prior Indian law. There's no way out of it."

Epstein stared at him. Then suddenly his head dropped. He broke into a torrent of tears. When he could talk, he blubbered, "You see, I knew when I heard all that good news, some new catastrophe was lurking just ahead! And it's arrived! It's been horrible enough, in the face of malignant fate, trying to bear up and take responsibility for myself. And now," a fresh torrent of tears, "I have to take responsibility for you, too!"

Heller laid the two one-hundred-dollar bills in his hand. Epstein looked at them forlornly. He got up and went over to his jacket. He put them in his empty wallet.

He sadly looked at Heller. "Meet me on the steps of High Library on the campus tomorrow at noon and I will have the plan of what we have to do."

"Good," said Heller.

Epstein picked up his coat and walked a little ways. Then he turned. "I am sure that, with my awful fate, you will live to regret the kind things you have done. I am sorry."

Head down, he trudged away.

Chapter 5

That evening, in the Gracious Palms lobby, Heller sat reading the *Evening Libel*. He was wearing his old, blue, too-short suit. The "throwaway" suit had really been thrown away after Heller's swim in the polluted river water. And evidently the tailors had not delivered any new clothes.

The story he was reading said:

In a strongly worded statement today, Mayor
Don Hernandez O'Toole censured the New York
District Office of the Internal Revenue Service.

"The IRS practice of blowing up perfectly
good tax-deductible property must cease," said
Mayor O'Toole. "It places all New York at risk."

The censure came on the heels of an explosion this afternoon on West 125th Street where an
IRS squad was visiting a tax-deductible apartment
house.

Dynamite found in the government cars was
clear proof of intent to dynamite, according to
New York Fire Commissioner Flame Jackson.

Premature dynamission was the stated cause
of the blast.

A U.S. Government spokesman said, "IRS
has a perfect right to do what it pleases, when it
pleases and to whom it pleases and New York better get the word, see?" This was generally
accepted as an evidence of cover-up as usual.

There were no lives of any importance lost in
the blast.

Heller had just turned the paper over and half a
strip of Bugs Bunny became visible and I was much
annoyed when he was interrupted.

Heller looked up. Vantagio was standing right beside
his chair.

"Did you get registered?" His voice was edgy. Hostile? "If you did, why didn't you call me?"

"Well," said Heller, "it's sort of up in the air. It's my

grades: D average and I'm asking to be accepted as a senior. It's possible I won't make it."

Had Vantagio gone white? Hard to tell as he was shadowed by a lobby palm. "What did they say?"

"It's 'under advisement.' I am to go back at nine in the morning."

"*Sangue di Cristo!* You wait until eight o'clock at night to tell me this!" Vantagio rushed off. He slammed the door of his office. Oh, he was angry.

Yes, I felt I could make, possibly, use of this jealousy for Heller.

But I made a more important observation about nine, New York time. Heller disengaged himself from some African diplomat he was talking to, got in the elevator and went to his suite. I could see that, down the hall, his door was wide open!

And down close to the floor, as though she were lying on it, a beautiful brunette girl was extending her hand out into the hall. In a musical voice she called, "Come along, pretty boy. We're waiting!"

A torrent of giggles came out of the room.

The interference went on. But I had made my observation. Heller never locked his door! Those women simply walked in whenever they chose!

A wide-open invitation to rob the place!

I myself had a very happy afternoon nap, contemplating it.

I must have overslept but there was ample excuse for it. I had not dared sleep for days. But things were running my way now. When I awoke, Heller was already disembarking from the subway at 116th Street. I watched tolerantly. His fate would soon be sealed.

He went directly to the temporary reservation area. There were quite a few students about, milling, finishing off their signups. I realized that it wasn't registration *week,* really. It had been registration day, per se, yesterday, judging from the crowd sizes.

I sat back to enjoy Heller getting his comeuppance. No way would this Miss Simmons let him into this school. Not with those grades. Heller's plans would be thrown into a cocked hat!

And there she was. She had just finished her last student. She ignored her short waiting line. She had a smile on her face but it was the kind you see on the female spider just before she has a meal of a male.

"Well, if it isn't the young Einstein," said Miss Simmons. "Sit down."

Heller sat down and Miss Simmons scrambled through her papers and then sat back with that horrible smile. "It appears," she said, "that they don't care who blows up the world these days."

"You called me 'Wister' yesterday."

"Well, times have changed, haven't they. Who do you know? God?"

"Has my enrollment received advisement?" asked Heller.

"That it has, young Einstein. Now, ordinarily we do not permit a transfer from another school into the senior class."

"I could make up——"

"Hush, hush. But in your case, it seems this is to be allowed. And into our competitive School of Engineering and Applied Science, too."

"I am very grate——"

"Oh, hush, young Einstein. You have not heard it all. Ordinarily we require a fresh American College Test that must average 28% or above. But you, young Einstein, seem to have had that waived."

"Well that's goo——"

"Oh, there's more," said Miss Simmons. "It has

always been mandatory that a student entering engineering school receive a Scholastic Aptitude Test and that the grade for verbal and written be above 700. But you are not being required to do any SAT at all."

"That's truly marv——"

"And more, young Einstein. Our requirement for a B average for such enrollments has been waived. Now, isn't that nice?"

"Indeed," said Heller. "It is very ni——"

"It is far *too* nice, young Einstein. I have direct orders here to admit you. As a senior. In the School of Engineering and Applied Science. As a candidate for a Bachelor in Nuclear Science and Engineering, graduating next May. And the order is signed by the president of the university himself."

"Really, I'm overwhel——"

"You'll be overwhelmed shortly," said Miss Simmons and her smile vanished. "Either somebody has gone stark raving loony *or* the reduction of government subsidies and the lack of a post-war boom makes them slaver for your twenty-five hundred dollars *and* they have gone stark raving loony! You and they are NOT going to get away with it. I will not have my name on the form registering you and turning upon the world a nuclear scientist who is a complete imbecile. Do I make myself clear, young Einstein?"

"I'm very sorry if——"

"Oh, don't waste energy on getting upset at this point," said Miss Simmons. "You are going to be upset enough later to need every calorie! Oh, I have no choice but to enroll you, young Mr. God Junior. But there are ways of enrolling and ways of enrolling. Now, shall we begin?"

"I really——"

"Now, to start with," said Miss Simmons, "you do

not have all the requisite credits in former schooling for this degree. There are four subjects here which are omitted and I am signing you up to take them IN ADDITION to the heavy engineering subjects you will be required to take for the semester."

"I am sure I——"

"Oh, don't thank me yet! There's more! Now, I very much doubt that with those D grades, you were firmly founded in the subjects in which you received them. So I am making your acceptance conditional upon special tutoring to bring those subjects up to the mark along with your regular class work."

"I think I——"

"I know you are grateful," said Miss Simmons. "So I will add another favor. Your Saint Lee's was a military school. And I adjudicate that your military science and study credits given there are not valid unless you continue on with and complete your entire ROTC—Reserve Officers' Training Corps—schedule in this, your senior year. You can really get a bellyful of how nasty war is! And the Army can be persuaded it is unpatriotic not to complete them. I intend to write them a little note. That means three additional class periods and one drill period a week. All on top of the extra subjects and tutoring. Now, isn't that nice, God Junior?"

Heller was just looking at her by now. Stunned, no doubt.

She had turned to her accordion-folded computer printouts of class timings and assignments already made. "But here is where you are really going to thank me, God Himself. When I received this order at breakfast, I worked it all out. There is no way to assign all these hours in such a way that the classes are consecutive. Several of them occur at the same exact hours. You have to be in two, and in one case three places at the same time.

And that is the way you have been assigned. You will be absent, one class or another, any way you want to look at it. The professors will rant. You will find yourself in front of deans. And it is they, not I, who will tell you that you cannot graduate and get your diploma next May. If they come back on me, I will say you just demanded it all, and you did, didn't you, Jehovah?"

Miss Simmons sat back and tapped a pencil against her teeth. Then after a bit she said, "Oh, I don't blame you for being over-awed in appreciation. You see, Master of All He Surveys and Creator Himself, I do not like INFLUENCE. Also, I am a member of the Anti-Nuclear Protest Marchers, its secretary in fact. And though the organization may be old and it may be suppressed and it may be that the New York Tactical Police Force is just waiting to bash in our heads again, the thought of letting a nuclear scientist as unqualified as you loose upon the world turns my blood to leukemia. Do we understand each other, Wister?"

"Really, Miss Simmons——"

"Oh, I almost forgot. Just in case you find time heavy on your hands—loafing about with this schedule— I have added another course to make up for a missing optional. It is Nature Appreciation 101 and 104. One goes out every Sunday, all day, and admires the birds and trees and learns, perhaps, what a nasty thing it is to make those world-destroying bombs! I teach this class myself, so I can keep an eye on your vicious proclivities. Now you can thank me, Wister."

"Really, Miss S——"

"And as they are so interested in money, all this adds another fifteen hundred and thirty-three dollars to your bill. I hope you don't have it. Pay the cashier. Good day, Wister. NEXT!"

Heller took the papers she had already made out. He took the invoice.

He went over and paid the cashier.

Aha! My heart had gone out to Miss Simmons more and more. What a sterling character! I toyed with the idea of sending her some candy "From an Unknown Admirer." No, on the other hand, a pair of brass knuckles would be more in her line. With maybe a Knife Section knife to keep on her desk. But really, did she need it?

Chapter 6

Just before noon, Heller came to the High Library. It was a very imposing building with a Roman look—ten huge columns stretched across the front, an enormous rotunda, a very noble façade. It was fronted with a vast expanse of steps almost as wide as the building itself.

He passed a fountain and then a statue with the words *Alma Mater* on it. He went halfway up the upper steps and slumped down on the stone.

And well he might slump. I had been kept laughing for the last two hours following his zigzag course around the enormous campus. He trotted here and he trotted there. He was locating every single one of the large number of classrooms, halls, armories and drill fields he would have to attend. He had constantly checked a copy of a computer printout and he had found that he had a schedule which went two classes at the same time, followed by no class for the next hour and then, in one case, three classes at the same time! I was kept in stitches. Not even the great Heller could cope with that schedule. And it went seven days a week!

As he sat there in the hot noonday sun, he must be realizing that there was no way on Earth he could get a diploma and carry out the silly plans he had undoubtedly made to carry his mission through just to spite me. And get me killed.

Students were drifting up and down the steps, no vast throng. Young men and women, not too well dressed. Heller must look younger than some of them, despite being, in fact, several years older in time and, in all honesty, decades older in experience. How silly he must feel, a Royal officer of the Fleet, sitting there amongst these naive creatures. Another joke on him and on them, too. I idly speculated what they would think if they knew a Voltar combat engineer was sitting right there, in plain view, a Mancoian from Atalanta more than a score of light-years away, a holder of the fifty-volunteer star, that could blow their planet to bits as easy as he could spit or could prevent an invasion that would slaughter every one of them. What a joke on them. How stupid they were!

A couple of girls and a young man drifted by. One of the girls said, "Ooo! Are you on the baseball team?"

"I didn't know they were still turned out," said the boy. "Why, you're wearing spikes!"

Heller looked at one of the girls. "You can't get to first base if you don't."

They all of them burst into screams of laughter. I tried and tried to figure out what they were laughing about. (Bleep) that Heller, anyway. Always so *obscure*. And he had no right to start currying popularity. He was an extraterrestrial, an interloper! Besides, they were pretty girls.

"Name's Muggins," said the boy. "This is Christine

and Coral—they're from Barnyard College: that's part of Empire but all women, oh boy!"

"My name's Jet," said Heller.

"C'm up'n see us s'm'time," said Christine.

They all laughed again, waved and walked on down the broad steps.

And here came Epstein!

He was dragging an enormously long roll of something behind him. It was about a foot in diameter and certainly over twelve feet long! He passed the fountain and then the statue. He stopped a couple steps below Heller. He was dressed in a shabby gray suit and a shabby gray hat and, in addition to the roll, he was carrying a very scuffed up, cheap attaché case. He sank down on a step, puffing.

"And how is Mr. Epstein?" said Heller cheerfully.

"Oh, don't call me that," said Epstein. "It makes me uncomfortable. Please call me Izzy. That's what everybody does."

"Good. If you'll call me Jet."

"No. You are really my superior as you have the capital. I should call you Mr. Wister."

"You have forgotten," said Heller, "that you are responsible for me now. And that includes my morale." Then he said very firmly, "Call me Jet."

Izzy Epstein looked unhappy. Then he said, "All right, Mr. Jet."

Heller must have given it up. "I see you found some clothes. I was worried that they'd all been destroyed."

"Oh, yes. I took a bath in the gym and I got two suits, this hat and this briefcase from the Salvation Army Good Will. They wouldn't do for you, of course, but if I dressed too well, I would attract attention and invite bad luck. One must never appear to be doing too well—the lightning will strike."

This Izzy Epstein was turning my stomach. It was quite obvious that he was a neurotic depressive with persecution complexes and had overtones of religio-mania, evident in his fixations on fate. A fine mess he would make for Heller. Neurotics are never competent. But on the other hand, it was really a break for me that Heller had run into him. The fellow couldn't even manage his own affairs, much less Heller's.

"Well, you look better, anyway," said Heller.

"Oh, I'm exhausted! I have been working flat out all night to prepare a proposal for you. The only building I could find open was the Art College, so I had to use their materials."

"Is that what that is?"

"This roll? Yes. All they had left out was studio paper—the kind they use behind models, twelve feet wide, a hundred feet long. And they didn't leave out any scissors. So I used that."

He tried to unroll it. But he didn't have enough arm reach. Heller started to help him but Izzy said, "No, no. You're the investor. You there!" he called out suddenly.

A couple of new students had come out of the library. Izzy stopped them at the top of the huge, wide stairway. "You hold this end," he said to one. "And you this end," he said to the other. "Now, hold it tight." The two stood there, twelve feet apart, holding the top of the roll.

Heller had followed Izzy up. Izzy took the roll and backed down two steps, unreeling it. At the top, in wild, garish ink, all along it, it said: *Confidential Draft.*

"You will probably find it too colorful," said Izzy, understating it like mad, for it was blazing in the sunlight, "but they had only left around old dried-up pots of poster paint and I had to mix it with water. And there were only some discarded brushes. But, it will give you the idea."

He backed down two more steps. Revealed to view were some odd lines and symbols. It looked like three wooden hay forks raking apples—and all of different colors, all bright.

"Now, that first row is what we call the mask corporations. We incorporate those separately in New York, New Jersey, Nevada and Delaware. They all have different, noninterlocking boards of directors."

He backed down another step unrolling the roll further. But there was a bit of wind. Two more students, eating sandwiches, were paused nearby. Izzy sent one to the far side and one to the right side and told them to hold it steady and they did.

Izzy pointed to the newly displayed mad thunder of color, lines and symbols. "Now, those are the bank accounts for those corporations."

He backed down another step, got two more students to hold the sides and two more to hold the extreme top which was buckling. "Now there, and notice the arrows as they intertwine, are the various brokerage firms which will handle orders placed with the mask corporations."

Izzy backed another step, unrolling the roll further.

"What is this?" one student, wandering up, asked another.

"Psychedelic art," said one already holding.

"Now, here we are getting to the more important stages," said Izzy. "The corporation on the right is in Canada. The one on the left is in Mexico. And these two corporations invisibly control the center one which is in Singapore. Get it?"

Izzy backed further. He needed more students and got them. Several were now up on a big stone parapet, looking down on it.

"Now, this series of arrows—the green series is the most important although the purple ones there are useful—transfer the funds of the above corporations in such a way as to bypass all reporting to governments."

"Is it a poster?" asked a student.

"Poster for some new riots, I heard them say," said another.

Izzy stepped down another broad step and unrolled it further. He got more holders. "Now, this is the Swiss-Liechtenstein consortium of corporations. You may wonder why these seem so independent. Well, actually they are not."

He unrolled more chart, got some newcomers to hold it. "The Swiss-Liechtenstein fund flow goes underground to West Germany and thence to Hong Kong. Do you get it? No?"

More of the chart was unrolled and held, "You can see why, now. The Hong Kong funds—see the purple arrow there—flow to Singapore, come back to Tahiti and . . ."

He unrolled more chart, ". . . arrive right in our own backyard in the Bahamas. Clever, eh? But look at London."

He unrolled more chart. One whole width was devoted to three corporations, three stockbrokers and three bank accounts, all in London. Orange lines radiated out and came back to Hong Kong. "And that is how we get the funds into the Bahamas from the City as they call it. But you will be interested in this."

He unrolled more chart and got more holders. There was an interlocking series of lines which stretched out to every bank account and brokerage house, a spider web of royal blue. "That is the arbitrage network. By means of a centrally controlled system, we can take advantage of the differences of currency prices throughout the whole network and every time we transfer any funds, we also make a mint! It requires telexes and lease lines from RCA, of course. But it will pay for itself every week."

He unrolled more chart, got more holders. The steps were pretty thronged by now.

"What was the artist thinking when he drew it?" asked a girl.

"Soul music," said a learned boy.

"I think it's quite lovely," said another girl. "It certainly makes one tranquil."

"And now," Izzy said to Heller, "I'll bet you've been holding your breath waiting until I got around to this." He waved his arm in a grand gesture at a single corporation marked with a circle and red arrows. "That," said Izzy, "is MULTINATIONAL! By reason of nominee shares, noninterlocking controlled boards, it orchestrates the entire conduct of the entire remaining chart. And listen, here is the best part: it calls itself a MANAGEMENT company! It isn't visibly liable for a single thing any other company does! Isn't that great?"

"But why," said Heller, "why all these different corporations and brokerage houses and bank accounts?"

"Now, I am responsible for you. Right?"

"Right," said Heller.

"If any one of those corporations goes broke, it folds all by itself and it doesn't do a thing to any other part of the entire consortium. You get it? You can go bankrupt to your heart's content! You can also sell them for tax losses, buy other corporations with them. You can also hide and vanish profits. Everything."

"But," said Heller doubtfully, "I don't see that so many——"

"Well, I will admit I haven't told you the real reason." He leaned over to Heller's ear. "You told me you had an enemy. Mr. Bury of Swindle and Crouch. He is the most vicious, unprincipled lawyer on Wall Street. With this setup, he will never be able to touch you."

"Why not?" said Heller.

Izzy leaned much closer and whispered much more quietly, hard to hear above the chatter of the crowd. "Because in every record, neither you nor your name will ever appear in any of this. And anything you are publicly connected with will not feed back into any of this. They are all private companies, all for profit, all controlled by actual stock shares. It is impenetrable!"

He stood back. "There is just one thing more I need your approval on. I didn't put it on this chart. An art student did it for me at breakfast."

Tucked in the bottom of the roll was another roll. It opened to a picture about two feet by three. It was a round, black globe. It had a little piece of rope or something sticking out of the top of it. Sparks were flying from the tip.

"What is it?" said Heller.

"It is my proposal for the evolving logo of Multinational! Actually, it is the old symbol of anarchy, a bomb! See the lit fuse?"

"A chemical powder bomb," said Heller.

"Now, we turn the poster over and we simply see a dark sphere with a wisp of cloud at the top. And that's what we will put out as the logo but you and I will know what it really is. Now do you approve?"

"Well, yes," said Heller.

"The chart and the logo?"

"Well, yes," said Heller.

"I know it is crude and hastily done. I haven't even filled in many of the names. I think it is very tolerant of you to approve it."

"What is this?" a newcomer asked Heller. "A work of art?"

"Yes," said Heller. "A work of art!"

"Well now, let's roll it up," said Izzy.

"No," said several of the crowd at once. One said, "A lot of people haven't been able to see it. We'll spread it out on the steps here and people can go up on the parapet there or climb the statue and get a real look."

Overruled, Heller and Izzy drew back and let them have their way.

"Did you get re-enrolled?" said Heller.

"Oh, yes," said Izzy. "That's why I was a little late. While I was doing all this, I got a brand-new idea for a doctorate thesis. And I saw them about it. It's 'The Use of Corporations in Undermining Totally the Existing World Order.'"

"And they agree to let you re-enroll and write it?"

"You see, the mistake I was making was getting off into political science and they kept telling me so. My doctorate is in business administration. But this new idea is perfect. It doesn't contain the word *government,* it does contain the word *corporations.* And *world order* can be interpreted to mean *capitalistic finance.* So unless some horrible, malignant fate overtakes me from some other quarter, I can get my doctor's degree at the end of this October."

"Then you paid your bill," said Heller.

"Oh, yes. You can have your two hundred advance back."

"But how . . . ?"

"Right after I left you yesterday, I went to the Bank of America. I showed them the two hundred which proves I had a job and borrowed five thousand dollars without collateral. I paid off the government loan and have far more left than I really need. I won't have to sleep in the park—I'm always afraid of being mugged. I can stay in a dorm a couple of nights until we get our offices. And, if you don't mind, I'll sleep there when we do."

I was speechless. How could this ragtag, mucked-up mess of a timid little man walk into a bank and borrow five thousand just by showing them a couple of hundred-dollar bills?

"Now wait a minute," said Heller, obviously having afterthoughts. "It will take a long, long time to set up all those corporations in Hong Kong and Tahiti and wher-ever. What do you have in mind as a time schedule?"

"Oh, that is my fault," said Izzy. "I have been under such a nervous strain lately. I didn't want to tell you because I was afraid you would balk."

"So, how long? Two months? A year?"

"Oh, heavens, no! I was shooting for next Tuesday! I thought you would want it Friday but there's a week-end..."

"Next Tuesday," said Heller. Then he seemed to rally. "You're going to need money for all this. So here is ten thousand to start with. Will that be enough?"

"Oh, heavens, yes. Too much, actually. I'll put it in a locker at the bus station to keep it safe. And then put it in the first bank account. And then, when everything is set, you can put your capital in the various bank accounts and it will get transferred around and start to get to work. Is it too much to ask to meet you here on these steps 4:00 P.M. Tuesday?"

And then I thought I had it. This Izzy was a sly, clev-er crook. He was going to take all of Heller's money, deny him any control and leave him broke. I cancelled any idea of interfering with Izzy Epstein! He didn't even give Heller a receipt!

Izzy got his chart back from the congratulatory crowd. Several even helped him carry it as he went away.

I laughed. Maybe that was the last Heller would ever see of him!

Chapter 7

I was quite heartened by the number of potential allies I was picking up in case everything else went wrong with my plans for Heller. Vantagio, Miss Simmons, this Izzy Epstein. I began to keep a list. When Raht and Terb called in, possibly I could greatly embellish my planning.

Heller spent the afternoon doing some more checking on class locations, obviously still trying to figure out how to be in two or three places at once and get tutored at the same time. And then he went around to the other side of what was labelled "Journalism" and found the college bookstore on Broadway.

All day he had been running into people and sticking his nose into professors' offices and making up a list. He had been using the back side of a computer printout with the staples removed and now had this yard-long sheet with titles and texts and manuals and authors scribbled all over it. He handed it to the girl behind the counter. She was obviously some graduate student doing part-time work to handle the current rush. Pretty, too.

"All this?" she said, adjusting her horn-rimmed glasses. "I can't read some of this writing. I wish they would teach kids to read and write these days."

Heller peered over at what she was pointing at. Yikes! He had annotated the list over on the edge with Voltarian shorthand!

My pen was really poised. Oh, I've seen Code breaks in my time. Maybe a whore and a tailor wouldn't know they were dealing with an extraterrestrial but he was in a college area and those people are smart.

"It's shorthand," said Heller. "The main titles and authors are in English."

They were, too. In very neat block print.

"What's this here?" said the girl, lifting her glasses above her eyes to see better. She was pointing at *The Fundamentals of Geometry* by Euclid. "We don't have any books by that author. Is it a new paperback?"

Heller told her she'd have to help him as he didn't know either. She went to her catalogues and looked up under "Authors." She couldn't find it. So she looked in a massive catalogue of alphabetical book titles. Then, cheered on by Heller, she looked up the author in the book titles. "Hey, here it is!" she said. *"Euclidian Geometry as Interpreted and Rewritten by Professor Twist from an Adaption by I. M. Tangled."* She went and found a copy. "You wrote here that his name was 'Euclid' when it was 'Euclidian.' You should learn how to spell."

They couldn't find anything by somebody named "Isaac Newton" and the girl decided he must be some revolutionary banned by the New York Tactical Police Force. But Heller persevered and they eventually came up with a book, *Laws of Motion I Have Rewritten and Adapted from a Text by Dr. Still as Translated from an Archaic English Newtonian Work by Elbert Mouldy* by Professor M. S. Pronounce, Doctor of Literature.

"You should have told me it would be in the literature section," said the girl. "You don't even know how to read a card catalogue."

"I'll try to find out," said Heller.

"Jesus," said the girl, "they teach card catalogues in

the third grade! God, didn't anybody ever teach you anything? There's a staff at High Library devoted to showing students how to do it. You ask them over there. I'm here to sell books, not teach kindergarten! But let's get on, this is an awfully long list! You're keeping others waiting!"

They did make progress, however, and the pile of books grew and grew. Finally the girl, peering between the columns of books and lifting her glasses to see Heller, said, "You can't carry all these. And I'm not going to wrap them. So you go over to the college store and get about five rucksacks while I get an assistant to add up this bill."

Heller did as he was told.

When he returned, he packed the five rucksacks and paid the bill. Then he began to adjust straps and finally managed to get the sacks hung around him. Other students who had been waiting made room for him disinterestedly.

"Can you manage?" said the girl. "That must be about two hundred pounds. Books are heavy."

"Just barely," said Heller. "But we haven't got everything on this list."

"Oh, the rest of that stuff. Well, take that one about thirty from the top, *World History Rewritten by Competent Propagandists for Kiddies and Passed by the American Medical Association,* that's fourth grade grammar school. We don't carry that sort of thing. You'll have to get them at Stuffem and Glutz, the city's authorized school supplier. They're on Varick Street." And she gave him the number. "My God," she added, "how'd you ever get here not knowing those texts?"

Heller turned to make his way through the backlog of student customers who stepped aside patiently. The girl said to the next student in line, "Jesus, what we get for freshmen these days."

"It says on your slip there he's a senior," said the student.

"I got it!" said the girl. I quickly and hopefully jacked up the audio. "He's here on an athletic scholarship! A weight lifter! Hey, call him back. I was awful impolite. I need a date for tonight's dance! Boy, am I dumb! He was cute, too."

Yes, she certainly was dumb! She had denied me opportunity after opportunity to file charges against Heller for Code breaks! And they had watched somebody heft two hundred pounds of rucksacks like they were air and I'm sure if they had looked out the door or window they would have seen Heller running along, clickety-clack, without a care in the world to the subway. My faith in the powers of observation of college students had suffered a heavy blow. Maybe they were all on drugs. That was the only possible explanation! An extraterrestrial right under their noses making all kinds of giveaways and they hadn't even blinked an eye!

Heller got right on down to Varick Street on the same subway. He got into the city-authorized bookstore. And he was shortly showing a half-blind old man his list. In the subway he had ticked off missing titles with a red pen and now he handed it over, Voltarian shorthand and all, for the red checks to be filled.

The old man bustled off to a storeroom. "You want thirty copies of each?" he called back.

"One will do just fine."

"Oh, you're a tutor. All right." And he came back in about ten minutes, staggering under a stack of books. "I'll get the rest now." And he went back and came out staggering under a second stack.

Heller checked off the titles. He got almost to the end. "There's one missing: *Third Grade Arithmetic.*"

"Oh, they don't teach that anymore. It's all 'new math' now."

"What's 'new math'?" said Heller.

"I dunno. They put out a new 'new math' every year. It's something about greater and lesser numbers without using any numbers this year. It was orders of magnitude of numbers last year but they were still teaching them to count. They stopped that."

"Well, I've got to have something about basic arithmetic," said Heller.

"Why?"

"You see," said Heller, "I do logarithms in my head and the only arithmetic I've ever seen done was by some primitive tribe on Flisten. They used charcoal sticks and slabs of white lime."

"No kidding?" said the old man.

"Yes, it was during a Fleet peace mission. They wouldn't believe we had that many ships and it was really funny to see them jumping about and counting and multiplying and writing it down. They were more advanced than others I've seen, however. One tribe had to use their fingers and toes to count their wives. They never had more than fifteen wives because that was all the fingers and toes they had."

The old man said, "A Fleet man, huh? I was in the Navy myself, war before last. You just wait there."

He went back and searched and searched and finally came out with a dusty, tattered text that had been lying around for ages. "Here's a book called *Basic Arithmetic Including Addition, Multiplication and Division With a Special Section on Commercial Arithmetic and Stage Acts.*" He opened the yellowed pages, "It was published in Philadelphia in 1879. It's got all sorts of tricks in it like adding a ten-digit column of thirty entries by inspection. Old-time bookkeeper stuff. Lot of stage tricks: they used to go on stage and write numbers and do complicated examples upside down leaning over a blackboard and get the answer in three seconds and the audience would flip out. Mr. Tatters said to throw it out but I sort of thought I should send it to a museum. Since they passed the law that kids had to use calculators in class, nobody is interested in it anymore. But as you're a navy man like myself you can have it."

Heller paid and the old man wrapped up the books into two more huge packages. Another two hundred pounds of books. I expected Heller to heft them up and walk off. It disappointed me when he found four hundred pounds too cumbersome. I'm sure he could have, with some strain, walked off with them. He had them call him a taxi. The old man even got a dolly and helped him load up. Heller thanked him.

"Don't throw that book away," said the old man at the curb. "I don't think there's a soul in this country knows how to do it anymore. I don't think they even remember it ever existed. When you're through with it, give it to a museum!"

"Thanks for piping the side!" said Heller and the taxi drove away leaving the old man waving at the curb.

Code break. "Piping the side!" It must be some Voltarian Fleet term. No, wait a minute. I had never heard the term on Voltar. But Heller wouldn't know Earth terms like that. Or would he? The Voltarian Fleet doesn't use pipes. A lot of them use puffsticks. Only Earth people smoke pipes. It was moving into the New York rush hour so I had a lot of time to work on this. I got as far as Earth sailors as well as spacers have a lot to do with whores when my concentration was interrupted.

A houseman was wheeling all that book tonnage across the lobby and Vantagio popped out of his office like some miniature jack-in-the-box.

He stared at the packages, tore a piece of paper off a corner and opened a rucksack to verify they were books. "They accepted you!" He let out a wheeze of relief and mopped his face with a silk handkerchief. He waved the houseman on and pushed Heller into his office.

"You did it!" said Vantagio.

"I think *you* did it," said Heller.

Vantagio looked at him with feigned blank innocence.

"Come on," said Heller. "They waived everything including having a head! How did you do it?"

Vantagio started laughing and sat down at his desk. "All right, kid, you got me. It was awfully late and I had an awful time getting hold of the university president last night but I did it. You see, at peak periods, we use some of the Barnyard College girls here. So I just told him that if you weren't enrolled in full by 9:30 this morning, we'd cut off our student aid program."

"I owe you," said Heller.

"Oh, no, no," said Vantagio. "You don't get off that easy. You still have to do what I tell you. Right?"

"Right," said Heller.

"Then get on that phone and call Babe and tell her you're enrolled!"

Heller turned the desk speaker phone around to face him and Vantagio pushed the lease line button. Geovani in Bayonne transferred the call to Babe in the dining room.

"This is Jerome, Mrs. Corleone. I just wanted to tell you what a great job Vantagio did in getting me enrolled."

"It's all complete?" said Babe.

"Absotively," said Heller. But I noted he did not tell

her, as he had not told Vantagio, that Miss Simmons had really set him up to fail. Heller was sneaky.

"Oh, I'm so glad. You know, you dear boy, you don't want to grow up to be a bum like these other bums. Mama wants you to have class, kid, real class. Become president or something."

"Well, I certainly do thank you," said Heller.

"Now, there's one more thing, Jerome," said Babe, a little more severely. "You've got to promise me not to play hooky."

That stopped Heller. He knew very well he would be missing in as many as two or three classes a day! Bless Miss Simmons!

Heller found his voice, "Not even one class, Mrs. Corleone?"

"Now, Jerome," said Babe, her voice hardening, "I know it is a terrible job bringing up boys. I never did but I had brothers and I *know!* Let down your guard for one second and they're off and away, free as birds, skylarking and breaking neighbors' windows. So the answer is very plain. I give it to you absolutely straight. No hooky. Not even one class! Mama will be watching and Mama will spank! Now promise me, Jerome. And Vantagio, if you're listening to this, which you are—I am sure you are as I can tell it's the speaker phone on your desk—you look at his hands; no crossed fingers, no crossed feet. All right?"

Vantagio peered at Heller. "They aren't crossed, *mia capa.*"

Oh, what a spot Heller was in! With his nonsense Royal officer scruples about keeping his word, I knew he was suffering agonies. He couldn't keep that promise so he wouldn't make it. And I was sure that, to Babe Corleone, the phrase "Mama will spank" translated more truthfully into "concrete overcoat."

"Mrs. Corleone," said Heller. "I will be truthful

with you." Ah, here it came! "I promise you faithfully that, unless I get rubbed out, or unless something happens that closes the university, I will complete college on time and get my diploma."

"Oh, you dear boy! That is even more than I asked! But nevertheless, Jerome, just remember, Mama will be watching. Bye-bye!"

Vantagio closed the circuit and sat there beaming at Heller.

"There's one more thing," said Heller. "Vantagio, could you get me the phone number of Bang-Bang Rimbombo. I want to call him from my suite."

"Celebrating, are you?" said Vantagio. "I don't blame you. As a matter of fact, he's right here in Manhattan and the parole officer is riding his (bleep) off." He wrote the number on a scrap of paper and handed it over. "Have fun, kid."

It left me blinking. Vantagio might be smart but he hadn't penetrated that one. Heller was full of surprises, (bleep) him. What was he going to pull? Blow up the university? That was the only way I could think of that would let him keep the promise he had just made to Babe Corleone.

Chapter 8

About an hour later, Heller came out of his room. The tailors must have delivered something, for in the elevator mirrors I could see that he was dressed in a charcoal gray casual suit—the cloth must be some kind of summer cloth that was very thin and airy but looked thick and substantial. He had a white silk shirt with what appeared to be diamond cuff links and a dark blue tie. For a change he wasn't wearing his baseball cap and in fact wore no hat at all. But when he crossed the lobby he was obviously still wearing spikes!

He clattered down the steps of a subway stop and caught a train. He got off at Times Square and was shortly clattering up Broadway past the porno shops. He turned into a cross street. I thought he must be going to a theater for he gave some attention to billboards of stage plays as he passed them.

Then he was looking up a flight of stairs. *K.O. ATHLETIC CLUB*, read the sign. He clattered on up and entered a room full of punching bags and helmeted boxers sparring around.

He was evidently expected. An attendant came over, "You Floyd?" and then beckoned. Heller followed him into a dressing room and the attendant pointed to a locker. Heller stripped and hung up his clothes. The attendant gave him a towel and shooed him through a door into a smoking haze of steam.

Heller groped around, fanned some steam out of the way and there was Bang-Bang Rimbombo, sitting on a ledge, streaming sweat and clutching a towel about him. The little Sicilian's narrow face was just a diffused patch in the fog.

"How are you?" said Heller.

"Just terrible, kid. Awful. I couldn't be worse. Sit down."

Heller sat down and dabbed at his own face with a towel. The sweat started to pour off him, too. It must be awfully hot.

They sat in utter silence, steam geysering around them. Now and then Bang-Bang would take a gulp of water from a pitcher and then Heller would take a gulp.

After nearly an hour, Bang-Bang said, "I'm starting to feel human again. My headache is gone."

"Did you take care of what I asked?" said Heller. "I hope it wasn't too much trouble."

"Oh, hell, that was easy. Hey, I can bend my neck. I haven't taken a sober breath since I saw you last." He was silent for a while and then apparently remembered what Heller had asked. "This time every week, Father Xavier goes down to Bayonne. He's Babe's confessor, knew her since she was a kid on the lower East Side. He has dinner with her and then hears her confession and then brings a load of hijacked birth control pills back to town. One of his stops is the Gracious Palms. So it wasn't any trouble. You'll have them later tonight. You don't owe me nothing. They wasn't no use."

"Thank you very much," said Heller.

"If all things was handled that easy," said Bang-Bang, "life would be worth living. But just now it ain't. You know, life can be pretty awful, kid."

"What's the matter? Maybe I can help."

"I'm afraid it's all beyond the help of God or man," said Bang-Bang. "Up the river I go next Wednesday."

"But why?" demanded Heller. "I thought you were out on parole."

"Yeah. But, kid, that arrest was very irregular. A machine gun is a Federal crime but the late Oozopopolis rigged it to be found by the New York Police and they got me on the Sullivan Law or whatever they call illegal possession. I didn't go to a Federal pen; they sent me up the river to Sing Sing."

"That's too bad," said Heller.

"Yeah. They're so crooked they can't even send you to the right jail! So when I was paroled, I of course went home to New Jersey. And right away, the parole officer dug me up and said I was out of jurisdiction, that I couldn't leave New York. So I come to New York and we don't control New York like we used to before 'Holy Joe' got wasted. So Police Inspector Bulldog Grafferty is leaning all over the parole officer to send me back to the pen to finish my time—they tell me now it's eight months, kid. Eight dry months!"

"Is it because you haven't any place to live? I could——"

"Naw, naw, I know a chick on Central Park West and I moved in with her and her five sisters."

"Well, if it's money, I could——"

"Naw, naw. Thanks, kid. I got tons of money. I get paid by the job and under the counter and that's the trouble. The parole officer made it a condition that I get a regular job. Imagine that, kid. A regular job, an artist like me! The job I do have nobody dares report and that leaves me bango right out in Times Square with no clothes on. Nobody will hire an ex-con. Babe said she'd arrange a regular pay social security job in one of the Corleone enterprises but that connects the family up to legit business—I'm too famous. I won't risk getting Babe in trouble, never. She's a great *capa*. So that's what I'm up against. They said, 'Regular job: social security, withholding tax or a charge of vagrancy and back you go this next Wednesday.' That's what the parole officer said."

"Gosh, I'm awful sorry," said Heller.

"Well, it made me feel better just getting it off my chest, kid. I feel tons better. Headache gone?" He shook his head experimentally. "Yep. Let's get a shower and get out of here and have some dinner!"

They were soon dressed. As they passed out through the training room, I suppose Heller just plain could not resist socking something—it's his vicious character. As he passed by a punching bag, he hit it. It flew off its springs.

"I'm sorry," said Heller to the attendant.

"Hey, boss!" the attendant yelled at somebody.

A very fat man with a huge cigar in his mouth came over.

"Look at what this kid did," said the attendant.

"I'll pay for it," said Heller.

"Hmm," said the fat man. "Punch this one over here, kid."

Heller went over to it and punched it. It simply vibrated back and forth—slam, slam, slam, slam.

"That other one just had a weak spring, Joe," said the fat man. "You ought to keep this equipment under repair."

I laughed. Heller couldn't punch so hard after all. He's always bragging and showing off. Good to see him come a cropper now and then.

The theater crowds had gone in. "Y'ever want to see the last end of a show," said Bang-Bang, "wait for intermission when the crowd comes out to smoke and then walk back in with them. You get to see the last acts but I always get to wondering how they got into all that trouble in the first acts, so I don't do it."

They came to a huge, glittering restaurant with a huge, glittering sign:

Sardine's

The maitre d' spotted Bang-Bang in the line and dragged him out. He led them to a small table in the back.

"Some of them diners," said Bang-Bang, "is celebrities. That's Johnny Matinee over there. And there's Jean Lologiggida. The theatrical stars all come here to eat. And after the opening night, when the stars come in, if it's a hit everybody claps and cheers. And if it's a bomb, they turn their backs."

The maitre d' put them at a small, secluded table and handed them menus. Heller looked at the prices. "Hey, this place isn't cheap. I didn't intend for you to invite me to dinner. I'll pick up the tab."

Bang-Bang laughed. "Kid, for all the glitter, this is an Italian restaurant. The Corleone family owns it. There ain't no tab. Besides, he'll just bring us antipasto, meatballs and spaghetti. Good, though."

Bang-Bang was hauling at his side. He brought out a full, unsealed fifth of Johnnie Walker Gold Label and set it on the table. "Don't look so surprised, kid. It's just going to sit there and be admired by me. I got cases of it left but I won't have any in Sing Sing for eight months. I just want it to tell me I'm not in Sing Sing yet."

The antipasto came and they got busy on the crisp odds and ends.

A waiter drifted by, a different one, with huge spiked mustaches. *"Che c'e di nuovo,* Bang-Bang?"

"All bad," said Bang-Bang. "Meet the kid here. One of the family. Pretty Boy Floyd, this is Cherubino Gatano."

"Pleased," said Cherubino. "Can I get you anything, Floyd?"

"Some beer," said Heller.

"Hold it, hold it!" said Bang-Bang. "Don't let this bambino kid you, he's a minor and they'd have our (bleep). Got to keep it legal."

"Hold it, hold it yourself," said Cherubino. "If he's a minor, he can still have some beer."

"Since when?"

"Since now." Cherubino went off and came back shortly with a squat bottle and a tall Pilsener glass on a tray.

"You're breaking the law!" said Bang-Bang. "And

me about to go back up the river. They'll add 'contributing to the delinquency of a minor' this time and never let me out!"

"Bang-Bang," said Cherubino. "I love you. I have loved you since you were a child. But you are stupid. You can't read. This is Swiss beer all right and the very best. But in this case they have taken all the alcohol out!" He pushed the bottle label at Bang-Bang. "Imported! Legal!" Then he poured the Pilsener glass full and gave it to Heller.

Heller tasted it. "Hello, hello! Delicious!"

"You see," said Cherubino, starting to take the bottle away. "You always were stupid, Bang-Bang."

"Leave the bottle," said Heller. "I want to copy the label. I'm so tired of soft cola I could burp!"

Cherubino said, "Bang-Bang and I used to stand off all the Greeks in Hell's Kitchen together, so don't get the idea we're not friends, kid. But he was always stupid and when he came back from the war they'd made him even stupider and that's impossible. See you around." He left.

Bang-Bang was laughing. "Cherubino was my captain in that same war, so he ought to know."

"What did you do in the war?" asked Heller.

"Me? I was a marine."

"Yes, but what did you *do?*" said Heller.

"Well, they say a marine is supposed to be able to do anything. They have to handle all kinds and types of weapons so they specialize less than the Army and get shot at with more variety."

"What training did you get?" said Heller.

"Well, it was pretty good. I started out real good. When I got out of boot camp, I went right to the top. They made me a gunship pilot."

"What's that?"

"Gunship, whirlybird, Green Giant, chopper. A helicopter, kid. Where you been? Don't you ever see old movies? Anyway, there I was dashing about shooting the hell out of anything that moved on the ground and suddenly they sent me to a specialist school."

"In what?"

"Demolitions." Their meatballs and spaghetti had arrived. "Oh, well, hell, kid. We're pals. I might as well tell you the truth. I crashed so many whirlybirds a colonel one day said, 'That God (bleeped) Rimbombo shows talent but he's in the wrong branch of the service. Send him to demolitions training school.' I tried to point out that choppers full of bullets don't fly well but there I went and here I am. Nobody else knows that, kid, so don't spread it around."

"Oh, I won't," said Heller. After a bit he said, "Bang-Bang, I want your opinion about something."

Ah, now we were getting to it. This Heller was sneaky. I knew all the time he was not there for nothing. I was alert. Maybe he would antagonize Bang-Bang. He sets people's nerves on edge. I know he does mine. Dangerous!

He was taking a form out of his pocket. It said:

> RESERVE OFFICERS' TRAINING CORPS

It was an enrollment form.

"Bang-Bang," said Heller, "look at this line here. It makes one promise to be faithful to the United States of America and support the Constitution. One is supposed to sign it. It looks like a pretty binding oath."

Bang-Bang looked at it. "Well, that's not the real oath. This next line here says you promise that when you graduate from the ROTC you will serve two years in the

U.S. Army as a second lieutenant. Hmm. Yes. This is the junior or senior year form. Now, when you get out of the ROTC, they make you take the real oath. You stand up, hold up your right hand and repeat after them and get sworn in for real."

"Well, I can't sign this allegiance form," said Heller. "And later, when I graduate, I can't take any such oath."

"I understand completely," said Bang-Bang. "It's true they're just a bunch of crooks."

Heller laid the form aside and ate some spaghetti. Then he said, "Bang-Bang, I can get you a job driving a car."

Bang-Bang was alert. "With real social security, withholding tax and legit? That would satisfy the parole officer?"

"Absolutely," said Heller. "By Tuesday I'll have a corporation, all legal, and it can hire you as a driver. And that will beat your Wednesday deadline."

"Hey!" said Bang-Bang. "And I won't have to go back up the river!"

"There are a couple of conditions," said Heller.

Bang-Bang looked even more alert.

"The driving itself won't amount to much. But during the day you'll have to run some errands. It isn't really hard work and it's actually in your line."

Bang-Bang said, "Do I smell some catches in this?"

"No, no, I wouldn't ask you to do anything illegal," said Heller. "There are lots of girls around the place of work."

"Sounds interesting. But I still smell a catch."

"Well, actually, it isn't much of a catch," said Heller. "You've been a marine and know all about this sort of thing, so it's no strain. What I want you to do, in addition to these other duties, is sign this ROTC form as J.

Terrance Wister, report to three classes a week and do the drill period."

"NO!" said Bang-Bang, refusing utterly.

"They don't know me by sight and I realize we look different, but if I know such organizations, all they're interested in is somebody to yell 'Yo' when the roll is called and somebody to march around as part of the ranks."

"NO!" said Bang-Bang. And of course he was right. He was a small Sicilian, a foot shorter than Heller, brunette where Heller was blond.

"If you keep telling people your name is Terrance, and if I keep getting people to call me Jet or Jerome, other students will think we are two different people but the computers will think there's just one of us."

"NO!" said Bang-Bang.

"You could give me the material they teach and coach me in the drills. I'd be earning the credits honestly."

"NO!"

"I'll pay you whatever you ask a week to do these other things and this and you won't be sent back to prison."

"Kid. It isn't the pay. A couple hundred a week would be great. But it isn't the pay. There are just some things one can't bring himself to do!"

"Such as?" said Heller.

"Look, kid. I was a marine. Now, once a marine, always a marine. The Marines, kid, is the MARINES! Now, kid, the Army is a hell of a downstairs sort of organization. It is the Army, kid. Dogfaces. I don't think you realize that you're asking me to throw away all my principles. I couldn't even *pretend* to join the Army, kid. I'd feel so degraded I wouldn't be able to live with myself! And that's everything, kid. Pride!"

They ate some more spaghetti.

There was a change of noise level. Bang-Bang looked toward the distant door. "Hey, a new show must have just let out. I think that commotion at the door must be the stars. Now watch this, kid. If it's a great show, this whole crowd of diners here will applaud and if it was a flop, they'll turn their backs."

Heller looked. Johnny Matinee was half out of his chair, looking toward the door. Jean Lologiggida was craning her pretty neck. Three of the Sardine photographers, that had been running around taking flash pictures of diners for personal albums, got ready to shoot a big scene.

The buzz at the door increased. The crowd there parted.

In walked Police Inspector Grafferty, resplendent in full uniform!

The diners turned their backs on him with a groan.

"That's Grafferty," hissed Bang-Bang. "Got his nerve walking into a Corleone place. He's in Faustino's pay!"

Grafferty knew exactly where he was going. He was coming straight through to the back. To Bang-Bang's table!

He stopped with his right side to Heller. His interest was in Bang-Bang. "The undercover cops in the street spotted you coming in here, Rimbombo. I just wanted to get one last look at your face before they sent you back up the river."

But Heller was not looking at Grafferty. He had picked up the corner of the tablecloth and was tucking it into Grafferty's coat pocket with a fork! What a crazy thing to do! Clearly showed he had a trivial mind.

"What's this?" said Grafferty. He was reaching out for the bottle of Johnnie Walker Gold Label. "Hooch without a revenue seal on its cap! I thought I could find something if I just came..."

Heller's voice cut into the speech and into the room for that matter. The drone of diners' voices vanished. "Don't try to pinch my friend for contributing to the delinquency of a minor!"

Grafferty let go of the Scotch and turned to face Heller. "Who's this? Haven't I seen your face before somewhere, kid?"

In that penetrating Fleet voice of his, Heller said, "This beer is legal!"

"Beer?" said Grafferty. "A minor and beer? Oh, boy, Rimbombo, you are in for it now! And this is a licensing matter! I can get the Corleone license revoked for this whole place!"

"Look here!" said Heller. "It's nonalcoholic beer. Look at the label!"

Heller was fumblingly, hastily, pushing the empty beer bottle forward toward Grafferty. It seemed to slip. Grafferty grabbed for it.

The beer bottle hit the bottle of Scotch!

The Scotch went over the table edge!

Grafferty grabbed for the Scotch!

The Scotch hit the floor with a splintering crash!

Grafferty was still going down. He seemed to trip.

The whole tablecloth was pulled off!

Bowls of spaghetti, utensils, dirty plates and red tomato sauce hit Grafferty in an avalanche!

Jean Lologiggida was half out of her seat, looking white, hand pressed to her bosom.

Heller was up. "Oh, my goodness!" he cried and raced around the table to help Grafferty. His spikes stepped on the broken glass of the Scotch. He looked down and kicked the cap and label far away with a twitch of his foot.

He was assisting Grafferty up. From a nearby table he grabbed a red-checked cloth. He began to swab at Grafferty's face.

What a horribly bad job of cleaning! He was smearing spaghetti all over Grafferty's face, in his hair, on his tunic.

Jean Lologiggida was pressed back against the side of her booth.

Heller took Grafferty by the elbow and led him toward the star's table.

The photographers were batting out shot after shot!

Heller got Grafferty to her table. "Oh, Miss Lologiggida! Inspector Grafferty demanded the right to tell you how terribly sorry he was to disturb your dinner. The tablecloth caught in his belt. And you are sorry, aren't you, Inspector?"

Grafferty didn't know whether he was up or down. He stared at the star. He said, "Oh, my God, it's Lologiggida!" Then he saw he was still trailing the tablecloth and plates. He tore the corner of it off his belt. And while the flashguns flashed, rushed from the restaurant.

Suddenly Jean Lologiggida burst into gales of laughter! She was doubled up with it!

Johnny Matinee rushed over. "Ye gads, I wish I'd been part of that. It'll make the front page!"

Somebody, evidently Johnny Matinee's public relations man, was grabbing the photographers and having a hurried consultation with the proprietor.

The PR man said, "It's nothing to you, kid," to Heller. "Do you mind if Johnny takes your place on the front page? We'll overpaste the shots they took."

"Feel free," said Heller.

They put Johnny Matinee where Heller had stood in front of Lologiggida, got him to assume the same pose. The flashbulbs flashed.

Heller went back to the table. The restaurant was still rocking with laughter. Somebody belatedly started to applaud and Heller turned and took a bow but indicated, with his hand, Johnny Matinee. This seemed even funnier to people.

Bang-Bang was sitting there, doubled over with laughter. "Oh, *sangue di Cristo!* That Grafferty won't come near a Corleone place for a while. And you bought the joint a million in publicity!"

Heller said, soberly, "And Grafferty won't connect that bottle up with the warehouse job."

Bang-Bang looked at Heller as Heller sat back down. "Hey, I never thought of that!"

Cherubino came over. He had another nonalcoholic beer. He was grinning when he set it down. "This a good kid you got here, Bang-Bang. I'm glad he's part of our family and not some other mob! Maybe you ain't so stupid as I thought!" He went off.

Bang-Bang sat there, looking at Heller. "You know, kid, I'm going to take you up on that offer. I'll even swallow my scruples and join the Army for you." He thought for a bit. Then he said, "It's not because it'll save me from going back to jail. It's just because you're kind of fun to be around!"

But I was not as impressed as they were. Heller's tablecloth trick was something we used to do at the Academy to dumb recruits. And any spacer has vast experience in handling barroom brawls. Heller was just taking advantage of the fact that Voltar technology was far higher than that of Earth's. Still, he was too tricky, too sneaky. And he was making too much progress!

Where the Hells was the communication from Raht and Terb? I couldn't abide the idea of seeing Heller fool all these people into thinking he amounted to something. All that (bleeping) applause!

PART NINETEEN

Chapter 1

Bright and early, Heller and Bang-Bang got off the subway at Empire Station. This morning Heller was wearing tailored gray flannel tennis slacks and a gray shirt with a white tennis sweater tied by its sleeves loosely around his neck. And he wore his inevitable red baseball cap and his spikes. He was carrying two heavy rucksacks evidently jammed with things I had no clue about.

Bang-Bang was something else. He had on some non-descript jeans and denim shirt. But on his head he wore an olive drab cap and across it in black was stencilled *USMC*.

They came up College Walk. Students were moving along, burdened with books, on their way to classes.

But Heller and Bang-Bang, much to my surprise, did not seem to be headed for a class. Heller striding along and Bang-Bang double-timing to catch up, they turned north past High Library and, threading their way around buildings, came almost to 120th Street. There was an expanse of lawn and a tree. Heller headed for the tree.

"All right, this is the command post. Synchronize your watch."

"Right," said Bang-Bang.

"Here is the schedule of plantings we took up last night in the suite."

"Right."

"Now, you've got to look at this from the viewpoint of timed fuses."

"Right!"

What in Hells were they up to? Was Heller trying to get out of his promise to Babe by blowing up the school?

"You put them in undetectably."

"Right."

"And what happens if you don't need an area mined anymore?"

"You pick them up undetectably," said Bang-Bang. "It's a secret operation. Run no risks of barrage."

"Right," said Heller. "Wait a minute. What does *USMC* mean?" Heller was looking at Bang-Bang's cap.

"Christ! 'United States Marine Corps' of course!"

"Give it to me."

"And leave myself under enemy fire with no moral support?"

Heller took it off his head. He removed his own baseball cap and put it on Bang-Bang. Of course, it was miles too big. Heller put the USMC cap on his own head. I couldn't see it but it must have looked very funny.

"I can't see," said Bang-Bang. "How am I going to plant a sensitive——"

"You're falling behind schedule," said Heller. He handed Bang-Bang one of the rucksacks. Bang-Bang sprinted away, lugging the filled bag and trying to keep the cap off his eyes.

Heller took out a ground sheet. Voltarian by the Gods—one of those inch square ones that open up to ten square feet! The kind that change color to match the ground!

It blended with the grass color. Leave it to him to keep himself neat! Bah, these Fleet guys!

He took out a gas inflatable backrest. Voltarian! It

puffed up. He upended the rucksack over the ground cloth. Books spilled all over the place!

Heller sat down comfortably against the backrest, pawed the books over and found one. Aha! If Babe only could see this! He was not going to class! He was playing hooky!

The book he had was *English Literature for Advanced High-School Students as Passed by the American Medical Association. Book One. The Complete, Rewritten and Abridged Works of Charles Dickens.* It was a quarter of an inch thick and had large type. Heller, in his customary show-off way, demolished it, turning the pages faster than I could see what the page numbers were. It took him about one minute. He turned the book over, seemingly puzzled that there was no more book there. Then he took out an erasable Voltarian pen—he's always so NEAT, it really gets on your nerves! —and marked the date and the Voltarian mathematical symbol that means "equation completed pending next stage."

He put the book aside and got another one, book two of the same series, *The World's One Hundred Greatest Novels Complete, Rewritten and Abridged.* It was also a quarter of an inch thick with large type. It took him another whole minute. He marked the date and the Voltarian symbol.

There was no book three so he opened a notebook and wrote *High-School English Literature.* And then the Voltarian mathematical symbol for "operation complete."

This must have made him feel good for he looked around. Most of the students were in classes, apparently, for there were only a couple of girls loafing along, maybe graduate students. They waved, he waved.

He found another book. It was *English Literature I for First Year College as Passed by the American Medical Association. The Complete Significances You Should Get Out of*

Literature and What You Should Think About It. He demolished that.

I was getting so dizzy watching the screen blur with turning pages that it was with some horror that I realized the worst. He was writing in his notebook, *First Three Years College English Literature* and the same Voltarian math symbol: "equation completed pending next stage."

I verified it twice on my watch. Only ten minutes had gone by!

Oh, I know disaster when I see it. (Bleep) him. When he went to get tutored on English literature he would just make a vulgar gesture with his thumb and say, "Yah, yah, yah!"

Bang-Bang came back. "I planted them."

"What took you so long?"

"I had to stop by the college store and get another hat. I couldn't work in your cap." And he had on a tasselled, black mortarboard. He gave Heller back his baseball cap, lay down on the Voltarian ground sheet and promptly went to sleep.

Heller had started on journalism, an unlikely subject that had been on his grade sheet. The book was *College Journalism First Year. Essential Basic Fairy Tales of Many Lands.* I was glad to see that it was taking him longer. He wasn't reading so fast. He seemed to be enjoying something, so I split the screen and still-framed the other one so I could read it. My Gods, it was the story of the lost continent of Atlantis!

He dawdled along and it took him a half hour to finish College Journalism. Then he saw that he was supposed to have written a sort of end-of-course paper. He got out his bigger notebook, the one he doodled in. He wrote,

CONTINENT SINKS
MILLIONS LOST

Circulation today was boosted by the timely event of a continent vanishing. Publishers ecstatic.

The event was further heightened by a conflict of opinion by leading experts.

However, an unknown expert leaked to this paper— sources cannot be disclosed despite Supreme Court rulings— that all was not known about this event.

The unidentified expert, who shall be nameless, declared that this colony had been founded by an incursion from outer space under the command of that sterling revolutionary and nobleman of purpose and broad vision, none other than Prince Caucalsia from the province of Atalanta, planet of Manco.

Some of the survivors, who emigrated immediately to the Caucasus, which is behind the Iron Curtain and human beings can't usually go there, were incarcerated by the KGB. Deportation soon followed and they arrived maybe in New York.

The public will be kept informed.

Heller punched Bang-Bang. "Read this."

"Why me?" said Bang-Bang, groggy in what must have been a warm morning.

"Well, somebody has got to read it and pass it. It's the end-of-course paper in Journalism. If nobody reads it and passes it, I can't have the credit for it."

Bang-Bang sat up. He read it with lip movement. "What's this word *incarcerated*?"

"Put in the slammer," said Heller.

"Oh, yeah. Hey, that's a good word. 'Incarcerpated.'"

"Well, do I pass?"

"Oh, hell, yes. Anybody that knows that many big words is a genius. Hey, I got to get going. Time for another line of charges!" Bang-Bang raced off, tassel of his mortarboard streaming in the wind.

Heller wrote, *College Journalism. Passed with In-the-Field Citation.*

Two more girls drifted by. They stopped to pass the time of day. "What's your major?" one asked Heller.

"It was Journalism. But I just passed it with Battle Honors. What's yours?"

"Advanced Criticism," said one.

"See you around," said Heller.

After a while, Bang-Bang came back. "First charges picked up. Second series laid." He went back to sleep.

Frankly, they were driving me nuts! What were they doing? Why didn't I hear some explosions as buildings went up?

Heller demolished a couple more subjects and passed himself in his notebook. Bang-Bang had come back again and was once again fast asleep.

Now Heller had gotten into high-school chemistry. But this time he was really tangled. I could tell. He was yawning and yawning. Tension! In fact, it was evidently too much for him for he laid it aside and picked up a text on high-school physics. He read for a while, yawning. Then he picked up the chemistry text again and began looking from it to the physics text.

"Hey," he told the texts. "Agree amongst you on *something*, will you?"

A clear-cut case of animistic fixation, his habit of talking to things. No wonder he couldn't understand clear-cut texts.

He finished up the chemistry including the college texts on it and then got going once more on physics. He kept going back earlier and looking again.

And then, I couldn't believe it! He started to laugh. He always was sacrilegious. Little spurts of laughter kept erupting. And then he read some more and he laughed some more. And then he got to laughing harder and harder and rolled off the backrest and beat at the ground with his fists!

"What the hell is going on?" said Bang-Bang, waking up. "You reading comic books or something?"

Heller got control of himself and it was time he did! "It's a text on primitive superstitions," said Heller. "Look, it's almost noon. Pick up those last charges and we'll have some lunch."

Ah, they were threatening the school! Demanding ransom?

Heller had everything gathered up and they went off and bought sandwiches and pop from a mobile lunch wagon.

"Operation right on schedule," said Heller.

"We made our beachhead," said Bang-Bang.

They enjoyed the view of girls as they strolled around. Heller bought a couple of papers. Then, "Time!" said Heller sternly. And Bang-Bang raced off again. When he came back, Heller had the command post all set up and Bang-Bang went to sleep.

If they weren't blowing things up, and I had heard no explosions, this was about the strangest way to go to college I had ever seen. You're supposed to go and sit down and listen to lectures and take notes and hurry to another class. . . .

Heller was halfway through trigonometry when Bang-Bang said, "I'll pick up the last series and lay the next. But then I got to go report to the Army and you'll have to take over."

Heller finished trigonometry and told it, "You sure go the long way round." But he entered it in his notebook as passed.

Bang-Bang returned and dropped the rucksack he had been racing about with. "Well, here goes the pig into the mire. You got the watch now."

Heller had gotten tired of studying, apparently, for he packed his books up. His watch winked at him in Voltarian figures that it was a bit after two. He opened up one of the papers he had bought.

He looked all through it. He couldn't find a trace of what he was looking for: he kept muttering, "Grafferty? Grafferty?"

He opened up the second paper. He got clear back to the photo section before he found it. It was a picture of an indistinct fireman climbing down a ladder carrying an unrecognizable woman. The caption said:

Police Inspector Grafferty last night rescued Jean Matinee from a burning spaghetti parlor.

Heller told the paper, "Now that I am a passed-with-honors journalist, I can truly appreciate the grave responsibility of keeping the public informed."

I heard that with some amusement. It just showed one how superficial he was. He had the purpose of the media all wrong! Its purpose, of course, is to keep the public *mis*informed! Only in that way can governments, and the people who own and use them, keep the public confused and milked! They trained us in such principles very well in the Apparatus schools.

And then an irritation of worry tinged my amusement. All this data he was getting, right or wrong, could be dangerous to me. It might accidentally make him think.

There was one field he mustn't study. And that was the subject of espionage. I didn't think it was taught in American public schools, even though I knew it was a required subject in Russian kindergartens so the children could spy on their parents. I knew that America often copied what the Russians did. I crossed my fingers. I hoped it wasn't one of his required subjects. I tried to read some of the text titles that were spread around.

Heller went back to his studies. At 2:45 he packed up all his gear, hefted the two rucksacks and trotted off. He paused in a hall, watching a door.

Ah, now I was going to find out what they had been up to!

Students streamed out of the room. The professor came bustling out and went up the hall.

Heller walked into the empty classroom. He went straight to the lecture platform. He reached down into the wastebasket.

He pulled out a tape recorder!

He shut it off.

He put it in the rucksack.

Heller pulled out a small instant recording camera, stepped back and shot the diagrams on the blackboard.

He put the camera away.

He left the room.

He raced over to another building.

He stepped into an empty classroom. He went to the platform, took a different recorder out of the rucksack, verified that it was loaded with 120-minute tape, put it on "record," placed it in the bottom of the wastebasket and threw some paper over it and then walked out of the room just as a couple of students were entering.

Outside, he leaned up against a building. He took the first recorder he had recovered, checked to make sure it had worked properly and removed the cassette. He marked the tape with date and subject, fastened the blackboard picture to it with a rubber band and put the package in a compartmented cassette box marked Advanced Chemistry. He checked the recorder battery charge, reloaded it with blank 120 tape and put it back in the rucksack.

Oh, the crook! He and Bang-Bang were simply

recording all the lectures! He didn't intend to go to a single class in that college!

Oh, I knew what he would do. He would speed-rig a playback machine as he had done with languages and zip a lecture through it in a minute or so at his leisure! Maybe even save them up and do the whole three months' course in under an hour!

What dishonesty! Didn't he know that the FBI arrested people for doing unauthorized recording? Or was that for copying and selling copyrighted material? I couldn't remember. But anyway, it was an awful shock to me! He had a chance of getting through college in spite of Miss Simmons!

I had a momentary glimmer of hope. There might be quizzes. There might be lab periods. But then I sank into a deeper gloom. Heller had probably figured those out, too!

(Bleep) him, he was defeating the efforts to defeat him! My hand itched for a blastick! I had better quadruple any effort I was making to put an end to him!

Chapter 2

Rucksacks and all, Heller went for a run. He went west on 120th Street, south on Broadway, east on 114th Street, north on Amsterdam, circumnavigating the whole university. He was obviously trying to kill time. I hoped he would look out of place and maybe even get arrested for something, but there were lots of other joggers or people late for something.

At 3:45, he began to drift back to the job of picking up and planting recorders. Then he went back to the original "command post" and looked expectantly around for Bang-Bang. He muttered, "The Marines should have disengaged by now. Where are you, Bang-Bang?" No Bang-Bang.

Heller went for a run on a path in Morningside Park and then came back and picked up what seemed to be the last recorder of the day.

He returned to the "command post." No Bang-Bang. His watch winked at him in Voltarian numbers that it was 5:10.

Heller found a shady place, spread his ground sheet again, reinflated his backrest and sat down. He didn't study. He just kept watching for Bang-Bang. The shadows grew longer and longer. He looked at his watch oftener and oftener. Finally it was 5:40.

And here came something!

It was approaching down a path. It looked more like a mound of baggage with two legs than a person.

Towering and unsteady, the mountain came near Heller. It tipped over and crashed on the lawn. It avalanched for a few seconds longer and then there was Bang-Bang, standing amongst the debris. He was out of breath from the effort. He moved over and collapsed on the ground sheet.

"Well," said Bang-Bang, "the engagement was bloody and prolonged. I will give you my battle report, Marines versus Army." He composed himself. "You presented yourself on time to the standard Army confusion of ROTC induction. You signed the form as 'J. Terrance Wister.' You then presented yourself to the first obstacle of the obstacle course.

"As you were new to this ROTC, you had a physical examination. Now, you will be horrified to know that you have incipient cirrhosis of the liver from overindulgence in alcohol. I'm glad it wasn't my physical. I have sixteen cases of Scotch left. So you were passed, providing you stop drinking.

"You then proceeded to the next obstacle. Uniforms and equipment. Those are them," he indicated with a disdainful hand toward a pile of clothes. "The quartermaster insisted everything would be a perfect fit. But I'll have to get them to an alterations tailor right away, get them taken in and let out to really fit me. I refuse to have you looking so *sloppy!* Even if it *is* the Army, there is just so much a Marine can take! So, you got over that obstacle.

"The next wasn't so easy. You know what those (bleepards) did? They tried to issue me a defective M-1 rifle! Now, you know and I know that a Marine can be socked a whole month's pay if his piece is found defective. And (bleep) it, kid, its firing pin was sawed off! Yes! Sawed right off! They tried to argue with me and I bench stripped it right there down to the last screw! They said ROTC trainees weren't allowed to have a firing pin. They said somebody might put a live round in the chamber and when they did inspection arms it might go off. And, boy, I let them have it. The *dangerous* thing is to have an inoperational weapon! You get charged, you can't shoot! And I said, 'What if you want to shoot some colonel in the back? How about that?' And that stopped them. They couldn't put the weapon back together and I refused to as I said it ought to be sent to the gunnery sergeant and repaired, and finally a Regular Army captain said he'd put in a request to allow you to have a nondefective M-1. So they'll issue the rifle later but you got by that. All right so far, kid?"

"Perfectly reasonable," said Heller. "Bad enough to have a chemical weapon already without its being defective. Must be an awful army."

"Oh, it is, it is," said Bang-Bang. "Dogfaces. Anyway, then you came to the swamp and no ropes to get over it so I had to make up your mind for you and I hope I did right.

"Some Regular Army lieutenant with glasses noticed it was your senior year and noticed in your prior military training at Saint Lee's that you'd never indicated preference for branch of service. Well, I hedged. But he said the classroom work in your senior year depended on it and you had to choose. And so he handed me a long list.

"Well, kid, I knew you didn't want to dig latrines, so the infantry is out. And I didn't want some dumb army jerk pulling a lanyard on a 155 when your head was in the barrel, so the artillery is out. And these days, all tanks is good for is to get burned up in, so that's out. I knew that you, like me, hated MPs, so that's out. When I finished the list, it left only one thing. I hope you will like it. G-2."

"What's that?"

"Intelligence. Spies! It seemed to sort of fit my job right now—a Marine infiltrating the Army. So I knew it would make you feel good, too."

I didn't feel good. I reeled!

Bang-Bang got to the books and pamphlets in the mountain. They were marked *Restricted* and *Confidential* and *Secret*.

"Look at this one," said Bang-Bang. "*'Codes, Ciphers and Cryptography.' 'How to Talk Secret.'* Look at these things. *'How to Train Spies.' 'How to Sneak Somebody Back of the Enemy Lines to Poison the Water.' 'How to Seduce the Wife of the Enemy General and Get Her to Give You Tomorrow's Battle Plans.'* Good, solid stuff! And look at the number of these manuals. Dozens! *'How to Tail a Russian Agent.' 'How to Select Sensitive Targets to Destroy Industrial Capacity.'* Good, solid stuff, kid!"

"Let me see those." And he got hold of one about

blowing up trains. And then another about the art of infiltration. Heller started to laugh.

"Are you pleased, kid?"

"Fantastic," said Heller.

"Oh, I'm glad you're pleased, kid. I just thought I was being a little bit selfish. You see, it makes me feel less degraded."

Bang-Bang recovered his USMC fatigue cap and put it on. Then he got an Army fatigue cap and put it on over it, hiding the Marine one.

Then Bang-Bang got down on all fours and crept to the other side of the tree and peered out with exaggerated care. He was clowning!

"Spies," said Bang-Bang. "A Marine spying on the Army! Get it, kid?"

Heller was laughing. He was laughing very hard. But I knew he wasn't laughing at the same thing Bang-Bang was.

Suddenly I knew how Izzy Epstein must have felt when the catastrophe he had dreaded struck. This Earth espionage technology was probably pretty crude. But it *was* espionage technology. It would make my job so much harder!

I hastily wrote another dispatch to the New York office repeating my earlier order to find Raht and Terb and promising torture along with extinction if they didn't comply! Heller had to be stopped!

Chapter 3

About the only thing different about Friday was that they had a different command post and iced soft drinks in a bucket!

What a way to go to college! Lying around on the lawn, watching the girls go by. Well, it was Bang-Bang who did most of the girl watching. Heller was getting caught up on grammar school and high school and college. But Bang-Bang did enough girl watching for both of them. Still, what an idyllic scene. How pastoral! Disgusting!

Saturday, however, was different. Bang-Bang had disappeared somewhere, some muttering about drilling. But Heller reported to some hall and began to take "counselling examinations" to determine which subjects and what part of them he should be tutored on.

I had slept late and when I did the scan through, I simply ignored his rapid pen movements on the exams he was doing. He is always showing off. I sped straight through to an interview he was having with some assistant dean.

"Agnes," the assistant dean was calling over his shoulder. "Are you sure that marking machine is in repair?"

A voice floated back. "Yes, Mr. Bosh. It has been flunking its quota all morning."

Mr. Bosh, an intense-eyed young man, fiddled with the big stack of completed exam papers he had and then looked at Heller. "There must be some mistake here. Your grade transcript said these were all D average and these exams are A average." A very severe glint came in his eye. "There is something unexplained here, Wister."

"Sometimes students have been known to date the wrong somebody's daughter," said Heller.

Mr. Bosh sat up straight and then beamed. "Of course, of course. I should have thought of that. Happens all the time!"

Chuckling to himself, he bundled the exam papers up and marked them *To be microfilmed for student's file.*

"Well, Wister, all I can say is, you're off the hook. There are no weak spots here to be tutored, so we will simply mark that completed in your admission requirements. All right?"

"Thank you very much," said Heller.

Mr. Bosh leaned forward and said in a low voice, "Tell me, just off the record, you didn't knock her up, did you?"

Heller leaned over and whispered, "Well, I'm *here* for my senior year, aren't I?"

Mr. Bosh went into howls of laughter. "I knew it, I knew it! Oh, priceless!" And with great camaraderie, he shook Heller's hand and that was that.

There was something in Bosh's attitude that irritated me. Possibly the way he was beaming at Heller. There was nothing that remarkable about Heller's passing: he had had several days and several long evenings in the lobby to review those subjects and, to him, it must have been a sort of ethnological study of how some primitive might view these things. There was nothing remarkable at all about a postgraduate combat engineer of the Voltarian Fleet passing a few lousy kiddie subjects like perverted quantum mechanics. It made me quite cross, really. Spoiled my faith in these Earth people—not that I'd ever had any. Just riffraff.

I walked around the yard for a while. Two of the children were picking grapes and I accused them of eating more than they picked and after I'd gotten them crying real good, kicked them and felt better.

I called the taxi driver and wanted to know when the Hells he was going to complete delivery of Utanc and he told me it was all on schedule. That made me feel a lot better. Watching that (bleeper) Heller being whistled into his room every night by gorgeous women had been getting to me more than I had admitted. And that I never

actually saw him doing anything with them made it even
worse! One's imagination runs riot sometimes!

Only the possible early arrival of Utanc gave me
morale enough to go back and watch what was happening around Heller. But all he was doing was trotting
around a track in a running suit, not even making good
time. He stopped and watched a football squad being
mustered up, apparently lost interest and resumed his
running. How can anybody just run for a couple of
hours? What do they think about?

I went outside again, and after a long delay in locating him, talked on the phone to the hospital contractor
who said the earth-moving was almost finished, the
water, electrical and sewage ready to place and he'd be
into pouring foundations tomorrow. So I couldn't find
anything to rag him about beyond being at the building
site working when I was trying to call him.

It was late evening, Turkish time, by now. There was
a sort of fascination about watching Heller. I desperately
longed for a time when I would see him curl up in a ball,
preferably in agony, and die and yet, so long as I did not
have the platen, he carried my life in his careless, brutal
hands. So I hung on to the viewscreen and raced the
strips forward to the present.

Heller was going down in the elevator. He was
dressed in a casual dark suit but there was nothing casual
about the way he was acting.

He rushed out of the elevator and burst into
Vantagio's office. "It's here! It's here! The car I want is
here!"

Vantagio was in a tuxedo, apparently all ready for a
Saturday night rush not yet started. "Well, it's about
time! Babe mentions it every day and ever since you spa-
ghettied Grafferty she's been insisting it be the best.
Where is it? Out front or down in the garage?"

"Garage," said Heller. "Come on!"

Vantagio needed no urging. He went rapidly out of his office, followed by Heller, and into the elevator they went and down to the garage.

"It better be a beauty," said Vantagio. "I got to get this action completed so I can have some peace. Been over a week since Babe told me to buy you a lovely car!"

At the garage elevator exit, there stood Mortie Massacurovitch. Heller introduced him to Vantagio. "I been workin' double shift," said Mortie. "I couldn't get here until this evening. But there she is!"

Standing in the middle of the vast pillared structure, surrounded by sleek limousines of the latest model, stood the old, shabby, paint-worn-off, cracked-window Really Red Cab of decades ago.

It looked like a piece of junk that had been shovelled in.

"Where's the car?" said Vantagio.

"That's the car," said Heller.

"Oh, come off it, kid. A joke's a joke but this is serious business. Babe will just about tear my head off if I don't get you one."

"Hey," said Heller, "this is a great car!"

"This was built when they really built cabs!" said Mortie.

"Kid, this isn't any joke? You mean you are really proposing I buy this piece of scrambled trash for you?"

"Hey," said Mortie, "the company ain't charging hardly anything!"

"I'm sure they wouldn't dare!" said Vantagio. "You ought to give the buyer twenty-five smackers to get it towed to a junkyard!"

"Oh, come on," said Mortie. "I'll admit she don't *look* like no limousine. But I had quite a time trying to get the company to agree to sell it. It's sort of a keepsake.

Like old times. Tradition! Of course, you can't keep it red or run it as a Really Red Cab in competition and you can't have its taxi license—that's expensive and stays with the company. But it's a perfectly legal car and the title would be regular."

Vantagio had looked inside. He backed off holding his nose. "Oh, my God."

"It's just the leather," said Mortie. "They didn't have vinyl in them days so it's real leather. Of course, it's kind of rotted and saturated a bit. But it's real leather."

"Please," said Heller.

Vantagio said, "Babe would kill me. She would have me whipped for two or three hours and then kill me with her bare hands."

"I got orders that you can have it cheap," said Mortie. "One thousand dollars and that's rock bottom."

"Quit torturing me!" said Vantagio. "I got a tough night ahead. This is Saturday night and the UN is hotting up—in just two weeks it is reconvening! Kid, have you got any idea——"

"Five hundred," said Mortie. "And that's absolutely rock bottom."

Vantagio tried to walk away. Heller got him by the arm. "Look, real quarter-inch steel fenders and body. Look, Vantagio, real bulletproof windows! See those stars in them? They stopped real bullets just a while ago."

"Two hundred and fifty," said Mortie. "And that's rock rock bottom."

"Kid," said Vantagio, "please, for God's sake, let me go upstairs and call the MGB agency, let them send over a red sports car."

"This cab," said Heller, "is a real beauty!"

"Kid, let me call the Mercedes-Benz agency."

"No."

"Alfa Romeo?"

"No."

"Maserati. Now, there's a good car. A real good car," said Vantagio. "I can get one custom built. Custom built and bright red, kid. A convertible. I'll fill it full of girls."

"No," said Heller.

"Oh, *che il diavolo lo porti*, kid, you're going to get me killed! I wouldn't even dare put that in this garage! It's just an ancient wreck!"

"It's an antique!" cried Mortie. "It ain't no wreck! It's a bona fide antique!"

Vantagio stared at him. Then he went on pacing.

Mortie pressed on. "You put that cab in the Atlantic City Antique Auto Parade and it'll win a twenty-five thousand dollar prize. I guarantee it! Antique cars are the rage!"

Vantagio stopped pacing. "Wait. I've just had an idea. If we put that car in the Atlantic City Antique Auto Parade . . ?"

"And filled it full of girls dressed in costumes of the 1920s," prompted Heller.

"And put guys on the running boards holding submachine guns," said Vantagio.

"And prohibition agents in 1920 costumes chasing it," said Heller.

"And painted 'The Corleone Cab Company' on the doors," cried Vantagio, "Babe would LOVE it! Tradition! And a million bucks' worth of advertising! Right?"

"Right," said Heller.

"Now, you have to do what I tell you, kid. Right?"

"Right."

"Choose this as the car."

"Like I was saying," said Mortie. "The price is one thousand smackers."

"Five hundred," said Vantagio, "providing you can get it to this address. And I'll buy its cab license later from your company." He was scribbling on the back of a card, *Jiffy-Spiffy Garage, Mike Mutazione, Newark, N.J.*

"Can I drive it and monkey with the motor?" said Heller.

"Oh, hell, yes, kid. It's your car. Just so long as you make it available for the parade and just as long as you let Mike Mutazione put it in new-car condition before you park it in here. You see, I can tell people it's for the parade and the UN diplomats will be happy on cultural grounds. They love to see tribal customs preserved."

A new voice was heard. "Hey, where'd this battle casualty come from?" It was Bang-Bang.

"That's the car you're going to drive," said Heller.

"Don't try to snow me under, kid," said Bang-Bang. "I've had a tough day trying to teach the Army the difference between their left feet and their (bleep)."

"Look, Bang-Bang," said Heller, pointing to a star in the glass.

"Hey, that's a 7.62-mm NATO round. See, it dropped down into the ledge outside. Belgian FN? Italian Beretta? Flattened the hell out of it. Bulletproof glass!"

"And fenders. Quarter-inch steel," said Heller.

Vantagio tapped Bang-Bang. "As long as you're working for the kid, go over to Newark with this cabby and tell Mike what to do. Use the same material but replace everything! New bulletproof glass, new upholstery, beat the body out, paint the whole car orange and put 'The Corleone Cab Company' on the doors. Make it all look brand-new. Even the motor. Tell him to do it in a hurry so the kid can have his car."

"I ain't supposed to leave New York," said Bang-Bang.

"It's Saturday night," said Vantagio.

"Oh, that's right," said Bang-Bang.

"I'll go, too!" said Heller.

"No, you won't," said Vantagio. "It's going to be a busy night and I want you in the lobby for a while. And I told two South American diplomats you'd be pleased to meet them. And there's something else you got to do."

Vantagio was signing papers that Mortie had been holding out. He counted five hundred into his palm.

Mortie and Bang-Bang jumped into the cab and with a roar, smoke and clatter were gone.

Vantagio and Heller got back into the elevator. "Now we got to go up," said Vantagio, "and phone Babe and tell her what a great idea I had. No, on the other hand, you phone her from your suite and tell her you thought it up. Tradition is the key to her character, kid. And when you mix tradition and sentiment, it's a winner every time. Old 'Holy Joe' got his start running hooch in cabs just like that!"

"You're a wonder," said Heller.

"Yes, you do what I tell you and you'll be in the money every time. Just remember that, kid."

I was baffled, utterly baffled. What was Heller doing with *two* cars? He already had that old Cadillac being specially rebuilt and didn't seem to be in any rush for it, yet here was this cab being rushed through. For once, some sixth sense—which you can't do without in the Apparatus—told me that this went beyond the Fleet toy fetish. I writhed. (Bleep) him, he was going too fast! Too fast! He could finish up and accomplish something and ruin me!

Chapter 4

Because I knew that on Sunday, coming right up, he was going to have his first Nature Appreciation class with Miss Simmons—who, I was sure, would do him in— I was not terribly interested in what happened to Heller the rest of that Saturday night and scanned him only lightly.

The two South American diplomats were completely unimportant. Vantagio brought them over to Heller and introduced them—they had names about a yard long. Heller was wearing a silk and mohair tuxedo with diamond cuff links and studs but these two South Americans put him to shame with black embroidery on their powder blue tuxedos and lace all over their chests: it heartened me to see Heller outdone.

They had an International Bank loan to build a lot of bridges and they'd heard Heller was a student engineer and they didn't think the bridges would stand up. So they showed him some drawings and he told them to float both ends of the bridges so the earthquakes couldn't affect them. He even drew them some little sketches to show their contracting firm. But I knew it was all silly—a bridge *crosses* water, you don't stick its ends *in* the water. But South Americans are polite and they went away beaming. Riffraff.

The only other thing that happened was also disgusting. Stuffumo and the *kris*-wielding deputy delegate that Heller had unfairly disarmed sought him out where he sat behind some palm fronds—he sat there often as it half hid him from the door.

They had an ornate box and they were both holding on to it. Both speaking English in chorus, they stood in front of him and said, "Thank you for your mediation on the treaty subject of Harlotta. Our two countries have united to give you a token of appreciation. There has never been such peace."

They opened up the box and there, in purple velvet, lay a Llama .45 caliber, large-frame automatic pistol finished in gold damascene and gold butt plates, with the coats of arms of their two countries intertwined with a heart. Some engraver had been working overtime at vast expense! It had extra magazines and fifty shells. It also had a back belt holster with a white dove of peace and *Prince X* engraved on it. Aside from the fact that it was all chased with gold instead of being black, it looked just like a gangster gun, an Army Colt .45.

Heller thanked them and they went away beaming.

It absolutely ruined my dawn sleep! The idea of getting a beautiful weapon like that for some petty, trifling, cheap trick! And he had obtained it unfairly, too! Masquerading under a false identity. "Prince X" indeed! He was just a Fleet combat engineer with middle-class origins like mine. I even outranked him! What an awful waste of a fine handgun!

So, as I say, I was really looking forward to Miss Simmons!

Around nine in the morning, New York time, the interference went off in his suite. But was he bustling out to go to his Sunday class? No! He was certainly taking a perverted angle on Nature Appreciation!

The first thing that came on the screen was the back of a girl's neck. She was a brunette and she was evidently lying face down on the sofa, head to one side, arm trailing limply to the rug, the very picture of exhaustion.

Heller was stroking the back of her neck, sort of working at it with his thumbs. There was a silver pitcher on a nearby table and, in peripheral vision, I could see that he was wearing a white bathrobe and sitting on the edge of the couch above the half-naked girl.

"Oh," she was groaning, "I think I'm going to die!"

Heller was working at the back of her neck with his thumbs. "There, there," he said soothingly. "You'll be all right, Myrtle."

She groaned again. "Seventeen times is too many!"

"Can you lift your head now?" said Heller.

She tried and groaned. "I feel like I've been raped by an elephant."

"I'm sorry," said Heller.

Suddenly I understood. This monster had really been abusing this poor girl! And she was a pretty girl, too, as I could see, now that she had turned on her side.

"It is better, honey," she said. "Jesus, I don't want another night like that!"

Aha, so he was not as popular with these girls as I had thought!

She got up unsteadily, got hold of her robe as an afterthought and half-heartedly covered her nakedness.

"You go get a bath," said Heller, "and a nice sleep and you'll be fine."

"Oh, Jesus, I hope so. Can I come back later?"

My Gods, I thought. He has effected a transference on this poor girl! Enslaved her into chronic masochism!

"I've got a Nature Appreciation class at one," said Heller.

"I've had all the nature I can appreciate for the moment," said Myrtle and stumbled, barefooted and half-clad from his room. The poor, abused creature.

Heller called down for some breakfast and while he was waiting, got on the phone. No wonder I couldn't keep track of him. He was transacting business under the cover of the interference. Sneaky!

A kid came on.

"Let me talk to Mike Mutazione," said Heller. And when the kid had put "papa" on the line, Heller said, "Sorry to bite into your Sunday, Mike. But did you get the cab?"

"Sure thing, kid. A beauty! Fix her up in no time!"

"Great. Now listen, Mike. I am sending you over a little bottle of stuff. I'll write the full directions. But I want you to put it in the paint as an additive. That's on the exterior body and in any of the signs you paint on it. It is easy. It just mixes into whatever paint you use. So when you get the motor and glass and body and upholstery work done, only use paint with this additive in it."

"Makes it shinier?" said Mike.

"Something like that," said Heller. "I'll send the little vial over. It'll be there by the time you're ready."

"Sure, kid, no trouble. The Caddy is doing fine. Bit of a holdup with the new engine but it's on its way. So are the new alloy pistons. She'll do 190 when we're done." Mike laughed. "You'll have to keep the brakes on to keep her from taking off for the moon."

"Take your time on it," said Heller. "The cab I'd like yesterday."

"You'll get it, kid. Want to come over and go to Mass with us?"

"Today is my day for Nature Appreciation. Thanks just the same, Mike. *Ciao.*"

Mass? These (bleeped) Sicilians would be converting him to Christianity next!

His breakfast came, starting with a huge chocolate

sundae. The waiter had no more than gone out the door when a gorgeous, slinky blonde came in.

"Hiya, Semantha," said Heller. "Have some breakfast?"

She shook her head and sat down in a nearby chair. She indicated the door. "Myrtle was just in here, wasn't she? Pretty boy, you've got to watch that Myrtle."

Heller laughed.

"No, seriously, pretty boy. You've got to watch her. She's full of wiles and tricks. I know her. Now, look, when she came in, did she do this?" Semantha loosened her robe. She didn't have anything on under it! Was this Heller's idea of nature appreciation?

She drew her legs to Heller's right. "And then did she sit sideways like this?" She made sure no robe was covering her legs. "And then did she show you her naked thigh like this? And then trail her fingers along it and say that it was bruised and please look?

"Oh, you have to watch that Myrtle, pretty boy. After she'd done all that, did she stand up like this and let her robe fall off like so?

"And then did she say she had an ache in her left breast? And, typically Myrtle, hold it up like this and ask you to see if there was a bruise there?

"And then did she walk real close like this and ask you to really examine it to be sure?"

Heller was laughing. "Watch it, you'll get ice cream on you!"

"And then," said Semantha, "did she sort of walk around like this? Oh, you've got to watch her! And pick up her robe like this? And pretend she'd just noticed she was naked, like this, and trail her robe behind her like this and go into your bedroom, looking back at you like this? You watch that Myrtle, pretty boy!"

"The bed isn't made," said Heller.

He could see what she was doing now from the multiple reflecting mirrors in the bedroom. "Then," continued Semantha, "did she poke at your bed like this? And then wonder if it was softer than hers and could she please get in it like this?"

Semantha had gotten in, but not under the covers. She was stretched out stark naked on the bed, legs apart. "And then did she stroke her body like this? Did she, pretty boy? She takes some watching, that Myrtle does! And then did she raise her arms toward you like this and move her hips around like that and tell you that she was feeling sort of empty and needed . . ."

"Semantha," said Heller. "Get out of that bed and come in here."

"Oh, pretty boy," she pouted. "You're going to make me stand up and hold that position while you . . ."

The interference came on. Well, I didn't need to see any more. It was obvious that he was one of those weirdos that liked odd positions.

Why the Hells couldn't that (bleeped) taxi driver rush up Utanc? I went out petulantly to call him. He didn't know what he was putting me through. I tried for quite a while and couldn't get him. I kicked around the yard and then had dinner.

Actually, I was outraged at Heller's idea of preparing himself for a Nature Appreciation class. How he could go from his dark den of vice into the bright sunlit world without his conscience withering, I did not know. He was not fit to associate with the dear little children and the charming Miss Simmons in their coming outing. But I knew I could count on Miss Simmons! Heller would catch it! A firm character, Miss Simmons!

Chapter 5

The first Nature Appreciation class was apparently being held in the United Nations park between 42nd Street and 48th Street and bordering the East River—just a few blocks from where Heller lived.

It was a beautiful September afternoon: the grass and trees were green and the sky and water were blue. The enormous bulk of the Secretariat Building reared its white slab behind the General Assembly Building and the Conference Building.

Some of the class had already gathered, as scheduled, in front of the Statue of Peace. They were college kids, mostly in jeans and rough clothing; some wore glasses, some did not; some were fat and some were thin. Heller looked them over. None of them were talking to one another or to him: obviously, they were all mutual strangers.

Heller was wearing, I knew from the elevator mirrors, very tailored brushed jeans, his baseball cap and spikes. He must look a bit out of place—neater and more expensively dressed aside from those two items, cap and shoes. He was also taller than the rest. And he carried a little brushed denim haversack while the rest had satchels or just big purses. It must make him stand out for an occasional eye flicked in his direction, especially the girls.

More class drifted up and now there were about thirty.

And here came Miss Simmons! She was marching with a purpose! She was wearing heavy hiking shoes and, despite the heat of the day, a heavy tweed skirt and jacket. She was carrying a walking stick that looked more like a club. Her brown hair was tightly swept back and imprisoned under a man's shooting hat.

She came to a halt. She pushed her horn-rimmed glasses up on her forehead so she could see them. She looked them all over. When she came to Heller, she let go of the glasses and let them fall back on her nose. Ah, this was a good sign. I had confidence in Miss Simmons. If all else failed, this was the one who would stop Heller cold! And her opening words encouraged me greatly!

"Oh, there you are, Wister," she said in front of the whole class. "How is the young Einstein today? Suffering from a swelled head? I hear you used more INFLUENCE yesterday to get out of further tutoring. Well, have no fear, you are not through the barbed wire yet, Wister. The war you so ferociously favor is barely begun!"

She raised her glasses again so she could see the class and proceeded to address them. "Good afternoon, tomorrow's hope. I always start our Nature Appreciation itinerary here at the United Nations park. The United Nations was founded in 1945 to prevent the further escalation of WAR and atomic war in particular. This hope was then entombed here in these great white mausoleums.

"It is of historical significance that this part of Manhattan was once an area covered with slaughterhouses. It is a very apt and fitting fact.

"The UN, this dark grave of all man's greatest hopes, has money, authority and POWER! Yet, I must call to your attention that, despite that, these greedy, self-seeking and egotistical MEN sit in these tombs all day every day, all year every year and do nothing but plot ways and means of avoiding their true duties, duties to which they were pledged by the most sacred vows!

"If these craven, base scoundrels had their way, they

would blow up the whole world with thermonuclear fission and fusion! Wister, pay attention." She lowered her glasses and scowled at him.

She raised her glasses and addressed the rest. "So, class, we start with a could-have-been, the United Nations. Everything you see alive throughout this course will soon be dead forever— destroyed by the vicious idleness, the indecision, the behind-the-scenes plotting and downright craven cowardice of the UN. Wister, what are you looking at?"

Heller said, "This grass is standing up pretty good despite the foot traffic. If they didn't water it with chlorinated water, it would do better."

"Pay attention, Wister," said Miss Simmons, severely. "This is a class in nature appreciation, not the use of poison gas! Now, class, and I hope you are taking notes of the important data I am giving you. Do you see that group of men there? I want to call your attention to the smug, maddeningly blithe expressions on the faces of those UN people stalking about the park."

Heller said, helpfully, "It says on their blue and gold caps and badges 'American Legion Post 89, Des Moines, Iowa.' Is that a member country?"

Miss Simmons quite rightly ignored him. "So you must note, class, and note with horror and indignation, the attitude of irresponsibility which prevails here. If these men would only do their duty . . . Wister, what *are* you looking at?"

"These leaves," said Heller. "All in all, these trees are doing pretty good in all these oil fumes from the river. I think the soil is probably slightly demineralized, though."

"Pay attention to your classwork!" snapped Miss Simmons. "Now, class, if the UN would ever do its duty, we could end utterly and forever man's lemming fixation on self-destruction."

"What's a *lemming?*" said a girl.

"They are hordes of horrible rats that go plunging in masses into the sea annually, committing mass suicide," said Miss Simmons helpfully. "If it wished, in a single, soul-stirring surge, the UN could rise up with clarion voices and cry 'DEATH TO THE CAPITALIST WARMONGERS!' Wister, what in the name of God are you looking at NOW?"

There were three seagulls lying along the concrete parapet. Their feet were stuck into black blobs of oil, pinning them to the concrete. Two were dead. The third, his feet stuck and his feathers saturated with oil, was still making feeble efforts to get free.

"Those birds," said Wister. "They got into an oil slick."

"And I suppose that will make it easier for you to trap them and blow them up with an atomic bomb! Ignore his antics, class. There is always some student who tries to get others to laugh." A helicopter was coming down the river very low and the sound blotted her voice out.

Heller was putting on a pair of gloves from his kit. He went over and verified that the two motionless ones were actually dead. Then he went to the third one. It feebly tried to defend itself with its beak.

Kneeling, Heller got a small spray out of his haversack. By Gods, he skirted on the edges of real Code breaks: it said *Solvent 564, Fleet Supply Base 14* right on it in Voltarian! I made a note of it. Somebody might notice!

He took out a redstar engineer's rag and protected the bird's eyes and air holes and rapidly sprayed its feathers. Of course, the oil vanished.

Then he unstuck its feet, wiped them off and sprayed them. He inspected the bird, found a couple of spots he had missed and handled those. He was always so maddeningly neat!

He took out a water bottle and filled the cap. The bird, head loose by now, started to strike, then thought better of it and took some water from the cap. The bird did it several times.

"You were dehydrated," said Heller. "It's the hot sun. Now take a few more sips." What a fool. He was talking to it in Voltarian and it was an Earth bird!

Then he took out half a sandwich and broke it up and laid it on the grass. The bird stretched its wings, doubtless with some surprise. It was going to fly away but saw the sandwich and decided to have lunch first.

"Now, that's a good bird," said Heller. "You stay away from that black stuff. It's oil, understand? Petroleum!"

The bird let out some kind of a squawk and went on eating the sandwich. I don't know why it squawked. It couldn't understand Voltarian.

Heller looked around. Of course, the Nature Appreciation class was gone. Heller listened intently. He heard nothing. He did a fast scout.

And then he was sniffing. What the Hells was he sniffing about?

He glanced back. The seagull was just taking off. It sailed by him and curved outward over the river and was gone.

Sniffing some more, Heller trotted ahead and was shortly in the reception center of the General Assembly Building, according to the signs. There was even an information sign but he didn't approach it.

He seemed to find the place very curious. The light

was coming through the walls from outside in a translucent effect. He went over to a wall and examined it to find out why, probably.

He went over into the Assembly Hall and there was the class.

Miss Simmons was lecturing. ". . . and here it is that the delegates could rise with one voice and in stentorian and noble tones denounce nuclear weapons forever. But alas, they do not. The men who occupy this place are silenced by their own fears. They cower. . . ."

Heller was examining some marble.

The class trailed out on Miss Simmons' heels and, with her still lecturing and totally ignoring the guide who seemed to have attached himself to the party, went into the Conference Building and were shortly in the gallery of a chamber labelled:

The Security Council

They gazed across the two hundred or so empty public seats—for, of course, nothing was in session and would not be for another couple of weeks—and Miss Simmons continued her lecture. ". . . And so we come at last to the lair of the powerful few who, even if the General Assembly did act, this fifteen-nation body would veto any sensible ban proposed. The five permanent members—United States, France, United Kingdom, Russia and China—each have the right to turn down, individually, the anguished pleas of all the peoples of the Earth! They block any effort anyone makes to outlaw nuclear power and disarm the world! Greed, lust for power, megalomania and paranoia cause these self-anointed few to surge onward and onward, closer and closer to the brink."

Heller had been admiring the gold and blue hangings and a mural. But at her last words, he spoke sharply. "Who keeps preventing a solution?"

Miss Simmons spoke out with a clarion voice of her own. "The Russian traitors who have sold out the revolution and asserted themselves the tyrants of the proletariat! Who asked that question? It was a very good one!"

"Wister did," said a girl.

"Oh, you again! Wister, stop disturbing the class!" Miss Simmons led them back outside.

Heller's eyes lingered on a huge statue of a muscular figure that was putting a lot of effort into something.

Heller asked, "What is that statue doing?"

Miss Simmons said, "That is a Russian statue. It is a worker being forced to beat a plowshare into a sword. It personifies the betrayal of the proletariat." She had looked back, moving her glasses off her eyes to see. "Ah, that was a good question, George."

Wister was looking around to see who George was and so were the other students.

She had gathered them together under the Statue of Peace. "Now, today, students, was just a start, an effort to orient this course for you. But I will review why we started here, so pay very close attention.

"All that you will see in our future Sundays of Nature Appreciation is *doomed* by nuclear war. It will make it far more poignant for you, as you admire the beauties of nature, to realize, as you look at every blossom, every leaf, every delicate paw and each bit of soft, defenseless fur, to realize that it is about to be destroyed forever in the horror and holocaust of thermonuclear war!"

Oh, she was right there! If Heller didn't win and a Voltar invasion got turned loose, those crude atomic bombs would seem like a picnic!

"So, class," she went on, "if you do not yet feel, individually and collectively, the craving urge to instantly sign up with the Anti-Nuclear Protest Marchers, I assure you that you soon will—New York Tactical Police Force or no New York Tactical Police Force. Class dismissed. Wister, please remain behind."

The students wandered off. Heller came up to Miss Simmons.

She lifted her glasses up to try to see him. "Wister, I am afraid your classwork is not improving. You were interrupting and disturbing the others. You were not paying attention!"

"I got everything you said," protested Heller. "You said that if the UN couldn't be made to function, the planet would destroy itself with thermonuclear weapons."

"Weapons made by such as *you*, Wister. My words were far stronger. So you get an F for today. If your daily classwork is a bad average, you know, of course, that even a perfect, INFLUENCED, final examination won't save you. And if you flunk this course, Wister, you won't get your diploma and then nobody will listen to you and you'll never get that coveted job of blowing up this planet. Small as it is, I do my bit for the cause, Wister. Good afternoon." And she stalked off.

Heller sat down.

And how pleased I was! Miss Simmons had him stalled. What a marvelous, brilliant woman! Her straight hair and glasses hid the fact that she was also quite good looking. And even though she obviously hated men, I felt a great tenderness for her, a longing to hug her and tell her what a truly magnificent person she was!

My ally! At last I had found one to give me hope in my sea of chaos!

Oh, it did me good to see Heller just sitting there, staring at the grass.

The fate of empires lay in the delicate and beautiful hands of a woman. But this was not the first time in the age-long histories of planets. I prayed to the Gods that her grip on fate would remain tenacious and strong.

Chapter 6

Heller glanced at his watch and it winked 3:00 P.M. He glanced at the sky: there was a pattern of cloud to the north and a stir of wind.

He got up and, at a fast trot, began to cover the long blocks home.

Suddenly he stopped. Something had caught his eye up ahead. Miss Simmons was just disappearing down a subway stairs, way up ahead.

Heller glanced up and down the street. It was Sunday afternoon and there wasn't anyone about. The usual midtown Sunday desertion. He trotted on. He seemed to be heading for the stairs. It came to me in a flash that maybe he was going to murder Miss Simmons! That is the first plan that would have occurred to me. Apparatus training is always uppermost.

But he passed on by the stairs.

A sharp voice from the bowels of the station! "No! Go away!"

Heller sprang over the rail and dropped onto the steps. He went down six at a time. He burst out onto the platform.

Miss Simmons was standing there, on the other side of the turnstile. A ragged wino was reeling back and forth in front of her. "Gimme a buck and I'll go away!"

She raised her cane to strike at him. He easily grasped it and yanked it out of her hand. He threw it aside.

Heller yelled, "You, there!"

The drunk looked around. He stumbled and scrambled for a more distant exit stair and went through a steel revolving gate.

Heller fished out a token and went through the turnstile. He walked over to the cane and picked it up. He came back and handed it to Miss Simmons.

"Things are pretty deserted on Sunday," he said. "It isn't safe for you."

"Wister," said Miss Simmons with loathing.

"Maybe I should see you home," said the insufferably polite and courteous Royal officer.

"I am perfectly safe, Wister," said Miss Simmons, acidly. "All week I work cooped up. All week I am mobbed with students. Today the class was finished early and it is the first time in MONTHS I have a chance for a quiet walk alone. And who turns up? YOU!"

"I'm sorry," said Heller. "I just don't think it's very safe for a woman to be walking around by herself in this city. Particularly today when there are so few people about. That man just now——"

"I have lived in New York for years, Wister. I am perfectly capable of taking care of myself. Nothing will ever happen to *me!*"

"You ever walk around alone much?" said Heller.

"I don't get a chance to, Wister. There are always students. Please leave me alone, Wister. I am going to have my walk in spite of you or anybody else. Go away somewhere and play with your atom bombs!"

A train roared up, the doors opened. She turned her back upon him pointedly and entered a car.

Wister trotted down the train a few cars and, steadying an automatic door before it could close, got aboard. The train sped along.

I was trying to figure out what his angle was. He lived only a couple blocks away from the station they had just left. She was definitely in his road on his way to a diploma. It would be greatly to his benefit if she were disposed of. The Apparatus textbook handling would be to do just that. Had I found a real ally only to lose her?

The shuttle train pulled into Grand Central. Heller had his eye on Miss Simmons, seen through intervening car doors. She got out of the train.

Heller also went out of the door.

Miss Simmons probably did not see him. She was following directions which took her to the Lexington Avenue line. Heller followed at a distance.

She got to the Lexington Avenue IRT uptown platform. Then she walked way on up the platform to where the front end of the train would stop.

She stood there, leaning on her cane, waiting for the next express.

A young man in a red beret walked toward her. Heller started to move forward and then stopped. The young man was a clean-looking youth. He had on a white T-shirt and it said Volunteer Guard Patrol on it.

He spoke to Miss Simmons. "Miss," he said politely, "you shouldn't be riding the front cars or the back cars of a train, especially on Sunday. Ride in the center where there are more people. The gangs and muggers are out real heavy today."

Miss Simmons turned her back on him. "Leave me alone!"

The volunteer guard drifted down the platform. He must have sensed Heller had seen the interplay. He said to Heller as he passed, "Rapes by the trainful and they never learn."

An express roared in and came to a hissing halt with a roar and clang of doors opening. Miss Simmons got into the first car. Heller stepped in to the middle of the train. The doors slammed shut and they roared away, lurching and banging at high speed.

A tough-looking drunk sized up Heller. Heller took his engineer gloves out of his haversack and put them on. It was an effective gesture. The tough one promptly staggered down the swaying train to the next car back.

White tiles of stations flashed by, one after another. They rode and rode and rode, all at very high speed through the dark tunnels, the sound a pounding roar. At each infrequent stop, Heller would half rise to see if Miss Simmons was alighting, would see that she was not and would then sink back.

After a very long time, the signs on the tunnel poles said:

Woodlawn

Miss Simmons got out. Heller waited until the last moment and then got out. Miss Simmons had vanished up a stairs.

Shortly, Heller emerged into daylight. Miss Simmons was striding along northward. He waited a bit. He looked at the sky. It was overcast. Wind was whipping stray bits of paper along roadways.

It was then I realized what he must be doing: he had probably read one of the G-2 manuals, the one about how to tail a Russian spy. He was simply practicing. He had not read any Apparatus manuals and so he would not be well enough trained to know that he should simply murder Miss Simmons. Having accounted for his actions, I felt much easier. Miss Simmons would be quite safe after all and I still had an ally.

Several picnickers were evidently going home, their hair blown about by the wind. Otherwise there was no traffic.

At least two hundred yards behind Miss Simmons, Heller followed along.

She went some distance. A sign pointed:

Van Cortlandt Park

She turned in that direction, striding along in her he ʼy laced boots, swinging her cane, the perfect picture ʼa fashionable hiker in the European style.

She made some more turns. They were well ʼ ʼ a kind of wilderness interlaced with infrequent ʼ dle paths.

The wind was rising and trees were bowing. Some belated picnickers fled toward civilization. After that it was a deserted expanse of thickets and trees.

Heller was closer to her now but still thirty yards or more behind. Due to the twists and turns of the trail, he was usually masked from her. She was not looking back.

Ahead was a vale. The path went down into a long hollow and then turned up at the far end. It was a totally hidden area, surrounded by large trees.

Miss Simmons got a third of the way up the far slope. Heller stepped forward to go down the path.

Abruptly, from the undergrowth around her, six men sprang up!

One leaped agilely into the trail in front of her, a ragged white youth.

A black jumped into the trail behind her!

Two Hispanics and two more whites blocked her way to right and left!

Heller started to go down the trail toward them.

A harsh, cold voice said, "Hold it, sonny!"

Heller looked back to his left.

Emerged from a tree but still behind it stood an old gray-faced, unshaven bum. He was holding a double-barrelled shotgun trained on Heller. He was twenty feet away.

Another voice! "Just stop right there, kid!"

Heller looked back and to his right. Another man, a black, was standing there with a revolver pointed at him, thirty feet away. "We been waitin' all afternoon for a setup like this, kid, so don't make any sudden moves."

The man with the shotgun said, "This is one time, sonny, when you don't get a piece all to yourself. You can have some later, if there's any left."

Excited laughter was coming from the men around Miss Simmons. They were jumping up and down.

She struck at them with her stick!

A black grabbed it and yanked it out of her hand!

The others screeched with laughter and the one with the stick started to dance with it, waving it. The others started to dance around Miss Simmons.

Heller shouted in a strong voice, "Please don't do this!"

The man with the shotgun said, "Take it easy, sonny. It's just a gang rape. Some fun for a Sunday. Me and Joe is a little too (bleeped) out to do more than watch, so you just get smart and be like us and maybe we won't have to kill you."

"What kind of beasts are you on this planet?" shouted Heller.

"You got any money?" said the man with the revolver. "The big H comes high these days."

The crowd around Miss Simmons was dashing in at her and dancing back. They were herding her into a flatter place more masked by trees. She was shouting at them to leave her alone.

Heller reached toward his haversack. "Hold it, sonny. Keep your hands in sight. This is a twelve-gauge and both barrels loaded in front of hair triggers. We can get his money later, Joe. Jesus," he said indulgently, "look at those young devils."

"Only the raving insane do things like that!" said Heller.

"What do you mean, insane?" challenged the man with the revolver. "Pete there taught 'em himself. He really knows his psychology. And every one of those kids got Grade A in psychology. How could they be insane? Jesus, would you look at how hard their (bleepers) are! Great stuff, hey, Pete?"

"Jesus, look at 'em," chortled Pete.

Heller was backing up, I suddenly realized. Inch by slow inch he had been backing up. He was going to use a standard solution. He was going to run away! He was smarter than I thought.

The half-dozen whooping young men, getting wilder and wilder with excitement, had herded Miss Simmons into the flatter area. A Hispanic leaped in and grabbed off her hat!

Another leaped past her and hit at her hair. It came loose and showered around her shoulders.

"Yippee!" screamed a black. "Don't she look wild!"

"Killing a bunch of hoodlums isn't part of my job!" Heller said. Then he shouted, "Please quit this and get away while you still can!"

"The only ones likely to be killed is you and that (bleepch)," said Pete. He shouted down, "Jesus! Start stripping her! Show me some skin! Oh, man, does this beat Sunday TV."

Two of them seized her coat, one from either side, and yanked it off her, danced away and threw it aside.

Two more dashed in past her flailing arms and tore at her shirt!

Heller was backing up, inch by inch.

"Blackie!" howled Joe down into the vale, "get behind her and get that bra off!"

"Ah," sighed Pete in ecstasy.

"Pedrito!" howled Joe. "Get the skirt! The skirt, man! Yank it off her!"

As if in ultra-slow motion, Heller moved back further.

"Heat her up! Heat her up!" shouted Joe. "Grab her from behind and heat her up!"

"Get her down! Get her down!" howled Pete.

Miss Simmons' foot lashed out at a man. He grabbed her shoe with a surging wrench, and tore it off her foot, laces and all. There was a crack.

Miss Simmons' face contorted in agony. "My ankle!"

Pete said, "Oh, Jesus, I like it when they scream!"

Inch by inch, imperceptibly, Heller was backing up. The angle made by two tree trunks was closing. He was getting out of the shotgun's field of fire. In a moment he would be able to escape. Smart.

Joe yelled, "Get her down! Get her on her back!"

Pete shouted, "Strip her total like I taught you!"

Joe let out a sigh. "Oh, wow! Look at that boy paw her!"

Miss Simmons' voice rose to the tops of the trees. "Don't touch me! Don't touch me!"

A Hispanic was watching avidly as Miss Simmons cried, "My ankle is broken!"

Joe licked his lips as Miss Simmons' scream lanced through the glade.

A wild-eyed white heard Pete's shouted order, "Get her begging for it!" He darted forward.

Pete yelled, "Grab her legs!"

Joe jerked as Miss Simmons' scream tore up from below.

"Let Whitey go first!" howled Pete. "The rest of you have got the (bleep)! Whitey first!"

Heller suddenly dived to the ground!

The shotgun blasted with a roar!

Heller was rolling to his left in a blur of motion.

A revolver shot racketed.

The man with the shotgun was trying to get around the tree which now blocked his aim. He pulled back.

Another revolver shot sounded and a spurt of dirt leaped near Heller's head.

Heller was rolling further.

A sudden glimpse of a tree. The shotgun man lunged!

Heller's hands shot out and grabbed the shotgun.

The man screamed, flailing back a broken hand.

Bark leaped from the tree! The racket of a revolver shot!

A sight down the shotgun barrel at the revolver man!

The buck of the shotgun!

The revolver man's chest spurted red and he flew backwards.

The shotgun man trying to get up!

The swinging blur of the stock. The crack as the stock shattered. The shotgun man didn't have a face! Just red flesh and bone splinters!

Heller sprang out into the path.

The group around the girl were spread out, facing up the path, crouched and alert.

A white youth yelled, "It's just one guy! Kill him!"

A black and a Hispanic rushed forward.

A switchblade flashed.

The other four spread out so they could encircle.

Heller's foot struck the switchblade hand. The knife flew. The man screamed!

A man seen between two others. He had a gun.

Heller's foot extended like a battering ram. The man's gun arm crumpled!

A whirl. Another knife! A foot up against the hand. The knife flew into the air!

Heller spun on one foot, the other extended like a scythe. The flat of the foot tore the man's whole face off!

Gods! Spikes! This was why Heller was wearing spikes!

A knife blade glittering. It slashed down on Heller's arm and bit.

A foot up toward the wielder. A down kick! The whole chest of the knife wielder ripped open!

Arms seizing Heller from behind. A darting back of Heller's head, his own arms rising and casting off the grip.

He spun!

Spikes stamped against a thigh and, ripping downward, that foot hit the ground. The other foot coming upward.

The whole throat of the man torn out!

A blur of three men trying to get at Heller.

A woolly head. A spiked foot driving at it. The grind of steel into bones!

A Hispanic face. The blur of a foot kick. The whole side of the head coming off.

A man's heels. He was running, trying to get away.

A rush. A horizontal thrust of two spiked feet. They hit the man in the back. He went down in a skid of leaves. Heller landed upright. Man's head two feet below the spikes. Down came Heller. The soles were held in a V. They stripped the skin, ears and two huge slabs of skull off the head.

Silence.

Heller started checking them. Five were dead, ripped to pieces. The sixth had his whole chest open. Veins and arteries were pumping.

The man came to. He screamed. He collapsed. The body went into the final twitches of the death agonies.

Heller went up the hill. Both Pete and Joe were very dead.

He walked back down, surveying the scene. It looked like a slaughterhouse. Blood was all over and leaves were churned into red mud.

I was terrified. I had never had an inkling as to why he was wearing spikes. But I knew now. In a primitive land where other weapons were not legal, he had been walking around on his! Supposing I had not known this! I myself might have been a target! Oh, I would stay a long distance away from this Heller if I ever had to talk to him. He was *dangerous!*

Miss Simmons, clothes torn, was lying there where they had left her at the first shot.

She was propped on an elbow. She was staring at Heller with wide, round eyes.

He went over to her. He tried to get her to lie back. It must have moved her leg. She screamed in agony! She passed out.

Heller examined her leg. The ankle was a compound fracture with a splinter of bone extending from it.

He got a knife out of his haversack, picked up a broken tree branch and quickly made a splint. He padded the ankle with wads of Kleenex he took from her purse and then taped the splints on with engineer tape.

He tried to get her torn clothes together. He got her

into her coat. She was still out cold. He found her glasses and put them in her purse and then tied the purse around her neck.

He gave the churned ground an inspection. His spike tracks were everywhere.

Heller looked down at his baseball shoes. They were coated with blood and fragments of bone and flesh.

He did a tour of the dead men. He chose one of them and took the shoes off the corpse. He took off his baseball shoes and put them on the dead man's feet. Then he pulled on those of the dead man.

It was a bad sign. He had already been reading G-2 manuals, obviously. As I feared, it was likely to make my work that much harder!

After a bit of search, he found Miss Simmons' stick. He went over the scene again—and a gory scene it was, there under the darkening sky, wind now tugging at the hair and clothing of the dead.

He picked up Miss Simmons and looked around again to make sure there was nothing left, apparently. Then he looked up the hill to where the shotgun man still lay, partially in view.

"I wish you'd listened," he said. "I'm not here to punish anybody." He looked down at Miss Simmons' face. She was out cold. Then he looked up at the scudding sky and in Voltarian said, "Is this planet inhabited by a Godless people? Has some strange idea poisoned them to make them think they have no souls? That there is no hereafter?"

Well, that was Heller. Stupid and theatrical. It served his best interests to just dump Miss Simmons and shove one of those abandoned switchblades into her. You could tell he was not Apparatus trained, so maybe G-2 wasn't going to do me as much harm as I had thought.

Yes. Stupid. He seemed to be casting about for compass directions. Then he began to move swiftly westward and south through thickets and trees, trotting along in a way that seemed to hold Miss Simmons level.

Eventually he emerged from what must have been a vast expanse of parkland. He was soon on some streets.

After quite a distance, a sign loomed ahead in the dusk:

Van Cortlandt Park Subway Station

He bought tokens and the person behind the glass didn't even look at him. He put two tokens in the gate.

He was shortly on a train. It roared along. There were hardly any people aboard. A security guard walked by. Despite the bloody trouser cuffs, the torn clothes on the girl and the splinted ankle, the guard did not even pause as he passed.

Empire Subway Station was there on the white tiles. Heller got off.

Carrying Miss Simmons with no bounce, he moved smoothly along. He was on College Walk. He turned south on Amsterdam Avenue and halted at a door marked:

Empire Health Service

There were no lights on.

He went across Amsterdam Avenue and walked into what must have been the emergency ward of a hospital. He waited a bit and a nurse passing through the waiting room saw him and came over.

"Accident," she said. "Sit right there."

She went off. She came back pushing a wheeled stretcher and patted it.

Heller put Miss Simmons down on it.

The nurse threw a blanket over her and tugged a strap tight over her chest.

The nurse led Heller over to a counter. She got out some forms. "Name?"

"She's Miss Simmons," said Heller. "Empire faculty. You can get the details out of her purse, probably. I'm just a student."

The nurse got Miss Simmons' purse and dug out insurance cards and so on.

A young intern came down the hall and looked at Miss Simmons. "Shock," he said. "She's in shock."

"Broken ankle," said Heller. "Compound fracture."

"You got a slashed arm," said the young intern. He was lifting Heller's sleeve. "Needs handling. Looks like a switchblade wound. Student?"

"Yes," said Heller.

"We'll fix it up for you."

Miss Simmons came to and started to scream.

Another nurse came along with a tray and a hypodermic syringe. The intern got hold of Miss Simmons' arm. The nurse put a rubber tube around the arm. Miss Simmons was threshing about and the nurse couldn't control the arm long enough to get the needle in.

"That isn't heroin is it?" said Heller. "I don't think she's on horse."

"Morf," said the intern. "The purest medical morf. Calm her down."

Miss Simmons was lunging against the strap. She had her other arm loose. She was pointing at Heller. "Get him away from me!" She struggled to draw backwards. "Get away from me, you murderer!"

The intern and the nurse managed to hold her still. The nurse got the needle into a vein.

Miss Simmons was glaring at Heller and screaming.

"You murderer! You sadist!"

The intern said, "Now, now, you'll feel better in a moment."

"Get him away from me!" screamed Miss Simmons. "He's just like I thought!"

"There, there," said the nurse.

"Grab him!" screamed Miss Simmons. "I saw him murder eight men in cold blood!"

"Nurse," said the intern, "mark that she's to be placed in an observation ward."

She threshed further. "You've got to believe me! I saw him kick eight men to death!"

"Nurse," said the intern, "change that to psychiatric observation ward."

The morphine must have been biting. She lay back. Suddenly she raised her head and looked venomously at Heller. "I knew it! I knew it all the time! You're a savage killer! When I get well and out of here, I'm going to devote my life to making certain that you FAIL!"

Oh, I was so relieved. I had been afraid all this time that she would be grateful to Heller for his preventing them from raping her, giving her the (bleep) and probably killing her for kicks. But she was true blue to the end.

The grimness was still on her face as she went under the full effects of the morphine and fell back.

I did some rapid calculation. She would not be able to continue as teacher of that course this semester but she certainly would be his teacher again in late winter and the spring. She had ample time to flunk him. Or—oh, joy—hang him sooner with a murder rap!

Bless her crazy, crooked and ungrateful heart!

How wonderful it was to feel I had a real friend!

And even if they put her under psychiatric care, that would change nothing. It never does.

*Does Simmons succeed in
ending Heller's mission?*

**Read
MISSION EARTH
Volume 3
*THE ENEMY WITHIN***

About the Author
L. Ron Hubbard

L. Ron Hubbard's remarkable writing career spanned more than half-a-century of intense literary achievement and creative influence.

And though he was first and foremost a writer, his life experiences and travels in all corners of the globe were wide and diverse. His insatiable curiosity and personal belief that one should live life as a professional led to a lifetime of extraordinary accomplishment. He was also an explorer, ethnologist, mariner and pilot, filmmaker and photographer, philosopher and educator, composer and musician.

Growing up in the still-rugged frontier country of Montana, he broke his first bronc and became the blood brother of a Blackfeet Indian medicine man by age six. In 1927, when he was 16, he traveled to a still remote Asia. The following year, to further satisfy his thirst for adventure and augment his growing knowledge of other cultures, he left school and returned to the Orient. On this trip, he worked as a supercargo and helmsman aboard a coastal trader which plied the seas between Japan and Java. He came to know old Shanghai, Beijing and the Western Hills at a time when few Westerners could enter China. He traveled more than a quarter of a million miles by sea and land while still a teenager and before the advent of commercial aviation as we know it.

He returned to the United States in the autumn of 1929 to complete his formal education. He entered

George Washington University in Washington, D.C., where he studied engineering and took one of the earliest courses in atomic and molecular physics. In addition to his studies, he was the president of the Engineering Society and Flying Club, and wrote articles, stories and plays for the university newspaper. During the same period he also barnstormed across the American mid-West and was a national correspondent and photographer for the *Sportsman Pilot* magazine, the most distinguished aviation publication of its day.

Returning to his classroom of the world in 1932, he led two separate expeditions, the Caribbean Motion Picture Expedition; sailing on one of the last of America's four-masted commercial ships, and the second a mineralogical survey of Puerto Rico. His exploits earned him membership in the renowned Explorers Club and he subsequently carried their coveted flag on two more voyages of exploration and discovery. As a master mariner licensed to operate ships in any ocean, his lifelong love of the sea was reflected in the many ships he captained and the skill of the crews he trained. He also served with distinction as a U.S. naval officer during the Second World War.

All of this—and much more—found its way, into his writing and gave his stories a compelling sense of authenticity that has appealed to readers throughout the world. It started in 1934 with the publication of "The Green God" in *Thrilling Adventure* magazine, a story about an American naval intelligence officer caught up in the mystery and intrigues of pre-communist China. With his extensive knowledge of the world and its people and his ability to write in any style and genre, he rapidly achieved prominence as a writer of action adventure, western, mystery and suspense. Such was the respect of his fellow writers that he was only 25 when elected president of the New York Chapter of the American Fiction Guild.

In addition to his career as a leading writer of fiction, he worked as a successful screenwriter in Hollywood where he wrote the original story and script for Columbia's 1937 hit serial, "The Secret of Treasure Island." His work on numerous films for Columbia, Universal and other major studios involved writing, providing story lines and serving as a script consultant.

In 1938, he was approached by the venerable New York publishing house of Street and Smith, the publishers of *Astounding Science Fiction*. Wanting to capitalize on the proven reader appeal of the L. Ron Hubbard byline to capture more readers for this emerging genre, they essentially offered to buy all the science fiction he wrote. When he protested that he did not write about machines and machinery but that he wrote about people, they told him that was exactly what was wanted. The rest is history.

The impact and influence that his novels and stories had on the fields of science fiction, fantasy and horror virtually amounted to the changing of a genre. It is the compelling human element that he originally brought to this new genre that remains today the basis of its growing international popularity.

L. Ron Hubbard consistently enabled readers to peer into the mind and emotions of characters in a way that sharply heightened the reading experience without slowing the pace of the story, a level of writing rarely achieved.

Among the most celebrated examples of this are three stories he published in a single, phenomenally creative year (1940)—*Final Blackout* and its grimly possible future world of unremitting war and ultimate courage which Robert Heinlein called "as perfect a piece of science fiction as has ever been written"; the ingenious fantasy-adventure, *Typewriter in the Sky* described by Clive Cussler as "written in the great style adventure should be written in"; and the prototype novel of clutching psychological suspense and horror in the midst of ordinary, everyday life, *Fear*, studied by writers from Stephen King to Ray Bradbury.

It was Mr. Hubbard's trendsetting work in this field from 1938 to 1950, particularly, that not only helped to expand the scope and imaginative boundaries of science fiction and fantasy but indelibly established him as one of the founders of what continues to be regarded as the genre's Golden Age.

Widely honored—recipient of Italy's Tetradramma D'Oro Award and a special Gutenberg Award, among other significant literary honors—*Battlefield Earth* has sold more than 6,500,000 copies in 24 languages and is the biggest single-volume science fiction novel in the history of the genre at 1050 pages. This *New York Times* and international bestseller was voted the number one science fiction novel of the twentieth century by the American Book Readers Association. Additionally, it was ranked number three out of the one hundred best English language novels of the twentieth century in the Random House Modern Library readers' poll.

The *Mission Earth*® dekalogy has been equally acclaimed, winning the Cosmos 2000 Award from

ABOUT THE AUTHOR

French readers and the coveted Nova-Science Fiction Award from Italy's National Committee for Science Fiction and Fantasy. The dekalogy has sold more than seven million copies in ten languages, and each of its ten volumes became *New York Times* and international bestsellers as they were released.

The first of L. Ron Hubbard's original screenplays *Ai! Pedrito!—When Intelligence Goes Wrong,* novelized by author Kevin J. Anderson, was released in 1998 and immediately appeared as a *New York Times* bestseller. This was followed in 1999 with the publication of A *Very Strange Trip,* an original L. Ron Hubbard story of time-traveling adventure, novelized by Dave Wolverton, that also became a *New York Times* bestseller directly following its release.

His literary output ultimately encompassed more than 250 published novels, novelettes, short stories and screenplays in every major genre.

For more information on L. Ron Hubbard and his many acclaimed works of fiction visit the L. Ron Hubbard literary Internet sites at: http://www.bridgepub.com, http://www.authorservicesinc.com and http://www.battlefieldearth.com.

"I am always happy to hear from my readers."

L. Ron Hubbard

These were the words of L. Ron Hubbard, who was always very interested in hearing from his friends and readers. He made a point of staying in communication with everyone he came in contact with over his fifty-year career as a professional writer, and he had thousands of fans and friends that he corresponded with all over the world.

The publishers of L. Ron Hubbard's literary works wish to continue this tradition and would very much welcome letters and comments from you, his readers, both old and new.

Any message addressed to the Author's Affairs Director at Bridge Publications will be given prompt and full attention.

BRIDGE PUBLICATIONS, INC.
4751 Fountain Avenue
Los Angeles, California 90029

Mission Earth

BY

L. RON HUBBARD

"A superbly imaginative, intricately plotted invasion of Earth."

— Chicago Tribune

An entertaining narrative told from the eyes of alien invaders, *Mission Earth* is filled with captivating suspense and action.

Heller, Royal Combat Engineer, has been sent on a desperate mission to halt the self-destruction of Earth—wholly unaware that a secret branch of his own government (the Coordinated Information Apparatus) has dispatched its own agent—whose sole purpose is to sabotage Heller at all costs, as part of its own clandestine operation.

With a cast of unpredictable characters, biting satire and interesting and imaginative plot twists, the two protagonists struggle against incredible odds in this intergalactic game where the future of Earth teeters in the balance.